# A DEAL WITH THE DEVIL

BOYS OF PRESTON PREP

ANGEL LAWSON

SAMANTHA RUE

# PROLOGUE

It's warm for late spring, even for the south, and it's the first time I've seen fireflies this year. They twinkle across the rolling green of the golf course, like tiny fairy lights beckoning me into the dark. I watch them for a long moment, transfixed, feeling the bloom of awareness that always arrives with the changing of the season, as if suddenly realizing the world has taken a gulp of time. Without thinking, I wander away from the patio, the dessert buffet, and my parents, to follow the blinking bugs in an attempt to catch one.

Even at thirteen, I'm still the kind of kid who's more interested in chasing fireflies than talking about gossip, looks, and boys. I'm just not into hanging out with the other tweens at The Club, which is not to imply that my parents would let me anyway. In a world of excess and privilege, I've been blessed with two obnoxiously overbearing parents who expect—no, demand—good, *appropriate* behavior. Especially for a girl. If others think I'm bland and boring, then it just means my parents are succeeding.

It doesn't really matter to me. I'm more comfortable on my own, anyway. I can't compete with the other girls my age, with their push-up bras from Victoria's Secret, or their high-heeled wedges that make them three inches taller. My best friend, Sydney, is all in the thick of it, a cornerstone of their whispered bathroom conversations about sneaking alcohol and giving guys blow jobs. Along with all the stuffed bras, I suspect they're making it up—well, I *know* Sydney is—but regardless, there has to be a certain level of confidence to even pretend to live that life. It's something I definitely lack.

The firefly slips through the cracks in the wrought iron gate leading out to the parking lot. I push through unthinkingly, continuing to follow it, but jolt to a stop when I hear a voice.

"I bet you can't do it," I hear a boy whisper.

No, not just a boy. My brother, Emory.

Someone else scoffs. "Sure, I can."

I freeze at the sound of *this* voice, my heartbeat stuttering at the low cadence. Reynolds McAllister is many things. He's our next-door neighbor. He's my brother's best friend. He's our neighborhood's biggest troublemaker. He is, I suspect, the focus of many of those whispered bathroom discussions among the girls. But most of all, Reynolds McAllister is this:

*My soul mate.*

Reynolds whispers, "I just need a distraction."

I shift a little so I can get a better view. It's already dark out—hence the fireflies—but the moon is bright and full enough that I can see both of their profiles in a thicket of sculpted bushes. They're crouched low, peering out at the parking lot, and I can just barely make out the confident, loose smile curving Reynolds' lips.

"Are you down, or what?" he challenges.

I watch as Emory gnaws at a thumbnail, silent for a moment, before agreeing, "I'll distract the attendant and you'll snag the keys."

Reynolds turns to him to say, "Remember what I taught you. Nothing too big. Don't draw outside attention."

"Yeah, yeah." My brother flaps a dismissive hand, adding, "And you can't just grab any key. It has to be something really nice, like a Porsche or Tesla."

"Hey, hold the fuck up. Now there's criteria?" Reynolds' voice is already deep for a fourteen-year-old. He makes my brother sound like he's still in middle school, with me—not a freshman at Preston Prep. His deep voice and penchant for curse words always makes Reynolds sound confident and a little commanding, like he's the one in charge, older somehow. It also frequently makes my cheeks heat, but that started long before he hit puberty.

Since as far back as I can remember, I've always had a crush on Reynolds McAllister. It isn't just his easy smile, nor is it the deep-set dimples on his cheeks, both of which are likely a useful distraction, as once he sets them loose, you're rendered temporarily unable to wonder what he's up to—though the answer is usually 'stealing something'. It's not his messy hair, or that he's got the dreamiest green eyes, or the way he always slouches when he sits, with his legs spread wide, like he's just too cool to care about anything. It's not even that he somehow knows a lot about things that fourteen-year-olds shouldn't.

It's about the way he looks at me sometimes, assured and trusting, like I'm not a child—like I'm more than the neighbor's bratty kid sister. Emory and the rest of his friends have no tolerance for me. I can't even count the amount of times Emory has wanted to do something and our parents have asked him to take me along. I can't ignore the way my brother and his friends react with deep groans and barely-veiled glowers.

But not *him*.

Reynolds will just give me one of those easy smiles, gesture with a nod at the door, and wait for me to follow.

"Bro, look," Emory explains, "if we're going to jack one of these cars, it may as well be worth it. We're both already on strike two."

I gape at their shadowy forms, knowing that one of the biggest reasons my parents are so overprotective is that my idiot brother can't seem to stay out of trouble. It's like a moth to a flame. Which is why, despite the fact I'm not the least bit surprised the guys are talking about stealing a car, I *am* surprised they're stupid enough to actually do it.

*Again*.

This has been going on for a year now already, and they're both close to getting into real trouble—the *serious* kind of trouble that can't just be wiped away with a phone call from our dad and a donation to whatever institution has fallen victim to their next antic. It comes as no surprise that Reynolds is orchestrating it, though. There are a finite amount of certainties in life; the grass is green, the sky is blue, and Reynolds McAllister will steal anything that isn't bolted down.

Not that bolts would stop him from trying.

It'd started as a running joke in the community—little Sticky Fingers McAllister—but Reynolds isn't little anymore, and no one is laughing now. It's grown obvious that this is more than good-natured pranks, more than material desire. Reynolds just keeps taking things, no matter the punishment. Whether it's for the fun of it, the challenge of it, or some weird compulsion, this is what it's escalated to, and he's dragging my brother along.

But Emory isn't stupid, and unlike many of our other friends' parents, ours would follow through on a serious punishment if he got busted one more time.

But I don't need to wonder why they're taking the risk. They've both been vying for a chance to be part of the exclusive group of Devils at the high school. The Devils are a bunch of popular jocks, which is something Emory and Reynolds already are, so it doesn't even make sense to me. They've already made the football team. They've dated the prettiest girls, have worn the matching letterman jackets, and have driven the expensive cars. They're already legendary, even by middle-school standards. But, from what I understand, trivial schoolyard shenanigans are far below the cruel caliber of the Devils' usual fare.

A prank like this would look great on their resume.

The second I decide to step in and do something, my heart starts pounding, palms growing sweaty, but I have to stop them before this goes too far. I don't want either of them to get a third strike—whatever that means, it doesn't sound good.

I take a deep breath and march down the sidewalk, having to cut around the shrubbery to meet them. But when I reach the bush, the only person I see is Reynolds, peering over at the valet attendant's stand.

"Where's Emory?" I whisper.

Reynolds jerks in surprise, whipping around to meet my gaze. When he does, he releases a slow exhale, shoulders slumping in relief. His green eyes sweep over me, then dart back to the attendant's stand where my brother has suddenly appeared. "Get out of here, Baby V."

*Ugh*, I hate when he calls me that. "I know what you're doing," I say, crossing my arms defiantly, "and you two need to stop."

"If you know what we're doing," he says, sparing me a rapid glance, "then you need to get the hell out of here."

From the attendant's stand, my brother suddenly shouts, "Goddamnit, Bryan!" sounding much older than fourteen. "There's a scratch on my father's BMW! Do you want to explain how that got there?"

We come to this country club often enough to know that Bryan is new. "A scratch? Where?" Bryan narrows his eyes suspiciously at my brother, but it's clear from the way they dart around that he's worried.

Emory gestures wildly. "Down the whole side panel!"

My teeth grind in frustration at having been blown off by Reynolds, so I give up and just march toward the valet stand instead. If I can't stop Reynolds, maybe I can talk some sense into my idiot brother.

"Why were you at the car, anyway?" the guy checked his clipboard. "I still have the keys here."

Emory's gaze jumps to mine as I approach, never flinching. "I was getting a sweater out of the car for my sister, and that's when I saw it. If you don't believe me, come see it for yourself."

Bryan argues, "I can't leave the stand and Jeremy is on a break."

Emory rolls his eyes, and I wonder if maybe he hasn't been

spending a bit too much time around Reynolds. He's putting on a really convincing act. "My sister will wait here and just tell everyone you'll be right back. Trust me, that's a better option than my dad being the one to see that scratch first."

I freeze.

Did he just drag me into this?

Bryan assesses me for a long moment, fingers carding through the papers on the clipboard, and must decide that I look trustworthy. Which, of course, I am. I'm just innocent little Baby V. Nothing to see here but an awkward thirteen-year-old giving her brother the stink-eye. Bryan mutters a curse under his breath but concedes to my worryingly persuasive brother. I'm left standing by the curb, arms crossed, as my brother walks toward the parking lot. He turns back to wink at me.

Before I can react, Reynolds darts out of the bushes, his dress shirt wrinkled and his club-mandated tie askew. He brushes past me without any acknowledgment, ducking behind the valet stand to run his finger down the clipboard. I watch uselessly as a slow, wicked smile appears on his face. A heartbeat later, he's snatched a set of keys bearing a Porsche logo from the board at his back.

"This is a bad idea," I say, wringing my hands to stop them from shaking. "I don't want you guys to get in trouble."

Every time Emory does something, my parents clamp down even more, and I'm usually the one who gets the brunt of their frustrations. It's not fair. It's not right. But that's the way it's always been.

Reynolds pauses just then, staring pensively at the keys in his hand, and for a moment I think maybe—just maybe—he'll actually listen to me. Instead, he turns his mischievous smile, dimples and all, right on me. "You should come with me."

I blink at him, gulping. "What?"

"Come on, Baby V." He reaches out, grazing the soft knuckle of a curled forefinger beneath my chin. I'm momentarily struck speechless. Breathless. Senseless. He cocks his head, watching me. "Aren't you tired of being the good girl who watches us have all the fun? Come with me, you'll have a blast." He holds out his hand, gesturing with a nod toward the parking lot. "It's just one joyride, it'll be fine."

Through the thick fog of my screeching internal '*oh my god, he touched me*', I'm only distantly aware of what he's doing. Reynolds wants me, at the very least, out of the way. And at the very most... *complicit*. Reynolds may be a thief and a troublemaker, but he isn't dumb. I'm a witness now, a liability. What better way to shut me up than to make me an accomplice?

Even more distant is the awareness that Reynolds *must* know how hard it is for me to say no to him. It always has been, and it certainly isn't the first time he's leveled me with one of those dimpled grins and found a convenient blind eye to his and my brother's antics.

It is, however,the first time he's asked me to go along for the ride.

I look at his outstretched hand, at long fingers that have picked pockets and locks and pretty high school girls, and I know it's not real, but this is Reynolds.

This is Reynolds picking *me*.

My heart bangs wildly as I slip my hand into his, finally meeting his gaze, and I wonder if I look as panicked and unhinged as I feel. "Okay."

"Sweet." He grasps my hand and turns, leading me away, and I follow without question.

Because the thing about Reynolds McAllister is that even when he's doing bad things—even if being nice to me is merely a means to an end—he still has a way of making me feel like I'm special.

Later—after the sirens and the pain and the tears—I'll look back on this moment and remember how it all began. I'll remember the way his smile makes me go all soft inside, and I'll remember the way he laughs—low and breathless—when I stumble over a dip in the asphalt. I'll remember the way my heart feels like a hummingbird when he squeezes my hand, and feeling scared and thrilled and like I'm finally a part of something. I'll remember all of it, and I'll wonder how I ever thought the beginning of my own personal nightmare had ever felt like a fairytale.

In my periphery, I see a firefly hovering just within reach.

I walk faster.

# 1

YOU'D NEVER KNOW from looking at me that I'm broken.

In fact, on the surface, I'm probably quite enviable. I've got long, blonde hair that isn't too straight, nor too curly. My teeth are perfect, the result of extensive adolescent orthodontia. My nose is thin and aligned. More than once my eyes have been described as 'strikingly blue', and spoken with tones of wonderment. I have a nice body. I know I look good in a one-piece bathing suit, when my scars are hidden. Once, over the summer, I caught the lifeguard checking me out by the pool. Even the basic school uniform is flattering on my figure. So yeah, on the outside—at least the visible parts—Vandy Hall is the kind of seventeen-year-old most girls want to be.

At least, I am until I walk.

There was a time during freshman and sophomore years that I used a cane, but I've gotten well enough to not need it. Even so, my limp is severe enough to draw stares. And if people could see past my normal exterior, and even further, past the stilted way I walk, all the way deep into the heart of me? It's ugliness, all the way down.

People somehow see it, regardless. I inspect my face in the mirror and try to find out how, but I don't really need to wonder. I'm not just the girl who survived the accident. I'm the girl with the scars. The girl with a secret. The quiet girl with the dead eyes who has to be treated ever-so-carefully.

"Vandy!" my brother shouts down the hall. "I'm leaving in five minutes! AIS or I'm leaving."

I roll my eyes at my own reflection.

AIS: *Ass In Seat.*

He'll do it, too. God forbid Emory miss the five minutes before the bell rings to ogle and flirt with girls on the quad before class starts. It's always been bad, but now that he's a senior, he's completely unbearable.

"I'm coming!" I yell, running my fingers through my hair one last time. Yes. Shiny hair, spotless face, and crisp uniform. Everything seemingly in order, I reach for the little pouch hidden in my jewelry box, pulling it open. I don't need to count, but I do anyway, like some kind of compulsion. Twenty-eight pills for fourteen days. Two per day. One in the morning, one at night. No more. No less.

Or at least, that's what I promise myself.

I'd spent all summer weaning myself to an acceptable amount of Oxycontin. Two pills isn't a problem—not when you've been through what I've been through. I swallow the small circular pill dry, then tuck the pouch back in the box, snapping the lid shut. I walk across the room, one leg refusing to function the same as the other, and grab my backpack, heavy with first-day essentials.

My mother waits in the kitchen, already dressed in her bright, camera-ready outfit. I know she has a big interview today—something to do with a collapsed multi-million-dollar utility project that has possibly been the front for some shady dealings. The thing about our mom being a big-time news reporter is that she's brushed fame a few too many times, but has never been able to really hold on to it. Instead, she has to constantly search for the next big scoop, hoping something juicy and significant will fall into her lap.

In many ways, I really respect that about her. My mom is the hardest-working parent I know who's also still involved in, like, *parenting.*

"I made your lunch!" She says as she closes the fridge. The stainless-steel door is covered in an enormous, post-it riddled, color-coded calendar. Every single activity has been micromanaged down to the minute, up to and including 'pick up lunch for the kids'. My mom cuts her eyes to the bag on the island. "Well, I *packed* your lunch. Spicy tuna roll, a little bit of rice, and that yogurt with the honey that you like."

"Thanks, Mom," I say, kissing her on the cheek. I take the bag and tuck it in my backpack. She leans over to help and I jerk around in a twist to prevent it. The horn blares from the garage, eliciting my groan.

"Your brother is anxious," she says, rolling her eyes as well. "You know how he gets."

"Oh, I know." I dig a fist into the small of my back, trying to reacquaint my spine with the weight of a backpack. "Now that Campbell's in college and they are 'keeping their options open'," I use finger quotes here, "he's on the prowl."

Mom's nose wrinkles. "Honey, don't talk about your brother like that. And Campbell is a sweet girl." She frowns as she says this, as if she could will it to be true.

"Uh huh."

Sometimes it's easier for my mom to live in a delusion than face reality, especially when it comes to my brother. Campbell Clarke is a bitch, through and through. She has my brother completely wrapped around her well-manicured finger. But if Mom looked beneath the surface of that choice, she'd have to acknowledge a lot of the other crap my brother does, and that would take the attention off me for a second. *God forbid.*

Preston Prep is everything to Emory. He'd been instantly accepted when he arrived as a freshman, his social status secured by his position on the football team and admittance into the quasi-legit fraternity, The Devils. He lived and breathed Preston Prep, the letterman jacket, and the older, more experienced girlfriend. He fully embraced the entitled, privileged attitude of the majority of our classmates.

He'd live in the dorms if he could—if he were allowed to. But there was no way my parents would allow *me* to live on campus, which meant there was no way he could live there either. Even for my parents, some tit-for-tats are just inevitable. Ultimately, that was probably a good decision. Last year, during Emory's junior and my sophomore year, the Devils outdid themselves, ultimately getting disbanded. The administration finally stepped in after a series of events that not only violated school policy, but brushed with illegal. To be honest, I wasn't paying much attention at the time. I spent my days trying to catch up on the schoolwork I fell behind on as a freshman, and my afternoons in physical therapy. I also spent the majority of time blissed out on painkillers, to the point that most of my classmates thought I was an idiot.

Or, so I learned over summer break. I'd been in the country club locker room when I overheard Amanda Brown ask Sydney if the accident had caused a brain injury. Apparently, she didn't remember me being *so slow.*

*Ouch.*

It was only through hushed talks between my parents and gossip at the swimming pool this summer that I learned what the Devils, including my brother, had really been up to for the last couple of years. None of it was necessarily good.

"I can't wait to hear about your first day tonight at dinner." Mom runs a hand through her hair, something she does when she's a little nervous. It's hard, sometimes, feeling all this bitterness toward her when she cares so much. She adds, "I'm making your favorite. Shrimp and grits."

I force a smile. "That sounds good." It seems a little much for the first day of junior year, but I've learned by now that if my mom wants to spoil me, the path of least resistance is to just let her.

The horn blasts again in the garage, and I roll my eyes, heading through the door.

"Finally," Emory says, as I climb into his truck. It's a beast. My parents only relented to getting it for him if he agreed to the lower running board so that I could step up to get into the cab. "I mean, what do you even do up there? It's not like you spend a bunch of time doing yourself up like the other girls."

*Double ouch.*

I scowl out the window. "You know Mom doesn't let me wear a lot of makeup." She also doesn't let me wear anything revealing, or go out with boys, or stay out past nine.

"Exactly," he replies, backing out of the garage and swinging the car around, "it shouldn't take you so long."

"My leg hurt this morning," I mutter, looking away. "I had to do some stretches."

"Oh." I notice how his fingers grip the steering wheel, his knuckles turning white. "Right, yeah." The 'sorry' is implied.

It's not totally a lie. My leg didn't hurt, but I did have to do stretches. I know from experience just how difficult it is going from a summer free of academics to suddenly having to haul books around on my back all day. The administration gives me plenty of time allowances to travel to and from my locker, but if I accepted all of them, I'd miss half of every class. Being stuck with back pain, a limp, and disfiguring scars the rest of my life was bad enough without throwing 'never graduated high school' into the mix.

Aside from that, I'd also been working on my newspaper proposal. Every year, Mr. Lee, the Chronicle sponsor, chose a student to do a deep dive for an investigative topic. This topic had to cover something current and gritty, something worthy of six months of focus, and something that was of interest to the Preston Prep community without actually offending anyone or making the school look bad.

I know people will assume I want to follow in my mother's foot-steps, and why wouldn't they? She's a moderately popular investigative journalist who's made quite a name for herself. But the reality is, I've seen what my mother does, and while she works hard and rails about things like justice and truth, her work is just a numbers game. The number of people who care, the number of viewers it can get, the number of ads they can run during the program, the number of dollars they can earn.

I don't want to follow in her footsteps.

I want to recreate them. The right way.

I'd been considering ideas all summer long and had finally settled on what I believe to be an amazing topic; the systematic classism and bigotry that has permeated a school like Preston Prep through the generations. I want to explore how that type of environment is a hotbed for racist and classist behavior—specifically the incidents leading to the Devils being disbanded. It's a tough topic, but one I think Mr. Lee, and the school at large, may finally be willing to address.

I keep my topic and the idea of proposing it to myself. This would be the kind of thing my family would cling to if I told them, feeding into their desperate hope that I'm doing more than just surviving. I don't want that kind of pressure.

I glance out the window as Emory drives past the McAllister house, next door. There's a black jeep in the driveway and it gives me a moment of pause. I wonder if Mr. McAllister got a new car. Seems a little juvenile for him, but he's been flirting with a mid-life crisis for years, part of which is likely courtesy of his delinquent son.

I shift uncomfortably, the pain in my back flaring, and divert my eyes. Although I don't like to think about Reyn, he's on my mind constantly. I can never forget that smile on his face as he held out his hand, daring me to go for a joyride with him. The way he confidently sat behind the wheel, peeling out of the parking lot. That moment, right before the world spun, with his wide eyes and locked jaw as he slammed on the brakes.

And, of course, I can never forget the last time I saw him—fighting through a wall of nurses, doctors, and emergency room security—pale-faced, covered in blood, eyes wild like a man possessed as he struggled to get to me. I still hear his screams in my nightmares, sometimes. *"What are you doing to her? Tell me what's fucking happening! Is she okay?"*

Emory cranks up the music as he drives the ten miles to school, and I let it drown out my thoughts. My brother and I don't talk much anymore. I don't blame him. The oxy made it easy for me to check out, and he's been focused on actually having a social life, unlike me. I know things kind of derailed for him when the Devils were disbanded. With most of the other guys—particularly Hamilton Bates—graduating last year, Emory had been in the position to take over the group. Even I had been stunned when Hamilton fell in love with his arch-nemesis, Gwendolyn Adams. The entire social ecosystem had been shattered. Emory no longer had a girlfriend, nor his group. He was understandably a little adrift.

*Welcome to my world.*

He turns into the Preston Prep parking lot, securing a spot in the senior section.

"Don't forget," he says, unbuckling his seat belt, "I have football practice."

I nod, gathering my bag. "I'm going to a meeting for the Chronicle, so I'll probably get out around the same time."

His nose wrinkles. I know he hates that I'm involved with "nerdy" stuff, but good grief, what does he expect me to do? It's not exactly like I can be an athlete or try out for the cheer squad with Syd.

"Okay." He commands, "Meet me out here when you're done."

Sydney's for me waiting at the edge of the parking lot. Her eyes are glued to her phone until she sees us walking over.

Well, until she sees *my brother*, which will always catch her attention.

"Heya, Em," she says, beaming at him. He gives her a quick nod and strides across the quad, unmoved by her batting eyelashes. Sydney turns to me, fanning herself with her phone. "If it's possible, I think your brother actually got cuter over the summer."

I grimace. "Hmm..."

Syd has had a crush on Emory since before we even got to Preston Prep. There's really no nice way to tell her that he's not interested, and frankly, he doesn't even like us being friends. But unlike him, I don't have a million people lining up to become my buddies, and sure, Sydney has issues, but she's also stuck by my side during everything. Even if it means I have to put up with a lot of her self-inflicted drama.

Speaking of, Syd's phone buzzes and she glances down. "Oh my god."

"What?" I ask, taking an awkward step over the curb.

"Fucking Caleb. He just texted me to say that *everyone* is talking about me."

"What now?" People 'talking' about Sydney is a common occurrence.

"Some insane rumor that I fucked two guys from North Ridge, *at the same time*, last weekend. As if." She laughs and shakes her head. "God, when are people going to stop being so interested in my sex life?"

I grip the straps on my backpack and don't reply to what is obviously a rhetorical question. Sydney's social life—her *sex* life—has been a constant source of gossip and fascination for years. She's either a slut, or a tease, or a sex goddess, or a virgin, at any given moment. I stopped keeping up years ago, and after the blow up with Skylar Adams, it seemed like maybe it would slow down, but nope. According to Syd, the rumors keep flying.

"Whatever," she mumbles, pushing her phone in her backpack. She turns to face me, her eyes searching my face. "How are you? You ready for this?"

Sydney is the one person who knows how much I've struggled the past few years. There's part of me that knows her interest in me is probably driven by a desire to be tragedy adjacent. But there's another part that's grateful to just have someone around. I haven't told her the truth about the painkillers—not exactly—but I have told her that I do have plans to get more involved this year. It all starts with the Chronicle.

I take a steeling breath, nodding. "I have my proposal ready."

"Awesome, I think you're going to kill it, and then next year you'll get to be editor-in-chief." I reluctantly accept her high-five.

We walk through the clusters of students and my eyes track them all. I see Emory and his jock friends, all in their letter jackets despite it still being hot outside. A few kids say hello before side-stepping to give me space. As we head down the sidewalk, I can't help but notice everyone taking great care to give me a wide berth. Their smiles are friendly, if distant. There's a twinge of pity on every face, and some people won't even meet my eyes.

I grab Sydney's arm to get her attention. "What's that all about?"

"What's *what* all about?" She's got her eye on Tyson Riggins, who is leaning against the brick wall by the main building. He's adorable, and if social media is accurate, very much already taken by a girl at another school.

"Everyone is looking at me," I explain, eyes warily taking in the students around me. "And they're all giving me room. I know I have the gimpy leg and all, but it's not like that's new."

"Uh," Syd says, looking around, "this is pretty much how people have always treated you. You were probably just too stoned to realize it."

I turn to her, mouth parted in surprise. "Seriously?"

*Wow.*

I'd known I was out of it. Almost all of my high school experience up to now can be described as just that—*high*. Months and months of sitting in the classroom, walking the halls, lost in a delicious fog of sweet nothingness, and this is probably only scratching the surface of things I've missed.

It's so much worse than I thought.

Before I can process this information any further, the bell in the tower tolls, signaling that we have five minutes to get to class. Syd gives me an apologetic smile and peels away, heading toward her homeroom. I do the same, taking the path toward the same homeroom I've had for three years now, but everything is different this year. My mind is clearer, like I can see things in a way I haven't in a long time. I run two rough palms over my cheeks, wanting more than anything to go back to my safe place, back to when I didn't realize how people looked at me. And the thing is, I could do it. I have enough meds stashed away in various hiding places in my room that I could probably medicate a small village. It would be so easy.

*No.*

The dead, nothing-eyed quiet girl isn't who I want to be anymore. I'd made a commitment to see this year through, clear-headed and decidedly *present*. For one reason or another, my life was spared that night.

It's time for me to start living it again.

# 2

Reyn

It's weird how things always look bigger in your memory.

For the first time in three years, I stand under the entrance arch to Preston Prep, and it seems strangely smaller than it had freshman year. Back then, the quad seemed fucking enormous. The halls felt infinite. The bell tower looked like a skyscraper. Sometimes I'd walk into this place and feel like it was indestructible, with its solid pillars and sharp steps.

Now, it all just looks like any other hunk of stone and mortar.

Like I could pull a hammer from my pocket and just start chipping this shit away, bit by bit, and watch it crumble.

The school is definitely old, but it's also a mixture of historic and new. From the ancient oak trees in the quad, to the stone bell tower, all the way to the shiny office furniture and state-of-the-art technology. Preston is two worlds merged into one. The end result is traditional, old-school elitism, combined with new world power. The students leave Preston with the ability to take over the world.

Now I have to see how, and *if*, I can fit back in.

I run my hand over the smooth mahogany railing as I climb the steps of the main building. I'm an hour early for my nine o' clock meeting with the headmaster, since I was already out of bed and doing pushups three hours ago. I was so sure my first morning back was going to be full of sleeping in, dicking off, and not doing drills for once, but it turns out to not be so easy. Nothing felt right or okay until I'd rolled out of bed, hit the floor, and started counting. There was a split second, right between my thirty and thirty-first pushup that I *almost* longed for the familiar feeling of some jackass instructor yelling down at me. I would have even gone for my old academy's customary sunrise run if Fucking Jerry, the captain of our gated community's security, hadn't parked his golf cart across the street and just sat there, waiting.

Jerry is the lovechild born of a slow-witted barbarian who fucked the very concept of spite. He's also a retired deputy police chief who's high as kite off his own little nugget of imagined power. Naturally, he's had it out for me since I drove through the gates. Messing with him would actually be a great time, if not for the fact that Fucking Jerry is a short fuse with ties to the local sheriff, and is also *stacked*. The guy could have me kissing pavement before I even had a chance to say 'dime-store police brutality'.

*Fucking Jerry.*

Since I still have some time to kill, I decide to reacclimate myself to Preston's hallowed halls. As I wander around, I get the same feeling of wrongness as I had trying to sleep in past five. Like someone should be watching me, telling me where to go, breathing down my neck, telling me I'm garbage. It's a crawling, slimy sort of feeling that gives me the impulse to stick close to the walls.

The main foyer of Preston Prep looks the same, with the wall of headmaster portraits looking down in stern-faced disapproval as I pass through. I note the steely eyes of Headmaster Hamilton—great-whatever of Hamilton Bates—and pause to raise a middle finger at his painting. In my brief stint as a freshman at this illustrious institution, Hamilton Bates had been only a year older than me, but was already the Prince of the Devils and Head Fuckboy by then.

I can only imagine how insufferable that sentient jerkoff got by his senior year.

I linger by the marble staircase leading to the second floor, trying to remember the layout, where the science wing is, the hall to the cafeteria, the restroom where I'd once drawn a crude stick figure on the red stall door. It's fucking stupid. It's been three years, but it feels like a lifetime ago.

I go straight instead, toward the main hall where large glass cases line the walls. They're filled with bragging rights I never had the chance to lay a claim to. Shiny gold trophies and mounted awards. Photos of championship-winning teams and distinguished alumni. The cases are big and flashy. Automatically, I try the door, testing the sliding glass with my fingers. It doesn't budge. Smart. Lock these valuable memories up tight. I duck down to check the lock and scoff.

I could have this shit open in three seconds flat.

I don't bother. My eyes skim for familiar names, people I knew from my freshman year here, before everything went to shit. Before the hospital. Before the three months of juvie. Before the years of Mountain Point Military Academy. I see the massive trophy from last year when the football team won State. There's a photo of the team minutes after the win, clustered together in celebration. If things had gone differently—I jab the tip of my forefinger into the glass—I'd be *right there*. Instead, I'd probably been scrubbing floors or doing drills until my arms felt like spaghetti.

The spike of envy is brief, feeble.

I shift away from football and move down the hall, perusing the various victories, hundreds of names and faces, people who have made their marks on this place. People who didn't fuck up and throw everything away. People who could still look at this building and think of it as big and scary and invincible, because they hadn't spent years at a military school that actually *was* all of those things.

It doesn't take long before I see Hamilton's name.

*State record holder in freestyle.*

*Beta Club President.*

*Class Salutatorian.*

I can't help my snide laugh, already imagining that fucker's reaction to *Class Salutatorian*. Just for the fun of it, I look to see who beat him for the title of Valedictorian. *Gwendolyn Adams. Ouch.* His well-known nemesis and, if the word on the street is to be believed, his current girlfriend. I snort spitefully, because even if he is getting a piece of that, I bet it still stings.

I wasn't here when shit went down with Skylar Adams at that party, but Emory and I keep in touch. In the summer, Mountain Point allows its students four weeks of supervised free time privilege. Mine were spent at the same football camp he attended. Aside from that, we were allowed our own phones and the occasional computer use—contingent on both behavior and performance—so we're in the same Discord gaming group.

He told me about Skylar because of our ties to the Devils, but when he explained how they were on a pretty short leash with the school at the time, all I felt was a hot surge of anger. *Pretty short leash?* There I was having my browsing history monitored, being woken up at five in the morning for drills, being told how much to eat, what to wear, when to go to bed, how to tie my shoes, how to make my bed, and this fucker was whining about a short leash? Try having some geriatric douchebag look over your shoulder while you piss in a cup for your monthly drug test, and then you can talk to me about a short fucking leash.

But apparently things imploded at Preston Prep, and now the Devils are completely defunct. Emory's pissed as hell about that, and maybe he's had it a lot better than me over the past few years, but I get it. He had the rank to take over Bates' position as leader this year.

Truth be told, I'm kind of relieved the Devils are finished. Better to not have the option at all than try to save face when I back out. That kind of thing is a slippery slope for a guy on probation. The more low-key I can keep it, the better off I'll be. Sliding back into the Devils wouldn't be a good move.

The rest of the awards case isn't that interesting; debate team photos, reading bowl winners, mathletes. Nerds, nerds, and more nerds. I unthinkingly pass the cheerleaders' showcase before hastily backing it on up.

One of the worst parts about the military academy was how much of a dick-fest it was. It was a sad state of affairs, three hundred some-odd teenage guys trying desperately to find ways around the academy's internet filter, just to get a taste of something even vaguely resembling porn. I'm not going to say I've jacked it to YouTube bikini try-on videos, but I won't say I *haven't*, either.

But *these*.

Fuck me, these are the real deal. I take in a few of the current classmates I'm looking forward to reacquainting myself with. Midriff. Cleavage. Legs. Shit, I'd almost forgotten how awesome a girl's thighs were. I want to drown myself in as much pussy as possible, but I won't front. I could legit fuck a girl's thighs right now and it might be the best sex I've ever had. That's how horrifically deprived I've been.

My eyes land on a familiar face. *Afton Cross*. I press my forehead against the glass as though that will get me a better look. *Yes, I'll take one of these, to go.* Huge rack, tiny little waist, long, tanned legs, and those *thighs*. Those are thighs I can imagine wrapped around my hips.

I shove a hand into my pocket to discreetly adjust a growing situation.

I take a furtive look around the hallway. Preston is nowhere close to resembling the ridiculous police state from whence I sprang, but you never know. Cameras are everywhere these days. Luckily, I don't see any, so I reach into my back pocket and retrieve the pin from my wallet. Crouching down, it takes almost no time at all to pick the lock. The photo is easy to remove from the frame and folds nicely, fitting right into the inside pocket of my jacket.

*Mine now.*

Setting everything to rights, I turn and head back toward the main door, aware that it's almost time to get to the headmaster's office. I'm halfway there when I stop abruptly, gaze caught on another photo. It's framed in a dark mahogany, sitting dead center in the case. A picture of a banquet. The engraved lettering at the bottom lauds student-athlete leaders in a rigid serif. In the photo, Emory is holding a plaque, posing happily with his parents, but that's not what makes my blood run cold.

It's the other person in the photo. Her hair is long and blonde, shiny. She's wearing a lazy grin and her eyes—eyes that I once thought of as a vast ocean of crystal blue—are unfocused and dull. Her hands are clasped behind her back, but her shoulders are sort of slumped, like maybe it's not the first photo that's been taken that night. I search her image carefully, for long moments, eventually hit with the realization of what I'm looking for.

Visible damage. Any sign of injury. Obvious scars.

I can't find any.

Maybe I hadn't completely broken Vandy Hall in the accident that night.

That's the only thing I'm thankful for.

It's a frail consolation. Even if she isn't horribly disfigured, it doesn't mean anything. Not really. I'd still hurt her. I know that. It's the shittiest, most unforgivable thing I've ever done. I've taken a lot of things in my life, but none more valuable than what I stole from her. I hurt myself, the stolen Porsche, our families, my friends...

But most of all, I'd hurt Vandy.

I'll never forget the way she looked on that gurney, bloody and frightened, as they loaded her into another ambulance. Later, at the hospital, they wouldn't let me see her. I don't even remember much from that night—all the sharp details lost in the haze of shock and desperation—but I remember running through the triage, so out of my mind from the adrenaline that my own injuries barely registered. I remember fighting, even though my wrist was fractured. I remember the look on her face when I finally found her, all strapped down, tubes and wires everywhere, the way her eyes were wide and wet and full of fear. I remember feeling like I could take every one of them down if it meant making that wild terror in her eyes go away—if it meant protecting her. Pretty ironic, seeing as how I was the reason she was there to begin with.

That was the last time I saw her.

I look at her again, trying to wash that bitter, gasoline-tinged memory away with this new image. The girl in the photo is older now, nothing like the awkward and gangly neighbor I used to know. She's grown up, no longer someone's kid sister. She's pretty much a woman now. Gorgeous, if I'm being honest.

It's a different look than Afton and the other hot cheerleaders. Vandy's beauty is all natural. She's wearing almost no make-up and has that same fresh, innocent face. Rosy cheeks. Flawless skin. Her smile is a little lopsided, her full lips furled to the side. She obviously came into her body, thin and curvy in all the right places. There's a hint of something going on underneath the conservative outfit, something just out of reach. *Ah.* There it is. The skirt that ends just above the knee, giving only the slightest peek at the creamy thighs beneath.

I jerk back, loudly clearing my throat.

*Jesus Christ, what is wrong with me?* Obviously, years of sexual deprivation have turned me into a fucking degenerate. That's the only excuse.

I shift my shoulders, feeling the tight pull of puckered scarring that covers most of my back. Guilt isn't something that usually comes naturally to me. I take what I want—get what I can. But what happened to Vandy was different. It was the one thing I'd never wanted to take. I pled guilty, because that's what I am. I didn't even fight when I was released from juvie only to be instantly sent away to Mountain Point. Point A to Point B. One prison for another. And I never expected to come back here.

But I guess shit changed when my mom left my dad for her personal trainer. I figured I'd just stay at the academy, but Dad called two weeks ago saying I had to come back home. My mom was taking him to the cleaners for his own 'indiscretions', and the legal bills were mounting. When he told me I was coming back to Preston Prep,

I was beyond reluctant. It would have been easier—more *just*—for me to remain at the academy. Not that military school was a bed of roses, but coming back to Preston? I don't deserve it, and neither does anyone else.

I'd outright asked him, *"What about the Halls?"*

He'd explained, *"I talked to Rob and Denise, and they understand our predicament. They're very forgiving people, Reyn. The biggest thing is that you follow the rules and don't give anyone a reason to question the second chance you're being given."*

I step back outside into the early fall air and think, *Here I am.* Deserving or not, I'm getting my second chance.

I have very little faith that I'm not going to blow it.

"I'll admit, when your father called me, I wasn't sure that your returning to Preston Prep was a good idea." Headmaster Collins sits behind a large desk, brass nameplate facing out. Next to that is a Devil's head, expertly cut into crystal. I drag my eyes away from it and see him nodding to the man behind him. "But Coach Morris came to your defense and said he's talked to your coach at Mountain Point. I'm told that you've done well there and have been an asset to their athletic program."

*Ah.* Of course.

Suddenly, everything clicks. Apparently, the Devils need a wide-receiver at the same time my father needs financial aid.

How auspicious.

Headmaster Collins continues, "That being said, I was still skeptical. In the past year, we've taken a hardline stance on inappropriate behavior at this school. We're zero tolerance on bullying and any kind of student harassment. I'll be honest, Reynolds, your history of pranks and petty theft do not fall into the current atmosphere of Preston Prep."

I blow out a hard breath. My dad had made this sound like a done deal. "So, what am I doing here, then?" I tap a rapid rhythm on the arm of the chair. "I can't take any of it back, and I think an apology would get some pretty bad mileage." After a beat, I tack on a habitual, "*Sir.*"

"Stealing that car was bad enough, but when you took that girl with you, it became very clear you were not only a risk to yourself, but other students, as well."

I do nothing but nod, even though I'm absolutely boiling inside. I don't have anything to prove to this guy. What's he looking for? Does he want me to prostrate myself before him? There are, at maximum, ten people who deserve to see that.

This dude isn't one of them.

Collins leans back, his large frame making the chair creak. "*But,* the Halls are a very generous, *very forgiving* family. It is only because of them and your record at Mountain Point that we're allowing you back on this campus on a probationary status."

*And because of the football season,* I want to add.

I don't.

"I understand, sir." My words are rehearsed and spoken a smidge too flatly to pass my own muster, "My behavior freshman year was unacceptable. I've had a lot of time to reflect on the choices I made that day and the severe consequences of such a short-sighted, irresponsible act." I dare a look at Coach Morris. "It would be an honor, not just to be readmitted to Preston Prep, but to also earn a spot on the team."

Some of the tension in the headmaster's face eases as I give my speech of contrition.

God, I had this idiot pegged.

Prostration, it is.

Coach Morris takes the opportunity to chime in. "I saw you during the regional game. You've got a lot of talent, son. Your biggest obstacle will be figuring out how to not squander it."

While the coach drones on about expectations for the upcoming season and repeating the championship, the ball of tension in my stomach slowly starts to uncoil. I can handle these guys. They're soft and malleable, nothing like the hardened, severe staff at the academy.

These guys sit up here in their ivory tower and think they can control student behavior with shit like 'difficult talks' and academic probation.

I bet I could have them eating out of my hand by next semester.

I find my eyes drawn back to the crystal devil, and my knee starts bouncing. It's about the size of a baseball and would fit perfectly in my—

"With that, we'd like to welcome you back to Preston Prep, Mr. McAllister." The tall man stands up and I snap to my feet—at attention—a touch too instinctively. I'd think I should really see about shaking these habits, but I can see from the satisfied gleam in the Headmaster's eye that he likes it. I shake the hand jutting toward me. His grip is firm, and I match it with a strong shake in return. "Mrs. Abernathy will get your schedule together and give you any other information you need to matriculate for your senior year."

"Yes, sir," I say, just to see the spark of sick approval in his eyes. *Easy.* "I appreciate you giving me a second chance, and I'm eager to get involved here, in whatever capacity you need me."

The nod he gives me makes it clear I've been dismissed, but when I reach the door, he calls out my name.

"Reynolds…one last thing."

I stop just short of doing an authentic about-face. Don't want to ham it up too much. "Yes, sir?"

"It goes without saying, but Vandy Hall?"

I feel my face shutter, something deep in the pit of my chest withering up at the way he looks at me.

"You do not speak to her, you do not look at her, you do not breathe anywhere in her general vicinity." A deep line forms between his eyes. "That poor girl has been through enough and she seems to finally be getting better. Just because her family has agreed to let you attend Preston Prep does not mean you can disrupt her world."

The words land like a punch in the gut. "Yes, sir. I have no problem with that." Except for the fact she lives next door and is my best friend's sister. That's not a goddamned landmine or anything. Even though my next words are spoken with the same fake deferential tone, they're no less sincere. "The last thing I want is to cause Vandy any more pain."

"Good."

The next moment finds me standing in the outer office, dismissed, trying fervently to stop my hands from shaking. I bury them in my pockets and take a series of deep, controlled breaths.

Mrs. Abernathy, the registrar, doesn't notice my discomfort. She types something into the computer and says, "I've got you all lined up, Reynolds. Let me just go get the copy of your new schedule."

I'm still rattled when she walks to the adjacent room, leaving me alone. I look around, searching her desk. Not much there except papers, a cup of pens, a souvenir figurine, a keyboard, mousepad, parking pass, and folders.

I look at it for a long time, hands fisting where they're buried in my pockets. No one is around. I inch forward, and reach out, the tips of my fingers gliding across the smooth surface of the desk. I pluck the figurine from its perch in front of her monitor—a jubilant Mickey Mouse—the rush of adrenaline swallowing the itch of discomfort from my meeting with Collins.

It's in my pocket only a split second before she returns.

*Mine now.*

"Here you go," Mrs. Abernathy says, strolling back in the room. "All set for you to start tomorrow. Do you have any questions?"

She holds out the file folder I'd brought to her with my school records. My schedule is on top. "I should be able to manage, but you'll be the first one I come to if I have any questions."

"Any time, honey."

I flash her an appreciative smile before walking out of the office and heading back into the empty halls of the school. The administration here is going to watch my every move—or at least, they think they will. It'd be a heavy weight on my shoulders, except that I know what having your every move watched is actually like. This won't be a cakewalk, but if I can curb my impulses until graduation, I can handle it. Probably.

I stuff my hand into my pocket, feeling the smooth ceramic figurine. Okay, maybe curbing my impulses will be a bit of a challenge.

And I'll have to keep my grades up while also working overtime to make sure I produce on the field. And I'll have to tiptoe around Vandy Hall.

Who am I fucking kidding?

I'll be lucky to make it to the end of the season before getting kicked out of here for good.

# 3

VANDY

"AS YOU CAN SEE, my proposal is to do a deep dive into some of the fallacies of the private school system, particularly the lack of diversity at Preston Prep." I take a deep breath. "As you know, a long-standing social club was disbanded last winter after a cover-up of illegal behavior, vandalizing school property, and bullying a member of the school community. The bullied person is black and identifies as genderfluid, making him a sitting target at a school that had previously ignored such behavior. I thought an investigation into why the school finally felt now was the right time to shut down the

Devils, and if that action will really make a difference if the school itself has or hasn't made any changes in welcoming diverse students."

I finish in a rush and my heart hammers in my chest, like I've just run a race. It's a bit strange, actually feeling things again. Without the pain pills, every emotion feels sharper and unused, clumsily rushing into all my cracks. I know the topic is risky. It's calling out the school on a long-held weak spot, but when the headmaster took action against the Devils, and Hamilton Bates made it clear he was finished with the group, it showed that maybe, *finally*, it was time for change.

With his elbow resting on the desk and his forefinger tapping on his chin, I wait for Mr. Lee to react to my story idea.

"It's an interesting concept, Vandy."

I breathe, shoulders losing some of that tight tension. "Thank you."

He pauses for a moment, seeming to choose his words. "You don't worry about this sort of topic coming from—well, to put it as delicately as possible—someone who's the exact opposite of a target for discrimination here?"

I raise an eyebrow. "You mean, because I'm white and cis and straight."

He makes a complicated head bob. "For starters. You also come from a wealthy family, particularly one that has significant influence in the world of journalism. You see where I'm going with this."

I only just barely stop my jaw from dropping. "Mr. Lee," I begin, battling down a bitter laugh. "First of all, I'm not able-bodied. Second of all, I'm not a guy. I'm not sure if you've been watching lately, but being a female student at this school can be actual hell." I level him with a look, and I don't need to say any names, but I could. The Adams girls. The Playthings. Even Sydney. "That said, you're absolutely right. Despite my adversity, I am incredibly privileged, which puts me in a position to put voice to these issues without fearing for my own security. So, to answer your question, no. I don't worry."

He nods, sighing. "You're not wrong about that, I suppose." His lips form a thin line. "The problem is, I'm just not sure it's the right...*tone*...for the Chronicle this year."

I frown. "What do you mean?"

He exhales and shifts in his seat. "What happened last spring was a wake-up call for the administration. As you know, it was a controversial move. The Devils were a long-standing tradition at the school and there were definitely some alumni who were not happy with the decision. Some patrons have even gone so far as refusing to support the school once the decision was made."

"You're kidding." I blink, processing that information. "Well, that just makes me think this is an even more relevant topic than before."

"I understand that point of view—and frankly, don't disagree with it, but..."

"But what?" I demand. "What is the problem?"

"The problem is that the administration wants topics like this to go away, not to be dragged through the school paper. They want the alumni happy. The donors content. Their endowment secure. They want a year without a scandal, or at least without a scandal being dredged back up."

I swallow, feeling gut punched. *Numbers game.* "So, you're saying you don't want a real investigative story." I smile tightly. "You want a fluff piece."

"What I want," he gently explains, "is for twenty students from unprivileged backgrounds to receive a scholarship here next year, just like they always do. That can't happen if donors keep pulling their funding. I know this must seem like a great injustice, but tell me. What's the best way of helping them? Because make no mistake, these are real kids we're talking about. They're more than just a story or a feather in the cap of your college application letters."

I bristle. "I don't think—"

He holds up a hand. "I didn't mean to imply you felt that way, I just want to be clear about where our priorities are. It's a good idea, Vandy. But it's just not something I can approve right now. In an institution like Preston, change must come slowly and quietly. I realize that must be difficult to hear." He pushes his glasses up his nose, smiling wistfully. "I was quite the activist in my day, too."

I carefully ease myself from the chair without even replying, gathering my things to leave.

Before I can, he says, "Miss Hall, you must know from your mother's work how these things go. Journalism is tricky. We have a duty to cover the facts, to give voice to injustice. But we also have to perform those duties responsibly, in a way that won't harm people who are already vulnerable. Do you understand?"

I swallow around the lump in my throat, managing a tight nod, and I know I should say something professional, like 'thanks for listening', or 'I'll try again later'. But I limp as quickly from the office as I can before the hot prick in my eyes turn to fat, angry tears. I'd waited an hour to present my idea, sitting behind three other students who were also competing for the piece. Had he rejected theirs too?

I cross the parking lot toward Emory's truck, thankful that the campus is empty enough that no one is around to see me. I'd spent the last three weeks of the summer working on the idea and in a few short minutes, my goal for the year—my motivation—is gone.

Just like that.

I unlock the truck and I'm so frustrated and unstable that it takes me three tries to climb inside. I stomp on the running board when I do, as if it were actually capable of feeling my wrath. Thankfully, Emory isn't here yet. I know him. He'd see me upset and get absolutely furious. He'd probably demand that I go back inside and try again—or worse, *he'd* go back inside and force Mr. Lee to reconsider. That's why I've been keeping this to myself. It's well known that everyone at school babies me. From the lunch lady giving me extra dessert, to my teachers allowing tardies or weak excuses for missing classes, everyone folds for me. That may be one reason I'm in such shock that Mr. Lee said no. Basically no one at Preston Prep says no to me.

Damn, it hurts.

The more I think about it, the angrier I get. This is what I get for trying something new, for weaning off the meds. The sharp sting of disappointment isn't something I'm used to feeling so acutely anymore. I run my hands up and down my legs, growing more and more agitated. The back of my teeth are clenched, grinding, and I'm distantly aware that part of this is the ever-present wane and ebb of withdrawal. I can't tell where one ends and the other begins, and it was supposed to be easy by now. I was supposed to be *okay.*

I don't even notice Emory walking across the parking lot. I jump in surprise at the loud clang of him tossing his equipment in the bed of the truck. I hurriedly swat my tears away, straightening my skirt and allowing myself one final, long sniffle.

He opens the door, and my nose is instantly assaulted by the sweaty stench of his practice clothes. My eyes prick again, this time from the odor. "God, you reek," I say, rolling down the window.

Hair all plastered to his sweaty forehead, he grunts in acknowledgment. "Yeah, you'd smell bad too if you'd just run twenty suicides." The instant the words come out of his mouth, his face pales, and it takes me a second to even realize why.

Vandy Hall can't run. She's lucky she can even walk.

"Fuck, Van." I can see the guilt in his eyes, even through my periphery. "I didn't mean—I'm sorr—"

"Stop," I say, shaking my head. "You know you don't have to apologize for saying normal stuff. That's...that's bullshit, okay? It's worse." I meet his gaze, willing him to see that I'm fine. "It's worse when you feel sorry for me."

He looks away, fidgeting with his keys as he puts them in the ignition, and I know he's looking for the right thing to say.

I get my sunglasses from the glove box and recline back in my seat. "Although, you're wrong about one thing."

He raises an eyebrow. "What's that?"

"If I'd just run twenty suicides," I slip on the sunglasses, flipping my hair over a shoulder, "I'd still smell like sunshine and rainbows."

His eyes crinkle when he laughs. "Knowing you, you probably would."

With the tension cut, he backs out of the parking lot. I try really hard not to get mad at Emory, even when he's doing dumb stuff like dating Campbell and getting caught up in Devil nonsense. He's just a really good brother. He's stuck by me this whole time, even after his best friend got sent away and I became the object of the school's pity.

Emory might pity me, too, but it's a different kind. Emory *hurts* when I hurt. It's another reason I'd wanted to get the newspaper position; I'd wanted to prove to him that I'll be okay next year on my own.

I calm down on the way home, the two of us talking about the first day at school. He has Dr. Ross, a notorious hard-ass. We both foresee him getting many detentions in the future. I have Art with Mr. Kent, which earns his side-eye. Kent is young, handsome, and by the intel gleaned from Sydney's social media stalking, *very* single.

"What about Campbell?" I ask, diverting the conversation. "Have you heard from her?"

"According to ChattySnap, she's having the time of her life at UVA." He shrugs, like he doesn't care, but I know better. I don't understand what he sees in Campbell. She doesn't treat him right. He should just drop her altogether, and her going to college seemed like the perfect opportunity.

"You should stop following her on there," I say instead, watching Emory lean out the window to punch in our code. Seconds later, the gate to our neighborhood opens. "It'll just make you crazy."

He gives me a smug grin, settling back into his seat. "I could, but then how will she see that I've got a date with Aubrey Willis on Friday night?"

I shake my head. "That sounds like nothing but a heaping pot of drama and heartbreak."

To be honest, I'm not sure how much Emory thinks with his heart. I'm pretty sure most of his emotions are ruled by another part of his body. Spoiler alert: not his brain, either.

Emory turns down our street, passing the other large homes in the neighborhood. The community is pretty idyllic, with tree-lined streets and wide sidewalks. The lots are big, with many houses, including ours, facing the lake.

Up ahead, there seems to be some commotion, however. The security cart with its rotating amber lights is stopped in the middle of the street. It appears that Jerry has someone apprehended, a man pressed up against the side of the vehicle, hands resting on the roof.

"Stress in the city!" Emory whistles. "Got us some serious piggy po-po action up here."

Emory and I both crane our necks as his truck crawls past. Jerry seems to be frisking whoever it is—a jogger, by the looks of his clothing—and the man has his head bowed as he stands akimbo, seeming to tolerate it all patiently.

Just as we pass, the man raises his head, his green eyes staring right through the truck.

"Holy shit," Emory says, foot stomping down hard on the brakes. My body lurches forward, and his arm flings out protectively, catching me.

Reynolds.

Brakes.

The screech of tires.

The world turning upside down, car flipping, the crunch of metal and glass, the heat of fire, the smell of gasoline, the rough scrape of asphalt as I slide and tumble, rolling—

Emory whips his head around to ask, "You okay?" and for a long moment, I can't breathe.

It's fine. Just a short brake. The truck is fine. I'm fine. Emory is fine. Reynolds is—

He's *right there*, pressed up against the security cart, green eyes staring emotionlessly forward as Jerry pats him down.

"Vandy!" Emory shakes my shoulder, eyes searching. "Hey, did I freak you out? I'm sorry, I just saw—I wasn't thinking."

"I'm fine." I don't even recognize the sound of my own voice.

Emory watches me for a moment, unbuckling his seatbelt. Whatever he's looking for, he must find it, because he gets out of the truck. He leaves his door wide open, showering the cabin in a rapid-fire series of *ding-ding-ding*s.

"Dude!" he says to Reynolds, face splitting into a wide smile when their eyes finally meet. "What the fuck? I can't believe you're back!"

"Yeah, you know what I was thinking?" Reynolds' mouth curls into a bitter grin, fingers tapping the roof of the cart. "I was thinking it's been a real long time since *Fucking Jerry* here has had my 'nads in his hand, so here I am." His stare is still flat, even when the corners of his eyes crinkle, squinting against the afternoon sunlight. "Home sweet home."

Emory clucks his tongue. "Come on, Jerry, this is just Reynolds."

Jerry walks around the cart, pointing his big Maglite at Emory. "Get in my way, it'll be you next." To Reynolds, he says, "We ain't through, boy. I got ten hours a day, right here, just waiting for ya. Want you to remember that."

"Sounds like a pretty shit life, but okay." Reynolds gives him a lazy look over the roof of the cart. "Am I free to go, *officer*?"

"Don't be giving me none of your damn lip, either, boy." Jerry drops into the seat, cart shaking as he pushes his dark Aviators up his nose. "Got the Sheriff on speed dial, and he's just dying to repay me a favor or three." Jerry drives off before Reynolds even steps away from the cart, hands stuttering against the roof as it zooms away.

"God, that guy's a prick," Emory mutters. They both watch Jerry's cart veer around the corner before Emory darts forward, slamming into Reynolds in a halfhearted tackle. "Dude! Holy shit! When did you get home?"

"Last night," he says, wrapping his arms around Emory in a tight hug. Over my brother's shoulder, he finally looks at me. From the way his eyes go shuttered, face paling, it's the first time he's even noticed me here. I can't even imagine how I look—wide-eyed and struck so frozen that it's hard to even pull in a breath.

Our gazes lock for a long, suspended moment. Even after Emory steps back, asking Reynolds something about school, we don't look away.

It'd be silly to call what passes between us, in that moment, understanding. Really, I don't understand anything. I don't understand the way my chest feels like it's collapsing in on itself, and I don't understand the way he stands rigid like that, like the barest twitch may shatter something. No, it's not understanding. But it's something.

Something only we share, that only we can know.

Reynolds looks away first, telling Emory, "I registered for school today. I'll be there tomorrow." His voice is flat and stilted.

"Fuck, man, this is going to be so—" Emory stops abruptly. Suddenly, it's like my brother remembers where we are, who he's talking to, and the fact I'm a few feet away. His eyes dart to mine and his face falls. "Hey, we'll catch up later, okay?"

"I'll be around." Reynolds looks away, gaze dropping. "Gotta keep Fucking Jerry busy somehow."

Emory gets back in the truck, slamming the heavy door. I'm still frozen in the passenger seat, reeling from what just happened. We don't speak, the cabin of the truck thick with a heavy, tense silence. He swings the car into the driveway and pulls it into the garage.

Before he reopens the door, I ask, "Did you know?"

Emory sighs, gaze dropping to the keys in his hand. "Vandy, look—"

It's enough. If he knew, odds are my parents knew, and if he'd been at the school, they knew, too.

Reynolds McAllister, the boy who broke me, is finally back.

And no one had the guts to tell me about it.

I STORM AS FAST as my defective leg will take me into the house, carelessly tossing my backpack on the kitchen table. Conveniently, both of my parents are standing near the island. Dad is still in his blue scrubs from the hospital. My mother looks up and obliviously asks, "Hey honey, how was the first day of—"

"When were you going to tell me?" I hate the way it comes out. Not angry, despite the way I feel. It comes out small and wounded.

My mother blinks and glances at my father, her expression confused. "Tell you—"

"She saw Reyn," Emory says from the garage door.

"Ah," my mother starts, but touches her neck, like she's trying to force more words to come. They don't.

"We were going to tell you tonight at dinner," Dad says carefully.

"So you all knew." I hug my middle, chest constricting with a tidal wave of something that's too big to be contained. I look at my brother. "Exactly how long have you been keeping this from me?"

"For a few weeks." Dad grimaces and the glint of guilt in his eye is almost enough to forgive this. *Almost.* "Warren came over and explained the circumstances surrounding the need for Reynolds' return. You know we've kept a friendly relationship with the McAllister's for years now. And it's just..." Dad sighs. "Well, it's seemed like you've been doing so much better."

I try desperately to swallow around the lump of betrayal lodged in my throat. "None of that explains why no one told me about it."

Mom circles around the island. "We wanted you to have a great first day of school, and we wanted to make sure Reyn was actually going to come home and enroll before saddling you with it all. There were a few things still up in the air about his re-enrollment."

"You were wrong." The tears finally fall, leaving hot tracks down my face. "You should have given me the chance to prepare myself for—"

My mom walks up and rests her hand on my shoulder. I jerk away. "Tell me what you're feeling? Are you only upset with us or are you worried about being back at school with Reyn? Do you need to talk to Dr. Cordell?"

My therapist. *Jesus.* "God, *no*. I'm just..." I'm holding in a sob. I press a hand into my chest, the thumping vibration of my heart so hard and fast that it feels like I've run a mile.

Dad coaxes, "What? Surprised? Annoyed? Freaked?"

"I'm sick!" I wail, grabbing the fabric covering my chest into a tight fist. "I'm sick of you not telling me stuff, I'm sick of being trapped here all the time, and I'm sick of you asking me how I feel and then never *fucking* listening!"

"Vandy Emilia Hall!" my mom shouts, eyes wide with shock. I've never once cussed in front of them before. Even Emory is gaping at me. "That language is unacceptable!"

I fling my arms out, helpless. "I'm sorry to inconvenience you with the feelings that you specifically *fucking* asked for."

My mom's eyes flash in anger. "One more time, Vandy, so help me..."

"What?" My laugh comes out slightly maniacal. "Are you going to ground me? That'll be rich. Maybe I won't be able to leave the house, or have friends, or talk to boys, or go to parties, or wear make-up. Oh, my mistake. Can't ground me from something you've never allowed me to have."

"Hey!" My dad steps forward, brows pulled together in anger. "That's enough. Maybe we made the wrong move not telling you about Reynolds, but you talk to us like the adult you want to be treated as. Apologize to your mother."

My ribs feel like they're strangling my lungs, and I can't even properly appreciate the irony in my parents wanting me to act like an adult when they treat me like a child.

I say, "I'm sorry," because I have to get away. "If you'd told me, then I could have—I could have just—"

It doesn't matter.

Emory's stricken eyes watch as I pass him, hobbling my way up the stairs.

What I want to say is that, if I'd known, I could have found out who to *be* around Reynolds McAllister. The last time I saw him I was whole, body and soul. I'm not that person now. I'm just this mangled, nervous mess of wanting and not-having. I'm the shattered glass and the crushed metal. I'm the long expanse of asphalt and the pungent spatter of gasoline. I should have had time to become something more than the meager sum of that night's parts. Because that's the kind of person who could have seen Reynolds and not felt like a broken thirteen-year-old all over again. That person could have been brave. Fearless.

That's obviously never going to be in the cards for me.

My blaze of glory would probably be a lot more effective if I could run, kick, or stomp my feet. Instead, I drag my defective leg behind me and do the best I can. I do manage a wall-rattling, vengeful door slam when I get to the room.

It doesn't help the way my lungs feel like they're being crushed. I just can't *breathe*. I keep gulping in air, but it's like everything is constricting me—my shirt, my skin, my bones. I frantically unbutton my shirt, no longer pressed and fresh like it'd been this morning, but eventually just grab the two sides and rip it open, flinging it away. I kick off my loafers and peel off the stupid knee-high socks that are required as part of the school uniform, despite the fact it's still in the eighties outside. Then I shimmy out of the uncomfortable wool skirt, stepping out of it bunched on the floor.

Crossing the room, I walk over to the bedside table, illuminated brightly from a ray of sunshine coming through the arched window beside it, and open the drawer. Inside is a tiny ring box. It's only one of many boxes hidden around this room that are filled with pills. I know I don't even need them anymore. Well, no more than the rationed allotment in the bathroom, just to get me by on a physical dependence level. But I like to know they're there, especially on a day like today. It's comforting just knowing. If things get bad enough—if I just can't take it anymore—then relief is only forty minutes away.

It helps.

I look at them and that overwhelming feeling of being crushed slowly starts to abate. I gasp in a short breath and release it slowly, counting them out in my head, palm pressed to my chest, feeling the choppy rise and fall.

*This is life*, I tell myself. This breath, this heartbeat, this is me being alive. I chant it like an affirmation inside my head, each exhale taking with it that debilitating panic until I finally stand there, drained and aching.

I trail my fingers over the uneven skin that slashes from just below my belly button around to my lower back. It's thick and gnarled, and the skin surrounding it is strangely numb. I turn my face to the ray of sunshine, eyes closed as I soak it in, exhausted and worn. Instantly, the guilt sets in. I should apologize to my mom and dad, to Emory. They don't know. They don't understand what it's like for me, weaning myself from the medication. That's all.

I open my eyes and Reynolds McAllister stands opposite of me.

He's still sweaty from his run, staring across the empty space between our houses from his own bedroom window—the one that's been dark for three years. His green eyes hold mine, and he's just as still and rigid as he was before, out in the street. It's different this time, nothing of significance passing between us, just a flat, cold stare.

It's not until his eyes drop that it comes to me in a rush that I'm half-dressed and staring at the boy responsible for all of this.

It should feel like a violation—like one more thing he's taking from me. Instead, it feels weirdly necessary.

*Yes,* look.

*Look what you did.*

He raises his gaze back to mine and I want to feel satisfied. I want to spread my face with a malicious grin. I want to break him as much as he'd broken me.

I reach for my curtain and let it fall, his haunted eyes disappearing with the light.

REYN IS the one who rolls down the windows. "It's better when you can feel the wind whipping around, you know?"

His face is bright, lit with the rush of stealing the car, illuminated in the soft light of the dashboard. My long hair whips across my eyes and my heart pounds like a jackhammer. For the first time, I get why they do this.

It's wild, crazy, *fun.*

His hand rests so casually on the gearshift that you'd think he's had years of experience driving a car, not that he's just a fourteen-year-old without a license. I'm envious of that confidence. Where does it come from? How can I get it? My hands twist in my lap, and I look out the window at the landscape rushing by.

"I knew it," he says suddenly, raising his voice over the loud rush of wind.

I glance at him, the swooping bangs of his copper hair blowing wild. "Knew what?"

"That you were cool, Baby V." He spares me a glance, cheeks dimpling with a grin. "That you were one of us."

He releases the gear shift and slides his hand down my forearm until our hands link together like pieces of a puzzle. He makes the move look so easy and nonchalant, but my stomach is bombarded with a stampeding burst of butterflies. Reynolds McAllister is holding my hand!

*Oh my god,* I can't wait to tell Sydney.

Reyn drives the car one-handed, coasting down the long road that leads back to town. It's a dark and rural, at one end of the lake. The Club is way out on a big piece of property. Out the window, I see a flash of light in the grassy fields lining the road. Fireflies, I think. But then, I realize it's something else. My stomach lurches and I sit up, twisting my hand from his. "Watch out! There's a—" I start, but it's too late. The next moment is a flash of pale brown fur, the squeal of tires, Reynolds fighting against the wheel. I throw my hands up, a scream bursting—

I bolt up, gasping for air, and instinctively look next to me.

There's nothing and no one there—just the empty side of my bed.

"Jesus," I gasp, hand shaking as I check the time on my phone; 2:47. Rubbing my clammy face, I try to shake the nightmare. The *reoccurring* nightmare. Or well, mostly. It's been a long time since I've dreamed it as it happened. Usually, it's off a bit. Sometimes I'm the one driving. Other times, Reynolds is next to me, and he's already bloodied up, mouth curling into a sick, malevolent smile. I haven't had the real memory in so long, that sometimes I worry I've lost the pieces, like they just dissolved inside my brain at some point.

I've fought the nightmares off for a long time, mostly with the meds, but now that I've cut back, they've returned with an unholy vengeance.

Without turning on the light, I ease out of bed. I learned a long time ago not to let anyone in the house know about my nightmares or insomnia. Mom can't stand thinking I'm alone and suffering. A thin coat of sweat makes my pajamas cling to my body and I take them off, dropping them to the floor and grabbing another pair out of my dresser. Once I've changed, I see the light coming from the house next door and push aside the curtain to take a peek.

The light is faint, coming from a lamp that's out of sight. All I can see from here are Reynolds' bare legs, stretched out on his bed with a book open on his stomach. His face is out of view, so I'm able to watch him for a moment, wondering what keeps him up at night. Is it the same nightmare that I have? Or is it guilt?

Whatever it is, I think, dropping the curtain and heading back to bed, there's a bit of satisfaction knowing that he can't sleep either.

# 4

STARTING BACK at Preston Prep is an avalanche of overload. It was only a few mornings ago that I was living the Mountain Point life, and now all of a sudden, there are all these *things*. Decisions, for one. What to eat. When to sleep. When to wake up. What to do. What to study. School and football give me plenty of structure, but even the structured time here is unstructured as hell. I keep finding myself paralyzed in the face of it all, as if a choice between writing the date above or below my name on my AP Lit report is some life-altering decision.

I tap the pen against my notebook, casting my gaze around to see what everyone else is doing.

"What was up with that Vandy girl's freakout in Art earlier?" The guy behind me whispers to his neighbor. "I straight-up thought she was about to *cry*."

His neighbor lowers her voice when she replies, "Well I can't believe Mr. Kent took it. It's just lipstick, give me a break."

"Do you think it's because of that dude being back? The new guy? I heard he kidnapped her or something, and that's why she's so—"

I spin around. George Whoeverthefuck, the gangly, pimple-ridden fucker behind me, is using a folder to hide his flapping mouth from the teacher. I snatch it from his hand and fling it down the aisle. "My name is Reynolds. Now shut the fuck up."

I can practically feel him gaping at the back of my head as I jot the date down in the opposite corner of my name. Who cares, anyway. This isn't Mountain Point; I'm not going to be doing ten push-ups because I put the date in the wrong place.

I hear George get up from his seat, and then watch from my periphery as he slumps across the room to retrieve his folder, face all pinched and sour as he returns.

*Try me, bitch.*

The remainder of class is spent in a blissful, George-free silence, which is good, because it takes me half of it to decide whether or not I should use the back side of the paper, or just get a new sheet. It'd be hilarious if I weren't so close to pulling my own hair out in frustration. Academically, Mountain Point was pretty competitive, which basically means I already covered most of this shit junior year. This should be a cakewalk, not a clusterfuck of indecision.

It's easier on the field. Coach tells me where to go and what to do. I'm in my element there, physically excelling at every practice. All those mornings of mandatory runs and constant training make it impossible for anyone to question my last-minute addition to the team. I can already see the gleam in the other guys' eyes, like they all know between me and the core team they already had, we're definitely going to make it to State this year.

I stick around when class ends, feeling flustered and pissed off when I drop the three sheets of paper onto the teacher's desk. "I didn't know which way to do it."

She picks up the pages, frowning in confusion. "You did the assignment twice?"

Once with writing on both sides of the paper, and again using the fronts of two sheets.

I chew out a terse, "Yes." For the record, I don't need her to look at me like that. I know it's stupid. Better to do something stupid than spend an hour agonizing about it, though.

"Okay," she says slowly, swivelling in her chair to tuck it all into the pile.

While her back's turned, I bend over her desk to swipe her personalized stationary pad in all its hideous pink glory. I tuck it into my pocket—*Mine now*—and am already halfway out the door before she turns around.

In the hall, I stop at my locker, pulling the pad from my pocket and writing a quick missive. I tear off the top sheet and leave the rest inside. That could come in handy someday.

Minutes later, I discover Mr. Kent is the easiest mark yet. "Yeah, I've got some extra colored pencils." He heads into a closet at the back of the room, raising his voice. "Are you all doing another book cover project?"

I nod as I rifle through his drawers. "Yep. It's uh—" Pens, highlighters, soy sauce, napkins, beads. "It's Fitzgerald."

"I hope you're doing some art deco!"

I open his bottom drawer, and there it is; a tube of lipstick.

*Mine now*.

"Here you are." Mr. Kent hands me three boxes of unlovingly used colored pencils. "You can just tell her to hold on to them."

I toss a lazy wave over my shoulder as I leave. "Sure thing."

I wait until I turn down the east hall to chuck the pencils into the nearest trash can.

My eyes jump back and forth between the macaroni and the mashed potatoes. They're both perfectly sufficient carbs. Although, the macaroni has more protein. On the other hand, potatoes have more vitamins. But who knows what kind of potatoes these are. They're probably bullshit rehydrated flakes. Does that make potatoes less nutritious? Does the macaroni even have real cheese?

I swipe a bead of sweat from my forehead. I wonder if it's just me, or if the lights in the lunch line are roughly the same temperature as the surface of the sun. Someone behind me in line exhales loudly and the sounds of their shifting feet distract me, breaking my internal debate. Now, I'll have to start all over. *Fuck.*

Thankfully, the decision is taken out of my hands when the lunch lady picks up a serving of each and dumps both on my tray. The ball of tension that's been rapidly growing between my shoulderblades suddenly releases.

I nod, muttering a thanks as I leave the line.

The person behind me huffs, "Finally," and someone else says, "Oh shit, that's the guy?" and someone else says, "Yeah, I think I remember him from before."

I'm not a fan of being the object of whispered talk in the hallways. In the classrooms. In the lunch line. In the seat *directly behind me*. It's hard to know what's basic 'new kid' chatter and what's gossip about what I've done and where I've been. At least having Emory by my side makes it easier. He might not be leading the Devils, but you wouldn't know it going by the way he's treated here.

It becomes obvious pretty quickly that scandals don't carry huge weight at a school like Preston. Wealth and access make it so that parents can get their kid out of any kind of trouble. Drugs, DUIs, vandalism, and—if the gossip is true—even bigger charges, like assault. If anything, my mysterious background and the fact I came back a foot and a half taller, boosts my image—something that no one cared about at military school. Over there, I was just another fuck-up sent away for doing something dumb enough to get caught.

In short, I can survive the gossip. It'll pay dividends. But you don't exactly need super-hearing in this place to realize that people are talking about Vandy, too. Without consciously realizing I'm doing it,

I've searched her out in the cafeteria. She's coming from the south doors, eyes trained ahead as she limps into the room.

Watching her walk is an exercise in masochism, much like having a knife buried into my gut, twisting sharply with each of her stilted steps.

I want to say it's not as bad as when I initially realized it, that first day back at school. The way her hand supported her back as her hobbling gait carried her across the quad, right leg faltering with each step, it was undeniable.

*That's what I did.*

I'd met up with Emory to walk to my first class and couldn't force a single word from my throat the whole way. I wasn't prepared, then. In photos, she looks perfect. And that day, standing in her window in nothing but a bra and panties, she looked... well, miserable.

Miserable, but also fucking breathtaking.

If fourteen-year-old Reynolds could see seventeen-year-old Vandy, he would have made a move so fast, her head would have spun. Of course, my crush on her back then was just a curious little hint of a thing. I never fully nursed it. Emory wouldn't have even let me. He's smart like that.

I expect it now, knowing exactly what it is to watch the consequence of what I've done. But in truth, even three days later, I still feel those vicious stabs just watching her.

My teeth are already tightly clenched when I finally find Emory's table, dropping into the seat beside him. "Fuck." I realize, "I forgot to get a drink."

Emory uses my shoulder for leverage when he rises from his seat. "It's cool, I need to get something from the vending machine, anyway. What you want?"

"I don't know." Choices, choices. Goddamn it. "Something wet."

Emory shoots me two finger guns. "I don't think they're putting pussy in the vending machine yet, bro."

I flip him a middle finger as he walks off. "Walked into it."

"So, what's the word on that?" Ben Shackleford asks through a mouthful of food. "You managed to score any yet?"

I don't know any of these guys well enough to talk about pussy with them. Even if I did, I probably wouldn't brag that there are a lot of choices. Well. Not *too much*. I've already gotten looks, had notes passed to me, girls asking for my number, girls giving me theirs. *Paying dividends*. It'd be like shooting cum in a barrel.

Uncomfortably, my mind instantly flashes to that moment of seeing Vandy in her window, the way her tits looked peaking over that bra, how soft her skin seemed in the evening light, the way my hands would probably fit perfectly on her narrow hips.

Even more uncomfortably, my mind flashes to how, thirty minutes later, I was in the shower angrily stroking myself off—gut-clenched and empty—just to make my erection go the fuck away. It was only a brief respite, because there's plenty of girls around here I can look at without feeling like sewer scum.

All these girls.

*And their thighs.*

Dozens—no, *hundreds* of pairs of thighs. This school's dress code might actually fucking kill me. Cause of death: erection lasting more than four hours. There are all kinds of girls here, in all shapes and sizes. Blondes, brunettes, redheads, even a few pushing the dress code with rainbow-colored hair. Everywhere I look, I see little hints of skin beneath skirts. The swell of perky tits under a tight button-down shirt. Firm asses swaying around all over the place. I feel like a pervert, twenty-four-seven.

It's a miracle I'm able to be productive at all. What was my dad even thinking, putting me in here? I'd just spent three years cooped up with sweaty, smelly, hormonally repressed boys. Mountain Point had reeked of feet and dried cum. Here? Every girl that passes smells like unicorns and dreams. Restraint, and a constant hard-on, has become my new normal. All I'd need to do is choose one and go for it.

The thought makes the back of my neck feel clammy.

I swallow a particularly dry bite of potatoes. "Still checking out my options."

"What was it like there, anyway?" Carlton Wade asks. He's a junior who plays running back on the team with us. He's also got this slimy grin that constantly makes me want to put a boot in his face.

"Was it just a bunch of dicks all the time? Circle jerks? On a scale of one to ten, how homoerotic are we talking?"

I swallow a mouthful of mac n' cheese and wipe my mouth. "Not half as homoerotic as the way you look at everyone in the locker room."

There's a chorus of loud whooping, but Carlton just shrugs. "I'm not ashamed. I might be pussy-eating straight, but my boys got some fine asses."

Emory returns with two cans of Dr. Pepper, tossing one to me. "Hell yeah, I do, and don't you forget it."

"But come on." Carlton makes a horrified expression. "Three years without any girls? That's some cruel and unusual shit."

"There were girls. Sometimes." The school administrators weren't idiots. They knew we had to be around girls occasionally or we'd burn that fucker down. "Few times a year, they'd bus in students from the sister school for social events. Plus," I add, popping the top on my can, "I had like a million hours of community service, and trust me, the kind of girls who are on probation?" I give him *a look.*

"Oh, shit!" Ben looks absolutely delighted. I don't know much about the guy yet, except that he plays drums in the marching band, and that's only because he's constantly got his drumsticks out, tapping them on everything. It's either monumentally stupid or completely genius that he's also an offensive linesman on the team. He almost never has to actually march. "You get some of that rough trade?"

I shrug, but that's basically the gist of it. "Had a semi-regular thing going on with an arsonist named Melody." By the looks on their faces, they can't decide if I'm jerking their chains or not. I won't bother saying one way or another. Quick, flustered hook-ups in bathrooms, utility closets, and port-a-johns aren't exactly brag-worthy. And that was only the summer before junior year. It's been a long time.

Thank god for contraband phones, social media, and girls with either the high or low self-esteem to send sexy photos. But, Carlton isn't wrong. Too many dicks and not enough tits. I glance over at a table of girls I'd seen the day before at cheerleading practice and feel the familiar tightening in my groin. "But yeah, but overall, it sucked. I'm glad to be back in the world of co-eds."

"So what I want to know is," Ben asks, gesturing with his fork, "is it true that you have a gnarly scar from the wreck?"

The whole table falls abruptly silent.

Emory slams his can on the table. "Jesus, Ben. What the fuck?"

"What?" Ben asks, totally clueless. "Chicks dig scars! I'm just saying, if it's bad enough, maybe it'll get you some ass."

Carlton jabs him in the side with his elbow and gives Ben a dark look. Looks like even that asshole gets the dynamic going on. Talking about my scar like that is so fucking far from being okay. Not in front of Emory. Not after what happened to his sister.

It's been the elephant in the room for days now—years, actually, if I'm counting all the calls and chats where we both completely ignore the issue at hand. But it's *our* elephant. Mine and Emory's. We don't need jackasses like Ben pointing it out.

Ben adds into the awkward silence, "Well, he never undresses in the locker room." And when that just makes it *more* awkward, "Probably because of Carlton checking everyone out all the time."

"Yeah. My scars are gnarly," I offer blankly, letting my fork fall onto my tray. My appetite is long gone. "And trust me when I say they're not getting me any pussy."

There's nothing cool or sexy about the way my back looks. It's hideous. A week in the burn unit and four skin grafts didn't do much to salvage anything. I have skin. That's about the most I could hope for.

After a long beat of silence, Emory stands, picking up his tray and striding away.

Ben mutters, "Tough crowd," and I gather up my own shit, suddenly feeling exhausted by the whole day. As I walk away from the table, I can hear Ben asking someone, "Have you seen my drumsticks?"

*Mine now.*

"Hey," I call out when I catch up to Emory. The hallway is empty, since most everyone is still eating. I fall into stride, jaw tightening. "Are we just never going to talk about it?"

He stops abruptly, mouth twisted into a hard grimace. "What's there to talk about, Reyn? It was an accident. Everyone knows it. Even Vandy says that deer came out of nowhere."

"Her being in the car wasn't an accident." I look away, still remembering how I'd held my hand out to her, coaxing. "And you're the only one who doesn't want to see me strung up for it, which is pretty weird, considering."

Considering that I've been privy to four days of Emory's vicious protective streak when it comes to Vandy. I've spent more time than I'd like to admit just waiting for the other shoe to drop.

"Yeah, well." Emory folds his arms and shifts, eyes diverted. "What happened that night was a fucking disaster, but it was my fault as much as yours."

I give him a look that I can only hope conveys how moronic that sounds. "How do you even figure?"

He explains, "I'm the one who didn't back off when she walked up to the valet. I lied and got her involved. You asking her to go with you was just...it made sense. Otherwise, she would have narc'ed. At the time, it was smart thinking." He runs his hand through his hair. "I don't blame you for that. Not any more than I blame myself."

"I got her into the car and then crashed it." My voice is flat, mechanical, matter-of-fact. "I crippled her."

Emory's eyes flash in something bright and livid, and it's almost a relief when he slams a hard palm into my shoulder, shoving me back a step. "She's not a fucking cripple. You don't know anything about it! The things she's done, the things she can do? She's fine. She's stronger than either of us. Don't ever talk about my sister like that, you fucking hear me?"

I watch him fume for a long moment, something hard and noxious settling miserably into the pit of my stomach. "You're right," I concede. "I don't know anything about it. Sorry."

It's almost a disappointment to watch the anger drain from his face. "Do you remember that night? When I came to see you, in the hospital?"

I stuff my fists into my pockets, shrugging. "Only a little." It'd been late—or maybe even early—and everything seemed fuzzy around the edges, indistinct, disorienting. Emory could have come to see me, or he could have been a hallucination. It strikes me that, until now, I never actually knew for sure.

"Yeah, you were out of it," he says, leaning against a column. "Your mom said they had to sedate you because you were in a lot of pain, but also—" He pauses, giving me a significant look. "But also because you kept trying to get to Vandy."

My jaw feels tense when I nod. "I remember."

"You were a mess. Busted up, like her. All it took was five minutes with you, and I guess I just knew." Emory nods, like this is something he's confident about. "I knew nothing I said or did could make you feel worse about it." After a moment of watching me, he asks, "Do you wish it'd been you? If you could take her place and—"

"Yes." No hesitation.

Emory nods. "Then that's enough for me. I'm not willing to lose my best friend over a horrible mistake. Are you?" He holds out a fist, and I know once I bump it with mine, this is it.

This is the last time we'll talk about it, and then we'll have to move on.

I bump my knuckles against his, a silent agreement passing between us as the bell rings. It's too easy to be forgiven, but then, it was never Emory's to give in the first place.

We head opposite directions, and as the crowd leaves the cafeteria, my eyes are drawn back to a head of shiny blonde hair, her body moving at its own, stilted pace.

I hope that Emory's right—that Vandy is stronger than either of us, that she's overcome it, that she's fine.

Because deep inside, I know that I'm not.

❧

MY ENTIRE BODY aches as I walk off the field. Coach Morris is serious about repeating the state win, even if we die trying. Emory, being captain of the team, barks orders at the underclassmen, making them do the brunt of the post-practice field cleanup. I stop and guzzle a bottle of water, waiting for him halfway back to the locker room. It doesn't hurt that the cheerleaders practice in the parking lot next to the gym. One of the girls spots me and gives me a little wave. I reluctantly lift my hand just as Emory walks over, carrying his helmet and a bottle of water. We're both so drenched in sweat it looks like we just got out of the pool.

"Hey, who's that?" I ask, nodding toward the girl. She's small, shorter than the rest of the girls, and has long, straight, dark hair.

Plus, a nice, thick ass.

He snorts, shaking his head. "That, my friend, is *trouble*. Stay away."

"She looks familiar." I squint, trying to remember. "Did I know her from before?"

"That's Sydney Rakestraw," he explains, lip curling in displeasure. "Vandy's friend."

"Huh." An image of a skinny, tiny middle-schooler with a mouthful of braces pops into my head. "What do you mean she's trouble?"

We walk toward the locker room, the back door hanging open. The voices of our teammates echo back outside. Emory stops before we enter, swallowing a mouthful of water. "I hate talking bad about her because she's been so loyal to Vandy the last few years, but real talk? That girl is a hot mess. There's always something going on, another rumor or accusation. She posts shit all the time on social media." He wipes his forehead with the hem of his practice jersey. "Trust me, she's tempting—and I promise you, she *will* try to tempt you—but make like Nancy Reagan and 'Just say no,' got it?"

"Loud and clear," I reply. "The last thing I need right now is trouble."

Emory's nose wrinkles and he scratches his neck.

"What?" I ask, getting a vibe.

"About that..." He gestures for me to move a little bit closer to the massive HVAC unit, away from the locker room. "There's something I'm involved with—something I want you in on—but I know you're on a really short leash here. I still want to give you the option."

I blink. "I'm going to need a little more information than that."

Two sophomore players walk off the field toward the locker room.

We both give them a nod in greeting, but Emory doesn't resume talking until they're inside. "Remember what I told you about the Devils disbanding?"

"About them getting kicked off of campus." I nod, wiping my forehead with a towel. "Yeah, I remember."

He grins. "Turns out the roots of the organization go deeper than the headmaster's directives."

"What does that mean?"

"If you want to find out, meet me at the Devil's Tower on Friday night after the game."

My eyebrows scrunch together. "You trying to take me to the stairway to hell? I'm telling you dude, military school did not make me gay."

He pushes me hard. "Shut up. Meet me or not. It's your choice, but if you want in on something truly epic, I can make it happen." The fact that I hesitate must mean that I've actually grown up a little bit since the last time I was here. When I don't respond right away, Emory adds, "Just think about it?"

I give a slow nod. "Okay."

"Oh," he says, as we walk back to the locker room door, "and you can't tell anyone about this. It's the kind of thing that could get everyone in serious trouble."

I freeze, watching his back as he disappears into the building.

*This doesn't bode well.*

*C*AT.

I look down at the orange ball of fluff currently occupying the stoop in front of my side door. I'd just come out to get my cleats, which had been drying on the step. It's almost ten at night, so the cleats are dry, only there's this cat curled up to them.

"Excuse me," I mutter, bending with the intention of easing my shoes away. But the cat peers up at me balefully, tail twitching, and I snatch my hand back. "They're mine," I inform the cat, gesturing lazily to the shoes.

I watch in surreal disbelief as this cat extends a paw, spreads its toes, and sinks five long claws into the top of a shoe.

"You gotta be shitting me."

The cat gives me a look that clearly says 'I'm not shitting you one bit'.

I sigh, peering around the yard, wondering who this jerk belongs to. "I've easily got a hundred and sixty pounds on you."

The cat doesn't even blink.

I'm still engaged in this staring contest when the side yard is suddenly flooded in a wash of porch light. When the door to the neighbor's house begins opening, I know there's only a twenty-five percent chance that it's Emory. Maybe I'll be lucky.

I'm not.

Because standing there in the doorway is Vandy Hall, sweater wrapped tight around her body as she crosses her arms. There's a long stretch of silence where we just stare wide-eyed at one another, nothing but the distant sounds of crickets and a purring cat filling the space between us.

She visibly swallows, eyes dropping to the cat. "Firefly, come." Firefly kneads a paw full of claws into my shoe and stays right where it is. Vandy makes a 'pss-pss-pss' noise and holds the door open, coaxing the cat into the house. Firefly is clearly having none of this shit, because the cat simply adjusts, making itself more comfortable.

Vandy meets my gaze again, and she probably tries to hide it— that reluctant, fearful thing swimming in her eyes—but I can see it. It's even worse than watching her limp across the distance between us, this agonizing realization that she's afraid of me.

"I'll just..." She gestures to the cat, but before she can reach down to pick it up, the cat springs to its feet and darts across the yard, disappearing right into the open door of Vandy's house.

*Asshole.*

Vandy tugs the sleeves of her sweater over her fists, eyebrows low in a surly expression. "Okay, then." She turns to leave and I jerk forward, like there's a fishhook in my chest.

"Wait."

She freezes, slowly turning to give me a blank look from over her shoulder.

And I'm not even sure why I asked her to. So many things need to be said that it feels like I'm drowning in the tidal wave of it. She could stand there all night, her pretty blonde hair rippling on every passing breeze, and I'd still only be able to scratch the surface.

I want to say that I'm sorry. I want to tell her what I'd told Emory before—that I wish it'd been me. I want to say that I think of her every night when I fall asleep and every morning when I wake up. I want to say that I spent the last three years paying for it in sweat and blood and isolation, and that it still isn't enough, and that I know it.

I want to say that I've missed her.

I release a long exhale, shoulders slumping. "Wait here." I don't catch her reaction as I turn back into the house, pulling my bookbag from a kitchen chair. I dig around in the front pocket until I find it, shuffling back to the door.

She's facing me now, something both defeated and defensive in the way she hugs her middle, eyebrows pulled tightly together. Her face instantly goes slack when I hold up the tube of lipstick, though. I broadcast the throw with a couple bobs of my hand before tossing it over the distance.

She catches it against her chest a bit clumsily, eyes wide as she inspects it. "How did you...?"

I shrug, turning to head back inside.

"Yours now."

# 5

I DON'T KNOW what's stunned me more.

Seeing Reynolds standing there on his porch—a pair of loose grey sweatpants slung low on his hips, threadbare black tee stretched tight over his broad chest—had been like a punch in the gut. The porch light just barely illuminated the sharp angles of his cheekbones, and with the way he was standing, so inhumanly still, he looked like a statue carved out of midnight and obsidian. In the low light, his eyes were nothing but two dark hollows of vacant shadow, but it didn't matter. I knew he was looking right at me, could feel myself pinned under the heavy weight of it, defenseless and paralyzed.

I've seen him around school for days, of course. And it's not like he's any less intimidating in the uniform, especially not with the way he's always sitting, slouched low, head down, as if there's no one around to pay attention to. Every inch of him screamed 'untouchable'.

Like this, he didn't even feel like that boy I once knew. That version of Reynolds was sketched from long summer days spent watching him, the wiry muscles of his back shifting beneath thin shirts as I followed him and Emory around the neighborhood. It was painted with short winter evenings spent in the treehouse, watching his sly smirk as he emptied a day's worth of loot from the pockets of his loose hoodie, Emory taking a studious inventory. The old Reynolds was a hurricane full of dimples and reckless abandon, and he was just as untouchable then, but there was a thrill in knowing I had a chance to find myself in the eye of it, if only I stayed in one place long enough.

This new version of Reynolds is hard-edged and quiet, obscured by the storm cloud of blankness that sets his features. It's almost scary to see, this new reserved stillness of him, as if he'd at one point shed his skin and floated away, and now something else is walking around with his older face and taller form.

But he had called out to me—*Wait*—in a voice that's deeper, rougher than it used to be.

Yes, seeing him there had stunned me. But *this* had stunned me more.

I test the weight of the lipstick tube in my hand. There's the panic that he's seen—that he knows what's inside—but louder than that are the questions. *How? Why?* I give the base two spins to the left and carefully pull the top off.

Three pills.

They're all still there. I'd had a miniature meltdown today in Art when Mr. Kent had taken it away, apparently irked by the way I kept turning it over in my hands, eyes focused on it like a lifeline. I hadn't planned to take them. But with the resurgence of gossip about me, I just needed the comfort of knowing I could. And then it'd been ripped away, and along with it, that soothing certainty that I had a way out if things got too bad. On top of that came the distress of knowing what would happen if Mr. Kent looked inside and reported it. Everyone would know. My parents. Emory. The administrators. Eventually, the whole school.

Reynolds had stolen it back, though. Had he done it because he knew it was mine, or was it just a coincidence?

I clutch the tube in my hand and turn back toward the house, unable to look a gift horse in the mouth. Reynolds stole it back because stealing is just what Reynolds *does*. The surety of that thought is almost as soothing as having the stash of pills in my pocket.

At least something about him hasn't changed.

MY PROPOSAL to Mr. Lee has an unexpected result. He'd shattered my ambition of investigating the years of systematic social inequality at Preston Prep, but he must have at least appreciated the spirit of it.

On Thursday, he stops me in the hallway and offers me a spot on the paper. "If you want it," he adds.

"What's the job?" I ask, as if I'm not going to say yes regardless of the position.

"Well, you got me thinking about some of the traditional roles here at Preston. While there are risks attached to certain topics, we definitely have a history mired in a deep patriarchy, and I think you're just the person to push the boundary." He pushes his wire glasses up his nose. "How would you like to be our first female sports reporter?"

"Sports?" The word comes out squeakier than I'd intended.

"Yep." His grin is warm, a touch satisfied. "You'd cover the different teams and their schedules. Obviously, football is predominant at the moment, given the time of year, but it's also girls' softball season. And actually, water polo is co-ed."

"I don't know a lot about those sports," I worry, flexing my hands around the straps of my bookbag. "Well, other than football. I guess

I've picked up a few things after watching Emory play all these years, but you know that I can't..." I feel my cheeks heat, "I can't play any of those things."

"And that's exactly what I mean by pushing boundaries," he says, scooting us toward the lockers when a group of students pass. "You'll not only be the first female sports reporter here, but also the first..." He visibly struggles to find a non-insulting term.

"...with a physical disability," I supply, grimacing.

"You don't have to play the sports to report on them," he concludes, "you just need to report the facts. Stats, a few highlights from the past games, and predictions for the next one. I'd also bet that you'd bring a refreshing angle."

The truth is that, even though sports don't interest me much, there's no way I'd say no to this offer. One, because Mr. Lee is actually going out on a limb to make a change, and however small it is, it's *something*. Two, because I'm determined to prove myself this year. It may not be the way I'd wanted, but it's better than nothing.

"Okay," I say, feeling a little nervous, "I'm in. Just tell me where to start."

He hands me a notebook with the Preston Prep Red Devil logo on the front and a very official-looking pen. "Tomorrow night. First football game of the season. Let's kick things off right."

I clutch the notebook in my hand and swallow. "Got it. Tomorrow night."

And that's how I end up, twenty-four hours later, standing by the fence that surrounds the field. It's my first time watching a football game anywhere but in the stands, next to my parents. I glance back at them now, decked head-to-toe in Devil spirit wear, eyes laser-focused on my brother out on the field.

Truthfully, I feel a strange sense of relief not having to sit with them. Sometimes it's almost like they're afraid to be too enthusiastic about these things when I'm around. *No fun allowed.* It never bothered me much before, but I'd been on the meds, the last three years spent blissfully unaware of their overprotectiveness. Now, I can feel exactly how smothering it's been. There's life here. The roar of the crowd. The booming announcer's voice. The crackling energy in the air. For once, I'm able to feel it all.

*No.* Not just feel it.

I'm able to be *a part of it.*

It's only a few minutes into the first quarter. I'm still dubiously inspecting the settings on the camera Mr. Lee let me borrow when the crowd suddenly jumps to their feet. The cries of excitement draw my eyes back on the field. I spot Emory's jersey number—quarterback, number 17—just in time to see him jerk his elbow back, sending a spiraling throw down the field. I fumble for a moment to position the camera, hoping to catch something good, and see the receiver through the viewfinder—number 32—glancing over his shoulder as he races toward the end zone. I press the shutter frantically when the ball comes to him. He leaps in the air, catching it effortlessly against his chest and landing perfectly behind the white line.

The stands erupt into deafening celebration.

The band kicks into gear, sending the cheerleaders into a flurry of dance. I cheer along with the crowd, albeit mainly because I'm almost positive I actually got a shot of the touchdown.

I'm crushing this.

Once the ref blows his whistle, Emory rushes over to his teammate and they move into a ridiculous and obviously over-choreographed victory dance that makes me honk an involuntary laugh. They bang their helmets together and do the ritual slapping of butts in celebration.

I get a picture of that, too.

The rest of the half continues in much the same way, and I might not be big into the sportsball, but even I'm impressed. Preston is absolutely wiping the floor with the other team. Any concerns that this year's team isn't up to last year's standards are sure to be crushed. I know from my brief but frenzied afternoon interviewing students about their predictions that there's been some worry about this. I guess when you win once, everyone wants it to happen again. On more than one occasion, I've overheard Emory lamenting the loss of a few integral graduating seniors and thinking it would be hard to fill their shoes. Clearly, these worries were unfounded.

When the buzzer finally blares, signaling halftime, I'm happy to put down my equipment and take a drag of the coffee I'd brought with me.

"Seriously, how many cups are you up to a day?" Sydney asks, bounding over from the cheerleaders. She's got glitter on her face, and I swear her skirt is an inch shorter than everyone else's, but she looks cute.

"I've been sleeping like shit," I admit. "Seemed like drinking a few extra cups could keep me alert for the game, although, with the way they're playing, that hasn't been an issue."

We both look at the guys running into the field house. I spot Emory with his helmet off. He catches my eye and waves. I wave back.

So does Sydney. "Your brother is so hot."

I grimace. "Shut up."

"Facts are facts." She shrugs. "Hey, do you think he'd go out with me now that Campbell is gone?"

The other team has a better chance of winning this game.

"You know he's hung up on Campbell," I say, shooting Sydney a sidelong glance. "I feel sorry for anyone he hooks up with while they're still attached."

"If that's your way of warning me off of being Emory's rebound, you're doing a bad job of it." Her eyes skim the rest of the guys as they trickle into the building. She nods at number 32. "Although he certainly grew up well."

"What?" I squint, trying to figure out, "Who?"

Right at that moment, the player takes off his helmet, revealing a sweaty head of hair and a hard-edged face that makes my stomach dip.

"Reyn," she says, "he's freaking gorgeous."

This is why I like Sydney. She doesn't apologize for saying what she thinks, and she doesn't treat me like I'm so fragile that one mention of Reynolds McAllister will shatter me.

Of course, it's true. If the Reynolds I knew at age thirteen was cute, then this new, harder version of him is something way too intense for such a juvenile descriptor. He's grown into his arms and legs, that sharpened face no longer bearing the blemishes or rosy cheeks of an adolescence that hadn't even been awkward for him. I can see from here that his arms and thighs are firm and sculpted, and he moves with a graceful, easy power that some of the other guys lack.

Just as I'm watching him, his green eyes pass over us, only to skitter back, gaze locking onto mine for a tense moment as he walks leisurely toward the field house. I don't even realize I'm holding my breath until he finally breaks my gaze, letting his head hang as he jogs the rest of the way.

I exhale in a rush. "I guess it's not a surprise. He's always been cute."

She nods, concern flickering in her eyes when she looks at me. "So, what's it been like? With Reyn being back and everything?"

This is another thing no one else would ask me. Sure, my mom and dad and Dr. Cordell want to know my *feelings* about everything, but this usually involves a long, in-depth analysis that leaves me feeling exhausted and vaguely like a specimen who's been placed beneath a microscope. Sydney, however, just wants to know what's happening. Talking to her never feels like a minefield.

"Once I got over the fact my parents kept it a secret from me, it's been... okay." I decide not to tell her about the yard—the cat and the lipstick and the obsidian. Something about it feels fragile and private, like it's a burden for me and Reynolds to carry alone. "I mean, it's weird seeing him on campus, but I'm pretty sure he's, like, avoiding me?" I glance at Sydney, unsure. "So, I don't really have to deal with him."

The truth is that I'm trying not to let him eat up so much head-space, but it's hard. He's suddenly everywhere. Loping casually down the hallway at school. Hunched over his lunch in the cafeteria, his forearm curled almost protectively around his tray. Here, on the foot-ball field with Emory. Standing like a statue on his porch, visible from the window overlooking the kitchen sink. And speaking of windows —also in the bedroom that looks right into my own. It doesn't help that his return coincides with my reduction in meds or the fact that the nightmares are back. His little glowing bedroom light is now the first thing I see when I wake up.

Okay.

Maybe I am letting him occupy *a little* headspace.

Sydney nods. "I think it's cool you're not letting him drag you down, you know? Preston Prep is *your* territory. The school obviously only let him come back because they needed him on the football team."

I shift uncomfortably at the thought of us being adversarial. Is that how other people see it? Is that how *Reynolds* sees it?

"Well, Emory's happy to have him back. You know he lost a lot of friends in the senior class last year, including Campbell. If Reynolds being back gives him a friend, and helps him have a winning season, it's worth it."

Syd tosses her sweaty arm around my shoulder and squeezes. "Even after everything you've been through, you're still amazing, you know that?"

I shrug and lift the camera. She instantly shifts into a seductive pose, pursing her lips and lowering her eyelids. "This is for the newspaper!" I laugh.

"Oh, I know." She flips her skirt. "I thought you were all about pushing boundaries this year!"

I take a few more photos of my friend, knowing good and well I am not going to submit these to the paper.

The buzzer on the scoreboard blares, a warning that the second half is about to begin. I wave to Sydney as she skips back over to the cheer squad, but I keep my eye on the fieldhouse door. She's right, this is a year for pushing boundaries.

I just haven't figured out exactly how far I want to go.

PRESTON PREP WINS BIG, setting a positive tone for the season. I snap photos of Emory's wide smile when the buzzer sounds, unable to stop my own grin at the sight of him like this, all radiant with the glow of victory. I try to take photos of the other guys, too, which is how I find

Reynolds's face suddenly filling my lens. He's at Emory's side, my brother's arm slung loose around Reynolds' neck as they walk. They're like an exercise in contrast—Emory's animated radiance and Reynolds' hard-edged stillness. His head's hanging down, something relieved and tired in the curve of his shoulders as he wipes his face with his jersey, but then Emory says something into his ear.

Reynolds lifts his head with a responding smile, those two dimples blooming like the sun over his sharp cheeks. My finger mashes down on the shutter, capturing an image so zoomed-in—so entirely irrelevant to football—that I know I could never submit it.

Just as quickly as it appeared, the smile is gone, replaced by something solemn and placid.

It's a tradition for the families and friends of the team to wait outside the stadium, congratulating the team for their win. I always hate doing it. Luckily, this time I have an excuse.

"Mr. Lee said I could drop the camera off at the desk in the boys' dorm," I tell my parents. Mr. Lee is one of the resident supervisors that lives on campus. "I'll meet you at the car when I'm done?"

Mom's face creases with worry. "Are you sure it's safe to walk across campus at night alone?"

I give her a peeved look. "Seriously?"

Thankfully, Dad squeezes her arm. "Hon, it's fine. Plenty of students are going back to the dorms anyway." He gives me an encouraging nod. "Just hurry back, okay?"

"Yes," I reply, and can't head off fast enough, before they can change their mind.

It's always depressing, after meeting the team. All of them are usually alight with excitement for their after-game plans, a whole night of fun teen antics spread out promisingly before them.

I just ride home with my parents, like a loser. Again.

Emory always has some post-game party or hang out. Last year, he would have gone wherever Campbell wanted, usually to a kegger at her parents' house on the lake. He'd said he had plans with Aubrey Willis this weekend, so God only knows what he'll get up to, but he'll probably come home reeking of BWS.

Beer, weed, and sex.

Whatever happens, I'm sure Sydney will have all the gossip in the morning. I never go to parties. For one, I'm never invited, and no one ever asks me to come with them. But even if all those stars aligned, my parents would never let me. God, Emory himself would shit a brick if I showed up at something like that. I can just imagine the look on his face. He wouldn't drag me home, he'd just end the party, right then and there, and these days? Emory absolutely had the power to do that.

I cross the quad toward Hayden, the boys' dormitory. Like Dad said, there are plenty of other students out. About half the students live on campus and most of those attend the home games. I follow a few guys into the dorm, thanking the one who patiently holds the door as I slowly climb the steps. I receive more than a few questioning looks, which is fair. Vandy Hall at the boys' dorm, at night? To see a guy?

Nope, just here on official Chronicle business.

God, I'm a loser.

I remove the memory card before leaving the camera in the office where Mr. Lee told me to, adding a note that I'd have my article written up by Monday. A weird feeling passes over me as I head back outside, the quad quieter than before. I close my eyes and inhale the late summer air. So, this must be what independence feels like— warmth and silence and calm—no questions or eyes or wild internal calculation as to how to justify what I'm doing. I'm still reveling in this as I approach the darkened area near the bell tower, the whole area shaded by the thick branches of ancient oaks.

I know all about the Devil's tower, particularly the rumors surrounding the Stairway to Hell. It's a stupid and cheesy name for a hookup spot, but the Devils love tradition, especially if it sets them apart from the rest of the student body. Obviously, I've never been up there—the thought alone makes me snort a laugh—but Sydney says that there's a beam across the top where the Devils carve their initials, adding slash marks underneath for each of their conquests. It's not the only way the Devils claim the girls they're with. There's also the Devil's Marks—strategically-placed hickies under girls' ears.

There's also some very specific rumors about 'tests'. With Emory in the group, I've done my best to completely avoid that winding path of gossip. The less I know about my brother's sex life, the better.

As I walk across the soft grass, I suddenly realize I'm not the only person in this part of the quad. Someone else is lurking around the base of the tower. I wait, feeling nervous about being out here alone. Now, all those absurd warnings my mother gave me about the buddy system come rushing back. What am I doing out here, all by myself? This is the perfect time and place to get snatched!

I stumble over a thick tree root, my lame leg faltering. I press my back against the trunk and wait. Whoever it is can't be hanging around long. What are they doing, anyway?

That's when I see the blue light of a phone cast over their face. My stomach clenches at the sight of Reynolds, leaning lazily against the stonework of the tower. His hair's wet and his eyes are blank, fixed to the screen of his phone. There's something wary in the way he holds himself, hand pushed tight into the pocket of his low-slung jeans, shoulders curling inward.

I wonder what he's doing there, but just as quickly as I ask the question, I know the answer. I'm not surprised that he's already found someone here to hook up with. I've been here for years and no guy has ever expressed the slightest interest in me, but him? I've over-heard enough bathroom conversations and whispered classroom discussions to know that Sydney and I aren't the only ones who have noticed that Reynolds is good-looking. Any number of Preston girls would be willing to bear a Devil's mark from him.

What does surprise me is the sudden boulder of disappointment that crashes into the pit of my stomach.

I instantly cringe away from it, heart twisting, because I refuse —*refuse*—to find where those breadcrumbs lead me. Even if I were jealous—and even if that night had never happened—it'd be laughable. Embarrassing. Pathetic. Wanting Reynolds is something my thirteen-year-old self would do, because that person was young and stupid and hopelessly naive. The person I am now feels physically sick at the thought of it.

I wait another few minutes before I leave, not wanting to run into him. He lingers around the door, and for a second I think maybe he's getting stood up. But that idea is heartily squashed when the door finally opens. It's hard to make anything out except a shadowy figure standing in the doorway, but Reynolds bumps fists with whoever it is. He vanishes into the bell tower a moment later.

I realize my heart is racing as the door closes behind him. I take a deep breath before walking as quickly as I can back toward the stadium parking lot.

One thing nags at me as I reach my parents.

Guys don't bump fists with a girl.

Who the heck was Reyn meeting?

I WAIT until it's late, house quiet and still, to flip through the photos on the memory card slowly, taking in every face, each moment, as if I'm not looking for one photo in particular. Determinedly—almost stubbornly—I take my sweet time clicking the 'next' arrow. I feel a swell of jubilation when I find the touchdown photo, a still frame of number 32 just as his hands make contact with the ball. It's not exactly framed professionally, but it's clear and crisp, a nicer snapshot of an action moment than I thought myself capable of, and I feel a bright spike of satisfaction.

*Crushing it!*

I flip through more—Emory, Sydney, Afton Cross, Ben Shackleford—until I reach The One.

The second his dimpled face fills the screen, I almost click back to the previous picture. Seeing him like this feels wrong somehow, like at any moment my parents are going to jump out of the shadows and start asking a whole lot of questions that I'm in no way prepared to answer. It makes me curl closer to the screen as I look at it, not at all unlike I've seen Reynolds curled around his lunch tray—a vaguely possessive, shielding move.

It's a fantastic picture. There's something strangely guarded in the way his eyes are trained off into the distance. Sweaty hair clings to his forehead in chaotic slashes, and his mouth is parted with his smile, like he's still trying to catch his breath.

It's a seemingly perfect mixture of the old Reynolds and the new.

I can only look at it for a few moments before the anxious fluttering in my stomach becomes too much. I close it all out before shooting a wary glance toward my window.

I blame the insomnia—or all the caffeine—for turning me into a nosy neighbor, or at least that's what I tell myself as I sit here on my bed, watching his dark window for signs of activity. It's already past midnight and he's not the only one who hasn't come home yet. My brother hasn't returned either.

I check social media, scanning Emory's account and even Aubrey Willis', but if they're together, they've kept it on the DL. I yet again restrain myself from seeing whether or not Reynolds has an account. That's like the isosceles triangle of slippery slopes. But I do scroll through a dozen other accounts of Preston Prep classmates hoping he'll pop up. He doesn't, even in the photos from a party where Sydney is claiming to have the time of her life.

I close the laptop and fall back on my bed, sighing.

I drum my fingers against my stomach. FOMO isn't something I'm used to feeling so acutely. The meds usually dulled those kinds of things. But now it's just frustratingly, achingly obvious that I'm the only one at home on a Friday night, sitting in my room, creeping on the off-limits neighbor I can barely even manage eye contact with. Jesus, the realization that I need a life has never been clearer.

I decide to risk going down to the kitchen. It's late enough that Mom and Dad should be asleep. Dad snores like a freight train and my mom has started sleeping with a noise machine. It's given me a little more freedom to move around at night, but I still play it safe, not even daring to turn on a light to illuminate my way down the stairs, through the house.

At the refrigerator, I open the freezer and stick my head in so that the cool air blasts across my face. I dig out an ice pop and am in the middle of tearing the package with my teeth when I hear a meow at the kitchen window. Firefly's climbed the flower box and is peering in at me with his shrewd eyes.

"Hey bud," I say, mostly to myself. It's not like the cat can hear me. He continues to meow, louder and a touch more obnoxiously than normal. At the door, I pause, because I know my cat. Usually, that much noise means he's brought a 'gift'. I ease the door open, just a crack, and look down. Sure enough...

"Ugh, Firefly, are you kidding me?"

Firefly is holding the brown, striped body of a chipmunk in his mouth. I know if I let him, he'll dart in, probably leaving the thing somewhere horribly inconvenient. Instead, I squeeze out to confront him.

"Let go of that!" I hiss. "Drop the chipmunk!"

Firefly isn't having it. As soon as I get near enough to grab him, he's jolting away. I chase him across the yard, grateful that no one's come home yet, because I can't even imagine how stupid I look, hobbling around after a cat and his chipmunk. I ultimately pick up a pinecone to chuck in his direction. Predictably, it misses, Emory having clearly sucked all of the throwing talent from our particular end of the gene pool. The yard is wet, coated in slippery dew. I throw another pinecone, which lands close enough to both alarm and piss the cat off. He gives me a surly, betrayed look, as if to say *I'm trying to feed you, woman!'*

Having done this song and dance before, I know from experience that, half the time, the chipmunks are still alive—just stunned into submission—which means if I can grab the cat, I can probably save the pitiful creature. I pick up one more pinecone and throw it. This one skitters across the driveway, producing a long hissing sound that scares Firefly enough to drop the chipmunk.

Once it's out of his mouth, that sucker dashes away.

*Knew it.*

"You're welcome," I mutter to its wake, working now to lunge for the cat before he can go after it.

I corner him behind an azalea, clutching the cat to my chest. Despite the loss of his prey, Firefly still deigns to bless me with an affectionate headbutt to my chin. "Yeah, yeah, you're a fierce predator," I pant, still catching my breath. That's about when I hear the sound of an approaching vehicle, unable to do much more than blink before the driveway is awash in a flood of headlights. My brother's truck—and I would recognize the bass from his sound system anywhere—comes to a slow stop.

Shit.

*Shit. Shit. Shit.*

I freeze, trying to decide what to do. Run? I physically can't do that—not well, at any rate. He's sure to hear my shuffle-limp across the driveway. I could just step out, admit I was out here with the cat. My mind runs through all the questions that will lead to; why were you in the kitchen, is something wrong, why aren't you asleep, do I need to tell Mom and Dad? It wouldn't even be a threat. It'd be concern. I realize it's stupid—insane, even—how ridiculously overbearing my family has become. But it's true, nevertheless. Getting up for a popsicle could land me back in twice-a-week therapy.

That's what leads me to option three: *hide.*

With the cat clutched to my pounding chest, I stay hidden behind the thick azalea and wait for my brother to head into the house. His door opens and shuts. Then... opens again? The second set of footsteps is what makes me realize he's not alone.

I close my eyes against the tide of horror.

"So what do you think?" Emory says, voice low but echoing in the silence of the driveway.

It takes Reynolds a long moment to answer. When he does, his voice is low and reluctant. "Collins made it pretty clear at my meeting that this kind of stuff is off limits."

"Well, that's what those assholes get for trying to shut down a long-standing tradition," my brother says.

There's a shuffling sound. The jingle of keys. Firefly twitches. "Come on, be straight with me," Reynolds says. "Is this just you being pissed that you couldn't be leader of the Devils this year? Because I've seen the way these people act around you, Em. You don't need it."

Emory scoffs. "Dude, fuck what the Devils used to be. The way Hamilton and the guys before him ran shit? It was petty posturing. This is how we reclaim it, don't you see? We'd be putting our own mark on Preston Prep, ushering in a new era for..." A thread of significance deepens Emory's voice, "for the people we *leave behind*."

Reynolds makes a soft scoff. "So that's what this is about."

"I'm not like Hamilton Bates," Emory says. "He left and never looked back, but I don't have that luxury. I know the Devils were stupid, okay? But I also know this school, and I know what the student body is like. Preston needs a group of upperclassmen—the *right* group of upperclassmen—to lead them. Because if they don't, someone else will, and those people won't be like us. It might be a bullshit power structure, but that's still what it is—structure."

"What it is," Reynolds says, "is full-on secret society shit."

"Which makes it infinitely cooler!" I dare a peek through the dense limbs and see Emory holding something in his hands. It looks like a book. "It's all here. Every ritual. Every tradition. The way it was always meant to be. This—" I see Emory hold up the book, "—is legacy. Don't you want to be known here for something other than..." Emory trails off, and the driveway fades into a tense stillness.

"Other than being a fuck-up?" Reynolds finishes, voice so flat and lifeless that it chills me.

"I didn't mean it like—" Emory sighs. "Look, I just know you're bigger than that. I *know* it."

"And if I get caught doing this, then that's all I'll ever be."

"No one is going to find out, that's the whole point. I'm not dumb, dude. Not anymore." Emory explains, "In here, there are precautions, okay? Insurance policies. I know what's on the line here." Emory shifts on his feet. "Bro, I need to do this. And I really want you to do it with me. It'll be like old times, you know? Before everything went to shit." There's another stretch of silence so long and loaded that I risk another peek.

"Christ, Em." Reyn's face is cast to the side, shadowed gaze trained off into the distance. I watch as his fingers flex around the strap of his equipment bag, knuckles going white, and I unconsciously mirror him, tightening my grip on Firefly. There's something dark and hunted in the curve of Reynolds' brow. Whatever struggle he's locked in makes his voice come out low and defeated. "I'll have to think about it."

"Yeah," Emory says, like this much is obvious. "We have some time, no problem."

I watch them bump fists before Emory walks toward the house, taking the sidewalk on the other side of the bush I'm hiding behind. The cat senses his presence and, being completely over my embrace, squirms right out of my arms.

I watch helplessly as the cat darts away, and now it's my turn to shoot him a surly, betrayed look. It's not long before I hear the door to our house open and close. My feet are wet and coated with dirt, and my leg is trembling, struggling to hold my crouch, but I stay there, listening for the sounds of Reynolds' retreat. I feel the surge of worry seizing my chest as I wait.

What the hell was my brother talking about? It sounded serious.

Like *serious trouble*.

"Guess old habits die hard," Reynolds' low voice suddenly rings out from the driveway. I cast my eyes around, wondering if someone else has arrived. Jerry, maybe. Or maybe he's just talking to himself. But then, he adds, "Isn't that right, Baby V?"

I stop breathing, eyes clamping shut in denial.

He sighs, voice is breezy and bored when he says, "I can see your foot."

My eyes fly open, shooting a glare to my dirty toes. I ascend slowly, carefully, in stages, forcing my bum leg beneath me. When I limp out from behind the bush, I see Reynolds leaning against the truck. His legs are crossed at the ankle, a gym bag slung over his shoulder. His dark eyes sweep over me.

"What are you doing." This is not phrased as a question.

"Uh." I pull my sleeves over my fists, gesturing weakly toward the yard. "I was just getting my cat. He had a chipmunk, and I—"

Reynolds is tall and thin, which is probably what makes him so fast on the field. He pushes off the vehicle, bringing himself to full height, and his face is that same shadowy, hard-edged blankness from the other night. "You're still a bad liar."

I feel a rush of indignation, Sydney's words floating back to me —*your territory*—and I pull myself to my own full height. "I'm not lying."

His face remains emotionless, even as his chest bounces with a silent laugh. "Lesson number one about eavesdropping; it's all about the cover."

"I wasn't—"

"Look," he says, the light from a distant lamppost bringing his tense features into sharp relief. "I know you're not happy about me being back. It's really obvious. And that's…" He works his jaw for a moment, fingers flexing. "That's fine. I deserve that. But I'm doing my best here to stay away from you, and let you be. You nosing around like this?" His dark gaze drops to my bare leg, something sharp and troubled in the curve of his brow. "It's just going to get you hurt again."

I feel the weight of his eyes on my leg so intensely that I actually stumble back a step, heel dragging across the ground as my muscles lag just a moment too slowly. I breathe in sharply, anticipating the tilt of the fall.

It never comes.

Reynolds, who only a moment ago was ten feet away, somehow manages to leap over the distance, lunging to catch me before I topple backward. His arm around my torso feels as solid as steel, pulling me upright, right into the wall of his warm body.

It takes me a moment to reorient myself, still half expecting the collision against the pavement. Instead, I feel Reynolds' slow, relieved exhale against my temple. Over his shoulder, I can see where he's dropped the gym bag, which is the last bit of sense I recognize before my lungs are filled with the clean, undeniably masculine scent of him. My belly twists in a humiliating tangle of bright-hot *want* that's so sudden, I immediately shove him away.

Reynolds instantly complies, lurching back with his palms up. His lips are pressed into a tight, grim line, and when he mutters a rough, "Fuck, sorry," I wrap my arms around my middle and turn away, eyes feeling hot and prickly.

I walk as fast as I can toward the house, and when I get there, I don't have to look back to know he's still standing in the driveway, watching. I don't turn around to confirm whether or not the heat of his gaze on the back of my neck is real or imagined. I just step inside, exhaling raggedly when the door is closed, and press my back against it.

I knew Reyn and I were going to have to speak to one another sooner or later.

I just didn't expect it to go like that.

# 6

EVEN THOUGH IT'S past midnight, I know there's no reason to be quiet when I walk in the house. My dad's car is gone. It hadn't taken me long to realize that he spends more time out than at home these days. It's just one more weird adjustment, going from being cramped up in tiny dorms with hundreds of other guys to finding myself constantly alone in this huge, silent house.

I slam the back door loud enough to wake up every dog in the neighborhood, which is probably not the smartest move coming from someone who's been ducking Fucking Jerry for three days. I run my hands through my hair, frustration thrumming through my veins.

*Goddamnit!*

Why'd I have to touch her?

It's not like I could just let her fall. It was instinctual, involuntary. The second I saw her stumble, I was clutched by panic, jumping forward to catch her. She was small and warm and solid, and I just wanted to carry her into her fucking house and tuck her meddlesome ass into bed, and then lock her in there. Safe. Away from all this. Away from me. Why does she have to make this so difficult? It's easy. She stays over there, I stay over here, and I won't get into trouble.

This is all for *her*. Emory hadn't come out and said as much, but he didn't need to. It should have been obvious from the moment he mentioned it. Only one thing would make Emory willing to ask me to be part of something so unbelievably risky. And here she is, sticking her fucking nose in it, just like old times.

I open the refrigerator. If it weren't for the three cartons of rank leftover Thai, a bottle of wine, and a bag of apples, it'd be completely empty. My father has clearly forgotten that there's now a growing boy in this house—one who needs protein and a caloric intake befitting someone currently engaged in required team athletics. Unless I count the sad protein bar I'd had before the game—stolen from Ben's locker —I haven't actually eaten since lunch. With a deep sigh, I grab an apple and take an aggressive bite. Deciding it could be worse, I carry a spare apple with me and climb the stairs to the second floor. The first thing I do when I walk in my room is check the window. Like every other time I've looked out, Vandy's curtains are tightly closed. It's kind of fucked, if I'm being honest, this way she has of closing me out of her world while simultaneously trying to nose into mine.

I shuck off my shirt before emptying the pockets of my jeans. There's a crisp five-dollar bill, liberated from the jacket pocket belonging to someone on our second string. A pair of dice my neighbor had been playing with in Chemistry. A little pickle-shaped button the girl beside me in History had pinned to her bookbag proclaiming '*Dill with it*'.

A bit of a disappointing haul.

I dump it all into the bottom drawer of my dresser with the rest of the things I've taken since being back. I push off my jeans and flop onto the bed in my boxers, chomping on the apple. The night had been a rollercoaster. First there was the game, which was aces. I fucking killed it. Emory and I clicked back together like pieces in a puzzle. Usually, other teams struggle with a good passing game, but us? We're like magic.

Then, I relented and went to Devil's Tower. What happened there was entirely unexpected. Worst case, I figured I was in for some kind of Red Devil hazing from the football team, and the thought was amusing. Best case, some girl wanted to be my welcome wagon, which worked out perfectly for me, considering that my molecular makeup at the moment must be something like fifty percent raging horniness and fifty percent crippling indecision.

It was neither of those.

When Carlton opened the door, I'd expected to go up the tower, because where else would we go? Instead, he'd taken a hard left toward an old wooden door. I didn't even remember it being there, but that's fair. It'd been a long time since I'd been to that place—the last time being accompanied by one very athletic Sheri Brown, the first semester of freshman year. It was the first time I'd successfully gotten under a girl's bra. Naturally, that's the only thing I remember about the place.

Behind the wooden door was a staircase that led down, winding under the one that led up to the bell. Carlton used a flashlight to light the way, and again, I wondered if I was about to get my ass beat in some good old-fashioned, Preston Prep hazing. I spent the whole way fighting a laugh, because seriously. As if whatever these spoiled little rich boys had in store could hold a candle to the hazing I'd endured at Mountain Point. Nevertheless, fight or flight began to kick in. My heart hammered, instinct driving me to look for an escape, and then toward fight when none could be found. I could take Carlton in a fight—no doubt about that. I was fast and strong. I was still plotting my preemptive attack when we reached the bottom of the stairs.

We came to another door, this one circular.

"What the hell is this?" I asked, frowning at the strange entryway. Carlton grinned and rapped a knock on the door. A moment later, it swung open, the hinges old and creaking. On the other side was a long room with a low ceiling. The walls and floor were made of concrete and it smelled a little musty, like old, dry dirt. Over a metal desk were some decorations—red felt Preston pennants, black and white photos, trophies. It was like the twisted basement version of Preston's main hall, with all the display cases. It was dark, only lit by a few flickering camping lanterns. Emory stood in the middle of the room, slightly hunched, arms open wide. A few other guys I recognized as part of the defunct Devils stood behind him.

"What's going on?" I asked, hoping I wasn't about to get outright murdered. Kids at Mountain Point might be harder, more vicious, but I tend to forget that rich kids like these have a tendency toward the batshit insane.

"History, my friend," Emory said, all dramatic and weird. "We're making history and here's your chance to get in on it."

Over the next hour and a case of room-temperature beer, Emory explained that what he wanted to do was to reestablish a straight-up, elitist secret society. Apparently, the Devils didn't start off as a bunch of jocks terrorizing underclassmen and scratching notches in the beam above the bell tower. It started a hundred years before the current incarnation; a group of high-powered individuals, male *and* female, who dominated the school academically, athletically, and socially. They had a strict initiation that went beyond drinking a gallon of vodka and screwing virgins. They had rituals, rites of passage, and—if Emory is to be believed—a civility lost on the current group of students.

How did Emory find out about this long-lost Preston Prep lore? Well, like he said, the Devils' roots run deep. Alumni, current faculty, probably even some administration were in on it. When they heard about the current group getting disbanded, they stepped up, reaching out to the strongest Devil, and suggested he lead the remaining members a new direction—or really, an old direction. They showed him the bunker under the tower, gave him the book of Devil's history, and ultimately gave him permission to restart the group.

I'd looked into the eye of his friends tonight—Carlton, Ben, and a few others I didn't know—and I saw the gleam of power in their eyes. They wanted this. The cred. The legacy. The power that had been yanked from them last year. Them I understood, but Emory already had all that. I couldn't figure out his angle, his motive.

But now I know for certain.

That's why I snapped when I saw Baby V skulking around the yard, eavesdropping on me and her brother. She'll blow this before Emory ever gets it off the ground. I'll get tossed out of Preston before that.

From the dark, fearful look in her eyes, she's probably already hoping I fail.

I turn the light off, slamming my fist into my pillow before rolling onto my side. I'm walking a tightrope here. One foot on the wire, holding myself above the fray. The other dangling, one bad move could send me tumbling. I do know one thing for certain; Vandy Hall is not going to be involved.

MY BODY WAKES LIKE CLOCKWORK, still attuned after years of early morning PT even after having been here a while. Every day, I'm still up at the ass-crack of dawn. I feel like hell, my body sore from the game the night before. Sore, but also good, and sort of proud. We kicked ass on the field. Me and Emory make a good team. We always have.

I try to train myself to sleep a little longer, at least until the birds are awake, but it's futile. Even if I could go back to sleep, my body craves a strong dose of caffeine and I feel the headache coming.

It's obvious the moment I walk into the kitchen that my father has been here. Seemingly, not alone.

Apparently, making up for being married to my mom all these years includes a lot of sleeping around. Not that he was loyal back then or anything. It's hard to tell with the way my parents always kept shit so tight behind closed doors, but if I had to guess, I'd say their biggest troubles started after the wreck. It was impossible not to notice the tension when they came to Mountain Point for visits. The strain on my mother's face and the twenty pounds she gained, most likely from binge-drinking wine, were glaringly obvious. For my father, this was a perfect excuse to fuck around with one or more of the recent college graduates that worked in his office. The weight gain and affairs ultimately led her to the personal trainer, who apparently thought working out in bed would be appropriate exercise. The night of the crash was like knocking over a domino, everything tipping over until there was nothing in this family left standing.

A bottle of wine is uncorked, ninety percent empty, on the counter along with two empty wine glasses. A black leather purse sits on the kitchen table—the table that, once upon a time, we sat at as a functional family.

The contents are painfully dull. Chapstick, tissues, keys, wallet, driver's license. Tammy Killian, same birth month as me, but seven years older, one hundred and thirty pounds, five-seven, brown eyes, brown hair, not an organ donor.

She has a crisp fifty-dollar bill in her billfold. Like, obviously that's...

*Mine now.*

I put it all away, eventually hearing the stirrings of an awkward morning-after occurring in the master bedroom down the hall. I snap alert and move to the counter, searching for the coffee. I didn't drink coffee when I left home. I was fourteen. My prime sources of energy back then were candy, soda, and masturbation. But six a.m. mandatory runs at school had made coffee an integral part of my diet. I open cabinet after cabinet, increasingly aware that at least half the dishes and glasses and everything else is gone. Did my mom come here and split everything down the middle? Did that include the fucking coffee? I go to the pantry and stare at the empty shelves. Where the fuck is it?

"Check the freezer."

Tension rolls up my spine, settling at the base of my neck. I close the pantry door and turn around. My father's opening a cabinet, pulling out a bottle of pain meds. From the look on his face, I'm confident in calling it a hangover. His hair is disheveled—a darker shade than mine—a scattering of gray at the temples. I guess he's what you'd call distinguished, although I can tell he's had some work done on his face since I saw him a few months ago. The fine lines around his eyes are smoothed, as well as the deep lines on his forehead that developed after I got sent away. He's fit, from hours spent at the gym or running. I get my athleticism from him—probably the lack of impulse control, too.

I go to the freezer and sure enough, among the mostly empty shelves is a container of coffee grounds. The frigid air feels good on my face, waking me up and cooling me off.

My dad sighs. "Shut the door, Reyn, it's not a goddamn air conditioner."

A heartbeat later, I ease the door shut and start making the coffee.

"You had a good game last night," he says, suddenly.

"You were there?" He wasn't out front with the other parents when we walked out of the locker rooms.

"For the first three quarters." He elaborates, opening another cupboard for coffee cups. "I had to leave early for a date, but you guys had a solid lead by then."

Ah, the date. The one I assume is upstairs sleeping off the bottle of wine and a night of gymnastics with my father.

"We had a few fumbles back on defense, but nothing we can't work out. A few of the guys need to work on their cardio," I say, rambling. I have no idea what to say to this man. We don't have a relationship. My mother is gone. There's a strange chick upstairs. I rake a hand through my hair.

He walks around me to set down three mugs, eyes sliding to Tammy's purse. There's a stretch of tense silence before he mutters, "*Christ*. Put it back." His voice sounds even more tired than he looks.

I give him my most convincing innocent look. "Put what back?"

He narrows his eyes. "Whatever you took from the poor girl's purse. Don't play with me, Reyn. I'm not in the mood for your bullshit this morning."

Yeah, I stopped being able to pull one over on my dad in about fifth grade.

I roll my eyes, pulling the fifty from my pocket and flinging it toward the purse. "Well since I don't have any money and you don't seem interested in the boring parts of being a parent like—oh, say, *grocery shopping*—does that mean my new mommy upstairs is going to find some breakfast?"

His nostrils flare angrily, but my dad doesn't respond. Instead, he stalks out of the kitchen and returns with his own wallet, plucking a credit card from it. "You know, you could try asking some time."

I take the credit card, feeling almost bored by it. Where's the thrill in *asking*? Where's the risk? Where's the satisfaction from getting away with it, taking it home, stashing it away? "Wasn't aware I needed to ask for food, my bad."

"You're eighteen, not eight."

I've also spent three years having every meal—as awful as they were—provided to me. The guys at school act like the lunch is some cruel form of institutional punishment, but the shit we ate at Mountain Point makes Preston lunch food look like gourmet dining. So, yeah. I'm not picky. I'm also fucking clueless where cooking is concerned.

"That card has a limit, Reyn. Essentials only," my dad continues. "There's a grocery delivery service, so order what you want on my account."

Thankfully the sounds of coffee brewing comes to a stop, and I have something to do with my hands besides pull out my own hair.

"Listen," he says as I start toward the hall, mug in hand, "I'll be gone for a few days this week. Conference in New Orleans. The maid comes on Tuesday. I told her to change your sheets."

I swallow the black, bitter coffee. "Got it."

He holds up the two cups and gives me a tight smile. "Guess I should take these up to Tammy."

Ah, Tammy. I roll the name around my brain a few times. Doesn't feel like the name of my new step-mommy. I won't get attached.

We go up the stairs, one after the other. Him back to Tammy. Me, back...alone. At the top of the staircase he pauses and says, "I expect you to be on good behavior while I'm gone. Leaving you alone right now isn't ideal but," his eyes dart to his bedroom door, "I have a life to live, and work to do, despite your return. No drugs. No stealing. No illegal behavior. Is that clear?"

I hold his eye for a long beat, wanting to tell him to fuck off, but I swallow it back and tell him what he wants to hear, "Crystal."

# 7

I'm already in the massage chair, feet soaking in hot water, when Sydney strolls into the nail salon. Her dark hair is twisted in a messy bun, like she didn't get a chance to brush it. Sunglasses cover her eyes and she carries a cup from The Nerd—The Northridge Diner—in her hand. She walks over to the wall and picks out a bottle of polish before climbing into the seat next to mine. It's only then that she pushes the glasses up and I see her red, exhausted eyes.

"Wow, late night?" I ask.

She programs the massage controller and leans back into the padded seat. "Be glad you aren't into the party scene, V."

I take a moment to chew on my lip before asking, "Why?" I already know this is going to be a thinly-veiled humblebrag, but maybe there's something there. Something that's so dreadful that my night at home, all alone, will seem less pathetic and lame.

"Because it starts out fun," she explains, eyes sliding closed, "like there's a million opportunities, you know? Boys. Booze. A hot tub. It's like anything can happen, yet every single time, nothing new happens." She exhales dramatically. "Just the same old hook-ups. The same fights. The same crappy alcohol that leaves a pounding headache."

Yep.

Just a humblebrag.

"I'm sorry?" I say, not really holding back my eye-roll. "I mean, you know what they say about repeating the same behavior over and over, and expecting a different outcome."

She glares at my insensitivity and shuts her eyes as the chair begins kneading her back. I look down at my feet, the water in the tub swirling around. This is the closest I've ever been to a hot tub. I've never been to a party. Never been invited. There's just this assumption that poor little Vandy Hall—Baby V—would never do something like that.

I lean back and let the massager pound into the tense muscles in my own back. I'm not even sure how the reputation of me being some virginal, angelic goody-goody even came from, but it follows me around like toilet paper stuck to the bottom of my shoe. I mean, for the most part, I really am a good kid. I don't seek out trouble like Emory. I don't go out of my way to flaunt myself like Syd. I don't steal like...*other people*. Truthfully, I'm a fan of the path of least resistance. That just so happens to mean not causing trouble.

But there's no doubt that it's all about the wreck. That's when my status was elevated from 'good girl' to 'tragic victim'. The only thing a group of school-kids loves to do more than rally behind a classmate after something terrible happens is to belittle them as subtly as possible. It didn't help that Emory went into overdrive as the protective older brother. He's gone way beyond the cliché. Even if a guy were interested in me—he wouldn't be—or if my parents let me go on a date—they super wouldn't—there's no way my brother would allow it to happen. His best friends were on the highest rung of the social ladder. If they weren't interested in me, no one was. And none of them would dare.

That's where the Oxy made things a little easier. I know it's wrong, and bad for me, and unhealthy, and is causing me more trouble now that I'd like to admit, but at least it's *mine*. With the pills, I can create my own world—one that's void of pain or sharp, harsh emotions. A world where I'm always okay and comfortable, and even if it can't give me happiness or the thrill of late Friday nights and their regretful morning-afters, it can at least dull the deep, aching sense of disappointment.

It's just really hard to care about being left out when you're high as a kite.

That being said, a few invites, even if I said no to them, would have been nice. Especially from my best friend.

"Hey," I say, tapping Syd on the arm. "Was Emory at that party last night?"

She cracks one eye. "No. Unfortunately. That would have made the night way more interesting." Her mouth pulls into a loose pout. "Why?"

"I heard him and...uh, Reyn," I look away, tripping over the shape of his name on my tongue, "getting home late last night. I was just wondering."

Her nose wrinkles. "Who knows. They were probably at some football circle-jerk. Wanking off to their win." Sydney makes a crude gesture with her fist, pumping it in her lap.

I snort. "Gross."

Sydney laughs quietly, wincing like it hurts to do so. "Sorry, I know he's your brother, but still. You know how tight those guys are. You can take the Devils out of the school, but you can't take the Devil out of the boy."

"That literally makes no sense."

She shrugs. "You know what I mean."

I do, which is why I'm suspicious of whatever it is those two were up to last night. Not only was their conversation a little cryptic and strange, but Reynolds' reaction to catching me out there? *Jesus.* Talk about intense.

*You nosing around like this? It's just going to get you hurt again.*

I still don't know if it was a threat. The truth is, I don't know this version of Reyn. I don't know the meaning behind his stillness, or his quiet, or the hard edges of his face. But I know he's trying to 'stay away' from me, and I know he feels my unhappiness at him being back is fair—*"I deserve that."*—and I know there's always something tight at the corner of his eyes when he looks at me. But I don't know him enough to recognize it as anything distinct.

*I know what he smells like*, my brain annoyingly reminds me. And it's true. I know the shape of his body against me, solid and strong. I know the warmth of his breath as it gusted against my hair. I know how it made me feel, like my skin was being stretched tight around a suddenly liquefied middle.

I know that I spent all night banging angrily against the sensations, willing them to leave.

The woman doing my pedicure sits on the little stool in front of me, gently lifting my foot out of the water. She starts the process of cleaning up my toes. From here, you'd never know I had a limp. It's not like it used to be, last year, back when I still wore a brace. Gait training has brought me a long way from that horrified thirteen-year-old girl who couldn't walk at all. Incomplete spinal cord injury, they called it. They said I was lucky. They said sometimes, bad things just happen to good people. They said if I worked hard and kept the faith, I could walk again—that I could be normal.

They said it wasn't my fault.

The truth is that I do carry my own blame for getting hurt that night. I'd followed the boys to stop them from doing something stupid. All it took was one smile from Reynolds, one peek at those dimples, and I happily went along for the ride. The sick truth of the matter is that I'd been elated for him to hold my hand instead of focusing on driving—a suspended moment of shiny girlhood glee that overrode all sense.

So, yes. I know what he smells like. I know the shape of his body against mine. I know the way it makes me feel. But I'm not the same girl who was sitting in that passenger seat. The image of his two dimples sitting on my memory card at home will not make me pliable, and neither will his words—threat or otherwise.

This time, I'll stop them before it goes too far.

It takes me until Tuesday to find an opportunity.

The rain comes in a sudden, rippling blanket of downfall. Everyone in the quad instantly scampers for cover, fanning out every which way. I don't bother trying to run like that—couldn't even if I wanted to—so instead I walk toward the closest awning, in front of the arts building.

It's there that I see him.

He's standing alone in the narrow, covered path that connects the old academic building to the athletic fields. I watch as his gaze slides down to his wet arms. He gives them two feeble shakes.

I walk toward him without giving myself a moment to think about it, shoes squelching in the wet grass as rain pelts my head and shoulders. Every step that brings me closer to him makes my heartbeat quicken, until it's a sharp, rapid percussion in my chest. When I reach him, he's turned away, and I spend a prolonged moment staring at the shell of his ear, stomach churning.

"I need to talk to you."

Reynolds tenses, shoulders hitching up just enough to be noticeable. He turns to peer at me over one of his wet shoulders, those green eyes tightening. "We're not supposed to be together."

I'd suspected as much. *Not* that anyone told me. "That's why I waited until I could catch you alone."

"Christ," he mutters, head shaking. "I'm not doing this." He moves to continue down the corridor and I reach out, grabbing him by the bicep. It's rock hard and bigger than my fist. He easily jerks away, eyes flashing as he turns to me. "Are you deaf?"

I swallow, and my voice isn't anywhere near as hard and sharp as I'd like it to be. "I just want you to answer one thing for me."

He chews out a terse, "What?"

"What is this secret thing you and Emory are planning?"

He snorts a humorless laugh, gaze jumping to a group of students in the distance. "So you *were* eavesdropping."

"No," I insist, grasping the straps of my bag in a tight, frustrated grip. "I was saving a chipmunk while you guys were loudly discussing something nefarious."

"Nefarious?" He rolls his eyes, the muscle in the back of his jaw going rigid. "Just leave it alone. It wasn't a big deal."

"No," I say, and there it is. The sharpness. The determination. *Finally.* "The last time I left something alone with you two, I regretted it."

His eyes finally land on mine, something dark and full of warning within his gaze. "Drop it, Baby V."

The nickname clings to the air like a memory of something painfully personal. He's the only one who ever called me Baby V. I see it now for what it always was; a way of putting me in my place. It's how he got me in that car. It's how he manipulated me.

Not anymore.

"If it's not a big deal," I say, raising myself to my full height, "then tell me what you were talking about."

His shoulder jerks up in a stiff shrug. "Can't."

"Why not?"

The curve of his brows pucker in annoyance. "Because, I promised your brother I wouldn't."

*Great.* Because stupid teenage boy loyalty always works out so well. "Tell me one thing," I demand, not flinching at the darkness in his eyes. "Is this going to get the two of you into trouble?"

His eyes hold mine. "Not if I can help it."

A flare of irritation runs through me and I hold up my hands. "God, why are you doing this? You just came back home! Emory is so excited that you're here. Last year was super shitty and a lot of bad stuff went down. Most of his friends graduated, his girlfriend gradu-ated..." I implore him with my eyes, "Why are you risking getting kicked out again?" I might not know this new Reyn, but one thing is for sure. "You're not this dumb."

Something in his expression shifts at my outburst, the crease in his forehead transforming to something seeking, confused. "It's not like that."

"How would I know?" I scoff, my anxious gaze tracking two passing students. I wait until they turn the corner to ask, "If it's not dangerous, then why can't you just tell me?"

With his hand clenched around the strap of his backpack, he turns away, face shuttering. "We're done."

"Wait."

He doesn't.

Moving as fast as I can to keep up with his long strides, I ask, "Why did you say we're not supposed to be together?"

At this, he stops, pulling in a hard breath. "Because it's a condition of my probation for coming back here." He uses fingers to quote, "Vandy Hall is off-limits."

*Off-limits.*

Story of my life.

"Why?" I blurt. "Because I'm so pathetic? So vulnerable? So—"

*Broken.*

The words won't emerge from the tightness in my throat. It feels like the last three years crashing back down on me and I'm drowning in it, fighting against a current I can't beat back.

He stares at me for a long moment, eyebrows pulling together. "What? That's not—" He waves a hand, something irritated and dismissive about the gesture. "I'm the one who's the problem. I'm like the bad fucking seed around here. Got to keep me away from sharp objects, you know. I'm a danger to pretty girls, sweet old ladies, and small fluffy animals." Despite the thread of levity to his words, the tight smile he wears is edged with bitterness.

Of course, all I can think about is the fact he kind of just called me... pretty?

I work so hard to push that thought away that I physically shake my head.

"You're not—" He looks away, that tight smile transforming into a stony frown. "You're not pathetic."

"Tell that to the rest of the school." I snort, following his gaze to where a puddle is collecting nearby. "They treat me like I'm a delicate flower. One swift wind or a hard rain, and my petals fall right off."

"Well..." He reaches up to rake a hand over his wet hair, back to front. "That's lame."

I laugh grimly. "No one seems to think so. Between Emory, my parents, and the school, I basically live in a bubble." *Except that if I lived in a bubble, I could probably breathe.* "No fun for Vandy. But hey, I can get a pedicure every now and then." I slide my gaze to his, offering my own bitter grin. "Without adult supervision, even."

Reynolds looks back at me, blank-faced but for the single eyebrow that curves upward. "I have to get frisked by Fucking Jerry every other day."

I counter, "I'm not allowed to go to parties."

A corner of his mouth tugs up. "I live next to someone I'm not allowed to even look at."

"If I'm in public and I need to go to the bathroom, my mom comes with me."

He shifts his shoulders, seeming to really get on a roll. "If I don't win enough games, they'll probably pull my scholarship."

I bob my head. "I've never had a boyfriend. I'll probably be thirty by the time I do, and Emory will probably scare him away before the appetizers arrive on our first date."

Reynolds looks away, pushing a long 'pssshh' from his lips. "I think if your biggest problem is that people actually give a shit, then that's probably a good problem to have."

"No," I say, nostrils flaring in anger. "My biggest problem is that I'm constantly suffocated and slowly dying of boredom."

"You work on the paper, right?" He suddenly says, brows drawing together. "I saw you taking pictures at the game the other night. That's..." He shrugs, seeming momentarily lost for words. "Well, I don't know. It's something."

"Nice try. I get to cover *sports*, which isn't even something I'm interested in." I roll my eyes heavenward, noting the emergence of the sun. "I actually proposed a topic for the investigative journalism spot, but the school is too scared to let me really dig into the seedy history of this place."

"What kind of history? Privileged, asshole white kids being institutionally molded to thirst for global domination?" He scoffs. "I think the jig is already up with that one."

I shake my head. "You missed a lot of crazy stuff over the last few years. There was an underage sexual assault scandal—one that was completely covered up by the administration and involved families, might I add. Besides the ongoing bullying of one particular senior, there was the homophobic harassment of her brother, a middle school student. Like, a legally legitimate hate crime. I'm not even including the pervasive sexism among the Devils. The way they treat girls, like they're possessions or something, is repulsive."

Reynolds makes a swooping movement with his finger. "Wheel keeps spinning."

"Yeah, well, not all of us are down with being cogs." I look around the campus, noting that students are beginning to filter out from the shelters. The air is humid and smells like damp concrete. "They don't want their dirty laundry aired, so my idea was instantly rejected."

He levels me with a look, and I'm not sure what's happened over the course of the conversation, but I think I'm beginning to realize that his face isn't actually always hard-edged and blank. He's harder to read than he used to be, more subtle, but if I look hard enough, I can tell.

Right now, he's looking at me like I'm an idiot. "Fighting a place like Preston Prep is futile. These people will never change, even if they pretend to. You should just lay low, get out of here in two years, and move on with your life."

"That sounds like what *you* need to do, not me." I level him with my very own 'you're dumb' look, thrusting a thumb at my chest. "Me? I've got a pristine record. Straight A's, no behavioral problems, the perfect picture of literal virginal innocence. I can risk ruffling a few feathers, and I'll come out unscathed." Because I'm slowly learning to read his bare expressions, I almost miss how he blanches at the word 'virginal'. *Almost.* "But you need to take your own advice. Stay out of whatever you and Emory are messing with, because if there's one thing I know about Preston Prep, it's that secrets rarely stay secret for long."

His eyes grow harder at this. "You're saying this like I have any control over what Emory does."

"Because you do," I insist, shifting to meet his gaze. "You might now know it, but he'll follow your lead."

Reyn just shakes his head. "Not with this, he won't."

It's obvious that I'm not going to change his mind, so I play my final card. "If you don't tell Emory to shut down whatever you're doing, then I'm going to the dean."

He blows out a puff of laughter. "You wouldn't."

"I would. Last time, I didn't stop you, and look what happened." Instinctively his eyes flick to my leg. I don't know if I'm bluffing, but from the hard set of his jaw, I'm pretty sure he believes me. "I won't make that mistake again." I turn away and have already made it halfway back to the building before I stop and add, "You have until tomorrow night."

# 8

"YOU READY?"

I shift my shoulders, settling onto the bench. "Yeah."

Emory stands over me to spot as I start my next set of bench presses. Preston Prep has an awesome training facility, including a weight trainer. He's created a specific workout to help improve my performance on the field. It's the little things like this that make Preston a cut above everyone else. Mountain Point had a sledge-hammer approach to most things. Nothing was targeted or focused. We all ran. We all ate the same shit, and the same amount of it. We all did the same exercises, day in, day out, rain, mud, or shine. We all had the same muscles, the same aches, the same conditioning. It was a conveyor belt of cattle.

But Preston is precise, surgical. If they want a wide receiver, they train him as a wide receiver. It's foreign, this feeling that I have something specific and useful, excelling at a skill that people actually want to see nurtured.

Probably because this skill is actually legal.

Lately, I've been finding myself—sort of embarrassingly—motivated at the mere thought of it. But not so much today. My arms strain against the weight of the bar, but I push through. Today, I'm pissed about Vandy and her little threat.

Was she for real? Would she really do it?

Well, that's what I get for letting my guard down around her.

I lower the bar and take a deep breath before pushing into the next rep. Squealing on her brother seems out of character, but do I even know Vandy's character anymore? She's always just been Emory's little sister—sweet Baby V, the girl I ruined—but maybe she's someone else now. Beneath the threads of fear and uncertainty in her eyes lurks something cynical and restless. Our earlier conversation made that much apparent.

It's not like I haven't heard the chatter. People like pimply-faced George seem a dime a dozen around here—people who see her as something to be gawked at and gossiped about. For them, she's entertainment. It only makes sense that people want to protect her from it. From assholes like George. From criminals like me, who are ultimately responsible for all of it.

Nevertheless, there's something ironically kindred there. Being gossiped about and watched, every waking second? Oh, I've got that shit down to a science.

My lips twitch as I think *'maybe we should start a band'*.

*Sensational and Surveilled.*

The parallels stop there, though. I'm despised and suspicious. Vandy is pitied, placed behind glass. *Look, but don't touch.* Seventeen, and never had a boyfriend? That *is* pitiful. God, she even dropped that she still had her v-card. Hell, I spent the last three years literally locked up, and even I found opportunities for action. Given the way she looks, all innocent and sweet, there should be a line of fuckboys just waiting to dirty her all up. Then again, maybe that's why Emory and everyone else are so quick to shut it down. Because it's true. She even looks pure as driven snow, and that shit definitely draws a certain type.

Up and down the bar goes. Sweat pools on my lower back. There's one more thing I learned about Vandy during that conversation: She's a shit stirrer alright, wanting to write that article about the skeletons in Preston Prep's closet. That takes balls. And with the knowledge comes a stark realization that I've been clutching to for hours now.

I hadn't broken that part of her.

The problem for her in all this is that, if what Emory said is true —that the school wants the Devils back, even in a new iteration— then what happens to Vandy if she narcs?

Nothing good, that's for sure.

Not for any of us.

My arms start to quiver, shaking under the weight. Sweat drips into my eye, but I can see Emory watching me, waiting for me to ask for help. I lower the bar one more time but just don't have the juice to lift it again.

"A little help," I grunt, feeling the weight pressing down on my chest. Emory moves quickly, grabbing the bar and lifting it back over the rack.

"Damn, son!" He looks impressed. "What the hell did they have you doing at that military school? I've been training my ass off all summer and I couldn't bench that much."

I lie flat for a few moments, my triceps stinging with exhaustion, before I get up to swap places. I wait until Emory's settled in my spot to say, "Hey, can I ask you something?"

He keeps his eyes trained to the bar. "Sure."

"What's the deal with your sister?"

His eyes flick to mine, lips pressing into a thin line. "What do you mean?"

"I don't know." I shrug. "I've just seen her around. She seems really quiet and introverted. Not like...well, you know."

His eyes narrow a fraction. "Not like she used to be?"

I elaborate, "No, I mean, not like you. Not popular, or outgoing, or uh..." I feel my eyes tighten as I try to find the least insulting way of calling his sister a coddled outcast. "Just not like you."

"Oh." Emory grips the bar, jerking his chin. I lift it off the rack, making sure it's steady in his hands. Emory tests the weight, voice strained as he explains, "Well, she had a hard time after the accident. You know, surgeries and stuff. Everyone just decided to give her a break. Make sure she had the space to heal."

Surgeries.

*Duh.* Of course, she'd have surgeries. I don't know why hearing about it makes something jagged rattle around in my chest, but it does. For some reason, I can't help but imagine it—Vandy on some table in a well-lit operating room, all opened up like a gaping wound.

I swallow around the nausea and watch as he completes only a few bench presses, struggling through the last two. I help him re-rack the bar, and he slings his legs over the bench, sitting up.

He tugs off the Velcro straps on his workout gloves. "Why do you ask?"

"I guess she just seems kind of..." I tug off my own gloves, trying to find the right words. "Sheltered?"

"Look, I'm not trying to—" Emory's eyes jump to mine briefly. "I don't want to make you feel bad about this. But dude, the wreck fucked her up. And then, after everything, she got kind of weird, which is to be expected, I guess. I'm not going to deny that I went into protective mode, especially at school. Not with the jackals lurking around every corner."

"Right." I nod, running my towel over my face. "That makes sense."

He frowns. "I know she feels a little stifled, but it's for her own good." He wipes the sweat off his own forehead with his shirt. When he meets my gaze again, his face is creased with a reserved, secret kind of concern. "Honestly? I'm worried about her being alone next year."

Finally. Maybe if I understood this, I can talk him out of this secret society thing.

"Why?" I ask, even though I already know.

"Because people here are fucking vicious, bro. Vandy's not like us. She's *good*." He looks down, fidgeting with his gloves. "She doesn't have that hardness. It's one of the best things about her, but it's also..." He pulls a face.

"It could make her an easy target," I guess. "If the wrong kind of people had the power here."

"Pretty much." Emory shrugs. "With me here, people know better. But after I leave? Who knows, you feel me?"

I change tacks. "She's got friends, right?"

He rolls his eyes. "Yeah, Sydney, for one. That girl is a fucking train wreck, though. I don't trust her as far as Vandy can throw her." I slide a weight from one end of the bar as he takes the other.

I keep my eyes fixed firmly to the task as I inquire, "What about a boyfriend?"

There's a long, tense silence as I rack the weight, but when I turn to get the other from Emory's hands, he's assessing me, eyes guarded. "Nah. She's not into dating." When I take the weight with nothing more than a mild nod, he seems to relax, letting out a laugh. "Thank god, right? We both know what all these guys around here want, and it's not to show her their stamp collection. Last thing I need is a murder charge."

"Wipes," I interrupt, fanning out my hands.

Emory rushes to the other side of the room to mimic our game-winning throw from last Friday. We spend a few minutes cleaning up, running the cleaning wipes over the equipment, heeding the big lecture we'd gotten from the trainer on the first day about MRSA and other such plagues.

I can't stop thinking about Vandy as we walk into the locker room. Is this my fault, too? Or would her brother and parents still have been this vigilant, regardless? She'd always been a little sheltered, truthfully, and Emory is right. Vandy doesn't have a hardness about her, never has. Back when we were kids, it used to be an almost fun trait to play with. Teasing her. Coaxing her. Getting her to cover for us, because she was such an honest face and an easy mark. When Vandy lied, butter couldn't fucking melt.

But the accident had to have made it worse. It's a question that nags at me, this sense that I have one more sin to add to my pile. Of course, Vandy is bored out of her mind, and why wouldn't she be? She's living in the land of gluttony at Preston. Everyone else is off partying, getting laid, spending mommy and daddy's money, making memories, and leaving a mark in that long corridor of glass trophy cases. And here Vandy Hall just wants to write some dumb fucking article—*that's* her pinnacle of significance here—and she can't even do that.

Instead, she wants to shut Emory's whole plan down.

I already know I can't talk Emory out of it—not if he's doing it for her. At the same time, I know I can't talk her out of getting in the way —not if she's doing it for him.

Goddamn siblings, man.

I thank God for making me an only child, but something begins brewing in my mind—some connecting factor. Emory needs the Devils. Vandy needs a project. I need to stop getting caught between it.

Maybe, if I handle this exactly right, all three of us can get what we need out of Preston Prep.

You'd think it would be easier to talk to the girl next door, but no dice. It's not exactly like I can go over, knock on the door, and ask her out for a chat. I don't have her cell number, and she hasn't touched the closed curtains on her bedroom window once. She has a couple social media profiles, but they're sparse enough that I figure she doesn't bother with them much.

At a loss for anything better, I do what all guys do when trying to catch a girl's attention; pretend to be doing something else, while lying in wait.

My chance comes after dinner. For me, that means a sad cheese pizza from whatever joint the HOA allows through their gate. And if the smells wafting from next door are any indication, then for Vandy, that means an actual home-cooked meal. The scent of it makes my stomach churn in longing as I take my empty, greasy pizza box to the trash can just outside the garage.

*Cat.*

The cat is clearly stalking something, crouched low to the ground in front of the bushes. Its fluffy tail flicks to the left and right, ears pointed forward as it listens intently.

"So we meet again," I tell Firefly, interrupting the cat's focus. "Come here, kitty-kitty." I bend down, fully expecting it to either hesitate or book it. It is a cat after all—they're suspicious as hell—but instead, it strolls right over and rubs a whiskered cheek across my outstretched hand. "What'cha doing out here, huh? Stalking chipmunks?"

The cat purrs greedily and stretches its front paws out, giving me space to scratch under its chin. Firefly is so pleased by the affection that it doesn't move when its owner comes outside.

"Firefly," Vandy coos. "Where's my sweet boy?"

"Over here," is my soft reply, knowing that I'm breaking all the rules by engaging her like this. School rules, house rules, best friend rules. At least what happened at school wasn't my fault. This is something else altogether, and it makes me antsy, nervous.

I hear the sound of her stilted footfalls before I see her. Vandy eventually appears around Emory's massive truck, and crouched as I am, the first thing I see is the creamy skin revealed by a pair of lounging shorts.

"Oh," she says, sounding vaguely startled.

I can't help the way my eyes slide up her calves, skitter over her delicate knees, and land on the pale expanse of her smooth thighs. I tear my gaze away to look up at her, jaw flexing. "He was on the hunt, again."

She chews on her lip for a moment while she regards the way I'm petting her cat. "It's dusk. The zombie hour. The best time to kill."

It's an odd, aloof statement, but I'm starting to think Vandy may be both of those things.

"So, uh." I pull my hand away from Firefly to scratch at the back of my own neck now. The cat looks vaguely put out about it. "Can we talk?"

Vandy eyes the driveway shiftily, peering over her shoulder to check her house. "You make a decision?"

I finally rise, glancing around in much the same way, neck prickling as I shove my fists into my pockets. "Is there somewhere we can go to talk?"

She points to the path between our houses. It leads up a hill and into a wooded area that we spent a lot of time in when we were kids, playing games and exploring. She says, "Meet me back there in fifteen minutes?"

Without further explanation, she lunges for the cat, grabs him, and vanishes back in the house.

Ten minutes pass, taking with it the soft glow of evening sunset as I watch from my kitchen window. Putting on my sneakers, I head out first, not wanting to be seen following her like some fucking creeper. One minute I'm on the well-manicured lawn, and the next I'm in the thicket of trees. I use my phone for a flashlight and wonder exactly where I'm supposed to go. Just then, the beam of my phone's light illuminates something old, familiar. I take a few steps forward and touch the weathered strips of wood attached to the big oak that straddles the property line. I point the light upward and see the tree house our dads had built when we were in elementary school.

A twig snaps behind me and I spin. Vandy stands a few feet away, the light from her own phone blinding me. I shield my eyes with my hand, glancing back to the tree house. "I can't believe this is still here."

She watches me for a long moment before her blue eyes follow my gaze. "I'm pretty sure they forgot about it."

We stand there for a suspended moment, just looking at the structure, before the sounds of her shuffling steps pass me. I watch as she tests the first rung of the ladder with her toe, eventually putting her weight on it and beginning to ascend.

I jump forward and burst, "Wait, we don't have to—" But she ignores me. Her steps are slow, deliberate, cautious, and my heart hammers as I track her form with the beam of light. If she falls and breaks something, I'm fucked.

No.

I'm *beyond* fucked.

I'm still locked in a whirlwind of panicky indecision about dropping the phone—I'll need both hands to catch her, but I'll also need to see if she falls—when she reaches the top.

"Come on," she says, face peering out of the door opening.

I still need to take a moment before my heart stops thundering, allowing some of the tension to bleed from my shoulders. I put my phone in my back pocket, and use her light to guide me. The wooden steps are old, but still perfectly sturdy, thank fucking god. Way to give a guy a heart attack.

Just as I crawl through the narrow door and get to my feet, the bright light of a camping lantern fills the room. I dust off my hands and glance around the space, surprised that even after all this time, it looks and feels exactly the same.

Professionally built, the structure isn't one of those slapped-together shacks perched precariously in the top of a tree. No, this shit is like the McMansion of tree houses. It was big enough for a whole group of us back then, and now, Vandy and I fit comfortably in the space together. An old hammock hangs catty-cornered against the wall, and a bookshelf filled with faded comics slouches under one window. There's a dartboard, two bean bag chairs, and the old futon that's seen better days. It smells a little damp, musty, but it's obviously still watertight.

"This is surreal," I say, absorbing it all. "Like a fucking time capsule." There was happiness here. Laughter. Crude jokes. Boyhood mischief. Long stretches of golden summer afternoons. Bright winter evenings spent huddled in sweaters and avoiding homework. Everything had felt so easy and certain, back then.

Now, everything seems grey and anemic, paltry in the face of recollection.

While I'm caught up in my own nostalgia, Vandy is all business. "If you asked me to meet you to try to talk me out of my ultimatum, forget it." The look in her eye tells me she's ready to call me on any and all bullshit.

I scoop a baseball from the shelf, testing the weight in my hand.

"I'm not trying to talk you out of it, but—" I meet her gaze. "I do have a proposal."

She stares back, face blank. "A proposal."

"A plan B, I guess." I shrug, tossing the ball from hand to hand. "Something that benefits all of us."

Her eyes narrow, hands settling on her narrow hips. "I don't think I care if it benefits all of us. I just want to protect my brother."

Another golden flash from childhood slams into me. Vandy, standing stubbornly in the tree house, same position she's in now, barking orders at me and her brother. Like the tree house, some things never change.

I thunk the ball back onto the shelf. "Will you just hear me out?"

Her arms move to cross her chest and her hip juts out. The position draws my attention to her chest, then down to her curves below her waist. Okay, maybe *some* things do change.

I run my hand through my hair and try not to blow the fact she's obviously giving me the chance to plead my case. "You said you wanted to write a big story about the school, right?"

Her eyebrows knit together. "Yeah?"

I nod, looking away. "What if I told you there's something big going on at Preston Prep. Something that falls right in line with what you want to expose about the school, like all the way down to the elitist foundations and principles of a place like Preston."

Some of the apprehensive tension leaves her face. "I'm listening."

I hedge, "I can't tell exactly you what it is—"

She huffs, "Are you kidd—"

"But!" I hold up my hands. "I think I can get you access. Like a real, undercover, deep dive into the bowels of the true culture of the school. You'll just have to give me a chance to get it together." Her face scrunches up and I tilt my head. "What? I thought you'd be into this?"

"I guess I am," she explains, "but I think I'm trying to figure out how you've been here like eight days and you know more about the school than I do."

I raise an eyebrow. "I suspect it has more to do with me being a white male football player than anything else."

She snorts. "God, you're probably right."

"So," I say, trying to get this ball moving. The way her and Emory made it sound before, it doesn't seem entirely unlikely that people might come looking for her. "Are you interested?"

She agrees, "Yeah, I'm interested," but that gleam in her eyes is pure suspicion. "But there's obviously a catch. You said this would benefit all of us."

"If we can make this work, I need two things from you."

She still looks skeptical. "Like?"

"First, you can't tell on me, Emory, or anyone else involved." She opens her mouth to speak, but I hold up two fingers. "And two, you can't turn in whatever you write to the school or paper until after he and I have graduated."

Her jaw sets as she thinks it over. I'm asking a lot from her. I haven't even told her what it's about. She's going to have to trust me —*me*. The guy who fucked up her life, and—although she isn't aware of it yet—is responsible for Emory needing to do this in the first place.

"Okay," she finally says, "but if you can't get me access to whatever this is, then I'm going straight to Dean Dewey, my parents, and your dad, and telling them you guys are up to something."

I know this is going to be a hard sell, on my end. I might not even be able to do anything at all. But if she agrees to this, then that's flexibility. I can work with this.

"Deal?" I hold out my hand. She looks down at it and hesitates for a second before sliding hers into mine, gripping it in a firm handshake.

She holds my gaze, her blue eyes full of something steely and resolved. "Deal."

~

"LET'S TALK ABOUT CHICKS," Carlton says, reaching for another piece of pizza.

"What about them?" Ben asks. "The fact you haven't seen one naked in over a year?"

Carlton shoves his hand out, slamming into Ben's shoulder. The baseball catcher falls off his chair, landing hard on his ass. Emory barks a laugh and I lean back in my seat, chomping on my own slice of pizza. It's steadily become ninety percent of my diet.

Personally, I'm still trying to figure out if Ben is actually as dumb as he looks.

"Shut the hell up," Carlton says, cheeks red. "I admit I'm in a bit of a slump, but that's because I'm picky. I'm not putting my dick just anywhere, unlike you indiscriminate fucks."

"Your loss," Ben says, righting his chair and flopping back into it.

We're seated in a small circle inside the bunker beneath the Devil's Tower. So far, it's only the four of us making up the Devils, which is kind of sad, if I'm being honest. Four dudes sitting in a dank dungeon eating room temperature pizza does not an elite secret society make.

Since we need a couple more guys, we've made a list of who we plan on inviting. Some new kid named Tyson from the swim team was tossed around and given approval. For the last guy, we needed a legacy—someone whose family is Devil-made—and that's how we settled on Sebastian Wilcox, Heston's younger brother. I don't know a lot about Sebastian, but I know just enough about Heston to feel like it's a bad idea.

Narrowing down the girls is a bit harder.

"I think the best thing to do," Emory says, propping his feet up on the small table in the middle of the room, "is to have each of us invite a girl to tryout to be a Devil's Plaything."

"Try out?" Ben asks, eyes flashing in excitement. "Like, we each get to fuck her?"

"Jesus Christ," Emory mutters, dragging a hand down his face. "No, fuckweed. They're not whores. They'll be our..." He rubs pensively at his chin, eventually landing on, "Our *contemporaries*. Every good fraternity has a sorority counterpart; girls to party with, both beautiful and smart. Think about Campbell. She ran those girls with an iron fist. The rest of the school revered them. Guys wanted to bang them. Girls wanted to be them. The Devils are nothing without a solid group of hot chicks by our side." He taps his pen on the pad of paper, mouth turning into a frown. "Unfortunately, most of them graduated last year, and frankly, Campbell may have done too good a job of isolating the rest of the girls at the school. We'll need to start fresh."

"I vote Afton Cross," Carlton says, using his pizza crust to point at Emory.

"Seconded," Ben instantly says. "Damn, she's hot."

Emory doesn't argue. "Yeah, that's pretty obvious. Because she's not *just* hot. She has influence and a good bloodline. See where I'm going with this?" After a few nods, Emory offers, "Aubrey Wills, too."

Everyone agrees, while Ben mumbles, "God, those tits," and makes a squeezing motion in front of his chest. Emory throws the pen at him and it bounces off his forehead. "Ow."

"Stop being a pervert," Emory admonishes, looking frustrated. "Aubrey is hot, but she's also smart and her family is loaded. Are you not getting the point of this?"

Ben stretches out his legs and rubs his forehead. "Fine, what about Sydney Tisdale?"

"Fuck no," Emory replies quickly.

"Why not? She's hot. Fun…"

"She's toxic," Emory explains, "and cannot keep her goddamn mouth shut. The whole school will know about this two minutes after she's invited, and there will be a video to prove it."

"That's fair," Ben admits. "Girl gives good head, though."

I snort a quiet laugh and Emory's attention turns to me. "What about you? Who are you going to nominate?"

I know he's expecting me to say that I don't know, that I haven't been here long enough to read the room or scout the options. He's not wrong. Nerves twist in my belly, knowing what I'm about to propose is going to be tough to sell. I take a calming breath and say, "Actually, I do have a suggestion."

"Wait, really?" His face shows his surprise. "Who?"

"Vandy."

The name is met by an uncomfortable silence, Carlton going still, mid-chew. All eyes dart to Emory, who stares at me for a long moment before bursting out with a loud, "Ha! Yeah, good one."

I cut my eyes to him. "I'm serious."

The tense amusement bleeds from Emory's face instantly. It's replaced by something dark and threatening. "You're going to want to get unserious."

I hold his stare, unheeding of the warning in his eye. "Why?"

He just grinds out, "Not going to happen."

"Why not?"

Ben and Carlton watch us closely. The back of my neck prickles like crazy, either in warning or annoyance. I'm not sure.

The irony might be lost on Emory, but not me.

The biggest reason I stole that car—and got Vandy hurt to begin with—was to impress the Devils and score myself and Emory a spot in the group. Now we're bringing the Devils back to life for pretty much the sole purpose of protecting her.

Emory looks at me like I'm an idiot. "Because she's my fucking sister, Reyn, and I said no. Vandy can't be involved in something like this."

I look at the others, lifting my shoulders in a loose shrug. "I'm still waiting for a reason why."

Emory's face is growing red now. "Because she's..." But he's at a loss for words.

I find them for him. "She's smart, pretty, and *your* family. She's a legacy, like Heston's brother, Sebastian. Plus, you trust her, right? If this is about building something, then adding someone like Vandy just seems like the right direction to go in."

Again, there's a long beat of silence. No one moves, other than Ben shifting uncomfortably in his chair and Carlton inspecting his phone.

Emory leans forward, elbows on his knees, and glances at them. "Guys, Reyn and I need a minute."

The guys don't have to be asked twice. They're out the door, feet echoing off the stone staircase, before vanishing completely.

I try my hardest to appear calm and collected when Emory shifts his attention back on me. "Dude, the fuck is this about?"

I wave my hand dismissively. "Nothing. You asked for a suggestion and I gave one. I don't even know that many girls here anymore."

"You're not even supposed to acknowledge my sister, Reyn. I know all about the rules Headmaster Collins set when he agreed to let you back on campus. Vandy is off limits—not just to you, but any guy at this school."

I raise an eyebrow. "So now you care about me staying out of trouble? Because I think being involved in this shit goes way beyond me maybe talking to Vandy every now and then, don't you?"

"That's not the point."

"No, the point is that when it comes to her, you don't think straight."

"I'm thinking just fine!" Emory exclaims, face flustered. "She's not that kind of girl. She's sweet and kind, and she's been through hell the last few years. This isn't something I'm getting her involved in."

"Well, that's too bad." I wipe my greasy hands on my jean-clad thighs. "Because if she's out, then so am I."

Emory is openly gaping at me. "What the hell is to you, anyway?"

"What is it to me?" I feel my eyes flashing in resentment. "It's my best friend willing to risk my second chance here because he refuses to let his sister out of his sight for ten minutes. It's superfucked, Em."

Emory rears back, face falling. "It's not like that."

"Yes, it is." I lean forward, as though getting closer could will him to understand. "And you know what the worst part is? I'd do it, just because you asked, even though it's a shitty plan with no guarantee to work. You think the next group of Devils are going to protect her, based on what, exactly? You think a Wilcox—" I press two fingers to my temple, incredulous, "—a *Wilcox*, of all motherfuckers, is going to stand between her and the assholes of this school? Fuck's sake, Em, we *are* the assholes of this school." I shake my head, falling back into my chair. "There's only one way she becomes untouchable, and that's to make her one of us, too. And if you were thinking straight, you'd see that."

I can see the moment he realizes I'm right. The tight pucker of his brows slowly eases into something slack and disappointed. He takes a deep breath and looks away. "The last time I got her involved in one of my schemes..." He rubs his hands nervously over his knees, head shaking. "I can't go through that again."

"So don't. But I'm out, too." I shrug, feeling weirdly empty. "I'm willing to do this if it's for Vandy, because I owe her that much. But anything else isn't worth it."

"This is all moot." Emory leans back in his own chair, arms crossing. "She'd never go for it, anyway."

I roll my eyes. "Dude, trust me. She'll go for it."

He challenges, "How can you be so sure?" and I feel my lips pull up into a hard smirk.

"I happen to know a thing or two about being locked up and never allowed to have any fun." I push an annoyed exhale through my teeth. "Em, the girl's bored out of her damn mind. You said it yourself, she feels stifled. If someone asked her to McDonald's, she'd probably break out into a Disney song."

Emory scoffs. "This is different. This is some serious rule-breaking shit. You know Vandy, she's a saint."

*Because that's all you ever allow her to be.*

"Just ask her," I say instead. "If she says no, then we can have a backup."

"You realize that some of this shit is going to pair us off—Devils and Playthings. Are you really telling me the thought of Ben or Carl or a Wilcox doing stuff with Vandy doesn't make you want to barf?"

Oh, it does more than make me want to barf. What it does it make me want to hit something, preferably a face, and preferably with my boot.

My hands are still reflexively fisted when I toss out, "So if that happens, I'll be her partner."

Emory seems to be mulling this over. "So you'll put on a show, if necessary, to make it legit as possible."

"Exactly."

"I can't believe I'm—" Emory rakes a hand through his hair before rising to his feet. "If I approve this, she's off limits to everyone in the club. That has to be a rule."

Part of me kind of balks at this on Vandy's behalf. Sure, she might be a bit naïve and goody-goody, but she's capable of making her own choices. Instead of saying this, I simply agree, "Fine by me."

As he begins pacing around the space, he adds, "And she has to agree to be okay with this. She may not even want to be near you, and I'm going to need your eyes on her. I don't trust the vultures around here, bro. I know my sister is pretty, and I know a few of them would love to sink their claws into her. That shit is *not* going to happen, you get me? She's immature, and has very little social experience. We'll have to keep tabs on her."

I feel my mouth slant, but still give a slow nod. "Yeah, that's... understandable." What it is, is pretty annoying. I don't want to be a babysitter, standing between Vandy and four other guys. The only thing I want between are this Afton chick's thighs. But I know I have to do it, to keep her mouth shut. At least for a little while. "You know me, dude. I'll look after Vandy like one of my own."

His pacing slows to pensive shuffling. "Since all of this is on the down-low and no one knows about it, you two being in the same group shouldn't be a problem, right? Like, the administrators won't find out. No one will find out."

I agree, "That's the idea."

Emory finally falls back into his chair, most of that crazy energy having drained out of him. "So, we can make this work." He sounds skeptical, but accepting.

"Yeah," I agree, refusing to meet his eye. When all this blows up—and it will, once Vandy gets the Chronicle to publish her paper—Emory is going to kill me. If she keeps her word, we'll both be long gone before that happens.

She corners me the same as last time, a quick exchange in the breezeway.

"What's going on? It's been three days." Her eyes are all shifty and annoyed, arms crossed over her chest. She's wearing her hair differently today, all tied up in a knot at the top of her head. A wayward lock keeps fluttering over her forehead, and she swats it away. Her eyes look tired, strained. "I'll go to Dewey."

Like usual, I can't tell if she's trying to be genuinely threatening. Honestly, I doubt her going to the dean with such limited information would do much harm, not when someone at the school wants the Devils active again.

But it's a risk I can't take.

"Calm your—" I swallow the word 'tits' before it slips out of my mouth. "Everything is good, but you're going to have to wait a little longer for details."

"How much longer?"

"If I knew, I'd tell you." Maybe. "But I don't. This thing... I'm in the dark about a lot of it, too."

The breezeway door opens and two kids, probably freshmen, walk out. Vandy and I stop talking while they pass. When they've gone through the other door she says, "But you worked it out? With Emory?"

"Yes. It's all good." She opens her mouth again, but I hold up a hand. "Just be patient, okay?"

She rolls her eyes. "You're one to talk. You've always been the most impatient person I know."

I stare blank-faced at her for a suspended moment, caught on a precipice between blowing it off and suddenly unloading the reality of my last three years on her. Impatience isn't sitting in two rooms all day, waiting for your hearing. Impatience isn't six hours spent on the track, doing drills every Thursday. Impatience isn't getting popped for contraband and cleaning five bathroom floors with a toothbrush. Impatience isn't knowing that the life you left behind is hundreds of miles away and not going so crazy with it that you do something dangerous and stupid.

I can't even remember a life where I could afford to be impatient.

But that's not her baggage to carry.

I smile tightly instead. "I've been working on it."

The look she gives me tells me she doesn't quite believe it. "Okay, if you can't tell me when I'll know, can you tell me how?"

"You'll know," I tell her, as another group comes through the door —this one a mixed group of juniors and seniors. I start walking away. "I promise."

I don't know how I know that, but I do. Something about the new Devils has that cloak and dagger thing going on, and I have no doubt that whoever is pulling the strings will make sure they leave an impression. Emory informed us he has a system set up. He leaves communication in a small box down in the bunker and whoever is orchestrating all of this picks them up. After we made our nomination list, Emory left that in the box. Now, we're waiting on the next step, like everyone else.

It happens on a Friday.

During football season, Fridays are a break in the monotony of school uniforms. Players still wear a button-down and pressed pants, but we wear black ties emblazoned with the PP logo and tiny devils stitched into the silk. The cheerleaders trade short plaid skirts for even shorter cheer skirts, and ramp up their hair and makeup under the guise of 'school spirit'.

Vandy may be onto something with her antiquated patriarchy stuff.

Not that I'm complaining. Two more inches of exposed thigh and black and red striped tube socks works for me. *A lot.*

Friday morning, dressed in my Devil tie and completely distracted by a sea of tiny, pleated skirts, I open my locker and see a black envelope taped to the inside of the door. Discreetly, I remove the envelope. There's no writing on the front, but the back has a red wax seal, a pitchfork pressed neatly into it.

The halls are busy, but I glance down the row and see Emory pulling his own envelope off the metal door. His eyes dart past me and I follow his gaze to the opposite side of the hall. Vandy's at her locker alone, and at first, seems like she doesn't even notice anything inside of it. My heart thuds, wondering if for some reason she didn't pass the nomination process. Did Emory take her name off? Did the people orchestrating this veto her?

I turn and make eye contact with him, but Emory just shrugs, obviously wondering the same thing. I grab my books and slam my locker door, looking back at Vandy one more time. That's when her eyes lift to the inside of her door, a quizzical expression lifting her features.

Slowly, she removes the envelope, and then begins darting her gaze around. Our eyes meet and I drag my backpack over my shoulder, give her a slight nod, and then do my best to vanish into the crowd.

My heart quickens as I walk toward my first class. Whatever this game is, it has truly begun. A game of secrets, danger, and a crossing of the boundaries I swore to stay away from.

I just hope like hell this doesn't backfire on us all.

# 9

GETTING out of the house isn't easy.

It's a Thursday night, so my parents and I are all in the den, watching the tail-end of an interview my mom had recorded with a local janitor-turned-hero. My eyes keep flicking to my phone, watching the time. I still have forty minutes before I have to be at the location, but my palms are already sweating.

I stand up.

Both of their gazes follow me.

"I'm heading to bed," I explain, slipping my phone into my pocket.

My mom frowns in that special, concerned way that more and more makes me want to scream. "It's still early."

I clench my teeth before willing myself to remain cool. Casual. Just any other night. "Honestly, I'm tired and bloated and a little crampy."

Well, Dad's out. He instantly focuses back on the screen. "Good night, then."

Mom's not so easily repelled by seedy underbelly of female biology. "Already? But you aren't due for another week."

I just stand there for a moment, too stunned to do much more than stare agog at her. "You're tracking my cycles?" Tagged, migratory birds are observed less than this.

"Well, I'd use the term 'tracking' very loosely here, Vandy-Bean. It's all over the place." She grabs her phone from the table, thumbs moving deftly over the screen. "I'm making you an appointment with Doctor Telsky this week."

It takes me a long moment to remember who that is. I have so many doctors, specialists, therapists, and old home care nurses that they've sort of congealed into a single unidentifiable blob of needles, pastel scrubs, and gentle bedside manner. It used to work in my favor, though. It's a lot easier to talk yourself into a prescription with that many chefs in the stew.

I groan when it hits me. "The gyno? Seriously? It's just a period, Mom!"

"I know you don't want to go on the pill," she insists, probably already texting the office, "but it'll help regulate it."

My poor dad looks like he's trying to melt into the couch cushions.

I'd argue with her, but time is quickly getting away from me. "You know what? Fine. Make the appointment."

She looks so pleased at my acceptance that I almost feel bad for what I do next.

It's not hard to make all the perfunctory sounds of me ascending the stairs, using the bathroom, and getting ready for bed. It's a touch more difficult to quietly make my way back down, but weeks of sneaking around during sleepless nights have made me a deft foot at navigating all creaks, every stilted footfall, each knob, any hinge.

Knowing that doesn't make my heartbeat any less thunderous.

I sneak out the garage door, because it's the farthest from the den and any visible windows. As soon as I hit the night air, something inside me all at once loosens and clenches, like a bird finally fluttering free of its cage. I start toward the boat ramp two blocks from my house. Everything in the area is connected to the lake. The houses, the town, even the Academy. The night is thick and humid, filled with a symphony of cicada, and the impulse to run is so intense that I'm buzzing with it, this need to get away, to go toward something. Thankfully there's no sign of Jerry, who's either nodding off in the gate shack or sitting outside Reyn's house to ensure he's not causing trouble.

Speaking of Reyn...

He's not on the boat ramp when I get to the top of the hill and look down at the water. No one is. I stand there for a suspended moment, panting more from exhilaration than exertion, and wonder why he isn't here, too.

I pull out the black envelope and squint at the card inside for the millionth time.

*Meet at the Cedar Shoals boat ramp, 10pm.*

*Come alone.*

*"No one can hurry me down to Hades before my time, but if a man's hour is come, be he brave or be he coward, there is no escape for him when he has once been born."*

*Elevatio Infernum*

I run my thumb over the embossed pitchfork stamped at the bottom. Because I'd searched online earlier, I know the quote is from the Iliad, and although the context is steeped in the grim fate of war, I also know what it means here; that there's no turning back. I'd googled the Latin, too.

*Raising hell.*

Ominous much?

I'm sweating by the time I get to the weathered floating dock, both from nerves and the humidity. There's a deep, tugging ache in my lower back, and as I gaze out over the dark water, I begin wishing I'd taken a dose before I left.

*No.*

No, it's better like this, sober and clear-headed, able to take in every detail. I gulp in the heavy air and feel it—that same exhilaration I'd felt on the steps of Cresswell after the football game. Even the tight ball of anxiety wedged beneath my ribs is something bright and swooping and so unapologetically alive that it makes my ears hum with the spastic pressure of it.

It's embarrassing how long it takes me to realize that *I'm* not the one humming.

I hear the motorboat entire minutes before I see the dark shape of it gliding across the glassy surface. Running lights reflect off the water the closer it comes, and when it's near enough to make out the driver of the boat, my stomach drops.

The person is dressed from head-to-toe in black, including the ski mask covering his face. It's a guy, I can tell that much from the broad shoulders and height. He literally looks like he's playing the part of a kidnapper in a thriller movie. He looks like a criminal. A goon. *A Devil.*

In conclusion, he looks scary as hell.

He docks the boat and cuts the motor, looping the tie around the post to keep it in place. He does this all in an easy, casual display of competence. I stare at that mask, the clothes, and am suddenly overcome by the insanity of this moment.

This is crazy. *Crazy!* I'm out here past curfew getting picked up on a boat by some large guy wearing a ski mask, and no one knows where I am. God, I can see my mom delivering the story in complete clarity. *Seventeen-year-old Vandy Hall was last seen in her own home on the night of September 15th.* My hands are shaking so badly that I'm almost positive Masked Goon Dude can see it, even in the dark. Why did I think this was a good idea?

I don't do things like this. Impulsive, brash, scary behavior isn't me. I stay home. I read books. I binge-watch ridiculous teen dramas on Netflix. I get stoned, but I don't do this—*whatever* the hell this is.

But...

That electric thrum of exhilaration keeps ratcheting up and up, and it's not the same—it's not the dullness and numbness of the pills —but I know a high when I feel it, and if this doesn't qualify as one, then nothing does.

The guy steps easily off the boat, takes a few paces in my direction, and extends a large, gloved hand. "Let me see your envelope." The tremors in my hands are all the more apparent when I reluctantly comply, handing it over to him. If he notices, he at least does me the courtesy of ignoring it. He skims the paper and tucks it in his back pocket.

*Note to self*: take photographic evidence of everything.

"Before we go anywhere, you need to know that there's no turning back. Once you step on that boat, you're in." I strain to recognize the voice, deep and gruff, but I can't. It isn't Emory or Reyn, of that much I'm sure. "You can't tell anyone what's about to happen. If you do—"

"I won't," I finally speak up, dusting my hands on my thighs. "Whatever this is, I'm in."

It's too dark to see the eyes of the boy standing in front of me, but I can tell he's assessing me closely, silently. Whoever he is, I'm sure he's wondering what the hell Vandy Hall is doing here. Who would invite this poor, broken, goody-goody girl to be a part of whatever this is?

He must come to some conclusion, because he pulls out another mask. This mask isn't like his. It's more like a bag—no eye holes— obviously meant to keep me blindfolded. He spreads it with both hands and holds it aloft, waiting. Every nerve in my body is screaming like an alarm, but I step forward, letting him slip the bag over my head anyway.

It's scratchy and a little too big, and if I thought the lake at night was dark, then I was sorely mistaken. This is pitch-blackness, and I'm unable to make out anything but the sound of his feet against the weathered wood beneath us. His hand closes around my elbow, guiding me to the boat, but with the lack of any visibility and my dumb foot catching on an uneven board, I stumble, having to hop a bit to keep my balance. I don't miss my kidnapper's deep sigh at this,

his hand tightening on my arm as he escorts me forward. I jerk away, determined to make it on my own. He lets me walk with only a hand on my shoulder to guide me, until I reach the edge of the dock. With surprisingly gentle hands, he helps me over the edge of the boat and into a seat.

A moment later, the motor cranks. He pushes the throttle so that the boat flies over the water, gliding over the smooth surface. I hold onto my hood with one hand and my seat with the other, and it doesn't matter that I can't see anything, because I can feel it all. The crickets as they wake. The wind across my face, damp and ripe. The tree limbs waving as we pass, leaves rustling in grim celebration. I can't see the moon overhead, but I can feel the pull of it, loud in its magnetism.

*You are alive*, it's screaming. *You are free.*

If I thought standing on a dark dock was exhilarating, then zooming over the onyx lake, blindfolded, in the dead of night, is on another level entirely.

I have too much time to think and feel as we buzz across the water. I wonder if my parents have discovered I'm gone yet. If they found my phone tucked under the pillow in my bedroom. I wonder what my brother's involvement in all this is. I wonder how desperate Reyn must be to agree to this arrangement, and if whatever is happening is worth the information I'm hoping to get. Both Emory and Reyn have a history filled with bad decisions and epic fuck-ups. Yet here I am, once again, willingly following them into the fray.

Yes, I'm an idiot.

My lips curl into a smile as the wind whips my hair around my arms, fluttering about me like an excited puppy who's missed its owner.

Well. At least I'm an idiot who's having fun.

There's more of that ratcheting thrill when the boat begins slowing, the sound of the motor decreasing to a hum before cutting off altogether. After the roar of the motor, the sudden silence is jarring in its loudness.

It doesn't last long.

"Get up," my captor says, and now that I'm listening more than looking at him, I can tell he's chewing gum—a subtle smack punctuating his words. I can also hear his feet as he exits the boat, so I struggle to follow, holding onto the back of the seat for balance.

Suddenly, a hand clenches around my upper arm. A low, velvety voice rushes against my ear, "I've got you."

A shiver runs down my spine.

I was wrong. I do know who's hiding under that mask. There's no doubt who that voice belongs to; Reyn.

My body should relax, knowing who's actually helping me off the boat and onto the dock, but it doesn't. I'm caught in a twist of emotions. Excitement, nerves, confusion, frustration. It's not like I didn't know he was involved. I mean, I'd even been looking for him at the boat ramp.

I guess it's the fact that he has the upper hand—again.

I look weak—*again.*

Reyn's hands clutch either side of my waist, and when he lifts me over the side of the boat, he doesn't even grunt. With his strong grip, he sets me down on the dock, hands lingering to make sure I've found my footing.

Before I can even think to feel embarrassed about this, someone speaks.

"Don't take off your masks yet." I instantly recognize Emory's voice. It's firm and assured, loud in the stillness around us. "You've all been hand-selected as the best of the best at Preston to pledge in an exclusive club." I feel more than see Reyn turning to look at me. Emory's voice turns mocking. "This isn't your garden variety Preston Prep spirit club. There aren't going to be any bake sales or dances. This will be physically, mentally, and emotionally exhausting. This will probably be perverse. This will, in all likelihood, be illegal as hell. So if you can't handle that, then raise your hand now, and we'll cart your ass off."

There's a long pause, and I wonder who's raising their hand. I'd be lying if I said that I didn't feel my own twitch of apprehension.

Emory says, "Some of you might not make it, anyway," I can hear his voice travel, like he's pacing the line of us, but at this, it seems closer, fixed toward me. "Just because you think you can handle it doesn't mean you can." His voice starts moving again. "If you have what it takes, then you're about to be a part of something that can't be dismantled. This is about leadership. Loyalty. Legacy. By pledging to this, you're swearing an unbreakable bond that transcends shitty little high school cliques."

"Last chance," another guy says. I don't know who. "Does anyone want to bail?" When no one makes a sound he says, "Well, alright then. Let the games begin."

It's a lot of dramatic fanfare, but my brother joined the Devils for a reason. Elitism, popularity, social dominance. That's why, when we're told we can take off our masks, I'm not surprised to see two other former Devils, Carlton Wade and Ben Shackleford, standing next to him. And of course, Reyn is no surprise, either.

He's still standing close enough that I lose myself in a suspended moment of drinking in his features. I seem to have this issue—this *thing*, bordering on fixation—with his silhouette. Like the times before, outside our houses, the night seems to cut his bone structure into something mysterious and sharp. In the daytime, at school, his eyes are guarded, and he still has that tense stillness about him. But like this, in the dark? The intensity is enough to make my insides flutter. It's like he's someone else—someone unreachable, hard like stone.

It's like a physical hurt to pull my eyes away, but I *am* surprised by the two non-Devils, Tyson Riggins and Sebastian Wilcox. And I'm downright shocked to see five other girls. Afton Cross and Elana Maxwell are the two seniors, then Georgia Haynes, Caroline Richmond, Aubrey Willis, and myself are juniors.

Their shocked and annoyed expressions make me feel a little more at ease. At least I'm not the only one who has no idea what's going on. Nevertheless, I'm clearly the odd one out. It's like one of those grade-school worksheets. *One of these things is not like the others.* All of these people are beautiful and talented, athletic and smart, popular and fun and skilled.

Sebastian, like me, had an older brother in the Devils. Heston was popular, good looking, and horribly mean. Unlike his brother, Sebastian plays lacrosse, which has the reputation for the absolute douchiest of the jocks. I don't know if he has the same mean streak, but there's no doubt he's intimidating.

As everyone looks around, sizing each other up, I feel the sweat beading on the small of my clammy back. It's impossible to ignore the reality of it all. I'm not here because of any of those things. I'm here because I used the leverage of knowing a secret to get an invitation.

God, I really am a loser.

We're on an old dock of some kind, the metal rusted from age. Thick tree branches hang over our heads, and although we're obviously on the lake, I have no idea exactly where we are. Emory holds up a camping lantern and spins on his heel, heading down the boardwalk toward shore. Once he gets there, he pushes aside heavy vines of ivy and reveals a door that looks like it leads straight underground.

I remind myself, as I follow my brother and the others into a dark tunnel, that I have a goal—a *cause*—and whatever risk I'm about to take will be worth it if it means that Emory doesn't get himself in too deep.

Reynolds doesn't speak.

~

"I swear to god, Emory! If I see a rat, feel a rat, or hear a rat, I am going to lose my shit."

The flashlight swings around, momentarily blinding my eyes before once again focusing ahead. "There aren't any rats," my brother tells Afton. In a lower voice, he adds, "Well, I haven't *seen* any."

"It smells in here," Aubrey adds, voice surly. "Like a coffin."

"Seriously, how much longer?" Sebastian asks.

"Jesus," a voice mutters behind me, "complain much?"

I turn and see Tyson Riggins' cute face in the dim light. His blond hair is fried from chlorine, skin a warm brown. He and I are the last two in the line and I know I'm holding him up with my slow gait.

"You can go ahead if you want," I tell him, stepping to the side while also trying not to touch the damp walls.

"It's fine." He grins. "I figure if I'm back here, there's less chance of running into rats or cobwebs. At least they'll warn us if they do."

When I turn back around, a bright light shines from the end of the tunnel. Emory stands in an open doorway, allowing everyone to pass. I pause at the threshold, shifting to navigate a step. Tyson offers me his hand.

"Oh, thanks," I start, but my brother's palm pushes into Tyson's chest. "Emory!"

"What?" he says, shooting Tyson a glare before clutching my elbow to steady me. "I was already here."

Jesus Christ.

When I turn to the room, Reyn is standing there, his dark eyes watching the exchange. He instantly looks away. I try to give Tyson an apologetic look, but he's already joined the others in a makeshift circle, situating himself between Caroline and Elana.

That leaves me between Emory and Reyn.

How appropriate.

The room is small, musty, and old. There are no windows, but the arched ceiling makes it a little less claustrophobic. Candles are scattered around the room, giving everything a hazy glow. I don't miss the Preston Prep memorabilia on the walls, some faded with time. There's little doubt that we're in some kind of Devils time capsule. As I take in the room and the people in the circle with me, my eyes meet Reyn's for a blink before he looks away.

Emory addresses the room. "As you know, the Devils at Preston Prep have been a long-standing tradition. But you may not realize that it started as something very different than the group it was when it was disbanded last year. Originally, it was a club for both guys and girls, and we've been invited by an anonymous alumni to restart the group under the original doctrine. There's an initiation process, rituals and rites. The four of us who were already Devils will still have to go through these with you, so this is even-footing, got it?"

"Headmaster Collins shut you down," Afton pipes in. "What makes you think he won't do it again?"

"Because he'll never find out," Reyn replies, and if his tone is dark with warning, then the way his eyes pass over each person is dark with threat.

It's a threat he looks like he could definitely deliver on.

Emory holds up a leather book—the one I saw in his hands the other night with Reyn. "There are six guys, six girls, and six rituals. When we complete the rituals, we'll be full members, bonded by sacrifice, experience, and legacy. There are other Devils out there, other societies—it's far-reaching—and when we finish, all of their access and influence will extend to us."

Slowly, the treasure trove of what Reyn is giving me starts to unfold. Preston Prep may seem like it's doing better, like they've taken a stand, but underneath it all—*literally underground*—nothing has changed. I don't miss what Emory isn't saying, that we're re-creating Devils and their Playthings.

*Holy shit.*

I'm about to become a *Plaything*.

What does that mean? He said perverted, right?

"What will keep someone from telling?" Tyson asks, unaware that I'm panicking. "You know how easy it is for shit to get around."

"Insurance," my brother says, holding up his iPhone. "The first ritual starts tonight."

"What is it?" Ben Shackleford asks, revealing that even the incumbent Devils are in the dark about this.

Emory's grin transforms into something wicked. "Each of us confessing our biggest sin on video, of course."

"What?" Aubrey says, eyes wide as saucers. "No way."

"Yeah-way, Aubrey. All of us."

Georgia might be the younger like me, but might also be the wisest. "That's stupid, Hall. Phones and clouds can be hacked. How are you even going to keep that safe?"

Carlton adds, "And how are we supposed to know that others are actually telling their biggest sin?"

Caroline agrees, "We could just make something up."

Emory only looks mildly annoyed. "First of all, this isn't connected to a cloud. Even the FBI can't get into one of these things. Secondly, you're right. You could make something up. I wouldn't know any better. But you know who would?" He levels everyone with a hard look. "The people in charge of this have eyes and ears."

I shiver at that thought, and it looks like Afton and Aubrey do the same.

Sebastian smirks, though, seemingly unfazed. Reyn stands with his arms crossed, still as a statue. There's no doubt everyone in this room has a secret. Including me.

Emory makes eye contact with each of us, mine a beat longer than everyone else. I know my brother doesn't want me here but Reyn talked him into it. It's obvious that starting with the first ritual, everyone will be forced to reveal something about themselves they don't want everyone to know.

Me? I'll be forced to tell my brother that I'm not the girl he thinks I am.

# 10

LOOK AT ALL THESE PEOPLE, squirming. Sitting with a group of my peers sharing my biggest sin? *Please.*

Been there, done that.

Counseling was mandatory part of my rehabilitation at Mountain View, a long string of weekly confessions where we all spilled our guts and made feeble promises to Never. Do. It. Again.

But this is different, and I don't just mean the black clothes, the kidnapping, and the candles lit for dramatic effect. I mean, I actually know these people—or knew them. I have to see them every day.

They're not a random group of boys sent away for badly committed crimes. It's my best friend, the hot girl whose tits I want to motorboat, the guys I played Pee-Wee with, and *fuck.*

Maybe worst of all, it's *Vandy.*

Am I really going to put her through listening to that shit?

I can tell from the expressions of everyone else in the room that they're not so into this either, but I have to hand it to whoever's pulling these strings. It makes sense. A secret society without the 'secret' is just a Friday free-period, with more steps. Knowing everyone's skeletons is the perfect way to start. Mutually assured destruction.

"I'll go first," Emory says, handing Afton his phone. She flips it around and presses pause when he nods. His eyes flick to mine so briefly that most of the people here probably don't catch it. To them, Emory probably looks assured, at best—indifferent, at worst. But that split-second look told me everything I needed to know.

He's pants-shittingly nervous.

"I'm sure most of you know about what happened with that party two years ago. With the Adams girl and the Northridge kids? Or at least you've heard rumors." He looks at Carlton and Ben, who nod. I'm assuming they were at the party. Emory's hands twitch at his sides, like he wants to rub his palms over them, but knows he can't. He's got to be the big fearless leader.

He's got to set an example.

"I participated in the blow job train on Skylar Adams."

I'm the only one who remains still. Everyone else's heads snap back on their shoulders, and it's like the oxygen gets sucked out of the room with their collective inhales.

I chance a sidelong glance at Vandy.

About five shades paler, face slack, she looks fucking *horrified.*

Emory explains, "I was there with Campbell, but she went out back to smoke up with her friends. I heard what was going on in that bedroom and just had to see it myself. I figured those Northridge guys were bullshitting, but sure enough, there she was. On her knees, waiting for the next guy to come through the room. When she reached for my pants, I just..." Something in him cracks. He reaches up to rub at the back of his neck, the tips of his ears suddenly growing red. "I let her do it. I mean, free blowjob, right? What did I know?"

The room is so silent that when Vandy shifts, crossing her arms over her chest, it draws every eye to the sound.

Emory goes on, "When shit hit the fan, there was no way I could fess up. You guys know how it was. Hamilton was on the war path, our parents were furious, the administration was fed up. I'd already had enough strikes to toss my ass out of Preston, and I'm pretty sure Campbell would have castrated me. If I had admitted it, the whole club would have been kicked out of school. The only thing keeping us in school was the fact we had not participated." He exhales and shrugs, obviously finished.

There's a long pause, so I guess it's someone else's turn, but that was a lot to digest. I know instantly that Emory has set the tone here. That isn't just some silly youthful indiscretion.

"I got pregnant Freshman year." Aubrey says, taking all the weird, awkward heat off Emory. Afton shifts the camera to her, but Aubrey's eyes are locked on Emory's as she speaks. "Twice, actually. These older guys—these two seniors—they used to bring me to hang out with them on the weekends. I used to feel so cool, you know? Because I was hooking up with these two popular jocks. Kings of the school. But they never wanted to use anything, and..." She looks away, shifting uncomfortably. "Well, anyway. I got rid of it. Both times." Her voice is bitter and cold when she adds, "They never even offered to help or sit with me, or...anything. It was like I was taking out their trash."

Georgia mutters, "God, what pricks."

And with that, Aubrey has augmented the whole game. This stuff doesn't have to be illegal. It just has to really mess up your life, were it to get out.

"I'll go next," Elana says, and Afton shifts the camera to her. "On the Fourth of July, I went to this party down at Wisteria Dam. I had this epic American flag bikini and this sexy cover-up. I decided my mom's diamond hoop earrings would look incredible with it—especially with my hair up, you know?" She looks to the other girls for confirmation and Elana nods. "Well, I knew she wouldn't let me wear them. She can be a greedy bitch when it comes to her jewelry, so I borrowed them." She rolls her eyes. "You know where this is going…I lost them in the lake. Joseph Miller was fucking around, dunking me and stuff—"

"Trying to get your top to fall off," Aubrey mutters. "Been there."

"Right?" Elana says. "Well, I hoped that my mom just wouldn't notice—it's not like she doesn't have enough to wear. But nope, her eagle-eyes caught it immediately." Her amused expression shifts, with jaw lifting and her arms crossing over her chest. "I thought for sure I was busted, which meant my trip to Costa Rica would totally be canceled, but I overheard my mother accusing our housekeeper of stealing the earrings. Marisol denied it, of course, and my mother had zero evidence, but it didn't matter. She fired her and I never said a thing."

*Note to self*, I think, as I reassess the girl with her dark hair and darker eyes. She's small—tiny, really—but holy shit, she's cut-throat. I'm not tangling with her.

There's an awkward silence while we wait for the next victim, and I hope it's Vandy, because one thing is becoming clear: The more awful bullshit that comes after yours, the better.

I'm about to open my mouth when Sebastian shifts in his seat, leaning forward. "So, I have this temper," he starts.

Ben scoffs. "That's not a secret."

Sebastian's dark eyes rise to his, tightening. "How about you shut the fuck up and not interrupt me."

Ben glowers back. "How about you make—"

Sebastian is already out of his seat, and I feel myself coil, back straightening at the wild look in his eyes. I'd know that shit anywhere. I saw it in my cellmate in juvie, in dozens of guys at Mountain Point, in the worn faces of my community service buddies.

"Hey," Emory steps in, probably sensing the same thing I am, which is that this Sebastian guy doesn't just have a temper. This dude is a rag soaked in gasoline. All he needs is a spark.

But just like that, it's gone. Sebastian quirks a knife-edged smile at Ben before falling back into his chair. After a moment of charged silence, he continues, "My family went upstate for the summer, to the Briar Cliffs." Everyone nods. The Briar Cliffs are a popular summering hole among the Preston elite. He sniffs, flinging his hair from his eyes. "I was out slumming it one night with one of my boys, and we got into some shit with a few townies. We took it out back, as you do." He says this like it makes him some kind of upstanding gentleman. "Had a few blows. Caught him in the jaw once, really good. Probably knocked out some teeth. But then..."

He reaches up to scratch at his jaw, an oddly shy gesture as he diverts his gaze to the floor. "This girl tries to get between us, break us up, right? She can't be more than like a hundred pounds, sopping wet. She came at me from the side, and I didn't realize—" His gaze jumps around the room. "I thought it was one of his boys jumping in, because they're all standing around, watching their buddy get creamed. I didn't even hesitate, I just." He buries his fist into a palm and doesn't need to elaborate.

He does, anyway. "I decked the shit out of her. She fell to the ground like a sack of meat, and for a second, we all just stood there, looking at her." He barks a dark laugh. "I thought she was fucking dead, to be honest."

"Was she okay?" Afton instantly pales at having interrupted him. "Sorry."

Sebastian watches her, maybe sees the fear in her eyes, and narrows his own. "Look, what happened to her was an accident. I don't hit girls. I fight people who can take me. I fight *fair*. I'm not like —" Whatever he's about to say is abruptly bitten off. "She was bleeding, but she was breathing. You could tell I rattled her lights, because her eyes kept rolling around, but then she started screaming." His throat bobs with a loud swallow, something dark passing over his face. "Like, I'm talking some serious blood-curdling shit. It was like she was possessed or something." He shakes his head. "I couldn't stick around. With all that noise, someone was bound to call the police. So, we all just...left."

I hear Vandy's sharp inhale, but am powerless to stop her screech. "You left her there?!"

I step in front of her about half a second before Emory does, but that just seems to piss Sebastian off more.

"Hey, I said I don't hit girls!"

"Who's next," Emory barks, looking around. This effectively ends Sebastian's confession, and everyone looks grateful for it—most of all me. I fall back into my seat and wonder if I could even take him. *Maybe.* I wouldn't want to find out, though.

Again, the room falls into silence, no one sure what to say. Then Afton thrusts the phone at Aubrey, who turns it on the cheerleader.

She flips her hair over her shoulder and says, "I've been having an affair with my dad's best friend." The confession hangs in the air, and her shoulders relax a little. "It started a year ago. We were at a family barbecue. I went with him to the garage to get some ice, and next thing I know, we're fucking on the tool bench." Her lips curve mischievously. "It was the best sex I'd ever had, and we've been hooking up ever since."

Elana's eyes bug out, and I can't help but wonder if she knows who Afton is talking about. Vandy hasn't moved an inch since I stepped between her and Sebastian, but I can hear her beside me, shifting more uncomfortably at this confession than the others. She may be too pure for this—too innocent—but then again, she's the one blackmailing me to be in this club in the first place. That's obviously what her confession is going to be.

"I'm really into it," Afton continues, "but I know if my dad finds out, he'll be devastated. Not just because I'm his daughter, but because it's his friend. I mean, they go way back, they're almost like brothers. It's a huge betrayal, which of course makes it even sexier. But I can't stop seeing him." She crosses her arms over her chest. "I won't."

Emory and I make eye contact, both of us having the same thought. Afton Cross has major daddy issues. *No thanks.*

We continue around the circle. Tyson, the new kid from Northridge, runs his hands through his hair a couple of times and admits, "I'm an atheist."

No one replies until Ben says, "That's not really a damning secret."

"Well, it is to my girlfriend, who's a seriously devout catholic." He reaches under his shirt and pulls out a chain with a sliver cross attached. "She only dates religious guys and her parents are super strict. I lied when I met her—like, created this fake persona for her and her family, thinking it was no big deal, and now I'm in love with her, so I have to keep up this whole phony life. If she found out, it'd be over. She'd dump my ass so quick."

I scoff, drawing a few stares, but I don't need to elaborate. Emory just confessed to a possible sex crime. Sebastian might have hospitalized someone. Poor Aubrey got used and abused by two jocks. Afton is fucking some old dude and she doesn't even realize how creepy and fucked up it is. Tyson is an atheist? It getting out might ruin a *high school relationship*?

What kind of weak shit is that?

"Well, that's all I've got," he finishes, sinking back into his chair.

I'm not sure how anyone else accepts this, but Caroline goes next.

"My mom forged documents and paid someone to take the SATs for me. 'I' got a 1540." Caroline rolls her eyes, shrugging. "She got a few wrong so it wouldn't look suspicious."

I narrow my eyes at Tyson. *See?* That's something with consequences.

Georgia is a cheerleader, like Afton, and from what I can tell, is a lot nicer than her pimply-faced brother, George. Emory wanted to make sure we had enough Juniors in the Devils to keep it going once we leave. She has wavy red hair and pretty green eyes. Her nails pick at the seam of her jeans when she says, "I told everyone that I went on a six-month foreign exchange program to France during Freshman year. Really, I was in a psychiatric facility for what they called a major depressive event." She wrings her hands in her lap for a moment, eyes cast down. "But I was just...well, there was this video going around."

Carlton springs up, "Oh shit! That was *you!*"

Georgia's eyes go wide and hunted, and she turns them on Emory. "This stays here, right?"

Emory looks about as confused as I feel. "Uh, yeah. That's the point."

Her gaze darts around the circle, and I think I can see what she must be seeing: varying degrees of recognition. I have no idea what it's all about. Everyone here has history, knows the in-jokes, understands the climate. But not me.

She continues, "I broke up with this guy, and he…well, you all know by now." She hangs her head. "He posted that video of us. I couldn't believe that he'd do that, and it's just always out there. It doesn't matter that you can't see my face, it's still—" She works her jaw, eyes growing wet. "It's such a violation. Most mornings, I couldn't even get out of bed, but when I did, I just wanted it all to end." She adds in a rough whisper, "I tried to hang myself."

Elana looks shocked and worried. "No one knew it was you."

Georgia just shakes her head. "But I did. I still see it sometimes, you know. All you guys share it around like it's this… *fun thing*," she spits. "But every time I see it, I just hate myself."

Emory must have seen this video, because he winces. Before anyone else can comment on it, Carlton cuts in.

"I sell drugs." The camera swings to him and he shrugs. "It's good money. Like…" He breathes out a laugh. "Fucking unreal money, you have no idea. Weed, uppers, codeine, oxy, Xanax, even some coke every now and then. I move a lot of weight, but I don't do it one-on-one anymore. I've got a few Northridge kids who sling for me down there, some more at Thistle Cove, a few here, a few there. It's not something I want to do long term," he insists, palm held up defensively. "I just want enough to coast after college without depending on my dad. Getting a scholarship is a given at this point. And once I get my degree, I'm done with him."

There's only three of us left.

Ben speaks up before Vandy and I can. "I went to camp over the summer, for band. We had these lame-ass dorms that were two to a room. My roommate was pretty cool, though. We hung out together for most of it, just screwing around, drinking, chasing tail. The last night of camp, we were packing up and getting wasted off shitty vodka, and we…" He pauses, but I already know what he's going to say, and it's a physical battle not to laugh aloud. He mutters, "We ended up fooling around."

Carlton obviously does not have my restraint. "You're always giving me grief for checking out guys' asses, and you're the one who's gay?!"

"I'm not *gay*." Ben glowers at him, but his face is beet red. "But I'm probably bi."

Caroline rolls her eyes, while Afton outright laughs. "Oh my god, it's the twenty-first century, who *cares*."

"My parents would care." His face just gets redder and redder. "I'm not getting sent to some fucking deprogramming camp just because I like a little dick."

"Only the little ones?" Carlton looks like he might have a stroke with all the laughter he's holding. "What a relief, mine is safe."

Ben flips him off. "*No one* wants your crusty dick, Wade."

It's a much-needed moment of levity, all of that back-tightening tension sapped from the room, even if only temporarily. Because it's just Vandy and me, now. I reluctantly turn to her, a question in my eyes.

*You or me?*

She meets my gaze. I'm not sure what she sees in mine, but hers is full of panic and *No*.

Suit yourself.

"Guess it's me, then." The camera turns to me and I lean forward, resting my elbows on my knees. I can feel them all waiting just a touch more intensely than they had for the other confessions, but it's no surprise, with all the gossip going around. The truth is probably a lot less interesting. Nevertheless, I keep my eyes trained to my linked fists as I begin, "Few years back, my buddy and I decided to steal a car." Vandy is so still and silent beside me that it's like a scream. I wonder if she's surprised that this is my worst. "His kid sister busted us, though. So when the time came to do it, I talked her into—" I squint at my hands, because that doesn't sound right. "No, I *persuaded* her to come with me, because..." I gesture to the room without looking anyone in the eye. "Well, if she's an accomplice, then she won't snitch on us. It was a really nice car, and it was dark, and we were on that old highway—the one down past the industrial park."

Sebastian interrupts, "Straight road."

I nod without looking at him. "Exactly, I wanted to get it up to speed, open it up. But I never got the chance. This fucking *deer* came running out into the road, and I didn't even have both hands on the wheel. I tried to swerve around it, and then—"

There's a soft, barely-there noise coming from my right—something small and strangled and pained—and I jerk my gaze to her. She's got a hand pressed lightly to her throat and her blue eyes are trained unseeingly across the room, angled away from me.

I work my mouth around a clumsy reply that never emerges. I want to tell her not to listen. To press her fingers into her ears. To go stand outside the door for a couple minutes. What the hell was I thinking, doing this? Even being detached and relaying it as mechanically as possible, I can barely stand to say it. Why did I think she could bear to relive it?

"What happened?" Georgia gently asks, ripping me away from my thoughts.

I look at Emory, but he won't meet my gaze, either. I continue, "It flipped. Four, maybe five times."

"Six." Vandy's ragged voice makes the back of my neck prickle. "It flipped six times."

I can tell a couple of them—Georgia and Sebastian, who must be out of the gossip loop—are just now putting all this together. I mutter, "Six times. Right. And she got," I sweep a hand toward Vandy, eyes diverted, "*hurt*. A lot worse than I did."

It's a nice, tidy summary. It's one I'm used to telling, back at Mountain Point, during those legally-mandated counseling sessions. Usually, I'd go on. I'd tell them how the road was so deserted that it took forever for anyone to pass by and see the fire. Rarely, but sometimes, I'd even go into how I kept walking, hoping to flag down the cops I'd called on my battered cell phone, but then always returning because I didn't want to leave her there alone, broken and barely conscious, on the shoulder of the road. I never say the other stuff—how the pain was so intense that it made me vomit, or how I kept wishing that I'd just died there, in the driver's seat, because it already felt like my life was over.

I never admit that I *moved* her.

"There was...fire," I explain, shifting my shoulders uneasily, "and she was in the middle of the road, so I had to move her away from the wreck, even though..." Vandy already knows this. I know she does. She was more conscious than not for that part. I can still remember the way she looked up at me, eyes dazed and full of agony as I carefully dragged her to the side of the road. It doesn't make it any easier to say this aloud. I wet my lips, finishing, "Even though you're not supposed to move someone with spinal injuries."

Everyone's quiet, and I know they're looking at her more than me. Looking at her leg. Thinking of how she walks. Maybe even remembering how much worse it used to be. I know at one point, early on, she couldn't even walk at all. I should feel relieved that she can. I should be able to see her merely limping and think *'thank fucking god'*, instead of the constant internal stab of *'I did that'*.

But I can't.

It's Carlton who ultimately breaks the silence. "Didn't you already do time for that?"

I finally lean back in my chair, knee bouncing. "Yeah, a little. I was in juvie for a few months, after the hospital. They let me plead down my sentence as time served, plus probation and community service, on the condition that I enrolled in Mountain Point for four semesters."

Sebastian rolls his eyes. "But you've already done the time. Everyone already knows."

"That's the best part," I say, giving him a bitter smile. "I'm having my record expunged when I graduate. Once I get out of here, it'll be like it never happened."

That's what the lawyer had said.

*Like it never happened.*

They must all sense the truth of it—that it isn't fair that Vandy has to walk around with the consequences for life, and that I can just move on and do anything I want. I could be a football star. I could be a doctor. I could be a lawyer. Sky's the fucking limit for me.

But if this video got out, that'd be a different story.

They seem to accept this as 'good enough', which is fortunate. It's not my fault my 'biggest sin' just so happens to be something I've already been caught for.

Everyone in the circle looks to Vandy, but my eyes are the last to land on her. She's still got her arms crossed, but her face is hidden from me now, obscured by a curtain of her pretty blond hair.

Emory sighs. "Vandy, you have to—"

"I know." She pushes her hair away from her face and finally I can see that she's not stalling. She's just slipping into some armor, building some defenses. Her eyes are guarded but resolute when she begins, "It started a few years ago."

Inside, I freak out a little, because I thought for sure being *here* would be her big sin, and it's suddenly occurring to me that a lot of these girls' confessions are about something sexual, and it's all been dubiously consensual bullshit, and I just...

I can't hear about someone doing shit to Vandy.

I can't.

Just the thought of it makes me want to get up and pace.

She goes on, voice soft, "I had a few surgeries that first year, and they had me on morphine for a while." *Fuck fuck, no.* Now I'm the one who wants to cover my ears. "Eventually, they put me on other painkillers. They were patches sometimes, but usually pills. I was almost always hurting, so I was almost always on them. It didn't seem like a big deal at the time." She takes a breath, and I can tell she's chewing the inside of her cheek. "At some point, the pain stopped being so bad. Or, at least, it wasn't bad *all the time*. I could have stopped taking them." She looks up, into the camera. "But I didn't." Her shrug is tight. "I kept telling them it hurt, and they kept giving me the pills. For a long time, it was really easy. Getting an oxy script was like asking for a drink of water. Everyone just automatically believed me. I can't even remember most of my Sophomore year, I was so stoned out of my mind all the time."

I chance a glance at Emory. He's watching her, wide-eyed, like she's someone he doesn't even know. I'm too busy being grateful that I'm not hearing about some doctor's bad touch to feel much of anything else.

Vandy looks down at her wringing hands. Her cheeks are red. "It's really hard to come off that stuff. The doctors tried to wean me in stages, last year. I acted like I was following the protocol, but I wasn't. I had built a nice stash over the two years, so I could keep taking them. And taking them. And taking them." Her smile is something tight and guilty. "Eventually, the stash grew a lot smaller. I tried playing up the pain, but it just led to more procedures and prodding and babying. I knew no one here would sell it to me, but I've even bought some off a couple Northridge guys." Her eyes move to Carlton, who's been watching passively. "Yours, I assume?"

Carlton's wide eyes snap to Emory. He points to her, voice insistent. "Bro, I didn't know about that."

"It was hard getting money, though," she continues, picking at a fingernail's chipped polish. "My parents would always ask what it was for, and it got easier to just steal it."

Emory runs a hand down his face. "*Jesus*, V."

She stiffens, almost imperceptibly. Her voice is harsh and biting when she says, "You don't know what it's like, okay? You have this whole life that has nothing to do with—" She swallows down the rest, exhaling in a hiss. "It was the only thing that got me through, and it's not like it's something you can just quit, cold turkey." She flattens her palms to her thighs, pushing her shoulders back. "It's taken me all year to get my dosage down to a point where I wasn't getting sick."

Caroline cautiously asks, "Are you still...?"

Vandy looks up at her, and then around at the rest of the people in the circle, Emory last. "No," she finally mutters, head shaking. "I'm done with it now."

There's something she's not saying. Maybe the others don't notice the slight crack in her voice, or the way her shoulders twitch when she says the words, but I've seen enough liars—*been* enough of a liar—to know when something's being held back. Maybe she's still addicted. Maybe she still gets sick. Maybe she still thinks about lying to the doctors.

It doesn't matter.

Among all those maybes is one certainty: Vandy's biggest sin is just another sick repercussion of my own.

One more thing I'm responsible for.

When the camera turns off, moments later, no one looks relieved.

# 11

THE RIDE HOME IS QUIET, filled with tension. Emory and I don't even look at one another. I remember a time, when we were kids, that Emory didn't always treat me this way—like something made of thin, fragile porcelain. We'd fight. We'd play together. We'd fight some more. We were always close, but we were still siblings at the end of the day.

Now, we barely seem to know each other.

When we get home, the house is dark and silent. I don't need to worry if our parents have discovered I was missing. Were that the case, things would look far more lively.

Emory just walks right into the house, because he can do this. He can stay out late. He can go to secret meetings, parties, get-togethers, without being asked much about it. I sneak, however. He jogs up the staircase with ease, and I tiptoe, avoiding the creaks. Worn out and exhausted from the night, I'm hoping he'll be locked in his room before I even get to the landing.

Unfortunately, my brother has other plans. His silhouette is framed by my door. I limp past him and kick off my shoes. The door clicks behind me.

His voice is quiet. "Why didn't you tell me?"

I don't want to face him, but I do. He looks weirdly hurt. "There was nothing to tell. I'm *fine*."

"Are you?"

"Do I look different than I did this morning? Yesterday or the day before?" I hold out my arms. "Why wouldn't I be fine?"

"I don't know, V." His jaw locks, nostrils flaring out. "Maybe because you just admitted that you're a fucking addict!"

I hiss back, "And you're a sex offender!" We both glare at one another, a silent agreement passing between us that we're waiting to see if our parents heard us shouting.

When it's clear no one is coming, he sighs, head dropping. "How did I not know about this? Mom and Dad—"

"Will *never* hear a word about it. I'm not using anymore." The lie feels heavy on my tongue. "And just like how I'm sure you won't be involved in anymore *sex crimes*, it's not fair for you to bring this up at home. You told Georgia that whatever was said in the dungeon *stays in the dungeon*. What happened to that?"

"It's not a dungeon," he mutters, thrusting a hand into his hair. "This is hard—having you in the group, treating you like—"

"An equal?" I bite out. "Like more than your innocent, crippled, loser sister?"

His face falls. "Come on, V, you know that's not—"

"Yes, it is." I snatch my pajamas from my dresser. "And maybe it's time you stopped looking at me like a broken little thirteen-year-old, and started seeing that I'm like any other girl at Preston Prep." I sarcastically elaborate, "Entitled, and filled with shit-loads of baggage."

"You could have told me."

I bury a groan into my hands. "You're not hearing anything I'm saying. I couldn't tell you, because you have this completely unrealistic view of me." I look him in the eye when I say, "You want me to be this quiet, innocent girl who's locked away, and I—" My voice cracks, and I shake my head. "I'm sick of being quiet for all of you, Em. I can't always be innocent, and I don't *want* to be locked away. I want to live my life, and that's not always going to be sunshine and rainbows, sorry to break it to you." I look down at my hands, feeling another wave of exhaustion. "None of you will even give me room to do anything *right*, let alone mess up every now and then. Are you really surprised?"

Emory certainly looks surprised. He also looks sad. "We're just trying to make things easier for you."

"Well, you aren't." I shuffle my feet, hiding a wince. It makes me breathe a strangled laugh. "All you're doing is ensuring that I hide every bad thing from you. My leg is so damn stiff right now, but I know if I let you see it, you'll just baby me for the next week. It's not easier, Em. It makes everything harder."

His eyes drop to my leg, and I can see him wanting to tell me to sit down. Instead, he rolls his eyes. "God, we're pretty messed up, aren't we?"

"Us?" I give him a sly look. "I mean, did you hear all that? Maybe we're not as fucked up as I thought."

"Or just as fucked up," he admits.

"Well, they wanted the best-of-the-best," I remark, leaning against the end of my bed, "I guess we're the cream of the crop; a group of thieves, sex fiends, liars, and cheats."

He rubs his chin with his thumb. "Sounds about right, actually."

My voice is soft and sounds as tired as I feel, "You have to let up on me a little, Em."

There's a long moment of silence where Emory does nothing but stare at my discarded shoes. "I'm not sure I know how to," he says, and I can see this strange, wild fear in his eyes. Sometimes I forget that, in a single moment, Emory almost lost his sister and best friend. Sometimes I'm too caught up in my own phantom grief to remember his own. Without warning, he reaches out and pulls me into a tight hug, mashing my face up against his chest. "But I promise I'll try. And you can tell me if you need help, okay?"

I sigh into his chest, squeezing him back. "I'm done with it, promise."

He must be convinced, because he releases me and exits the room without another word. I wait a beat before going to the bathroom and locking the door behind me. I open the tiny drawer on the jewelry box and pull out the pouch, hooking a shaky finger around one of the pills.

Reyn had been right about the secret. This business of reestablishing the secret society at Preston Prep is no small matter. It proves that the roots grow deeper than I ever realized, and an exposé would be earth-shattering to the entire institution. What I didn't know was that I'd have to reveal my own secrets to be involved, which means when I write my story, I'll open myself and my family up to scrutiny.

But I can see the whole picture with crystal clarity now. The Devils are bigger than just one person—bigger even than a group of people, or the ones behind the curtain, orchestrating it from the shadows. The Devils are a body—mind, heart, and twisted soul—and it breathes in all of us. Reyn, Emory, and I all have our own share of the blame, but the guys only stole that car because that's the kind of thing you do when you're being courted by the Devils. And the more I think about it, the more I can see a little bit of the red and black behind each of those bitter confessions.

The Devils' strongest legacy lives in all of us. It's a long, multi-generational string of pains and hurts that will just keep growing and spreading. I think of the look on Reyn's face that night, in the hospital. I think of the wild fear I'd just seen in my brother's eyes. I think of the other initiates, quiet and solemn during their confessions. I think that thrusting my family into the fray by exposing it all is a bitter pill to swallow.

I smile brokenly at the white oval in my hand, before popping it into my mouth.

Well.

I'm pretty good at that, anyway.

IF SOMEONE TOLD me that being part of a club, a sorority, or secret society would change my entire perception of school, I would've called bullshit.

But now I see that it's true.

I mean, on the outside, nothing has changed. I still listen to Sydney, wearing her cheer uniform, as she discusses the rumors flying around her that day; someone posting a photo of her measuring the length of her skirt compared to the other girls. It's all, she tells me, very tragic and desperate. While she goes on about this, I still notice everyone giving me a wide berth as I walk past. I still register the looks of pity and disinterest. From their perspective, I'm still just Vandy Hall, the broken girl with the hot older brother.

Except…

I make eye contact with Sebastian Wilcox, who's propped up against the statue in the quad. It's brief and fleeting, and I know when others look at him, they might see a rough, disinterested goon with cold eyes and a hard expression. But I can see the flatness of regret now, something haunted and aged looking back at me. He gives me the smallest nod, an almost imperceptible dip of his chin, and there's an understanding there. I know exactly where he got those scrapes on his knuckles.

It's a surprising weight, knowing the deepest, darkest secrets of the most popular people in school. It's more than just a responsibility, but also an odd, patchwork union.

"Hold on a sec," Sydney says, grabbing my arm. "Afton!"

Afton turns. Her long hair has been styled stick-straight, a red and black hair bow jacked-up three perfect inches from her hairline. Her gaze darts from Sydney to me and lingers a bit longer than it should. There's no doubt what we're thinking simultaneously:

*You're fucking your dad's best friend.*

*You're a junkie.*

"Yeah?" She focuses back on Syd.

"What time are we meeting tonight? I need to run home after school."

Afton snorts, something caustic in the curve of her mouth. "Why? To hike that skirt up another inch?"

Sydney rolls her eyes. "Oh, you saw that, huh? For the record, I do *not* make my skirts shorter. My legs are just that long."

"Uh huh." Afton looks away, already seeming bored by her. "Bus leaves at five."

"Are you riding the bus?" Sydney asks once we walk away.

My eyebrows pull together. "Why would I ride the bus?"

"Because you're the newspaper chick now. You're part of the team!" She says the last part with an overly cheesy fist pump. "But seriously, you should. It's kind of fun."

I wrinkle my nose. "I'm not sure my mom will let me."

"Just tell her that you're looking for all the deep, behind-the-scenes action for the paper. The gritty details. Like those women reporters who go into the locker rooms." She gives me a wink.

Honestly, it's not a bad idea. Even Mom can't resist the allure of getting a good scoop.

"I'll see if I can pull it off."

The bell tower chimes, so we head into the school, parting to our separate lockers. I pause when I open the door to mine. There's no note inside, but there is a small box. Discreetly, I open it up and see a long leather cord inside. A key and a silver devil's head are attached. Quickly, I loop it over my head and drop it under my shirt. I have no idea what it's for, but I do know who it's from.

And, as I close my locker door and start down the hall, I suspect I'm not the only one who got one.

When I asked Emory for a ride back to school for the game, I didn't realize Reyn would be riding with us, too. He pauses when he sees me standing by the truck—for just a fraction of a second—so it must be news to him, also.

"Hey," he mutters, walking over with his bag of football gear. He's wearing a dark blue baseball cap, and he pulls it low enough as he approaches that it almost hides his tired eyes. His gaze doesn't linger on me for more than a second, but he grabs the door handle before I can, jerking it open. "I'll take the back," he says, crawling through the gap between the front seat and the back. His shirt snags on the seatbelt as he wiggles his long body through the space, revealing a narrow swath of tanned skin and the top of his boxers.

His lower back is muscular, sloping down to his waist. There are two indentations just above his boxers. I guess he has four dimples—two on his face, two on his lower back. I'd seen Reyn shirtless a million times as a kid, but this isn't that. This is a man's body, strong and capable. As he situates himself, I try to shove aside the swooping sensation that knowledge gives me, but it's difficult. I get the strongest vision of what it'd feel like to touch that skin, to have him hovering over me, moving.

I take a clumsy step back, willing my face to stop heating. Reyn McAllister has always made my body do things I couldn't control. It's unnerving to know that, despite everything, that hasn't changed a bit.

Emory starts the truck and glares at me out the open door. "AIS, V."

I blink and scramble into the cab, flipping the AC on blast the instant I slam the door.

"What the hell?" Emory readjusts the dial. "Don't touch my settings."

"It's hot." I fan my face, refusing to look at the back seat.

"What? Are you having some kind of teen-girl menopause?"

"Shut up," I shove him with one hand and flip the AC up again with the other.

He turns it back down, batting my hands away as I bat his. "My car, my AC!"

I mock, "*My car, my AC.* You're such a baby," and turn it back up.

He thrusts a finger at me. "I will take you down, kid."

"I'd like to see you try, *kid!*"

A snort bubbles up from behind us and we both look back. Reyn's resting his head back against the seat, looking down his nose at us, and his mouth is curved into a crooked smile that's big enough to reveal a single dimple. "Good to see you two are still status quo."

I turn back around to hide my smile—and my reddening cheeks—because Reyn probably doesn't realize just how *un*-status quo that little scene has been lately. Maybe Emory had taken our talk last night to heart.

Emory adjusts the AC to the middle position, which is slightly higher than he keeps it normally.

Wow, a compromise.

He backs out of the driveway and asks, "So Mom really gave you permission to ride on the bus?"

"Yeah," I say, checking the camera in my lap and making sure I didn't forget the list of game notes Coach Morris sent for the newspaper. "She wasn't happy about it and kept aggressively 'offering' to drive me, but I think she's just ecstatic that I'm involved in something at school."

My brother glances at the rearview mirror and says to Reyn, "Until last night I thought Vandy was just a boring nerd hiding out in her bedroom all the time. Now I realize she was just getting high."

I jab him with my elbow. "What happens in the dungeon stays in the dungeon," I snap.

He holds up a hand defensively. "Last time, I promise!"

My eyes flit up to the rearview mirror, checking to see Reyn's expression. The smile has faded. I have no idea what he thinks about my confession, but I'm not going to let anyone judge me, least of all him. I was in pain for a long time. Sometimes, I still am.

Emory talks about the game the rest of the drive, but Reyn's responses are all rote and quiet. When we get out of the truck I call out, "Good luck," before walking over to the non-player bus. Emory raises his helmet in response and Reyn meets my gaze, offering a tight smile that's nowhere near the dimpled easiness as before.

I bite back a sigh and look for Syd.

The bus I'm riding on is filled with cheerleaders, members of the dance team, and their coaches and sponsors. Micha Adams is standing in a grassy area behind the bus with a cluster of cheer-leaders showing off his backflip. Sydney glides up to me the instant she sees me, eyes focused toward the field house.

"Did Reyn ride with you?"

"Yes." I dig in my bag for a pen.

"Oh." She frowns, eyes following them to the bus. "So, you two are like... cool now?"

"Um." I chew on my lip for a moment, thinking. "I don't know if I'd call it that. We're neighbors, and he's Emory's best friend. Civility just seems the best way to handle it."

She looks at me, eyebrow curved upward. "I heard he's not allowed to have anything to do with you—per Headmaster Collins."

"Well, Headmaster Collins can stuff it." My bristling tone is only half meant for Collins. Some of it's reserved for Syd's snarky tone. "It's not a big deal. I mean, we weren't friends before he left. We just had—" A life changing event? A shared tragedy? An epic failure? "Well, nothing really. He's back. I'm me. We definitely don't reside in the same social circle. Other than rides to school with Emory, I doubt our lives will even cross."

As I say it, she glances at my neck and says, "What's that? A new necklace?"

I touch the metal hanging at the center of my chest. "It's nothing." But right when I say it, Afton walks by, dolled up in her cheer uniform. She does have a necklace on, but it's a delicate chain with a cursive 'A' hanging in the V of her top. But then she raises her hand high into the air and I see it. The black cord is wound around her wrist.

And like that, we're connected.

"Devils!" Afton shouts, fingers snapping. All the girls—plus Micha—focus on her intently. "Gather all the stuff and get in the bus, we're leaving in five! No dawdling, got it? You all know what it's like when the players get there before us."

"Well, I don't think you can sit with the squad on the way there," Sydney says, giving me an exaggerated frown, "Afton likes us to do this whole 'bonding' thing before the games. It's super lame. But we can talk at halftime, okay?"

"Yeah." My smile feels a little tight. "Sounds great."

She skips off, her little skirt flouncing behind her. I know by now that climbing on the bus and navigating the aisle will hold the people behind me up. I'm waiting for everyone to file on first when Elana walks up in her black and red sparkly dance leotard. She stops next to me and bends to tie her shoe.

"So listen," she says, and it says a lot that it doesn't even register that she's talking to me, "some people are coming over to my place tonight. You're invited if you want to come."

I look around, blurting out a confused, "Me?" and her eyes jump to mine.

She's looking at me like I'm dumb. "Yes, you."

"Uh, yeah." My reply is somehow both too enthusiastic and overly flat. "I'll um... think about it."

"Cool," she says, tightening the bow of her lace and walking off. She gets onto the bus and I'm left standing there, wondering if it actually happened.

I'm still wondering, minutes later, as I pass her and her friends for one of the last available seats on the bus. I look over and see the black cord tucked just beneath her leotard, and on impulse, I reach up to touch the key under my own shirt. I have no idea what the key actually goes to, but one thing is clear.

It's definitely opening doors.

MY MOM DIDN'T *EXACTLY* GIVE me permission to go to the party, but she did say I could hang out with Sydney after the game. In her mind, that probably meant milkshakes and cheeseburgers at The Nerd, but hey. To-mayto, to-mahto. *Technically,* it's not a lie. She didn't ask for specifics. This only makes the guilt a little stronger when I take the glass of red punch from Sydney. My mom trusts me not to be a liar.

All I do is lie.

I tip the plastic cup back and swallow a gulp of the concoction Sydney gave me. It burns my throat and I fight a gag. "Jesus," I cough. "What the hell?"

"Grain alcohol." Syd makes her own face after taking a sip. "You get used to it."

"Yeah," I peer down in the cup, "not sure I want to."

What I'd give to be high right now. Pills are so much better than this. Only one swallow, no flavor, and hours of melty goodness. A waft of skunky smoke rolls past us and I observe a circle of kids passing what I assume to be a joint. I mean, hey. Maybe if I wanted to branch out...

Across the room another group of boys—all in letter jackets—get rowdy and a shout comes too late, not enough time for me to get out of the way as a body slams into me. I lurch forward, a big wave of punch leaping from the side of my cup. It hits the floor with a messy splat by my feet.

"Oh god," I groan. *Smooth fucking move, Vandy.* I stare at the red mess, knowing my cheeks are just as bright, semi-frozen. I look around. "Is there a rag? Uh, paper towels?"

I have a moment of silent, chest-clenching panic. I can feel it, sense it. Someone ran into the crippled girl. Everyone is staring at me, down at my leg, back at my face. *This* is why I'm not invited anywhere. I'm a liability. A buzzkill.

I search for Elana, but predictably, she's nowhere to be found. I can't just let people drag toxic punch through her parents' house.

"Here." A roll of paper towels suddenly appears, offered by George, the guy from my art class. "Let me help."

He yanks off a stretch of sheets and hands them to me, then pulls off another bunch. We both drop to the ground and start mopping up the mess.

"Thank you," I breathe.

"Sure," he replies with an easy grin. George is one of those guys that have been in my classes for years, but I know very little about him. He seems nice enough. He's the best in the class with pastels. He's a bit reserved, like his sister, and has a really unfortunate acne issue, but that's about the extent of my knowledge. Like everyone else, I've kept him at a distance. He holds the soaked towels in his fist and offers, "I think there's a trash can in the room off the kitchen."

He stands and I follow him, walking past a series of increasingly curious eyes. *Oh, nothing to see here, folks.* Just the loser limping around with dripping paper towels. *Ugh.* When we arrive in the kitchen, he pushes a pedal on the floor. A silver trash can opens and he dumps in his wet towels. I toss mine in next. The room is quiet, dark, and I take a moment to catch my breath. I don't know why it bothered me so much. I know it's dumb. I know it's not as bad as it feels. But for some reason, my body is just not getting with the program.

I feel like I just ran ten laps.

"You okay?" he asks, watching me closely.

"Yeah." I nod, pressing my palms to my warm cheeks. "I just feel stupid about making such a mess. Way to make an entrance, right?"

He laughs. "Well, you know the saying, 'it's not a party until someone spills the punch'."

I stare at him. "Is that really a saying?"

He laughs again. "No, but it is now."

I drop my head in my hands. "Oh god, what a disaster. My first party and I'm a punch-line."

He bursts out laughing, but when he sees my not-so-amused expression, he stops abruptly and frowns. "Wait. That wasn't a joke? The punch-line thing?"

I grimace. "Unfortunately, no."

"It's really not that bad." George rolls his eyes, leaning back against the counter, next to me. "Jason Floyd puked all over Campbell Clarke's pool table last year at one of her parties. *That* was a disaster."

An image of Jason Floyd, lead in all the Preston Prep musicals, hurling on Campbell's pool table appears in my mind. Then, a picture of Campbell losing her shit. That makes me smile. "Okay, yeah, that beats me. But still, I think I've confirmed the party scene isn't for me."

I cross my arms over my stomach, inhaling carefully. My heart has been racing ever since we got here, and the spilled punch only made it all worse. Obviously, I need to find Sydney or Emory and get out of here, cut my losses.

George places a hand on the counter between us and says, "I can hang out with you for a while, if you want."

"That's okay—" Another commotion comes from the other room. Someone shouts "Thistle Cove can suck my dick!" which is met with a round of cheers and applause. "I think I should probably just—"

Without warning, George swoops in, eyes falling closed, hand cinching around my waist. I throw up two hands and shove him back before our mouths connect. "Dude, what the hell?"

"What?" George blinks at me, gesturing at the space between us. "I thought there was some chemistry."

"You thought wrong, dumbass." The words come out fierce, but inside I'm crumbling. I push past him to get out of the small, secluded room, and reenter the kitchen. At least two dozen more people showed up while I was with George and I skim the crowd for Sydney or Emory. I can't find either of them.

Too many people. There are arms everywhere, and it's loud—so loud—and the air feels thick with smoke and sweat, and is it just me, or does this room seem smaller than it had ten minutes ago?

Spinning on my heel, I make for the front door but slam into a hard body. I look up into Ben Shackleford's surprised face. Peeking out of the top of his shirt is the black cord. Now, all I can think about is how he knows the truth about me—my secret. The feeling of being exposed is so overwhelming, it's like I've been flayed open.

*Fuck.* I need to get the hell out of here. Now.

"Vandy?" Ben frowns down at me. "What's—"

I shove him aside and weave through the crowd. I end up in a back hallway, passing a line outside the bathroom, and turning the corner. There's no one back here, and I can finally take a breath, trying to choke down some air. I press my back against a closed door, and it gives, dumping me into the room.

Immediately, I realize I'm in an office, or maybe a library due to the rows of books on the wall. But it's quiet here, so I shut the door behind me, blocking out the noise from the party. I shudder out an exhale, willing my lungs to contract, and start to take a step into the room.

I freeze when I realize I'm not alone.

Sitting behind the desk, flicking a cigar lighter in his hand, is the last person I want to see me like this.

# 12

I HEAR the music before I can see the house. The slow thump of bass bouncing off the tall pine trees is a nice change from the oppressive nothingness going on at my place. Elana's house is on the far end of the lake, so I take the path behind my own, the one that leads past the treehouse, through the woods and out to the other end of the neighborhood. At least I know Fucking Jerry can't get his golf cart through the woods. Not that he wouldn't try. Fucking Jerry might be stacked as hell, but I've got running legs. No way he'd catch me.

At first, I'd begged off, thinking all I wanted was to relax after the game. It'd been a tough one. Those assholes down in Thistle Cove play dirty and we'd sustained a few injuries. Still kicked their asses, though. I guess once their old coach got arrested, the team fell apart, leaving a spot for Preston to slide in and take the championship. Looks like they're not any better this year.

Once I got home and took a shower, I realized I was tired of sitting at home alone. Dad's off doing something—or *someone*—and god only knows when he'll be back. That's something else I'm not used to. At Mountain Point, there had always been people around. While you slept, while you shit, while you jerked off. My whole time there, all I wanted was some peace and quiet. But now that I have it, 'round the clock, it's driving me up the wall, making me restless and overly-vigilant. When things got quiet back at Mountain Point, it meant some serious shit was going down. It's a hard feeling to shake.

This is why, when I enter the party, squeezing between a cluster of girls by the door, I brace myself for the comfortable lull of voices and too much energy.

"Hey, Reyn." A girl I don't recognize touches my arm and I look down at it. "Good game tonight."

I flick my eyes up to her face. She's cute. She's got a Devil sticker on her cheek, left over from the game, and a quick glance downward tells me she definitely isn't wearing a bra.

I could tap that.

"Thanks." I don't know her name, and I don't ask.

"There's beer on the patio and punch in the kitchen," another girl adds helpfully. It's a sketchy sort of feeling, everyone knowing who I am while being total strangers to me. A few faces are vaguely familiar, and I figure that maybe I knew them when I was a student at Preston the first time around. It doesn't matter. Everyone has changed a lot.

Especially the girls.

"Great." I give them a tight smile and work my way to the kitchen, pulling my baseball cap lower in hopes of hiding a little. I might be twenty-four-seven horny, but I'm not stupid. I don't know how old that girl is, or if she has a boyfriend or an Emory-esque brother, or if she's going to run around telling everyone about it tomorrow. Party hookups require a hell of a lot more recon that I've come equipped with.

Carlton, who is standing over the sink, grins when he sees me. "Dude," he says, holding out a cup. "Try that."

I tilt the cup to my lips and feel a caustic burn at the back of my throat. "Jesus Christ," I mutter, looking at the red punch. "This shit could peel paint."

Carlton laughs. "It's nasty but it'll fuck you up."

"Well, there is that," I say, taking the cup and turning around. My feet stick to the floor and I lift one up, looking to see if I stepped in something.

"Oh yeah, watch your step." Sydney is leaning against the island, hip jutting out. "Vandy spilled punch all over the place."

My eyes dart down to her tanned legs, tracing up to her thighs. Even I've heard the rumors and jokes about her short skirts. She's an attractive girl. Sexy, if you're into the overt stuff, which I'm sure many guys are. The warning Emory gave me flashes in my head, but it's not even necessary. Normally, I'd be all about seeing what it might be like to feel my hands between those legs of hers, but there's just something about Sydney that's off-putting. She's trying just a little too hard, and it takes away a lot of the appeal.

I'm still a guy, though, and it takes me a stretch of silent leg-ogling to register her words.

"Vandy's here?"

I force myself not to look for her.

"I know, I'm surprised, too. She *never* wants to come, but she asked for a ride and I was like, yes! Let's do this!" She lifts her foot, which makes a ripping sound as it separates from the sticky floor. "Poor thing. She's barely here for five minutes when she commits the ultimate party foul."

"Hm." I absently bring the cup to my mouth again but stop when the smell hits me. Aren't rich people like the Maxwells supposed to have good liquor? "So, where did she go?"

"Being *Vandy*," her eyeroll doesn't look nearly as fond as she probably thinks it does, "she tried to clean it all up. George was helping her and then they vanished. Not sure."

"George?" Fucking pimply faced fucker. *I swear to god.*

"Holy shit." Her face lights up, oblivious to my irritation. Oblivious to a lot of things, really. She grabs my forearm. "Do you think she's like, flirting with him or something? That would be *amazing*. It's high time my girl started seeing some action. You know, things have been really shitty for her since that wreck." Her eyes suddenly widen, her hand popping over her red mouth. "Oh shit, sorry. I didn't mean—"

I'm not ungentle when I pull my arm from her grasp. "No worries."

She doesn't look put out. "I get it, you know."

My eyes narrow. "Get what?"

"What it's like to be the center of all the rumors. People love to talk about me. It's non-fucking-stop. It's like, just live your own damn life, people. Why are you so interested in mine?" Her mouth runs like a freight train, barreling forward. "I just try to focus my attention on Vandy. She's really needed my support these last couple years, so I've done everything I can to really stick by her side. Even when things were bad." She leans forward. "I mean, *really* bad." She looks like she's dying to tell me specifics.

"Uh huh." Jesus, this girl. Emory was right. She's a piece of work.

"Anyway, I know that you're not supposed to be spending time with her because of your probation and everything," she touches my shoulder, "but that doesn't mean *we* can't hang out." My eyes flick to her hand and the way her thumb is rubbing against my shirt.

"Right." I reach for my phone in my back pocket, acting like I'm looking at an incoming call. "Know what? That's my probation officer. I need to go take this."

Her eyebrows shoot up her forehead, but she nods solemnly. I stalk away from her, making an easy escape down an empty hallway. I expect that by the time I get home, rumors will be flying about the 'call' I just received. I don't even care. I slip to the back of the house and pass an open door. A lamp on the desk casts a dim light through the room, but it's enough to catch my attention.

I step inside and push the door closed. The room itself is a show-case of leather-bound books, shiny trinkets, and collectibles. While the party rages on down the hall, I take my time, running my hands over the spines of books, inspecting a solid silver figurine in the shape of a bear, an elaborately carved humidor and various cigar paraphernalia. I bypass the photographs of Elana and her family, but linger over a curio cabinet, the central focus being a gold pocket watch.

My body hums like a diviner searching for water.

The watch is too pricey to steal, though. Obviously, a family heirloom. Too flashy, too much attention. I sink into the deep leather chair behind the desk and peruse the cigar offerings instead. I don't smoke, but the cigar lighter is *rad*. It's heavy and flares to life in a billow of brightness and butane when I press the trigger.

Like always when I see a flame, I feel that old background nudge of *'get away'*. I stare into the blue and yellow of it, letting the wrongness of it slide over me like melted wax. It doesn't give me the same back-sweating panic that it used to, and sometimes I think my little stint with Melanie The Pyromaniac was more about *this* than the sex. The way she handled fire was a thing of beauty. I'd watch her from afar, too proud to admit that the sight of flames made my stomach roil and my back itch. Given the gentle way she kept bringing it closer and closer, I'm pretty sure she knew. Complete lunatic, and the sex was... *fine*, but that's the biggest thing I took away from my time with her.

This thing—this light and heat—only has as much power over me as I give it.

I press off the trigger, kicking back leisurely in the chair.

I'm assessing my prize, testing the weight of it in my hand, when the door falls open and a girl stumbles in.

Not just any girl.

Vandy turns around, her long hair falling over her shoulder, and our eyes meet. I know instantly that something's wrong. Her eyes are big and wild, and when she reaches up to push her hair behind her ear, I can see a little tremor.

We silently take each other in. She's wearing a clingy little jumpsuit with thigh-grazing short-shorts, and I don't even know what it is about this place. It's like every bit of female clothing in this town was designed to torture me.

Her eyes flick down to the object in my hand and back up to my face, but I'm focused solely on her expression. Her face is drawn and ashen, and I know the way she's breathing. I'd know that shit anywhere. It's the same way I used to breathe when Melanie first started setting shit on fire in front of me. All I can think is that the last person she was seen with was George.

"Are you stealing that?" she asks, the judgment thick in her question.

"Just browsing." I don't miss her knitted eyebrows, but at least she's being distracted from her panic. "What? That's not a crime."

"Picking through people's personal belongings without their permission is pretty damn close to a crime, Reynolds."

"Close, but not quite." I pick up the cigar cutter and balance the two in my hands. "I'm wavering between the guillotine and the torch. What do you think?"

She stares at me, aghast, unaware that I'm successfully drawing her out of her panic attack. Her arms cross over her chest. "I think you and every other guy in this place should start keeping your hands to yourself."

I hold her eyes as I lean forward, carefully setting the items back on the desk. "Is someone bothering you?" There's a threat in my voice that I'm all too ready to deliver on.

"No." She visibly struggles to take a deep breath. "Yes. *No*. Well… it's less about the guy and more about me. I told you before, I don't do things like this." She gestures wildly, babbling, "I don't go to parties. I don't mingle and drink and *not* embarrass myself. Elana only invited me because," she gives me a significant look, "well, you know why she invited me. But I'm sure she's regretting it. I'm clumsy and slow, and I spilled my drink, and everyone is watching me, and I don't know how to talk to people, and George didn't even do anything wrong, except… except pick the *worst girl* in school to try to kiss, and *god*, this would all be so much easier if I'd taken an oxy tonight." She punctuates this by rattling the door when her head bangs back against it, nostrils flared out with her breaths.

That may be the most I've ever heard Vandy say in her life.

"Hey." I keep my voice low, waiting for her eyes to meet mine. "Hey, come on. Parties suck. Why do you think I'm in here?" I stand from the chair, burying my hands into my pockets. "And look, everyone does embarrassing stuff. Fucking ChattySnap will be full of hormonal teenage regret by tomorrow. And George?" I swallow back rising irritation and try to come up with the right words to say. "George is a fucking idiot, but I'm pretty sure you're not the worst girl in school to try to kiss."

Her cheeks turn the most delightful shade of pink, spreading down her neck and to the V of her shirt. I notice the black cord and instinctively feel for the one in my pocket. I'd spent half the bus ride to and from the game wondering what it goes to.

Now I'm wondering if hers is the same.

Vandy shakes her head, eyes dropping. "He's an idiot because he picked the one girl at this party with zero experience." She presses her palms to her cheeks, giving me a wincing look. "I completely panicked when he tried. I didn't even have time to think about if I wanted it or not. I mean, god, it would have been my *first* kiss, and I just shoved him off and ran away like a coward."

I let out a slow, relieved breath. *Halle-fucking-lujah*, I won't have to pummel that kid.

Her face turns inexplicably red and I try to come up with an appropriate answer for that. Appropriate in the way her brother's best friend might be, an answer that doesn't slip into improper territory because, well...

When I first saw the photo in the trophy case, I'd noticed how pretty she was, but in person? In the dim light of this room, with the red cheeks and the short-shorts? It's more than obvious. She's stunning. A little low-key, especially compared to girls like her friend Sydney, but cute in a whole different way.

Not in the big-brotherly kind of way, either.

"Doesn't seem like a big loss." I eventually say, shrugging. "Do you really want your first kiss to be with some chicken-shit pizza face, next to the keg?"

I'm not sure why, but she looks vaguely embarrassed by this. "He's not so bad."

It occurs to me that she might actually *like* that douchebag. I have a lot of opinions on this, but don't voice a single one. I just grit my teeth, reaching out to finger the cigar lighter again. "Whatever floats your boat, Baby V."

Her eyebrows furl into something dark and combative. "Well, *some people* don't have prospects throwing themselves at us all the time."

I feel my lip curl at this, because I've seen the way guys look at Vandy—far better guys than George—and seriously? This is the culmination of Emory's bullshit efforts to keep them away? I can see it perfectly. She's going to go for the first guy who has the balls to make a move. All it'll take are a few generically pleasant words, the right place, and some gentle coaxing, and he's in there. Just like that. It could totally be George. It could be Tyson, who already lies to a girl every single day, just to get into her pants. It could even be Sebastian, who legitimately seems one misspoken word from an assault charge. It could be anyone.

She'd just... *settle*.

The thought makes me boil inside.

Before I can decide how to even voice any of that, the sounds of distant sirens begin swelling beyond the house. I instantly recognize it as the howl of Fucking Jerry's golf cart. I walk to the window and take a furtive peek through the curtains, and sure enough, his amber lights are flashing up the drive.

But blue lights follow close behind.

"*Fuck.*"

It's not just him this time. He's called for back-up from his buddies, two police cruisers rolling up behind him.

I glance over at Vandy, and all of that restless, wide-eyed panic has returned with a vengeance. "Oh my god, I can't get caught here."

"You and me both, Baby V." There's no Mountain Point at the end of this road. There's just probation violations and more time in juvie, for me. I snatch the lighter off the desk and put the guillotine carefully back in its place. Then, I walk over to the opposite side of the room and push back the sheer white curtain, revealing French doors that lead to the side yard. "Come on," I tell her, holding out my hand.

She blinks and stares at it, frozen still as a statue.

It's like I'm transported back in time. Suddenly this room is a parking lot and I'm watching the glow of stadium lights playing across the softness of her young cheeks and bright eyes. It takes me a moment to blink myself out of it, but when I do, I snatch my hand away.

I swallow and ball my fist, shoving it in my pocket. "I can get you home safe. I promise."

The words ring hollow, even to me—even knowing that I can. That I will.

For a moment I think she's going to turn and run, and for a longer moment I'm thinking that she should.

She *should* run like hell.

Instead, she braces herself and walks across the room, following me out the door.

It's the second time Vandy has put her faith in me to get her somewhere safe.

This time I'm not going to fail.

# 13

I STARE at that hand for a long, hard moment, fear licking up my spine. The last time I followed Reynolds McAllister, it destroyed my life and his. But the sirens are growing louder, and outside the library door I hear frenzied footsteps, kids shouting, "Cops!" and I know that if I get caught here, that's *all she wrote*. My mom will never let me out of the house again.

I also know if I don't make a decision quick, Reyn will leave me here. He'll have to, I wouldn't even blame him. He'd be facing a prison sentence that's a lot worse than the mere parent-mandated house arrest I'm looking at.

Self-preservation kicks in, and before I can change my mind, I've followed him out the door. The entire front yard is chaos, blue and yellow lights casting a swirl of color across the front yard. Reyn heads toward the woods, away from the light and noise. He darts ahead, fast, clearly unfamiliar with how much my halting gait holds me back. He vanishes into the tree line, but reemerges instantly, a deep line slashing his forehead.

"Sorry!" I whisper, struggling through the grass, "I can't—"

He turns, squats and says, "Get on my back."

A twig snaps and it startles me into action. Despite a gazillion reservations, I steady my hands on his firm, broad shoulders and hop. His hands catch my thighs and hitch me up, and he straightens easily, hooking his arms under my legs.

"Good?" he asks, although he's already moving.

"Go go go!" I urge and without any more hesitation, he takes off through the woods. He moves just like the athlete he is, steady and sure. The jostling makes me clench my knees around his waist, and when I press my cheek against the side of his neck, his skin is warm and a little clammy. As he darts through the forest, I'm overwhelmed by sensations. The scent of him, soapy, clean, and masculine, fills my lungs. I find myself breathing it in curiously, filing it away. The hard lines of his muscular body shift against me with the raw power of his movement.

Once we're away from the lights of Elana's house, he slows, striding quietly through the dark, but he doesn't release me, and I don't stop clinging to him. I readjust my grip to something less strangling and he ducks his head, bouncing once to buck me up a little higher.

A different set of lights appear, but these I recognize as our houses in the distance. He spins for a minute, reaching out and touching the trunk of a tree. The treehouse, I realize. He clutches my legs against his sides and I feel his pulse hammering beneath my cheek. His breath comes out in low shudders, his chest heaving from exertion, and there's a moment when it becomes acutely awkward that I'm still hanging on his back.

I unlatch my hands and slowly slide down the lean slope of his tall body. The chirp of the early fall crickets fills the air, and the lights from our backyard cast far enough back here that we're not completely swallowed in the dark.

He lets out a low, breathless laugh, collapsing against the trunk of the tree. "And here I thought I was done with ruck marches."

I watch his chest rise and fall. "Ruck marches?"

He nods breathlessly, leaning forward to rest his hands on his knees. "Ruck marches are... like..." He tilts his head, but the bill of his cap obstructs his eyes. "Travelling a certain distance, in a certain amount of time, with a certain amount of weight strapped to your back. My old school had them twice a year. It's always a big deal."

It's the first time I realize that I don't actually know much about what Reyn's life was like, wherever he was. I knew he was in a military academy, of course. Everyone knew that. I'd known about juvie. I'd even known about the week he spent in the hospital, after the accident. But I guess I'd never given it much thought beyond the bare fact of it.

"That sounds terrible."

"Nah." He straightens and gives a dismissive wave. "They test you first, build up the weights and the distance depending on your conditioning and endurance. There's PT for it every week. There are some people in the military that have to do it all the time."

But Reyn didn't go to that school because he wanted to be in the military. It was punishment.

Punishment for what he did to me.

He breathlessly adds, "Who knew it'd come in handy, huh?" and smiles at me.

It's *the* smile. His eyes still look tired, and he has that same stillness about him, but now his lips are pulled back, revealing both of his dimples.

It *kills* me.

"Thank you," I say, having to look away from it, "for getting me out of there."

"Well," he says, his voice a slow drawl, "I did owe you one."

I smile despite myself and I'm glad he can't see me fully. "Yeah, I guess you did," I reply, and start down the hill toward our yards. I don't get far before I feel his hand holding me back.

"You know, you did the right thing tonight."

I turn to look at him, but I can't make out much about his eyes. "Running from the police and climbing on your back like a monkey? As embarrassing as it was, I agree."

"No," he says, voice gruff. "With George. Shoving him aside. A guy like that doesn't deserve your first kiss."

"Oh." My cheeks instantly flame. "Yeah, well, if it takes me another seventeen years to get that kiss, I'll probably regret it."

"It won't." He looks away, and for a second, I think that's it. I wait, but when he remains silent, I turn to leave again. His voice stops me. "I don't know where you got it in your head that you're not..." He pauses, and when I turn back to him, his expression has hardened. "That you're not, like... *desirable* or whatever, but it's not true."

I stare back at him, too stunned to form words.

Did Reyn just say I'm desirable?

"I know it's my fault," he continues, voice rough with an emotion that hurts to hear. "That your life got so fucked-up, and that you think you're broken. That your parents watch you like a hawk, and Emory thinks he's gotta carry the key to your chastity belt. But they almost lost you. It scared the hell out of them." He rubs a palm over his forehead and it tips his hat up enough that when his hand drops, I can see the way he's looking at me. It feels like a fist is tightening around my heart. "It scared the hell out of me, too."

It's a loaded confession, and I'm no more prepared to hear it than I am to see that pained, haunted look in his eyes.

I wring my hands together. "Reyn—"

"So, I know, okay? I know you missed out on a lot of firsts because of what I did, and," he exhales like he's trying to fold in on himself, "that you might feel...pressure. To just take something because it's there, for the sake of having done it. But you shouldn't do that, V." He pins me under his stare. "You shouldn't just settle for anything."

I choose my words carefully when I start, "The way my family is has nothing to do with you." He scoffs, looking away, and I can't stand it—the way his features go so stony and dark, hidden from me again. "It *doesn't*, Reyn. They were always going to be like that. I mean, do you even remember what it was like for me in middle school? I couldn't even go to that stupid Valentine's dance." I roll my eyes, remembering the epic fight that had spanned an entire week. "The accident gave them a reason, but let's be real here. There was always going to be a reason, however big or small. This one just happened to be big. But the first time I came home crying about a boy, they would have thrown away the key."

His mouth curves into a sharp smile, and I can't help but mirror it.

I add, "Honestly, it's my fault more than yours. I never pushed it." I shrug, shifting my feet around in the leaves. "I never had that moment, you know? Where I just...showed them I was my own person. I spent so long—" *High.* "—not caring, that it's never seemed worth putting them through more worry. In a way, I guess I coddle them as badly as they coddle me."

And yeah, this isn't the most comfortable realization to have.

"You Halls sure do have a way with that." Reyn stares toward our houses, standing bright behind me. His jaw goes tight. "It could be worse."

I nod. "I know."

He nods back. "Just...things might get intense, with all these Devil rituals, so I need you to know that you can count on me if you need someone to help you get through them. You shouldn't feel just stuck with someone."

"Because you owe me," I reply slowly.

"Right."

"So..." My mind runs a million miles a minute, and I'm only half-joking when I say, "If I wanted to have my first kiss—just to get it over with—you're offering to take one for the team?"

His chin pulls up and he's looking at me blankly. I'm filled with a sharp panic that the half-joke came out far too earnest, and maybe the thought hadn't even crossed his mind. I basically want to crawl into a hole, right here. The forest will be a good home. It's quiet out here. Forward my mail, Mom, because I can never show my face again. My cheeks burst into a crazy heat, but before I can backtrack and explain that I was just being funny, *ha ha*, he shrugs.

"If you mean the team of ready and willing teenage boys, then sure."

My low laugh has an edge of hysteria to it, because he's agreeing. *Agreeing.* It's insane. Maybe he doesn't realize how wrong he is. There is not a team of teenage boys lined up to do anything with me. Regardless, this whole idea is wrong on more levels than that. He's Emory's best friend, which makes him unilaterally off limits. He's a senior, and gorgeous, and popular, which makes him completely out of my league. And he's... well, he's the boy I shouldn't even be out in the woods with, or talking to, let alone kissing, because we could both get in huge trouble.

But foremost, he's Reynolds McAllister, and it strikes me uncomfortably why my mind had leapt there. It has very little to do with him being gorgeous and smelling amazing. It was all that stuff he said about not settling. It just makes a perfect kind of sense. He was the first boy I ever fell for. If I had a choice for my first kiss, it'd be him.

It'd have to be him.

"Okay," I say, trying to sound more casual than I am, because my insides have just imploded. I feel a little faint. "Ready?"

"What?" His head snaps back. "You mean now?" his voice rises, eyes roving around the forest like my brother or Jerry or someone is about to jump out.

Once the words left my mouth, I couldn't take them back. I try to sound cool. Aloof. This kind of thing happens to me every day. Talking gorgeous seniors into kissing me is boring stuff. "Why not? I just went to my first party, drank nasty punch, committed a party foul, and escaped from the police. What better night to get my first kiss?"

He reaches back to rub at his neck, and I remember vividly the way it felt against my cheek. "Point taken."

"Cool."

He runs his hands down his thighs, and this is all so antithetical to his usual stillness that I unconsciously mirror his fidgeting. I wonder if his palms are sweaty like mine, and if they are, if it's because he's nervous, too. Probably just worried about what Emory will say to him if he finds out. No, what Emory will *do* to him. Shit. Emory can *never* find out.

While I'm caught in a mental whirlwind, Reyn has stepped forward, closing the gap between us. I look up and see the angle of his jaw, the faint line of stubble dark against his chin. "Are you sure about this?" he asks, head tilted down.

I nod, because my words are not working right now.

He stills for a heartbeat, looking down into my face, and reaches up to his ballcap. He spins it around on his head, and I feel another one of those grand stomach-dips. He's doing that so it won't bump my forehead. Because we're going to be that close. Kissing.

I wet my lips, and since the bill of his cap is no longer in the way, I can see when his eyes dart to the motion. He inches forward, tip of his toes bumping into mine. He seems a little unsure, mostly about what to do with his hands, which is not normal. Reyn never seems unsure, especially with his hands. They're always touching, stealing, catching or throwing. He finally places one on my hip, holding me in place.

I feel it like a brand.

He meets my gaze. "This is just to make sure you don't end up kissing a jackoff like George by mistake, okay?"

My voice is thin. "Okay."

He reaches up to sweep my hair away from my temple, and his hand trails down the side of my face. His lips are dark pink, a little chapped, but soft-looking. I push up on my toes and the hand on my hip moves around to my back. Our bodies are pressed up against one another, and I can't feel the same raw power as before, when his muscles were shifting against me, but I still know it's there in the solidness of him.

He continues, "You don't have to—"

I don't let him finish. I press my lips against his because I don't want to hear him keep rationalizing this, like it's something that needs talked into being nothing. I don't want nothing, I want *this*: The way his lips give against my own, reluctantly pressing back, and the way it's suddenly not so reluctant anymore. It's soft and surging, the way he pinches my bottom lip between his own, face tilting to get closer.

His hand cups my cheek, fingers weaving into the hair behind my ear, and he pulls me closer, like... like maybe he wants more. Like maybe he's getting more out of this than just some favor to a dumb girl. Like maybe when his mouth parts, his wet tongue slipping between my lips, it's because he likes doing this.

My stomach bottoms out and my fingers curl into his shirt, looking for something to hold onto as I try to mirror his movements, tongue meeting his. The kiss is *wet*, and warm. He tastes like air and something ripe and alive, and when he sucks a soft retreat, only to dip back into my mouth, my chest feels like it might cave in.

My breath hitches and he stills.

He pulls away gently, his hands slowly dipping back into his pockets as he steps away. The light from the houses reflects off his lips, shiny with our kiss.

I've gone from boiling to tepid, from the warmth of his body next to mine, to standing awkwardly alone in the woods.

"That was—" I start, because someone has to say something, and from the shell-shocked look on his face, the expression that no doubt precedes deep and sudden regret, he is at a loss for words. "Okay."

His eyebrow shoots up. "Okay?"

"Okay," I repeat, giving my lips a quick suck. "That was... okay. Good. Done. Mission accomplished."

Oh my god, Vandy, shut the fuck up.

I give him a double thumbs-up.

And because things couldn't get worse... he slowly, reluctantly, gives me a double thumbs-up in return.

"I'm just going to go in now. You should probably wait—"

"A few minutes. Yeah, I agree." That same dumbfounded expression is on his face and wow, that is *not* the look you want a guy to give you after you jumped him in the woods. *Jesus.*

I take off after that, hobbling down the hill as fast as my leg will take me. I don't look back until I'm all the way at the back porch, hand on the doorknob. I can barely see him up on the hill, but I know he's there, watching to make sure I get in the house, probably mentally scrubbing what had to be the worst kiss of his life out of his mind.

$$\sim$$

"It's better when you can feel the wind whipping around, you know?"

I look down at his hand on the gearshift, confident and sure. I think about what it would feel like on my hip. The pressure of his thumb against my skin. I look down, feeling a flicker of a memory, then look back up at his face.

Fourteen-year-old Reyn is gone. A more mature, more handsome boy sits next to me. But boy isn't exactly the right word. Not for the stubble on his chin, or the strong muscles that line his forearm as he shifts from third to fourth gear. This is a man.

"I knew it," he says suddenly, raising his voice over the loud rush of wind.

"Knew what?"

"That you wanted to kiss me."

My stomach flip-flops. He knew? How did he know? That was a secret I'd carry to the grave. My cheeks burn with heat and I dare a glance at him again. He's smirking at me from the driver's seat.

"What?" I laugh nervously. "I don't want to kiss you."

I play it off, or try to, but he's leaning over the center console, one hand sliding behind my neck, the other still on the wheel. He dips his head and brushes his lips against mine, sweet and soft. He pulls back, smiling *that* smile.

"How was it? Was it worth it?"

I turn away and look out the window, seeing the glow in the dark. Fireflies, I think. But then, I realize it's something else. My stomach lurches and I sit up. "Watch out! There's a—" But it's too late. It's always too late. The next moment is a flash of pale brown fur, the squeal of tires, Reynolds' fighting against the wheel—

I jolt awake, a scream strangled in the back of my throat. My hand moves to my lips, which feel different. They tingle with the memory of Reyn's kiss, from the dream.

No.

The *real* memory of Reyn's kiss in the woods.

God, that's the real nightmare.

I stand, tugging at my sweaty T-shirt. I can't believe I kissed Reyn McAllister. I can't believe I basically played on his guilt to get it. I'd been wrong before, about not settling. At least if I'd settled, it would have meant the guy actually wanted to kiss me back. It would have meant I could look back on it with something other than this awful churny feeling in my stomach.

He'd looked so horrified. So regretful. I don't even blame him. He still thinks I'm a kid, and even though we laughed about him owing me one, the root of this is guilt. Reyn feels guilty about the fact I'm a pathetic, crippled, virgin loser and yeah, he took one for the team.

I cross the room and change, trading out one shirt for another. It's a nightly ritual, as is my habit of sneaking a peek out my bedroom window to see if Reyn's awake. I carefully slide the curtain aside and look across the gap in our yards. Sure enough, his light is on. The difference is that he's not sprawled on the bed, like usual. Tonight, he's sitting on the edge, his profile in full view. He's wearing a shirt with the sleeves torn off, and one arm is reclined back, propping him up. His jaw is locked tight, and from here, it looks like he's in some kind of pain. His other arm is moving lazily in his lap, and I furrow my brows at it.

*What is he do—*

Oh my god.

*Oh my god!*

My heart thuds in my chest as I realize what's happening and I drop to my knees, chin level with the windowsill. He's *jerking off.* Talk about horrified. I glance away, but barely a second passes before I look back again, my eyes drawn to his motions. He isn't facing me, so I can't see that much of him.

At least, not until he falls back on his elbow.

Abruptly, I get an eyeful of his erection—his *cock*, Sydney would call it—standing alert. Even from a distance it seems huge, obscene, but his hand glides up and down the hard length of it, like he's exceptionally familiar with the territory. Reyn isn't afraid or in pain, he's very much in control.

The pounding in my chest vibrates down my body, spreading warmth from the center of my belly. I feel like I have multiple heartbeats, one in my chest, one in my ears, and another pulsing hot between my legs. I can't tear my eyes away from him. His motions aren't frantic, they're unhurried and precise, more than some mechanical means to an end. He's enjoying it. He starts at the base and strokes upward, pushing toward the head. He rolls that in his palm, before tugging at the tip, jaw easing slightly. A shiver runs down my spine, which is in direct contrast to the heat I feel building beneath my skin. I shift, intending to ease the weight on my leg, but my body has a mind of its own, begging its own relief. A shaky sigh emerges when my hand pushes under the fabric of my panties, down to the warm heat below.

It's with surprise that I find that I'm already wet.

Unlike the guy across the way, this is not familiar territory for me. I'd been too numb, too drugged up to worry about feelings like this for a long time. Like everything else, cutting back has given me an awakening for almost all things, physical and mental. As Reyn continues his pattern; *stroke, push, roll, tug*; I create my own, running the pads of my fingers over the slick nub, alternating between deep pressure and barely touching. A coil twists in my lower belly, spurned on as much by my own actions as what I'm watching. It's terrifying, real, and distressingly beautiful. Reyn's speed increases and his jaw slacks entirely, mouth hanging open. Other than the hand in my panties, rubbing and rolling against my slippery clit, I'm nearly frozen, watching as he pushes himself closer and closer to the edge. His eyelids shutter closed, and his nose wrinkles, while his teeth sink into the bottom lip I'd just been kissing hours earlier.

*Oh god*, the memory of his mouth on mine, the feel of his hand on my lower back, the press of his body is all it takes to send a ripple of pleasure through my core. I force my eyes open while the orgasm wracks through me, struggling to watch him because I know he's close. I don't know how I know, I just do. It's in the way he's biting his lip, head falling back on his shoulders. It's in the tension in his arms, muscles flexing. When he falls back on the bed, free hand groping for the sheet, and *seizes*, I lean forward, nose pressed against the glass, breath fogging the window. When he erupts, I clamp my legs tight together, feeling the ripples course through my own body as if we were connected by more than the distance between our bedroom windows.

I watch as his hand slows, and then falls away. His chest lifts up and down and he arches his back to stretch. I take in every detail when he grimaces, using the sheet at his side to wipe his release away. I'm still unable to move when he stands and walks across the room. His bare ass moons me without a care in the world when he enters his bathroom.

When he's out of view, I pull my hand from between my legs and turn around, sitting with my back against the wall. I can already tell I'll be chasing the thrill of that for a long time.

Kissing Reyn, seeing him like that, coming with him?

It's the best high I've ever had.

# 14

Reyn

By the grace of god, I manage to sleep past dawn. Two thoughts enter my mind when I roll over, impaling myself on morning wood: The girl next door and having jerked off to her. I swore to myself that I wouldn't do that again. There are generally three categories of girl in direct relation to my libido—the ones I can fuck, the ones I *can't* fuck, and the complete void only reserved for family members. I'd tried to put Vandy in one of those last two, only as much I promised Emory I'd treat her as one of my own, that shit just wasn't happening. My brain—and dick—saw Vandy Hall as a lot of things, but 'sister' wasn't anywhere near to being one of them. That put her firmly in the 'girls I can't fuck' category, and that's always a tricky designation.

Of all the things I want, the ones I can't have burn the brightest.

Getting off to Vandy broke a thousand rules, but here I am again, not just fantasizing about her but *remembering* her. That kiss was fucking *electric*. I can still feel her hitched breath when I deepened the kiss, and I'm no idiot. That wasn't a gasp of surprise. It was pure sex.

I groan and adjust my boner. It was one thing to see Vandy from afar and think about her. It's a whole other ballgame now that I know what she tastes like. How she feels under my hands. How, even though she's innocent and inexperienced, it was hands down the hottest kiss of my life.

And what had I done about it?

Nothing. Gawked at her like a fucking moron. Too busy thinking that I'd just stolen her first kiss—*mine now*—to ease an awkward situation, unable to even offer some trite welcome into the world of face-sucking. Oh yeah, then I came home and beat off like a thirteen-year-old who just discovered his parental internet filter had a back door.

I knew I was playing with fire the minute she walked in that room at the party, looking all frail and vulnerable. I *felt* the panic rolling off of her. The urge to distract her, to protect her, was like second nature. Maybe I'm as bad as Emory.

Except Emory wouldn't have taken advantage.

I scrub a hand over my face. That was the real crime. There I was telling her not to settle, not to just take whatever came along, and I basically led her right into settling on me.

The only thing that eases the gnawing guilt is that I didn't kiss her. She kissed *me*. Of course, I kissed her back. I'm not made of stone here.

Well, my dick might be. None of this is making me less hard, but before I can do anything about it, my phone buzzes on the bedside table. The caller is unknown, but the message comes through loud and clear: a devil graphic followed by a time; 11 a.m.

I guess it's time to get up and see what the powers that be want us to do next.

I ARRIVE at the bell tower with a coffee in one hand and a breakfast burrito in the other. Campus is quiet. Most people are still asleep, or maybe over in the dining hall for breakfast if they live on campus. I look both ways before I slide in the door, eyes and ears alert as I try the handle to the basement stairs.

I wrench the knob when the door doesn't give.

"The fuck?" I'd assumed this is where we're meeting, even if the details on the message were vague. Wasn't this supposed to be our base of operations, or... what had Vandy called it? Our dungeon?

"Try your key."

I turn and see Caroline standing in the doorway. She's wearing leggings and an oversized hoodie, and it's weird. I'm not sure I've ever seen her out of uniform. Her hair is in two long braids, and she pushes thick-framed glasses up the bridge of her nose. I stand there for a moment, trying to figure out what she's talking about.

She rolls her eyes and exhales loudly, pulling a key similar to the one I'd found in my locker from her pocket. She makes a big production of shoving it in the keyhole, like I'm a complete idiot. A few jiggles later, it opens.

So I'm still half asleep, give me a break.

"Maybe you deserve that high score on the SAT after all," I say, pushing the door wide and letting her go in first.

"For the record," she says imperiously as she passes, "I *did* get a high SAT score. 1400 just wasn't good enough for my mom. She didn't even give me the chance to try for anything higher."

I nod in understanding, because I can believe it. If there's one unifier at Preston Prep, it's that everyone has massive amounts of parental baggage.

We walk down the winding stairs and enter the bunker. Most of the initiates are here already, and I'd been preparing all morning for seeing Vandy here, but the sight of her on the couch still makes me vibrate with nerves. The plan had been to approach the situation as if last night had never happened. She's sitting on the couch next to Tyson, and the flicker of emotion that sparks in me when I see her smile at him, friendly and open, isn't something I want to examine very closely.

Emory's standing by a table, scribbling on slips of paper. I was sort of torn on the prospect of telling Emory about the party. On one hand, I want him to know that I'd gotten her out of there safely. It's a weak concession that doesn't even come close to making up for what happened three years ago, but it still settles something inside of me. On the other hand, I'd have to skip over the whole kiss situation, which I figure sort of cancels out any 'attaboy' I'd be due.

In the end, I decide that it doesn't matter what I want. If Vandy wants him to know, she'll tell him herself. She's the one who has to live with him.

"So listen," Emory says, drawing my attention. I can see the slips of paper, two names on each. He's written Vandy's name on one and holds the pen poised over the second space. "I know we talked about you teaming up with V for all this stuff, but I was thinking of putting her with Tyson tonight."

Against my will, my eyes fly over to him. He's telling Vandy some kind of story that apparently necessitates a lot of animated gesturing. She laughs at something he says—not a big, flashy laugh, just a quiet chuckle. It still makes my eyes narrow. Perfect, squeaky clean, nice, friendly, smart, and athletic Tyson, whose biggest flaw is lying about believing in God.

I look at Emory. "Why?"

"It's like this," he starts, and I can see the tension in his eyes. Whatever this is, it's stressing him out. "This is going to require a few quick and dirty B&E's, and you're the only one here who can get into Thistle Cove. They've really upped the security since that girl went missing and their coach was fired for being a fucking pervert. You'll have to pick a couple locks, probably. But Northridge is easy, and Tyson's a transfer, so he knows that place like the back of his hand. He'll be able to get in and out, no problem."

I bristle at this. "I can get in and out of Thistle Cove." In no fucking world is Tyson better than me at this. Maybe he's better at being a 'good guy', and maybe he's better at deceiving stupid girls, but breaking into places he doesn't belong? *In no world.* "A couple locks aren't going to stop me."

"Here's the thing..." He grimaces, and I know he's holding something back. "Thistle Cove has a fence."

*Ah.*

I shift my gaze back to Vandy, considering. I wonder if she's ever going to make eye contact with me. I probably fucked things up last night. I mean, things were already tense between us, adding in another uncomfortable situation was piss-poor thinking. "What kind of fence?"

"Chain link," he explains. "Maybe eight feet?"

"I can cut it."

He shakes his head. "This has to be completely non-destructive."

"So I can pick the padlock."

"Can't." He shrugs. "Padlock's out front, full view of the cameras. The only way in there is to jump it."

I roll my eyes, thinking of Vandy scaling the tree house. "I don't think you're giving either of us enough credit." It might be a little sketch, but I can feel it in my bones. She can handle an eight-foot fence.

He still looks doubtful. "Even if you can get her over the fence, she won't be able to run if shit goes south."

This would be a really great time to tell him about the successful party escape and inspire some confidence. Instead, I say, "Well either you trust me to get her out of there safe, or you leave her alone with some random dude who swears his biggest crime is *atheism*."

Emory's eyebrow arches skeptically, and I know it's shitty, playing against his crazy-protective nature, but *shit*.

I promised her.

I *said* I'd help her get through this. Can Tyson run with her on his back for a mile? Fucking doubtful. He's a diver. Not a sprinter. All that aside, Vandy's clearly got a thing or two to prove to her brother, and she deserves the chance to do it.

He peers over at Tyson. "What, you think he's suspect?"

"I think no one is that *clean*. And we both already know, for a fact, that he dupes innocent girls into getting with him."

Yeah, that does it.

Emory's jaw clenches. "Point." But then he meets my gaze, eyes tight, and I realize that whatever's coming next is the actual source of his stress. "It's just that you'd have to drive her."

My lungs constrict in an exhale that doesn't seem to end. Well, what the *fuck* am I supposed to say to that? My, "Oh," comes out flat.

Emory sighs. "It's not that I don't think you'd be careful or anything."

"I get it."

"No, you don't," he says, looking annoyed. "I know you'd be more careful with her than literally anyone else on Earth. I know that, Reyn. But it'd be putting both of you in a really fucked up position, and when I asked her, she said—"

I interrupt him, "If you already asked her, then why are we even having this conversation? If she wants to go with Tyson, then I get it." And I do. Who could blame her?

But Emory just gives me a look, and maybe it's the subtle thread of guilt within it that tips me off, but either way, I know.

I *know*. "She chose me."

"The thing about V," he slowly adds, "is that sometimes she bites off more than she can chew. I was just kind of hoping to ease her into something like that."

I bite back an irritated reply. "Maybe you should let her make some of her own choices, Em. She's seventeen, not seven." Okay, maybe I *don't* bite back an irritated reply, because his face goes a touch stony. Also, maybe I just got that line from my dad and I want to hit my own face a little bit. Still stands. "Come on, man, have some faith." I bury a playful punch into his shoulder, trying to dissolve the tension. "You know I work best under pressure. It'll probably just make it go smoother. If she thinks she can handle it, then give her a chance."

Emory looks at me for a long moment. "You really think it'll be fine?"

"Yes." No hesitation.

After a minute of nervous shifting and overly dramatic sighs, he nods slowly, like he's warming to the idea. "Well, if you're both really sure you can pull it off, then maybe…" He glances back at Vandy. "Maybe it can be a good thing. Maybe you two can work out some of your shit. Things are tense enough around here, you know?" He rubs a hand over his drawn face. "I mean, fuck, I don't exactly enjoy staying up until four in the morning stressing over this shit."

"Right, that's what I'm thinking."

Lie.

What I'm really thinking about is that she had a choice between me and Tyson, and she didn't choose pretty-boy Tyson.

*She chose me.*

He scribbles my name on the piece of paper and finishes up the rest. By this point, everyone has arrived. Apparently, no one else had a problem figuring out how to unlock the door. I sit on a musty armchair and take another bite of my breakfast, assessing the group.

Sebastian, who looks about as tired and stressed as Emory, has a new shiner swelling under his eye. Afton is next to him, studying her nails like she's bored, and maybe she is. This is probably kid's stuff to her. Georgia is sitting with Ben, talking about the game last night, and Elana's animatedly telling Carlton about the cops showing up at the party the night before.

In the middle of Elana's summation of events, it finally happens.

Vandy's gaze flicks to mine.

She doesn't *look* nervous, but her cheeks instantly begin blooming a soft, warm pink. If she were any other girl I'd just kissed, I'd be smirking at her, or winking, playing it up, putting it on to build the promise of more. But because it's Vandy, I just dip my chin in a nod and lift my cup of coffee to my lips.

I don't miss that her eyes follow it.

We both look away when Emory gathers everyone's attention.

"Tonight is the second ritual," he says, reading from a slip of paper. "Now that we've had to entrust everyone with our deepest, darkest secrets, it's time to prove our loyalty to the Devils and our school." He starts handing out the slips of paper. Vandy looks at hers, tucks a strand of hair behind her ear, and peeks at me quickly before looking away. "Each slip of paper has your partner's name on it, along with a rival school on the back. Each school has their thing, like how the Devils have the pitchfork over the stadium entrance that everyone touches for luck. Sparrowood has the crest that hangs by the gymnasium wall that they bring to each game. You catch my drift. You'll each have until tomorrow at dawn to complete your assignment and prove your loyalty to Preston Prep."

It takes a moment for everyone to find their partners. I've got a mouthful of egg and bacon when she stands over me, holding up the slip of paper. "Looks like we meet again." She narrows her eyes at her brother. "Though I'm sure he tried to stick me at the kids' table."

"Northridge is the kids' table?"

"Absolutely," she says, eyes rolling. "But I told him to ask you, just in case..." She's wearing a purple cardigan, and she tugs the sleeves of it over her fists, expression uncertain. "I know I'll probably slow you down."

"Nah," I say easily, looking around. "No more than any of these other people."

She gives me a doubtful look. "I'm kind of surprised he's letting me do it, honestly."

I swallow my breakfast and crumple up the foil. "Maybe he just wants his best friend and his sister to get along."

"Or he wants to keep me away from every other guy here." Her blush, which had begun to fade, comes back with a vivid, red vengeance, and I know exactly what she's thinking.

I'm the only guy here she's kissed.

"What's the assignment," I ask, hoping to distract her from the ugly truth of that.

"Thistle Cove," she says, smoothing the paper. "We have to replace their Viking helmet with devil horns. The helmet's in their trophy case just inside the gym, so we just have to get in there and take it. Sounds like he picked the perfect task for you."

I take the slip and read it for myself. "To be fair it says 'replace', not 'steal', but if we have to break into something, I'm your man."

We strategize for a bit, coming up with the supplies we'll need to pull it off. Thistle Cove is an hour away, which means we'll need to leave early enough to scope it out before dark. We spend a while pulling up photos of the school on our phones. She points out to me where the cameras will be, but doesn't know the interior of the school well enough to guess which doors we should take. A PDF classroom map, internet aerial view, and a trip down a few of the students' ChattySnaps reveals enough photos and videos to make a crude estimate. We huddle over the slip of paper and I grid it out, mapping the way.

While we talk and plan, my gaze keeps being drawn to her mouth, like a magnet. Her lips are pink and only marginally glossy, like she's wearing Chapstick. They look as soft as they'd felt last night, and if I allow myself to really sink into the memory, I can still recall the texture of her tongue when it greeted mine, the way she tasted like that bad grain alcohol and something so warm that it ignited my spine.

I spend just as much time fighting the urge to look down at her bare legs.

By the time we've roughed out a general path, I'm half hard and most everyone else is gone. Only Emory and Aubrey remain, still jotting down notes across the room. There's no doubt he specifically chose her as his partner.

"Do me a favor?" I say, slipping my phone into my pocket. She looks at me questioningly, openly, but I can't help it when my gaze finally travels down to her bare legs. She probably catches it. "Wear some jeans tonight, okay?"

"Oh." She blinks, following my gaze to her shorts. "Yeah, sure."

"Because of the fence," I explain.

*Yes*, because of the fence. *Not because your thighs are hardcore distracting.*

"My parents are going to have questions," she says, casually slipping the paper into her back pocket. "I'm not sure how I'm going to get out of there."

I think on this for a moment. "Tell them you're going to cover something for the paper. Football isn't the only sport that's in-season, right?"

"True," she replies. "Softball and water polo."

"Just pick one and tell them it's at another school. Emory can cover for you and say he's driving. He'll be gone all night anyway." She gives me an odd look. "What?"

"It comes so easy for you, doesn't it?"

"What comes easy?" Because nothing in my life feels easy right now.

"The lying, I guess." She ducks her head, fidgeting with the volume on her phone. "I feel really bad whenever I do it."

"Like with the drugs?"

Her expression shifts and she straightens. "It didn't feel good hiding that from them, but they were so worried about everything. I couldn't add something else to the list."

I try to choose my words carefully. I'm not trying to sound like an after-school special or anything, but it nags at me. "Opioids are serious shit, V. It's not like with weed or something where you can just do it casually on the weekend." Way too many of the kids at Mountain Point were in there because of that crap.

"You think I don't know that?" she says, eyes flashing. "Like I said before, I'm clean now. It's not a problem."

"I'm just saying, I've seen people kick it, and I've seen people 'kick it', and then I've seen people *kick it*."

"What's it to you?" She's awfully defensive for someone claiming it's no big deal. She stands, signaling that she's ready to go—or rather, ready to get away from me and this conversation.

"Hey, come on," I say quietly. "I'm not trying to judge you. I just... I guess I'm trying to understand you a little better."

"There's not much to understand. I used to do it, now I don't." She slings her bag over her shoulder and calls out to Emory, "I'll meet you at the truck."

He looks up and nods, eyes darting over to me. I pick up my trash and wait as Aubrey follows Vandy up the stairs. Emory turns off the bunker lights, voice low when he says, "I'm trusting you with my sister. Do not fuck this up, okay?"

I look him in the eye and give him a promise I hope I can keep. "I won't."

⁓

I WAIT at the gas station for a good twenty minutes before Emory's truck pulls into the parking spot next to mine. I hop out of the Jeep, feeling erratic with all of the energy building inside of me. I wasn't lying to Emory before about doing best under pressure, but that pressure usually didn't include having to drive with Vandy for the first time since almost killing her. I blame this restlessness for going to the truck and opening Vandy's door for her. She's wearing a black top and dark skinny jeans, and I'm relieved she heeded my request. Whatever sour note we'd left things on this morning isn't going to interfere with what needs to be done.

A large canvas bag sits in her lap. Hesitantly, I reach for it, and she lets me. Inside is a large, flashy pair of paper mâché devil horns.

"Where did you get this?" I gesture to the horns.

"From last year's homecoming float," she says. "Each class gets a storage room at the school to keep supplies for the next year. I figured it would work."

I nod appreciatively. "Good thinking."

"Hey," Emory calls to me from the driver's seat. "I'm going to get Aubrey and we're heading up to Sparrowood. I doubt we'll be back before midnight."

Vandy steps down on the running board. I offer her my hand, but she just shoots it a glare and hops down on her own. She looks back at her brother. "We'll text when we're done to coordinate getting home at the same time."

"Be careful," Emory calls to her. His eyes dart to mine. "If anything goes south, both of you get the hell out of there. At *any* cost."

"Got it."

I follow her around to the other side of my Jeep under the guise of putting the bag in the back. I reach around her for the door handle, but she stops me and shoots me another glare. "What the hell are you doing?"

I stare at her. "Opening the door?"

"I can do it myself. I know my leg is a mess, but my arms work just fine."

I want to say that the Jeep isn't like her brother's truck. I don't have running boards. But hours earlier, I'd been making a big case about her ability to scale an eight-foot fence, so there's no way to justify helping her that isn't some form of the truth--which is that the thought of driving with her in my car is making me fucking crazy.

"Okay," I say instead, taking a step back. The Jeep is high off the ground, but she manages all the same. I hand her the bag and back away slowly. Even though I don't deserve to feel annoyed and sort of cast off, I do.

Emory drives away as I get into the driver's side and shut the door. Vandy and I are very much alone now, and our positions are not lost on me—me behind the wheel, her in the passenger seat. Her thighs are primly pressed together and her fingers curl around the edge of the seat.

*Here we go.*

I crank the engine, place both hands on the steering wheel, and stare out the windshield. "Are you sure you're okay with this?"

There's no need to push what 'this' is.

Her voice is clipped. "I'm fine."

"Because it's normal to be anxious," I assure her. "I mean, it took me a long time before I was comfortable behind the wheel. My therapist used to—"

Her head whips in my direction. "You have a therapist?"

"I did." I blow out a breath, just grateful for the lack of bite in her tone. My insides feel twisted enough. I wonder if she even realizes how big of a deal this is for me, too. "At Mountain Point. One-on-one, plus group therapy. It was a condition of my release and enrollment."

Her fingers relax a little. "Me, too. Well, not the group, but the individual." She looks askance at me, mouth lifting into a small grin. "Sucks, huh?"

"Yeah, it does." I grin tightly back. "But I have a feeling they'd both think it was pretty valid for the two of us to be freaking out right now."

Vandy looks at me for a long moment, eyes searching. "Well, you seem like you're handling it fine."

I hold her stare, and I don't think I've ever been more honest in my life. "Before you got here, I threw up in that trash can. Over there by the Redbox." She follows the direction of my nod, as if she could see it. "Trust me, I'm freaking out."

"Do you think those therapists would support us doing it?" Her face blanches. "I-I mean, this? The driving thing? With everything we..."

"God, probably not." I run my hand down my face. "At least not without a shit-ton of reflection and mindfulness exercises. Probably some deep dives into our psyches about why we're insisting on hanging around one another again, and hey, what's with the deep-rooted need to join this group, anyway? Are we flirting with self-destructive tendencies by putting ourselves in all these risky situations? And then we'd probably need to do some controlled breathing and talk about how our mothers were mean to us once in second grade, and now we don't know how to safely process our attachment issues or whatever."

Vandy lets out a laugh, and it's nothing like the laugh she had with Tyson. This one is bright and sharp. "You're right, that's exactly what Dr. Cordell would say. Minus the second-grade thing. Mine was probably the Valentine's dance."

I flinch when she reaches across the center of the car and gently pries my hand from the steering wheel. I watch in a silent stupor as she places it on the gear selector, closing my fingers around the lever.

"But I have a better idea, Reynolds." She looks at me, her hand warm and so heavy on mine that it feels like every point of my body is pinned beneath the weight of it. She breathes, "Just drive."

My exhale escapes in a measured gust. "Yes, ma'am."

I put the car in reverse and take one last glance over to make sure she's okay. Her eyes are forward but she seems less tense, at least. There's a lock of hair hanging over her cheek and the instinct to reach over and sweep it away, tuck it behind her delicate ear, is so powerful that it's nearly an ache not to.

Slowly, using every single lesson from Driver's Ed, I ease the Jeep from the parking space.

I can do this.

*We* can do this.

Without another thought about why we're drawn to one another, I pull onto the street and head to Thistle Cove.

# 15

THE FIRST TWENTY minutes of the drive are excruciatingly quiet, but without even having to ask, I know that he wants to focus. He'd seemed so cool at first, when I first got into the Jeep, but I can see it now—the tension in his hands where they grip the steering wheel at perfect ten and two positions, the way his eyes keep jumping to the side of the road, the tight, ticking muscle in his jaw as it clenches. His weird new stillness is in fine form. The top of his back doesn't even touch the seat, he's sitting so rigidly.

He's wearing darker, casual clothes—a black hooded sweater pulled over a shirt that, from the looks of the collar, is soft and worn. He dressed for comfort and utility, but it's maybe not working out for him.

His forehead sparkles with a fine sheen of sweat.

He waits until we roll to a stop at an intersection to roll his window down, and he probably tries to hide it, but I can tell he's sucking in these little breaths of the fresh air. I can tell that it's relaxing him.

But once the Jeep starts moving again...

*"It's better when you can feel the wind whipping around, you know?"*

"Reyn, I can't—" My voice is all choked, and now I'm the one sweating, eyes squeezing shut. "I *can't*—the window." He instantly rolls it up, no questions asked. Maybe he understands.

Softly, he says, "Sorry."

"It's okay." I fumble for the AC controls, and this time we both breathe relieved sighs when the cool air hits us. "That's better."

"Yes," he agrees.

I can't stop my mild laugh. "God, we're a mess."

I feel better when he grins, even though it's still strained. "Hey, talk to me."

I look over at him, confused. "About what?"

"Anything." He grips the wheel tighter. "Tell me about this Thistle Cove drama."

I realize that his silent focusing technique probably isn't panning out as effectively as he'd intended. So I settle into my seat and start to tell the story of how the idyllic little town turned into a Lifetime movie complete with sexy school girls, illicit sugar daddies, and murder.

Ten minutes later, Reyn seems appropriately distracted. He's no longer stick-straight in his seat, strangling the steering wheel. "Wait, you're telling me that the coach was having an affair with his student —also his best friend's daughter—and her father was like, the king of the SugarBabies online match-up site?" He raises an eyebrow.

"Yep," I reply. "Oh also? The girl's father? He was the mayor."

"Damn."

"Right?" I relax a little into my seat. "You know, I kind of wonder if that's what Afton's doing with her dad's friend?"

He lifts a shoulder in a loose shrug, both hands still on the wheel. He's been a very conscientious driver this whole time, even after he began relaxing. Eyes forward, hands steady, speed level. "It doesn't sound like it. Whatever Afton's got going on seems a little more passion-driven than an arrangement."

"True," I admit, although the thought of Afton with a guy that old still grosses me out. "You really never heard about that whole story?"

"We didn't get much news at military school."

"There was this whole episode about it on Crime Nation." I shift in my seat, feeling a little embarrassed to admit my guilty pleasure, but I can't contain my enthusiasm. "God, I love a good true crime story, and this one was so close by!"

His head tilts when he says, "Sounds like you just really like journalism. Like you've already found that thing you're passionate about. Like your mom."

"I guess." I chew on my lip, thinking. "Although, my mom's got a drive that I don't think I could ever have. For her, it's less about the story and more about the glory. I'd be perfectly happy if no one ever looked at me again."

His forehead creases as he turns off the highway. Daylight is fading, and we need to get to the school before it's fully dark to do a little recon. The small town of Thistle Cove is in the distance, the river on one side and thick trees on the other. My mind wanders back to the girls seeking affection and money from older men, back to Afton.

"You think she's pretty," I say suddenly.

His eyes jump to me and back to the road so fast that it seems involuntary. "Who?"

"Afton," I answer awkwardly. "I've seen you looking at her."

There's a long stretch of silence where I cringe internally. It isn't until we hit a stoplight that Reyn flicks his turn signal and finally answers. "I spent three years in military school. I think a lot of girls are pretty."

"Well, she is." I focus out the window at the sinking sun, feeling self-conscious and strange. "Pretty, I mean."

He looks away to turn, face neutral when he responds, "Yeah, but she's not really my type.

"No?" I hate how quickly it comes out. "From the looks of it, you can probably take your pick. Who is?"

"I don't know." His hands grip and release the steering wheel. "I guess I'm still trying to figure that out."

"I saw you go into the Devil's tower after that first game," I admit. "I thought you were going to meet a girl."

"Sneaking around again?" he says teasingly.

"No." I narrow my eyes. "If anyone was sneaking around, it was you."

"As you know, I was meeting your brother." He comes to a stop sign—we're getting close now—and while the car idles, he gives me his attention. "The Stairway to Hell isn't really on my radar right now."

"Whatever." I flap a hand dismissively. "I bet your name is already up there."

His expression is guilty enough for me to know that it's true, but he says, "I wasn't here long enough to really make a mark."

I idly wonder, "Do you think that, because the other girls and I are officially Devils—well, Playthings, I guess—we'll get to put our names up there? Assuming there's opportunity for any of us." Not that there'll be any for me. Who would I even go up there with? What would we even do? That train of thought brings back some of the tension I'd had from earlier.

"I'm not sure," he says slowly, eyes going inexplicably tight. "I don't know the rules about that—for girls. We're in new territory, I guess. Before, the Playthings were just..." He pauses here, and I know he's editing. "Just the girls who hung out with us. But now you're a member." His eyes dart over, eyebrow quirking. "Look at that, you're already shaking up the patriarchy. Maybe you *should* get your own spot on the beam."

"Yeah, right. Like anyone would want to." I scoff. "And anyway, I'm not doing this for me. I'm in this for the sake of the community, our peers. A secret society isn't really opening doors for anyone."

I've been diligently taking notes and collecting evidence for my article. I take screen captures of the meeting times, photos of the box and key in my locker, the envelope, all of it. I've even saved the slip of paper telling me and Reyn what to do tonight. I felt a twinge of guilt as I did it, though. The Devils are so important to my brother, but he's also graduating this year. Honestly, all three of us need to move forward and leave this kind of trouble behind.

We cross the bridge into Thistle Cove, and I point to the scrubbed remains of what had been a memorial. "That's where she jumped. Rose Waller? They thought she was dead, but she wasn't. She was just in hiding from her crazy dad."

"It should make me feel better that Preston isn't the only fucked up place in the world, but I'm not sure it does."

The GPS leads us to the school, but it wouldn't be hard to find, anyway. The campus takes up a central location in the middle of town, a historic three-story school building, and a big stadium ablaze with Viking pride is visible from the street. My nerves increase the instant we turn onto the property, then heighten even further when Reyn drives around back, locating the gym. The sky is little more than a blot of deep gray as he backs his Jeep into a spot by the edge of the lot and cuts the engine.

Silence fills the cab. We both unclip our seatbelts, and he rests his head back against the seat, eyes falling closed. It occurs to me that the drive here was probably the most stressful part of the night for him. Meanwhile, I'm still looking at a long stretch of tangled nerves.

He takes a breath and finally opens his eyes, looking more settled in this moment than I've maybe ever seen him. He says, "I want to wait until it's totally dark," and twists, stretching toward the footwell of the back seat. I watch curiously as he pulls a brown paper bag into his lap. His eyes look less crazed than they had while he was driving. Now, they're just heavy, tired-looking. "I brought snacks," he explains.

I take the bag and look inside. Chocolate, buttery croissants. I shake my head, "No thanks."

"What?" he frowns into the bag, and I almost feel a little bad. "You don't like them?"

I press a hand into my stomach. "Honestly, I'm too nervous to eat."

His eyes flick to the gym. "You're worried about breaking in? Because you know that's not a problem."

"I'm not questioning your thieving superpowers." I roll my eyes. "It's the 'not getting caught' part that worries me more."

He takes an aggressive bite from a croissant, jaw shifting as he chews it down. "Not getting caught is one of my superpowers, too."

I watch him scarf down an entire croissant in two bites. "Boys," I mutter.

"Hm?" He's got a crumb hanging on the corner of his mouth and my fingers twitch.

"You all eat like animals," I explain.

I immediately regret it when he stops mid-chew, furtively swiping at his mouth. Suddenly, he seems to adopt some manners, grabbing a napkin from the console. "Sorry, I've been hungry all day. There's nothing to eat at my house."

Now it's my turn to frown. "Your dad doesn't buy groceries?"

"We have grocery delivery," he confirms. "But it's all shit that needs to be prepared. For the record, that's *not* one of my superpowers."

I'm torn between ribbing him for being a cliché and asking what he eats every night when I see the patrol in the distance. "Oh! There's security!"

Reyn grabs his phone from the dash clip, noting the time. "We'll see how long it takes him to make another pass."

Thirty minutes is the answer. Reyn wants it to be darker, though, so we sit through two more passes. When he starts pulling things from his pocket and fiddling with his phone, I know that the security guard's next pass will be it.

"Make sure your phone's on vibrate," he says, watching as I do it. "And if you have an ID on you, put it in the glove box." He watches as I do this, too, putting his wallet in next to mine. Next, he hands me a pair of leather gloves.

Stupidly, I guess, "Because of fingerprints?" Like they're going to have CSI out here dusting for prints on account of a great helmet caper.

Reyn gives me a look that suggests he's thinking the same thing. Generously, he merely explains, "For the fence."

When the guard comes into view for the final time, I try to breathe in and out calmly. This is nothing. No big deal. What had Emory called it? Just a light B&E.

Softly, Reyn says, "Hey," and leans forward until our eyes meet. "Don't worry. Thirty minutes to get from here to inside the building? Piece of cake."

"Easy for you to say. I should have practiced climbing a fence or something." I run my palms across my thighs, looking across the lot at the fence. "Don't you need time to pick the lock? What if I'm really slow?"

"You won't be," he assures. "We've got this."

By then, the guard has disappeared, and there's really no way I'm wasting my precious climbing time whining about it. I'd wanted to do this. It's time to woman up.

I pull the handle to the door and Reyn follows suit.

While he goes around to the back of the Jeep, I skulk around the side and have a miniature meltdown, heart pounding. When Reyn returns, he's holding a big sheet of cardboard and the license plate from the car.

"In case we need to make a speedy getaway," he explains, throwing the license plate in the back seat.

The sheet of cardboard, I discover, is for the top of the fence. I watch as he slings it into the air, draping it over the pokey bits up top.

"You'll climb up first," he whispers, watching me put on the gloves. "When you get to the top, just straddle it and wait for me." I nod, but he still asks, "You good?"

Instead of answering, I grab onto the fence and test it, wedging the toe of my shoe into a knee-high diamond. My good leg lifts me up easily, and I can feel him at my back—'spotting' me, Emory would call it. My other foot slots into a space that's only a couple diamonds above the first one, and I think I can see the pattern I need to take—the unevenness of it.

When I pull my good foot from the diamond, nothing but my hands and bad foot holding me up, Reyn's whisper catches my attention.

"Hey, I'm not trying to cop a feel, okay?" Before I can ask what that means, one of his hands is on my ass, holding me up, steadying my quivering leg.

My face blooms into a fierce heat.

I get my foot into another knee-high slot and do it all over again, and this is fine. A little precarious, but *fine*. I'm doing it. And in about four hours, I'm going to totally die over the fact that Reyn is *touching my ass*—oh my god—but for right now, I just clamber up the links.

When I reach the top, I shakily swing my good leg over the edge and do as he instructed. I wait.

I watch as he watches me, an understanding passing between us.

*All systems go.*

He scales the fence so fast that I can only watch in disbelief. All this fanfare to get me over the edge and he does it in like three steps and a single drop. *Showoff.* Once he's on the other side, landing easily on his feet, he moves beneath me, gesturing me forward.

The trip down is a bit harder.

It's difficult to swing my weak leg over the edge, and I spend a moment trying to find the best way to brace myself. I can hear Reyn down below, shifting, like maybe he's anticipating having to catch me. I don't exactly have time to tell him that I'm fine, I just have to strategize. I clamp down on the top bar with one hand so that my other can grab a handful of my jeans and yank it up.

Once it's over, I carefully turn, putting my chest to the cardboard. I grab onto the bar with both hands and carefully lower myself, hanging. It's about three feet to the ground—an easy drop for anyone else, but not for me. Obviously sensing this, I feel Reyn's hands come up to my hips, clutching me in his sure grip.

"I've got you," he assures, but I still take a deep, steeling breath when I let go.

He lowers me to the ground without so much as a grunt.

When I turn to him, still feeling a little winded, he's smiling—dark eyes and dimples and all. He holds his phone up. "Five minutes. See? Piece of cake, Baby V."

I laugh breathlessly, too high on both the victory and the sight of Reyn's signature smile to form anything coherent.

We take the cardboard with us as we hurry through the tennis court toward the first door. We decided the best way into the gym was through the girls' locker room. When we arrive, a quick peek at his phone tells us he has about twenty-two minutes to pick the lock.

Reyn crouches down, pulling a black roll from the pouch of his hoodie. When he flips it open, there are all kinds of tools inside—picks, I suppose, though some look crude, fashioned from thick, stiff wire. Maybe even just regular paper clips. I chew on my lip as he takes one of the flatter-looking tools and eases it into the lock. Next, he takes one of the thinner, hooky-looking tools and puts that in.

It's too dark to make out more than the sharp silhouette of his face, but I can tell his eyes are laser-focused as he works. I don't know exactly what he's doing, but his fingers—skilled and sure—are doing it gently, fingertips easing the rod through the keyhole, back and forth.

I step away for a moment to look out over the court and toward the large air conditioners on the other side of the building. I don't see or hear anyone, and the time on the phone tells me we still have twenty minutes. I try not to jitter around, because I assume it'll be distracting, so I go back to watching him.

He's quiet, and the curve of his back as he crouches, combined with the easy movements of his fingers, begins to make something inside me go a little bit liquid and hot. It takes me too long to realize why. The memory of him on his bed, using that same hand to skillfully stroke himself, tramples right through my thoughts. I stare at those fingers for far too long, mentally pasting them into the memory, since he was too far away for such distinct details before.

"Time?" he murmurs, never taking his eyes off the task.

I fumble with my phone. "Ten minutes."

He spits a low curse, slowly removing one of the rods from the keyhole. He ducks his head to wipe his face on the shoulder of his hoodie, but then hangs it for a moment, holding the other tool inside the hole. "Left or right."

"What?"

He looks at me, jaw tight. "If I turn the tension wrench the wrong way, it'll reset the pins and I'll have to start over. I need you to choose, left or right."

I panic. "Why me?" We only have ten minutes left. There's no way he does all that again in ten minutes.

"I just need you to do it," he grits out, and he looks so inexplicably frustrated that I hastily throw something out.

"Left."

He turns it left.

His posture suddenly deflates, and I think for a second that I'd chosen wrong. But then he levels me with that dimpled smile again and turns the knob. "Lucky charm."

We get inside the locker room with nine minutes to spare.

The room is dark and smells exactly like a locker room. I can make out Reyn's outline as he shifts beside me, putting away his tools.

"One down, one to go."

He precedes me through the row of lockers at first, but then seems to hang back, waiting to walk at my side. When I get there, his hand comes up to the small of my back, leading me the rest of the way. I always hate when Emory or my parents do that, but when Reyn does it, it just makes me feel all viscous inside.

*Stupid.*

The second door—the one that will lead us into the gym—goes much like the first. Reyn crouches down and gets to work, while I keep track of the time. Chances are, we won't make the guard's next pass and will have to hang around a bit.

When he whispers, "Left or right," I don't even hesitate this time.

"Left."

The door opens easily.

"Damn, girl." It's too dark to see his smile, but I can hear it in his voice. "Two-for-two on this shit."

I don't say that it's just common sense that they'd have the same sort of lock, but it's true. There is absolutely no basis for the swell of pleasure I feel at his words and the way he says them—like I've done something impressive, special.

"Okay," I say, "the trophy case is through the lobby."

We stalk along the bleachers, and I don't even try to contain my smile. He can't see it, anyway. When we reach the lobby, there are lights shining right in the trophy case, and it's like something out of a movie. The Viking helmet shines under the light, our illicit treasure.

But the trophy case is locked.

"Damn." I jiggle it, but it's no use. "He said there were only two locks."

Reyn gives me a look, crouching down once again. "*Please*. A toddler could open one of these things." He once again removes the flat-edged thing—tension wrench, he'd called it, although it looks nothing like a wrench—from his roll of tools. But this time, he extracts one of the cruder picks. He holds both tools out to me. "You were watching earlier, right? Put the tension wrench here." He points to the bottom of the keyhole.

"Wait, me?" I punctuate this by jabbing a finger into my chest. "I don't know how to do this."

"Just think, this will be the last time you can say that." Reyn give the glass a tap. "Come on, we've got like thirty minutes to kill. You picking this thing will probably only kill five of them."

I give him a dubious look, but crouch down beside him, slowly taking the tools. "This thing? Here?"

Reyn nods when I insert the wrench, his eyes watching me so closely that my neck prickles. "You're going to put some light tension on the plug, like you're turning the lock, but you're not. Just kind of rest your fingers on it."

"Like this?"

"Exactly." He shifts a bit, so close that I can smell him, voice a rough murmur. "Now put the pick in, hook-side up. All the way to the back. Good, now..." He shifts impossibly closer, his shoulders almost curled around mine. "Drag it out, really slowly. Try to feel the pins. You feel them?"

I furrow my eyebrows, trying. "I don't think—oh. Yeah, that little bump?" I can even kind of hear the click when the pick runs over it. "I feel two. No. Three."

"Sounds about right. You're going to press each of those pins in," he explains, miming the action. "One at a time, click, click, click." I do what he says, but it's harder to catch the pins than he makes it sound—and look. "Just take your time, it'll take a few tries, but—"

*Click.* "Oh, I got one."

I can see his grin out of the corner of my eye. "Wicked. Do the next one."

The second one is just as hard, but I have a better feel for it now. It only takes a handful of stabs before the click comes. I lose the third pin for a moment and have to kind of shift around. I feel more than hear Reyn's silent puff of laughter.

"You're out too much, go in a bit."

*Ah.* There it is. I prod at it carefully, and I realize just how precise Reyn needs to be when doing this stuff. The smallest slip could mean starting over. No wonder he's learned to be so still.

When I get the third pin, Reyn shifts again, and I can hear him lick his lips. "Okay, take the pick out, but not the wrench. There you go. Now you need to choose which way to turn it."

I almost think of making him choose. It only seems fair. But I'm sort of weirdly attached to the idea of picking this lock all by myself now. I choose left, because it's been such a pal tonight, and I'm nothing if not loyal.

The lock springs open.

"*Sweet,*" he says. "You're a natural, Baby V."

I look at Reyn and he graces me with another one of those dimpled smiles. You'd think if he showed me enough of them, I'd begin building a tolerance, but that is clearly not the case. Especially when he's as close as he is now. Without my permission, my eyes glance down at his mouth, and it's an idle thought—that it'd only take a few inches to clear the space—but it's enough to make my cheeks heat. When my eyes flick back up to his, I find that his gaze is fixed on my lips, too.

It would be so easy, but...

We both quickly stand, shuffling away from one another.

Reynolds McAllister doesn't think about me like that. Even after our shared kiss. How many times has he called me 'Baby V,' tonight?

I'm just a kid, and bringing me along tonight was just another night of babysitting.

I gesture to the helmet. "You want to do the honors?"

Wordlessly, he nods, easing the trophy case open and extracting the Viking helmet. "Heavy," he notes, rubbing the pads of his fingers over the engravings. "Your turn."

I put the Devil horns on the shelf, adjusting them just-so, and carefully close the door.

We have to kill a few minutes in the locker room, waiting by the door. Both of us have our phones out, watching the time, but there's been this weird shift in energy all of a sudden, like neither of us wants to talk. It's a formless impulse, and I'm not sure if it's born of an apprehension to build on the moment or completely shatter it.

Either way, Reyn is solemnly quiet when we finally exit the door.

We get to the fence and he throws the cardboard up. I try to fight against the strange sinking feeling. I can't exactly put a name to it, but it feels kind of like a worse version of disappointment. Like maybe there could have been a *moment* back there. Like maybe we could have—

But we didn't.

Reyn stands behind me as I ascend the fence, but he doesn't put his hand on my ass this time. Instead, he holds my hips, pushing me up.

Definitely a worse version of disappointment.

"So what'd you do last night?" Sydney asks. She's lying on my bed, flat on her stomach, scrolling through ChattySnap. Every few seconds, she snaps a picture and sends it off to one of her followers.

"Not much."

It's killing me not to tell Sydney where I'd been the night before—and with *who*. Keeping all of this from my best friend feels more like a betrayal than any other part of this whole thing. Is it wrong that I feel less guilt about stealing the Viking horns from Thistle Cove than I do about keeping it a secret from her? Reyn's questionable moralities may be rubbing off on me. After all, I do sort of know how to pick a lock now. Easy locks, but still.

"I called you," she says, "around nine. I was bored and wanted tacos."

"You did?" I ask, instinctively picking up my phone off my desk. I pretend to scroll. I had a vague recollection of seeing her missed call when Reyn and I got back in the Jeep. The adrenaline rush combined with the swooping dissatisfaction kept me from caring too much, at the time, but obviously now I'd have to face it. "I must have been in the shower or something. I passed out early."

She looks up from her phone, eyes sweeping over me. "Are you using again?"

"What? No." The truth is that I'd actually gone all night without a nightmare. I think doing something other than moping around my room probably wore me out for once. "I was just tired."

Syd rolls over and pulls up the hem of her shirt, fingers grazing her flat stomach. "I really want to get a belly piercing but it's against the rules for cheer. It violates some appropriate dress code or something. Which seems totally sexist and oppressive, don't you think?" She turns her head to face me. "Maybe you should write an article about *that*. All the bullshit dress code stuff. I mean, guys wear pants and button downs and ties. Fully covered. We're out there like some kind of perverted fantasy of knee-socks and plaid skirts."

I lean back in my desk chair. Sydney thinks I'm working on my sports article, but I've really been uploading all the documents I've been collecting about the Devils onto my laptop. The paper files are in a folder tucked in my desk. "So in order to not be as objectified, you want me to write an article about how you should be allowed to wear a belly ring, but not forced to wear knee-socks?"

"Duh."

In theory, she's not wrong, but I know that, ultimately, Sydney just wants to be able to show off her belly ring in her cheer uniform. I open my mouth to tell her that I'll consider it when she gasps and jolts up suddenly. "Oh my god!"

"What?" My pulse quickens. "What happened?"

She holds out her phone but it's too far away for me to see it. "Holy shit! Someone broke into the Thistle Cove gym, stole their Viking helmet, replaced it with Devil horns, and *then* delivered the helmet to the quarterback's house."

"Really?" My heart is about to launch out of my ribcage. With a shaky hand, I quickly 'X' out the file and go over to her. "Where did you see that?"

"I follow a few kids that go there—I met them at a party last summer—and one of them posted it. That is an epic prank." Her thumbs fly over the keypad and she smiles gleefully. "Who do you think did it?"

I feign innocence. "I have no idea. Probably just some jocks or something. Trying to stir up the rivalry, maybe?"

"You know what?" she asks, dropping her phone into her lap. "This reeks of the Devils."

The wind gets knocked out of me. "There are no Devils anymore."

"Sure, I know." She flaps a hand. "But don't you think this has the Devils' hoofprints all over it?"

Pranks were a big part of the Devils' wheelhouse, so it's not a bad theory, but here I am, part of this group—this *secret* group—and my instinct is to protect it.

"Emory has been pissed about the Devils getting disbanded for months. Trust me, I'm pretty sure I would know if it had started up again. Plus, there's just not many of them left, anyway. They had too many seniors."

"True," she says, twisting her hair around her finger. "I'm not gonna lie, I'd had my eye on being a certain Devil's Plaything this year. But it looks like someone got there first." She shoves the phone in my face and this time I see Emory and Aubrey in a selfie together. I can't tell where they are from the photo, but I already know regardless. Emory told me this morning that they'd successfully removed the Sparrowood shield from the stadium and mounted it over the front door of the Academy.

Not wanting to get into another conversation with Sydney about Emory's lack of interest in her, I offer to get us some drinks from the kitchen. My brother has his head in the refrigerator when I get down there.

"Did you see the picture on ChattySnap from Thistle Cove?" I ask, getting two glasses out of the cabinet.

"Yep." He straightens, holding an armful of food. "Gotta hand it to you, V. You guys killed it."

It's almost embarrassing how much pride I feel in getting his approval. "Any word from the others?"

"As far as I know, everyone pulled it off." He shrugs. "I think Georgia and Tyson may have had a hang up at Northridge, but since Tyson used to go there, they smoothed it out."

"Good." I fill the cups with sparkling water. "Sydney's in my room. She already speculated that this had the Devils' 'hoofprints' all over it."

He laughs. "I dare her to prove it."

"I'm just saying." I return the water bottle to the refrigerator and grab the glasses. "People are going to ask questions."

"Let them, V." He rolls his eyes, propping his arms on the counter. "You know I don't care, and you shouldn't either. If no one squeals—and they won't, because then we'll be forced to reveal the secrets they recorded—then we're fine."

I have no doubt that the threat is real. There's someone else pulling these strings—someone I'd love to find out the name of—who is obviously mega-invested in the Devils' reinstatement at Preston Prep. Whoever that person is, I wouldn't put it past them to ruin a life or two along the way.

Back upstairs, I walk into my room. I look for Sydney on the bed, but she's over by my computer instead. My first thought is a frantic attempt to remember whether or not I'd left up the exposé file.

"Hey," I say, trying to keep my voice even. "Here's your drink."

"Thanks," she says, stepping away from the desk. "I was just trying to check my email real quick. My stupid phone has stopped loading emails. I think it's because I have like sixty-thousand that need to be deleted."

"Sure," I say, assessing her expression to see if she saw something.

There's nothing there, and she just takes a sip from her drink, but I'm not altogether settled. "Anything else show up about the prank?"

"A bunch of comments. Everyone's dying over it and trying to speculate who's behind it. Apparently, whoever got the Viking helmet had to break into the school, because there wasn't a single thing out of place. No sign of forced entry. Not an easy feat." With her eyes glued to her phone, she sits back on my bed and crosses her legs. "Oh damn, see? Now they're dragging me into it! I swear they can never leave me alone." She shakes her head, sighing long-sufferingly. "See Vandy, this is why it's good that you don't go out. Now I'm going to have to prove where I was last night."

I slide back over to my desk, discreetly clicking the screen over from Sydney's email account to the Devils file. When I open it, I'm happy to see that the file itself is closed. I slouch back in my seat, marveling over the fact that while Sydney is trying to insert herself into the current drama at Preston, for once I actually am part of something big at the school.

It feels better to be included, even secretly, than I'd ever imagined.

# 16

BEFORE THIS WEEKEND, the hottest thing I'd ever seen was Kaylee Killian laying on a pool chair at The Club, spreading her thighs open for me. Underneath her yellow sundress, Kaylee hadn't been wearing her bikini bottom. To be fair, I was fourteen that summer, and Kaylee Killian was the sixteen-year-old goddess of the Junior class, so it was like the height of eroticism. That moment has taken up some prime real estate in my fantasies for almost four years now. Like any other memory, however, the allure of it started to fade after so long, like a photograph that's been handled a few too many times. It's only natural that my libido is looking to step shit up.

Why it's decided to laser-focus on Vandy Hall is beyond me.

Only that's not so true, is it?

I look across our driveway as I dump my school bag into my backseat. She's standing over there, waiting for Emory at his truck. The thing about Vandy is that she's just so fucking *cute*. Always was, honestly. Really sweet-looking. *Pretty*. V looks like the type of girl you take out on a date only after impressing her parents. She is no Kaylee Killian.  She looks like the kind of girl who doesn't put out until she finds 'the one'.

She doesn't look like the kind of girl who can pick a furniture lock in four minutes flat, either.

That's the real stain on my sheets.

At the time, I was just thinking that thirty minutes in that gym was probably going to be boring. I was *not* thinking of her crouched down in the dark, diligently following my instruction, and deftly breaking a lock. I wasn't thinking of the way she looked, with her lip between her teeth, nibbling. I definitely wasn't thinking that the way she looked at my mouth, eyes all hooded, cheeks blooming red, would make my dick rock hard.

Suddenly, that moment in the gym, corrupting cute Baby V and knowing for a fact that she was down for it—ready to get messy and anything *but* sweet—had overtaken Kaylee's spread legs by a landslide. Isn't even close.

Vandy meets my eyes then, over the distance. Her smile is a slow, knowing thing, and it's doing nothing to help the issue currently coming up in my pants. The thing is, I could have taken it. She wanted me to kiss her. No experiment this time, just two people in the same place, high off adrenaline, falling into place like a clicked pin. I can see it so clearly, the way I would have taken it—*mine now*—grabbed her by the back of her head and thrust my tongue into her willing mouth. It would have been scorching fucking hot, so much better than the first one.

I give her a nod and wrench my door open, because that's the real problem here. It was just the heat of the moment, and it'd be too easy to push something on her that she'd regret. I've never been on a date in my life, I'll certainly never impress her parents, and I'm not 'the one'.

To V, I'm nothing more than the bright allure of danger.

Rebellion might be hot, but I know better than anyone how badly it can burn.

THE PHOTO from Thistle Cove was just the first. Next came Sparrowood, then Northridge, and then every other school we hit. The timing was tightly coordinated, no one was caught, and after a few days, the delighted chatter dies down into a sort of collective awe. We'd pulled off something epic.

If I were some normal fucker who was doing this for normal reasons, then I would have felt an acute sense of pride as I walked down the halls, knowing that some of that collective awe was meant for me. Instead, I feel it for Vandy. None of these idiots even realize. Their wincing eyes watch as she limps across campus. Their gossip, little more than a long string of pedestrian clichés, follows in her wake. They all part when she passes. They see some poor, pretty, innocent girl who they'd never suspect.

If I feel any pride at all, it's that I'm possibly the only one in this school who knows the true Vandy Hall.

I stop at my locker between second and third period, shoving my math book inside and searching for my bio lab notes. A shadow crosses over me and leans against the next locker.

"Did you hear about the assembly?" Sebastian says, looking forward.

"What assembly?"

"After lunch. I was in the nurse's office earlier. Apparently, the admin is pissed about the pranks." Sebastian smiles wolfishly. "Collins is prepping a stern lecture."

A coil of tension winds in my stomach. "Do they know anything?"

He sniffs. "Nah, it feels pretty CYA. After the Devils went down for making fun of that middle-schooler last year, they want to present a united front. Too bad they've got jack shit for suspects."

I find the notes, but when I shut the door, Sebastian is already gone, sucked into a crowd of passing students. At lunch, the rumor is confirmed when Dean Dewey's voice crackles over the intercom. "All students report to the auditorium immediately following lunch for an assembly about recent events that involve the Preston Pep community."

I look across the table at Emory, who's sitting next to Aubrey, their feet intertwined under the table. Down at the other end, picking at salads with a few other cheerleaders, Afton and Georgia exchange a look before shifting their gaze down the table at us.

"They know nothing," Emory says in a low voice, ignoring everyone. Aubrey nods in agreement and they gather their things. "Just be calm."

I know he's right. If any of us had been busted, they'd have dragged all our asses straight out of class. Preston isn't the type to make a big show. The term 'handled quietly' is probably in the disciplinary guidebook. Unfortunately, it only takes a quick look across the dining hall to see that one of us doesn't get that.

Vandy was obviously sitting with that Sydney chick at one point, but abruptly stands, her chair making an obnoxious screech across the linoleum floor as she lurches to her feet. Her movements are jerky, nervous, eyes flickering anxiously around the room. Luckily, her friend is turned, cluelessly flirting with a guy at the table behind her, else she'd be seeing the worry plain as day on Vandy's ashen face. I glance back for Emory, hoping he's witnessing this, but he's already filtered out the back door with Aubrey.

My response is instinctive, although tightly controlled. I stand and gather my trash, quickly dumping it in the bin. I keep an eye on Vandy every step of the way, careful to keep my distance. At school, she's still completely off limits, but we have a secret together—*several* secrets—and neither of us can afford some Vandyesque wave of morality. Part of doing shady shit is being able to withstand the pressure of scrutiny. I'm not convinced Baby V is ready for that.

Allowing a few people between us, I follow her out the door. She starts down the main hall toward the administrative offices. That particular hallway is barren, quiet, free of the dining hall bustle. I furtively scan the doorways, quickly locating one labeled 'Tech Storage', and close the gap. I thread my fingers through hers and she looks up with a gasp, eyes wide when she realizes who has her hand. Pushing open the door, I pull her inside and shut it quickly.

My heart pounds erratically, because *fuck*. This could get me in so much trouble. George's words float through my head, unbidden, and I wonder if it counts as kidnapping to pull a girl into a room without asking.

Vandy looks up at me with questioning eyes, voice a half-whisper. "What are you doing?" Now that she's only a few inches away, I realize that she doesn't seem as upset as I thought. Her cheeks have color and her eyes, though suspicious, lack all of that frantic energy I'd seen before. She also smells really good, but in that nebulous way pretty girls often do. Something chemically floral and delicate, clean.

"I, uh..." I scratch my neck, feeling stupid now. "You left abruptly after Dewey's announcement. Just making sure you're okay."

Her blue eyes watch me, searching. "Why wouldn't I be?"

"I don't know, because..." Fuck, her eyes totally just looked at my mouth. "Because you looked nervous, and I know nervous people sometimes have the tendency to..." I can't find a delicate way to accuse her.

I don't need to. "You're afraid I'll squeal," she realizes, eyes wide with disbelief. "You're *handling* me."

"What?" I try to play it off. "No, it's not—I know you won't narc on us. I mean, you also broke in and picked a lock, so that'd sort of be suicide, but I just know how—"

Her expression shifts into something so shuttered and cold that I almost take a step back. She breathes out a low, "Fuck you," and it somehow sounds *worse* than her rigid posture and icy expression.

It sounds like she just got slapped in the face.

Whatever just happened, I try futilely to fix it. "Hey, come on. I just know you're not usually in this kind of situation because you're..."

"A good girl? Sweet? Innocent?" Her eyes are like ice. "I stole, hid, and kept a drug habit secret for years, *Reynolds*. I know you think I'm some baby who needs to be handled, but I'm not. I can handle myself."

I recoil at the way she said my name there. Not Reyn, but *Reynolds*, all dripping disdain. I watch her, confused. "Why are you so mad?"

Her gaze is so full of razor blades that it takes me too long to realize how wet her eyes are becoming. "Next time you want to trick some idiot girl into committing a crime with you, do me a favor and just take Afton. She doesn't know you yet, so *her* legs still work fine." Before I can respond, she's out the door.

Not that it'd matter.

Any words I might have had are trapped by something dark and heavy, wedged into the pit where my lungs used to be. I move fluidly to a seat and carefully lower myself, shifting my gaze to the window.

I sit there for an hour.

It's quiet and peaceful, and it's almost a relief now to know. It was too easy, everyone forgiving me, acting like I was just coming home from summer camp or something. It's worse now than it might have been that first day, seeing the sharp, bitter resentment in Vandy's eyes. But it also feels so necessary, the inevitability of her hatred.

Still hurts like a bitch.

I SPEND the rest of the day going through the motions, trying to make myself stone. Essay for English. Worksheet for Bio. Problems for Trig. It's one seat after another, just waiting, even though I don't know what for. Everything feels too loud, too bright, and I'm caught in a chasm between wanting the day to end and not wanting to go home, either.

Speculation continues during football practice, mostly because it was obvious our biggest rivals had been targeted.

"Hey." Emory corners me on the line of scrimmage. "What's up with you?"

"Nothing."

"Bullshit," he says, giving me a look. "Are you worried about what he said at the assembly?"

"I skipped it."

His forehead creases. "Well, it was nothing. Like I said, they don't have anything. It was just a bunch of posturing about school reputation and the obligation of the student body to uphold it."

My quiet scoff feels like the first expression I've made since Vandy left the tech room. I'm not sure the administration really understands the true reputation of Preston Prep, which is that a bunch of spoiled rich kids are going to do whatever the hell they want.

Em calls the play, an easy one we've performed dozens of times this week alone, but I'm slow. My arms don't cooperate. My legs drag and as Emory's perfect spiral sails into the stands, my error gives the defense an opening and they jump on me like a loose ball. The feeling of being crushed beneath seven football players is almost negligible, seeing as how I haven't been able to reliably breathe for at least four hours now, anyway. The sharp, crushing pressure on my shoulder as they all clamor to their feet is another story.

I lay there for a moment, wincing, wallowing in some seriously pathetic self-pity, until Emory's hand comes into view. I take it, but lift myself carefully, unable to hide the pain.

He calls the medic over, but I wave him off. "It's fine."

Nevertheless, I walk stiffly off the field, feeling completely done with the entire fucking day. I'm walking past the bleachers when I see *her*, sitting four rows up. I only look at her for a split-second, but I can tell she's halfway out of her seat, like she's about to come down.

I hurry past.

I GET HOME JUST before dark, relieved my dad's car isn't in the garage. Sometimes, him being home is almost worse than him not being here. Every now and then, I half-expect him to charge me rent, because we're more like roommates than father and son. When he's present, we orbit one another suspiciously, simultaneously hoping for and dreading the silence being broken.

I have a good view of the Hall house. It's clear that Mr. and Mrs. Hall's vehicles are gone, but Emory's truck is in the driveway. I'm only standing by my car, but I can still smell the mouthwatering scent of a home-cooked meal wafting over from their house. My stomach growls and I can't help a surge of envy, knowing that even when their parents aren't home, Mrs. Hall makes sure they're fed.

Must be real nice.

Inside, I grab a container of leftover Thai out of the refrigerator, along with an ice pack for my back. I don't bother flipping on any lights. I just flop down on the couch in the dark of the living room and feel for the remote control. I've just marginally managed to lose myself in a basketball documentary when the doorbell rings.

I heave a loud sigh.

I guess that cold Thai won't get any colder.

Adjusting the ice pack, I lumber to the door, thinking that Fucking Jerry better not be interrupting my dinner with some contrived bullshit. It'd be the second time this week. I school my face and swing open the door.

I freeze at the sight of Vandy on the doorstep, a foil-covered plate in her hands.

She chews on her lip as our gazes lock. "I brought you some dinner."

"Thought we weren't supposed to be seen together." To compound the point, I look over her head toward the driveway and street, making sure that no one is watching.

She frowns and looks back herself. "Can I come in?"

I should say no, because she was right before. About all of it. The one who's going to get in trouble here is me. I step back though, holding the door open, and try to stand still as stone as she walks past me into the kitchen.

"Where are your parents?" I ask. "Emory?"

"Dad's at the hospital. Mom's covering a town council meeting. Emory is up in his room, eating his dinner and video chatting some-one. Campbell, Aubrey, take your pick." She stands in front of me, looking small in a pair of cotton shorts and an oversized Vanderbilt T-shirt. The Halls named their kids after their college alma maters, Emory and Vanderbilt University. It's fucking ridiculous, but it's been ridiculous for so long that I couldn't imagine the two of them being named anything else.

She cradles the plate against her chest, eyes dropping. "I wanted to say that I'm sorry for all that stuff I said before. I was…harsh, and unfair." She sighs, tucking a piece of hair behind her ear. Her eyes look red-rimmed. "Honestly? I *was* a little nervous." Her eyes fly up to mine, and I can see the conviction in them. "Not nervous enough to snitch about it, though. I just needed to get away from Sydney, who *cannot* stop talking about it. I'll lie to her—I can—but I don't enjoy it." She swallows, eyes going tight when she adds, "And then you said all that stuff, and it seemed like maybe that whole lockpicking lesson was just to make sure I was as culpable as you, and it brought back some bad mem—"

"Wait."

Her mouth clicks shut, but I don't need her to elaborate. I can see it in her eyes, in the slant of her lips, the curl of her shoulders. Whatever that moment had meant to me, it'd obviously meant something to her, too. Maybe enough that the thought of some ulterior motive behind it had stung.

"I wasn't doing that to make you culpable." I gesture toward the driveway and my ice pack falls to the floor in a sad, sweating heap. "In the car, on the drive up, you just seemed really into all that crime journalism stuff. I thought—" Well, I was thinking that I actually had something to offer her, to teach her. Something valuable. Something we could share. All of that feels stupid as hell now. "I thought it could be useful or whatever, and I wanted you to see that you could do it."

Some of that rigidness in her posture deflates. "Oh."

"It wasn't like when I stole the car," I add, because there's obviously something wrong with me. But I see the relief and guilt in her eyes, and it all feels *wrong*. "That night, I knew you'd come with me if I asked. You were always a soft touch. It was the best way to keep you quiet. That's really all it was."

She says, "I know," but despite this, the hurt is evident in her eyes.

It's disappointing. I'd been hoping for fire or frost, not this flat, cynical understanding. The apology she's due sticks in the back of my throat, sour like bile. I don't want to give it. I don't want her to stand there and feel like she needs to say it's okay. That first day back, seeing her in Emory's truck, a silent understanding had passed between us. I've been clutching onto it ever since, this *thing* that only the two of us know. It's acrid and full of grief, but it's ours.

*It'll never be okay.*

"I think I even knew it at the time. I was just..." Her laugh is a small, broken thing. "I was just hoping you'd like me being there anyway, because I was so crazy about you."

Now it's my turn to say, "I know." Thirteen-year-old girls aren't generally subtle with their affections, although she obviously tried. Even now, I can see her cheeks flush, a spark of cringing embarrassment in the cast of her eyes. I shake my head, because I'm the only one here who should feel ashamed.

It burns to admit that I'd taken advantage of it. It burns worse to know that it hadn't been entirely unrequited, even if I was too loyal to Emory to really let it grow into something worth pursuing.

"I did, you know." I look her in the eye when I say it, because this is all I can give her. "I did like you being there."

She smiles sadly. "That's nice to know."

I'd be lying if I said I hadn't spent the last few weeks fighting the urge to wonder 'what if'. What if that night had never happened? Would we have eventually ended up together? Where would we be right now, and what kind of people would we have become, in that impossible alternate reality? Better people, for sure. Unbroken people.

I reach down to retrieve my ice pack, pushing a hiss through my clenched teeth at the pain in my shoulder.

She steps forward, like maybe she's about to grab it for me, but steps back just as quick. "I saw you at practice, while I was waiting for Em." Matter-of-factly, she notes, "You got hurt."

"Just a bruise." I press the ice pack to my shoulder, but I can't quite reach it. "Courtesy of Shackleford's cleat."

She follows me into the living room, where I'm finally able to wedge the ice pack between my shoulder and the back of the couch. She shifts around uncomfortably for a moment, still holding the plate. Whatever is under that foil smells like meat, cheese, and pure ecstasy. Any other night, I might actually have an appetite for it.

"I brought you some leftovers, because..." She sets the plate on the coffee table, gently lowering herself to perch on the couch beside me. "Well, just because."

I know the truth. Because I never have food. Because it's an apology. Because Vandy is better than me, able to stand here and give me two apologies for something I deserved when I can't even bring myself to apologize for almost fucking killing her.

I'm the living embodiment of scum.

My small, "Thank you," comes out rough and inadequate.

"Can I see?" She goes for my sleeve, her hot fingers grazing my skin.

I jerk away, abruptly. "See what?"

Her hand freezes midway between us. "Your bruise. It looked like it hurt pretty badly."

The thought of her seeing my back makes me feel physically ill. It's a permanent reminder of what happened that night, less visible than her limp, but still my cross to bear. It's horrific, gruesome, and in no way should usurp her own pain and injury. I don't want her pity any more than she wants mine. "I can't," I say.

Her forehead creases, hand dropping to her lap. "Why?"

My hair is already a mess because I hadn't washed it after practice. I run my fingers through it now, agitated, thinking that it makes me sick, but that if anyone is entitled to see it, it's the girl sitting next to me. It's not an apology, but maybe it's... *something*, this evidence that I didn't come away from that night without its gnarled mark upon me. I grab the hem of my shirt and elbow it up my chest, pulling it roughly over my head. Her eyes follow the motion, darting down to my chest, my defined stomach. I hold her gaze for a long moment, seeing her confusion at the resignation I'm wearing.

I twist around, presenting it to her like some disgusting gift.

Her sharp intake of breath is so soft, that if I hadn't been waiting for it, I might not have heard it at all. She's still on the couch, and I can feel the heat of her eyes taking it in. I know what she sees. A wide swath of deformed skin, gnarled like melted vinery. There's a three-inch square on my right shoulder that's smoother than the rest, but no less grotesque. Near my collar, there's an indentation where the tag of my shirt had melted into my skin. It's hideous.

I feel her move, and even though I know what's coming, I still flinch when her fingertips graze the scar. "I didn't know," she breathes, voice strained. "No one told me it was this bad."

"It wasn't." It's all at once the truth and a lie. The scars are bad. The injury was nothing. Not in comparison.

"Is this...?" She touches my right shoulder, and I nod.

"Skin graft."

"Where did they—"

"My thigh."

She asks, "Does it hurt?" fingertips, trailing to the left shoulder.

My tongue feels stuck to the roof of my mouth. It's been years since anyone's touched me there, that I've allowed anyone to touch me skin to bare skin. "I don't have much feeling in most of it."

I don't tell her about the other stuff, like having to wear compression bandages for months. Or how sometimes the nerves will randomly flare to life, and how it feels like an electric shock. Or how I had to do stretches during the healing process to get any kind of elasticity back, and how that PT was cut short on account of life at Mountain Point, and how the scars could probably be better if it hadn't been.

Her hand falls away and I feel her shifting. I gather the courage to look over my shoulder, prepared for whatever I see in her expression —disgust, pity, revulsion.

I am not prepared for the sight of her topless.

She's shucked her shirt off. My eyes instinctively fall to her chest, to the dark outline of her nipples beneath the delicate fabric of her bra, before I whip my head back around.

"Christ, V."

"Look." When I don't, she stands, turning to me. "*Please.*"

When I turn, her pale stomach is right there. Because of this, the long scar slashed across the skin is the first thing I see. It's not like mine. This one is thick, raised, and precise. Surgical. There are little dots above and below it, staples having at one point held the skin together. Someone could walk into my house and cut me open in the same place, and I'd probably feel less gutted than I am right now, looking at this.

"My pelvis was shattered," she explains, turning so that I can see how it goes all the way around to her back, stopping at the base of her spine, where there are other obvious surgery scars. "I have some metal in there now." She turns back to me, but I can't tear my eyes away from the raised flesh, two shades lighter than the skin the rest of the world sees.

She doesn't flinch when I curl my fingers around her waist. I rub the pad of my thumb against the scar, as if I could smooth it away, wipe the damage clean. This used to be flawless, this skin. She used to be sound. Pure.

"I'm sorry." My voice is gravel when it gives her this, rough with my quiet secret. I don't mean to say it—I never wanted to—but I find that I don't regret it. It's not sour, like I thought it'd be. It's as easy as the space between one breath and the next, and suddenly, the thought of *not* saying it feels like absolute agony. I barely have to tip forward to bury my head into the warm, marred skin of her stomach. My hands clutch her waist, holding her close, as if I could press the truth of this into it. As if it could hide the way the corners of my eyes sting. "I'm so fucking sorry, Vandy."

I feel her hitched breath in the jump of her stomach below my face. "Reyn..."

"It's my fault." I can't bear to hear her say it's okay. "I'm sorry." Like a floodgate opening, now I can't seem to stop saying it, over and over, "I'm so fucking sorry." I think I'm shaking, and I'm holding her too tight, but she doesn't push me away.

Her fingers thread through my hair, holding me to her, and she doesn't say it's okay.

Softly, she says, "I forgive you."

"Don't." That single word holds multitudes. I want to tell her to take this and just leave it. Let the silence hang. It's what I deserve, we both know it.

"Reyn," she insists, voice thick with tears. "What happened to us was an accident. A horrible accident. We both suffered because of it, but you didn't mean for that to happen. I know you didn't."

I have to let go of her then, because I definitely can't take her consoling me. *Fuck.* As if I don't feel sick enough. I jam the heels of my palms into my eyes, just as much to hide the redness of them as to not see her crying. I'd used up my tears for that night years ago, in the scant privacy of my hospital room, dark bunks, and shower stalls. It's not fair that she still has some left.

Her voice sounds close enough that I can feel the heat of her breath on my knuckles. "I shouldn't have said that, about Afton and everything. I didn't mean it, I just wanted to hurt you. But the thing is...I knew it would." When my hands drop, I realize she's kneeling down in front of me, mere inches away from my face. "I knew it would hurt you, because I already knew you were sorry."

Vandy tips forward and our mouths slot together too easily. This isn't the tentative kiss of experimentation beneath the tree house, nor is it the searing, rebellious tongue-fuck that the kiss at Thistle Cove might have been. The way our lips eagerly part, tongues sweeping wetly together, is a sigh of reprieve. The way her hands fist my jeans, pressing closer, is a frantic kind of mercy. When I reach up to grasp her face in my hands, it's a grief so acute that it'd choke me if she weren't giving me her own breath.

This kiss is solace.

It's also frantic and too hard, teeth and noses clashing. The room is full of the sounds of our harsh breaths, and my blood feels electrified with the way she surges into me, seeking. She tastes like summer and sadness and life.

It hurts like hell to break away.

I grab her shoulders and push, though. She's flushed all the way down to her chest, which is heaving just as much as my own. I hold her there for a moment, heedless of her stricken eyes, trying to shake the unexpected fog of *sex-sex-sex* from my brain.

My throat feels full of everything I want to say, but all that emerges is a hoarse, "That was a mistake."

She's not crying anymore, but the wet tracks are still on her cheeks. I give in to the impulse to lift a hand and brush my thumb over the wetness there.

Her eyes flutter closed. "Why?"

I sigh, letting my hand fall away. "You know why."

Just then, my stomach decides that it's done with all this. A loud rumble breaks the stillness and Vandy's eyes fly open. We stare at each other for a moment, and maybe it's the shattered moment, the overload of emotion, but a peal of abrupt laughter bursts from her throat. She immediately looks horrified, clamping a hand to her mouth and falling back on her heels.

"Sorry."

I fall back too, grateful for the space between us. "Don't be." I idly wonder if my smile looks as tired as I feel. "I think my stomach is smelling your mom's food."

"Oh, she didn't make it. I did." She looks around for her shirt, quickly pulling it over her head. Her cheeks are red and she's not meeting my gaze, and I don't know how to tell her that it's okay. She looks like she's about to bolt.

"Hey, no." I grab her wrist before that spark of flight realizes itself. "You can stay." She finally looks at me then, mouth pinched into something awkward and uncertain. Gently, I add, "Please?"

I'm pretty sure she's going to say no. She should. But when she agrees, the rush of adrenaline feels like sheer relief. Nevertheless, she still looks deflated as she settles next to me again. "It's probably cold now," she says of the plate.

I lean over to reach for the plate, and any other time I might feel horrified that she's probably getting an eyeful of my back again. But I'm so sapped of everything. It feels like I've been hollowed out and then packed back together messily, like shit's just rattling around inside, looking for a place to settle.

I peel back the foil and look down at the meal, the careful way it's been prepared. There's thick layers of pasta, and salad with little pieces of nuts and some dried fruit. I'm not even sure when the last time I had a home-cooked meal was, but knowing that Vandy prepared it for me makes my stomach twist in an unfamiliar way.

"You cooked this?"

"Yeah." She's sitting with her limbs all tucked in close, like she's afraid of leaving a mark on anything. "When everyone's out of the house in the afternoons, I like to cook."

I extract the fork from my discarded box of Thai and try a bite of the lasagna. I instantly know this is going to be embarrassing, because once I taste it, it's like one of those rattling pieces inside of me finds its place.

My appetite returns with a vengeance.

"Don't judge me," I mutter to Vandy, shooting her a glance. "What you're about to witness won't be pretty."

Briefly, she looks confused.

And then, I eat.

"Oh my god, you're going to choke." But it works. She watches me and laughs, and even if her eyes are still sad, it's such a relief that I almost *do* choke. "I can see that we're going to have to adopt your cause. These are some serious Oliver Twist vibes you're putting out."

"I'll eat you out of house and home," I warn.

She rolls her eyes. "I live with Emory, okay. We're familiar with the bottomless pit known as teenage boys."

I spear my fork into the salad, making sure to get some of the goat cheese. "Maybe you can teach me how to cook something. Probably not this, though. It looks a little beyond my microwaving skills."

"It's not that hard," she insists, finally losing some of that dejected tension. "What were you watching?"

I look at the TV, still paused from earlier. "Just a sports documentary. I won't force you to watch."

"Hey," she says lightly. "I'm the Chronicle sports reporter now. Maybe it's something I need to watch."

"It's a doc on Dennis Rodman, actually." I gesture to the TV with my fork. "It probably won't help your sports writing career, but he's definitely one of the more interesting subjects."

She nods. "Well then, let's watch it."

I press play.

We watch while I eat, and Vandy is silent next to me. Sometimes I'll peek over at her and she looks tired, too. Sapped, like me. Sometimes she'll see me glancing over and catch my gaze, giving me a small smile.

For the first time since I got back, the house feels like something other than an empty place I stay on my own. There's life here—a life I almost extinguished on that dark night so long ago. As we sit side by side, I realize that Vandy may be broken, but she's here, and I'm more thankful than ever for that simple fact.

# 17

I DREAM, but it isn't one of the crash. Instead, I'm standing on the floating dock, looking out over the surface of the lake. It's night and fireflies twinkle all around me, floating over the glassy water and weaving toward the trees in the distance. It's a warm, indistinct feeling of comfort and stillness. I'm safe here, but I'm also waiting. I'm not sure what for, but the frisson of excited anticipation settles like a cloud around me. It's not an impatient feeling. I just know that soon, I'll have something really amazing.

I wake with my cheek pressed to a warm, bare shoulder. It takes me a moment to shake out of the dream because I want to go back, to the fireflies and the stillness and the thing I was looking so forward to. My eyes feel gritty and sensitive, like I've been crying, although I don't know what I'd have to cry about. It's so warm and comfortable here. I flex my hand and open my eyes just in time to see it sweep against a smooth, defined abdomen.

Reyn's lower belly caves inward and he shifts, free arm sliding around my back, pulling me toward him. I realize that he's reclined against the side of the couch, his elbow propped like a pillow, and I'm curled up against his side.

It comes back to me in a rush. Bringing him food. Seeing his scars. Feeling his forehead pressed into my belly as he shook, hands clutching my hips. The kiss. Oh god, *the fucking kiss*. Him telling me that it was a mistake. The stinging plunge of rejection. The relief when he asked me to stay. The bright satisfaction of watching him eat my meal.

Falling asleep on his shoulder.

I blink hazily at the faint line of hair that begins at his belly button and disappears beneath the waist of his pants. It's two shades lighter than the hair on his head, and never in my life have I wanted to touch something so badly just to see if it feels as soft as it looks.

I'm staring at that line of hair when he shifts, his fingers curling against my back. A jolt of pure electricity runs down my spine. I'm working out how to extract myself from this position when I feel him gently press his nose into my hair. It's a slow, testing sort of gesture. I know he's awake. I can feel it in his inhale and the twitch of his fingers against my back. Even so, he doesn't pull away.

Not until the pounding comes at the door.

Reyn jumps, jostling me as he shoots upright. "It's almost midnight." The clock on the wall above the TV confirms this.

The booming door-pound comes again and I lurch to my own feet, knowing instinctively who's at the door. Reyn must too, because his eyes are sharp and full of dread as they dart around the room.

"Fuck, *fuck*, where's my shirt?" He's pulling at the cushions, face wild.

"It's okay," I say, trying to calm him, even though my own heart is pounding almost as loudly as the door. "It's okay. I'll explain."

Reyn doesn't answer. He's fixed on his task of finding the shirt, and his movements are growing jerky and panicked, so I help. I find it on the floor behind the couch, all balled up into a sad lump, and he catches it easily when I throw it to him.

He doesn't look any less scared. "Maybe you can sneak out the back," he says, wild eyes holding mine.

I shake my head, though. "I'll take care of this. Don't worry."

But when I get to the door, Reyn hovering halfway between following me and bolting up the stairs, I'm secretly not feeling so confident.

Especially when the pounding comes again. "Reyn!" Emory calls. "Open up."

Reyn spits out a low curse, and when I look back at him, his fingers are running agitated circuits through his hair.

"Just let me talk." I take a calming breath, trying to remember the stillness of the lake, and open the door.

Emory and my mom are both on the porch.

"Oh thank god," my mother exhales, then lunges forward to pull me into a hug. "We were so worried."

"We were looking everywhere!" Emory growls, but the spark of terror in his wide eyes belies the anger of his voice. "What the hell, V?!"

"It was my fault." Reyn's voice is still thick with sleep as he steps up behind me. "Or I guess, technically Dennis Rodman's."

"No," I state quickly. "It was no one's fault. It was just a mi—" I start to say mistake, but that excuse isn't going to work here, not without dredging up a lot of bad memories. "I had extra food from dinner, and I thought maybe Reyn and Mr. McAllister would like some. Reyn was alone when I got here, and we fell asleep on the couch, watching TV. I'm sorry." I'm relieved to know that Reyn and I both look the part, eyes heavy and squinting against the porch light. He even has a sleep line pressed into his cheek.

"I'm just glad you're okay," Mom says, stroking my hair. Her hands feel needy and possessive. "I got home, and you weren't in your room and Emory hadn't seen you. I panicked, but your brother remembered the phone tracker app and it said you were here."

I try to hide my embarrassed recoil at being lo-jacked. "I didn't mean to worry you." I keep my eyes off of Reyn. "I didn't mean to stay, really. I think it was just a testament to how tired I was."

My mom frowns. "Are you not getting enough sleep? Should I make an appointment with Doctor Cordell? Maybe he can prescribe you something."

Emory replies with a sharp, "No!" at the same time I warn, "*Mom.*" This is exactly why I tell her nothing.

My mother doesn't catch the censure in Em's voice, but I do. I'm sure it's not lost on Reyn, either. "Okay, okay. Let's get you into bed, then."

"Wait," Reyn pipes in, suddenly disappearing. When he returns, he's holding the empty plate, looking rueful as he extends it to my mom. "Sorry, Mrs. Hall."

We're at the driveway when I look back and see Emory having a low conversation with Reyn. This is why I tell *him* nothing, either.

Once we're in our yard, Mom says, "That was very generous of you to take the McAllisters dinner. I know things have been strained between the two of you. Understandably."

"Reyn and I are fine," I say, adding quickly, "you know, for the limited amount of time we've seen one another. It was no big deal. I had a lot of extra lasagna and I know with Mrs. McAllister gone, there have been a lot of delivery cars coming in and out every night."

"Well, considering everything, I think it's very generous of you to look out for them like that." She squeezes my shoulder. "I'm proud of you."

The thing about my parents is that they'd initially rallied for Reyn to be charged. I'm not sure how they went from wanting him locked in juvenile detention to this strange sort of pity they feel toward him now, but I know that it happened after his hearing, three months following the accident. Neither of them would tell me the details.

I follow her into the house, scooping up Firefly on the way. I glance back once more, and my brother is walking back, Reyn standing alone now in the doorway. Our eyes meet for a moment, sending a spark across my nerves, before he steps back into the house and out of sight.

Before I can disappear into my bedroom, Emory catches up to me. "What the hell, V?"

I give him a tired look. "What?"

"Why didn't you tell me you were leaving?"

"Does it matter?" I look at him accusingly. "Apparently I can be tracked anywhere."

He rolls his eyes. "As if Mom and Dad couldn't track my phone, too."

"But they never do!" I storm into my room, heedless of him entering behind me. "You can accidentally fall asleep at a friend's house and it'd be no big deal. This is exactly what I was talking about."

"What do you expect? You just walk out, no note, gone 'til midnight. Do you have any idea—" His voice cuts off with a choked sound. "When it's the two of us here, I'm responsible for you. I'm *always* responsible for you."

If Emory were any other sibling, that might have sounded bitter. Instead, it just sounds sad and exhausting.

I look at his slumped shoulders and drawn face, and can't help but feel bad. He's not lying. Our parents put way too much pressure on him to look after me, as if he doesn't already put enough on himself. "It really was an accident. I thought I'd just be in and out."

"Just tell me next time," he pleads.

I flop onto my bed and make the only promise I know I can keep. "I'll try to be more considerate, okay?"

He's pacified by this enough to leave, which is good because I can't put this uncertain feeling into words. This new thing we're doing...it's so hard to know what normal even is. Would any other girl tell her brother she's popping over next door? Would any other girl have to explain why? Would any other girl have to hide that she'd kissed a guy tonight, and that it didn't matter, because he'd brushed her off.

*The kiss.*

God, just remembering it makes my insides plummet in equal

parts excitement and humiliation. The latter is tempered by the knowledge that he seemed just as into it as I was. That was easily the hottest thing about it, although the feeling of his mouth sliding against mine, those hands holding me to him, is a close second.

*That was a mistake. You know why.*

But there are too many reasons hidden behind that truth to grasp at a single one. Was it a mistake because I'm his best friend's kid sister? Because we have this whole complicated history? Because we're both too messed up? Because the people around us would never be okay with it?

Or was it a mistake because Reyn doesn't want me that way?

Reluctantly, I lift myself from the bed and walk toward the window, pulling the curtain aside. Even though I'd been looking for him, I'm still surprised to see Reyn. His window is open and he's leaning out, elbows resting on the sill, turning his phone over in his hands. He doesn't see me at first because his head is hanging, face hidden. A full minute passes before he looks up.

He straightens and pauses for a moment, watching me. Then, he lifts his phone, and holds up four fingers. Realizing what he's doing, I take my own from my pocket and slowly program in the numbers.

I hit the call button.

There's a few seconds of delay, but Reyn finally picks up, pressing the phone to his ear. I watch his lips move. "Are you in trouble?"

I shake my head. "No, it's fine. My mom was cool and Em and I hashed it out."

He resumes his earlier position, forearm propped on the sill. "Sorry."

"What for? It's not your fault." I smile sadly, burning with the question that keeps running through my head. I ask him another one, instead. "What did he say to you?"

"Nothing," Reyn answers, shrugging. "I think he was just wondering if you were here on Devil business, but couldn't say because of your mom."

"I guess it's just that thing, you know? About me needing to push it sometimes, show them that I want to have a life. I knew it wouldn't be easy."

His eyes dart up to mine and whatever he's about to say, he looks hesitant about it. "You should be careful, with all these rituals. Having your phone tracked and everything."

"I know."

"If you want, I can…" He trails off though, eyes watching my house.

"What?"

After a moment, he answers, "I can show you how to disable it."

"Oh." I don't tell him that I could probably figure that out myself. "Okay."

He gives a heavy nod, and then looks toward the street. "Well, good night."

I try not to feel disappointed. "Night, Reyn."

I watch him hang up and follow suit, and when I close the curtains, I try not to memorize the tired curve of his shoulders.

That night, I want nothing more than to dream of the lake again. I lay in bed and try to remember the glow of fireflies, the calming stillness, the anticipation.

Instead, I dream of the two of us inside that car again. It's anything but still here, with the wind whipping my hair around. It's loud and dark, and my stomach feels full of the bad kind of expectation. Reyn looks older again, almost exactly like he did when I'd closed the curtain. There's something hard and complicated swirling in his eyes. He keeps his gaze on the road, shifting gears every now and then, but doesn't speak over the roar of the wind.

I keep waiting, but the crash never comes.

Even with the commotion, the deep sleep I got at Reyn's house makes me more alert than I've been in weeks. At least Emory doesn't seem to be holding a grudge, meeting me at the car with his usual barked, "AIS!"

I meet Sydney before classes start. "Wait, so you're telling me that you fell asleep at Reyn McAllister's house? That's where you were when your mom was calling all over the place?"

Apparently before she remembered the location app, mom made a few desperate phone calls.

"Yes. By accident," I stress.

"Uh huh." Her eyes flick over to where I know he's standing with my brother and the other jocks. Luckily, whatever issue Emory took with me last night didn't seem to extend to Reynolds. Emory smiles at something Ben says, lobbing a playful smack into Reyn's shoulder. "Maybe I need to show up at his house with dinner so I can sleep over by accident, too."

I'm not expecting the vicious stab of jealousy that explodes in my chest. Sydney has zero boundaries. To her, all guys are an opportunity. If she tries to make a move on Reyn...

God, I don't want to even think about what would happen. I remember the tired curve of his shoulders last night, his stillness and silence and the complicated darkness of his eyes, and it makes me *burn*. She'd chew him up and spit him out. I think of his scars and how Sydney would see them, like some kind of curiosity. I think of her telling everyone about them, and every fiber of my being screams *no*.

Luckily, I don't see Reyn ever being interested in her.

At least, I don't think so. I don't even know what kind of girl he likes. Maybe he'd be into that—a one-and-done with a girl like Sydney. But he could get that from plenty of girls here, and he still hasn't gone out with anyone since he's been back. In fact, with all the Devil rituals, the one person he seems to be hanging out with the most is me. The thought instantly soothes away the sharp pang in my chest, even though it shouldn't. Like Reyn had said, kissing me was a mistake.

I just don't know which mistake he's scared of making.

It's so frustrating, not knowing how to approach this new shift between us. When we woke up, he was so soft and sweet. But he pushed me away when we kissed, so does that mean he just wants to be friends? I've never been friends with guys before, and I've certainly never been *more* than friends with a guy. How do girls navigate all these nebulous signals?

This is the sort of thing I'm supposed to have Sydney for, but she's clearly not an option, and not only because of the Devil secrets. She'll know instantly who I'm asking about, and by the next day, half the school will, too.

These thoughts linger in my mind as I make my way to my locker, but vanish as soon as I open the door. Inside, I discover a new black envelope, my name printed across the front, same wax seal on the back. I don't get a chance to open it until I'm tucked away in a bathroom stall two periods later. Inside is a card with instructions.

*We commend your trust and loyalty, but neither can be wielded without a pledge of permanence.*

*Meet your partner at Cain's Ink, Thursday at 4pm.*

*"The devil's agents may be of flesh and blood, may they not?"*

*Elevatio Infernum*

Well, that's vague.

Inside the envelope is a flimsy slip of paper bearing a Devil's pitchfork, about the size of a quarter. The paper looks familiar to me, like one of those temporary tattoos we used to get when we were kids.

Cain's Ink.

*Ink. Permanence. Flesh. Blood.*

Oh my god, they want me to get a tattoo? On my body? Of a pitchfork?

Emory has lost his damn mind!

I find him outside the science lab talking to Aubrey. "Can I talk to you?"

He shrugs at me before nodding a farewell to Aubrey. He pulls me next to the water fountains and asks, "What?"

"Do you really think I'm going to get a tattoo?" I try to whisper, but it still comes out sounding loud and shrill.

Frowning, he shifts me over and looks around to make sure no one heard. "I think you are if you want to be part of this."

"A tattoo! That's, like, insane."

"It's the rules, V. If you walk, that's fine, but know the whole school will find out about your pill addiction."

I gawk at my brother. My brother who has protected me, always. "You'd seriously release that video."

"I don't think you get it." His hand clenches around my arm. "I'm not in charge of this, Vandy. I don't even have the video. There are powers that be. I'm a recruit, just like you. Christ, I told you what we were getting into. I told you this is for life. What were you expecting?"

Something about this stuns me. I'd gotten into this to get information, to make a point, to establish myself as a serious writer, but now I'm supposed to permanently brand myself with the symbol of this group. Isn't that a step too far? And using the video to make me compliant and keep my silence—that's outright blackmail.

"Look, I tried to keep you out of this." He looks frustrated when he steps away. "But I thought this was what you wanted—to make your own choices."

"It is," I weakly insist.

"Well, this is how that works." His shrug is hapless. "Sometimes, you make a choice and you have to stick with it, even when shit gets dicey." Before he walks away, he adds, "You better get it somewhere seriously invisible, because if Mom or Dad sees it, they will have an entire herd of cows."

I'm still stewing over this when I walk into the science wing's bathroom, later that day. Afton and Elana happen to be at the sink, reapplying makeup. Afton's eyes catch mine in the mirror reflection. "What's up with you?"

Even though there's no one else in the bathroom but the three of us, I'm not really expecting her to speak to me.

"Nothing, just...." I pump soap into my hand. "Well, did you get your envelope?"

Elana says, "Yep," and Afton nods while coating her lips in a shiny gloss.

"Don't you think it's going a little too far?"

Elana shrugs. "I'm putting mine on my hip." She touches the spot she means.

"I think it's sexy," Afton declares, snapping the gloss cap on and dropping it in her purse. She turns and sits on the sink. "Plus, it'll be nice having a little memento. In ten years, when I'm married to someone disgustingly rich and starting my own designer label, I'll be able to look at it and remember the glory days. I mean, all of us just broke into rival schools, unnoticed. We're bad ass, gorg." She finishes, expression pensive, "Let's face it, being a Plaything will probably be the most meaningful thing I've done at Preston."

Despite the arrogant elitism of the school, it is involved with some good projects. Habitat, food drives, tutoring in low income communities. The fact a secret society is the most meaningful thing Afton will do here is a little concerning.

"Are you scared?" Elana asks, turning to me. "Of the pain?"

"No," I reply. "I've handled my fair share of needles."

I expect a reaction, an apology about being insensitive, but Elana just fishes out her mascara wand and says, "It's not as big a deal as it seems. Look at these things, they're tiny. You could cover it up with something else, or hell, it'd probably take less than three sessions to have it lasered off. My cousin has three. She says it feels like a low-level burn." She coats her already inch-long eyelashes in black. "She also says it's kind of erotic. Like pleasurable pain. That's why it's so addictive."

Obviously, these girls are all in. Emory is all in. I'm the one who's not because I got into this with ulterior motives. But just talking to the girls makes me reconsider. If I'm doing this, really doing it, I need to be all-in. Getting the tattoo will be proof that I went all the way, that I'm committed. Maybe Elana is right. Maybe I'm making too big a deal of it.

I watch Elana apply her makeup as Afton's feet swing against the counter, eyes fixed on the screen of her phone, and something occurs to me.

I'm currently in the combined presence of more boy experience than Sydney's ever had.

My voice still comes out nervous and reluctant. "Can I...ask you two a question?"

Elana's curious eyes jump to mine through the reflection. "Shoot."

"I kind of need some advice about...guys."

Elana takes this in stride, casually listing off, "No matter what they say, boners don't hurt, pulling out isn't effective birth control, and it's never *just* the tip."

"Good to know." I say slowly.

Afton says, "But I'm guessing you had something more specific than that."

I nod, dropping my bag with theirs, underneath the paper towel dispenser. "So...say there's this guy."

In unison, they both slowly turn to me. "Isn't there always?" Afton replies.

I nod stiffly, suddenly unable to meet their eyes. "Say there's this guy and you kissed, but then he said it was a mistake."

They both give twin 'ughs'.

"Those guys are the *worst*," Elana mutters, fluffing her hair.

But Afton tilts her head. "But it was, though. Emory would absolutely crush him."

Elana grimaces. "Yeah, good point."

"That's exactly what I mean," I groan. "How do I tell if he thought it was a mistake because of Em, or if it's because he's just not into me like that."

Afton's looks at me thoughtfully. "Well, who kissed whom?"

"I kissed him," I admit, but hastily add, "he seemed really into it, though."

"Okay, wait." Elana's hands make a timeout signal. "We're going to need details. Where were his hands?"

I think. "On my face?" The same face that is now bright red.

Afton perks. "That's a good sign."

"It is?"

Elana agrees, "Totally. How long did it last?"

"Just like... I don't know. A minute?" They both frown and I quickly amend, "Maybe two. Time kind of stopped."

Elana gives me a knowing grin. "That hot, huh?"

Afton offers, "I think you're free to test the waters," and I remember that she's with someone who had probably—hopefully—told her the same thing. That it was a mistake.

"How do I do that?"

Elana gives a slow smile. "This is a detail-oriented endeavor. You need to see how he acts around you."

Afton agrees, "See where he looks, how he stands, the way he treats you."

"I'm not really sure what to look for," I admit, feeling embarrassed.

"Well, we'll start with how he treats you," Elana begins. "If a guy is really into you, he'll act like you're the only one in the room when you're around. His eyes will keep finding you, know what I mean? And speaking of eyes…" She smiles wisely. "Every guy loves tits and asses, so that's a complete bust, but if he's doing it a lot, you might be onto something. Some guys have a 'thing' though. You just have to find their kryptonite."

Afton pitches in, "Sebastian and lips."

Elana nods. "You can tell when he's into someone because his eyes are totally glued to her mouth. A little strategic lip gloss could bring that guy to his knees."

"And then there's Carlton and his hair thing," Afton adds, twirling a lock of hair around her finger. "Tyson has a fixation with necks, you can tell whenever you wear your hair up. And then there's Reynolds." Afton and Elana lock gazes before their eyes roll.

In unison, they say, "*Legs.*"

"Wait," I say, heart skipping a beat. "What?"

"Don't you notice?" Elana asks. "He's constantly looking at girls' thighs."

"Constantly," Afton stresses. "I swear, my salon should throw that boy a bonus. All the girls around here scurrying to get waxed and exfoliated just to catch his eye? They're having a good fiscal quarter."

I turn that over in my mind, trying to remember if he's looked at my legs, but instead I'm just wondering if any of those other legs have 'caught his eye'. *Legs?* Why haven't I been paying attention to this stuff? I've totally thrown away weeks of important analytics. I guess, "So you just wait and see if the guy focuses on that thing when he's with you?"

Afton tosses her head back, laughing. "Oh, my sweet summer child."

Elana grins wickedly. "No, Vandy. You flaunt it in front of him."

"Mercilessly," Afton adds.

The bell rings just then and Afton slides from the counter as Elana packs her purse.

I pick up my bag, my head still flooded with this knowledge. "It probably goes without saying, but can you—"

"Not tell your psycho over-protective brother?" Elana says, smirking. "It does go without saying."

I exhale in relief. "Thanks."

Now I just have to figure how to mercilessly flaunt my thighs in front of Reyn without making a complete fool of myself.

Truthfully, the tattoo seems less painful.

MY STOMACH ERUPTS in feral flutters when I arrive at Cain's Ink and see Reyn's Jeep in the parking lot. I linger a bit before going inside, finding him curled over the reception desk, flipping through a binder. His head turns just enough to peek over his shoulder, eyes locking with mine. The flutters turn into wild twisting when he gives me a small grin.

He turns back to the binder, finger tapping against the counter. "I see we're paired up again." He sounds perfectly neutral about it, neither approving nor disapproving.

"I thought you had practice." I'd come straight from school, still in my uniform. I'd had to catch a ride with Elana since Emory was tied up in football duties, and I was half expecting to find someone else here waiting for me.

"I got the afternoon off to let my injury heal," he explains.

"My brother's work, I suspect." I know Emory. He'd flip out if he knew how close Reyn and I had become, but he also trusts his best friend to keep an eye on me more than any of the other guys.

I'm relieved.

He nods and I watch him closely, prepared to mentally document where his eyes go. But he's not looking at me anymore. "Any fallout from the other night?"

We hadn't really spoken since our accidental sleepover. It's weird, but sometimes it's like Reyn is everywhere, and other times, he seems to just be nowhere. This week has been one of those instances where I didn't see him around the quad or in the driveway. My furtive peeks through my curtains have been met with an empty room, as well.

"Not really," I reply, grabbing another of the binders and opening it. I flip through it unseeingly. "Mom and Em are a little more hovery, but that's just business as usual."

Quietly, he asks, "And the sleeping pills?"

I glance at him in confusion before I remember my mom's comment that night. My face heats. "My mom's just obsessed with fixing every little thing wrong with me." I roll my eyes and mirror his pose, elbow propped on the counter. "But no, I don't need that."

He nods again, muttering, "Good," and that has to be a sign, doesn't it? Someone who didn't care wouldn't give my addiction that much thought. It's a weak concession, admittedly.

I flip through the images in the book; peace signs, half-naked women riding tigers, daisies and snakes. I barely process any of it. Instead, my ears slowly and intensely fixate on the buzzing coming from the other room. Suddenly, all my musing about whether or not Reynolds likes me seems completely idiotic. It hits me why I'm actually here.

I push away from the counter. "This is a bad idea."

Reyn eases his binder closed. "What's a bad idea?"

"This. The tattoo. I thought I could do it, but I can't."

He finally looks at me, languidly twisting to watch me pace by the door. "Freaking out, huh?"

"You think?!" I try to keep my voice low. "I'm becoming a Plaything to get access for my article, but I didn't think I'd have to..." I wave spastically.

He studies me for a minute, tongue swiping out across that bottom lip. Every time I look at his mouth, my stomach bottoms out. If he's watching me for signs, then they have to be clear as day. "Is it about the pain?" I give him a look and the corners of his eyes crease. "No, we've both been through way worse than this. It's about the permanence."

I wring my hands. "I know it's good proof. Like, indisputable. It'll be great for the piece, but *god*. It's forever." Even if I cover it up, even if

I laser it off, it'll still be a part of me, *flesh and blood*. "Aren't our scars enough?"

He gives a lazy shrug. "You're looking at this all wrong."

My eyebrows fly up. "How do you figure?"

"The scars are..." He goes still in that odd way of his, looking away. "They remind us of a mistake. There's no making them into something pretty. But maybe in ten years, you'll look at this tattoo, and you won't even remember all this stupid Devil stuff. You'll just remember why you did it. The people you did it for." When he meets my gaze again, there's something heavy and significant in his eyes. "If you think of it like that, it's not a such a scary thing to immortalize, right?"

I chew on my lip as I try to see it from that angle. Can I do that? Can I make this tattoo less about being bribed by some shadowy cabal, and more about the reason I did it? The more I think about it, the more it grows on me. I don't want to be forcibly branded like a piece of cattle. But the memory of being able to protect Emory for once, of feeling passionate about something—about justice and truth —for the first time in my life, of doing all this with Reyn at my side, becoming two people who are more than just the product of a terrible accident?

Suddenly, I *need* this damn tattoo.

I cut my eyes at Reyn. "Oh, you're good."

A slow smile dimples his cheeks. "Am I?" His eyes drop. It's only for a split second. If I hadn't been watching him so closely, I probably would have missed it, the way his gaze locks on the bare skin just below my skirt hem. I watch his gaze flick away just as fast, and now I'm flooded with all kinds of memories of him doing that. At the party, when I first closed myself in that room. In the bunker, when he asked me to wear jeans. That time in the driveway, the moment that started all this, when he accused me of eavesdropping.

Reynolds McAllister has been looking at my thighs.

Before I can formulate a response, a skinny guy walks out from a back room, arms covered in tattoos, a series of earrings glinting off the shell of his ear. "I'm finishing up with my other client," he says, "but if one of you wants to wait in the other room, I'll be with you shortly."

"I'm ready," I blurt, walking in the direction of the room. I enter the small space, the walls covered in a mix of colorful and black and white art. In the middle of the room, there's a long chair-slash-table convertible combo, a lot like the deck chairs at the pool, except this one is padded and sturdy. Next to it stands a stainless-steel table filled with supplies. My eyes linger on the containers of ink, the small squeeze bottle of water, and the clean cloths. The nervous flutter sparks in my belly again, but it's a different kind of anticipation than it had been before. When I turn around, Reyn is in the doorway, leaning against the frame, arms folded over his chest. He looks tired, but there's a softness to his eyes as he watches me that I'm not quite used to.

"Where did you decide to put it?" he asks.

"I haven't," I admit, taking the temporary tattoo from my bag. "Somewhere bulletproof invisible, that's for sure." When I look up from the paper bearing the pitchfork, I catch it again—his eyes rapidly flicking away from my thighs.

"I haven't decided, either," he offers.

I rub my thumb over the ink on the paper, mind blooming with an idea. Just thinking about it makes my skin feel a little too hot, but I can hear Afton and Elana in my head, *flaunt it*. But I'm not someone who flaunts, mercilessly or otherwise, and I'm already certain that I'm about to make a fool out of myself.

"I was thinking," I begin, backing myself up to the chair. "I could do it here." I watch him as I lift the side of my shirt, tapping the soft patch of skin over my ribs. His eyes follow the motion. "It's above my scar, so I already have a whole wardrobe built around hiding it."

He meets my gaze again. "Looks good."

"Or..." I scoot myself up, onto the chair, and plant one of my feet in the middle of it. "... I could get it here." I have no idea how the hell I manage to keep my voice even as I hike up the hem of my skirt and spread myself open, exposing my inner thigh.

His eyes drop to the spot, face going slack. I watch as he stuffs his hands into his pockets, piercing green eyes taking it all in.

I wet my lips, explaining, "Because no one ever sees this." It isn't like the other times, where his eyes immediately dart away. He takes two steps into the room and freezes there, lips parting. "What do you think?"

"Me?" he asks, eyes flying up to mine before snapping right back down. His voice is husky, rough. "I don't know."

His eyelids are heavy now, and my thighs erupt in vicious tingles at the weight of his stare, this awareness of what I'm doing to him. I pull my hem up a little more, ignited by the way his jaw tightens. "You choose."

His breath escapes in a loud exhale, eyes lurching away. "This is about you, V. You *really* shouldn't let me choose."

Softly, I ask, "Why?"

"Because." From my periphery, I can see his fists clenching inside his pockets. His voice is quiet, accusing. "You know what I'll choose."

I drag my lip through my teeth. "*Choose.*"

We both know what I'm asking, and it has little to do with the tattoo. I'm completely twisted up inside as I watch him go still, eyes darting from the paper to my thigh, to my eyes, to the table.

He knows exactly what I'm asking. "Hand it over."

I give him the paper, and although I'm preparing for him to approach my leg with the wet towel he's preparing, I'm equally as prepared for him to tell me to lift my shirt. So when he turns to me, reluctantly approaching the chair, and rests a hand on my knee, I shudder out an exhale.

"Here?" he asks, pressing the paper to my skin.

It's all I can do to stop myself from squirming under the light pressure. "Higher."

He looks at me through his lashes, skittering the paper up an inch. "Here?"

I swallow and reach down, fingers loose around his wrist as I tug it higher. "There."

His eyes watch this, and the way he's clenching his teeth makes his features sharper, severe. "You're sure."

"Yes."

He presses the towel to the paper and holds it there, thumb pushing it into my thigh. I lean back on my hands as we wait, watching him watch me. His eyes are all over them, crawling up one thigh and then the other. It's *killing* me, the way the air is practically humming around us, charged with something heady and electric. I'm hoping he doesn't notice how shallow my breath is, how heavy my own eyelids have gotten, but inside, I'm a complete mess of molten hot *want*. The way he looks, leaning over me, hand clamped around my thigh? I've never been so wet in my entire life.

We both exhale when he eases the towel away, peeling the paper back. A droplet of water glides down my leg and he wipes it away with his finger. I take a break from watching him to look down and see it for myself—a perfect little pitchfork pressed onto my inner thigh, six inches above my knee.

I don't have to wonder how I'll be able to look at this for the rest of my life. It'll be a reminder of all the things I'd thought about before, but now it's a reminder of this *thing* that passes between Reyn and I when our gazes meet.

I don't think I'll have any problem immortalizing the heat in his eyes.

# 18

Reyn

IF THIS GIRL doesn't close her legs right now, I might have to just walk out, or find a bathroom, or close myself up in the car and lose myself in some seriously deep breathing.

She looks like absolute sex, sitting there with her foot kicked up on the table and her skirt hiked so far up that a little sliver of panties is actually visible. In like five seconds, Vandy Hall took my top ten erotic moments and just swept them all into the trash can. I'm sure part of it is that I've been ragingly horny since stepping off the bus from Mountain Point, but the big picture is a high-resolution shot of her legs parting, those blue eyes watching me hawk-like.

She knows just what she's doing.

My eyes zero in on this stray drop of water from the towel, running down her inner thigh, and look. I'm trying really hard to be stone here. Inside, I'm fucking losing it. I rub at the damp sweat springing up on the back of my neck.

"What about you?" she asks, her other foot swinging casually. "Where are you going to put it."

"I don't know." I should tell her to close her legs. Instead, I pull the tattoo design from my pocket. "You should choose for me, too."

That's probably the most senseless thing about this. I couldn't even choose which jeans to wear two hours ago, but apparently whatever's messing with my executive function is completely immune to a choice between Vandy's smooth, open thighs and *literally anything*. Maybe I could make that choice because there really wasn't one.

I watch as she chews on her lip for a moment, eyes roving over me. Finally, she swings her leg back around, hopping off the chair. I look at her thighs when she stands, just to make sure it's really not visible.

She approaches me, cheeks tinted pink, and pushes up my sleeve with a delicate touch, holding the tattoo against the curve of my bicep. Before the night at my house, I wouldn't have let her touch me like that—afraid she'd see the scars—but that's moot now.

"You can get away with it," she notes about the tentative location, "jocks always get leeway." But she drops my sleeve, her eyes darting down to my stomach. "Can you lift up your shirt? Just a little."

I do as I'm asked, because if she touches my stomach, things are going to get out of control. This is very different from our 'I'll show you mine, if you show me yours' scar exhibit the other night. That had been about revealing the painful secrets that only we share. This is very much about now, like there's this charged, sex-fueled bubble surrounding us. I'm silently begging my body to behave, something I know is mostly futile. I'm already half-hard.

I pull up my shirt and watch as she stares at my stomach, those blue eyes drinking me in. For once, I'm grateful for the years of mandatory sit-ups. I'm not stupid. I know exactly how I look.

Her eyes dart to mine briefly, and there's a question there. Like she wants permission. I look back at her, an answer in the curve of my brow. *Whatever you want.* Worshipping at the altar of Vandy's thighs is the closest I'll ever get to an organized religion. She has no idea how much power she has over me.

She takes the permission for what it is, and two fingers bury themselves beneath my waist band, hooking into the denim. I gnash my teeth—*stone stone stone*—but there's no calming down with this girl. That's the problem. I knew it when I was fourteen. I knew it when she kissed me under the shadow of the tree house. I knew it when I woke up and found her asleep on my chest. All these things I feel for Vandy can't just be locked away, and the more I try, the worse shit gets.

She tugs at my pants, the waist loose enough to get over my hips. I bite my bottom lip as she explores the area. There is zero doubt about her inexperience, because she's toying with all the hot zones like it's nothing for her to ghost over the hair of my happy trail. Her thumb settles on my hip, just outside the cut of muscle I've worked so hard to possess. She rubs a small circle and says, "There."

I look down as she presses the paper to it, testing. It's sort of halfway between my hip and stomach, easily hidden. I have to wet my lips before I rasp out a quiet, "Yeah?"

"No one will ever know it's there, and also…" Her fingers graze the muscle, eyes growing heavy when my stomach twitches. "*This* is your second hottest feature."

My eyebrows shoot up my forehead. "Really now?"

Her face is flaming red, but she just meets my gaze and gives a casual shrug. "Absolutely."

I have to ask. "What's the first?"

Her grin is this slow, sort of wicked thing that I never really thought her capable of. "Wouldn't you like to know."

She reaches for the damp cloth and pours fresh water on it. I watch with my belly caved in and my cock hard as a motherfucking rock, as she carefully applies the tattoo right where she wants it. There's no way she's not seeing what she's doing to me.

We wait for it to take hold, her hand clamped around my hip, pressing the towel into my muscle. She's looking at my abs again, and she's so close that I can see the way her eyelashes flick and twitch as her gaze climbs and dips. She's not particularly trying to hide it.

This is totally an eye-fucking.

She carefully peels the paper away, skimming her fingers around the Devil's mark. She says, "All good," and her voice is this breathy, trembling thing that makes me want to push her against something sturdy and vertical.

She steps back, but my hand impulsively curls around her neck, fingers threading in her hair, keeping her close. She freezes, watching me, but my eyes zero in on the delicate patch of skin beneath her ear. I think about marking her there too, this time for all the world to see.

*Mine now.*

It's a seductive falsehood, but it doesn't make me want it any less. I rest a thumb under her chin and lift it, searching her eyes to see what this is. Is she toying with me for the fun of it? I wouldn't hold it against her. I'd play along, shrug it off. Or does she want to feel whatever this thing is between us spark and catch fire?

The answer is clear in her eyes.

The door swings open and skinny McTattoo-face strides in, focused on a tool in his hand. "Alright then, I think I'm all set up." He looks up at Vandy. "You ready?"

"I am," she replies, steadier now. She pulls up her skirt, flashing the pale flesh of her inner thigh and the temporary tattoo at him. "This is what I want, where I want it."

McTattoo looks at her thigh and *oh, fuck no.* Hot, possessive fury boils under my skin at the sight of his eyes fixed there. I didn't think this through.

My flash of rage is instantly soothed when Vandy slips her hand into mine. She doesn't let go as she sits in the chair, the artist gently positioning her legs apart. I take a deep breath and try to loosen my grip on her hand. The last thing I need is to crush her bones with my irrational jealousy.

She jolts when he tests the gun, giving it a few rapid buzzes.

"It's important you don't move," McTattoo says calmly. His fingers hover over her thigh and I consider breaking each and every one.

"How bad is it going to hurt?" Vandy asks, but she sounds more curious than scared.

He shrugs. "On the scale? Not that bad, but I'm not sure what your tolerance for pain is."

"High," she admits.

"Then you'll be okay. But if you're worried about it, don't watch." He looks at me. "And you—distract your girl."

*My* girl.

"I'm about to start. Is everyone ready?"

Vandy nods, and I watch as her teeth press down on her bottom lip. The ink gun turns on, buzzing with life, and her eyes meet mine. All my life I've taken what I've wanted, and right now, all I want is to make her feel safe. I bend until I'm inches away from her face, eye to eye, breath mingling with breath, and I know when the needle makes impact, because she gasps. I watch as her eyes tighten with the pain of it and my chest clenches.

I mutter, "Fuck it," and capture her lips in a kiss. She freezes at first, but then slowly relaxes. I lick her lips apart, and her tongue meets mine. She needs to be still for the ink, and she's got some random guy messing around between her legs, so I keep the kiss gentle, slow, but it barely matters—at least, for me. The harsh buzzing is washed away by the warmth of her breath, and I hope she feels this too. This feeling that nothing else exists besides the point where our mouths meet.

More than once she sucks in air, a sign that the needle hurts, but I do my best to soothe it with sucking pecks at her lips, wet sweeps against her tongue.

It's over so fast that I could almost be disappointed.

Almost, if not for her sigh of relief that it's over. "That wasn't so bad," she says, glassy eyes darting down to the tattoo. If she's feeling regretful about it, she doesn't show it. She just nods along to his care instructions, glazed eyes watching him cover it up.

"You're next, Romeo." The artist rips off his gloves for a new pair, running an astringent-smelling wipe over the chair once Vandy slides off it.

She watches me take her place, eyes widening when I unbutton my jeans and fold them out of the way.

"You're the one who wanted it there," I remind her, grinning at her pink cheeks.

Vandy is right, the pain isn't so bad. At least I don't have to worry about sporting wood as the artist inks my skin, because pain has never done it for me. Nevertheless, when she takes my hand in hers, holding it in her lap as she cringes along to the harsh sound of the gun, I don't say anything.

FRESHLY INKED and armed with written instructions on how to take care of our new tattoos, Vandy and I walk out of the parlor into the cool night. My Jeep is the only vehicle in the lot.

"Do you need a ride?"

"Actually, yeah," she says, gripping the strap of her bag. "I'm supposed to call Emory, but that's probably out of his way."

This time, when I open the door for her, she accepts it. She also takes my hand, which sends another wave of electricity across my skin.

"So, listen," I start, rocking back on my heels. I have no clue how to handle this moment. How do I tell the girl who's off-limits, who's a one-way-ticket back to military school, who will destroy my relationship with her brother, that my brain isn't going to start working until I kiss the shit out of her again? Repeatedly. "I think—"

"I'm hungry," she blurts, cutting me off. "Starving, actually. Do you want to get something to eat?"

I assess her quietly. "Like, at a restaurant?"

"Do you have any food at home?"

The image of a bare refrigerator comes to mind.

"No." I run my hand through my hair. "Sorry."

"I could go for a hamburger. Actually, the bacon avocado cheeseburger at The Nerd would be amazing right now." She looks at me expectantly, normally, like we hadn't just gotten secret society tattoos and made out while doing it.

"Yeah," I say slowly, trying to find my footing and failing miserably. "I could eat. I mean, I can always eat."

The hum of electricity continues to crackle between us as I drive across town. I want to hold her hand. I want to reach out and touch that strip of leg again. I want to look at her and have her look at me. I have this policy, though. Whenever Vandy is in my car, my attention is on the road, hands fixed at ten-and-two.

I take a left, into the abandoned K-Mart building that's a few miles from The Nerd. The parking lot is enormous and bare, and when I roll into a spot and put the Jeep in park, I have to sit there for a second, hands clenching tight around the steering wheel.

The cabin is quiet enough that I can hear her soft inhale right before she speaks. "What's wrong?"

I look at her, too many answers swirling in my head—none of which I can give her. That my insides feel like they're magnetized. That my blood feels like lava right now. That my balls ache, and my chest hurts, and I'm not safe to drive, because I have this gorgeous girl in my car and all I can think about is burying literally any part of myself between her thighs, and that all of that is the easy part. Because being horny is one thing, but whatever I'm feeling right now is some crazy mess of nervous want that I have no idea what to do with.

There's no doubt the tension rises the longer I stay silent. I'm just not sure what the tension means. Regret? Fear? Want?

I know what it means for me. I feel it every fucking day, the impulsive urge to take what isn't mine, an urge I rarely push back against. I didn't resist at the tattoo parlor, and I can't resist now.

The faint shred of control doesn't slip away so much as it plummets.

The kiss is borderline embarrassing. We're flying at each other over the console, lips meeting hungrily, but our seatbelts are straining against us, pulling us back. It takes me three tries before I have it unlatched, but once I do, my hand is in her hair, tugging her closer. If I'd taken that kiss back at Thistle Cove, it probably would have been ice in comparison to this—the way I fuck my tongue into her mouth with greedy kisses.

She makes a sound deep in her throat, this quiet little whine that has me pushing closer so I can swallow it, keep it for myself. *Mine now.* I know I'm being too rough, that I'm pulling her hair, and she probably can't even breathe with how desperate my mouth is against hers, but instead of pushing me away, she grabs back, hand fisted tightly into my sleeve.

I break away to suck at her neck, only just barely cognizant enough to not leave any marks. She tastes so sweet here, this little patch of skin under her jaw, and I can feel the thrum of her pulse beneath it, frenetic and alive. She gulps in these big inhales, and there's a soft, unspoken approval in the way her fingers wind into my hair, holding me there.

When I plunge back in for a kiss, she meets me readily, like she'd been expecting it, hoping for it, and I can't help myself. I want everything right now, all at once. I want to mark and have and consume, so badly that I'm shaking with it.

I push my hand up her skirt, wedging it between her thighs.

She gasps into my mouth, and the sound is so gentle—such a stark contrast to the way I'm kissing and groping her—that it shakes something loose inside of me.

I pull away, crashing back into my seat. Hands at ten-and-two. Eyes closed. Chest heaving. Deep breaths.

*Fuck.*

After a long moment of our harsh breathing, Vandy's reluctant voice breaks the silence. "Reyn?"

I suck in a long inhale. "I just need a minute."

She answers with a soft, "Okay," and my eyes are still closed, but I can practically *feel* her chewing on that lip, and it's not helping my situation much.

I say my ABCs backward in my head, and it takes more than a minute, but eventually I can let go of the steering wheel and rake a hand through my hair. "Sorry, that got a little out of hand."

Her mouth is red when she smiles, but her eyes are soft. "Yeah, I was about three seconds away from coming over that gear shift."

A rough chuckle escapes my chest. "I won't even say what I was three seconds from doing." She laughs in response, and her eyes look so bright—so calm—that I almost feel dumb for asking, "Are you okay? Did I freak you out?" *With my massive, throbbing libido.*

Some of that radiance dims a bit. "Of course. I'm not made of spun glass, Reyn."

I want to tell her that I know she's never done this before, that I don't want to be the scary front-seat groping-guy she tells her friends about at some college sharing circle in four years. I want to be that other guy, the kind of guy who takes her out and treats her right and doesn't push his hand up her skirt in an abandoned K-Mart parking lot, even though I am apparently *totally that fucking guy.*

Instead, I drive.

Like most nights, The Nerd is packed. Familiar cars with Preston Prep stickers on the back windows line the parking lot. Emory's truck is, unfortunately, right by the door. I grip the wheel, staring at the neon sign. She sits quietly for a minute, her forehead creased in thought.

"Maybe we should get takeout," she suggests, shifting in her seat. Her skirt rises, giving me a view of the edge of her tattoo, kick-starting my heart. I tamp it down, not wanting another demonic boner possession situation on my hands.

"Yeah, I think that's a better idea."

The food doesn't take long, Vandy waiting in the car while I dip inside to order it. When I return to the Jeep and get back on the road, we're both quiet. I know from the drive to Thistle Cove that she doesn't like for the windows to be rolled down. She knows from the same trip that I don't like music playing when I'm driving. In other words, by the time I park at the clearing overlooking the lake, the silence has grown into something charged and uncertain.

"Reyn?" she asks quietly, eyes looking over the lake. "What is this?"

I turn to look at her, the way the lights play against the soft curves of her face, the delicate bow of her lip, the fan of her lashes. I reach across the center of the car and gently cup my hand behind her neck.

"That kiss wasn't just to distract you," I admit. "I want this." Quieter, I add, "I want you."

She swallows and eases the bag of greasy food onto the floorboard. "Wanting what isn't yours is kind of your thing, Reynolds McAllister." Her voice is soft. "Just promise you won't toss me into a drawer or leave me on the side of the road when you're done."

I sigh, thumbing that patch of skin below her ear. "That's the problem, Baby V, I haven't been done with you a day in my life." What she doesn't understand is that it's different with her. It's easy to steal, but so much harder to take something willingly given, because those things are more than conquests or shiny trinkets. They're precious, a responsibility.

"I'm not the kid I used to be, Reyn." Her eyes flutter closed, and if I look hard enough, I can see the shadow of that girl who used to look at me like I hung the moon. But she's right. She's not that kid anymore.

"Neither am I."

The kiss that follows is slow and quiet, like a secret.

# 19

Vandy

"What's wrong with you?"

"Huh?"

Sydney points her fork at me and swirls it in front of my face. "You've been a space-cadet for two days."

Well, she's not wrong. I haven't found myself alone with Reyn since that night in the Jeep, after the tattoo, so I keep running over the memory to sate my thirst. It's not like it was anything earth-shattering. We kissed, we ate, we kissed some more, and then he drove me home.

Still, it was the perfect date.

And now I keep finding myself wondering if that's what it even was—a date. There was kissing and food and scenery, and that all seems pretty date-like. There was also Reyn's hand around my neck, thumb rubbing into the spot behind my ear as he licked lazily into my mouth. It's like now that I know I can have it, it's all I can think about. Reyn's mouth. Reyn's hands. Reyn's rough fingertips skating across my jaw. The sound of his breath every time we pulled apart. The way his eyes looked, glazed and yet sharp, like he was drunk and sort of frustrated about it.

Of course, then we'd stepped out and meticulously cleaned out the Jeep to free it of any hamburger-related messes. This new Reyn, I've found, is a bit anal retentive, and if I didn't know the source of it, it'd be painfully cute. As it stands, I could see the anxiety creasing his forehead as he picked a piece of lettuce from the console.

Sydney brings me crashing back to the present when she looks at me, eyes sharp and accusing. "Oh my god, are you high right now?"

I balk, casting furtive glances at the people around us. "Excuse me?"

"The way you're acting today?" She raises her eyebrows. "That's sure what it seems like."

I grip my fork and want to tell her that the only thing I'm high on is the boy who just walked into the dining hall. Obviously, that's not happening. "Well, I'm not," I snap, face heating. "And maybe you can ask that a little louder next time. I don't think they heard you over in *Canada*."

She shrugs. "No one's listening to us."

I sigh, eyes moving back toward where Reyn is waiting in the lunch line. "You can't ask me that every time you think my behavior is a little off."

Before I can think to be more careful, her eyes are following mine. She looks at Reyn, then back at me, eyes full of pity. "Please don't tell me your delusional crush on Reynolds McAllister somehow managed to survive despite *everything*."

Now, I outright drop my fork. *Delusional?* "What are you talking about?" *DELUSIONAL?*

"Oh, come on. The way you're looking at him right now?" She rolls her eyes, looking at him again. "Everyone always knew you were crazy for him, and it's not like you were alone. None of us were being realistic back then, even when the competition was mediocre." When she meets my gaze again, her face is full of sympathy. "Is that what has you so spacey this week? Because if it is, then we need to find you someone to shake it off. That way lies a path of rejection and relapse."

Sydney Prescott has literally stunned me speechless, because I can't even tell her how wrong she is. Instead I have to sit here and be told that I don't have a chance with Reyn, despite having had his hand between my thighs two nights ago. The pressure inside my head rises until I can finally grind out a quiet, "Did it never occur to you that I might just have stuff going on?"

She purses her lips, considering me. "Like what? Newspaper stuff?"

"No, not—" I bite off my growled response, because this is the thing about Syd. To her, I can easily be boiled down to two things; my injuries and school. She really believes that encompasses me. "For the record, you don't actually know everything about me. And given how completely careless you are with other people's secrets, I'm starting to think maybe that's not such a bad thing."

Her eyes flick up, flashing in equal parts anger and hurt. "That's a really shitty thing to say to someone who's stuck by your side for three years."

"Look," I start, drawing in a calming breath. "You know I appreciate you being my friend and everything, but when you talk about it like that, it's like you see it as some form of charity. And then you hold it over me, like I have to tell you everything because you're my only option."

She gives me a blank look. "I *am* your only option, Vandy." She doesn't even say it meanly—maliciously—but it still feels like a slap in the face. "I'm your only friend because you spent years doped up on painkillers, limping around like a zombie. That's your fault, not mine."

Now, *that* was said meanly.

"You know what?" I say, throwing my things haphazardly onto my tray. "I think I'm ready to expand my options."

"Me, too." She pushes her chair back dramatically and grabs her lunch tray. It's game day and the glitter accenting her uniform makes it all that more theatrical. She doesn't look back as she storms off to a table filled with a group of lacrosse players, including Sebastian, who pats the bench next to him for her to slide in. A few people nearby notice the commotion and turn to look at me, but once they see that it's just Vandy Hall, their eyes glaze over and they go back to the business of eating lunch.

I push my tray away, suddenly void of anything resembling an appetite. My eyes prickle, and it's dumb. It shouldn't hurt like this. I know that. Whatever I've got going on with Reyn, it's between us and no one else. Sydney is clueless. This should slide right off me, because I know better.

*Delusional.*

Instead, that single word just keeps looping around in my head.

"Over here," a voice calls, and I look up to see Aubrey beside my table. She's waving Emory over, and I cast my eyes around in confusion. Emory doesn't exactly ignore me at school, but he doesn't actually engage me much, either—not unless it's some hyper-protective move that's sure to annoy me.

But Emory isn't the one deciding to approach me. It's Aubrey. It's a testimony to his interest in her that when she takes the seat just vacated by Sydney, he drops into the one next to her without a second thought.

A few feet behind them, Reyn lopes across the room, eyes finally landing on me. My whole body rushes with heat and I'm pretty sure this is headed for some of that rejection stuff Sydney just mentioned. He's not even *allowed* to sit with me. The muscle in the back of his jaw tenses, but before either of us can figure out how to handle the situation, Emory slides the chair out next to him and tells him to sit down.

Problem solved.

Reyn sets his tray on the table across from me and slings his backpack over the chair. I pull my plate back toward me and focus on the lettuce as he shoves his long legs under the table.

His knee bumps into mine. "Sorry," he mutters, picking up his fork. When our eyes meet, he stares at me, forehead creasing. There's a question in his eyes, lips parting as if he wants to verbalize it, but then his gaze pings to Emory, and he doesn't.

I just shake my head in response.

"How did y'all's appointment go?" Aubrey asks. "Mine hurt more than I thought it would. Well, not hurt, exactly. It felt strange."

Emory says, "Reyn won't tell anyone where he got it. We have a pool going."

Reyn answers, "It's not on my ass."

"Oh, that was Ben's guess. Mine was tramp stamp."

Reyn pelts him with a green bean. "You're not even being creative."

No one ever asks me where mine is. Thankfully.

Emory opens a bag of chips and Aubrey casually plucks one from inside, which is interesting. Emory and food sharing? Must be serious.

"I got mine on my ankle," Aubrey says, and I already know Emory got his on his shoulder.

Under the guise of gathering my hair over a shoulder, I glance toward where Syd is sitting. She's looking right at me, blank-faced and guileless, and I get this white-hot stab of resentment as her gaze shifts to Reyn.

She rolls her eyes at me.

*Delusional.*

I look back at Reyn, who's watching me, that question in his eyes again.

Instead of answering, I bump his knee, holding it against his. My own question.

He responds by pressing back, studying his lunch carefully. There's no mistaking the way his lips are flirting with a smirk. I spread my fingers over my knee, and a second later feel the graze of his fingertips on mine.

Heat burns the tip of my ears and I squeeze his fingers, laying them on my knee. Sitting with me at lunch could get him in trouble. Flirting with me in front of Emory could get his ass kicked. But as usual, Reyn has a better read on the situation than I do, because my brother is fully entranced with Aubrey. He's placed his hand around her back, on the seat of her chair, leaning as close to her as he possibly can, speaking quietly in her ear.

Reyn takes the opportunity to reach those long fingertips up my bare thigh and toy with the hem of my skirt. Every other sound in the loud cafeteria vanishes. I'm focused on the way his skin feels against mine. His pouty bottom lip. The memory of making out with him in the front seat of his Jeep, our lips salty from fries, windows fogging over.

As the seconds pass, I get more and more overheated—overwhelmed, worried about getting caught. This boy is fire and I've always been attracted to his flame. With my heart pounding, I abruptly push my chair back and announce, "I need to go to the library before next period." Emory's barely paying attention, so I'm able to give Reyn a significant look as I leave.

The crisp fall air relieves the heat, sort of, and the quiet of the library settles my heart rate. I stroll through the stacks, past the librarian's desk. Ms. Cowen gives me a small smile. The library is a common haunt of mine. For the past three years, I'd spent a lot of time here, pretending to read a book in one of the comfortable chairs along the back wall, while really being high as a fucking kite.

I'm good at pretending, and right now, strolling through the stacks, I'm pretending that I'm not waiting—*dying*—for Reyn to come find me.

I find myself back in the biographies, the quietest row in the building. The only sound is the drag of my feet on the carpeted floor. I run my finger along the dusty spines, trying to settle this crazed, energized thing inside of me. I'd lived so long with dulled feelings, but now everything hits against me sharp as knives. Scary. Dangerous. Thrilling. I've had it bad for Reyn since as far back as I can remember, and I told him that I wasn't disposable, something he could toss away once he was done with the thrill.

But even I know I don't mean it.

It's not a good feeling, knowing that I'd just take whatever I can get. But the thought of not having it at all is so much worse.

I stop, spotting a shiny new cover among the older titles, and pull a Ronan Farrow book off the shelf. Now *this* guy knows how to investigate and reveal a scandal. I tuck the book against my chest, turn the corner, and stop short, my hand reaching out to the tall bookshelf for support.

He stands down at the other end, red and black football tie slightly askew. His hands are in his pockets—no pretense of even looking for a book—and his eyes are focused on me, green, alert. He's looking at me in a way that makes my stomach flutter anxiously.

"I wasn't sure if I was supposed to come find you," he says, voice low enough not to carry back out to Ms. Cowen. His words might be uncertain, but the heat in his eyes as they drag down my body are anything but.

"That was the idea," I admit.

He stalks toward me, propping his shoulder on the shelf in a casual lean. His eyes are intense, searching. He has this way of pitching his deep voice where it seems like anything he's saying is just meant for me. "You looked upset before."

"It wasn't important," I insist, mirroring his pose.

He reaches out to tuck a strand of hair behind my ear, and it makes me shiver. "I probably shouldn't have touched you like that, not in front of everyone. Definitely not in front of Emory. Sorry."

I can still feel the warmth of his fingers on my leg, like they never left. "Don't be. I wanted you to." Quietly, I confess, "I've always wanted you to."

He looks down at me, his wide shoulders casting me in a shadow. I think about the scars and how much I'd wanted to touch them that night he showed them to me. How much I want to touch him right now. Reyn has never been one to resist, and although his interest in me is still a surprise, the fact he reaches for me, touching me just under the chin, isn't.

Every nerve in my body alights and only increases when he speaks. "Seeing you all day and not being able to get close to you is killing me," he confesses, inching closer, like we're magnetized. "Knowing that mark is on your thigh. Knowing what your lips taste like." His hand settles on my hip. "It's making me reckless."

He turns me so that my back presses against the bookshelves, his hand dropping to fist the hem of my skirt. His knuckles graze the skin there, teasing, pressing. He kisses me, coaxing my lips apart with little licks. His tongue tastes sweet, like the juice he drank at lunch.

*Delusional.*

Warm insurgence grows in my belly and I grab at his tie, tugging him down so I can reach him better, sliding against his hot mouth. He makes a sound deep in his throat, something guttural and barely restrained, as the kiss swells in intensity. I run my hands down his biceps, feeling them flex as he surges into a deep, sucking kiss. Heat pools between my legs, and I push my hips into him without thinking, pure instinct.

His kiss sort of skitters and he pulls back. "I like you like this," he whispers. His eyes bore into mine as he carefully wedges a thigh between my legs, like he's testing my reaction.

The length of him, hard and pressing beneath the front of his pants, slots up against my hip. The shock of the pressure against my middle is just as intoxicating as the knowledge of what I'm doing to him. I'd seen it through the window, but actually feeling it? *Jesus.*

Who needs drugs when you can have this?

"Like what?" I ask, distracted.

He rumbles, "Bold." *Kiss.* "All worked up." *Lick.* "Mine."

He's the Devil alright, always there with an open hand, always ready to drag me with him into trouble. His lips burn against my neck, stubble rough against my skin. The pain feels good, grounding, just like his thigh, which I can't help but buck against. He spits a low curse into my throat when I do, mouth dropping to the edge of my collar. He pushes with his leg, a hand coming down to the small of my back, grinding me harder against his thigh.

I gasp at the friction, hands clamped around his shoulders. "Oh god." It feels so good and solid against me that I legitimately worry there might be a wet spot on his pants when he pulls away.

He mutters a sharp, "Fuck, V," and takes my mouth again, his movements hungry and almost as desperate as my own.

My hips move of their own accord, chasing the friction and heat, and this could be enough. I could ride Reyn's leg and probably have the best orgasm of my life, and from the way he's pushing into me, I think it wouldn't be so bad for him, either.

Then the bell tower chimes.

His lips pause and he looks down at me, chest rising and falling. Next class begins in ten minutes. We both freeze with the awareness that Ms. Cowen will do a sweep to get all the students hiding out during lunch back to class.

"We should…" I start and he nods, fingers still making lazy circles down on my outer thigh. I straighten his tie and he smoothes down my skirt. I have no doubt his heart is hammering as hard as mine.

He looks at me and smiles with those abused, red lips, like I'm some kind of prize he's just swiped off the headmaster's desk.

"Will I see you at the game tonight?" he asks, glancing down to the end of the stacks where a student passes by, oblivious to us being there. Regardless, he adjusts his body so I'm blocked from view.

I shake my head, trying to calm myself down. "The paper's double booked. Mr. Lee assigned Dustin Brown to cover the game tonight. I have to go with the softball team over to Eastside. It's a region game."

"Oh," he says, eyes dropping. "We'll figure something out."

He kisses me one last time, then releases me, walking one way down the aisle while I go the other. At the end of the row, I turn the corner and rest my back against the endcap, taking the first deep breath since I saw him standing there.

Reyn loves a shiny object, something new and off-limits, but wanting to make plans? That's not a quick grope in the stacks.

That's not delusional.

SYDNEY: **Heard Reyn was kissing someone in the stacks at the library. Guess he's back in the game.**

I stare at the text for a long moment. We hadn't spoken since our fight earlier in the day, but Syd obviously can't resist what she thinks is a harsh blow.

"Who's that?" Dad asks, glancing away from the window. He came to pick me up from school after the softball game was over.

"Just Sydney."

"How's she doing?"

"Oh, you know," I say stiffly, "drama never stops chasing her."

He smiles. "She does seem to have a penchant for that, doesn't she?"

There's a weird prickle of pride that runs through me when I look down at the message. I was the one kissing Reyn. I'm the one that got a tattoo and was asked to join a secret society. I know that Sydney thinks I'm still the same boring girl she's always stuck by, but I'm not. Not anymore.

The message stares at me, and although the last thing I want to do is encourage a discussion about who Reyn was kissing in the library, ignoring it seems like a defeat.

**Vandy: Reyn in the library? Sounds like mistaken identity if you ask me.**

Dad passes Jerry, who waves us through the gate. It makes me think of Reyn and his ongoing feud.

Honestly, *everything* tonight has made me think of Reyn.

He pulls into the driveway and I notice that Emory's big truck isn't there. Dad said they won their game, 76 to 12. I'm sure he's out celebrating. After he parks the car in the garage, I get out and see Firefly's tail in the hydrangea bush. I look over my shoulder and say, "Just a minute. Let me go catch the night stalker."

The garage door shuts behind him and I drop my bag on the driveway. Poking my head into the bush, I see Firefly, then a set of hands pulling him out the other side.

"Looking for this guy?" Reyn asks, holding the cat against his chest while stroking down his back.

"I was." I tilt my head. "What are you doing out here?"

Reyn pauses, and it's too dark to make out what his eyes hold, but I can see the silhouette of his parted lips. "I'd probably seem a lot cooler if I said I was getting something out of the car, but I was actually just waiting for you to get home."

Those warm butterflies spin in my stomach again. I take a step closer and open my mouth to tell him that I'm glad he did, but the garage door opens again.

Dad calls out, "Everything okay? You find the cat?"

"Yes, Dad!" I yell, a little too loud. Firefly jerks back, offended at my volume. "Coming!" I turn to Reyn, grimacing. "Sorry. I have to go."

I see the flicker of disappointment—irritation, maybe—in his eyes. I push up on my toes and kiss him quickly, hoping to soothe it away, and then take the squirming cat from his hands.

"Night," I whisper, hoping maybe he'll kiss me again, but he just nods, eyes settled on the house behind me.

*Great*, I think, dropping Firefly by his food bowl and refreshing his water. He's probably pissed off, or frustrated, or realizing that I'm basically a prisoner and having second thoughts. No—*third* thoughts. Maybe even *fourth* thoughts. It's hard to forget that this thing I've got going with Reyn is fragile. Any little thing could burst the bubble.

I tell my parents goodnight, pulling out my phone as I ascend the stairs.

**V: Sorry. I told you my parents hover.**

I wait for a moment on the staircase, hoping for a response. It never comes.

Paranoia nags at me as I walk into my room. I'd told him that I'm not a kid, but sure enough, that's exactly how everyone is treating me. Now, I look like some silly girl with no freedom, home on a Friday night, locked up tight by her well-meaning parents. I kick off my shoes, push down my jeans, and look at the tattoo on my inner thigh. Earlier, I'd felt so brave and special for having it. *Chosen*. But that's not actually the case, is it? It's just another symbol of pity, one that Reyn had to secure for me out of fear of getting in trouble. And who even knows. This thing we're doing could easily be a ploy to make me forget about the exposé. If there's one thing my brother and Reyn know how to do, it's making me complicit in their crimes.

Suddenly, I feel like a complete fool.

The wave of insecurity takes my breath away. It's abrupt and engulfing, a tidal wave that I haven't felt in a long time. I hate it. I hate it so goddamn much. In the back of my mind, a little voice is telling me that it's not rational. Emory would never sign off on something like that. But it makes a perfect kind of sense. What other reason would someone like Reynolds McAllister be interested in someone like me? Maybe I'm being careless, having all these feelings for him. Maybe it's all a joke.

Maybe I'm delusional, after all.

*There's a way past this, you know...*

The impulse settles over me like a heavy cloud. It's a justification, an excuse. The sad thing is, it's not even hard to rationalize when I go into the bathroom and approach my jewelry box. I open the top and fish out the small drawstring bag inside. There's three pills left—one for tonight, two for tomorrow. I restock from my hidden stashes on Sundays, and lately, I've tried really hard to ignore how small that's probably getting. I drop one pill in my hand and contemplate another. Maybe I should take an extra today, just to get past the hump, the insecurity, to calm myself down. Who could blame me?

I'm shaking the second into my hand when I hear three sharp raps. I jump, the two pills falling out of my hand. Worried that it's my mom, I hastily fish them from the counter and put them back into the bag, locking them away.

But when I get to my door, no one is there.

*Tap-tap, tap.*

As soon as I realize where it's coming from, I know it's Reyn. There's nothing special about the raps to give anything away, but clues so obvious are unnecessary. Somehow, I just... know.

I feel him.

He's crouching right outside my window, but it's too dark to make out anything but the ambiguous shape of him. "Hey, it's me, don't freak out," he whispers when I've wrenched my window open.

I watch, stunned as he climbs inside. He's wearing a loose pair of gray sweatpants and the same Preston Prep football shirt he'd been wearing the day we got our tattoos. He gets inside easily, shirt lifting when he reaches up to grab the window, swinging a leg inside. I catch a quick flash of dark ink disappearing beneath his waistband and my fingers itch to touch it.

Once inside, he quietly slides the window closed and turns to me, dusting his hands off on his thighs. His face spreads into a wolfish grin, cheeks dimpling. "Hey."

"How did you get up here?" The awe in my voice is apparent and I peer around him to see out the window.

"You've got that little overhang just below the window that covers the side door. I pulled myself up." He inches forward, and his hands fit perfectly on my waist, thumbs sweeping gently beneath my shirt. From here, his eyes look tired, a little bit strained. At my incredulous smile, some of that falls away, softens.

"You pulled up?" I gape at him. "Twelve feet?"

He shrugs and tightens the grip on my waist—my bare waist. I'm still not wearing pants, something I slowly realize as my heart rate shifts from shocked to...well, something nervous and undeniably wanting.

He ducks his head to press a slow, soft kiss to my neck. "I may have been the pull-up champion of Dixon Hall for three years running." His kiss travels up the spot below my ear, sending a shiver down my spine. "Had no idea it'd be so useful."

I accept his kiss enthusiastically, our mouths parting, tongues gliding against one another. He tastes like warmth, a lot like how he smells. Something complicated and new and undeniably masculine. His hands drag down my hips, fingertips skating across my outer thighs so gently that it's as if they're merely flirting with the idea of touch.

I break from the kiss with a sharp inhale, feeling too exposed. "I'm glad the training paid off, but..." I bite down on my lip when he noses behind my ear, breathing me in. Scared of putting him off, I reluctantly ask, "Can you give me a second? I was just cleaning up in the bathroom."

Luckily, he takes it in stride, pressing a deep, "Sure," into my neck. His fingers drag as he steps away, eyes dropping to my legs. "Want me to lock the door?"

My throat clicks with a loud swallow. "Yeah, good idea."

I close myself in the bathroom, and sure enough, my reflection is telling me what I already know. My face is beet red, eyes a little bit wild around the edges.

I brush my teeth and look down at the white bikini panties, a little horrified there's nothing sexier in my drawer. All those trips to the mall with Sydney and never once did it cross my mind to buy something to be prepared.

Not like I'd ever have been prepared for Reynolds McAllister. In my bedroom. On a Friday night. With my parents downstairs.

I reach in my drawer and tug on a pair of soft cotton shorts, unhooking my bra. I take one glance back at the jewelry box, nerves craving a hit of something to chill me out, but I know one thing for sure.

Whatever is about to happen with Reyn, I want to be able to remember it. Every little detail.

I walk into the room and find him sitting on the cushioned chair by the window. Distantly, I'm surprised that he's not on the bed. But it's hard to focus on that when his sharp green eyes drink me in, roaming from head to toe and lingering heavily on my thighs. The tattoo is completely visible in these shorts.

"Is this okay?" he suddenly asks, gaze fixing to mine. "I know I just barged in. I probably should have texted you first."

"No, it's good! Great, really." Quieter, I admit, "I wanted to see you."

He smiles, fingers tapping the arm of the chair. "Yeah, I wanted to see you too."

I step in front of him. "I just...I'm not sure if I'm ready for..." I make a gesture that's meant to encompass the very concept of sweaty sexual relations, but instead is just a spastic jerking. "*That*. Yet."

His forehead creases—for about three seconds. Apparently, my gesture was informative enough, because his face goes slack in realization. "I didn't come here to have sex, Vandy." His voice is low, and despite his words, he barely has to reach forward to brush his fingertips over my legs. "Just what kind of guy do you take me for?"

I give a nervous smile. "The kind of guy who has a lot more experience than me?"

His hand drops, fingertips dragging away. "Not with this," he says, eyes boring into mine. "It's not like I've exactly had an active dating life. I was trapped in a school with three hundred other guys."

*Dating life*, my brain screams.

I relax, nudging him with my knee. "That's a good reason not to date."

"Yeah," he reaches out and grabs my hand, pulling me close, "but there were other reasons, too."

He wants me to ask and, like a fool, I do. "Like what?"

"Like," he says slowly, looking up at me through his lashes, "this girl I knew was still back home. I hurt her pretty bad, and I wasn't going to be satisfied until I saw she was better." He lifts my hand to his lips, and he kisses me on the back of the knuckles. "And then when I saw her, suddenly I knew why I'd waited. She was even prettier than before. Funny. Determined. Sexy." He drags me, stunned, between his knees, hands stroking my legs. "I'm not here to pressure you, V. I just want to hang with you, and if we can't do it in public, we're going to have to make our own opportunities."

His left hand trails from my thigh to my hip, pushing at the hem of my shirt. He stares at my stomach and rubs his fingers over the numb ridge of the scar. The surgeries left me with little feeling there, too much nerve damage, but I can feel his touch, the warmth of his breath as he kisses the puckered skin.

"Tell me about it."

I swallow, already knowing my voice is thick with unshed tears. "You were there." I wasn't expecting him. Not like this. Not sweet and soft and the way he looks at me, like I'm something special. *Chosen*. I hope he understands that the wetness in my eyes isn't bitterness or hurt. It's an ache, for sure.

But a good one.

"Not really." He shakes his head and looks up at me, eyes brilliant and sure. "Not for what happened after. In the hospital, at home. I want to know." His voice is so soft that I can hardly make out the words, "I need to know."

I reach out to touch his cheek, cupping it in my palm. "Are you sure?"

I ask, because it's ugly and I know it'll stab him in the heart, but he nods and says, "I'm sure."

I take a deep breath. "Will you tell me about yours, too?" I ask, thumb rasping against the stubble covering his jaw. "Where you've been?"

"If you want."

"I do," I say, taking the hand he has on my hip. I tug, reluctantly explaining, "Eastside's softball bleachers weren't very friendly to my back. Can we just..." I nod toward the bed.

His eyes follow and he nods, standing to follow me to the bed. He perches on the edge, untying his shoes, and leaving them there, lined up perfectly, laces tucked inside. "Do your parents come to check on you?"

I watch his gaze ping nervously to the door. "Once I'm in bed for the night, they generally leave me be. How about you? Where's your dad?"

He scoots up against the pillows, stretching out next to me. "God knows." He wedges his arm beneath his head, eyes fixed on my ceiling. "Probably some hot date. How the hell he manages to pull so much trim is beyond me."

"Trim?"

He looks at me. His mouth is pressed into a thin line, but his eyes are smiling. "You know, tail? Pussy?"

"Oh." My face heats, but once his smile finally breaks to the surface, I can't help but bury a laugh into my hands.

He tugs a hand away from my face, dimples shining at me. "You're so fucking cute, sometimes it kills me."

I playfully bat his hand away, but something warm and joyous radiates from the center of my being, and he'd have to be blind to not see it. "The feeling is mutual."

"Good to know," he says, smirking at me. With his arm up behind his head like that, his shirt has risen up the scantest inch.

I ask, "Can I see it?" and reach tentatively toward his stomach.

He looks down, realizing what I'm requesting. "Can I see yours?"

Mine isn't exactly hidden, but I lift my knee anyway, putting it on display. It's pretty much healed, no longer red around the edges. He lifts himself up on an elbow to look, teeth pulling at his lip as he reaches out to graze a rough fingertip around the ink. He makes a couple of those shiver-inducing loops before his fingers start roaming out a little further, grazing up and down in slow circuits.

He whispers a soft, "Fuck," and then falls back, hand pulling away. "God, that drives me crazy."

"Yeah?" I ask, even though I know it does.

He looks at me, and then down his body, lifting an eyebrow. "Yeah."

The outline of his half-hard erection is so visible through his sweatpants that it makes my mouth part in surprise. Reynolds McAllister is in my bed, with a *boner*. It doesn't even feel real.

"Your turn," I say, reaching for his waistband. He watches, but doesn't stop me, letting me tug it down until the pitchfork is revealed, as if my hand isn't mere inches from the hardening length of him. His tattoo is healed as well as mine, the ink settled in well amongst all his hard muscle. I brush a thumb over it and his stomach flexes, twitching. I push his shirt up a little, revealing more of his toned stomach. It's just crazy really, how perfectly he's cut. I get this crystal-clear vision of myself climbing on top of him, slotting that hardness under his pants right up against my core.

I groan, falling onto my back. "That drives *me* crazy," I confess.

Jesus, when did it get so hot in here?

I feel more than hear his chuckle as he turns on his side, watching me. "Good."

I mirror him, rolling to pillow my hot cheek on my hand. I blow a lock of hair from my face. "Seriously, I've never felt so—" I cut off, not knowing how to explain it without delving deeper. But that's what he wanted, wasn't it? He's looking at me curiously, waiting. "When I was on the pills, I didn't feel stuff like this," I admit.

Gently, he asks, "Like what?" and tucks that piece of hair behind my ear.

"Well, I didn't feel much of anything back then, but especially not..." I have to look away, already cringing. "... horny?"

He puffs a surprised laugh. "*Baby V.*"

I give him a weak shove. "Shut up. Like you don't know the effect you have on girls."

He blinks at me, and if I didn't know better, I'd say he looks almost *bashful.* "I haven't been around girls for a long time."

I remember now how Reyn got all those cut muscles, and my smile slowly bleeds away. I'm almost afraid to know the answer when I ask, "At your school...did they hurt you?"

His forehead creases at the abrupt change of topic. "At Mountain Point?" When I nod, he brushes a thumb over my jaw. "Not in the way you're thinking."

I frown. "Then how?"

He sighs, looking away. "It's not really about rehabilitation there. It's about...scaring us. Telling us that we're nothing, making us feel small, worthless. Tell us that, despite the therapeutic mumbo-jumbo, we *are* defined by our actions. The more you feel like an individual, the more you start feeling rebellious, or falling into your old habits. It's shitty, and a bit of a mind-fuck, but I don't know, it's probably effective for a certain type of kid. Some of those guys made me seem like a fucking do-gooder comparatively, but they didn't know how much damage I'd done. How much penance I owed."

I watch him talk, his face growing into that same stony stillness I've alternately come to love and loathe. "You didn't," I say, capturing his hand in mine. "It was a mistake."

He looks at me again, eyes dark. "Yeah, I did."

I shake my head. "I don't think so."

"Vandy." His gaze flicks across my face; cheeks, mouth, nose, chin. "Your turn."

But suddenly, the thought of telling him makes my stomach hurt. In a small voice, I confess, "I'm scared."

He tilts his head. "Of what?"

"That it'll make you believe what all those people at Mountain Point told you," I admit. "That I won't be able to have this again." I pull his arm around my middle, reluctantly meeting his eyes. "That you'll pull away because you feel guilty and responsible."

"I am guilty, V." He pulls me closer, arm tightening around me. "But that's not going to happen."

I fidget with the sleeve of his shirt. "Promise?"

He presses a kiss to my forehead and holds it there, muttering against me, "Promise."

Quietly, I tell him everything. About the first surgery, and how it was the scariest. How I woke up in recovery alone, and I thought I had died. And then the second surgery, weeks later, and how it'd been painful to recover from and ultimately ineffective, and how blindingly angry I was. Not at Reyn, but at the surgeons, for making all these promises they couldn't keep. For putting me through something so traumatic, for zero gain. Then I tell him about the third, and how it was better after that. The years of PT, the gait training, how slowly I got my strength back. How much work has gone into where I currently am, able to walk without crutches or braces. I tell him about the party Emory threw for me the first time I spent a whole day walking on my own, without any tools to help me, and how he even bought me a cake and balloons. I tell him how high I was through all of it, and how badly I feel about it now, looking back, being unable to muster a fraction of my brother's enthusiasm.

"He was so happy," I remember. "He was happy enough for both of us, I guess."

I hear Reyn's swallow. "Em's a good brother."

"He is," I agree, nestling my head into the curve of Reyn's shoulder. "I'm always caught between never feeling grateful enough and always feeling suffocated by him. It's hard. But I know I'm lucky."

Reyn whispers, "He's going to fucking kill me."

I pull back to look at him, at the dread swirling in his eyes. "Reyn, I can't—" I touch his face, coaxing him to look at me. "I can't keep not living my life just because my family is like this. I can't." My voice is full of an old, secret fear. "It's like every day since the accident, I've faded, and I've just become this ghost of a person. Part of it was the pills, but I know that isn't all of it. A bigger part is just not being allowed to grow into the person I'm supposed to be. It's crushing me."

He looks at me for a suspended moment, gaze moving back and forth between my eyes. He finally sighs, reaching up to cup the back of my head, pressing it back to his shoulder. His voice rumbles beneath my ear. "I didn't say it wouldn't be worth it."

We fall asleep like that, wrapped up in each other, breaths evening out. When I dream, it's just like before—on the floating dock at night, with the fireflies and the calm and the anticipation.

Only this time, I can see Reyn on the shore, silhouetted by the twinkle of lights, watching over me.

# 20

"GET CLEANED UP," Dad says when I walk in the kitchen. I'm dripping with sweat from a morning run that was supposed to be one loop around the neighborhood, but ended up turning into four.

I grab my water bottle off the counter, still breathless. "Any particular reason why?"

"Because we've been invited to watch the Vanderbilt game at the Halls'."

I freeze with the bottle halfway to my mouth. "We've *what*?"

"You know how they are about game day," Dad says, finishing

breakfast as he flips through his mail. It's started stacking up. "They've invited people over. Including us."

"Including *me*?"

I know my father and I resemble one another. The green eyes, the sharp cheekbones. The hint of arrogance and impulsivity. It's a little unnerving to look at him sometimes.

"Specifically you, as a matter of fact. Denise made sure I knew you were welcome." He carries his plate over to the sink. "It's an olive branch. We're going to take it."

What my father doesn't realize is that the branch has not only been extended, but the tree has been climbed. Vandy and I are good —better than good—like, 'slept in the same bed all night for the best sleep I've had in ages' good.

I left before dawn, sneaking out the way I came in, through the window and off the small overhang. I crept back into my house, ignoring the woman's jacket on the coat rack and going for a run instead. I didn't want to lose the feeling from the night before. What it was like to have time with Vandy. To touch her scars. To hold her in my arms. To wake up and watch her sleeping, face placid and soft, and run a careful fingertip over the curve of her delicate cheek bone, unable to fight the awful awareness that I could have destroyed this.

But I hadn't.

She says she's not ready for sex and I'm okay with that. I wasn't as careful with her as I should have been. I won't make that mistake twice.

An hour later, I follow my father into the Halls' house. It's a midday game and we come bearing gifts; a six-pack of locally brewed beer and a bag of organic chips. I scan the room, eyes peeled for my girl, but I don't see her. I do take in the foyer, full of shoes and keys and old mail, and then the formal living room, which looks elaborately unused. It's been a long time since I'd been in this house—at least not through the upstairs window.

Nervous about meeting with the Halls again, I linger in there, looking at all the photos on the mantle. I remember when some of these were taken. Emory, in the eighth grade, holding up an MVP trophy. That year had been crazy, with everyone vying for a good spot in Preston's underclassmen programs. In another, more recent photo, Emory and Vandy are posed for one of those boring professional shots that never quite look natural. It's taken outside, probably by the lake, and it looks warm, bright. Spring maybe, going by the dress she's wearing. Half of Vandy's blonde hair is pulled back, clipped above her ear, and everything about it is picture-perfect. Hands folded neatly on her knee. Shoulders straight. Not a single hair out of place.

Her smile is as flat as her eyes.

She's absolutely stunning, but beneath the pretty face, nice dress, and shiny hair, there's something dark swimming under the surface. The more I look, the more I can spot it in the other recent photos, too.

"Hey dude." Emory startles me, sidling up, following where my eyes just were. He scowls. "I know what you're thinking."

I doubt he does. "You really didn't know?"

His voice drops to a low murmur. "That she was high for most of these? Not really." He gives me a sidelong look that seems a touch defensive. "She'd just been through a lot of difficult shit, dude. It's hard to know what's normal and what's not."

I shake my head. "No, I get it."

There's a roar of laughter from the family room, shattering the stillness, and Emory smiles easily. "So hey, I wasn't sure if you'd come."

I follow him into the kitchen, explaining, "Warren didn't give me much of a choice." I drop the chips on the counter, and from here, I can see my dad giving Mrs. Hall a hug. "But it's okay. I guess it's time to finally break the ice or whatever." Despite my words, my hands feel clammy. I keep rubbing them on my thighs.

He snorts. "I think you did that the other day when Vandy fell asleep at your house."

"Fair point."

He nudges me toward the patio. Once we're outside, I grab a soda out of the cooler and pop the top.

"How are things going with her, anyway?"

I've got the can halfway to my mouth when I freeze. "What do you mean?"

He rolls his eyes. "With the rites, duh. You two have been partnered up so far. I know the tattoo was hard on her, but it sounds like it went okay?"

"Right, yeah." I rub my thumb over the condensation on the can. "She came through like a champ. I told you, she's a lot stronger than she seems."

He bumps his can against mine. "Well, I appreciate you looking out for her. I know things have been tense for you two, but I don't trust anyone else." *Wince.* "And also, you were right."

"About what?"

"About the Devils maybe being good for her. She needed to do something, and she already seems more involved this year. I mean, obviously it may be the fact that she's not using anymore, but she seems invested in school, the club, her newspaper gig." He glances over my shoulder and lifts his chin. "I do wish she'd stop hanging with Sydney so much, though."

I turn to look, seeing Vandy and Sydney in the kitchen. Whatever they're talking about, they both seem tense and look kind of annoyed. My eyes take in Vandy's clingy black sweater and gold pleated skirt slowly. It's easy to notice that she looks well-rested, easier still to notice that she looks hot as hell. She catches my eye and her face instantly flushes. It's enough of a hello for me. Sydney glances my way and greets me with a small, flirty grin.

*Yikes.*

I exhale. "Yeah, I'm not a fan either. She seems pretty hung up on what an amazing friend she's been to you sister, but I'm not sure I get that vibe."

"Nope," Emory agrees. "That girl is all about herself, trust me." When he looks over again, his expression perks up. Aubrey's here.

I watch the way his face changes, realizing, "You really like her, huh?"

"Yeah, I guess I do," he says, straightening his Vanderbilt-gold oxford. "She's way less complicated than Campbell."

I remind him, "That's a pretty low bar, considering Campbell is a controlling bitch."

"She is." He laughs. "Actually, that's one of the things I liked most about her, but I won't lie. It's nice to be around someone who's not scheming world domination all the time."

He claps me on the shoulder and walks through the patio doors and into the kitchen. Aubrey beams when she sees him—seems like everything there is mutual—and he slips his hand around her waist. A spike of bitterness runs through me. What I'd give to walk up to Vandy right now and kiss her hello, mark my territory while everyone watches. *God.* Her parents would flip out. My father would send me back to military school. And Emory? He wants his sister to have a babysitter, not a boyfriend.

I know my place here. The troublemaker. The criminal. The one who isn't good enough. I'm welcome in this house, under supervision. What would they say if they knew I'd spent the night upstairs with their daughter? That she'd had her warm body pressed up against mine? That I'd woken up that morning to her soft thigh thrown over my morning wood?

They'd call Fucking Jerry, that's what they'd do, and it would be the last time I'd see her.

My instinct is to swipe something, quell the impulsive urges that heighten when I'm feeling shitty, but if something goes missing, I'll be the first one they question. Vandy seems semi-tolerant of my habit, but not necessarily in her own home.

Plus, it's not an expensive object I want in my hands.

It's her.

I walk back inside, skirting the crowd forming around the TV. Kick-off just started and Mr. Hall corners me, beer in his hand. His other hand looks like it wants to ruffle my hair, but I'm probably an inch taller than him now. Instead, it lands on my shoulder, heavy and loud in that aggressive way old guys always like. "Little Reyn McAllister! I'm glad you could come. I know you're not a Vandy fan, but it should be a good game."

I give him a smile. "You know, I think as I've gotten older, Vandy has started to grow on me."

He gives a surprised laugh. "Denise will be excited to hear about that."

As he continues to talk, asking me a little about school, some about Mountain Point, and a lot about football, I keep tabs on his daughter across the room. She's standing behind the couch, where Sydney is trying to engage Aubrey in conversation. My girl looks so fucking good in that sweater and skirt, it's killing me to know how close we'd been just six hours ago. That I'd had my hands on those legs, that skin, my mouth on that neck. From here, I can see that she's wearing little black boots with a raised heel, and I'm starting to think she knows how much I love her legs. And fuck, now my dick is getting hard and I'm talking to her dad and, "Excuse me, sir. I, uh, need to use the restroom."

"Go ahead. I need to get focused on the game. I have quite the wager with Mark Bradshaw over the point spread. You know where it is, right?"

I nod and toss my soda can into the recycling bin, but I'm diverted by my dad, who takes to parading me around the circle of clean-cut adults gathered in the family room. It's all artificial, small-talk bullshit that makes me want to punch myself in the face. Everyone here already knows me, but you wouldn't know it by the way my dad keeps gesturing at me with his beer, rattling on about my rushing yards. It's not like he can be genuine, anyway.

*Allow me to reintroduce you to my son! Yes, he is a criminal. We have his juvenile detention release papers framed, right next to his sixth-grade perfect attendance certificate, isn't he swell? Yes, he stole your watch. And your wife's garden gnome. And your daughter's phone—twice, because she's incredibly fucking stupid. He also hasn't spoken to his mother in three weeks. No, she didn't want him. But he's tidy and quiet, and isn't a massive cockblock, so I let him sleep in my house. Don't we look so much alike? If you ever get locked out of your house or car, you should totally give him a call.*

Mark Bradshaw asks, "So what schools are you applying to?"

*Way to lead with the easy questions there, Mark.* I vaguely remember him falling victim to my middle school hood-ornament spree. I'd managed to collect six Mercedes, thee Jags, and my crowning

achievement, one off a classic Rolls Royce belonging to a state sena-
tor. Never got caught. They're still buried in a box at the back of my
closet.

I answer, "I don't think I'm going to apply this year."

My dad whips his head toward me. "What's that mean?"

*Duh*. It means that I have no idea what I'm doing next week, let
alone the rest of my life. "I'll probably just take a year."

My dad barks a cold laugh. "Take a year for *what*?" I give him a
look. *Do you really want to do this in front of all your rich buddies?*
Apparently not. "Well, there's still a lot of time. Why don't you go
check out the spread in the dining room?" The words sound perfectly
casual, but I can tell from the sharpness of his eyes that this conversation has only just begun. Nice selective parental tendencies.

A quick look around tells me Vandy is no longer by the couch, but
Sydney, who's standing between me and that dining room spread,
catches my eye, and gives me a wink. So that's a no on the food, then.

A few moments later, my phone buzzes with a text from Vandy.
It's nothing but two emojis; a tree and a house.

I can't get away from this place fast enough.

It's a little cooler outside, less stifling, and the path into the tree
line stretches out before me like a lifeline. I feel around in my pocket
as I walk, fingers finding the money clip—sadly empty—I'd swiped
from Mark Bradshaw's pocket, easy as pie.

*Mine now.*

When I reach the treehouse, I climb the ladder and pop my head
through the door, searching.

She looks back at me, all wide-eyes and long legs.

"Hey," I say, taking the hand that she's offered me. I don't let go
when we're face to face. "What are you doing out here?" I reach out to
the hem of her sweater, adjusting it just so. She looks even better up
close, the fan of her eyelashes sweeping down when her eyes track
the gesture.

Her smile is soft. "I needed some air. Sydney wouldn't shut up."

"About what?" I abandon the sweater to tuck a strand of hair
behind her ear.

"You, actually." I raise an eyebrow, and she continues, "How hot you are. How off-limits. How she heard you were secretly dating someone and that's why you ditched the post-game party last night." Her cheeks turn red and she looks away. "How she'd like to meet you in the Stairway to Hell and give you the kind of welcome you deserve."

"Oh." I grimace. "That's...a lot."

"*She's* a lot."

"What did you tell her?"

"Nothing." She shrugs, this time reaching out to adjust the hem of *my* shirt. "I said I had to go get more ice from the freezer in the garage and ran out here. I saw you before, with your dad. You looked like you were about to bolt, so I figured I'd give you somewhere to run to."

"I didn't even know I was coming here today." I run a hand through my hair, feeling the last of my agitation slip away. "Did you know about this?"

"You and your dad coming? No." She rolls her eyes. "Well, they told me about ten minutes before you got here. You know, to keep me from 'worrying'."

"Sneak attack, huh? They seem to do that a lot."

"Well, this is a surprise I can handle." Her eyes are stunningly blue, up close like this. I watch as they drop to my mouth. "So, who are you hiding from?"

"Everyone." I hook a finger under her chin, tilting it upward. "Well, everyone but you."

She bites her lip on a smile. "Good."

I snake a hand around her waist, leaning in to quietly confess into her ear, "You've been making me crazy from across the room."

Her breath hitches when my lips graze her soft earlobe. "I know the feeling."

She turns and we kiss slowly and carefully, like maybe we're both wondering if this thing we've got going on still works in the harsh light of day, and the thing is?

It really fucking does.

Whatever this is, it's doing it for me; night, day, any time in-between. Every time we kiss, I think that this hungry, desperate mania for her will start to fade, but it doesn't. Not even close. I can feel it now, this crazy-hot thing sliding through my veins. It's daunting, sensing how much I need to hold myself back, taking this slow when all I want to do is *take.*

"How long do you think we can get away with staying out here?" I ask, my hands sliding over the curve of her ass.

"Long enough to take off the edge?" she replies, and her words come back to me from the night before, about being horny. They'd turned my blood molten then, and the memory does it again, feeding this feral thing inside me. It's still a surprise, knowing that Vandy *has* an edge. Mine is razor sharp and currently trying to stab her in the lower belly.

She places her hands on my chest and pushes me backward. There's an old musty futon that Mr. Hall donated from the attic when they first built this place. Emory and I slept on it a few times when we were kids. My calves hit the edge of the cushion and I fall back, pulling her with me.

She lands in my lap, her legs, her *thighs*, straddling around me. I'm somehow both putty in her hands and so rigid that my bones feel like they could rattle with the slightest movement. She looks me right in the eye when she descends, pressing herself against my cock.

I suck in a measured breath, eyes falling closed. This could be fine for me. Just the weight of her against me, the pressure and the stillness. It's hardly anything, but it's almost enough to topple me right over.

And then this girl rises over me, dragging us together, and my jaw locks with my groan. "*Fuck.*"

She puts her hands on my shoulders and does it again, rocking into me. Her voice is barely a breath. "Is this...?"

I answer by grabbing the back of her neck and slotting our mouths together, licking into the seam of her lips. Her tongue meets mine and she rocks again, the friction so sweet that it has my blood thrumming.

When I was coming home from Mountain Point, I had this idea of what things would be like at this point. I'd be neck-deep in pussy, face buried between someone's legs every weekend, so fucked out by

Sunday that I'd have to sleep the day away. I was sorely disappointed when I couldn't actualize any of it, but now?

Her little punch of breath when she grinds into me, the way her fingers thread through my hair, the heat of her eyes when they open, the softness of her lips.

This is so much better.

I kiss her like I'm drowning, and maybe I am. I try to hold it back, to reel my hands in, but they shove beneath her sweater and run over the soft, warm skin of her back instead. Vandy has the perfect skin there, a long swath of girl-soft smoothness that tempts my fingertips to go higher, lower. She arches her back in response, making a quiet sound into my mouth as she rocks against me.

I freeze when she pulls away, worrying that I've gone too far. But in one swift movement, she peels off the sweater. She sits before me, chest heaving, eyes burning into mine, and I gently finger the strap of her bra. She wears these basic little white things and *holy fuck,* they're hot as hell. It's insane, this isn't the first time I've seen her topless. It isn't even the second time. But it's the first time I've seen it like this, her red flush blooming down the swell of her cleavage, inviting me. She grinds down on me, a move that has to be pure instinct, and I carefully close my palms over her tits, testing.

"Yeah?" I ask, sweeping my thumbs over them. They fit perfectly in my hands—not too big, not too little, just fucking right.

Her eyes fall closed and she exhales, sighing against my touch. "*Yes.*"

That's all I need to push the fabric aside to thumb her hard, pebbled nipples. Her mouth parts on a breathy little gasp when I do. Like a button, every time I touch her, she grinds down harder on me. So responsive that it's driving my hips up, meeting hers in a needy thrust. The action makes her face screw up, like it hurts, but she does it again and again. I move a hand to her thigh and sweep it up, raising her skirt. I want to let her take the lead, but Jesus. She's driving me crazy.

"Does that feel good?" I ask, because I don't want to hurt her. Never again.

She nods, eyes clenched tight.

I touch her chin and force her face to mine. "Does it feel good, V? I need to know."

Slowly, her eyes open, blue blazing back at me. Her words escape in a frantic rush, "It feels so good."

"That's what I want," I tell her, and I can barely recognize the low octave of my own voice. "I just want you to feel good."

I plant a hand on both her hips and drag her against me. I'd give anything to shuck these jeans and coax her into riding me bare and hard. I bet she's wet for me, and the thought alone is enough to make my balls tighten. But she's not there yet. *We're* not there yet. Slow, steady. I am not fucking this up.

But I can make her feel good, and I focus every ounce of energy I have on it. I push the cup of her bra aside and take her into my mouth, licking and sucking on her peaked nipple. She arches into it, fingers threading into my hair and holding me there, no question that this is doing it for her. I hum when she touches me in return, hand pushing my shirt up, fingers teasing the hair below my belly. *Jesus.*

Such a little touch to make me feel so crazy.

I wonder, "Can you come like this?" and tip my face up to hers when she doesn't answer. Vandy isn't very good at holding a conversation when she's like this—chasing, hungry, *horny.* It's like fire in my veins to know this about her, a knowledge that no one else has. "Can you?"

She's looking at me with glazed eyes, hips never ceasing. "Yeah, I think—*yeah.*" And then she asks, "Can...can you?"

I look at her tits, spilling out over her bra, and then at the way her skirt is riding up her thighs, the starkness of her soft skin against the rough denim of my jeans. "Definitely."

Her lips press against mine, wet. Her tongue tangles, hot. Little pants coat me in her breath, and it takes everything not to cave to my instincts. To *take.* It becomes clear that Vandy needs this. That she's desperate for release. I let her ride against me, hips thrusting more and more frantically, and this is *it.* There's no way I'll ever feel this good again, Vandy using my body to chase her own orgasm.

I can feel it approaching in the stutter of her rhythm, the way her legs tremble around me, in the sound she makes, these choked-off little whines against my lips. I guide her hips, working her against my cock, and whisper, "Yeah, that's it," and, "Come on, baby."

Her fingers pinch into my shoulders, like she's holding on as she falls over the edge. I watch as she falls apart, teeth sinking into her lip, brow furled. I sweep the hair from her cheek as she whimpers, and when I press a soothing kiss to her jaw, she pushes her nose into my temple, body shuddering one last time. The motion of her hips grows less frantic, more controlled. Intentional. Giving instead of seeking.

I'm so close, I push my hands up her skirt and clutch her hips, falling back to look at her. She looks like pure sex. Her eyes are still glazed over, but there's a sharpness in them. Something bright and satisfied. She surprises me like this. I guess I always figured Vandy would be shy and reluctant, but she's shameless and soft here, so willing that it makes my chest clench.

"God, look at you." I wet my lips as I take her in, her skirt riding up around my wrists as I drag her against me. She doesn't even play it up—doesn't even need to. She looks into my eyes and my thumbs sweep inward, grazing the softness of where her legs meet her body, dangerously close to finding out just how wet she is, and that's it.

My hips buck forward and I groan as the hot, sticky release spreads inside my boxers.

I take her face in my hands and rub a thumb over her puffy bottom lip. "You okay?" I didn't miss the way her leg shook there at the end, even though I was doing most of the work. The realization that all that trembling from before could have been something *bad* startles the shit out of me.

"You don't have to ask me that." She swallows, eyes boring into mine. "Please don't... don't treat me like that, okay? Like everyone else does, like I'm fragile. I'm a big girl, Reyn. If we're going to do this, I need you to know that."

"I hear you," I say, understanding that this is what she needs from me. The one person that treats her like an adult. "Just don't ever..." Only I don't quite know how to say it. How to ask her not to push herself too far because she's afraid that I can't handle facing the truth of her injuries. I try, "You can tell me, if there's something you can't—I mean, something that's hard for you to..."

*My fault*, my brain screams. *I did it.*

I'm the reason I have to ask this, in every single way, and it makes my stomach roil.

Luckily, she understands what I need from her. "I know my limits, don't worry." If I was afraid of pissing her off, then I'm pleasantly surprised when she gives me a soft smile. "I told you last night, didn't I? That I wasn't ready for sex."

"Right." I do my best to tamp down the sudden sick feeling. Kind of shitty, if I'm being honest, wanting her to be open and honest, and then not being able to handle it. "Sorry."

She grins. "As long as we keep doing things like that, I'll give you a pass."

A surprised laugh bursts from my chest and I right her bra, fingers lingering. "You're fucking gorgeous, you know."

Now, she gets bashful, exhaling a dubious, "Pshhh."

"Really," I insist, fingers dragging down her chest, stomach, landing on the scars there. "All of you." If I were in that Devil confession circle right now, my biggest sin, my darkest secret, would be how touching that scar makes me feel. Because there's anger and shame, a regret so acute that it burns the back of my throat, but there's something else, too. It's possessive and unsettling, looking at this mark I've made on her. No one else would understand, but Vandy probably would. It's not that I've marked her with this pain, it's that no one but the two of us really gets it. No one else can ever know what it was like, that night on that road, waiting for help. Something like that—those moments are what define you. Shape you.

And I was a part of hers.

I know it's fucked up. It's something I try not to look too closely at.

I watch as she finds her sweater, pulling it over her head. I help her tug it down, covering up all that skin. I just came my brains out, but when she tugs my shirt down, her knuckles grazing low on my belly, my dick is thinking that it's already down for another go.

Never done until it goes twice.

"Oh, I brought this," she says, clambering off my lap. I reach out to steady her waist when she wobbles, but she waves me away. "It didn't look like you were able to eat." She pulls a plate from the shelf, setting it on my lap.

It's a little hard to ignore the mess happening inside my boxers, but when I pull the towel off the plate, it's a near thing. "Fuck." *Yes.*

"I remember how much you used to like cornbread," she says simply, dropping beside me. She looks blissed out, the good sort of tired. "Mom was totally laughing at me because it didn't gel with the spread, like there's ever a bad time for cornbread."

I already have a mouthful of it when I realize, "You made this for me?"

She blushes, eyes narrowing playfully. "I made it because cornbread is good. But knowing how much you liked it *may* have provided some of the motivation." She lets out this airy, carefree laugh as I shove it into my face. "Plus, it was nice waking up with some energy."

I admit, "I ran like four miles more this morning." Part of it was that Fucking Jerry was nowhere to be seen—must be on the afternoon shift today—but a bigger part of it was just waking up well-rested.

"I may have seen some of those," she says, eyes sliding to mine.

*Christ*, a few more looks like that and I might start adding to the mess in my boxers. I keep eating instead, watching Vandy extend her leg, stretching. She reaches out to grab her toes, exhaling as her leg flexes.

I swallow painfully. "Are you—"

"Yes, I'm okay." She huffs, eyes rolling. "It's just like this sometimes. After PT, or a long day of walking at school, it gets a little weaker. It doesn't hurt, I just want to make sure I have range of motion for when I climb down the ladder. Stop freaking out."

"I'm not," I lie, eyes tracking as she massages the back of her thigh. "Can I help?"

"Reyn." Her voice is sharp with frustration, but when our gazes lock, her face softens. "Sure." I set the plate aside when she puts her foot on my knee, propped back on her hands. "Just push against my toes, make it flat, okay?"

I nod, clutching the bottom of her boot in one hand, and the toe in the other, flexing it. She pushes against the resistance. I watch her for signs of pain, but there aren't any. She does this for a few minutes, alternating between reclining back and bending over her knee, stretching the muscles. After a few of these passes, she goes to take her foot away, but I stop her, running my hands up her leg.

She sighs when I reluctantly dig my fingers into the muscles of her calf, doesn't protest when I sweep them up to her thigh. "That's good," she says, face going slack. I go higher and then back, to the place she was massaging before, and she groans, "*God*. Right there."

When she opens her eyes and meets my gaze, I think maybe she understands what it means to me, being able to do this. I can't fix what I did. I can't fix *her*. But making it better, even in this tiny, inconsequential way, is like a balm to the burn of that truth.

"Reyn?" The dread pooling in her eyes makes me go still. "Can you promise me something?"

I don't even need to think. "Anything."

She watches me watch her, and I don't know what this is, the heaviness here, but I know that this is important. "Whatever this is or isn't, just... Not Sydney, okay?" Her voice is a small, quiet thing. "Never Sydney."

My head snaps back when I realize what she's saying. "I'm not interested in Sydney."

She looks away. "I don't think she cares."

It's obviously ridiculous, but it doesn't matter. I knead my fingers into her muscles and it's easy to say, "Never Sydney." I wait for her to meet my eyes again. "Promise."

I wish she didn't look so relieved. I wish she wasn't sitting here thinking of what this *isn't*. I wish I could tell her that she's my girl and have that mean something beyond these fleeting secret meetings.

But I can't.

Minutes later, I wait at the bottom of the ladder. If I can't be anything more to her than this, then at least I can catch her if she falls.

# 21

VANDY

SO THIS IS what a walk of shame feels like.

Not that I feel shame, because I feel a lot of things—good, satisfied, happy, and kind of boneless—but shame isn't among them.

Nevertheless, having to collect myself and walk back down to the house in broad daylight without anyone noticing is definitely a new experience to me. So is the fact my panties are soaked.

God, that was epic.

Sure, it was just a dry-hump, but it was my first dry-hump and it was with Reynolds McAllister, of all people. Talk about starting from the top. And it wasn't done out of some convoluted situation, or after too many shots, or with any hint of regret. Reyn, I've realized, actually *likes* me. I knew it when we were together in my room last night, and I definitely knew it just now, watching his face flush with desire, his jaw going slack as he came beneath me. I'd seen that look before when he pleasured himself in his room, but this was different. Just for me. I'm the one who made him fall apart. *I* did that.

No, I don't feel shame. I feel a little proud, though.

He left the treehouse first, face twisted in a grimace, telling me he had to go change. He didn't take the path down the hill, instead taking the long way around to his house by cutting through another neighbor's yard. I spend the walk down the hill smoothing my hair and making sure my skirt is aligned. I'm at the edge of the driveway when I see Jerry's blinking yellow lights. As I get closer, I realize that the person standing spread-eagle, palms flat against the top of the cart, is none other than Reyn.

*What the hell?*

I storm across the yard. They must both hear the scrape-pull of my steps at the same time, because they look over in tandem. Reyn's expression goes from annoyed to something darker, that storm cloud passing over his sharp features.

Jerry's shoulders ease when he sees me, obviously unconcerned about my presence. "Nothing to worry about Miss Hall, just caught this boy trespassing."

"Trespassing?" I say, not trying to keep the incredulousness out of my voice. "What are you talking about?"

"I caught him red-handed, climbing the Reed's fence." He focuses back on Reyn, hand shoving his head down. "Empty your pockets, *boy*." I hate how he says that, like Reyn is just some juvenile scumbag. Like he's *less*. I hate even more the way Reyn just takes it. He trains his eyes on the hood of the cart and just stands there, scowling.

He looks embarrassed.

"He wasn't trespassing," I hotly insist, hoping I can put him off. God only knows what Reyn has in his pockets. Possibly something from my house. "He was with me."

Reyn's eyes shoot up to mine, head shaking slightly.

"With you?" Jerry chuckles. "I doubt that a sweet girl like you would spend time with a punk like him."

A streak of fur races across the front yard. "He—he was helping me find my cat."

Jerry's eyes narrow. "Your cat."

"Yes." My heart hammers. I don't know why I'm so nervous. I guess because Reyn is on the line and Jerry has such a hard-on for busting him. He always has, ever since we were kids, but these days it's worse. Maybe it's the higher stakes. Maybe it's that Reyn is technically a legal adult now, and Jerry is free to handle him like that, rough him up. It makes me hot and angry. "Firefly got out during our football party and Reynolds was helping me find him."

"And you thought it was okay to go into the Reed's yard to search for a cat?" His words are skeptical, but I can see the deflation in his eyes. He knows his opportunity to bust Reyn is slipping right through his fingers.

Reyn gives a tight shrug. "Cats don't understand the laws of property lines."

I add, "Why don't I just go and give Mrs. Reed a chat? She'll tell you it's fine." They both know I'm right. No one around here would be anything less than perfectly hospitable and courteous to Vandy Hall.

Jerry assesses the two of us. He, like everyone else around here, knows all about our history and the accident. Because of that, he probably thinks he knows what we are to one another. After all, why would Vandy Hall falsely vouch for the boy who hurt her *so terribly*? She wouldn't. I can tell that's what he decides. "Fine. If Miss Hall says you were helping her, then I believe it." He grabs Reyn by the shoulder and lurches him back, away from the cart. I can tell from the way Reyn holds himself that the motion is rough and jarring. A pathetic attempt at intimidation. "But you just stay on your own property from now on, is that clear?"

"Crystal," Reyn grinds out, meeting Jerry's gaze directly.

The security guard climbs back into his cart. He gives me a look. "The next time your cat goes missing, call me. There's no need to put yourself in an uncomfortable situation."

I open my mouth to speak, but Reyn's hand tugs at the back of my sweater. It doesn't matter anyway. Jerry's already zipping down the road away from us, off to terrorize someone else.

I face Reyn. "*God*, he's such a—"

"Douchebag. I know." He takes a deep breath. He still won't meet my eyes. "Well, I need to change, and you have a party to get back to."

I nod but grab his arm and say, "You know that's not true, right? I don't feel uncomfortable with you. I never have, even that ni—"

"I know," he says sharply, not letting me say it all the way. Quieter, he adds, "I know you don't, V. Thanks." He walks away and I stand there watching, not knowing what to say.

Disappointed, I walk toward my own house, stopping to pick up Firefly on the way. He's pissed about all the people being inside, getting in his space. I carry him into the kitchen and drop him in the laundry room, shutting the door behind him. When I turn, Emory is waiting for me.

I freeze. *Shit*. Did he see what happened outside? Does he know I've been missing? Once again, I run my hands over my hair and tug at my sweater. He gives me a weird look.

"Where were you?"

"Oh, I uh," I give an ambiguous wave toward the window. "I was just outside with Firefly."

His mouth forms a line. "I've been looking for Reyn. Have you seen him?"

I decide to tell some of the truth, admitting, "Jerry was giving him a hard time out front."

"What?" His eyes widen and he starts toward the door. "That fucking prick."

I grab him. "No, it's fine. I vouched for him and Jerry let it go."

"You did?"

"Sure," I say, my stomach twisting anxiously. "Isn't that what you do for another Devil?"

"Yeah, actually, it is." His expression smoothes. "I'm not saying Reyn never did anything wrong, but it's hard for him, you know? He just has this need to take things that aren't his."

I fight a smile. "Yeah, I do know."

"Well, I needed to talk to you, too. I just found out Sebastian is in a fight tonight. Seems semi-organized. Some dick from Northridge is starting a bunch of shit with the Preston crowd, so I thought maybe we could go as a group. Watch that kid get his ass handed to him."

My eyebrows shoot up. "Go to an illegal fight?"

He shrugs. "It's not like any of us have clean hands these days. I know it's not something you'd normally do, so you don't have to. I just thought it'd be cool for all of us to have his back."

"It is," I say. "I think it's a cool idea."

"Awesome." He gives me a grin. This is new for us, doing things together—as equals, not just Emory looking out for me. "Let me go find Reyn and tell him." He jerks his thumb toward the main room. "You go figure out how to ditch Sydney, because this shit is for Devils only."

I nod, and watch my brother head out the side door. There's a swell in my chest at the words, *Devils only*, a foreign feeling of finally belonging somewhere, with other people. I glance at my friend across the room. It sucks I have to cut her out of this. She'd absolutely flip over it. But there have been too many times she's left me out, and like Emory said, this is for Devils only.

And I, like the tattoo on my leg says, am a Devil.

"How did you find out about this?" Afton asks when we meet up in the dark, gravel parking lot on the other side of town. She's wearing jeans with a wide leg and a tank with lots of straps. She looks like a bad ass. I check out the other girls—they're also dressed appropriately for the night. Jeans. Boots. Sexy tops. They all look like fashion models.

I glance down at my sweater and skirt—different from the one earlier today, but just as prim and proper—and immediately feel out of place. See? This is why I need Sydney. She wouldn't have let me go to an underground fight looking like a massive dork.

"I keep up with Heston," Emory says, tugging on his jacket. He stretches his arm over Aubrey's shoulder and pulls her close. "He told me he'd be here tonight, and since it was actually planned ahead of time, that I should come."

"What about the rest of us?" Carlton asks. "Is it going to be a problem for a whole contingent from Preston to show up?"

Afton nods. "Especially a group that would probably never hang around one another if we weren't in a secret club together."

Even though no one is looking at me, I feel like that comment was a direct hit.

"We're supporting him," Elana says, defensively, "and no one gets to determine who we hang out with."

"Yeah," Ben says, reaching into his pocket and pulling out a roll of cash, "and some of us are here for other reasons. I'm betting on Sebastian to win."

Caroline asks, "What are the odds?" and the two of them start off toward the dirt path, trading numbers. Carlton removes a cooler from the trunk of his car. He opens it and Elana and Afton both take a beer. Emory grabs the other side of the cooler and they carry it down the path.

"What is this place anyway?" I ask. We're in a wooded area off one of the city parks. Lights glow through the trees, but there's not a lot of traffic in the distance. This place is deserted and quiet—or would be, if not for the couple dozen cars that litter the lot.

"You've never been here?" Tyson asks. I shake my head. "It's the old water-works building. It's been abandoned for decades. Now all that's left are the derelict remains."

"Everyone comes here," Georgia declares, which makes it only that much more obvious how sheltered I am. "There's a bunch of walls to graffiti, people build bonfires, smoke a lot of weed."

"Skateboarders," Carlton adds. "All those empty pools."

"Come on," Tyson says, nodding toward the path. "It's pretty cool."

Apparently, he had to lie to his girlfriend to get here tonight. I know the feeling. I told Sydney I had a headache and wanted to just crash early. We're technically speaking again, but it's awkward and strained. It's hard to forget the way she called me delusional, and even harder to tolerate all of her slavering over Reyn.

If nothing else, at least I have his promise.

As everyone walks toward the building, the object of my thoughts appears in my periphery.

I spot his Jeep and turn to Tyson. "Yeah, I'll be there in a second. I just remembered that I need to put something in the car."

Tyson waves and he and Georgia walk off toward the others. I hold back, eyeing Reyn, who's leaning against the side of his car. He's wearing a black leather jacket and a clean pair of jeans, and I can't help but think, *Damn*. I was *on* that. He watches the others get a few feet away before pushing off the car and walking over.

He looks in a better mood than he had after the Jerry incident, at least. His features still have a touch of that stony darkness, but his eyes are soft as they take me in. "Hey."

"Hi," I reply, wanting to reach out and touch literally any part of him. We're in uncharted territory. Public, but not public. My brother approves of us being Devils together, but beyond that...

Emory's distant shout shatters our stare. "Are you two coming?" We both turn to the sound. He's waving a hand in the air, suspending it there in the universal gesture for 'what gives?'

Reyn takes in a slow breath, muttering, "Fuck, I thought people keeping tabs on me was bad. He has a gorgeous girl right there and he's worrying about you."

"Welcome to my world," I reply with a smile. I can't get mad. I'm here and he's here. It's not like I'm a big fan of PDA anyway. Yuck. I've had to sit through too much of that in my life with both Sydney and Emory.

I start down the hill, following the others who are already in a line at a makeshift entrance. Absurdly, there's a fee to get in, ten dollars a head.

"Who gets the money?" I wonder.

Over his shoulder, Tyson says, "The winner, duh."

"So basically, we're giving this guy money, and it's entirely possible that it'll go to the person who kicks Sebastian's ass. That doesn't *seem* very supportive." Not that a Wilcox of all people particularly need money.

Emory hands the burly guy a stack of twenties and points down the line of us. "These ten are with me."

He nods and waves us past. The scene unfolds as we get closer. Lanterns light up the shells of old buildings that co-mingle with nature, roots and vines growing over the cement walls. Spray-paint covers everything, and I feel like I've entered a magical, secret world. It even smells different here, musty and astringent, kind of like gasoline and cigarette smoke. It's also a bit crowded, which is the worst environment for someone with a leg like mine. When I was first hurt and having all the surgeries, people were really nice. I got free tickets to the Taylor Swift concert and the Atlanta United games, but I didn't have to walk. I was still in a wheelchair back then. Here, I have to fight against the uneven terrain. With the dubious exception of Preston's dining hall on pizza day, it's been a long time since I've been to something with this kind of crowd, and I feel panic tightening in my chest. What happens if we need to get out of here quickly? What if someone gets pissed I'm taking too long?

From the tattoos and piercings and dyed hair, the whole group looks a little temperamental. These kids are *not* from Preston Prep. I doubt they're even from Northridge. These are the kinds of kids who just go wherever they can find trouble.

I fight to take a breath and absently feel my pockets for a stray pill. I know I didn't bring any, but maybe? I pat for back pockets that aren't even there—this is a skirt, duh—and feel fingers hooking over my waistband. I look over my shoulder and Reyn is there, warm against my back. My anxiety instantly dissipates. I'm not here alone.

"Sorry I'm holding us up."

He touches my hand. "Never apologize for that."

It's empowering to hear him say that. "I won't."

"Also?" his fingers graze the back of my thighs, mouth moving close to my ear. "Keep wearing these skirts. They're making me crazy, in a very, very good way."

I shiver at the feel of his breath against the shell of my ear. "Oh, I know."

His expression morphs, from sexy and in-control, to stunned. Suddenly, I'm less regretful about this outfit.

We arrive at a clearing, the grass tamped down. The foundation of an old building marks the ring, a large, open expanse of concrete framed by a low retaining wall. We find the others staked out close to the edge, sipping beer and huddled together. Talking. Laughing. I sidle up to the group and Reyn takes his place beside me, propping his elbows on the wall. Unlike me, he looks totally in his element here, the line of his long, lean body curved almost lazily. I notice the other people—the non-Preston people—eying him.

Carlton offers him a beer, but he shakes his head. "I'm driving."

Carlton shrugs at this and pops the top to drink it himself.

I confess, "I've never seen two guys really fight before," and Reyn turns to look at me. "I mean, on TV, sure. But not in real life." Even when we were younger, back when they'd get into scraps with the other neighborhood boys, Emory would send me away before anything physical happened.

"I've never been to one of these," Reyn says, nodding into the 'ring'. "But it's all the same, probably. Testosterone overload. Posturing. A bunch of circling. Only like three actual blows before someone comes to break it up."

Elana adds, "And they take off their shirts."

"Yeah, what's with that, anyway?" Georgia asks, squinting into the distance. "Have you noticed that guys always start undressing when they fight?"

Reyn gives her a blank look. "It's so the other guy will have less to grab onto."

"Yeah," Ben adds, "you want to be uncatchable."

"Sweaty and slippery," Afton laughs.

Emory leans over the wall, clearly having heard the debate. "It's like when girls fight. They always put their hair up and take out their earrings."

"I don't know." Georgia shrugs. "Seems kind of sexy to me." She looks instantly embarrassed about voicing this though, face going pink.

Aubrey raises her beer in agreement. "Hell yeah, it is!" Elana bumps the necks of their bottles together in solidarity.

"Well, well, well," comes a voice from behind us. We all turn in tandem to see Heston Wilcox ambling up to our little group, tall and handsome, cigarette between his fingers. "All the degenerates are here, I see." He and his brother favor one another, sort of. They both have strong, striking features. But where Heston oozes privilege, Sebastian gives off a darker, more frenetic vibe.

Elana makes a disgusted sound. "If you're here, I know that's true."

"Just coming to watch my little bro besmirch our fine family name."

Emory snorts. "I think you do that enough for the both of you."

Heston doesn't seem bothered by this, running his gaze over all of us. "This is a weird little group. Aren't you that mathlete nerd?" Caroline flicks a pigtail over her shoulder and ignores him, but he's already moved on. "Shackleford. Wade. Riggins. Holt shit." His eyes stutter when they reach Reyn. "Sticky-fingers McAllister? I thought you were in prison or something."

Reyn gives him a look that's dripping with disdain. "Military school."

Heston lets the chill of Reyn's voice pass without mention. "Didn't realize they'd released you back into society."

"How's college?" Afton asks pointedly, and I use the veil of my hair to hide a grin. It really is pretty pathetic of him, still hanging around the high school crowd.

"Good," he says a little stiffly. If anyone thought Heston would suffer real consequences for what he'd done, they didn't understand the power of his family. He pulls out a notebook and a bag, and asks, "Okay, who's putting money down? The bets so far are on first blood, KO, and winner. Street fight rules, first one down loses."

"You're the one taking bets?" Ben asks, looking about as uncomfortable as I feel. It seems like Heston isn't just taking bets. It seems like he's the one *organizing* it.

"Yep." Heston taps the notebook. "Personally, I've got three grand on the Northridge kid to win, but a grand on Bass drawing first blood. Kid's all temper, no strategy."

Emory gapes at him. "You're betting against your own brother?"

Heston shrugs. "Why not?"

"Because he's your brother!"

"So?" Heston takes some money from Carlton, who glares as he puts it on Sebastian to win. "Doesn't mean he's not a twat."

Emory shakes his head. "Dude, that's fucked up."

It's beyond fucked up. Heston doesn't think Sebastian can win, but he's still willing to make sure he fights?

Heston's eyes suddenly land on me. "Not all of us can have a sweet little thing like Vandy as a sibling. Finally let the princess out of the castle, huh? Who'd you let down your hair for, sweetheart?" He reaches out, like he's going to touch my hair, and I can feel Reyn stiffening beside me, radiating tension. I duck out of the way before his fingers make contact and he clucks. "Aw, don't be like that."

Emory barks a sharp, "Back the fuck off, Heston," but he just smiles at me.

"Don't sweat it. Baby V and I have a whole rapport."

I recoil, snapping, "No, we don't. And don't *ever* call me that." My neck prickles in sudden, scorching anger. Only one person here is allowed to call me Baby V, and it's certainly not Heston Wilcox. I've always hated him most, and not just on account of our 'rapport'. Reynolds might have gotten Emory in trouble, but friends like Heston? They made Emory *mean*. I know Heston was the one behind the vandalism about Micha last year. Well, everyone knows, because Hamilton Bates beat the shit out of him for it. Too bad I couldn't have been a spectator to *that* fight.

Heston's grin turns predatory. "Sure, we do. Remember? The Christmas party?"

Emory's eyes shift suspiciously between us. "What the fuck does that mean?"

God, what an *ass*.

He thinks he has something over me, is the thing. He thinks I'm scared, that I'll stand here and let him look at me like that. He thinks I'll back down.

I don't.

I look Heston right in the eye when I tell Emory, "It means that he sold me a bottle Oxy last year." Heston's face goes slack at my easy admission.

Emory pushes off the wall, face hard and stormy. "Did he now?"

Heston recovers quickly, giving a casual shrug. "She was basically begging me, bro. You know what they say about friends in need. I was just doing her a solid."

"By selling my little sister narcotics?"

He gestures to my leg. "She said she was hurting."

Emory looks at me, but I can't lie. That's all true. "Your scene's gotten real old, Heston."

"And what's your scene now, exactly?" Heston gestures to the lot of us. "Sluts, nerds, druggies, jocks, and delinquents?"

Reyn steps in front me. "You say that like it's any different from before."

Heston's eyes move to Reyn, giving him a slow, aggressive onceover. "Hey, at least the Devils were good at what we did."

We all share a quick look, and in that moment, I know we're thinking the same thing.

*We still are.*

Emory pushes a stack of money into Heston's chest. "Put that on your brother to win. Unlike you, he can actually hold his own in a fight." Ben throws in a couple hundreds, Caroline tosses in her own stack, and even Afton manages to produce some money from the inside of her bra. Suddenly, the *new* Devils are in for a pretty penny on Sebastian winning this thing.

Reyn flings his own wad at Heston. "Northridge kid for first blood." Some of the others frown at this, but I understand instantly what he's doing.

"Your daddies' loss," Heston says before walking away.

Emory meets my gaze, something firm and annoyed in his eyes, and I know what it looks like—like I've been accosting his friends for drugs. But that's not really how it went down. Heston had approached *me*, offering me one. I just asked for more.

"Em—"

He shakes his head at me. "Later."

My stomach churns uneasily at the brush-off and I turn away, back to the ring.

Reyn assumes his earlier position, but ducks his head, trying to meet my eyes. "Hey."

"It's not like how he made it sound," I insist.

Reyn just says, "I know," and bumps me with his shoulder. "Want to watch him lose a grand?"

I look at him, something unwinding in my chest at the sight of his dimpled grin. "Definitely."

SEBASTIAN LOOKS different when he walks up and takes off his shirt—to Elana's delight. He's still handsome, but his face is blank and hard as he tucks the shirt into his back pocket, letting it hang there. He keeps shifting his shoulders, wiry muscles rippling beneath his tanned flesh. He's restless and agitated, but most of all he looks scary as hell.

I can see the pitchfork tattoo placed neatly on his chest.

The Northridge guy is bigger, without a doubt. His arms are huge and he looks a couple inches taller. I chew nervously on my lip as they watch each other, and it starts exactly like Reyn had said. Posturing, circling.

People are pressing closer now, and it's louder. The whole crowd is charged with adrenaline, pushing and pressing closer to the ring. I don't know if it's some kind of blood lust, or something more feral, but it's triggered my biggest fear; not being able to move quickly if I need to. I can feel the crowd up against my back and it makes me feel like Sebastian looks—twitchy and sweaty.

An arm wraps around my waist, making me jerk in surprise, but I look over and realize that it's just Reyn. He's not looking at me, but he presses closer, muttering, "I've got you. Just look ahead, okay?" I nod, trying not to focus so much on the press of people at my back. When Sebastian circles closest to where we're all standing, Reyn raises his voice. "You get how this betting thing works, right?"

Playing along, I stutter, "Ah, no—not exactly."

"If he wins and doesn't draw first blood, his brother will be out some serious money."

Sebastian goes still only for a split second, long enough to tilt his head toward us, and both of us know that he heard.

I say, "Oh," but it's lost in the frenzy of the first punch being thrown. Sebastian's head snaps to the side, but he easily swerves away. He doesn't even look like he needs to shake it off. I wince, knowing that mine and Reyn's little stunt had given the Northridge guy an opening.

Despite that, Sebastian is grinning—if you could call the tight, feral thing on his face anything of the sort. His lips are pulled back, eyes burning, and his teeth are stained red with blood.

I stiffen in anticipation of the next blow, because maybe we hadn't distracted Sebastian after all. Now that the other guy has drawn first blood, Sebastian goes all-in, fists flying, feet moving. This part, at least, is nothing like Reyn had said. The blows keep coming. No one tries to stop them.

Between blows, the Northridge guy gets in a solid hit, and the crack of his knuckles against Sebastian's temple makes me rear back in alarm, hands coming up to cover my eyes before I can see him fall.

Reyn's voice is warm and soft in my ear. "He's alright, just rung his bell a bit. Still on his feet."

Despite that, I can only peek through my fingers to watch as Sebastian retaliates, looking slightly less agile than before, but no less full of rage. I have no idea what Heston was talking about before, about his brother being all temper and no strategy. Sebastian's fists land every time, and when he grabs the guy by his hair, bringing his face down into his knee, it's such a precise, practiced motion that it barely looks like it takes any effort at all.

Even though I want him to win, it still hurts to watch the other guy get pummeled. I have to turn my face into Reyn's shoulder, away from the blood and the sickening crunch of bones and flesh. It's nothing like it is on TV. This is painfully human, what's happening here. Like sacks of angry meat banging around.

I might be sick.

Reyn spits a low curse, hand coming up to cradle the back of my head. "Em! I'm taking her out."

I don't hear what Emory says in reply, but I feel Reyn's hands clamp around my hips. He pulls me close and his football player physique plows through the crowd, not stopping until he gets us away from everyone. The fresh air feels good against my hot cheeks, but my stomach's still churning.

"Hey," he says once we stop, sweeping my hair back. "You okay?"

I nod uneasily. "I don't think I'm into that," I admit.

"That's okay," he says, eyes searching me carefully. "You look a little green."

"That was..." Violent. Nauseating. Scary. "... sure something."

He sighs, lips pressing softly against my forehead. "Can I get you something? Water? I think Carlton had some in the cooler."

I nod. "Yeah that would be good."

"Stay here. I'll be right back."

He ducks back in the crowd and I stick by the wall of another falling-down building. There's a little creek nearby, I can hear the water rushing downstream. While I wait, my heart rate slows, and I wonder why it made me so sick. Part of it was the intensity Sebastian showed in the ring. It was scary, and it felt like the anger was barely a peek under the surface. Another part was just the memory of hitting the pavement, the sounds of a body breaking. Yet another part was recognizing the stillness of Sebastian's face, just before the fight really got started. The same kind of stillness I see in Reyn sometimes, but have never been able to explain.

It's the look of someone bracing for impact.

Suddenly, the noise of the crowd erupts into a climactic cheer. I don't have to wonder for long who won. The sight of Heston's angry face as he and his friends stalk toward me tells me all I need to know.

# 22

REYN

I GET THERE JUST as Sebastian lays the Northridge kid out, so it takes a while before I can even reach the cooler. Everyone is losing their damn minds. If anyone from Northridge is even here, you wouldn't know it going by the cheers and excited screams.

Not my scene, if I'm being honest.

I manage to catch Emory by the wall, laughing something into Aubrey's ear. "Hey, V's all good."

Annoyingly, Emory just shrugs. "Okay." He's trying to act like he doesn't care, even though it's obvious that some of the tension in his shoulders eases.

I roll my eyes. "Whatever. Where's Carl?" I follow where he points, having to squeeze between a group of rowdy guys before meeting up with the rest of the Devils. The water is buried deep enough under the beer that I'm up to my elbows in it when Sebastian jumps over the retaining wall, joining up with all of us.

"Winner gets squatter's rights," he says, grabbing one of the beers I'd set aside. He sits on the wall, a swollen bruise already blooming over his eye, and spits off to the side. "Y'all want to build a fire and get baked?"

The others agree, even though Caroline says, "I have curfew in two hours."

"No problem," Sebastian says, throwing an arm over her shoulder. She blushes and does a really bad job of hiding her smile. "We'll have you home to mommy at eleven sharp."

The crowd is already starting to thin out some. There's probably something else going on by now, judging by the way the non-Preston people are checking their phones. The entertainment here is done, anyway.

I emerge from the cooler with the promised bottle of water, and look at Sebastian. "We didn't fuck you up before, did we?"

He flings his sweaty hair off his forehead, scoffing. "Nah. Had that shit on lockdown."

Despite that fact, he still looks a little battered and unsteady. "Well, we were just—"

My words cut off sharply, because over Sebastian's shoulder, I can see a group of guys clustered around the exact spot I'd left Vandy. It's too dark to make out who they are, but it looks like one of them has her boxed in against the wall. I can't see the details of her face—her expression—but the silhouette of her posture is radiating discomfort.

"*Hey!*" I'm over the wall, through the ring, and over the opposite wall in an instant. I'm so laser-focused on getting to that mother-fucker in front of her that the steps behind me barely register. The closer I get, the more I realize who it is.

I get a big fistful of his shirt and yank Heston back sharply enough that he grunts. His three buddies all step forward, but Heston just laughs it off, watching me shoulder in between them.

"Relax, tough guy. We were just having a little discussion." From the flushed, uncomfortable look on Vandy's face, it couldn't have been about anything good.

I take my jacket off and hand it back to Vandy. *See, Georgia?* It's not about abs, there's less to grab onto. "She's not yours to talk to," I say, jaw clenched tight. "Not now, not ever."

"Oh, this is rich." He turns to one of his friends. "See, Reynolds here is the reason her leg's all fucked up like that. Almost killed her in a car accident. Now he's trying to be the big hero. Used to be, you treated a girl like shit and she'd leave you alone. But Preston girls? No self-respect."

My blood pumps hard as I step forward. "I know you wouldn't say that with Emory around, and you're dumber than I remember to say it in front of me."

"I'm not scared of Emory," Heston says, sneering. "And what are you going to do, McAllister? Steal my wallet? You were never anything special. Heard your daddy lost all his money in the divorce settlement, so now you're just one of Preston's scholarship charity cases. They really like collecting the trash these days."

My fist is already tightly clenched when I lunge forward, spine buzzing with the anticipation of slamming my knuckles into this asshole's face. And then Vandy grabs my arm, tugging me back. I'm not proud of it, the way I coil angrily against her grip, but if I throw the punch, it could hurt her.

We both know I won't.

"Don't," she says, voice reedy with panic. "Reyn, your probation. It's not worth it."

Heston laughs, mocking, "Yeah, *Reyn*, your probation. It's not worth it."

"Might be, actually," I respond, still feeling that crazy itch rushing through my blood. "Wouldn't be much of a challenge. I hear even Hamilton's little punk ass could take you down."

Heston scoffs. "Hamilton only beats me when I let him."

"What's all this about?" Sebastian ambles up to us, face red and bruised, but still just as hard. The guy just spent a solid twenty minutes in a fistfight intense enough to rival even the hazing shit I'd seen at Mountain Point, but he doesn't even look tired as he takes a lazy drag from a cigarette.

He doesn't look any less like a bomb about to detonate, either.

Heston levels him with a cold glare. "This is about you apparently throwing fights now. What the fuck, Bass?"

"Throwing fights?" He gives a razor-sharp laugh. "You can't throw a fight by *winning*."

"Since when do you not draw first blood?" Heston's icy gaze moves between Vandy and me. "Since these two are feeding you bullshit?"

Sebastian looks bored now. "Don't know what you're talking about. I took the first hit to throw him off his game. It worked."

"Want to know what I think?" Heston nods to Vandy, still clutching at my clenched arm. "I think Baby V doesn't know when to mind her own damn business."

Before my own fury can even properly flare, Sebastian is there, stepping up to his brother. "And I think you need to back the fuck off my girl here."

Heston says, "*Your* girl?" and it's such a mirror-perfect echo of my thoughts, derision and all, that I actually think I'm the one saying it aloud. Heston's eyes shift to Vandy, and I can't stand the way he's looking at her—greedy and cutting. "So, *he's* the one you let your hair down for, Princess? Slumming it with my brother? I guess that makes sense. The defective Wilcox and the defective Hall."

Vandy's grip goes slack enough that it's almost nothing to jerk out of it, but I'm not sure I could have stopped myself if it hadn't. My eyes go so suddenly blind with rage that it's almost like I lose time. One second, I'm there in front of Vandy, and the next...

I'm watching Heston stumble backward, hand clutched to his face. "Fuck!"

For a brief moment, I wonder why my knuckles don't hurt, and then I realize my punch never landed.

Sebastian's did.

Heston pulls his hand away, face all screwed up in an angry

grimace. He says, "I'm going to make you regret that," and I don't put much stock into anything Heston says. Never have. But it sounds like, for Sebastian, maybe he actually could.

Nevertheless, Sebastian just takes a drag of cigarette, voice as dry as his stare. "Look at that." He points to Heston's nose. "First blood."

Heston looks at us like he's trying to decide if it's worth his pride and pretty face to fuck with us any longer. He makes the right decision. "Whatever. I don't have time for your dumb high school bullshit." His eyes sweep over Vandy. "Not really into chicks with a masochistic streak anyway."

I PULL up the hood of the sweater I'd taken from the Jeep and cross my arms. We're at the lake now. Apparently after all that shit went down with Heston, Ben and Sebastian decided to take the party elsewhere. We're on the north side of the lake, otherwise known as the Jerry-free zone, and it's a lot more relaxed here.

Or would be, if not for the roar inside my head.

Vandy's huddled with some of the girls across the small clearing as Sebastian shows off, teaching them some fighting moves. He's inspecting all their fists, saying stuff like, "Don't tuck the thumb. That's how you break it." She's got my jacket zipped up around her, watching dubiously as he taps her knuckles. "Straighten your wrist, though."

She keeps shooting me these little worried glances, smiling when I meet them. And I always do. Because the sight of her swimming in my jacket is seriously *doing things* for me.

This, and the fact that she looks loose and chill, soothes some of the sharp edges that could only be the result of not giving an ass-kicking that's clearly owed.

I'd parked my car at home and walked over, hoping it might settle the firing impulses of my nerves, but it didn't really work. When I arrived, they already had a crude bonfire going, flames crackling and hissing, making my back prickle and itch. Elana's car is parked close, windows down, music blaring from the speakers.

I'm tending to the business of downing as many of these beers as I can.

Carlton is at my side, carefully separating seeds from a makeshift notebook-tray of weed. It's a nice break from the incessant clicking of the pocket knife he's been playing with all night. "Usually," he's saying, "people want something, I don't ask questions. It's not like I knew Heston was selling it to her."

I give him a sidelong look, raising the bottle to my mouth. "Sure."

I'm not pissed at Carlton, though. I'm pissed at Emory for taking Vandy out there and leaving her to fend for herself. For making me take on a duty that I can't even fucking honor. I'm pissed at Heston, and I'm pissed at his brother for being able to do what I can't, because Sebastian can clock that asshole and still be fine come morning. Sebastian can ride around with a beer in his system. Sebastian can call Vandy his girl.

He didn't even say it like that—not the way I mean it. He said it in the same way I call Emory, Carlton, and Ben my boys. It's the same way all of us call the Playthings our girls. It wasn't like that. I know it's irrational.

The thought is still pinging angrily around in my head when Carlton offers me the joint, and yeah. I'm pissed about this, too. "Can't," I say, jaw clenching. "Got a piss test next week."

Carlton just says, "Bummer," and lights it up for himself.

The fire, coupled with this sudden hurricane of impulses I can't cave to, has me tense and all coiled up, and there's nowhere to put it. So when Emory drops down next to me, giving a quiet, "Sup," it's all I can do to not reach over and bust him in the face.

I give a tight nod instead, emptying my beer.

At least Carlton can read the room. He instantly hands me another.

Emory says, "Sorry for that shit with Heston. Told that asshole to lose my number."

"Don't apologize to me," I say, nodding over the fire. "Apologize to Vandy for letting him get in your head." Another addition to the long list of things I'm pissed about is Emory ever being friends with tools like him in the first place. I know it's not fair. If things had been differ-ent, I probably would have been part of the same crowd.

"I did," he says. "V and I are cool. Thanks for having her back."

I close my eyes, rubbing my fingertips roughly into them. "I can't be her babysitter, Em." It stings to say, because I know how it sounds. Like she's a burden. Like I don't want to protect her. Like I'd rather do anything else than be at her side. Even if all those things aren't true, the words are. "If I'd decked that prick, I'd be sitting in county right now. I don't know what you expect me to do." I take a long drag from my beer.

"I don't expect you to do anything," he says, sounding incredu-lous. "I just asked you to look out for her. I never meant you had to throw fists to do it."

"Yeah," Carlton adds, passing the joint over my lap to Emory, "we already have a fighter. It all worked out."

I scowl across the distance, to where Sebastian is now teaching them something with their knees. Vandy's edging back, looking awkward about it, but Aubrey threads their arms together.

"Sebastian makes a lot more sense now," Carlton says, nodding in his direction. "Can you imagine growing up with an ass like that? I didn't even know Heston had a younger brother until junior year. Guy's got 'single golden child' written all over him."

Just then, a loud peal of laughter rings out, drawing our eyes to Vandy. The fire is playing sharply against her face and it makes some-thing inside me thrash instinctually at the contrasting sight of wrong and right. She presses a hand to her mouth, like she's embarrassed about being so loud, but then ducks in close and says something that makes Aubrey giggle back.

It's weird how easily something loosens within me at the sight of her smile, bright and happy.

Still in my jacket.

"She looks like she's having fun." Emory sounds glad. "That's really all I wanted. I mean, if you want, I can pair her with someone else for the rites."

"What?" I say, whipping my head around. "Why?"

Emory gives me a look. "You said you didn't want to be her babysitter anymore."

"No, I didn't." Only I can't exactly explain the difference between 'don't want to' and 'can't'. Instead, I just say, "That's not what I meant. It's fine. We're fine." Without the rites, we'd hardly have any Emory-approved reasons to hang out anymore. I know she's not over there all laughing and happy because of me. But I had to have contributed to some of it.

Didn't I?

He looks confused, but he takes a drag from the joint and passes it back to Carlton. "You don't seem fine. You look pissed."

"Not about Vandy," I insist. I look into the fire, the cinder and sparks, and distract myself with catching the panic. Gathering it up and packing it away, bit by bit. I tell him, "I could have kicked his ass," and tip the bottle to my lips.

"That's what you're so pissed about?" The tone of surprise in Emory's voice is jarring. It's getting really weird that I can feel something so enormous, and no one can just look at me and somehow *know*. "Of course, you could kick his ass. *Georgia* could probably kick his ass. Heston isn't the physical kind of guy, you know that. He's all about fucking mind games."

"I should have," I say, finally looking my friend in the eye. "If you heard some of the shit he was saying about her, you'd wish I did."

Emory jabs a playful elbow into my side. "Look at you, getting all big brotherly. Now you're getting a taste of how I feel all the time."

Big brotherly is *not* the way I'd describe it. I give him a tight smile, elbowing back. "You know V's my girl." I say it just like Sebastian did—totally casual—but it rings too true in my own ears.

Emory just looks pleased.

We both look in her direction, toward where Sebastian is assessing her. "This is your dominant leg, isn't it?" I track him carefully as he bends down to tap her bare knee. "What's the deal with this thing? What's your range of motion?" It's her bad leg, and I'm not sure what makes me tense more; the question itself or the easy way he just touched her leg.

Devil or not, I will break this fucker's fingers.

She darts her eyes toward Emory and me, shifting uncomfortably. "Uh, I don't know. It depends on the day, I guess. Maybe fifty percent, on a good one?"

"How high can you get it?"

She draws out a long, "Um," and braces her grip on Aubrey's arm to lift her knee. "It's not—I mean, I can't—not without something to hold onto."

Sebastian seems to consider this, and I feel Emory going still as stone beside me, as well. "How's your balance on it? Can you lift the other one?"

Her face is turning red now. "Not great. Really, it's just...weak."

"But you do PT, right?"

"Yeah, once a week now." She looks self-conscious and uncertain, ducking her head, but Sebastian takes it in stride.

"Then here's what you do." He takes her hand and puts it on his shoulder, tells her to use the attacker to brace herself before driving her knee into his groin. "You'll be close enough, just try it out. Grab and spike it."

She gives Aubrey a sidelong look but does as he says, grasping his shoulder and jerking the knee of her leg upward—

Slamming it right into his crotch.

Sebastian lets out a winded 'oof', doubling over.

Vandy stumbles back, hands clamped around her mouth. "Oh my god, I'm sorry!"

Sebastian flaps one hand while the other cradles his balls. "It's fine, it's cool."

Emory and Carlton are howling with laughter.

"Damn dude, she just racked you!" Ben's pointing as he laughs, doubled over almost as far as Sebastian.

"I'm so sorry!" Vandy puts a hand on his back, eyes wide and alarmed.

Sebastian finally straightens. "Well, I did tell you to try it."

"This must be one of the good days," she laments, pulling a face. "I never know what it's going to—I'm *sorry*."

"V," he says, already looking completely recovered. "It's cool, I'm good."

Despite that, when he turns his back to her, facing the rest of us, his face crumples enough that I finally crack up, too.

That effectively marks the end of the fighting lesson, and the rest of them come to the little circle by the bonfire to grab beers and hit the joint. Vandy sulks over to us, telling Emory to, "Move over," and plops down between us. She's warm and solid at my side, her thigh pressed up against mine, and the urge to throw my arm around her shoulders is so strong that I have to lace my fingers tight around the neck of my bottle, hanging loose between my knees.

She's wearing this tight, haunted expression, so I make sure to tell her, "Hey, we weren't laughing at you," just loud enough for the others to hear.

Ben's head snaps up. "No, we were laughing at him! It's a total bro rule."

Emory nudges his shoulder into hers. "Yeah, if a guy gets hit in the nuts, you have to laugh. Because it's…you know."

"Hilarious," I finish.

Ben says, "Exactly."

She finally cracks a smile, some of the tension in her shoulders falling away. "I didn't mean to."

Afton takes a hit from the joint Caroline just waved off and asks, "Hey, Emory, are you going to go all psycho caveman if I offer this to your sister?"

"Yes," he says without hesitation. Vandy scowls at him but he doesn't back down. "Absolutely fucking not."

"I wouldn't have taken it," she says, even though I can see the curiosity plain as day in her eyes.

"If you don't let her try it where you can supervise," Carlton pipes in magnanimously, "she's just going to pick it up off the mean streets."

"I think I've heard enough about you supplying my little sister with drugs for one evening, thanks."

Carlton winces. "Ouch."

"Emory," she warns, and he backs off.

Carlton's playing with that annoying knife again, and Caroline keeps hinting around about maybe wanting to jump into the lake, even though it's going to be cold as a witch's tit. Vandy grows quiet as the others talk and drink and smoke, staring wistfully into the fire. She doesn't look upset that Emory won't let her partake, but she's also not laughing like she was before.

*Fuck it*, I think and sling my arm around her neck, giving her a light jostle. "You okay?" This doesn't look like anything, could easily pass for brotherly affection.

She looks at me, a flash of trepidation in her eyes, and then back at Emory.

He sees, but doesn't seem to care.

She gives me a secret smile that makes me want to take her behind a tree and kiss the hell out of her. "Yeah, just getting tired."

Emory overhears. "Need me to take you home?" Despite the effortless words, he looks disappointed.

I let my arm fall away, standing. "I'm out, too. I'll walk her home."

He gives me a grateful look, taking out his phone. "I'll text Mom, in case Jerry gives you some shit."

I grimace, but don't ask him not to, instead making my goodbyes to the others, slapping palms, picking up my bottles. I've only had six, so I'm not even drunk, just pleasantly buzzed. I wait, fidgeting impatiently as Vandy does the same, saying goodbye to the girls and apologizing to Sebastian one last time.

All night, I've just wanted to get her alone.

She finally sidles up to me, letting me lead the way down the shore. "Are you mad at me?"

I feel my eyebrows draw together as I look at her. "Of course not."

She wraps her arms around her middle. "You've just looked really mad. Like, all night."

I glance over my shoulder, wondering if we're far enough away yet, before reaching out to put my arm around her the way I've been wanting to all night. "Not at you. Just Heston, living rent-free inside my head."

She leans into the touch. "He's a fucking jerk."

My eyebrows shoot up my forehead. "*Baby V*. Such language."

She whacks me playfully in the stomach. "Well, he is!"

We reach the footbridge that takes us across the west side of the lake, and I keep taking peeks back at the bonfire, watching it grow smaller and dimmer in the distance.

"Hey," I say, pulling her to a stop and touching her chin. There's no way they could see us here, but I still dart a nervous glance toward the orange glow behind us before ducking in to lick at the seam of her lips. Vandy meets me with enough gusto that I stumble back a step, having to clutch at her hips.

I pull away when I realize the beer is almost as strong on her tongue as it is my own. "Violence, strong language, alcohol. What's next?"

She hooks her fingers into the waist of my jeans, watching me through the fan of her eyelashes. "Adult content?"

I shake my head. "How much did you have?"

She rolls her eyes. "Afton let me take two sips of her beer. Don't worry, it was super gross and I'm definitely not in any hurry to have more."

I exhale slowly, feeling relieved when I dip back in to kiss her again. I'm not like Emory. Annoyingly, I probably fall more on Carlton's side of the argument. If Vandy wants to try something, she should be able to do it around the people she trusts and feels comfortable with. People who want to keep her safe. People who'll know if things get out of hand, like with the pills.

But I need wherever this kiss is heading to be nothing but legit.

Her cheeks are red when she asks against my lips, "Can you come over again? Like last night?"

I let one of my hands drop, fingertips grazing the outside of her bare thigh. It's risky, doing that two nights in a row. "I don't know if my dad's home."

"If he isn't?" She looks up at me, her puffy bottom lip trapped between her teeth, and I just keep thinking about what we did in the treehouse earlier. Her on top of me, riding me, coming for me. My dick aches with the memory of her tits in my hands—my mouth— and I was ready to do it again *hours ago*.

"Come on," I say, capturing her hand and heading toward home.

～

GETTING up Vandy's roof is fine when I'm sober, but when I've had six beers, it's a comedy of errors. It takes me half a dozen tries, and by the time I get to her window, my elbow is bruised, my muscles are stinging, and my pride is even more injured.

If the boys at Dixon Hall could see me now.

She said it might take her a little while to get up here, so I slide the window open and carefully climb inside to wait. The room looks almost exactly how I'd left it. It's weird being in here. Everything is bright and girly, the picture-perfect princess oasis. It smells like Vandy though, all floral and clean. Her bed is this absurdly comfortable monstrosity that calls to me like a siren.

Her pillows smell like her hair and I lay my head on one as I wait. I reach into my pocket and take out Carlton's knife—*mine now*—Afton's mascara—*mine now*—Sebastian's cigarette lighter—*mine now*—and yes.

Heston's fucking wallet.

*Mine now.*

*Prick.*

I can't hear much happening downstairs, which is good. Means they can't hear us much, either. Briefly, I think about looking around and finding something in here to swipe. It doesn't have to be anything big or important. Just taking anything from here and carrying it to my own room would satisfy the twitchy impulse.

But the thought of taking something from here—something soft and bright and *Vandy*—and putting it into my dark dresser drawer alongside Heston's wallet feels *wrong*.

I'm lingering somewhere between sleep and wakefulness when her door finally opens. I spring to my feet, alarmed even though I'd been expecting her to come.

She shuts the door softly behind her, fingers turning the lock. "Hey," she breathes, cheeks a soft pink. She's still wearing my jacket.

"Hey." We watch each other for a long moment, and I feel compelled to say, "We don't have to do anything. It's okay if you want to wait." My dick twitches tragically, but it's been a long fucking day.

"I really don't," she says simply, stepping forward to curl a palm around my neck. She pulls me down and kisses me with her hot, quick tongue.

I groan in approval.

"Tell me what you want," I say, pushing her hair aside and kissing her neck. Her body is arching into me, making contact in a variety of good places. "Tell me what you need."

Her hand brushes against the outside of my pants, more tentative than necessary. I pull back and look at her. The innocence flickers in her eyes. "I want to feel good. I want you to feel good."

She can't lead here because she doesn't have a map.

"We can just..." I back up toward the bed, dropping down on the edge and guiding her into my lap. "Like last time."

Her lips part on a sigh when my mouth kisses down her neck, bumping into the cool leather of my jacket. She rocks against me hard and I can't help it when my hands go lower, sliding up her spread thighs. I've been thinking about them all night—that pale, soft skin where she got the Devil's mark. I've been thinking about how much I want to mark her myself, so that guys like the Wilcoxes don't dare think of touching what's mine again.

Her hips roll to a stop, and I almost pull away when one of her hands closes over mine, worried I'm pushing it too far. Instead, she guides my hand to stroke upward, beneath her skirt.

I meet her heavy eyes, swallowing. "Like this?" I ask, running my fingers over that tattoo and then inching up and up, until I'm touching the cotton of her panties.

She nods, eyes fluttering closed. "Like this," she decides.

I press my thumb to the middle, testing, and her hips chase it, bucking forward. My breath escapes in a loud gust and I trail my fingers deeper, lower. I hiss a low, "Shit," when I feel the wetness that's soaking through.

I wrap an arm around her back and flip us, scooting her up the bed. She helps, digging her heels in, pushing to the center, and the sight of her spread out beneath me almost makes me bust a load right there. I can see the tattoo here, and she lets me sweep her skirt up, revealing the same place I'd just been touching. I lick my lips and meet her gaze when I return my fingers, pressing slow, firm circles around her clit.

Her hips press up into it, expression crumbling. "Oh, *god.*"

I don't even recognize the sound that comes from my chest, something rough and hungry, but I brace myself over her to duck in for another kiss and she meets me open-mouthed, eager.

It's completely an accident when my fingers slip—pure drunken lack of coordination—dipping in beneath the edge of her panties. But the sound she makes into my mouth is full of equal parts shock and approval, so I pull back to watch my hand push clumsily under the fabric. I feel, hear, see her chest hitch, hips squirming beneath me as I finally touch her, skin-to-skin.

"Fuck, you're so wet for me." My fingers slip around in her folds until they find her clit, and she bucks into it, mouth falling open so invitingly that I have to lick into it. She's fighting to stay quiet. I can hear it in the tense little bitten-off whimpers she makes into my mouth. Her hips keep working against my hand and it's driving me fucking *crazy*, how badly she wants it.

Alcohol always makes me lazy and loose-lipped, and that's exactly how I feel when I breathe into her mouth, "God, I want to eat your pussy." It's just pure, trashy truth. I love eating pussy, and I'm good at it, and in that moment, I want so badly to taste what my fingers are doing, to make her fall to pieces on my tongue.

But even though her face screws up in pain-pleasure at the words, she doesn't ask me to.

That's fine.

I hold her eyes with mine, wanting to know she's okay but not daring to ask. Asking that pissed her off last time, and all I want is to make her feel good. Her legs spread just a bit wider, sensing what I'm about to do, opening for me. I circle around her core and slowly, carefully, sink a finger into her.

"Oh," she whispers in a sharp intake, but she doesn't withdraw. No, she pushes her hips against it, making it sink in deeper, shoulders tensing, breath caught.

Yeah, she's better than okay. She's tight and beautiful and perfect. Her head grinds back against the bed, pale hair glowing like a halo around the long column of her throat. I rub my thumb over her clit as she fucks herself on my finger, pushing in another, and the sounds I can hear her trapping in her chest are making my dick throb with the rhythm of them.

"Don't stop," she cries in a rushing exhale, hand gripping my arm as it moves against and inside of her. I don't stop. I'm so fixated on needing to see her come that my wrist is trembling under the strain of it. I want to watch her feel it—feel *good.* I want to know that it's nothing but our two bodies doing it. I want to know that it's something *I'm* giving her.

And then it happens, the wave of release rolling up her body, starting somewhere deep inside, clenching around my fingers, mouth parted, lips red, eyes slamming shut.

"Oh my god, oh my god, oh my god," she chants, jaw going slack. I can't stop myself; I kiss her. I kiss her hard, deep, furious. I want to taste all the good she's feeling. I want to breathe it into my lungs like secondhand smoke and hold it there, because it's ours.

She shudders beneath me, hips writhing around, and then whimpers herself still.

Somehow, I'm just as breathless as she is, like I'm the one still shaking with the aftershocks. The fine hair framing her face is damp with sweat and I push it back from her forehead, pressing a kiss into her temple.

"Fuck, I'm sorry, I've got to...." I reach down to fumble with the fly on my jeans, because I am *not* climbing down from the roof with a wad of jizz in my boxers.

Vandy blinks like she's coming back into her own body, movements languid as she reaches for me. "I can—"

I gently push her wrist away. "No, that's not—" Not the point, I want to say. Not important. I'm pretty sure I just jumped ten spots on my 'steady and slow' sex-with-Vandy risk management plan. If we jump any further, I might as well just shred the damn thing.

She pouts, watching my hand disappear into my pants. "Or I could watch you do it." Her gaze rises slowly to mine. "It wouldn't be the first time."

My hand pauses. "Wouldn't be the first time you *what*?"

She squints one eye in a grimace. "Watched you...jerk off?"

"Wait," I say, incurably confused. I'm an eighteen-year-old degenerate, sure, but it's not like I'm whacking off all over the place. "When did you see me jerking off?" Her eyes jump to the side and mine follow, a slow sort of understanding falling over me when I see the window that looks into my own. I look back at her. "You're fucking with me."

She groans into her hands, but she's fighting back laughter. "I'm sorry! You never close your curtains."

I'm stunned speechless. Or, almost speechless. "Liked what you saw?"

She's smiling back at me now, her lip trapped between her teeth. "Clearly."

I wet my lips just imagining it—her watching me. "Full disclosure here. I'm not really in a position right now to give you much of a show."

She looks back at me, face puckered in confusion. "What do you mean?"

I look between us, slowly working my pants and boxers down my hips. I feel more than see Vandy rising up on her elbows to watch as my cock springs free, bouncing lewdly over her spread legs. I take myself in hand, glancing up at her, and she's staring at it intensely. God, this is probably the first cock she's ever seen up close and personal.

That risk management plan is *so fucked*.

"Show me," she breathes, blue eyes blazing back at me. "Show me how you like it."

I sit back on my heels, eyes dragging down her body as my fist starts pumping. She's still wearing my jacket, and it's lame. I *know* it's lame. But I feel this hot spike of possessive *want* shoot right to my cock. Her skirt's still pushed up, revealing her wet panties and *all* of her thighs, and I really wasn't lying before.

This is going to be quick.

My jaw clenches hard as I look, eyes roving from her thighs, to her panties, to her hot, eager gaze, and then back again. My hand moves on its own, slow and languid, trying to draw it out, even though I know it's futile.

"Does it hurt?" she asks, watching my every move.

"No." I bite my lip, stroking up the shaft, rolling the tip in my palm. "It feels fucking fantastic."

"It feels good when I do it, too," she admits, which causes me to skip a beat. "But the best time was when I did it while watching you."

"Oh, Jesus Christ."

I focus on her legs, unable to really process what she's telling me. It's too much, too intense. Already, I can see her hips subtly wriggling with me, like they're magnetized to the rhythm I'm setting. I watch the tattoo as it moves with her, her legs still spread open for me like they want to cradle my hips and take me in and—

I fall forward on my palm, hovering over her as the coil finally snaps. All of the tension I've been holding in all day seems to erupt with it. "Fuck," I growl as I watch my come paint the skin of her thighs, my fist wringing it out.

Vandy makes this airy little, "Oh," sound as she watches—as she feels it fall on her.

"Sorry." I feel like I'm half-wheezing from the force of it, sitting back on my heels to commit the vision to memory. I swipe the back of my hand over my mouth. "Sometimes I can't control where it goes," I lie.

She gives me a look that tells me just how much she isn't buying this. "It's okay."

It's probably not, but I'm too wrung out to beat myself up over it. Instead, I fish around in her bathroom for something to clean it off with, offering her an apologetic glance when I do.

She spends a long time in the bathroom—cleaning herself up, I guess—and I set myself to rights and linger around the window. I shouldn't stay. A cautious glance out her window tells me that my dad isn't even home, but it can't be a good idea.

But when Vandy walks out of the bathroom in a thin shirt and a pair of shorts, eyes pinging between me and the window, I know before she opens her mouth what she's going to ask.

"Stay?"

I know I'm going to give in.

"Okay."

She rests her head in the crook of my shoulder when we lay down, and it's a different quiet in here than the one in my room. This quiet is full of Vandy's soft breaths, the rustle of the sheets when she moves her legs, the gentle sweep of her fingers against the hair on my forearm.

I break it with a soft, "Hey, V?"

She looks up at me, but I can't bring myself to tear my eyes away from her ceiling. "Hm?"

"Remember earlier," I ask, "when you made me promise?"

Her hand goes instantly still. "Yeah," she says reluctantly, voice small and full of something I don't want to think about.

I swallow. "Never Sebastian, okay?"

There's a long stretch of silence, and I'm afraid for a moment that she's going to ask why, and I won't know what to tell her. It's not that I don't like him. It's not that I didn't see the way he treated her back there, like she was just any other girl—like the way her leg is was nothing to him. It's not even that I think he'd hurt her.

It's *because* of all those things.

It's not until she repeats, "Never Sebastian," and presses a small, "I promise," into my shoulder that I can finally close my eyes.

# 23

Vandy

"Don't forget the meeting tonight," Emory says, wiping his mouth with a napkin. Our lunch table has grown into something crowded and curious. My brother and Aubrey were one thing, but after the fight—the bonfire—most of the other Devils and Playthings began drifting to our table, too. People around us notice and I can feel their probing gazes, because Vandy Hall does *not* sit at the popular table.

Except suddenly, I do.

If someone had suggested this possibility on the first day of school, I would have thought they were high. Or that I was.

It's not without its conflicts. Emory has made it clear that Sydney isn't welcome. She pretends she doesn't care, sitting over with the lacrosse boys, but the pointed looks directed my way are laced with tension and a bitterness that makes the back of my neck prickle.

Then there's Reyn.

He's not supposed to be anywhere near me, but the merging of our worlds has made that a challenge. And after those two nights in my room, it's almost a physical ache to not be around him. It doesn't help that he hasn't been to my room since that night. It seems like his dad is always home now, so I've had to settle for the moments like these, clustered around the other Devils, watching him, pretending I'm not over-warm and restless and impatient, and yes.

Tired.

Sleeping without Reyn *sucks*.

It's only been three times, but *god*. I already miss it. I miss the good dreams, the lake and the fireflies and the stillness. I miss the warm, solid weight of him beside me. I miss the way he looks when he's sleeping, face slack, lips just barely parted. I miss the way he kissed me when he left those two nights—a soft, feathery touch to my forehead—believing I was still asleep, even though I was listening to him put his shoes on.

Admittedly, sleep is a doomed endeavor when night is the only time I can really talk to him. For the past week, we've met at our windows, phones pressed to our ears, voices low across the distance. It's painfully insufficient, but at least I have that—the sound of his voice as he leans over the sill, face shadowed.

Sometimes, if I really work for it, he'll raise his face into the light and give me one of those patented Reyn McAllister smiles.

"I'll be there after practice," Afton says. "We're working on homecoming stuff."

"I have a shit-ton of homework for Dr. Ross due tomorrow, but," Emory says, lowering his voice. "I have the next rite."

I discreetly glance across the table at Reyn. His intense green eyes are already fixed on me. It's a thrill to know that maybe he shares this chaotic, bone-deep need to touch and clutch and *have*. He's a lot better at this thing than I am, stealing his covert glances at the perfect times. Of course, Reyn is always good at stealing. His expression is always schooled into something aloof, disinterested, but I know better. He's definitely interested. I can tell when those eyes roam to my mouth, my chest, my waist, my *legs*.

He's infatuated with my thighs, and it isn't fair. The thought that I can't just give them to him, feel his hands grazing up my skin there, claiming it, marking it, is killing me. if I wasn't being watched twenty-four-seven by my family, I'd get utterly lost in letting him fawn over them as much as he wants.

Unfortunately, that's not how life works. Just figures that I'd finally find a guy who wants me, a guy I want back, and I'm not allowed to even be around him. I try to steal another glance, but this time, he's not watching me. His gaze is trained across the room, face set into that sharp stillness. He's got one hand on his backpack and he's already halfway out of the chair. I turn to see what he's looking at. Not 'what', but 'who'.

Dean Dewey.

I glance at my brother, who has also noticed what's going on. "Dude," he says to Reyn, "let me say something to him. We can deal with this."

"My problem," Reyn says with a shrug and, a blink later, has already eased himself into a group of passing students.

"Is everything okay here?" Dean Dewey says, eyeing the empty chair. A water bottle sits on the table, half-full. It's not the first time Dewey has scared Reyn off. It's like they're hoping to catch him in the act, just to have something to pin on him. Maybe Jerry and Dewey are trading notes or something.

"Everything's fine," Emory says, speaking for the group. Afton gives him a smile. Tyson focuses on his lunch. I feel the hot spike of anger building in my chest, but swallow it back until the Dean, and his penetrative eyes, leaves.

"We need to fix this," I say to Emory, fed up. "It's not fair that he can't sit with his friends."

"He can sit with his friends," Carlton says. "Just not when you're around."

The words sting like a slap, even though I know Carlton didn't mean for them to. "You're right. Reyn should sit here, and I—" I look around, deciding, "I'll go somewhere else to eat from now on."

"What?" Emory grabs my arm before I can stand. "No way. That is not how we're handling this shit. You're my sister. He's my best friend. There has to be a solution." He sighs. "I'll talk to Mom and Dad, maybe they can do something."

I nod but wait a few minutes before leaving the cafeteria anyway, explaining that I just don't have an appetite anymore. It's not a lie. I search the hallways, but can't find Reyn. I fire off a few texts:

**Where are you?**

**Are you okay?**

**I'm sorry.**

Finally, just before the bell rings, my phone buzzes.

**I'm fine. See you at the meeting tonight.**

I know better than to press, and there's nothing I can do about it right now, anyway. Every time something like this comes up, Reyn tends to fall into some silent, blank space that I can't seem to reach. I'm just hoping that someday he'll let me help him the way he's helped me. I know there's a lot of pressure on him with Jerry and Dewey always following him around, not to mention his dad and the combined expectations of Preston's football program heavy on his shoulders. He's finally found acceptance with me and it's a secret wrapped in another secret.

All of that is still on my mind when we meet in the bunker that night. When I take my seat in the circle, he's already there, sweaty and flushed from practice. His face is still set into that eerie stillness from earlier, jaw sharply clenched.

"We're halfway through the rituals," Emory says, holding the black book in his hands. "And we've had advance notice by the Devil 'Powers that Be' that there's an endowment fundraising dinner at the club to kick off homecoming. Plan on being there."

Reyn speaks up, voice flat. "Might be a problem, considering I'm not allowed on club property anymore."

Afton's eyebrows shoot up and Sebastian gives a deep little laugh. For once, no one looks at me.

"Don't worry about that," Emory says. "We'll figure it out."

"Any news on the next ritual?" Tyson asks.

"Yes," my brother says, holding up a piece of black cardstock. He flips it around so we can see the silver handwriting. "Our next challenge is getting into the Preston Alumni House and leaving the Devil's mark inside somewhere."

"We're doing another break-in?" Georgia asks, eyes darting around.

"Not exactly." He reaches into his pocket and pulls out the key that is identical to the one we all have. "These keys open a lot of doors at Preston. The Alumni house is one of them."

He goes on to explain the specifics. The Devils mark—the D with the pitchfork—needs to be stamped somewhere discreetly in the house. Apparently, this was done for years before it fell out of tradition. "Like the other rites, you'll work with a partner. There's a caretaker on site and we're instructed to leave the marks between nine p.m. and three a.m. this Tuesday."

"On a school night?" I blurt. All their eyes shift to me in varying degrees of amusement. One sentence just confirmed my excruciating lameness. It's just hard getting out of the house at night with my parents watching. "Never mind. I'll figure it out."

Emory calls the meeting to a close and I stand, grabbing my bag. I turn to Reyn, excited that we have an excuse to finally talk, but he's already filtering out the door behind Caroline. I watch, stomach twisting in disappointment as he leaves. It's almost as bad as that night of the bonfire, wondering if I've done something wrong. Even if I hadn't, it just always feels like all of Reyn's problems are because of me.

"Hey." Emory bumps our shoulders together once everyone else has left. "I can probably talk to Mom and Dad, try to get you an alibi."

"Oh." I try to play off my sullen mood. "No, it's okay. I can wing it." He's already talking to them about Reyn. If I want to be treated as an equal, I can't keep counting on Emory to have all my difficult discussions.

"Well, other than myself, Reyn is the most likely to get in and out of there with no trouble." We walk toward the staircase and he turns to lock the door with his key. "I'm going with Aubrey."

"You really like her, huh?"

His cheeks tint but he shrugs like it's no big deal. "She's cool. Way less demanding than Campbell. Less mean, too. Plus, she's..." he looks at me and I see him mentally shift gears from whatever other compliment he was going to give her, "... uh, *cool.*"

"Right." My eyes narrow and for a split second, I wonder what he was about to say. What do guys like in a girl, anyway? Of course, then I'd have to live with the knowledge of my brother *liking* something about a girl. *Blech.* "Well, for what it's worth, I like her, too."

He gives me a small grin. "Honestly, that's worth more than you'd think."

There's a beat where I want so badly to tell him about Reyn. To share this enormous, all encompassing, life-changing thing I'm going through. The confession is like fire on the tip of my tongue. Maybe he wouldn't really care. We're all friends now. We're Devils. Emory *likes* Reyn.

But I know better.

Emory's approval has limitations. He's getting something out of this—his best friend back. And I'm getting something too—the article. If he scratched the surface on my relationship with Reyn, god knows what else would come out.

"Reyn and I will do fine," I say. "The odds of getting caught are pretty slim."

"He's uniquely skilled for this type of prank." We reach the top of the stairs, but before we go outside, he says, "One thing, though."

"What's that?"

He turns to me, face serious. "You guys need to get in, leave your mark, and get out. Don't let him take anything. I know for a fact they inventory everything in there. It's a historic home, filled with historic Preston Prep artifacts. It's like putting a fat kid in a candy shop, but he needs to keep his hands to himself."

The snort happens without warning, and I slap a hand over my mouth and nose. It's not the candy shop comment that gets me laughing. It's the idea of Reyn keeping his hands to himself. I know for a fact that's something he struggles with.

"I'll try to keep him in line," I reply, "or distract him somehow."

He grins. "Thanks V. You know, I'm really glad we're doing this together. The three of us? It's like old times, before—"

"I'm glad, too," I finish before he can wallow in the memory of what happened. It's the first time that the thought of actually completing this article gives me pause. Emory and I have built this fragile, new trust with one another, and the thought of breaking it makes my chest ache. He's opening up to me, about Aubrey and Reyn, and who knows. Maybe if he had a little more time to get used to the idea, I could open up to him about Reyn, too.

Am I really ready to burn that all down?

I'm still thinking about it that evening as I add the details of the new rite to my notes, staring at all the material I've collected. Because of my access, there's a lot here, and it's solid stuff. The invitations, the notices about the rituals, photos I secretly took of the bunker, the tattoos. All of these things were meant to bond us together, and I have to hand it to them.

It's worked.

I think of Sebastian jumping to my defense, Georgia and her shy smiles, Afton and her badass attitude. I think of Aubrey and the way she looks at my brother, hopeful and soft. I think of Tyson's easy smiles and Carlton's ridiculous comments. I think of Ben and Elana's laughter, people who I used to think mean and elitist, but who I've found nothing but kindness. I think of Caroline sitting at our table and all the awed looks she gets for doing it.

We're nothing like we were on that first night, sitting in the circle, confessing our sins. We were all a little broken then, shiftless like flotsam. This thing—these Devils—have always been a cruel, ugly thing. Maybe the havoc of the legacy breathes in all of us, but maybe I've been too quick to write it off.

Maybe we're turning this into something better. Something *good*.

But just as soon as the thought comes, it passes. If it were only the twelve of us calling the shots, maybe it could be like that. But we don't hold the power here. Whoever's behind the resurgence of the Devils do.

~

THANKS.

I keep scrolling up, reading my texts with Reyn. A couple hours ago, I'd left him a plate of fried chicken in the front seat of his Jeep and shot him a message telling him where to find it. Hence, the *Thanks*.

And then, nothing.

I'm trying not to be 'clingy.' I might not know a lot about being with boys, but I've heard enough from Emory to know that's not something a girl wants to be. It's hard, but we're still an hour away from when we usually meet at the window for a call. That's what I keep telling myself as I stare at the text on my screen.

**Thanks.**

Suddenly, there's a text below it, though.

**Warren's gone.**

I sit up, thumbs flying as I type in a response. The same moment I send it, I get one from him, too.

**Can you come over?**

**Can I come over?**

I smile so wide my cheeks actually hurt.

**Yes!**

He doesn't answer, but he doesn't need to. I spend a moment in the bathroom, making sure my hair doesn't look stupid, before I hear the subtle sound of his footsteps outside my window.

He enters quietly, like Firefly slinking though the garden. I smile when I see him look up, but it fades quickly. He's wearing a senior class shirt with a smirking devil on the front and soft, loose sweats. He looks tired. Hard-edged. Still.

"Hey," I say, reluctantly reaching for him. "Are you okay?"

He takes my face in his hands and kisses me. It's deep and intense, biting, full of his harsh breath and insistent tongue. The spark in my belly ignites into a disorienting inferno. I grab two handfuls of his shirt and try to meet his fervor, but somehow I suspect that's not what he needs. This is frustration and anger. Catharsis. Reyn kisses like he's trying to give something to me, and that's exactly how I kiss him back. Like I'm accepting it, taking it into myself and packing it away, nice and tidy.

Just as suddenly as it came, it's gone.

He pulls back and sweeps the pad of his thumb against my cheek, all of his hard edges softening. He smiles. "Am now."

Still reeling from the kiss, I watch his red lips form the words, but take a second to actually parse them. "And before?"

His hands slide away, smile falling. "Shitty day."

"What happened?"

He turns, eyes taking in my room. "Started with Fucking Jerry pulling me over on the way to school to 'check my paperwork', which made me late as fuck, so Dr. Ross gave me detention. Then that bull-shit at lunch with Dewey. And Coach was on a rampage about the detention because it proves I'm not 'taking the team as a whole into consideration', which is not fucking true. I'm busting my ass out there for the team." His jaw clenches. "And don't even get me started on the food situation over at my house and the fact my father cannot bring home any fucking dinner, but he sure can bring home *another* chick, and she's usually closer to my age than his." His chest rises with a hard sigh, fingers raking through his hair. "Thanks, by the way. For dinner. You didn't have to do that."

"I didn't mind." I reach for his hand, relieved when his fingers instantly lace with my own. I confess, "I thought you might be mad at me. It felt like maybe you were avoiding me earlier."

He sweeps my hair from my shoulder, green eyes tracking the motion. "Would you believe me if I said I was avoiding you so you wouldn't think I was mad at you?"

I search his eyes, finding nothing but truth there. "Yes."

His forehead creases with a frown. "I don't play games, V. If I'm mad at you..." His cheek pulls up into a crooked grin. "Well, I wouldn't be, but if I were, I'd just tell you. That's sort of how I operate."

I nod. The exhaustion and irritation make more sense. "I'm sorry you had a bad day."

His face falls. "I didn't want to dump all my shit on you."

"No, dump away," I insist. "Please?"

His hand slides up my side, thumb setting just below my breast, and I think he must understand what I'm asking. "I meant it before." He kisses me again, mouthing against my lips. "With you, I'm good. None of that shit matters."

If this is what he needs, I can gladly give it to him. I like knowing that I make him feel good, that I soothe the impulsivity of his fingers and elicit the hard arousal in his pants. I love the rush that he gives me. The way my skin, my nerves, my body blaze beneath his touch. It seems like the past few weeks have been all about things we've taken from one another, but there's also *this*.

There's the give.

Reyn's hands move behind my thighs and he lifts me off the ground, my legs latching around his waist. I plant kisses on his neck, tugging the shirt aside to suck on his collarbone. My core heats against his hard, taut belly, craving more. I want *so much* more—more than I know how to properly express. When he carries me to the bed, I exhale in relief.

We haven't talked about it, but I want it.

I'm ready.

He lays me on my back and stands over me, staring at me as though I'm already naked. I'm not, I've got on a T-shirt and shorts, but my nipples peak under his intense gaze and every inch of my skin pebbles with goosebumps. I remember what I was thinking earlier in the day, about wanting to give him what he likes most, and I spread my thighs, toes curling at the look on his face at the sight of it. He's caught mid-expression, like he's trying to decide if he should take what he wants or control himself.

"Don't," I say.

His forehead furrows at my incoherence. "Don't?"

"Don't control yourself." I lift up on my elbows and get an eyeful of his long, lean body.

His lips twist into a dimpled grin as he bends to meet me, voice hot in my ear. "I always knew you were cute, Baby V, I just didn't realize you'd be this incredibly sexy."

Sexy.

Not pathetic. Not weak. Not broken. Not *defective*.

Reynolds McAllister sees the real me, the girl underneath all the history and hurt. A rush runs through me and we reach for one another. He pulls off his shirt and drops it on the floor, giving me the hard expanse of his abs to kiss. His breath sucks in, just as a loud knock bangs on my bedroom door.

"V," Emory calls, jiggling the doorknob.

"Shit," I say, instinctively pushing Reyn off as I scramble off the bed. "Shit. Shit. Shit."

"V—I need to ask you something." Again, the knob twists. "Why is your door locked?"

"Bathroom," I whisper, shoving Reyn out of the room. He's already two steps ahead of me though, eyes blank as the door shuts in his face. I cross the room and open the door.

"What?" I ask this with a perfect façade of calm, as though my heart isn't about to beat out of my chest.

Emory assesses me. "Why was your door locked?"

"Because it's my room, Emory. Sometimes I want a little privacy."

He huffs, like the thought of me expecting a grain of autonomy is downright absurd. I can't even recall the last time I went into the dungeon he calls a bedroom. He frowns, studying me. "And why are you so sweaty?"

"I, uh." Shit. *Why?* Because your best friend was about to ravage me on my bed, that's why. Have you seen him shirtless? Logic prevails. "Because I was doing my PT."

*That* seems to appease him. "Well, I thought you'd want to know that I talked to Mom and Dad about Reyn."

"Oh," I try to compose myself a little, furtively straightening my shirt. "About him sitting with us at school and stuff?"

"Yeah." Without an invitation, he steps into the room, pushing past me. "I told them things have chilled out a little with everyone and you two were getting along—which they knew, since they invited him and his dad to the football party. I said neither of us wanted him to be excluded at school."

"What did they say to that?" I ask, realizing that my bed is completely rumpled, from the foot up. My eyes bug out when they land on Reyn's shirt, still discarded on the floor. Damn it.

"They agreed that any kind of social isolation was probably not in his best interest, but most of all, they're just worried about what you think."

I fight a snort. *Now* they're worried about someone's social isolation? Where was this concern when I had no friends and sat at home alone all the time? "Did you tell them that I'm okay with it?"

"I did, but you'll need to tell them yourself." His eyes sweep over my room and I shift to block the messed-up bed, foot covertly extended to kick the shirt beneath the dust ruffle. "Hey!"

"Huh?" Heat spreads up my neck. "What?"

He reaches down and grabs the shirt, holding it between two hands. "Is this my senior shirt?"

"Oh, uh, yes." I nod. "Must have gotten mixed up in the wash."

He scowls. "Damn it, V. You know I don't like it when you steal my shirts."

"I'm sorry, seriously. I didn't realize I had it."

He balls the shirt in his hand and continues with our prior conversation. "They think I'm just backing Reyn up because he's my best friend. No one cares about what I think here."

"Yeah, okay," I agree, nodding. "I can do that. I'll talk to them tomorrow."

"Thanks," he says. "I can tell he's struggling a little. This has been a big change for him. Not just school but all the other stuff. Girls, the Devils, Fucking Jerry riding his ass all the time."

For some reason I blurt out the one thing my mind held onto, "Girls?"

He gives me a conspiratorial look. "Yeah, not that he's told me anything, but there's a rumor going around that he hooked up with some chick in the library. Plus, he was looking pretty damn satisfied the morning after the bonfire." He raises an eyebrow. "Did you see him with someone?"

"No." I shake my head. "He, uh, walked me home and left. I'm sure Mom told you. It was a short walk."

"Right." He finally moves toward the door. "Well, talk to Mom and Dad tomorrow, okay?"

"Sure. Happy too."

He pauses and rests a hand on the door jamb. "All this stuff with him has really sucked. I know if people just let him prove it, they'd see he's not a bad guy. So thanks, I guess." He knocks his knuckles into my shoulder. "For giving him another chance."

I feel my face soften. "Yeah, of course."

He knocks on the door jamb before pushing away. "Night, V."

"Night, Em."

When he's left, I press my ear against the wood, not moving until I hear the soft click of his own door down the hall. I relock my door and pad to the bathroom, swinging the door open.

Reyn is standing at the counter, his back is to me. All I see are the muscles spread across his broad shoulders, that wide swath of dark scarring that always makes my own itch.

I say, "He found your shirt, but luckily, he decided it was his shirt, so we're all good. I mean, you're out a shirt, but..." I sigh, eyes dropping to my feet as I admit, "It's hard deflecting him, especially when he's trying to do all this nice stuff. I hate lying."

That's when I notice the jewelry box open in front of him. The velvet pouch is in Reyn's hand, a small pile of pills gathered in his palm. My breath catches in my throat, our gazes meeting in the mirror's reflection.

"Do you?" he asks, turning to face me. "Hate lying?"

I swallow heavily, all the blood draining from my face. Even now, just seeing the pills makes my heart skip a beat.

"You told me you weren't taking pills anymore." His voice is low and flat, those green eyes watching me, searching. "For the record? This is me, being mad at you."

"I haven't been." The lie is heavy. Stupid. "I'm not—I'm not using. Those are just old." My mind runs frantically, latching onto the first thing it sees. Apparently, that's indignation. "And what are you doing digging through my stuff, anyway? Feeling impulsive? Trying to steal *my* things now? Is nothing off limits?"

His fist closes around the pills and he crosses his arms over his chest. "I was poking around, sure. But only because I was stuck in here." His green eyes bore into mine. "I wasn't going to take anything."

"And I'm not using anymore." Bitterness coats my tongue at the thread of anger in my voice. I exhale slowly, measured, trying to rein it in. "But, when you first got back, I'd had myself weaned down to two pills a day. Even that was..." I laugh miserably, looking away. "Such a fucking struggle, you have *no idea*, Reyn. Then we fell asleep that night at your house, and we started hanging out more, and we kissed, and now we're..." I swallow. "We're doing whatever this is. And it's been... good. It *feels good*. It's easier to do it now—to just stay away from it. Being with you makes my..."

"Your what?" he prompts when I stumble. His eyes are less harsh and he's listening. Thank god he's listening.

"It makes my craving for it almost like background noise. Honestly, I haven't even thought about them until just now. It's been a while."

"But you were before?"

I beg him with my eyes to understand. "That night we recorded our confessions, I knew Emory would flip out, and he did. He lost it when we got home. But I was down to *two*, Reyn, and I know you don't get it—how big of a deal that already was, but it's true. Emory wouldn't have seen that for what it was, either. I just needed some more time to step myself down to nothing, and I got it. I'm done with it now."

He watches me closely then holds out his hand, revealing the pills. With his other hand, he opens the toilet lid. "Then toss them."

The request hurts. It's scary, the thought of not having them here like a life preserver—*just in case*. But the thought of losing Reyn over something stupid like this? I take the pills and drop them into the water. "There—happy?"

"Is that all of them?" he asks, catching my gaze. "Are there more in your room?"

I pause, thinking of how he'll look at me when I begin pulling pills from my desk drawer. My shoeboxes. My purses. My nightstand. The lipstick tube he'd stolen back for me, all those weeks ago.

"No," I lie. "That's it. No more. I'm telling you, I'm done."

I'll get rid of the others later.

He closes the gap between us, tucking me into the curve of his body. I mold gratefully against his chest. "I'm just worried about you," he says into my hair. "That shit is scary, V. I can't stand the thought of you doing that to yourself."

"I'm sorry. I should have tossed them before." Tears prick at my eyes and I cling to him, panic gripping a tight fist around my heart. "Please don't leave me."

"What?" He pulls back and touches my chin, tilting it up for our eyes to meet. His eyes sharpen in alarm at the look on my face. "Why would you think that?"

"I don't know." The tears flow now and I'm powerless to stop them. "But I've spent so much time alone, I don't know if I can do it again."

"Hey, no, that's not—" He tips forward to press a gentle, lingering kiss against my lips. "*No.*"

I sigh in relief, but cling harder. "Thank you."

"I'm sorry for going through your things. Sometimes, when things get bad, I just—I want to say I can't help it, but that'd be a lie." He pushes a lock of hair behind my ear and cups my face. "I get it, bad habits are hard to break. I'm not exactly a saint here. But if shit gets hard, you can tell me, okay? I'm not going to bail."

"You, too," I say, leaning into the touch. "When things get hard, when you feel like you need to take things, you can tell me."

His lips meet mine a second time, and it feels like a promise. An absolution. An understanding that we both have these demons inside of us, and they're always right over our shoulders, waiting for that perfect moment to twist us up.

For the first time, I feel like I may truly not be alone.

# 24

Reyn

"Put both feet on the ledge, crouch." I whisper, keeping a sharp eye toward the road, "Sit, and then you'll just ease off. I'll catch you."

I peer up at Vandy, positioning herself on the side of the small overhang under her window. When it came time to get out of the house for the fourth rite, V wanted to legit sneak out. Now that we're here, I see the fear in her eyes.

"You don't have to do this," I say, hating that spark of terror in her eyes. "You can go back. Tell your mom Sydney is having some kind of crisis, and just get Emory to drive you to the school."

"No," she says with a determinedly set jaw, "I want to do this on my own, the right way."

I'm not sure she knows what that means, but everything we do is backwards, so I get it.

"Then jump." I shift on the ground beneath her, holding out my arms. "I'll catch you."

She wiggles forward, until she's almost dangling. She peers over the edge, eyes widening. "What if I fall and I can't walk, and I won't have any explanation when—"

"Come on, baby, look at me." I make sure I look like I'm patiently waiting, but patient is the last thing I feel. If her dad comes out here, or if Jerry drives by, I'm fucked. I wait until her apprehensive eyes meet mine to say, "I promise I won't let that happen. You've got this. Remember the fence?"

She sucks in a shuddering breath and I see when she finally crosses that line, eyes clenching closed. Despite everything I just said, I still feel this sharp spike of panic when she releases her grip, pitching forward and falling.

I lunge, catching her with both arms, body folding quietly around hers.

Her face is still tightly scrunched, bracing for impact. "Did I hit the ground?"

"Nope."

She opens her eyes and looks up at me, face smoothing into a soft, relieved smile. "Thank you."

I ease her feet to the ground, hands on her hips, making sure she's steady. "They don't call me a wide receiver for nothing. Catching stuff is my job."

Her head tilts. "Did you just call me wide?"

"If I'm calling you anything," I press a kiss to the tip of her nose, "it's beautiful."

She rolls her eyes, and I love it. I love that she doesn't put up with bullshit.

We don't linger, hopping in the Jeep and heading out to the school. I'm less nervous driving her now—less anxious in general, I suppose. Maybe it's the better quality of sleep, or the fact that Vandy keeps leaving me food in my car, or maybe it's just *her*. Things are going really well with Vandy. The rituals are almost over, and homecoming is around the corner. In a perfect world, I'd ask her to go as my date, but my world isn't perfect.

I'll take what I can get.

Finding the pills was pretty fucked up, though. She looked so panicked when she saw them in my hand, like her whole world was crashing down. I hate being judged on shit from my past and I'm not going to do it with her. Jesus, if she looked in the drawer in my room at all the shit I've nicked since I've been home? I don't want to be on the other side of that judgment. My girl may not be perfect, but she's perfect for me and that's all I care about.

"Did you bring your stamp?" she asks, pulling the small box and the little card that came with it out of her hoodie pocket.

"Yeah." I gesture toward the storage area behind the gear shift. "So, miss investigative journalist. Any leads on who's leaving this shit in our lockers?"

"Or even making them up." She turns the stamp around in her hand. It came with a small inkpad and instructions about where we were specifically supposed to leave it. For us, that's on the back of a framed photograph of Martha Preston, the founder's wife, which is located in the Langford room. "It seems like all of this would take a fair amount of organization. And work. And influence."

"Someone is definitely committed to the Devil legacy."

"Yeah," she says, but she's shifting uncomfortably, not looking my way. "I actually have to talk to you about something."

I give a quick flick of my eyes. "Sounds ominous."

"No, it's not—" She pushes out this huge sigh that isn't very reassuring. "This place is on the historical register or whatever, and the things inside are artifacts. Like, super rare, well documented. If something goes missing..." She trails off, but I don't exactly need a billboard to pick up what she's putting down.

"You think I'm going to take something," I slowly realize. "I can control myself, you know."

"No, I know that," she argues, and I can see her head shake in my periphery. "I actually read this article about kleptomaniacs, and it said if there's a chance of you getting caught, then the likelihood of you—"

I bite out a sharp, "I'm not a fucking maniac."

Her mouth snaps closed and the car goes quiet, my hands tightly clenched around the steering wheel. Well, I was right about one thing. Being on the other side of that judgment shit really does suck.

*Christ.*

"I'm sorry. I didn't mean..." Her voice is small and low, and I hate it. It makes my fingers flex around the leather. "I just wanted to understand what it was like for you. Why you do it. I thought maybe if I did, I could help you. You know, like how you help me?"

I roll to a stop at a deserted red light a few blocks from the school. It casts her face in a worrying glow when I finally turn to meet her eyes. "You do help me, V. Trust me, it's been days since I took something. And it's not...it's not simple, okay? It's not something that can be summed up in some fancy term and written down in an article by someone who's never met me. Yours couldn't, could it? The way you feel about the pills?"

Her eyes are wide and so guileless that it makes me want to take her back home. "Probably not."

The light turns green, but I idle there, trying to find the words. "There isn't one reason. Just sometimes, the only thing that makes me feel good is taking something and getting away with it. I know it's stupid."

She puts her hand on my leg. "It's not stupid."

"Yes, it is," I argue. "It feels good for a few hours—maybe even a whole day—but the trouble it causes for me and everyone else? It lasts a hell of a lot longer than that." I give her a significant look. "I'm trying, V."

She studies me closely, and I can tell from the sadness in her eyes that she gets it. My family is in pieces. My future is up for debate. I can't take a jog without being watched. But what happened to her is the worst consequence of all.

The fucked-up part is that, even despite all of those perfectly valid reasons, resentment burns hot at the thought of giving it up. Why should I? Aside from Vandy, it's not like I have much else going for me. Why can't I have something that makes me feel good? The idea of a life without that rush seems like nothing more than a dull expanse of tedium. Sometimes I wonder what the point would be.

"I meant what I said before. You can tell me if it gets bad, if you feel like you need to do it. I won't think any less of you." She echoes my words from the other night, "I won't bail."

"Seriously, I can handle it." I finally press the gas, rolling over the intersection.

I drive past the main campus entrance to the service road that runs behind the dining hall. It's darker back there and easier access to the Alumni house, which is settled on a hill at the back of the property. Although everyone on campus is familiar with the house, it's not frequented by students. It's strictly for guests and donors.

I park the car and grab my stamp, then walk around to open the door for Vandy. I help her out, not because she needs it, but because she's my girl. It also gives me a chance to kiss her in apology, soothing the tension from earlier, before taking her hand and slipping into the dark shadows of the campus.

"The Preston House was built by Gerard Preston for his wife, Martha," Vandy whispers. I've conditioned myself to walk at her slower pace. "They bought the property to build a school and lived in the house. The first headmasters lived here, but eventually they turned it into a guest house."

"You sound like a Preston history textbook."

"Well," she looks away, "it's a required mini-semester in tenth grade. You kind of missed it."

I tighten my grip on her hand. "Good thing I have you to give me a primer."

She grins and veers us slightly off course. "You're right about that, because we learned that there's an entrance to Preston through an old tunnel that starts in the old water-well shed behind the building. All of these tunnels go back to the Civil War. Like the one that leads from the lake to the bunker."

We go to the small brick building that I don't think I've ever noticed before. She extracts her key and slides it into the lock, twisting it to the side. The door opens and cool, musty air rolls past.

"Creepy." I take a look back to make sure no one notices us, and then duck inside. Vandy shines her phone's light and I notice fresh footprints on the dirt floor. "Guess we weren't the first ones here."

Vandy uses her key to unlock a second, barely noticeable door and then, hand in hand, we enter the tunnel and walk the stretch underground toward the house. It's cool and damp, and the ceiling is low enough that I have to duck not to hit it. It's a little claustrophobic and I'm glad when we get to a staircase that leads up. The air is cooler up here and at the top is another door. This one leads inside the house—to a dark storage pantry. I push open the swinging door to the hallway and see a dozen frames mounted to the wall.

My eyes scan them tiredly.

Shit. Needle in a haystack.

"Did your class happen to tell you where the Langford room is?" I whisper. The caretaker is in the house somewhere. Asleep, probably. And it's possible some of the other Devils are here as well. I'm not sure what would happen to any of them if they got caught, but my own fate might as well be spun on an elaborate wheel of misfortune: swift expulsion, arrest, hard time, you name it.

"I'm not sure," she says, chewing on her lip. "But I think that the guest rooms are named after former Headmasters, and Langford was a headmaster. So probably upstairs?"

"What about the caretaker? Where are her rooms?"

"Off the kitchen." She snorts. "Like they let the help sleep upstairs."

She's right about that, so I start down the hall, away from the faint light of the kitchen, toward the staircase. We pass a formal living room and adjacent dining room. I keep my eyes diverted from the shiny trinkets and collectibles in the antique furniture. It'd be a lie to say I'm not tempted as we pass it all.

Together we climb the narrow stairs, my hand settling on Vandy's lower back, fingers slipping under her shirt to touch her skin. This need to touch her all the time, it's even more intense than my compulsion to take. The only thing I want to take from Vandy is something she wants to give—and that has to be on her terms.

I thought it was going to happen in her room the other night. It felt right, but then fucking Em had to barge in and interrupt us. He'd probably be proud of his cockblocking efforts if he knew about it. Right after he skinned me alive, that is.

I've sneaked into her room twice since then, but aside from some heavy kissing, I've managed to keep things PG-13. Pretty easy thing to do with the possibility of Emory knocking on her door again hanging like an axe over my libido.

The truth is that I need to slow down, anyway. Vandy is more into all this than I really expected her to be, but sex is a big step. You don't get that back. There are too many ways for her to get hurt.

The stairs spill into a wide landing, decorated in more antiques. She turns left, heading down a hall with thick, carpeted runners that muffle our footsteps. Vandy reaches the first door and peers at the small sign next to it. "Hamilton," it says. Clearly, this room was named after the headmaster, Bates' great-grandfather. Her fingers are paused against the crystal doorknob and she lifts them, ready to walk on, but a thud comes from inside and she jumps back, slamming into me. Over the sound of my heartbeat I hear a giggle, followed by a too-loud, "Shhhh."

I reach past Vandy and slowly open the door. Two figures stand by a dresser. The light of the flashlight reveals Caroline and Tyson. Caroline's eyes widen when she sees us, and Tyson shrinks back a little. "Fuck," he mutters, "you scared the hell out of us."

"Maybe don't make so much noise?" Vandy hisses, echoing my thoughts. These idiots in here are going to get us caught.

Caroline's gaze darts down, and I realize she sees our clasped hands. Instinctively, we both drop one another's hand and step away. *Stupid.* So fucking obvious. "This isn't the room we're looking for."

I forge ahead, flashing my phone light on the sign by each door. Langford is at the end and I open it quickly, stepping inside. The room is big, with a massive four poster bed in the center. Marble-topped tables sit on either side of the bed, and I don't hesitate to search the frames for the one we're looking for. Hearing the soft click of the door closing behind me, I glance up and see Vandy's eyes looking everywhere but at me.

"Do you think they saw?"

I sigh, trying to shove down the wild anxiety at knowing they did. "We can probably play it off." Maybe I was just helping her up the stairs. Maybe it could be like that night at the lake—just brotherly.

She says, "I wish..." but trails off, eyes wistful and averted.

"Yeah," I agree, knowing what she's thinking.

"Are we just going to keep this a secret forever?" When she finally meets my gaze, she doesn't look angry. She just looks disappointed. "If this is real—"

"It's real," I assure her, tilting her chin so I can brush my lips across hers. "Very real." There's a long silence where we watch each other, the air heavy and charged with all the things we won't say. I try to get us back on track. "It's probably one of these." I flash my phone over the photos by the bed. "Any chance that history lesson told you what Martha looked—"

The words die on my tongue when my light flashes over something hazy and solid. It's sitting on the antique dresser, angled just-so, a crystal devil a lot like the one on Headmaster Collins' desk. Only now that I'm seeing this one—old, veined, flawed—I'm realizing that his is a lackluster replica.

I want it so bad, I'm fucking *shaking* with it.

"What?" she asks, sensing my shift.

I clear my throat. "Nothing. I was just wondering what she looked like."

But her eyes follow the beam of light before I can jerk it away. "Oh."

"I wasn't going to take it," I burst, my shoulders feeling tight and tense with the defense.

"But you want to." She studies me carefully, curiously. "It'd make you feel... better. Good."

I give a shrug that looks looser than I feel. "Yeah, sure. It's not a big deal."

"Does that mean something to you? Like, symbolically?"

"No," I scoff, but deep down, I know that's not the whole truth. I'm just not sure how I'd explain seeing it on the headmaster's desk that day, and the way I'd felt then—wild and uncertain and sick inside with all the change happening.

Softly, she says, "Reyn," and I deflate.

"Fuck, V, I don't know." I drag a hand roughly down my face. "*Maybe*, okay?"

"Okay," she replies, like that's enough of an answer. "But you know that's not the only thing, right?" She steps in front of me, the backs of her knuckles grazing over the front of my pants. "It's not the only thing that can make you feel good."

And then she kisses me. It's one of those slow, deep, sexual things that fuzzes my mind out enough that it takes me an absurdly long time to understand why she's suddenly trying to unbutton my fly.

"What?" I breathe, grabbing her wrists.

Her throat bobs with a swallow. "It'll make you feel good," she explains.

"So will a milkshake from The Nerd."

She quirks an eyebrow. "Call me ambitious, but I'm sort of hoping getting a blowjob from me is better than a milkshake."

My eyes scan the room. I feel like I've missed about twenty very integral parts of this discussion. Dumbly, I repeat, "What?"

She backs up to the bed, perching on the foot of it and dragging me along. "There's a link to sexual impulsivity that I won't go into, but mainly? There's this whole thing where you've never let me actually touch you, and it's driving me crazy."

I gape down at her, at the way she brings me between her knees, eyes shining up at me, so hopeful. So trusting. I argue, "You can't just give me head in Martha Langford's bedroom," but it's a weak rebuff.

She tilts her head. "Why not?"

"Because we're in the middle of committing criminal trespassing." I watch as she stares up at me, tipping forward to mouth at the button on my jeans. I swallow thickly. "And because other people are here." Her mouth moves lower, grazing closer to the obscene bulge pressing against my pants. "Because it's not—" She presses her mouth to my cock, her hands holding my hips steady when I buck into it.

I completely forget what it's not, because mostly all I'm thinking of are her red lips and the way my dick would look disappearing between them.

Apparently, she totally *can* give me head in Martha Langford's bedroom, because when she unbuttons my fly, I don't stop her. Couldn't, really.

I mean, *fuck*.

I'm just one man with well-documented weak impulse control.

Her hand is warm and soft when it dips into the waistband of my boxers. I inhale a slow hiss at the contact, stealing a quick glance over my shoulder at the door. This is fucked. There were already about thirty ways this night could have gone wrong. Adding some impromptu head in the mix is probably way up there on my list of poor executive decisions.

She obviously wants it and god knows *I* want it. This just isn't the kind of thing you ask a respectable girl—a girl like Vandy—to do. But, as she pulls me out of my shorts and looks at my cock, her red tongue slowly peeking out to wet her lips, I'm not asking her to do a damn thing. Her choice.

All this thought is moot, because if I thought I couldn't get any harder than when she pressed her mouth to it over my jeans, then I didn't fully actualize the feel of her hand around me, the sight of her mouth *right fucking there*. I'm throbbing.

She sinks her teeth into her lip, thumb coming up to caress the tattoo on my hip. She licks the mark and my hips jerk forward. God damn. Her eyes flick up to mine, and I know what this expression means now. Glazed. Heavy. *Horny*. "I've never done this before, so tell me if I do something stupid, okay?"

Little late for that, but, "Just..." *Hurry*, I want to say, as if that'll be a problem—but the words get swallowed when she sinks her mouth down around the tip of my cock. My teeth click shut, jaw grinding at the sensation of her soft, wet mouth. God, how many times have I thought about this? Too many to be acceptable.

My breath feels like it's being yanked from my lungs when she pushes forward, her tongue slicking the way. I try to find something to do with my clenching hands, settling one loosely on her shoulder while the other ducks beneath her hair, gently cupping her neck. Her heavy eyes raise up to mine and there's a question in them—a need for criticism or praise.

All I can offer is a surprised, "Oh, fuck," as the blood rushes from my brain. She's looking up at me so sweetly, but what's happening with her mouth is anything but. She sets an unhurried rhythm that feels more about being indecisive than trying to draw it out. If we were somewhere else, I'd let her hear all the tortured noises I'm trapping in the back of my throat. Since we're not, I just rub her neck, hoping that's enough encouragement.

It's not long before I begin feeling the telltale tug of my orgasm approaching. The room is filled with my hard breaths and the sucking, wet sounds that make my toes curl. Vandy's got a hand fisted into my jeans and she never lets up. Not once.

I wind my fingers into her hair, trying to ease her off. I feel her disagreement more than I hear it, high and desperate-sounding in the back of her throat, and I know it'd be better to just let her swallow. Less mess. No fuss. But I need her to know, so I manage to grind out a low, "Baby, I'm gonna…"

She pushes back down, taking me all the way in.

It's that determination that's always drawn me to her, and I know better than to fight her. Not that I want to, because the coil in my balls unwinds and rushes through me like a tidal wave. I gasp and let it go, hitching out a strained, *"Ahhh,"* as I pulse hard and hot between her slick lips. My hand grips a tight fistful of her sweater, twisting it up. "Jesus, V."

When our eyes meet again, hers are satisfied. Mine are probably crossed.

My knees feel like jelly and there's this deep buzzing sensation happening in the pit of my stomach that is the very opposite of unpleasant. There's a reason I didn't want to do this in a rush. The urge to touch her is overwhelming, but instead I'm tucking myself back into my pants, eyes tracking the way her chest rises and falls, nearly as rapid as mine. I pull her off the bed and tell her, "You didn't have to do that."

She shrugs and straightens her sweater, but I can see how flushed she is, the way her eyes keep dragging down my body. "I told you, I wanted to."

There's no such thing as an appropriate thank you in a situation like this. I mean, there totally fucking *is*, but there just isn't time. I do the only thing I can; I kiss her on the mouth, slow and gentle, tasting myself.

"Now that we've confirmed you're a thrill junkie," I say, which elicits a smug grin, I fumble in my pocket for the stamp. "Let's find this fucking thing and jet."

She quickly agrees, eyes scanning the room for the portrait. "I think this may be our girl," she says, nodding to a framed portrait that looks similar to one we passed in the hall. It's quick work to take it down, flip it over, and add our two stamps to the back. After that, I grab her hand and lead her hastily out of the room.

It never even occurs to me to look back at the crystal devil.

# 25

Vandy

Reyn puts the Jeep into park and cuts the ignition. The parking lot is dark and deserted, nothing but the tall rise of buzzing sodium lights scattered here and there. Fleeing the Alumni house was easy. We hadn't made a sound. But inside, I was a tangled mess of want, praying that Reyn wasn't just going to drive me home.

I can't believe that twenty minutes ago, I had Reynolds McAllister's dick in my mouth.

I guess I always expected that giving a guy a blowjob would be tiresome and unpleasant. The reality was much different, though.

Reyn pulsing hard between my lips, the way his hips kept hitching forward, like he couldn't help it. The way his hand felt on the back of my neck, not pressing or insistent, but just there to make contact. The *sounds* he made—*God*—like something was torturing him. *I did that.* I made his knees tremble. I'm the reason his face collapsed into that agonized expression of ecstasy. I'm the one who tasted his release, the one he kissed so sweetly afterward with that wrung-out look on his face.

All of it coalesced like a lightning bolt striking right between my legs, and now I'm squirming, my core still throbbing in distressed wait.

Fortunately, he'd pulled the car into here.

Now we're sitting in the dark, a sea of cracked concrete spread out all around us. He'd pulled his hood up to leave Preston House and it's still like that, shielding his expression from me. I have no idea how to ask for what I want, because I can't totally parse it myself. I just know if he doesn't touch me soon, I might *die*.

I look over at him, but he's already unbuckling his seatbelt and turning to me, pushing a sucking kiss to my mouth. I meet him in the middle, fingers tangling in his sweater, holding him close.

"Christ, you're so fucking—" He sighs, hand coming down to cup me, right between my legs. He never finishes and I *need* to know what he was about to say, but the world seems to narrow down to the heel of his palm, rubbing rough and insistent against me. "Want me to...?" He trails off, fingering the button of my jeans.

My breath escapes in a loud gust. "*Yes.*"

He makes short work of it, pulling down my zipper and then stuffing his hand inside. I raise my hips into it, the feel of his fingers sliding through all my messy wetness. I take in his breath as our kiss stalls.

His eyes fall closed on a jaw-clenched groan. "Fuck, I love how wet you get."

I'm too slack-mouthed and breathless to answer back, but when my eyes drop to his hand, I gasp a sharp, "Reyn." His wrist is trapped beneath my panties, hand disappearing inside, and I can see the way he's moving it beneath the denim, these tight little circles over my clit. The sight of it makes my brow screw up in pleasure.

"Don't," he says when my chest hitches with a bitten-off sound. "Let me hear you, baby."

It's easy to forget that we can be loud here, that no one is around to catch us. I brace my hand on the fogged-up window, leaving a smudged print, and finally moan the way I want to. It's shrill and frantic, laced with an embarrassing amount of urgency.

"Yeah," he breathes. "You like that? Does it feel good?"

Reyn, I've found, is a *talker*. It drives me crazy, the way his smooth, deep voice sounds in my ear when we're doing stuff like this. It drives me crazier that I'm never coherent enough to meet it.

I nod dumbly, tongue wetting my lips. "Y-yes."

I know he doesn't have much space to work with here, and I briefly consider lifting my hips and pushing my pants away. But with a jerk of his hand, a slow slide, he somehow manages to sink one of his fingers into me, knuckle deep.

That already has me barreling toward the edge, legs trembling when I buck into it, moving my hips with his rhythm, chasing the sensation.

And then his lips come up to my ear, voice gruff. "Is it my turn to give you head now?"

I clamp my hand hard around his wrist when I come, pressing it close as I grind up against it, crying out. Just the thought of his face buried between my legs, those green eyes burning up at me, has me falling. 'Earth-shattering' is such a cliché, but that's exactly how it feels, like the ground is quaking beneath me as I fall over the edge, thighs clenching. It's almost better than the last time he did this, and that's...

That's saying a lot.

Reyn buries a warm chuckle into my throat. "Maybe next time."

It takes me a ridiculously long time to shudder through the aftershocks, lungs sucking in these frenetic little gasps. I can't seem to let his wrist go. "Oh my god, you're so good at that." I'm not sure where Reyn got the nuclear launch codes to my vagina, but here we are.

"Yeah?" he asks, his palm giving me another one of those crazy-making grinds.

I whimper in response, over-sensitive, but somehow unwilling to let him go. "So good," I emphasize.

It's difficult to let his hand slide out of my pants, but the way he licks soft and slow into my mouth soothes the loss.

He sighs when he pulls away, resting his forehead on mine. "I was trying really hard not to be that guy."

I frown. "What guy?"

"The guy who fingers you in the Kmart parking lot."

I reach up to touch his jaw, fingers rasping on the day-old stubble there. "Better than Martha Langford's bedroom." We share a quiet laugh, and I feel boneless and fizzy by the time he pulls away.

"What can I say?" He turns the keys in the ignition, fixing me with a deadpan smile. "I'm a romantic."

"You look like hell."

"Thanks," I grouch, resting my face on the art table. "I didn't get much sleep last night."

As I say it, there's part of me that wants Sydney to ask why, to question why I didn't get any sleep, to declare I look different, more mature, less...virginal. And then I can tell her that I got fingerbanged. Twice. By easily the hottest, most off-limits guy in school. And then I can finally tell someone about this thing that keeps growing in my chest, every time I see him. It's heavy and hungry, but it's also full of excitement and delight. I think I know the name for it, even if I'm too cowardly to say so.

But she doesn't ask.

In fact, what I notice the most about Sydney these days is that she never asks me about myself, at all. She never wonders what I'm doing or what's going on in my life. I realize now that she never did. It took me having something to tell to really recognize that our friendship has always been about *her* social life—the gossip that swirls around her, the boys that like her, or wish she would like them back.

My relationship with Sydney is completely one-sided, and now that I have more going on in my life—*real stuff*, with an actual, albeit secret, boyfriend—the reality of it sinks heavily in the pit of my stomach.

Sometimes I wonder if she even really likes me, or if this has always been about the spectacle of it all, nothing more.

"I texted you at midnight," she says, suddenly, pulling out her sketch pad. We start each day with a pen and ink sketch of an object on the front table. Today it's a stuffed owl. "If you were awake, why didn't you answer?"

I blink at her. "I uh—well, I had my phone turned off." I pick out a good pen, averting my eyes. "You know they suggest turning off all screens when you're having a problem sleeping? The light is bad for you."

"Mmhmm." She starts drawing the owl at the beak. Syd isn't a bad artist—she's just kind of sloppy and rushed. Much like she is with everything in her life. "That's weird, though."

"What's weird?"

"That your phone was off. Because I was scrolling though the location feature of ChattySnap and your phone was...well, *here*."

"Here?" I'm unsure if it's an accusation or a question or what. Maybe Syd has been paying more attention than I realized.

She turns to look at me. "Yeah, here. And interestingly, it wasn't the only phone showing up on campus. Emory. Aubrey. Caroline..." She watches me intently. "Even Reyn."

"That's, uh, really weird." Screw ChattySnap and its stupid tracking features! "Because there's no way I'd be on campus in the middle of the night."

"That's what I thought. Especially with Reyn—who, you know, is not allowed to be near you." This isn't actually true—not anymore— but I don't bother to correct her. She adds an eye and some details. "But then I thought about it some more, and you've been distant lately. And not in that 'too much Oxy' kind of way, either."

"Shhhhh!" I glare at her before making sure no one overheard. Our table is to the side of the room, but Syd's voice has a way of carrying. "What the hell, Syd?"

She puts down her pen, turning to me, and through the firmness in her eyes, I can tell there's also some hurt. "No, Vandy, what the hell is going on with you? You've been ditching me at lunch, blowing me off for getting our nails done, and something is obviously up. I'm not stupid. It's not the first time I've noticed your phone isn't where you say it is."

I gape at her. "Are you seriously stalking me now?"

"No. I'm trying to figure why my best friend is keeping secrets from me."

"I'm not."

She laughs and rolls her eyes, "Yeah, okay. Sure."

I push past the panic I'm feeling. I need a way out of this. She can't know about the Devils or Reyn or any of it. "I'm just...having my own life for once. I'm not sitting at home alone and feeling sorry for myself. I'm..." I glance around the room, buying time. "I'm working on something for the newspaper."

Her eyebrow raises. "Your article?"

"Yeah," I admit, my pulse thrumming. "I got a lead on something and I've been following up on it."

She leans forward, demeanor shifting from stiff to eager. Syd can't resist juicy gossip. "What is it? What did you find out?"

I shake my head. "I can't say. Not yet. No one knows."

She's quiet for a moment, and I can see the gears turning. Her eyes widen. "Does it have something to do with Reyn? Is he in trouble again? Or your brother? I love Emory, but he's got a history of not making the best decisions." She bites her bottom lip, eyes pensive. "You know, I had a feeling something was up. Things have been weird lately. Afton's more aloof than ever. Suddenly Tyson's hanging around all those former Devils..."

I freeze, panic blooming even more fiercely. *Shit.* Sydney is a nosy, selfish bitch, but she's right. She's not dumb. "Look, I can't say, Syd, but hopefully one day I'll be able to reveal it—the right way—in a big flashy exposé in the school paper."

"Okay," she says slowly, looking down at her sketch. "I wasn't trying to stalk you, I was just..."

I shrug. "No, I get it. You're used to me sitting at home all the time doing nothing. It's a change." She probably doesn't miss the bitterness in my voice.

She sighs. "It just sucks that you're never around anymore. I miss you, you know?" The words sound so sincere that, for a moment, I feel guilty. She's right, we used to be joined at the hip. And it's not like I don't think about her, too. Having all of this stuff, these feelings and new experiences bottled up inside me and not being able to tell her is hard. For a moment, I really miss her.

She turns to me, eyes sparking in delight. "I can be your partner in crime. You and me, hitting the streets, digging up the dirt. Come on, it'll be awesome!"

I shake my head sadly. "This is something I need to do on my own, you know? It's the only way to prove to Mr. Lee and everyone else that I have it in me."

She rolls her eyes. "But like, what if you don't? You need someone to do the physical stuff, and hey. Cheerleader here. I'm totally agile, like a cat."

And all my guilt is gone.

Just like that.

"I can handle it," I respond, smile so tight that my own face feels brittle.

There's truth to that statement. Truth to all of it, really. And I feel a little better about adding more deceit to the piles I've been building lately. Even if I wanted to let Sydney in on this I wouldn't, I couldn't, and I don't. Ironically, the idea of exposing the Devils has started to lose some of its appeal. I'm working on the article less and less, because among all the lies and deceit are a couple hard-earned truths.

One of them is that I'm more interested in being part of the group than taking them down.

WITH MY PARENTS' approval, Reyn is now allowed to sit with us at lunch. For the past few days, I haven't had to worry about being seen with him. That's the good news.

The bad news is that it's harder and harder to pretend everything is normal between us. That we're just part of the same social circle. That he's just my brother's best friend. That we don't kiss when backs are turned, or steal little grazing glances beneath the lunch table, or as we leave our driveways, or as we pass in the halls.

And it's getting downright impossible to ignore that I'm falling in love with him.

We sit across from one another in the bunker, along with the other Devils and Playthings. It's only been a few days since breaking and entering into the Preston House, but Emory holds another card in his hand, the fifth rite.

We're almost done.

"The next rite is one the Devils managed to maintain through the years, even if it was a little bastardized." His eyebrows raise. "A test. Seven minutes in Hell—the *Stairway* to Hell, that is. Like the tattoos, it's time to get marked. Only this time, by someone in the group."

"Wait," Afton says. "I've already been marked. Freshman year. Well, and junior year. Does that count?"

Elana nods next to her.

"No dice," Emory says, shrugging. "You have to be marked by a current member or pledge, but for those of you in a committed relationship, there's some leeway. The official Devil's mark is under the ear." Right, the famous hickey. Many girls have sported them proudly over the years. Last year, Sydney herself had supposedly scored herself one, although I sometimes suspect it wasn't made by a Devil at all. "Other than that, it's up to you and your partner how far you, uh, want to take it."

I can't help the way my eyes snap to Reyn's, but he's already watching me, slouched low in his chair, eyes dark.

It's awkward listening to my brother vaguely talk about blow jobs, especially when he thinks I have no experience with them. I have no doubt Emory and Aubrey have already gone there, if not further. Emory doesn't take stuff slow. And Campbell? She built her entire reputation around being the blow job queen, just like Hamilton Bates had his little test. I guess I shouldn't be surprised this is the one rite that managed to stand the passage of time *and* they managed to work it in the guys' favor.

Perverts.

"How are partners going to be established?" Caroline asks, eyes darting around the group.

"Playthings choose their Devils." The fact that his eyes seem to jump over me gives me an uneasy feeling. "You'll write down the name of the Devil you want to go to the Stairway with, and turn it in. Since there could be overlap, I may have to make some executive decisions." He smirks at Aubrey.

Slips of paper are passed around, followed by stubby pencils. My heart pounds in my ears and I stare at my hands. You'd think that with the decision in my hands, it would be a no-brainer. Reyn, obviously. But if I write his name down, if I choose him, Emory will know. Everyone will know. Why would I pick the guy who'd done irreparable damage to me as my partner in this? But my brother had tossed us together over and over again, so could he really be surprised?

"Okay, Devils, let's give the girls a few minutes to make their decisions. You'll be notified of your meet-up time and partner by our usual methods of communication."

"Wait, wait. I think I need to campaign a little here," Sebastian says, a wolfish grin on his lips. "For the record, my favorite song is *The Devil Went Down on Georgia*." He gives Georgia a lewd wink.

All eyes shift to Georgia, and I think we're all expecting her to blush or brush him off. Sebastian flirts with her and Caroline pretty indiscriminately, and it's obvious that it flusters them—which I suspect is part of the draw. But to everyone's surprise, Georgia simply smiles back and openly writes "Bass" on her slip. Sebastian is giving her a look full of raised eyebrows when she drops it into the box.

"Put up or shut up, Bass," she says, flouncing gracefully from the room with the other guys.

He mutters a pleased, "Good shit," and follows them out.

I feel sick with nerves, watching each girl consider the name of the Devil they want on their paper. Aside from Aubrey who, let's face it, is putting my brother's name down, any of these girls could choose Reyn and be paired with him without a second thought from Emory.

Afton stands and holds up her slip, announcing, "I've put down Tyson, so hands off. He's the only other Devil involved in a long-term relationship."

I want to point out that her boyfriend is also in a long-term relationship—with his *wife*—but I'm actually a little scared of Afton and don't want her to kick my ass. Plus, she's right. It gives Tyson an out which I think he'd appreciate.

Elana taps the pencil against her chin as though she's deep in thought, which seems unlikely, but soon writes a name in loopy cursive. I peer over, trying to catch a look, but she quickly folds it over. Caroline looks a little pale. I'm not sure how many boys she's dated—if she ever has. She's always been notoriously focused on her academics. Math geek, everyone calls her, even though she's incredibly pretty. For a moment, I think that this could be the rite that breaks her, but eventually she writes down a name and turns it in.

She leaves looking assured and determined.

That means I'm last.

I know in my heart whose name I need to write down on the slip of paper. Not need—want. The thought of putting anyone else down is physically repulsive to me. And seriously, screw my brother. Screw the rules. Screw everything.

For the first time, even if it's in secret, I write Reyn's name down and claim him for my own.

# 26

I HAVE a physical reaction when I see the black envelope taped to the inside of my locker. I know Vandy had to have written down my name, that she's got to be willing to take the risk of Emory figuring out what was going on with us, because any other option—for her or me—doesn't sit right. It's a relief to have that confidence. I don't want another guy touching her any more than she probably wants another girl touching me.

*That,* we're in agreement about.

But I open the envelope anyway, checking for the time of our date in the Stairway.

*Loyalty to a collective many is creditable. Now you must prove your loyalty to one. We form our wicked chains with the links of flesh and temptation.*

*Meet Miss Afton Cross in the Stairway to Hell at 7p.m. A Devil is a gentleman, and a gentleman does not leave a lady waiting or wanting.*

*"To live and burn in everlasting fire,*

*So I might have your company in hell"*

*Elevatio Infernum*

Afton Cross?

I skim the front, eyes jerking up and glancing down the hall. Emory's leaning against the wall, tucking a piece of hair behind Aubrey's ear. I glance back at the name on the card again.

*AFTON CROSS?*

What the motherfucking *fuck*?

The envelope burns in my pocket all day, as does the question. Through lunch, I keep shooting sharp looks at Vandy, but she just smiles back at me, like nothing is amiss. I wait until right before practice, as Emory laces up his football pants, to hold up the card and say, "Afton? Seriously?"

I deserve an Academy Award for my stunning portrayal of Man Who Isn't About To Fuck Some Shit Up.

His expression turns sympathetic. "Look, dude, I'm sorry I saddled you with a chick who won't put out. But she's dating that gross old guy, and I figured you would at least respect her decision not to go too far. I don't trust the other guys not to throw down about it and cause a problem."

He's worried about *Afton* all the sudden?

"What," I say, struggling to keep an even tone, "about your sister? I thought maybe since you'd put us together for the other challenges, you'd do that again."

He pats me on the shoulder. "Yeah, well, I let you off the hook for this one. Way too awkward." He snorts and grabs his practice jersey. "It'd be like you hooking up with your little sister, right?"

My teeth hurt from all the grinding. "Was Afton the only one who put down my name?"

Emory barks a laugh. "The funny thing is that Afton put down Tyson, and Vandy chose you. I guess she didn't know who else to write."

The relief is short-lived. "So, you changed it," I say slowly.

"Yeah, I gave her Tyson instead. He's dating that religious girl, so he's used to playing it safe." His jaw goes tense. "I don't like the idea of her with anyone, but I know he'll keep it in his pants. I threatened to chop that fucker's balls off if he did anything besides give her a hickey, so I think all is safe on that front."

He's oblivious of my stare, continuing on with dressing-out. Mechanically, I open my own locker, thinking of what it's going to be like giving Afton Cross a hickey. Thinking of seeing Tyson's mark on *my* fucking girl. I'm halfway through unbuttoning my shirt when I turn to him and say, "She deserves to have a choice."

He looks up from where he's adjusting his cup. "What?"

"Vandy," I say, shutting my locker too hard. I know I'm probably being obvious here. I don't care. "She deserves a choice in who she marks and who marks her."

"Hey, I'm just doing you a solid here. The idea of her being involved in this at all makes me want to puke. None of these guys are worthy of her." He eyes sweep over me. "She just picked you because she had no idea who else to put down. She has zero experience, dude. None."

Emory is such a fucking idiot that it's a physical battle not to fly over the bench and throttle him. So utterly damn clueless. He has no idea that not only has his sister kissed a guy before, she's sucked the brains out through one's dick. And, also? She's good at it. My cock twitches just thinking about her hot mouth and tight pussy.

If I thought I was horny all the time before, I was wrong. Knowing how good her mouth feels, what she looks like staring up at me as I come? It makes my dick hard and my brain foggy. That has to be why I don't hesitate to say, "I've learned a few things about Vandy over the last few weeks, Em, and it's time for you to stop interfering with her life. She's smart and strong. She knows what she's doing and she knows what she wants. She's done every single one of the challenges you've thrown at her and if she wants to go up in that tower with me, or," I swallow, "anyone else, you should let her."

"What's it to you, anyway?" He says, eyes narrowing.

"Maybe she put my name down because I'm the only one she feels that comfortable with, did you ever think of that? It's not about me, it's about Vandy." And truthfully, I mean it. If Vandy had chosen Tyson, it'd fuck me up inside, but I'd find a way to deal.

"It sure seems like it's about you." His eyes flash angrily and he steps over the bench, chest puffed out. "You want to be the one who marks her? Trust me, you've already done that. You left the only mark on her that can't be taken away. Even the fucking tattoo can be removed, but not the scars. Not the limp. Not the surgeries that apparently turned her into a fucking junkie. Now you want to add another one?"

If he'd punched me, it would have hurt less.

It isn't that he's wrong. We both know he's right. Can't argue with that, can I? I take and take and take from that girl and she just keeps giving. But it isn't that he's right, either.

No, what hurts is the realization that Emory had never really forgiven me for what happened. That it could be years and years down the line, no matter what, and he'd still have that old wound to hang over my head, to use against me.

And if it means keeping me away from his sister, he will.

I'm rendered speechless for so long that the sharp burn of anger begins fading from his eyes. It's replaced with something cold, but wary. "Dude, look—"

I cut him off. "Do you think I care about this juvenile Devil bullshit? Do you? Do you really think for *one second* I'm in this for the legacy and prestige of being pinned by some rich cocksuckers as worthy?" My nostrils flare and I meet him over the bench. "No, we were supposed to be doing this so that, next year, some high and mighty asshole doesn't get put in the position to tell Vandy that what she wants doesn't matter." My nostrils flare, voice low and hard. "If *you're* that asshole, then what the *fuck* am I doing here?"

He's watching me, face gone shuttered, but I'm ripping off my shirt. I never change with the guys, too ashamed of my scars to let them become something whispered about between jocks. I don't even fucking care anymore.

Vandy isn't the only one who's been marked for life, and I might have been the one driving, but Emory wanted me to do it.

I turn to my locker, shoving my shirt inside, and I know he's staring at my scars. After a suspended moment, I hear some of the other guys go quiet, too. It makes my stomach roll painfully, but I thrust my arms into my gym shirt and yank it harshly over my head like it's not making me sick to be seen like this.

When I slam my locker, turning around, Emory's back on his side of the bench, pulling a roll of tape from his locker.

We don't speak to each other for the rest of the day.

I'VE NEVER BEEN SO tired as I am walking across campus toward the tower. It's early evening, which means there are a lot of people around. Kids are walking to and from the dorms for dinner. Homecoming week begins Monday, which adds a new dynamic to the climate. The cheerleaders spent the afternoon painting giant banners for the game and are just now walking to their cars. Coach Morris wants a blow-out and he kept us late, running a million fucking suicide sprints. Vandy could probably out-run me at the moment. With a quick glance around, I duck into the tower when no one is looking and head up the stairs.

I made a decision during practice. I'm not going to give Afton the mark or let her give one to me. I can't do it. There's no other girl I want to be with. I won't hold it against Vandy if she's marked by Tyson and I'll *try* not to kick his ass.

Try.

No promises.

*Shit.* This is a clusterfuck and there's only one person to blame. Emory.

If he'd just let things be and trust his sister to make her own decisions, maybe he'd see that she's not an idiot. She's not *him*. God, the fucking irony of him believing he can make better decisions for *anyone*, let alone someone as strong-willed as his sister. Regardless, I'm going to have to reject Afton, which will probably cost me my spot in the group. Hers too, unless he'll give her another Devil on account of me bailing on it.

It sucks, because despite what I'd said to Emory, I have grown to like the club. Everyone is pretty cool. The rites are stupid and childish, shit you'd expect a fifteen-year-old to get up to. But at fifteen, I was locked away, forced to become another subordinate in Mountain Point's faceless, unfeeling mass. I never got to do shit like this. So yeah, I won't lie. It was sort of fun, too.

But most of all, it brought me and V together. I know leaving the group won't change that, which is why I'm willing to accept the consequences. Whatever we've got, it's bigger than the Devils. She's the only part of this I can't do without.

I make my way up the spiral staircase, somewhere I haven't been in years. As I approach the landing, I glance up and see the beam that holds the bell and eye the notches. Despite what I'd told Vandy, I know that beam has my name on it. Three notches. Kind of pitiful, but I'd barely been a Devil for more than a blink. I know it's a dumb tradition, but back then, I was different. I still bought into the hype. I'd been proud of being added to the legacy, the notoriety.

But this isn't the way I want to add to it.

As I round the curve, I see a pair of scuffed loafers, ankles peeking out just above white socks. The owner is sitting on the spiral steps, face just out of sight. Like a traitor, I follow the slope of toned calves and rounded knees. I will myself to stop, because this has to be close to cheating. But fuck-it-all, I'm still a guy and there's nothing, *nothing*, that turns me on like the hem of a short skirt grazing an upper thigh. My gaze inches upward into the beckoning space between those sexy knees. They shift slightly, revealing a dark circle on the pale, inner thigh.

Ink. *My* ink. I jolt up the steps and there she is, my girl, lounging back on her elbows, waiting for me.

"Thank fuck you're here." I drop my bag and drop next to her, wrapping my arms around her body.

She laughs, her chest vibrating against mine. "What do you mean? You didn't really think I'd put down anyone else's name, did you?"

Em. He must have listened and fixed this. I open my mouth to explain, but I stop myself. He did the right thing and she doesn't need to know how close he was to fucking this up for her, for me, and the club.

"So," she says, leaning back. A shout from below bounces in the open, arched window in the bell tower above. No one can see us, but we can hear them. "I've never done this before. Any advice?"

"It's just a kiss," I reply, bending to kiss her under the ear, lathing my tongue on the thin skin. "So soft that you don't even realize it's leaving a mark."

Her pupils dilate and her hips shift. "What about the other stuff?"

I reach down to her skirt, fingering the hemline. "What other stuff?"

Her hand slides down the front of my pants, where my cock has been at the ready since I saw those ankles. "The other tests." There's a smile in her voice. "I know the only test we're required to pass is the mark, but I know the other traditions—about what couples do up here—how they got those slashes under their names on the beam."

*Ah*. The blowjobs.

"V, you and I have passed a million tests already. Pain, pleasure, distance, fear." I press my forehead to hers. "You don't have to get on this dirty floor to prove anything to me."

Her lips turn downward, into a soft, sexy pout. "But I liked it."

"Actually," I say quickly, "you're a Devil now. You were talking about the Playthings having their own notches, right?" I smirk as comprehension comes over her features. I've been thinking about doing this for weeks now—practically begging her to let me—and just the possibility has me straining against my pants now. I inch my finger up her thigh. "Do you want it?"

She looks into my eyes, face flushing, voice a fluttery breath. "You know I do."

I kiss her hard, stomach igniting at the permission—the promise. My lips move down her jaw, mouthing at the curve leading into her neck. I choose my spot right beneath her ear and gently suck my mark into the skin there, feeling her chest heave at the sensation

My hands travel on their own, fingers deftly plucking the first four buttons of her shirt. I dip my hand inside, grazing the swell of her fantastic tits, cupping them. She makes a soft sound when my thumb rubs over her nipple, already hard and pebbled. Her moan is sexy, perfect, and I work the spot under her ear until I'm sure it'll leave a nice, dark bruise.

"That mark is for them," I tell her, sweeping her hair back to inspect it, fingertips skating over the damp skin. Fuck, the sight of my mark on her makes my chest clench.

I drop two steps, positioning myself in front of her and nudging her to lean back on her elbows. I finish unbuttoning her shirt, revealing the rest of her body. I pay attention to the slash of pale skin on her torso. I kiss the scar—the mark I never wanted to leave— wishing more than anything that I could make it fade forever. But she's not the only one marred by that night. We've both been broken. What people like Emory can't see is that we've both been put back together, too. Maybe it's not pretty, not tidy and clean, but it's ours.

After I dote on her belly, I shift to my knees, eyes level with her thighs. I run my fingers over the tattoo and give it a ghost of a kiss. Then on the opposite side I nip her with my teeth, sucking another mark into the skin there. Her hips writhe as I pull the skin with my mouth, rubbing my palm up her other leg, soothing the nerves she'd deny having.

I pull away, admiring my handiwork. "This mark is for me."

I skate my hands up her thighs, catching her skirt as I go, revealing all of that soft skin. I look up at her, making sure she's okay. Her hands grip the edge of the step, and she swallows thickly, eyes locked with mine. Yeah, she's more than okay. I'll never understand how anyone could look at Vandy and see someone who's *less*.

She's perfection.

Hooking my fingers in those crisp white panties, I hold her eyes, waiting. She lifts up in response, bracing her hand on my shoulder, and I pull them down and over her hips. Her knees wobble as I drag them down each foot, before tucking them in my back pocket.

*Mine now.*

"Are you sure?" she asks, cheeks flushed red and her knees slowly closing. "I think our positions are supposed to be reversed."

"I'm so fucking sure," I say, pitching forward to press my lips against her mouth. "I've been thinking about this for so long." I punctuate this by touching her there, fingers easing sightlessly through her folds, getting her ready for my mouth. I watch as her gaze goes heavy, eyelids sliding closed, and take the opportunity to look down. I take a long, enthralled moment to watch my fingers working against her. "Just relax, okay? I'm going to make you feel so good."

She shudders out a slow, "Okay."

Despite that, when I drop back down, cupping her knees, I have to whisper, "Open your legs for me, baby." She exhales, eyes glued to mine, and lets her legs fall open. I gather her skirt up at her waist and duck between her thighs, pressing a long, open-mouthed kiss to her pussy.

She gasps, fingers thrusting suddenly into my hair. When I flick out my tongue, her fingers clench, tugging hard, and it feels so good that I groan against her and feel her responding shudder. I hook my hands around her thighs, letting my palms run up and down as I finally—*finally*—taste her. At some point, the taut, tense thighs beneath my hands begin relaxing, slowly falling open. The nervous, inexperienced girl vanishes as her hips rise, bucking forward into my ministrations. Her breathing turns from deep inhalations to these sharp, quick hitches that have her chest jerking up and down. I can't stop touching the soft skin of her inner thighs, my hands skating up and down, squeezing, kneading.

I raise my eyes to lock with hers, cock throbbing at the wrecked expression on her face.

"Oh my god," she cries, and I smile against her, keeping a smart remark about being a god to myself. She's the goddess, writhing under me, yanking my head closer by my hair, riling me up in a way I never knew was possible. Someday, I'll get to tell her that it's not just about sex. That she makes my dick hard and my balls ache, but that there's also something new and terrifying in the pit of my chest, and that's the thing driving me forward here, desperate to elicit a smile from her just as much as these blissful sounds she's making.

Lofty cries echo up the tower, and when she comes, it's like she's ringing the damn bell with her voice. She trembles, legs weakly clamping around my ears, until they fall to the side and I lift my head, seeing that she's flat on her back, eyes closed, facing the ceiling. I smooth down her skirt, wipe my mouth, and lie next to her. Her chest rises and falls, and I rest my hand over her belly, covering her scar.

"Are we okay?" I ask, hoping I hadn't crossed a million lines.

She turns her head. "Why would you ask that? It felt—amazing. Did I do something wrong?"

"Fuck no, you did everything right."

It's dark when we leave the tower, both freshly marked. It sucks that I can't hold her hand, but I give her a kiss before I push her out the door and onto the quad. It feels wrong having any kind of distance after what we'd experienced in the Stairway. Like what we did was shameful. I'm definitely not ashamed to have the taste of Vandy on my tongue.

I give her five minutes to get across the campus, to the parking lot, before I walk into the cool, fall air. I'm passing the main building when I see Sydney leaning against the wall in a pair of black, skin-tight booty-shorts that barely cover her ass. Her eyes narrow briefly when she sees me, but then her lips quirk into a smile.

"Reyn, hey."

I don't slow my stride. "Hey, Syd."

She pushes off the wall and rushes to catch up. "My car's in the shop and my sister was supposed to pick me up. According to Chatty-Snap, though, she's at the Nerd with her boyfriend." She rolls her eyes. "Any way I can catch a ride home?"

At this point, we're in the parking lot, a few feet away from my Jeep. Saying no would be rude as hell, and despite everything, she's Vandy's friend. "Yeah, sure." I unlock the doors. "Hop in."

I toss my bag in the back and get behind the wheel. Sydney slides in the front seat as I crank the engine. She lifts her foot and rests it on the glove compartment, eyes searching her leg. "Shit. I knew it."

I glance over. She has a huge black mark on her inner thigh. "Damn, what happened?"

She grazes her fingers over the bruise. "Oh, collateral damage from being on top of the pyramid. I have bruises *all* over my body." She grins. "But you'd know all about that, being a football player."

"Yeah, I guess," I mutter, pulling out of the parking lot, as she starts to go into a rant about how cheerleaders are real athletes despite everyone just thinking they're for show.

"You wouldn't believe how hard we work. There's cardio, tumbling, strength training... it's a serious workout." She pulls up the hem of her shirt. "Check out my six-pack."

I nod, but barely look. I'm still humming from my time in the Stairway. Whatever this girl is selling, I don't want any.

"Uh," I say, pulling up to the four way stop. "Where do you live?"

"Cedar Grove," she replies pointing to the left. "You haven't been to my house before, have you? I have a pool. You should come by sometime for a swim."

It feels egotistical to assume a chick wants on your dick, because let's face it, usually they don't. They want a compliment, or a little flirting. But Sydney? I have a feeling she'd be into road head if I suggested it. Which I'm not. What I want is to get her out of my car. Despite having done this out of respect to Vandy, it suddenly feels like anything but.

"I have this new bikini," she continues, unaware that I'd stopped listening to figure out if it would be bad form to toss her out at the next stop sign. "It's white with black stars. Luckily, our pool is heated so we can use it all year. My dad also installed a new hot tub that is so relaxing after a long workout." She pauses and then adds, "I've been trying to get Vandy to come hang with me, but she's busy all the time. Plus, you know how she is about bathing suits."

I turn into the Cedar Grove entrance and frown. "What do you mean?"

"God, she's so self-conscious. About the scars. Like, I would die if I had to wear a one-piece forever, especially if I had her rockin' bod."

Talking to Sydney is like trying to decipher a puzzle. One sentence is a compliment. The next an insult. She digs and pokes and soothes, all at the same time. No wonder Emory is so lukewarm about their friendship.

"I don't know," I say, hating the game she's playing. "Scars can be kind of sexy."

I can feel her stare hot on the side of my face, and I know she's trying to come up with something flippant, something to shift the conversation back to her. She snaps her mouth shut, and after flipping her hair over her shoulder, gestures to a large brick house coming up on our right. I pull up to the curb, making it very clear that I am *not* going inside.

I already know she's going to ask.

I'm staring out the front window, waiting for her to open the door when I feel her hand on my thigh. "Thanks for the ride. Let me show some appreciation, yeah? My parents aren't home, if you want to relax in the hot tub. I bet your muscles could use a little heat."

"Thanks," I tell her, gripping her hand and removing it off my leg. What I really want to say is that I'm dating the most beautiful, sexy, amazing girl in the world. But that's a secret and Sydney definitely can't keep one of those. Instead, I say, "But things are really busy right now, with football and catching up on schoolwork. It doesn't leave a lot of time for social stuff."

"Right." Her chin falters. "Well, you let me know when you're ready to start... *socializing.*"

"Bye, Syd," I say, raising my eyebrows. Normally brushing off a girl would be no big deal. But she's Vandy's friend and I'm not going to interfere with that.

"Bye," she says, well aware she's been rejected. Evidently undeterred, she gives me a beaming smile as she steps out.

I exhale the instant she shuts the door and drive as fast as I can to get away from certain trouble.

# 27

---

Vandy

"Ms. Hall, can you come in my office for a moment?"

I stop when I hear Mr. Lee call my name, and awkwardly cut through the crowded hallway to get to his room. He leans against the door jamb, glasses slipping down his nose. I follow him into the office.

"Next week is Homecoming," he says, as though this isn't already well known. The whole school has started to get the buzz—the dance proposals, girls sharing photos of dresses, guys wagering over the game. There's a big banner two doors down from Mr. Lee's room announcing ticket sales at lunch. "I just wanted to make sure you know that you'll be on duty all week."

"Other than the game?"

"The game, the pep-rally, the parade." He sits behind his desk. "Really any and all activities. It's kind of an all-hands-on-deck scenario. If you're there, take some photos and write it up. We always put out a special edition of the newspaper."

Something niggles at my mind. "What about the Alumni Fundraiser?"

Emory mentioned that it's a mandatory event for the Devils. Why? He hasn't said yet, but I suspect it has something to do with the final rite.

He looks surprised. "That event is traditionally for just the alumni and special guests. They'll hire a PR person and their own photographer for the event. You don't need to worry about that. The teachers don't even get an invite," he adds with a mutter. "Just make sure you get photos of the football team and the cheerleaders. That's what brings in the most donations anyway. Then, if we're lucky, they'll toss us a few bucks for new software."

Of course the football team and cheerleaders bring in the most donations, I think, walking down the hall. Everything in this place circles back around to the same groups promoting the same things; football, cheerleaders, doting on alumni. Preston Prep is like a snake eating its tail.

I push into the bathroom and hear Sydney's voice before I round the metal partition. I stop, not wanting to get into it with her today. Things have been tense and weird between us lately, especially after I rejected her offer for 'partner in crime'. She's too nosy for her own damn good. I saw her last night when I was leaving the tower. She must have been waiting for a ride. I managed to avoid her only by going all the way around the building to get to the parking lot.

I start to turn, but before I can get out of the door, I hear someone say, "So, is it true?"

"Is what true?" Syd asks.

"That you and Reynolds McAllister hooked up last night?"

My stomach bottoms out and my hand clenches the door handle. I recognize the second voice as Fiona Davidson, another cheerleader.

"Where did you hear that?" Syd asks, not denying it.

Please deny it.

*Please.*

"Regina Beckwith told me in second period. She said someone saw you get into Reyn's Jeep last night after practice. And then he comes to school today with a hickey!"

I feel a little better then, knowing they're talking about *my* mark. I'd put it on him in the Stairway. The relief is short-lived, though.

"Well," Syd says teasingly, "he did give me a ride home."

"And?!" Fiona's chomping at the bit.

"And I may have invited him to hang out in the hot tub as a thank you."

"Oh my god. You were in a hot tub with Reyn? He's so fucking sexy."

"Mmhmm," she replies.

"Tell me everything."

"Oh, come on, Fi, you know I'm not one to kiss and tell."

Sydney is literally one to kiss and tell. She's one to kiss and shout. She'd kiss and hire a fucking skywriter. I feel like throwing up.

"Reyn was a gentleman," I hear the smile in her voice, "but let's just say he was concerned about the bruises I got at practice and wanted to make sure I was okay."

"That nasty one on your inner thigh?"

A tight fist constricts my lungs, stealing my breath, and *god*, this hurts. I've experienced a lot of pain in my life, but nothing is like the razor-sharp blade of anguish that buries itself into my stomach right now.

"Yep."

She dissolves into giggles, and I bolt from the room, trying to keep the bile from rising in the back of my throat. The hallway is jam-packed and my slow entry into the stream of walkers is halted and awkward, causing me to slam into the back of another student. His shoulders throw back. "Watch it!" he shouts, spinning around and throwing his arms out. The action forces his hand into the books I'm carrying, flinging them across the hall and knocking me against the lockers. It might hurt, but I can't feel anything besides this stomach-churning sickness. He's still yelling. "God damn it, if one more underclassman rams into me in the hallway, I'm gonna—"

His words cut short and I think it's because he's realized it's me—the poor crippled girl—but then I see the large hand on his shoulder yanking him harshly back. I see the tuft of blond hair next.

"You're going to what?" Sebastian asks, palm slamming hard into the guy's shoulder. "What the fuck were you going to say, Pierce?" His eyes are hard as stone as he steps up to him. Pierce, whoever he is, looks like he may wet his pants. So do some of the guys inching around them, even though I can see the anticipated buzz on their faces. Sebastian icily challenges, "Well? Go on, I'm dying to hear it."

"N-n-nothing," he says, glancing over at me, awareness finally dawning on him. He looks around desperately, but Sebastian just smiles, sharp and cutting, like this is the best day of his life. Pierce swallows. "Nothing, dude. I swear."

"Apologize to my friend." His gaze darts to mine and I know he sees the tears in my eyes, completely unaware that I'm not hurt—not physically. My heart is aching, betrayal lodged like barbed wire in my throat. Sebastian adds, "You're going to want to speak up, fuckwit. Enunciate clearly. And trust me when I say it'd better be sincere as hell."

Pierce turns haltingly, like he's afraid looking away from Sebastian will tempt him to pounce. From the look on Sebastian's face—cheerily murderous—he's right to be wary. "I'm sorry. I know it was an accident. I shouldn't have lost my temper."

"Everyone clear the hall!" Dr. Ross's authoritative voice fills the corridor. No one wants to be the subject of her wrath, so the crowd disperses quickly. "Mr. Wilcox, I know you aren't involved in any kind of hallway altercation."

"No ma'am," he says, posture and face shifting to perfect politeness. The southern drawl slides back into place. "Just looking out for my fellow classmates."

Her dark eyes meet mine. "Ms. Hall, are you okay?"

*No. Yes. No.* I manage a jerky nod. Her eyebrow arches and I grind out, "Yes ma'am."

Sebastian walks over, having collected my books from the floor. "I'll make sure she gets to class," he says to Dr. Ross, and for some reason, she seems satisfied leaving me in the care of a possible psychopath. The weird thing is that I'm okay with it, too.

I follow him, only halfway aware when he pushes open the girls' bathroom door and leads me inside.

"Uh," I pause. "Sebastian..."

He doesn't stop, just continues in. Thoughtlessly, I do the same. This time the room is empty—Sydney no doubt having seen the dramatics in the hallway and has probably already posted video of it online. He stops by the sink and reaches in his pocket, pulling out a cloth handkerchief. He douses it with water and directs, "Here, wipe down your face."

I do as I'm told. I'm caught somewhere between epic embarrassment about what happened in the hall and still aching at this empty pit my chest has become. While I clean up, Sebastian leans against the sink, studying the room.

"So, it's true. You girls have way nicer digs than we do." He crosses his arms over his chest. "Want to tell me what's going on?"

I avert my eyes. "You saw what happened."

"I did, but I also saw you right before that asswipe threw a tantrum. You were already upset."

I exhale and look at my face in the mirror. My eyes are ringed with red and there's still a smear of mascara across the bridge of my nose. I wipe it again and my hair shifts, revealing the poorly concealed Devil's Mark under my ear. Quickly, I pull my hair back over it, hoping that people can't see the other, less visible marks he's left on me. I confess, "I overheard some gossip about... well, someone I know. And it bothered me."

He snorts. "Gossip? Why are you letting gossip bother you? Do you know how much bullshit goes around this place? None of it is ever true."

"But Sydney said—"

He barks a sudden laugh. "Sydney said?" I nod and he shakes his head. From here, I can see the Devil's mark that someone—Georgia ostensibly—gave to him. "Come on, you were her friend, weren't you? I know you know her better than this. Definitely don't listen to a word that comes out of her mouth, because trust me. Nothing she says is even remotely based in reality."

This is Sydney's reputation, and Sebastian's right. No one understands that better than me. But the thing most people don't get about Sydney is that her lies are always full of little truths. He notices my hesitation and runs an anxious hand through his hair.

"Look, did she ever tell you what went down between the two of us?"

I frown. "You and Sydney?"

He groans. "First, there is no 'me and Sydney', but yes, we had a brief... situation."

It's not like Sebastian to hedge, he usually tosses everything out there for the world to see. "What kind of situation?"

He twists the ring on his finger. "It happened last year—a few times. We'd end up at the same party, drink the same shitty beer, get a little high, make out a bit. Some...other things."

"Oh, Sebastian. No."

"I know! Stupid fucking move, V. So stupid, but I was drunk, high, and definitely horny." He holds up three fingers. "The trifecta of bad decision-making."

I wrinkle my nose. "So what happened?"

"I blew her off—big time. Total dick move." He shrugs. "But then I started hearing all these little rumors. Shit about how things went a lot further than they did. Stuff about us fucking, and then actually dating."

"Did she get the wrong impression?"

"Not a chance. I was clear—crystal, fucking, clear." He gives me a level look. "She's a clinger, V. Stage-five. She doesn't always take no for an answer, and if it suits her, she'll create a situation that resembles fantasy more than reality."

I nod, feeling a little better, but then I circle back around to what I'd overheard her say to Fiona.

"She said something that—"

"Is this about Reyn?"

I whip my head toward him, eyes wide. "What? Why would it have anything to do with Reyn?"

He raises an eyebrow. "Now who's not telling the truth? I know about you two."

My mouth forms an argument that my voice can't seem to vocalize. Instead, I deflate, wondering, "How?"

He lifts a shoulder. "Intuition. That, and the fact I saw you two leaving the Preston House the other night after your B&E. I forgot my key in my car and saw you two getting into his Jeep." I try to think back about that night—but my mind is a foggy void of anything that happened after I sucked him off. Sebastian happily fills me in. "You were holding hands and well, let's just say guys don't kiss a girl like that unless he likes her. A lot."

I groan, slumping against the counter. "Please don't tell—"

"Your brother? Yeah, no worries. I like a fight, but overprotective brothers who are also quarterbacks? Not the one I'd pick." He tilts his head. "Is that what this is about? Reyn? Did Sydney say something about him?"

I try to swallow, but my throat feels like sandpaper. "She said that he... that *they*..." I can't quite get the words out of my mouth. The image is hard enough. "That they were together."

He rolls his eyes, pushing a loud 'pshh' from his lips. "Total bullshit. I'm talking free-range, cage-free, locally-sourced, one-hundred-percent organic *bullshit*. I might not know him that well, and I'm not saying guys aren't assholes, because we are." A flicker of guilt crosses his face—possibly thinking about his confession of hitting that girl. "But Reyn? Nah. Take it from someone who's used to measuring other dudes up. McAllister's the ride-or-die type. I've seen you two since Preston House. The guy looks at you like you're the sun. Holding your chair out for you? Always touching you beneath the table? Eyes glued to you every time you're in the same room? *Jesus Christ.* If that's not a sign of a boy who's whipped..."

I watch him, feeling alarmed. "If you noticed all that—"

"Then your girl Sydney probably has, too." He shrugs loosely. "And we both know she's the jealous and vindictive type. Let me guess, she's had it bad for McAllister since school started? Mad at you for blowing her off for the Devils? Are two and two making four yet?"

That information hits almost harder than the gossip about Reyn. Is Sydney saying all this to hurt me? On purpose? Sure, she's been fishing around for information lately and admitted to tracking me on the ChattySnap app, but the thought of her deliberately making me feel like this stuns me.

Sebastian takes the handkerchief from me and tucks it, dirty and wet, in his back pocket. "If I were you, I wouldn't worry about Reyn getting side action. I would worry about the atomic bomb that's going to go off when your brother finds out. That's going to be a kick in the 'nads."

I nod.

"And V?"

"Yeah?"

"You're a Devil now. You don't have to hang out with shit-stirrers like Sydney anymore. You've got us." He tosses his arm around my shoulder like a protective cloak and leads me back into the hall. He's right. I don't need Sydney the way I used to. I'm starting to worry that she's not going to let me go so easily, though.

Although I've been a student for three years at Preston Prep, this is the first time I've actually been truly aware of Homecoming. Before, it was always a buzz around the edges. Something bright and shiny that tried, and failed, to break through the stony-haze of drugs. Nothing—not the hand-painted banners, or the elaborate and cheesy HOCO proposals happening all over campus—ever penetrated the fortified armor I numbed my mind with.

But not this year.

This year, I'm clean. This year, I'm involved. This year, I've got the Devils. And yeah, this year, I've got Reynolds McAllister, who, at almost all times, has his eye on me like one of those shiny objects he can't help but steal.

*He promised*, my mind keeps repeating like a mantra, *never Sydney*. I don't have any reason not to trust him.

It almost makes up for the fact he doesn't ask me to the dance. He can't, I know that. Because of Emory. Because of Headmaster Collins. Because of the final initiation. The Homecoming dance is held at the same time as the Alumni fundraiser. The deck is stacked against us. Always has been, probably always will be.

"Well," I hear Sydney say, three lockers away, "I haven't decided what I'm going to do about the dance yet. Reggie asked me—via text." I hear the disdain in her voice. Lazy move, Reggie. "Andrew left a poster on my desk in French." Better, but not quite up to Sydney's flair. "But I'm really holding out for someone else to ask me, you know? Someone I really like."

I glance down the bank of lockers as she says it and our eyes meet. Hers are hard and hold none of the warmth for me they used to. I still don't know how she can be so angry at me. Because I've been busy? Because I have my own life now? There are a dozen reasons, but what I've noticed most is that cutting her out of my life has been a blessing more than anything else. Maybe Emory's been right all these years.

The locker door closes, and I see Fiona's profile. That's who Syd's around all the time now. Fiona's younger and obviously enthralled by Syd's dramatic life.

"There's still a few days," Fiona says. "He's pretty notorious for being impulsive, right? Maybe he'll ask you last minute."

"We'll see. I'm not sure school dances are his scene." Sydney grins wolfishly. "I'd be more than willing to ditch it for other activities."

As hard as I try not to think about it, an image of Reyn and Sydney together pops in my head. In it, they're at the dance, in his car, in that parking lot, making out, touching. My throat constricts and my palms suddenly feel clammy. Maybe Heston wasn't so far off-base about me having a masochistic streak, because why? Why would I think of that?

I reach for the little pocket on my backpack where I keep my lipstick tube—the one with the little compartment that I know has two pills inside. But before my fingertips can even make contact, I yank my hand back.

*No.*

I won't let her fuck with my head, and I'm certainly not breaking a promise to Reyn over it. I will not let her drag me back to that place. She'd want that, is the thing. She'd prefer the old Vandy who relied on her. The sad girl who walked at her side, whose whole life revolved around her. The girl who made Sydney feel superior.

I start down the hall, away from Sydney and her drama, steeling myself against the lure of oblivion. It'd just hurt so much less if I had it.

A hand cinches around my waist and drags me behind a pillar and stone bust of one of the founding fathers. Reyn towers over me, fingers pressing into my hips. He kisses me before I can say a word, and it takes my breath away.

This isn't a tender kiss. It's full of teeth and tongue and a desperation that I don't quite understand, but meet all the same. I tangle my fingers into his hair and hold him close, kissing back with a startling kind of abandon, and all I can think is *mine.* This man and the way he kisses me, it could never belong to Sydney. He could never surge into her like this, like he's magnetized and so hungry for it that his movements grow jerky, barely restrained.

He pulls away with a hard punch of breath, green eyes blazing into mine. "Come on," he says, tugging me to the side, into the little alcove beside the industrial air conditioning units. It's louder here, difficult to hear the students milling around on the other side.

Reyn casts a furtive glance around before cupping my face in his hands. "Hey, they said you were crying."

I reach up to touch his wrists, hypnotized by the way he's looking at me. "Who said?"

"Everyone is." His jaw ticks. "Apparently some dick hit you in the hall? Your brother is on a fucking rampage."

I can't help it. I laugh. Sebastian really had it right before. So much bullshit goes around this place. "He knocked my books out of my hands, and yeah, he was a jerk to me. But it really wasn't as violent as all that."

Reyn's hands slide away. I tangle our fingers together as they drop.

"Sebastian Wilcox to the rescue again?" He looks away, scowling, but I strain up on my tiptoes to press a kiss to his cheek.

"I didn't need to be rescued." Even Dr. Ross was right there. "But yeah, he put the fear of god into him, I think. It didn't mean anything, if that's what you're worried about. We're just—"

"Devils, friends," he says, meeting my gaze. "I know. And I know you don't need to be rescued. It'd just be nice to be the one who gets to do it every now and then." Despite knowing that, he probably also heard about us disappearing into the bathroom together, he doesn't look worried. He just looks pissed off.

Because I promised.

And he trusts me.

Suddenly, I feel so *stupid*. "No one rescues me as much as you do, Reyn." He rolls his eyes, but I can see some of that tight tension leeching away from his eyes. "Also, it was nice of you to give Sydney a ride home yesterday." I'm not even digging. Not prodding. I already know in my bones that there's nothing to find.

His face screws up. "Yeah, I probably won't do it again. I know she's your friend, but honestly?" He gives me a vaguely questioning look. "I'm not entirely sure why."

Instead of answering, I give him a kiss of my own. This one is slow and sweet—an apology for letting her get into my head.

"Think you can get away after school?" he asks. His fingers are playing at the hem of my skirt again. It always drives me crazy. "I got all that stuff we talked about." He smiles at me so softly when we're close like this, faces tipped together, that it's a physical impossibility to not smile back.

"I'll be there at five sharp."

# 28

"WHAT'S ALL THIS?" my dad asks, walking into the kitchen. I can tell from the way he's dressed, pulling on a jacket, that he's about to leave for the night. It used to annoy me, but now it just makes me feel grateful. I'll be able to sneak over to Vandy's tonight.

I roll my eyes. "Remember? You talked to Mrs. Hall?" It's ridiculous all the shit we had to go through to get a single parent-approved evening hanging out together. There were, in fact, *three* phone calls, a stern talking-to from my dad, and an email from Vandy's mom containing her contact info 'just in case'. Just in case what? Who fucking knows.

Comprehension dawns over his features. "Oh, that's today?" He looks around at all the shit I've dragged onto the counter. "Should I stay?"

I shoot him a narrow-eyed glance over my shoulder. "I think I can manage to not almost kill her for a couple hours."

My dad does not look impressed. "You know how the Halls are about that girl. I'll just push my meeting a little later." He takes off his jacket and I determinedly do not think of the way he skittered out the word 'meeting.' As if whatever booty call he's putting on hold is some sort of business symposium.

It doesn't matter, though. Vandy and I had already agreed that a successful parent-approved hang-out could only open up the possibility for future... *meetings*.

I watch from my periphery as he takes out his phone, thumbs tapping over the screen. Apparently, dad is in the stage in his life where he can postpone booty calls by text alone. Classy fella, my old man.

Out of nowhere, he lets out this long sigh. "I hope you're using rubbers."

I think a drop of saliva becomes permanently lodged in my windpipe. "*What?*"

He looks up at me, gesturing to my neck. "Rubbers. Wrap it up, Reyn, or so help me god..."

The hickey, I realize. I resist the urge to press my fingers into the mark Vandy made beneath my ear. I mutter, "I think I'm a little old for the rubber talk, so why don't you just cross that off your list and pretend we did."

"God damn it." He slams his hand down on the counter, almost startling me. "I mean it, Reyn! The last thing you need is to knock up some idiot girl—and a Preston girl, at that. Your life is going to be hard enough. You want to be saddled with some princess's snot-nosed brat for the next eighteen years?"

It takes me a long moment to form words, but when I do, gripping the counter at my back, all I can manage is an awed, "Wow."

"What?" he snaps, watching me.

"Oh, don't stop now." I sweep my hand out magnanimously. "Why don't you tell me how you really feel? It's not like I don't already know, what with the way you can't even stand to stay in the same house with me for more than three hours. Though, I've got to say, adding '*some princess's snot-nosed brat*' to those college applications will really give it a certain flair. So, thanks for that, I guess."

I barely catch the look on his face when I sweep past him, but it's slack and surprised, and I want to tell him, *Yes*. I know. Of course, I already knew all of this. It's just different, hearing it all laid out like that.

It stings.

I drop on the couch in the den and try not to let it bother me so much. I'll be out of his hair soon, and he can have his house back. We'll probably end up rarely speaking to one another. Holidays. Birthdays. I can see it now, me calling him on Father's Day and faking through it, pretending he's still the same guy who built me that treehouse and taught me how to catch a football.

I don't turn when I hear him walk into the room, keeping my eyes fixed to the TV. Strangely, Vandy's mom is there. She's covering a story about fraud down at the board of education. Sometimes watching Mrs. Hall makes me wish I'd turned out to be a better kid—like I could have a mom like that, with warm eyes, who actually gives a shit.

And then I remember the stuff her own kids are getting up to.

My dad picks up the remote control, turning the TV off. The room goes silent, darker, thick with awkward tension. "Reyn," he starts, and he's standing there shifting around, hands planted on his hips, looking anywhere but at me. "You've got it all wrong."

I snort bitterly, wishing he'd just go away. Vandy will be here in thirty minutes.

"You were just a boy when you went away," he goes on. "You came back this angry, quiet man, and the truth is, I don't know you anymore. I don't know how to talk to you. I don't know how to be a dad to someone who's—" he lifts a hand, gesturing at me like I'm something baffling and foreign. Maybe he's right. Maybe I am. "You grew up when I wasn't even looking. Sometimes I go into your room and look in that damn drawer." He nods when I gape at him. "Oh, I know about the drawer. I also know you haven't been adding to it quite as much, so I thought maybe... maybe you were working it out on your own." He falls on the couch beside me, heaving a big sigh. "I don't know what else to do about it. When I was your age, I was just fucking everything that moved."

My face screws up. "Gross." And then, "As if you ever actually stopped."

I see his nod through my periphery. "I did, once. When I was with your mom. For... for a long time." He looks around the room, the silence still charged with that uncomfortable silence. "This is her house, you know. Your mom's? She's the one who chose it, furnished it, decorated it. Everywhere I look, there she is." He drops his head to the back of the couch, admitting, "I hate it. I was going to move, but they said I shouldn't. They told me you needed some normalcy when you came home, the home you remembered. I thought I could handle it, but I guess I was wrong. You're right; I don't like being here. But you're wrong if you think it's got anything to do with you."

"You miss her," I realize.

He smiles sadly. "Like you wouldn't believe."

"Then why?" I wonder, my reality shifting. "Why did you fuck around on her? She would have stayed."

"Christ, Reyn." He drags a hand down his tried face. "There's no easy answer to that. Just sometimes, when things get rough, that's the only thing that..." He trails off, waving his hand, but I don't need him to finish.

It's such a carbon copy of what I'd told Vandy that night—about why I steal—that it guts me. "Jesus."

He must realize I'm drawing the dots, because he nods. "Your mom used to say McAllister men had a sickness. That we sabotage ourselves. That we couldn't handle things going good, we just had to mess it all up. She never understood. Not like we do."

I finally look at him, and I know she was wrong. It's not about self-sabotage. But it doesn't really matter. That's the outcome, every time. "Sometimes I really hate how alike we are."

"Me, too." He doesn't look upset about it, but his smile is rueful. "It's not all bad, is it?"

It's easier than I thought it'd be to give him this. "Not all of it." I pluck idly at a spot of fuzz on the sofa. "Plus, grandpa still has all his hair, so we've got that going for us."

"You take after him, you know." He nods when I meet his gaze. "Oh yeah, that man would steal the ground right out from under you. He just became a CFO and called it acquisitions."

We share a small laugh.

"I'm not sure that's for me," I admit. Then, quietly, "I can't go to college next year, Dad."

Instead of arguing with me about it, he asks, "Why?"

I shrug, falling back against the couch. "I'm not Emory, okay? I didn't spend the last three years at a nice school, finding out who I am and what I want. I only just recently learned how to drive with someone else sitting in my car. I know I'm too old to be a kid anymore, but..."

"But you're not ready to be an adult. I'll let you in on a secret, son. No one ever is. It's just something that comes and we deal with it, because there's no other option." To my surprise, he adds, "But if you think a gap year is going to give you time to become an eighteen-year-old, then I think I understand."

"You do?"

"One year," he stresses. "And I want you to work hard, Reyn. Get your GPA up. Keep performing on the field. Use that year for something good. Become an attractive applicant." He claps me on the shoulder, standing. "I know I can't tell you not to steal, but would I still be a hypocrite if I asked you to try?"

I look at him, deciding to be honest. "I'm already trying."

"Good. And I know you're different than I was at eighteen, but for Pete's sake," He hands me the remote, eyebrows raised, "wear a rubber."

"Flour, corn meal, salt…" Vandy lists out, sifting through the supplies I'd added to the grocery list. "Baking soda?" She shakes the box at me. "We need baking powder, not baking soda."

I'm sitting on the counter, and if my dad weren't in the next room, I'd be pulling her between my legs right now, licking at that mark she's hiding beneath her hair. As it is, I watch her lean against the island, her skirt grazing her thighs. "They're not the same thing?"

She starts pulling open cabinets. "What are the chances you have baking powder?"

"Slim," I confess, watching the way her skirt sways when she stands on her tiptoes.

She eventually shuts the cabinets, admitting defeat. "I'll go get some. Break those eggs."

I do as she asked, but I wasn't lying before. Cooking isn't one of my superpowers. There are shells all in this bowl. I try to pick them out, grimacing at the feel of it.

When she returns, holding up the can of baking powder victoriously, my hands are slimy. I glare at her. "Why did you give me the hard job? I thought I'd just be stirring or something. Stirring, I can do."

She doesn't relent. "Try it again. That's why I told you to get a dozen eggs. Trust me, it's a vital skill." I throw the eggs out and try again.

That's when Emory suddenly walks in.

He doesn't knock or anything, apparently just walks right through the front door, waltzing into the kitchen like he owns the damn place.

We both freeze in place, looking back at him as he narrows his eyes at us.

"Dad said you were over here," he says to Vandy. And then, "The fuck is this?"

Vandy and I share a look. We'd put so much energy into getting parental approval that we'd forgotten her third parent. Things with Emory have been quiet since the Stairway to Hell rite. He made it right by letting V choose her own partner, but he hasn't been particularly chummy with me since then, regardless.

"Guess we're busted," I say, setting the bowl aside. "Your sister is teaching me to cook."

Vandy corrects, "This is baking, not cooking."

I give Em a long-suffering look. "Your sister is teaching me to *bake*."

"Why?" he asks, eyes taking in the scene. Somehow, despite not even having everything mixed yet, there are dishes everywhere.

"Because I don't know how?" I answer slowly. "And because her cornbread is slamming."

Vandy jumps in, voice sharp and defensive, "Mom and Dad said I could."

I point toward the den. "Warren's here, too."

Perfectly legit, thank you very much. *Asshole.*

Emory's eyes shift toward the den, neck craning. "Oh."

Vandy pushes a lock of hair behind her ear, revealing the mark. I think she must sense the tension between us, because she adds, "You could probably use a lesson, too."

Emory scoffs. "I can cook."

"You can cook?" Vandy throws her head back and laughs, loud and bubbly. "Stop, *my sides*."

But Emory's relaxed now, strutting up to the island, bracing on his forearms. "Fuck off, I make plenty of stuff."

"Hot dogs and hamburgers?" She gives him a look. "Yeah, you're basically a culinary mastermind."

I show the egg bowl to Vandy, asking, "Does this pass?"

She peers into the bowl. "Yep. Now for the part you've been waiting for. Stir that into this."

Twenty minutes, nine eggs, and five dirty bowls later, we're all sitting around the island, waiting for it to bake. Vandy's scrolling through her phone, sending me these little glances that have my leg bouncing impatiently. Emory's running the recipe card over a spot of wayward flour, sweeping it into a line like it's cocaine.

It's not like we hadn't already planned for this situation to be void of kissing or touching, but having Emory sitting here like a supervisor is kind of grating on my nerves.

"You hear about that Pierce fucker?" he suddenly asks, tapping the card. He looks up at me, quick and casual, but I see it for what it is.

He's trying to move past our little spat.

Vandy sighs. "Let it go."

I nod, jaw clenching. "Prick." The way everyone talked, you'd think he'd body slammed her in the hallway. She swore up and down it wasn't that bad, but I could see the redness in her eyes, knew it'd been bad enough.

"Bass scared the shit out of him, though." Emory smirks, kicking back on his stool. "Saw him in fifth period. He looked like he was crapping his pants."

I rest my chin on my fists. "I broke into his locker."

Vandy's head whips back. "Reyn!"

I roll my eyes. "Relax, I just transferred everything into his gym locker. He'll spend most of the day tomorrow freaking out, but he'll find it. If anything, I did him a favor. That shit was a pig sty."

Emory laughs. "This is awesome. It's like V's got five more big brothers now."

Inwardly, I cringe. Does that mean I'm going to have to deal with four other angry jocks if this gets out? As if Emory isn't bad enough.

"Great," Vandy mutters, echoing my thoughts. "Just what I need."

"Aw, come on." Emory reaches out to pat her wrist. "Look at it like this; more people to haul you around, right?" His expression turns pensive. "Not that I'd trust Carlton to drive you around. Or Ben. Or Tyson. Probably not Sebastian, either."

"Or," I suggest as the hottest take yet, "she could just get her own car and drive herself."

Emory shakes his head. "V doesn't know how to drive. She can't learn."

I push back in my seat, suddenly feeling ill. "Because of...?" I drop my gaze to her leg. *Jesus.* Had I really taken that away from her, too?

She must see the dread on my face because she gives a sharp shake of her head. "No, I probably *can.*" She looks away, cheeks blooming a warm pink. "I'm just not allowed to."

I cut my eyes to Emory, voice full of disbelief. "She's not allowed to *learn* to drive?"

I've learned a lot about Vandy over these last few weeks, and one of the subtler wisdoms I've gained is that she's terrified of not being able to move. Of being unable to get away fast, if she needs to. Of being trapped. Of needing other people to save her. They have no idea what they're taking away from her with that.

Emory shrugs, hapless, and I'd push it—I really would—but look what that little Stairway to Hell disagreement had caused.

Just then, the timer dings for the cornbread. Vandy looks grateful when she hops off her stool and goes to the oven to get it out. She's embarrassed. I can tell in the redness of her cheeks and the way she won't meet my eyes. I think back to my dad's words—*give you time to become an eighteen-year-old*—and wish that Vandy could have that, too.

While Vandy's prodding the cornbread, Emory leans in to say, "Look, my truck's too big, anyway." I watch as he thumps his knuckles onto the counter, three soft raps. "We'll have to use the Jeep."

My eyes snap up to his, dubious. He can't really be saying...

Emory smirks back at me. "Yo, V. Wrap some of that up, then we're AIS."

I LET Emory take the passenger seat.

Vandy's looking at the dashboard like it's something out of a NASA control center as she jerkily pulls the seat belt around her torso.

I'm in the backseat, pitched forward between them. I spin my cap around backward, watching her face. "Move the seat up if you need to," I instruct, watching as she follows. "And adjust the mirrors."

She fiddles with the rearview mirror, eyes meeting mine in the reflection. There's fear there, but also something else.

It's energized and excited.

Emory says, "Press down on the brake."

"Okay," Vandy says, glancing down. After a beat of silence, she asks, "Which one is the brake?"

Emory and I both look at her, wide-eyed.

Emory opens his door. "Okay, get out."

I grab his arm. "No, just—it's the one on the left, V. The bigger one."

She shoots her brother a glare, but he sinks back into his seat, closing his door. He shoots me a nervous look over his shoulder. "Maybe we should have given her a strictly stationary primer first."

Deadpan, I say, "Gas makes it go, brake makes it stop."

"What now?" she asks, foot planted firmly on the brake pedal.

"Now, you put it in drive."

I watch as Emory points out the gear selector, instructing her to press in the button. She plants both hands back on the steering wheel, waiting.

"Okay, ready to move it?" he asks. "Just ease your foot off the brake. Don't press the gas, just coast for a bit."

I'd taken us back to the Kmart parking lot, which is awkward as fuck—V and I had shared a glance when I pulled in that had made me half hard—but it's deserted and perfect for the task.

She lets her foot off the brake and the car slowly begins rolling forward. "Oh," she breathes, and I can see her fingers easing up on the steering wheel. "This isn't so bad."

I suggest, "Try braking again, get a feel for the—" but before I can finish, she has her foot on the brake, jerking us to a sudden stop. "—sensitivity."

Her hands clench back around the steering wheel, throat bobbing with a swallow. I can tell that made her anxious, panicky, and it isn't helped when the car suddenly fires off a rapid bout of dings. Her eyes widen in alarm, hands flying off the wheel. "What's wrong? What'd I do?"

I snake a hand around the driver's seat to touch her hip where Emory can't see. "It's fine, relax. It's just doing that because Em isn't wearing his seatbelt."

She whips her head around. "You're not wearing a seatbelt?!"

Emory gestures out the windshield. "We're in an empty parking lot."

"Emory!" Then she peers back at me, shrieking, "Reynolds!"

We both sigh, pulling on our seatbelts.

She coasts for a bit longer, getting more and more used to the tension of the brakes. Every time she pushes the pedal too hard, jerking the car to a stop, her shoulders get higher and tighter, chest hitching to a still.

I say, "Breathe, baby," and tack on a hasty, "*V.*"

*Shit.*

I jerk my eyes toward Emory, but he doesn't notice anything. "Ready to try the gas?" He looks nervous too, but he's doing a better job of hiding it than Vandy is.

My hand, still wedged between her seat at the driver's side door, grazes her hip. "You've got this. Remember the fence? And the roof?"

"The fence?" Em looks at me. "The roof?"

I pause, wondering if it'll piss him off to know how she got out of the house for the fourth rite.

Vandy just breezes out, "Yeah, I jumped off the roof and Reyn caught me."

Emory gapes, gaze pinging between us. "When was this?"

"How do you think I snuck out to go to the Alumni house?" She presses the gas and the car lurches forward.

Emory's hands fly out to clutch at the dash. "Slowly!"

She smirks at him out the side of her mouth. "I'm guessing I use the wheel to turn, right?"

It takes her about ten minutes to get a feel for the gas and brake, working them together to make the stop and accelerations smoother. I watch the spark of excitement return to her eyes when she starts turning down the old, faded parking aisles. She's gorgeous like this, the fading evening sun casting a warm glow over her cheeks.

Even Emory seems to relax, watching her with a soft smile. "Hey, you're doing good." It's patronizing, but Vandy takes it as it's meant to be, shooting him a grin.

"Want to learn how to reverse?" I ask.

By the time she puts the car in park, it's almost dark out. We all get out, trading seats, but Emory stops me around the front of the car, pressing a palm to my shoulder.

"So, maybe you were right before," he says, not meeting my eyes. "I think this Devil stuff kind of got away from me."

I watch him skeptically. "Yeah?"

He nods. "I have to remember why we're doing this. This isn't about being cool or popular. It's about giving Vandy something to hold onto next year." He looks over to where she's kicked back in the passenger seat, sliding my sunglasses up the bridge of her nose. "She should have stuff like this. And I know it's better to do it while I'm still here, where I can watch over her, be a part of it." He finally meets my gaze, finishing, "I might need someone to keep reminding me of that."

Vandy calls out, "Guys!" She's poking her head out of the window, hand raised in the air. "Not to interrupt this touching bro-ment you've got going on, but I have to be home in ten minutes."

I bury a playful punch into Emory's shoulder. "Will do," I promise, jogging back to the driver's seat.

I give Vandy a wicked smile when I get behind the wheel, wishing she wasn't wearing those sunglasses so I could see the way her eyes glaze over when I do. For the first time, I begin feeling a little hope. It'll take time, but maybe Emory won't be so hard to convince, after all.

# 29

"AFTON AND AUBREY, you're in charge of supplies. No one will think twice about the two of you carrying around a lot of red and black on Homecoming Week." Emory turns. "Elana, you're on logo design. Caroline, we need your tech savvy. Sebastian…"

My brother continues giving out orders, and it's weird seeing him like this. Commanding, organized, assured. He's captain of the football team, so most of these guys are probably used to it, but me? I'm used to sitting at the dinner table next to the guy who uses his bread as a napkin and then *eats it*. But here, he effortlessly orchestrates where and when we're pulling off this epic prank for the fundraiser.

I look down at the black card that had appeared in our lockers four hours ago.

*A Devil should know how to make an entrance. You will gather at the ninth hour to announce your presence. Consider this your homecoming.*

*"All men speak in bitter disapproval of the Devil, but they do it reverently, not flippantly."*

*Elvatio Infernum*

I've barely heard a word of what Emory's saying, however. I'm sitting in the middle of the couch, Sebastian on one side, Reyn on the other. His knee, thigh, or arm occasionally touches mine, and it's perfectly benign. Innocent. But every single nerve in my body feels each touch like it's the Fourth of July.

Between school, Devil meetings, and my evening driving lessons —five so far, and I even got to practice on the neighborhood roads last time—it seems like Reyn and I spend more time in the company of Emory than alone with each other. Every now and then, he comes through my window, sometimes to sleep over, but it's frustratingly void of anything but light kissing and sleep. Ever since Emory tried to barge in that one time, we're too skittish to push it.

My gaze keeps wandering to Reyn's forearm. He's got his sleeves pushed up to his elbows, and sometimes he'll shift or reach forward and I can watch the corded muscles there flex and tighten.

I tear my eyes away and try to focus, not just for my role in the prank, but also because it's the ultimate rite. This will be, as the card says, our homecoming. Our public announcement that the Devils are not dead, but alive and active.

Emory suddenly turns to me. "V, you'll be in charge of alibis."

"Uh," I stutter, brain rushing to catch up. Damn Reyn and his distracting forearms. "Wait. How exactly am I supposed to alibi twelve people?"

"With your position on the newspaper. You're going to provide documentation that we're all at the dance while the prank goes down." He mimes pressing a shutter on a camera. "Snap, snap."

Well, that sounds easier said than done.

Emory's already onto the next thing. "Reyn, you'll be the one who gets us in and out unnoticed, okay?"

Reyn nods. "No problem."

"I have a question," Ben says, holding up his hand like we're in class. Emory waves him on. "What's the point of all this? I mean, we're not even making fun of anyone."

Emory looks like he's about to slap him upside the head. He reins it in, pushes his shoulders back, jaw tight. "How are you still not getting this? Being a Devil isn't just about picking on underclassmen anymore. The point is to prove that the faculty can't stifle tradition or legacy." He turns his sharp gaze on the rest of us. "This is about showing them that the Devils are here. We're in their school. We're on their sports teams. We're at their country club. We're inside their institutions. The point isn't to be a thorn in their side. Thorns can be pulled out." His smile is dark and sharp. "But not us. The point is to be the blood that's pumping through the veins of this place. It's about power, and showing them who has it."

I'm a little stunned by the outburst, and I can tell some of the others are, too. My brother is completely, disgustingly into this. His eyes search the rest of us, wanting confirmation that we understand how important this is to him—to us. When they meet mine, I give him a small smile of approval, although I taste bitterness on my tongue. Really, all he's doing is proving exactly why I'm doing all this; to bring down the smug assholes that think they're better than the rest of us—even if I am one of them at the moment.

"This prank is complicated," Emory adds, "but all the other rites have led us here. We have the skills to pull this off, we've already proven that. It's time to let the Powers that Be know we're back in the game." He rubs his hands together. "This one will go down in infamy."

"And if we get caught?" Georgia asks.

"Then we're screwed," Emory says, eyes jumping from mine to Reyn's. "We'll get expelled, made an example of, and become an embarrassment to our families."

"Which is why none of that can happen," Reyn says, leaning forward, his arm brushing against mine. "There's no other option. We pull this off, and we do it clean. I'm not going down for this and I'm not letting anyone else go down either."

Emory levels his dark grin at Reyn. These two are always on the same page, with the same goal; stirring up as much trouble as they can and getting away with it.

I just hope they can pull it off, because we all know what can happen if they fail.

THE REST of the week passes quickly. Academics are replaced by spirit week. Theme days allow us a break from our uniforms, which is something that's embraced with a truly telling amount of enthusiasm from the student body. There's College Day, which turns the hallways into a veritable sea of ivy league sweaters—an easy choice for me and Emory. Then there's Iconic Preston day, where you dress up as your favorite founder, teacher, or headmaster. Then there's Red Devil Day, which I'm pretty convinced is just a ploy for the office to sling school spirit merchandise. It all goes smoothly, other than 'Twin Day'.

Twin Day is something I've participated in before. Every year, Sydney talks me into wearing a matching outfit. But this year, since we're not really speaking, that's off the table. That doesn't mean I don't have someone to match with—or *someones*. Afton and Elana got together and decided the Playthings needed to match.

I know that morning, as I look at myself in my bedroom mirror, that walking into school like *this,* with *these* girls is going to be a seismic shift in the social framework of Preston Prep. Sure, things have already changed in small ways—the lunch table, the hallway greetings, even the way people treat me in the hall. People at Preston seem aware that I've suddenly leveled up on the popularity scale, but Emory is my brother. Why wouldn't I climb a few rungs?

But this...?

I stare at the tight black T-shirt with a winking Devil on the back, eyes descending to the skin-tight, painted-on jeans that are leaving none of my curves to the imagination. Aubrey dug through my closet last night and pulled them out herself. I've knotted the shirt as she directed, which shows part of my stomach, including a small sliver of my scar. It's something I never show. *Ever*. But the only person I care about has already seen it.

*Kissed* it.

Somehow, it just doesn't feel as ugly as it used to.

I tie a red, glittery ribbon in my ponytail and slide on a pair of red sneakers. It's a concession I know the rest of girls made for me. Red, ultra-high-heeled boots were floated briefly as an idea, but instantly shot down in favor of something flat, comfortable, and easy to walk in. Afton barely gave me time to feel bad about it, explaining that it'd look amazing, but none of them want to lug ten pounds of books across campus in heels all day, anyway.

She probably has a point.

The self-consciousness doesn't kick in until Emory does a double take as I walk across the driveway. "What the hell are you wearing?"

I cross my arms over my stomach, but then drop them awkwardly at my sides. "It's twin day. This is how all the Playthings are dressing." I fight the urge to run back inside. "Aubrey picked out the jeans herself."

"That's not—" He stares at me like I'm an alien. "That's not appropriate!"

"Oh, really." I prop my hands on my hips, forgetting my shyness. "Would you tell Aubrey that? Or Afton? Any of the other girls?"

"The other girls aren't my sister!"

We stare obstinately at one another, caught in a power struggle.

A door slams from Reyn's house.

"What's up?" Reyn asks, rounding the bed of the truck. When I look up, he's frozen in place, those green eyes drinking me in. Swallowing thickly, his Adam's apple bobs. "Oh, uh."

"Emory is horrified at my outfit." I raise my arms, challenging, "What do you think?"

"I think, uh," His eyes dart to my brother's and he rubs the back of his neck. He shrugs off his letterman's jacket and holds it out. "I think that maybe you should wear this. As a compromise."

The jacket is new and smells strongly of leather. There's a hint of Reyn in there too—something soapy, clean. His fingers graze my neck as he helps me drape it over my shoulders and I fight a shiver.

Emory shakes his head, cranks the engine, and barks out, "AIS, V. I need to go by Coach's office before school."

"Chill out," I mutter to my brother, struggling worse than ever to get in the front seat with the skin-tight jeans and oversized jacket. I'm about to topple backwards when strong hands cinch around my waist and push me inside. The sensation of Reyn's hands on me isn't surprising. By now, it's familiar. One look at my brother makes me think he knows it. "Thanks," I say to Reyn and he quickly shuts the door.

Emory stares out the window at his retreating form for a moment longer.

"I thought you were in a hurry," I say, buckling my seat belt.

"I don't like the way he looks at you."

"How, exactly," I ask, tired of this game, "does he look at me, Em? Like I'm a girl? Like I'm a real person? Like I'm not broken?"

"No." His jaw tightens and he shifts the truck into gear. "Like you're a shiny object and he can't wait to steal you."

"VANDY, I wanted to talk to you."

I pause, fork halfway to my mouth, and look at my mother. The worry lines run deep across her forehead. It's just the two of us eating dinner tonight. Dad's at the hospital and Emory is at a late practice. Coach Morris is hardcore about winning tomorrow night.

I hedge, "About...?"

"A few concerns," she starts, abandoning her fork. "Dr. Cordell says you cancelled your last two appointments. I noticed your grades are slipping in Bio and French. You're hiding in your room a lot, and well," her eyes sweep over my outfit, "you just seem different."

"Anything else?" I ask, spine going rigid under her scrutiny. "Is my period off schedule? Is my bra size too small? Maybe my baths are too hot?"

She looks taken aback, but quickly schools her expression. "I just want to make sure you're okay. Things have been different this year. You're more independent. Your brother says you've been fitting in better with the kids at school, which I know involves certain types of pressures you haven't experienced before."

*What?* I want to ask. *Like drugs? Now you're worried I'm going to be a stoner?*

That ship has fucking sailed.

"And," she continues over my silence, "there's Reyn."

My eyes snap up. "What about him?"

"Just that he's back. He's around quite a lot. I know you and your brother have both been spending more time with him. Is that awkward for you? Does it make you uncomfortable?"

I force—no, *plead*—with my body to not react to her questions about Reyn. But just his name makes me flush hot. It makes me remember what his mouth feels like and his fingers. What I did to him at the Alumni house. What *he* did in the Stairway. My cheeks burn so hot that I can feel them, and there's no way my mom doesn't notice.

I look at her, willing her to see *me* for once, to see the truth about her daughter. To see that I'm more than the weak, injured girl she's protected and sheltered for so long. To see that I'm strong, brave, and occasionally a little bad-ass, if only I have the space to try. I want her to know that I'm *good* at driving, and I like it. I like the freedom, the taste of independence, the feel of Reyn and Emory at my side, there to catch me if I need it, but just as fine with watching me figure it out on my own. I want to tell her I can climb a fence. I can pick a very rudimentary lock. This whole journalism thing? I'm into it, and I could be really, really good at it, too.

And yes, I'm in the middle of falling head over heels for the boy next door.

Our eyes meet for a long moment and I'm about to tell her every-thing—well *almost* everything—when she frowns.

"Are you feverish?" she asks, leaning over the table, the back of her hand poised to check for a temperature. I twist away, but she's already up, searching for the thermometer. "You know that's the first sign of infection. Any aches? Pains?"

I sigh. "I'm not feverish, Mom."

"Sometimes it's hard to tell, especially if you're run down from other things. I know you're dedicated to the newspaper, which thrills me, but I also know adding in any kind of extra-curricular activity can be a burden on a compromised system. You're just not used to—"

"Mom, stop." She shoves the thermometer toward me. I push it away. "Stop!"

She blinks. "Vandy, stop fighting me. You're flushed and agitated, something's wrong!"

I lurch from the table, chair clattering over behind me. "Nothing's wrong, Mom! For once in my life, everything is right! I've got friends. I'm involved at school. My grades are slipping because I'm not sitting around with nothing to do!" My voice echoes off the vaulted ceilings. "And Reyn doesn't make me uncomfortable. He makes me..." Her eyebrows knit anxiously, but I keep going, "He makes me feel right, Mom. He makes me feel good about myself. He's the only person who makes me feel strong!"

"What are you talking about?" She shakes her head, exasperated. "We've given you every support you've ever needed. Every resource!"

"You have." I nod, laughing bitterly. "And each and every one of those is built to enable and keep me under control. But Reyn? He's the only one who doesn't treat me like an infant."

Her mouth purses angrily. "Because he's careless."

"No," I say, backing away.

She insists, "He's a careless, angry, confused boy."

"That's not true! You don't know anything about him."

Her eyes narrow. "How much are you seeing of him? Because it's one thing for him to be Emory's friend, it's another for him—"

I know then and there that I can't tell her the truth, and it *hurts*. Any other girl my age could talk to her mother about this feeling growing inside of her chest, so big that it can't be contained. She'd be able to be happy about it, to share that joy.

Reyn and I are alone in this.

My mom and Emory will never understand what we are to one another.

"I'm not," I say quietly, voice flat. "Just... just with Em. I just wanted to make it clear that he's not bothering me."

She blinks, the cognitive dissonance, the false reality she's created where I'm happy being alone and protected, shifts back into place. And with the same ease, I do the same thing. "You know, maybe I do feel a little worn out. I think I'll head to bed."

"Good idea," she says with a tight, approving grin. My mother may want to dig out the truth in her reporting, but she definitely doesn't want it at home.

I go to my room like a good girl, but that's not me anymore. Honestly it never *was* me, but the last few weeks have made that simple fact real. Concrete. I try to think back to that nervous girl who started the school year, but it's as fuzzy as back when I was using. It's lost to the life I lead now, the one filled with shine, excitement, and a touch of danger.

The one that gives me the courage to sneak out of my room on a Thursday night and break into my neighbor's house.

I'm a pro now, grabbing the letterman jacket, locking my bedroom door, and then slipping out the window to the small overhang. My heart pounds as I ease off the edge and I drop to the ground, but even though my landing is stumbling and sloppy, I still have both my feet beneath me. There are so many things I didn't think I could do—or would ever do—yet here I am, creeping across the space between our houses, digging the McAllisters' spare key out of the wilted, potted fern beside the door.

Fall is officially here and the night air is cold. I tug Reyn's jacket around my shoulders. I'd worn it all day, feeling bold in my outfit that matched the other girls. It's an antiquated notion, but it still holds up. Wearing the jacket is a visible sign of Reyn marking me as his own. People definitely noticed. Emory waved off questions at the lunch table, grumbling about my outfit and Reyn doing me a service, but I think almost everyone, save my brother, knows what's going on. Sydney's eyes followed me across the cafeteria. She was dying to know why I was wearing it, but her bitterness is what drove us apart. Let her keep guessing.

Suddenly I'm out of fucks to give.

I enter the side door, into the dimly lit house. I know I could have just called, and Reyn would have happily invited me in, but as it turns out, like him and my brother, I have a thing for risk. Maybe that's why I got into the car all those years ago. I'd wanted to taste what they tasted. I wanted to feel that thrill.

Crossing the kitchen, I see a suit jacket on the back of a kitchen chair and a woman's purse. Reyn's father must be here—with a date. I've seen the cars come and go, the women entering in the evening and out the next day. My pulse quickens, knowing there are other people in the house. For a minute, I consider backing out and running back home, but stop myself.

Laughter floats in off the back patio and I notice the flicker of the fire pit. I stay away from the windows and sneak up the stairs. At the landing, I orient myself, figuring out which closed door would match up with my own bedroom. I pick the one at the end and try the knob. It opens, and I step into Reyn's room.

It's the first time I've been here, and a wildly different view from my window across the way. The room is smaller than mine, but he also has a bigger bed, one more suited to his long arms and legs. I'm a little surprised to see the bed covers straight, the pillows flat and smooth. His shoes are lined up against the wall next to this closet and the open door shows me a clean line of shirts hanging in a row.

I guess those military school habits are hard to break.

Shutting the door behind me, I notice that the bathroom door is closed and hear the sound of the shower running. I sit on the bed, feeling the adrenaline from the altercation with my mom waning, and wonder if showing up here was the dumb thing to do.

The shower cuts off and yeah, this was a mistake. What am I doing? Sitting in his room, wearing his jacket. Desperate much?

The door swings open. Steam spills out, billowing forth until it clears, and then there he is. Reyn stands in the doorway, towel slung low around his hips. Water drips down his neck, traveling over his chest and torso. His hair is a wild tangle of damp chaos, still being rubbed with the towel he's holding in his hand.

When he sees me, he goes still. Eyes boring into mine, his mouth parts in surprise, but he doesn't speak.

I wait for him to ask why I'm here—to ask what's wrong.

He doesn't. His mouth pulls into that sexy, dimpled smirk, and he doesn't look confused to see me sitting on his bed. He just looks pleased.

Maybe this wasn't a mistake after all.

# 30

Reyn

It's worse when I'm bored.

I spend all evening kicking around the house, restless and full of too much energy. Even though he's busy getting ready to 'entertain' a guest, I can tell it's driving my dad nuts.

"Can't you go take a run or something?"

I stare at him blankly. "It's dark."

He gives me this look like I'm the idiot here. "So?"

"So..." I say it really slowly, drawn out. "There's this little issue where the HOA, care of Fucking Jerry, doesn't like me roaming the streets of their precious gated community past—"

"Okay, okay," he says, flapping a hand. "Then go do homework."

I pause. "I'd rather face Fucking Jerry."

He whirls on me. "Reynolds."

I heed the warning in his voice. Pops hasn't had any action in five nights, which is practically a dry spell for him, and I'm fine dealing with his ire, but sexual frustration? Disgusting.

My room is just as boring as downstairs. I hear Dad's lady-friend knock and thank whatever deity is listening for the fact his room isn't within hearing distance. Really did me a solid there.

It's not only because I haven't stolen anything in two weeks. That's obviously a factor in my massive amounts of boredom, but mostly it's the lack of challenge. Thrill. Adrenaline. It's embarrassing how worked up I'm getting over this idiotic Devil prank. It's juvenile, sure. But it's also something to fucking *do*. It's a risk. It's something I'll need to use my skills for, something that I can get away with.

Something I can help *eleven other people* get away with.

I spend some time going over the plan in my head, but I'm only a minor part of it, and truthfully, getting into the tech room is kid's play, anyway. It's all about time management. Instead, I decide to do what any bored eighteen-year-old guy does. I take a shower and jerk off. I really draw it out, too. Make a night of it. Show myself a good time. I think of Vandy and the way she looked in my jacket today. I think of how everyone saw it, and the expression on their faces—the aware-ness—is enough to make me want to sneak over there and get my hands on her.

I'm still thinking of that when I come.

Okay, so maybe some of my restlessness is because Vandy and I haven't been alone in days. Whether it's seeing her from afar or sitting next to her in the car with Emory, the result is the same: Biting, acute *want*. Emory is seriously getting on my fucking nerves. Always there, always watching. I know there was a time I was happy to see him, to hang with my best friend, but the memory is being all fogged up by the way his sister is making my dick hard, twenty-four-seven.

Breathless and too hot in the steam, I cut the water and dry my face, prepared to retire to my bed for a lazy round two.

But when I walk out of the bathroom, there she is.

On my bed.

In my jacket.

Alone.

I'm not going to bullshit myself and pretend a dozen different fantasies don't start like this. I walk into my room to a hot girl sitting on my bed. In my mind, she's usually in some kind of lingerie, something sexy and easy to rip off, but seeing my girl, dwarfed in my jacket...

Yeah, that works too.

*Really* works.

We stare at each other for a long moment, and I'm not sure what my face is saying, but she's got this wicked little smile that's making me think I need to lock my door.

I do that.

"I needed some air," she finally speaks, standing. "Dinner with my mom was kind of..."

I turn to her, rubbing the towel over my face. "Kind of what?"

"Like, an interrogation? A wellness check?" She shrugs, shoulders falling low. "Whatever it was, I didn't want to be there anymore."

"So you came here." Fuck, I like that. I like the fact she relied on me. That she feels comfortable enough to just come over. "Did my dad or... whoever he's with, let you in?"

"Nah," she grins, stepping toward me, "those B&E skills came in handy."

I raise an eyebrow, gaze dropping to her mouth. "I didn't mean for you to use them against me."

Her eyes track where the towel in my hand falls on the floor. "So, you want me to leave?"

"Not a chance." I wrap my arms around her waist and pull her close, trailing my nose over the shell of her ear. "You've been teasing me all day, in that shirt. Those jeans. Wearing my jacket." I bend and lick that little patch of skin beneath her ear, where the mark has faded, feeling her squirm against me. "I've been fucking dying to get you alone."

Her hands splay across my chest, and I slide a hand behind her neck, intent on kissing her long and slow. Deep and unrelenting. There's not enough time for us to be alone—not with our schedules, her brother, the Devils. She meets my kiss with a vigor that's causing a situation my towel can't hide. Her tongue is hot and persistent against mine, and when I lick into her mouth, she surges into me. The movement brushes across the towel and I choke on a groan at the feel of it. Her breath is hot and quick and I push the jacket off her shoulders, dropping it carelessly to the floor.

My fingers tug clumsily at the knot in her shirt, pushing beneath the fabric as we kiss, wet and loud in the stillness of the room. I know it was brave of her to wear this—to show her scars. I never needed Sydney fucking Prescott to tell me about those insecurities. This is something only Vandy and I can really know, having the proof of that night branded into us forever.

She sways towards me when I bend, planting a slow, sweet kiss on the pale flesh.

"Reyn." Her breath catches, hands grabbing at my sides.

I catch the towel before it falls completely and say, "You keep messing with me, I'm going to lose the towel."

"Then lose it." Her tone is daring, eyes lit by a brilliant spark.

I let out this embarrassing half-laugh, half-groan. "Trust me, I am losing it."

She reaches for her shirt and yanks it over her head. It's a move so sudden that I have to blink a few times to really process all the skin standing before me. She's not wearing a bra, and her tits are perfection, soft and round. She watches me back, wetting her lips. "Let's just... get lost."

This isn't a fingerbang in the front seat of my Jeep. It isn't head in the Alumni house. It isn't eating her out, quick and dirty in the Stairway. It isn't even that night in her room, when I went up her skirt.

This is both of us, here, alone, practically naked.

Absolutely nothing is stopping us.

I exhale slowly, lifting a hand to gently graze the side of her breast. It's warm and just as soft as it looks, and I instantly just... know.

I know I can *take* it.

"We don't have to—I mean, we can wait," I say, thumb brushing across her nipple. "There's nothing wrong with taking things slow."

She shudders in a breath, blinking slowly. "We did take it slow," she whispers, catching my wrist before I can pull it away. Her blue eyes bore into mine. "I did wait."

My body says to go for it, and despite having just jerked off, my cock's already hard again, ready, two seconds from exploding. My brain is a jumbled mush. My eyes won't stop staring at her tits. At her flat stomach. Then down at the scar.

Guilt.

It washes over me. Always. I can't shake it. I can't get away from it.

I take a step back, but she moves with me, eyes imploring. "Hey, I want this. I want you."

God, I want her too.

"Then take me."

Did I say that out loud? Fuck. "I just need to—" I need to *think*. I need to make sure I'm doing this right. I need to consult the risk management plan.

Some of that spark in her eyes dims. "Unless you don't want to?"

"No, I do," I burst, taking her face in my hands. I can feel the heat of her cheeks beneath the pads of my thumbs. "So badly, you have no idea. I just thought I'd have more time to plan."

Her eyebrows knit together. "Plan what?"

"How to do this without hurting you."

"Reyn," she says, mouth quirking into a grin. "It's totally fine. I talked to Afton, Elana, and Georgia about it. They all say it hurts, but only a little and not for long. Come on, you know I'm not scared of a little pain."

"No, I don't mean *that*." I shake my head. "Obviously that'll hurt, and that... that sucks." I get lost in this little brain-loop of awareness that, yes. I'm going to hurt her. With my dick. It's not a good feeling to have. "But mostly, I meant..." My eyes drop to her leg. "Sex is physical, and I wasn't sure if—"

"Oh," she cuts me off, blue eyes full of realization.

I rush to assure her, "Not that I think you can't do it or handle it. But if there's a way I can make it easier or better, then I wanted to know. Before."

There's a moment of pensive silence, and I worry that I've pissed her off. There are few things Vandy hates more than being babied. Luckily, she just looks at me and says, "It's not like I have any experience, but I don't think that's going to be a problem. We can just work it out, right? Together."

This is the scariest thing about it. The trust. She has this faith in me to make it good—to make it worth it. This girl—the girl I love and want and obsess over constantly—is offering to do the one thing I think about three times a second, and here I am, scared shitless. Eventually, she's going to realize that I'm not good enough.

I really don't want that moment to be now.

"Yeah," I say, mustering a confidence I don't feel. "We'll work it out."

The skin over her ribs is warm and smooth when my fingertips drag over it, mouth taking hers in a slow, long kiss. She winds her arms around my neck and her tits press into my chest. It takes my breath away, this heavy feeling swelling in my throat. It's full of things I already know I won't say. That I love her. That I'd die for her. That being with her like this is better than stealing. It's better than drugs. It's better than anything.

I try to tell her with my kiss, with the way my hand cups her tit in my palm, gentle and testing. I swallow the sound she makes and wrap an arm around her waist, steadying her as I move us toward the bed.

I glide my hands down her back, over the curve of her ass, and lift her, placing her on the bed. She sits before me, eyes staring into mine, and softly drags her nails down my chest, traveling below my belly. They hook into the towel that's honestly barely hanging on at this point. I just watch her back as she tugs it away, letting it fall around my feet.

Her eyes dip down, taking me in slowly, reverently. Her hands touch me like she's not even nervous about it. Like she knows this is hers. Like she owns it. Her palms drag down my hips, eyes fixed to where I'm hard and eager, cock flushed and ready.

I suck in a deep breath when she wraps a hand around me, giving my cock a soft stroke. A tremor shudders through my body. She's watching her hand on me, interested, inquisitive, and I let her play with it for a few moments before capturing her wrist.

"Keep doing that and this'll be over before it begins."

Her eyes jump up to mine, flashing in gratification. I slide my forearm under her lower back and gently ease her up the bed before dipping back in to capture her lips. Vandy kisses like it's still something new. She takes her time, patient and curious, and gives me that same frission I feel when I'm breaking into something. No one else has this. Kissing me like this is all she knows. *I'm* all she knows. Beyond the layers of crushing anxiety I feel about it all, there's definitely something satisfied and possessive lurking beneath.

Her mouth chases mine when I pull away, but I sit back on my heels, fingers tugging at the button on her jeans. She's flushed all the way down her chest, hips lifting as I tug them down her thighs. When I don't pull her panties down with her jeans, she reaches down to do it for me, sliding them down her hips.

"Fuck, V." I look at her spread before me, and it's almost surreal. Her hair's fanned out on my pillow, mouth parted as she watches me in return. There's something nervous and soft in her eyes, and her knees graze against my bare hips when she tries to close them. I soothe my hands over her thighs, running them up to her hips. "You're so fucking gorgeous, you know that?"

She sinks her teeth into her lip when I bend down to press an open-mouthed kiss to the tattoo on her thigh. I linger there for far too long, lathing it with my tongue, licking up one thigh, and then the other. I suck and nip, embarrassingly self-indulgent about it, before I crawl on top of her, kissing her hips, her scars. Her hair fans behind her like a golden halo, and it only slams it home that I'm defiling her, claiming her, taking something that can never be given back. She must sense my hesitation because she pushes up and captures my lips, coaxing me into a searing kiss. A kiss so good, combined with her roaming, curious hands, that makes the doubts vanish and my lust rush forward.

She makes a sharp sound when I take her peaked nipple into my mouth. "Reyn…"

I hum as I palm the other one, spine going liquid at the feel of her squirming beneath me. Her hips cant upward and the soft skin of her thigh brushes the tip of my cock. I unthinkingly chase it, ultimately grinding down into her center, thrusting mindlessly against all of her warmth.

"Shit," I rasp, pulling away. We're getting ahead of ourselves.

"Sorry," she says, but she doesn't look it. "You're just really good with your hands. Catching footballs, swiping keys…" I dip my fingers between her legs, and she shivers. "And that. You're good at that."

She's already wet for me, mouth falling open as I sink a finger inside. I take some time opening her up, swallowing the little sounds she makes with aborted, distracted kisses. At some point, her leg hitches over my hip and I have to clench my teeth against the wave of frantic want that explodes in me. I want to feel every inch of her skin pressed against mine.

Quietly, she asks, "Do you have a condom?" and I pull away.

It already feels like I just ran suicides. "What kind of Devil would I be if I wasn't prepared?" I fumble for the drawer by my bed and shake a condom out of the box. I'm impulsive, but not stupid. I didn't need my dad to give me his gross horny teenager talk to know better than that. I tear the package with my teeth, intensely aware of her leaning back on her elbows, staring.

I pause, dick in hand, rubber at the tip. "What?"

Her eyes jerk up to mine, heavy-lidded and inquisitive. "I want to watch."

I laugh. "You like to see the monster that's coming?"

She lifts an eyebrow. "It's big and all, but it's not a monster, Reyn."

I'm not talking about my dick. I'm talking about myself. It's hard to see myself as anything else. But the girl below me, the one watching my every move, doesn't look at me like a monster. She looks at me like—*fuck*—like I'm the moon and the stars, the sun that rises. Or maybe I'm projecting, because that has to be how I'm looking at her. Like she's the shiniest damn thing I've ever seen and god, I want her.

*Mine now.*

The words are on the tip of my tongue. I've known them forever—felt them my whole life—but I don't want to be that guy. My girl deserves better than to just belong to someone. She deserves to get what she wants. Vandy doesn't want to be coddled, and the very least I can give her is that, which is why I look past the way she tenses her belly, the rigidity in her thighs, and I take control. *Not* that I have much of it at this point. My balls ache and I'm probably at risk of being a two-pump chump, but I kiss her lips, steady her hips, and press the tip into her warm, wet pussy.

I freeze there, wide eyes seeking hers, terrified that she'll hate me forever if this hurts too much.

But she just exhales against my lips. "I'm fine, Reyn. I'm fine. Please..."

I push, rocking inside past the resistance. That's the thing about *stealing*, about *taking*, you can't hesitate. There's no time for it. So I take her, caving to the urge to invade and *have*.

She's so warm, so tight, so soft underneath me. I have to take a second, pressed deep inside her, to pull myself back from the edge. Not fucking brainlessly into her wet heat is harder than running an entire afternoon of suicides. Harder than ruck marches. Harder than just about anything.

Soft exhalation blows across my face, and I feel the tension in her stomach easing, her thighs releasing their tight clutch around my hips. When I open my eyes, I see the curve of her parted lips, the soft fluttering of her lashes.

I cradle her cheek. "Are you—" My words choke off into a rough noise when she rocks up against me, spurring me on.

"Yes," she breathes, fingers pressing divots in my shoulders.

She's okay. We're okay.

And fucking hell, I'm going to take this girl and really make her mine.

# 31

Vandy

I'VE FELT a lot of pain in my life and I've numbed the hell out of myself to keep it at bay, but having Reyn inside of me, stretching me, pushing my body past the point of pain toward the rush of pleasure, is something I didn't anticipate.

At first, I thought there was no way he'd fit inside of me. No way his cock, with the length or girth, would be able to get past my entrance. But it was the noises he made that broke down my defenses. The little grunts, the hum of pleasure, the set of his jaw as he tried to control himself. It was the look in his clear green eyes, the tightening of his stomach and god, how safe I felt in his arms, even as he pressed into me.

"Breathe," he whispers, mouth hot near my ear.

I do it, sucking in air and with it, the clean, masculine scent of him. Slowly that fear, that insecurity, all melts away. I want him more than I fear what comes next and when he sinks into me, rocking his powerful hips, all I want is *more*.

It's not just my body, it's my heart, my mind, my skin, my core. That feeling that was almost bursting out of me before finally spills over, and I can't do anything but pant against the wave of it. My nails drag down his back, wanting him closer.

"*More*," I whisper, because what Reyn doesn't understand is that I'm not afraid of pain. I've lived with it for so long that this other side of it is deliriously intoxicating.

My demand breaks the tight concentration of his façade. He laughs.

"What?" I ask, panicked that I'm doing it wrong.

"You." He grins down at me. "I need to stop underestimating you."

Our eyes meet and hold for a long, precarious beat. I run a hand down the curve of his bicep and shift my hips, planting my feet on the bed. He sinks in deeper, a teeth-clenched grunt wiping away the smirk.

I've been afraid of feeling for so long, but now I can't get enough of the tug in my chest. I can't get enough of *him*. The long cords of muscle down his back, the pebbled scars that unite us, the curve of his ass, his breath, the sweep of his tongue. Sweat builds between us, and it's sticky, messy, noisy, and god, so very real.

That's what I've been scared of: real.

The way Reyn McAllister's hips drive into my body is achingly real. The way he sets my nerves on fire, the way he tastes, the way he touches me—*god,* the way he looks at me, so soft and intense, like I'm the only thing that exists here and he's so grateful for it. His thumbs hold me down, anchoring my body so that my desire can build.

The sounds coming from me are unexpected; grunts and moans, words I can't place, sharp fricatives. Slowly, we fall into a rhythm —*our* rhythm—one that's coursed between us from the beginning. It all led to this. To this pounding. This pain. This pleasure.

His hips buck harder, frantic, and I know he's close. I can see it in the pucker of his brow, the tremor in the arm that's holding him up. "Baby," he groans through gritted teeth. His sweaty forehead lands on my neck, mouth hot on the skin of my collarbone. He pushes out a long, raggedly whispered, *"Fuuuuck,"* before coming, back ramrod straight.

He collapses on me with heaving breaths, and I swear I can feel his thudding heartbeat against my chest. Before I have a chance to process the weight of him, solid and sure, his hand dips between my legs, circling my wet, aching clit. My body shudders from the sensitivity. It's overwhelming. Too much.

"It's—" I start, wanting to beg him to stop, to say that it's enough for one day, but he leans over me and swallows my breath with a kiss. I sink and just when I think I'm going to drown, he pulls away and travels down my body, ultimately replacing his hand with his mouth. My hips buck, and his hands slide under my ass, tilting me upward. This, god *this*, is nothing like I've ever felt before. My orgasm, coiled tight, releasing like a pounding heartbeat, is so close, so near, that when it finally happens it's like a breaking wave, crashing hard. My head presses into the pillow, heels digging into the mattress. My nails sink into his skin, needing something to hold onto so I don't get washed away.

When I open my eyes, he's looking down at me, lips shiny, curved into a smirk.

The feeling in my chest, in the pit of my stomach, I recognize it. It's fear.

Not of pain. Of how much I love Reyn McAllister. I'd always thought we were connected, linked. But now? Now there's no going back.

~

HOMECOMING FRIDAY IS A BIG DAY. There's a tangible buzz in the air of Preston Prep. Dates are set, dresses are bought, and the pep rally scheduled, and even if it only means getting out of last period, what's not to love?

But none of that matters to me.

I'm flying high. So fucking *high*. Way better than any drug I've ever taken. I'm high on Reynolds McAllister and from the smug look he gives me when I pass him on the way to Art, he feels the same way.

I pass Caroline on the way to my seat and wave hello, while ignoring Syd's too-loud laughter coming from the other side of the room. She'd moved to another table last week, which leaves an empty chair next to mine. The bell is about to ring when a body slides into it.

"Hey, Vandy," George says. "No one's sitting here, right?"

I look around, shrugging. "Nope, it's all yours."

"Cool, cool, cool," he mutters, pulling his sketch pad and pencil pouch out of his backpack. He zips and unzips the pouch a few times, dipping his fingers inside, yet never retrieving a pencil. I get my own pencil and eraser out and start on the morning assignment.

"So, I was wondering," George says, finally having chosen a pencil, "if you're going to the dance with anyone?"

Half-focused on the assignment, shading technique, I glance up. "Uh, yeah, I'll probably swing by."

"Swing by." He moves the pencil wildly in and out of his fingers, until it flies across the room. "Oops."

He scrambles to get it and all I can think is that Reyn was right. Not only did I do the right thing not giving this awkward, clumsy boy my first kiss, I probably dodged a bullet.

"Anyway," he says, jumping back in his seat. "I thought, you know, maybe we could go together?"

"Together?" I slowly repeat. Shit. How did this happen? I glance back and see Caroline smiling in amusement.

"Right. I'd pick you up. We'd get some food. Then head to the dance." He taps his pencil on the table, a rapid tattoo that's drawing annoyed stares. "Together." He looks at me hopefully. So very hopefully that I feel a little bad for him even if he's been a touch too presumptuous in the past.

"That—" I spot Sydney from the corner of my eye. She's focused on her sketch pad but it's obvious she's listening. Screw her. "That's really nice of you to ask, but I've got to cover all the homecoming activities for the newspaper, and I don't think I'd make a great... uh, date."

"The newspaper." He nods rapidly. "Right, right. I get it. Duty calls and all that."

"Yep," I tuck my hair behind my ear, feeling oddly embarrassed. "Mr. Lee's a hardass. Deadlines and all." Even I can feel the weakness of my smile.

Caroline, two rows back, gives me a thumbs up. It's pretty obvious from George's fidgeting that he's regretting his seat choice right about now.

Two hours later I'm at lunch, Reyn on the opposite side of the table, tipping a can of soda to his mouth. He's been eating cookies out of a bag that was left in his locker by one of the cheerleaders this morning. It doesn't exactly make me jealous. It's just some dumb homecoming tradition, cheerleaders showering the players with locker goodies on game day. But it does make me want to snatch the bag out of his hand and throw it across the room.

Okay, maybe it makes me a *little* jealous.

I could have left him food in his locker. And it would have been good food, too. Something other than empty calories. Protein, because Reyn is an athlete. Something with a sauce, because he likes stuff in a sauce. It's bad enough I have to sit all the way over here, unable to touch him, do I really have to watch him eat some other girl's food, too?

He's not near enough that it completely rattles me—not close enough for me to accidentally brush up against his leg under the table. Or, you know, lick that sugary soda off his lips. Conversation floats. The guys are deep in discussion about the game. The girls are gossiping about who's taking whom, some muttered worries of the weather possibly being bad and ruining hairdos. None of it penetrates. I just keep thinking about the way those hands of his were on me last night. The way he—almost obsessively—showered my inner thighs with obscenely wet, open-mouthed kisses. How his mouth felt between my legs. How his hard cock was—

"What about you, V?"

I blink, head whipping around. "What?"

Georgia's eyebrows are raised. "What does your dress look like?"

I struggle to become coherent. It's not really working. "Dress?"

"For the dance," Afton adds.

"Oh, well, I didn't get one." My mind had been on other... things. I lower my voice so only the Devils and Playthings can hear. "We're just kind of making an appearance, right? Does it matter?"

Elana rolls her eyes. "Of course, it matters. It's a new dress," she says, as though that clears it up. "And you can't just walk in all casual like a total rando. That'll be more obvious."

"Oh, well." I frown, trying to think if I have a dress that wasn't just bought for Easter portraits. "I guess I can figure something out."

"You can borrow something of mine if you want," Aubrey says. "We're about the same size, and my mom's already started shopping for sorority rush next year. Or at least that's what she says. Seriously, I have things I've never even worn."

My eyes dart next to her, where my brother is sitting. I didn't realize he was listening, but he gives Aubrey an appreciative smile for her generosity. Damn, she's working this hard and he's buying into it. Not a single one of his prior girlfriends even looked in my direction except for their rare moments of slight pity.

Her voice grows commanding, assured. "Come over tomorrow and dig through my closet. We'll find you something."

Although I appreciate the offer, I can't help but feel like this is one of those moments where everyone is well aware of the fact I've never been to a school dance. And even though my social life has changed tremendously over the last few months, due to the secret nature of my relationship with Reyn, I'll still be walking into this dance alone.

"Speaking of the dance," Caroline says, her gray-blue eyes twinkling, "poor George looked completely heartbroken when you said no to his invitation."

"I, uh..." The sound of an aluminum can crumpling comes from the other end of the table. I look down at the soda can crushed in Reyn's hand.

"Dude. What the hell?" Ben shakes his head at the soda that's spilled from the can and all over his notebook. He grabs a napkin and wipes it off.

"Sorry." Reyn's jaw tenses, and he sets the can down gently.

I turn back to Caroline, eyes rolling. "Heartbroken seems like an exaggeration."

"I don't know," she teases. "He's been watching you a lot in class lately."

I push a doubtful 'psh' through my lips, but I don't miss the way Reyn has gone still, green eyes watching me.

"Hey, guys!" Sydney suddenly appears at the end of the table, all sparkly and bright in her cheer uniform. "I overheard talk about the dance. Everyone excited?" There's a feeble response from the girls. The boys simply ignore her. It's clear no one is really into talking to her. I stare at my half-eaten sandwich. She ignores being ignored and continues on, "What about you, Reyn? You taking someone?"

Reyn's chair is tilted back and he slows the chocolate chip cookie he's about to shove in his mouth. His expression remains impassive, but I can see the tick in his jaw. "I haven't decided if I'm going yet."

Of course he's going. We're all going, our alibis needing to be airtight. But if Reynolds McAllister is too cool to commit to a Homecoming dance, he's certainly too cool to commit to a date.

"Oh," Sydney says, bending over to adjust her knee sock, which serves to give a flash of her cleavage. "Me either." She flips her ponytail over her shoulder. "Maybe I'll see you there."

He does that guy thing, where he lifts his chin in acknowledgement but never makes actual eye contact. She walks off, ass swaying under that tiny skirt, and I snap my gaze toward him, because if he's looking at her legs, at her *thighs*, I swear to god—

He's looking at me.

"Damn that was cringy," Georgia says, breaking the awkward silence that's settled around the table. "Right? Just coming out and basically asking Reyn to the dance?"

"Straight up thirsty," Afton agrees, tossing her trash on her tray. "I really wish she wasn't such a good tumbler, or I'd toss her ass off the squad." She gives Reyn a look. "Don't even think about it, Thigh Master."

Ben mouths a confused, "*Thigh Master*?"

"Seriously?" Reyn tosses his hands. "Why does everyone think I have such bad taste in women? You're like the fourth person to tell me that."

"Because you were locked up for three years," Carlton replies, shrugging. "Desperate times, my friend."

Aubrey shrugs. "I don't think you have bad taste, Reyn." Her lips curve and her eyes dart toward me. "In fact, you probably have pretty outstanding taste in women."

"Alright, that's enough," he says, pushing his chair back. He grabs his trash and backpack. "I'll see you later."

But inside, I am *freaking out*. Aubrey knows.

*Aubrey knows!*

I meet her knowing gaze with my own panicked eyes, but she just mimes zipping her lips and goes back to eating. I'm hoping that means she won't tell Emory. She obviously hasn't yet. I can tell by the lack of Reynolds being all *dead* on the lunch table.

The bell rings, saving us all from further dance conversation, but Aubrey grabs me on the way out of the room.

She clutches her hands together, begging, "Seriously, please come by tomorrow? Let me help you pick out a dress." She grins. "I have something I think Reyn will like."

My shoulders tense and I glance around. Maybe I can just deny. "Why would I care about what Reyn will like?" My laugh is half-hearted and full of dread. "We're not going together."

She gives me a look that says just how much she isn't buying this. "Yeah, well once he sees you in this dress, he's going to wish he staked a claim on you. Publicly."

"Aubrey," I start, stomach flipping anxiously.

She must sense the doom in my voice, because she puts a gentle hand on my arm. "Hey, it's fine. I'm not going to tell Emory, okay? That's your business."

I release a hard breath and don't ask her how she knows. It's more of a mystery to me how anyone could *not* know. "Thank you," I say instead.

ARMED WITH A NEWSPAPER CAMERA, I enter the gym a few minutes before the pep rally starts. Mr. Lee gave me a pass to get excused from class early, and so far, the room is filled with athletes, spirit teams, and a section of the marching band already mid-rehearsal. The drumbeat echoes off the high, metal ceiling. It's one of those environments that a short time ago would have sent me running—or well, limping—away. It's too noisy and over-stimulating. Now, behind the shield of my camera, I scope out the room, determining the best spot to get photos of the event. I know from past rallies that the coaches and team will be up on the stage, and the cheerleaders just below them. The dance team will perform on the gym floor and the band will stick to their corner of the bleachers.

I move backwards, camera in position, toward the stacked steps to see if I can get a decent shot of the stage and floor from this angle. I bump into something hard and steady.

"Hey," Reyn says from behind me. "Got a minute?"

I don't, not really, and neither does he. But I don't fight him when he pulls me under the bleachers, fingers laced with mine as we traverse the narrow space. He stops and pushes my back against the wall. I notice his expression is tense.

"What's up?" I ask, running a hand over his black jersey.

"George?" he blurts.

I blink, trying to follow his non-sequitur. Then I see the answer on his face. Jealousy.

"Seriously?" I ask, fighting the urge to laugh.

But Reyn's face is stormy and hard. "He's been sniffing around for weeks now. I mean, he already made one move on you."

"Which I rejected," I calmly remind him. "Full Heisman."

He barks an abrupt laugh, eyes softening. "You know what a Heisman is?"

I roll my eyes and hold my hand out to his chest, blocking him, like on the coveted Heisman trophy. "I live in the south with a foot-ball-loving family. Of course, I know what a Heisman is. But that's not the point. Why are you being weird?"

He swallows, fingers coming up to fidget with my hair. "I just don't like it—him. George."

I watch him brush my hair over my shoulder, and he does it so carefully. "Saying no is all I can do, Reyn. Plus, it's not like..." I trail off.

"Like what?"

"Like I can say I have a..." Again, the words don't fully form, but this time I clamp my mouth shut.

He eyes me. "A what?"

"Nothing." I cross my arms over my chest and don't miss his gaze dropping down. "You know, it's not like I don't see girls flirting with you all the time."

He looks taken aback. "No one's flirting with me."

I scoff. I refuse to bring up Sydney. That's partly out of fear. What if the rumor was true? It would crush me. And if it's not? It's not worth bringing up. It'll only feed her need for rumors and gossip. "I'm just saying, scantily dressed men aren't leaving baked goods in my locker."

It's his turn to scoff. "Come on, you know that's just a stupid foot-ball thing. I don't even know which one left it in my locker." His fingers squeeze my hip and in a quieter voice, he asks, "What's this about?"

"It's about..." I look down to the end of the stands. Students are filing into the gym now. "It's about labels. About what we are to one another." Reyn and I had both made promises. Never Sydney. Never Sebastian. It hasn't escaped my attention that we've never made promises about anyone else. The ambiguousness of it has this way of rattling me at completely random times.

He studies me, like he can see right through me. My skin prickles under the intensity, but his free hand grabs mine, threading our fingers together. "I don't know what you want to call this, Baby V. It's twisted and caught up in a bunch of bullshit and secrets—which, for the record, goes against all my instincts." He hooks a finger under my chin, forcing my eyes to his. "All day, all I want to do is let the whole goddamn world know you're mine." His voice is low and rough in a way that makes me shiver when he says, "I've marked you. I've been inside you. I've made you come three different ways." His mouth hovers over mine. "And god knows you've done the same for me. If you don't know that I'm already yours, then you're not paying attention. Because I am—completely."

All of that is raw and real, I can hear it in his voice, see it in his eyes. I push up on my toes at the same time that he bends, mouths meeting in the middle. It's a different sort of kiss, less horny, more determined. This kiss is a promise, and it's about more than just two people. This is a pact. This is us agreeing to be in this together, and when he pulls back, the wild anxiety rolling around in my chest has abated. Something warm and so happy replaces it, that I'm almost sure he can see it in my smile.

He thumbs my lip, sighing. "We're going to have to tell him, aren't we?"

"Eventually," I concede, because Reyn is right. As much as we want to belong to each other, it can never fully happen until we cross that bridge. "We'll make a plan."

He nods, brushing the hair off my cheek. "Maybe soon we can…"

I watch curiously as he trails off, eyes going dark. "What?"

"Maybe we can get together again," he answers, and from the spark in his eyes, I know exactly what kind of 'getting together' he wants to do.

"*God*, please," I groan, letting my head fall back. I watch him through slitted eyes. "Maybe tonight?"

His lips curl into a slow smirk. "Maybe." And then, the smirk falls. "This isn't just about sex for me. You know that, right? I can't ask you to go to the dance with me, but I would if I could."

I shake my head. "I don't need a dance."

"I do have something to give you, though." His voice is slightly raised. The gym is filling quickly and above us, students are climbing the bleachers. He shuffles closer. "I've been meaning to. I've been carrying it around for a while." He shoves his hand in his pocket and looks at me, forehead creased. "And for the record, I did not steal it."

I laugh, confused but happy. "Okay."

He holds out his hand and a small silver charm sits in the middle of his palm. At first glance, I think it's a butterfly or maybe a dragonfly, but then I notice the small, glassy bulb at the tail. He cups his hand to block the light and a faint glow comes from it.

"It's a firefly," I say, shocked. My hand trembles when I take it from him, thumb running over the charm. He can't possibly know the significance—probably just thought of my cat. But this? I meet his gaze, eyes prickling. "Reyn, it's… it's perfect."

He looks down at it in my hand, eyebrows knitting together. "It's nothing special or expensive, I just—"

I shut him up with a kiss. "Thank you."

It's way past time for us to go back out to the gym floor. Hands linked, we make our way through the narrow path under the bleachers, back toward the exit. For the first time in a while I feel settled, secure, whole. I've got Reyn, the Devils, the Playthings. I'm focused and have a solid position on the newspaper. I'm clean, healthy, madly in love.

Life is actually good, for once.

"Hey," he says, pushing me against the wall and flattening his palm next to my head. "One last kiss?"

There's no way I'll say no. I've never been able to, and when his lips meet mine, warm and soft, I know why. Reynolds McAllister owns me. Then and now. The kiss isn't sweet and slow, like the ones we just shared. This one is fast and hard, full of the 'maybe' we're waiting for, tonight. Maybe we'll find a way to be alone. Maybe we'll do it again. Maybe this time, I'll find out what it's like to have Reyn inside of me without all the nervousness and fumbling and pain.

We break apart with heaving chests and heavy eyes, but not before a shadowy figure appears at the end of the bleachers. Reyn must notice him a moment before I do because he drops my hand like it's on fire.

It doesn't matter. It's too late.

Emory just caught us.

# 32

"Dude, talk to me."

Emory stops midway down the row of lockers, his shoulders as tense as his fists, which are notably balled tight. Without turning, he says in a low, apocalyptically angry voice, "Reyn, if I even look at you right now, I will kick your motherfucking ass, and I can't do that. Not with this game on the line. But tomorrow?" His jaw locks tight, neck cracking. "Tomorrow, you better watch your fucking back."

He continues through the empty locker room, flinging the metal door open so that it slams hard against the one next to it. The rest of the team is still eating the pre-game, pot-luck dinner brought to us by the booster club. Emory made an appearance—he's captain after all. That had been a blast, trying to get him alone, only to be met with a red-hot, dagger-glare. If looks could kill, I'd be dead. But if looks could nuke this town, we'd all be dust right now.

The second he could leave, he bolted. Stubbornly, I followed.

Now I'm standing between the banks of lockers, the scent of sweaty jockstrap in the air, trying to figure out how to fix this. How to salvage what I can of our friendship. I broke a cardinal rule. The *only* rule.

"Well, if you won't talk," I reason, "you can at least listen."

He yanks his gear out of the locker, slamming it on the bench. His voice is sharp through gritted teeth. "Don't fucking test me, McAllister."

Stupidly, I push. "Whatever you're thinking is going on is worse than reality."

"You can have any girl in this school. *Any fucking girl.* Could have just taken your pick, but no. That's not good enough for you, is it? It's so typical Reyn, I don't know how I'm even surprised. You saw her, shiny and clean and *innocent*, and you thought to yourself 'I'm going to take that'." The anger rolls off him in waves. "I trusted you! I really fucking trusted you, with the most important thing in my life. Do you even understand that? Do you even fucking care?"

He still won't look at me and I'm not sure I want him to. Guilt bubbles in my gut, hot like acid. "If you'll let me explain—"

He snaps his face in my direction. "Fuck no. You don't get to explain or manipulate your way out of this one, Reyn." When he finally meets my eyes, I wish he hadn't. The anger was one thing, but this is something new. This is hurt. "Did you set this up? Was it all a scam? Did you talk me into letting Vandy into the Devils so that you could get close to her and try to fu—" the word stumbles on his tongue.

"That's *not* how this started. I was looking out for her, just like you were. But—"

Fuck. Shit. I can't tell him the *but.*

*But she knew we were up to something and was going to narc.*

*But she was tired of being treated like a baby and I told her I would help.*

*But she was drowning and needed something—someone—and that person, against all fucking odds, was me.*

Good thing Emory doesn't even want to hear my 'but'. "But then you decided to use her?"

"I'm not using her!" I insist. "See, you're already twisting this into something—"

He slams his fist into the locker, the sound reverberating harshly in the room. "I know my sister, Reyn! I know how she felt about you, and I saw the way you always fucking played on that. You made a promise!"

It takes me so long to understand what promise he's referring to that by the time it dawns on me, he already has his shirt ripped off. I gape at him. "You can't actually be serious."

His eyes bug out, fists clenching. "Ask me again how serious I am. I dare you."

"We were ten!" I laugh in amazement, remembering a promise made on a balmy Halloween night, eight years ago. "We didn't even have pubes yet, Em. You think maybe shit's a little different now?"

"I think maybe you're a little different now." He doesn't want to hear a word I have to say. He walks up to me, chest heaving with restrained anger. "If you go near her again, I will fucking end you, Reyn. You're never fucking my sister, so I'm telling you now, if you know what's good for you? You'll move the fuck on." I'm not sure what my face is saying, but it seems to be broadcasting loud and clear, because Emory suddenly lurches back, face slack. "You already did," he realizes.

"Em, wait," I try.

"You fucked her? You fucked her. You *fucked* her!" Every time he says it, his eyes get a little wider, voice a little louder. There's this vein in his forehead that bulges with each sentence, like it keeps feeding this feral, apoplectic rage into his bloodstream, and I'm powerless to stop the freight train behind it. He lunges at me, fist balled tight, swinging at my face. He pulls it before it can make contact, fist shaking with the force. "You're so lucky there's a game tonight."

I never even flinched.

"When was it?" His voice is being pushed through his clenched teeth like a sieve. "Was it that night, when you said you'd walk her home? Keep her *safe*?" He spits the word like venom. "Was it at Thistle Cove? Huh? Or did you just have no self-control and fuck her the day after you got back?" His raging eyes ping back and forth between mine. "Answer me, pussy!"

"Last night," I answer honestly.

"Bullshit!"

"What exactly do you want to hear, Emory?" I raise my voice, tension rolling up my spine. "You want a play-by-play? You want to hear about how I fingered her two weeks ago? You want to know when she sucked my dick? You want to know what we did in the Stairway for the fifth rite?"

Bad move.

Real bad move.

"I knew it!" He slams his fist into the locker beside my head. "And you stood here and made me feel like the bad guy for suspecting anything! What else, huh? How many times have you lied to my fucking face so you could get into her pants?"

I laugh bitterly. "You're insane. You can't handle the thought that Vandy has been out there making choices you don't agree with, but instead of being angry at yourself, you're just taking it out on me. News flash, Em! You have massively disturbing control issues! I can't believe they have her in therapy and completely failed to realize that you're fucked in the head."

He pulls his fist back again, but I'm not going to just stand here, this time.

I square my shoulders. I'm taller than Em. Stronger. He's a pussy quarterback, all protected and coddled. I've spent my life getting piled on. I can take him in a heartbeat.

"What the fuck is going on in here?" I hear Carlton coming down the row of lockers, but I don't break Emory's gaze.

"Why don't you tell him?" Emory says, nostrils flaring. "Come on, Reyn, don't be shy. Tell him how you almost killed my little sister, then came back three years later to take advantage of her like a fucking—"

I plant both my palms into his shoulders, shoving him with enough strength that he stumbles back into the lockers. "That's not what fucking happened!" I can take a lot. If Emory wants to be pissed at me? Fine. I'd let him hit me, if that's what he needed. But I can't take this thing I have with Vandy being dragged through the mud like that—all twisted up into some ugly, hurtful, monstrous thing.

Emory gains his footing and is immediately flying toward me, but suddenly Carlton and Ben are there, separating us.

"What the hell, you guys?" Ben shouts. "This shit ain't buddies!"

Red-faced and irate, Emory thrusts a finger in my face. "This gutless asshole fucked my sister!"

Carlton lets out a slow, "Aw, shit," and looks at me wide-eyed.

Ben winces. "Jesus Christ."

"She's seventeen!" I shove Carlton's hands away. "If she wants to be with someone, that's her business! You're not going to stop her."

"Watch me." His voice is low and deadly.

"You're going away next year, genius!" I press my finger to my temple. "V and I are staying right fucking here."

His eyes narrow. He knows it, which is why he adds, "I will tell my parents, your dad, and Headmaster Collins that you took advantage of her. I'll tell them you broke into Thistle Cove. I'll drive my fucking truck off a bridge and tell them you did it. Try me, motherfucker! I'll have your ass tossed out so fast, you'll wish you never stepped foot back here."

"Whoa," Ben says, arms extended between us. "Can't we just talk this out? I mean, Reyn doesn't seem like the kind of guy who'd—"

"What do you know?" Emory spits.

"I'm just saying," Ben tries, voice calm. "Maybe we need to just cool off for a bit, let Vandy clear this up."

"Shit is perfectly clear," Emory replies, cutting his eyes at me. "You and me? We're done. You're never going near her again."

I scoff. "You need to figure out how to tell your sister that, because I don't think she's going to take it very well."

He shoves a finger at me. "You leave Vandy to me. She has never been, and will never be, any of your fucking concern. That ship sailed three years ago, when you almost killed her. Or have you forgotten that?"

He turns back toward his locker and grabs his stuff, carrying it past me toward the door. Carlton and Ben are looking between us, wary.

My nerves are still firing, and I'm pissed off, but beneath that is the same thing I'd seen in Emory's eyes before. It's hopeless and sharp and wants to strike back. There's only one thing I know that'll hurt him as much as I want to, so I call out, "I want my senior shirt back, asshole!"

Emory takes two steps and freezes, slowly turning to glare at me over his shoulder. "I don't have anything of yours."

"Yeah, you do." I swear, Ben and Carl must sense that whatever's about to come out of my mouth won't be good, because they start inching between us. "You picked it up off her floor."

I can practically see the words hit him. "You piece of—" He tries to fly at me, but the others are already there, pulling him back. "In my house? Under our fucking roof?"

If I thought it'd make me feel better, then I was wrong.

OUR FIGHT DOESN'T MUDDLE the game. Emory won't let it. He's stone cold, flinging ball after ball in my direction, like he's daring me to fail.

I don't. I *won't.*

I score touchdown after touchdown. I'm a fucking machine out there. Adversity isn't a problem for me, I thrive on it. But that's me. More than once, I catch sight of my girl in the stands, camera clutched in her hands, eyes red, forehead worried. This isn't the kind of situation Vandy flourishes in. The gaping chasm between Emory and I hurts, but he's her brother. She has to live with him. She loves him.

No one can tell everything is crumbling. Not during halftime when Headmaster Collins announces Emory, coated in a sheen of sweat, and Aubrey, cute and sparkly, as our newly crowned Homecoming King and Queen. Or when Sydney lunges at me for a post-game, celebratory hug. I peel her off without another thought and head toward the showers, stopping at the fence where she's waiting for me. Vandy smells so sweet and fresh that I just want to wrap her up in my arms and bury my face into her neck.

The firefly charm is hanging around her neck.

"We'll figure this out," I tell her. "Don't panic."

"I'm not," she lies. It's not even half-hearted. It's like one-fiftieth-hearted. Her face is drawn and she looks all at once sad and terrified.

I mutter a low curse and wipe my face with my jersey. "Let's give him a chance to cool off, get through tomorrow night, and then we'll deal with it, okay?"

She nods and I beat a hasty retreat, knowing that if he catches us talking, shit will escalate fast. If Em squeals, I'll get sent packing, and at this point, I'm not sure I'd call his bluff.

What he doesn't get is that Vandy has leverage of her own. She's documented everything about the Devils since the beginning. If he pushes her... well, she may just take the whole thing down. Including herself.

People are talking when I get into the locker room. Emory's still on the field, taking pictures, but the rest of the guys are in the room, sweaty and tired.

Some junior I barely know is saying, "So McAllister's hitting that shit?"

"Apparently," Ben says.

Another senior pipes in, "Well I hope he keeps banging her and fighting with Hall about it, because those two were killing it out there."

The junior agrees, "It was like McAllister was possessed."

Carlton's sharp voice drifts in. "This is serious, okay? You know how Emory is about his sister."

"Do you really think Reyn..." Ben trails off, voice low and uncomfortable, but I can't see him yet.

"Nah," Carlton says. "I know Em. That girl could have her consent signed and certified in a court of law, and he'd still find a way to ignore it." I slump, exhausted and relieved, against the wall. At least these guys don't think so low of me. So low of *Vandy*. "This was always going to happen, sooner or later. The fact it was his best friend?"

"Fuel to the fire," Ben agrees.

They all go quiet when I walk in, eventually changing the subject to this game's point spread. I rip my pads off mechanically, barely seeing what I'm doing. It's not long before Emory walks into the room. I don't see him, but I can feel the shift in the energy, the hush and tension.

His locker's right beside mine, which used to be a good idea.

Now, not so much.

I don't look at him, but my anger has already fizzled. It's been replaced by something cold and tired. "We didn't do it to hurt you." I keep my voice low, but I know he hears me. I can tell by the way he goes still before jerking his pads from his shoulders. "And it's not just a physical thing, it's—"

He slams the locker closed and walks toward the showers, ignoring me.

Ben gives me a look from the other end of the row, but I just shake my head, resigned.

I think back to that promise I made eight years ago.

*"Do not be fucking with my sister, Reyn."*

*"What?" I asked, stuffing a candy bar into my mouth. Emory and Vandy had gone trick or treating, but I was content to swipe my candy from the other kids' bags. "Why would I mess with Baby V?" She was so cute that night in her little angel costume, silver halo bobbing along as her wings dragged the ground. "I like your sister."*

*Emory scowled. "If you try to make her your girlfriend, I will kick your ass."*

*I choked on the chocolate. "Gross!" At the ripe old age of ten, girls were only sometimes tolerable when they were the same age, but nine-year-olds? That was a completely insurmountable age gap. Entirely different worlds.*

*"I mean it," Emory pressed. "I'll fuck you up."*

*"I don't want a girlfriend," I said, but I could see he was bothered. So even though the thought outwardly grossed me out—and inwardly did*

*things I couldn't even understand yet—I loftily added, "I promise, I won't fuck with V, okay?"*

I hadn't even thought of that night in the treehouse in years. There should really be some law of limitations regarding promises made by ten-year-olds. What the fuck did I know back then? *Nothing.*

All I know now is that everything is fucked up and there's a lot more to lose than my freedom. I can handle losing Preston Prep, the Devils, maybe even Em. But after getting Vandy back? That's a loss I'm not sure I can survive.

# 33

I WAKE up the next morning with the same pit of dread in my stomach that was there when I went to sleep. Only now, it's joined by something else. It'd be stupid to call it anger. Anger is messy and confusing, and what I feel is a very tidy, simple thing. It's strong as steel and just as unforgiving. It's sure and confident—things I'm not used to feeling.

Emory didn't get home until late, so we haven't talked. But I know it's coming. Up until now, I don't think I knew how to even approach it. It all seems very clear this morning, as I get dressed, carefully and efficiently.

When I come across three pills tucked into an old bra, I know I'm doing the right thing. Things are muddled and scary right now, but looking at them, I barely feel the pull to bliss out and escape. Whatever Emory thinks of Reyn and me, he's dead wrong. Being with Reyn makes me better. Stronger.

Fuck what Emory thinks. Screw what my parents think, for that matter. To hell with Mr. McAllister, who's never around. Headmaster Collins, Jerry, Dewey—all of them can suck a fat one, for all I care.

I know it's not that easy. I can rail against everyone and come out the other side just fine. Reyn doesn't have the luxury. He has Jerry riding him. The school. His dad. His future.

The best thing is for me to do as Reyn asked; wait. Let Emory cool off and we'll talk it over. And if not? I'll get my revenge with my exposé. It's all sitting on my laptop, locked behind an encrypted file, tucked in my room. It's also backed up on a flash-drive I've started carrying on my person. Every letter, every instruction, every photo.

If Emory wants to burn my life down, I can do it right back. And I will. No regrets.

The flash-drive sits warm in my pocket as I walk into the kitchen. Emory looks up from the counter, bagel in his hand, cream cheese on his bottom lip. "You ready?" he grunts. "Because we need to talk on the way."

The final meeting is in thirty-minutes, at ten—or as Sebastian declared, "The ass-crack of dawn," when I called him to ask if he'd pick me up.

"I don't have anything to talk to you about," I coolly respond, popping two slices of bread into the toaster. "In fact, if you know what's good for you, you'll probably avoid talking to me at all today." There's a long stretch of silence and I don't bother turning around to see the annoyed expression he's probably wearing.

"So, it's going to be like that?"

"Yes," I answer simply. "It's going to be exactly like that."

I hear his glass of orange juice slam down harshly on the counter. "Well, tough shit, V. You can act like a baby about it, but—."

"Oh, that's rich." I laugh darkly, finally turning to look at him. "You want me to stop acting like a baby? Maybe you should try not treating me like one for once."

"You want to do this here, *fine*. You and Reyn? Not happening." Whatever's in my eyes makes him toss the bagel aside. He dusts his palms off with two pointed whacks against one another. "I'm doing this for your own good."

I tilt my head, watching him. "Maybe that's how it started. Maybe there was a time this was all about what was best for me. But now?" My smile feels tight and wrong. "Now, it's something else, and you know it."

"You're wrong."

"Emory," I start, staring calmly into his eyes. "You have two girl-friends." I hold up two fingers. "*Two* of them. I never said a word when Campbell dragged you around school by your balls. I kept my mouth shut when she kept you chained to your phone. I didn't say a thing when I watched her tell you how to dress, how to talk, how to *exist*. You know why? Because for some crazy reason, being with her made you happy. If I want a boyfriend—"

He cuts in with a clipped, "Not him."

"Then who?" I wonder, lifting my chin. "Not Reyn. Definitely not Sebastian, or Tyson, or Carlton, or Ben. Go on, then. Tell me who meets your standards. Give me a list of names, Emory."

Instead, he just grits out. "You're not seeing him again, and that's final."

Right.

*Here's* the anger.

Despite feeling like I'm shaking with the force of it, I keep my voice low and controlled. "I'm only going to say this once, so you'd better listen. You're not my father. Even if you were, you'd still have no say over what I do with my time, my feelings, or my body."

"Oh, I'd love to see what Mom and Dad would say about this." He crosses his arms, eyes shrewd. "You think this is a *bad reaction*? Wait until they get wind of it."

"You're threatening to tell them?" Having seen this coming miles away, I just shrug. "Go ahead. I don't give a single solitary fuck."

Pure disbelief fills his eyes. "Jesus, he really got into your head, didn't he?"

"You still don't get it!" My toast pops and I completely ignore it. "This is me, Em! This is who I am, without the pills, without feeling like I'm some defective loser, without my family constantly breathing down my neck and telling me how to feel. This is the *real* me. Get used to it."

"Oh, he's good." His laugh is completely without humor. "So that's how he's playing it, huh? Got you going on some little independence kick? Open your eyes, V, this is what he does. He manipulates situations for—"

"Give me a break." I roll my eyes so aggressively, I might have pulled something. "Look at his life, Emory. Who exactly is he manipulating with these superpowers of his? He can't even leave the house without getting frisked. He has to go through three layers of procedure just to have me in his kitchen for an hour. He couldn't even eat at my table until Mom and Dad *un-manipulated* their own situation."

"Poor Reyn," Emory sneers, nostrils flaring. "He's such a *victim* for committing a felony and almost killing you in the process. We should throw him a pity party. In fact, you know what? I'll design the banner myself." He sweeps his hand high. "It'll say '*that's what you get, asshole*'!"

I push off the counter, feeling my eyes flash red. "Don't even act like you haven't been worried about him all this time."

"That was before he fucked my sister!"

"I know you. If you really thought Reyn was everything you're saying, he never would have been your best friend."

He scoffs derisively. "Please. Hamilton Bates was one of my best friends for three years."

"And look at him now." I pull out my phone, swiftly navigating to his ChattySnap. I angrily swipe through, shoving the phone in his face. "Building homes in other countries, working at the soup kitchen with Gwen, teaching cello to disadvantaged youth." Emory just snorts, pushing the phone away. I continue, "Because deep down, you knew Hamilton was a good guy." I can't even say that with a straight face. "Okay, he's an *alright* guy." That doesn't quite feel right, either. "Well, he's not evil!" Yeah, that's about as good as I can do.

"This has nothing to do with Hamilton."

"You're right," I agree, stuffing my phone back into my pocket. "This is about you being a complete coward."

He stares at me unblinkingly, voice low and deadly. "Excuse me?"

"If you weren't," I explain, snatching my toast, "then maybe you could face the truth."

"And what truth is that?" His voice turns mocking. "That you're in stupid, schoolgirl puppy-love with Reyn?"

I'm not expecting the way the words fall like lead in the bottom of my stomach. It momentarily takes my voice away, trapping it into a lump at the back of my throat. He doesn't even know it, but hearing it said like that—having these colossal, exhilarating, once-in-a-lifetime feelings diminished so callously—is probably the most hurtful thing he's ever said to me.

I'm still caught in the trap of it when a rumble echoes off the pavement, followed by a solitary blare of the horn. I grab my stuff while Em's eyebrows draw angrily together. We both look out the window. Sebastian's shiny blue muscle car sits in the driveway, engine purring like Firefly on my lap.

"Is that Sebastian?" I move toward the door, but he blocks my way. "What the hell is he doing here?"

Finally finding my voice, I flatly explain, "He's giving me a ride."

Emory balks. "Like fucking hell he is. First of all, this conversation isn't over, and secondly, there's no way in hell you're getting into a car with a Wilcox."

I glare at him. "Get out of my way, Em."

"Jesus Christ, V." He looks at me like it's dawning on him that he doesn't even know who's standing in front of him. "I don't know what you're doing, but I know you're going to get hurt."

I swallow hard, hand flexing around the strap of my bag. "The truth I was talking about before? The one you're afraid of facing? It's that you're so worried about some guy manipulating my life to fit his own pleasure, taking away my happiness and hurting me, that you're missing a very essential point." I look him in the eye and feel the steel in my veins. "It's you, Emory. You're the guy."

I barely watch the words land, using the opportunity to skirt past him. I walk to the car, wrenching open the heavy door and sliding inside. Sebastian looks over at me. He's wearing dark sunglasses, hair a mess, and sporting a thick layer of stubble over his jaw. I don't know how I look, but it must be pretty bad, too, because he says, "You okay? Someone's ass need kicking? Reyn?" He turns to look at the house next door, forehead puckering pensively. "Yeah, he's strong and fast, but I can take him."

I sigh and sink down into the leather seat. "Just drive, Bass. Just drive."

Becoming the master of Ignoring Things, I brush off the stares as Sebastian and I walk into the bunker together. Reyn stands quietly in the back and my eyes instantly search him out. The cup of coffee in his hand is about the only put-together thing about him. He looks terrible—dark marks under his eyes, rumpled shirt, unshaven like Sebastian. His green eyes track me closely as I come in, like maybe he's assessing me the same way.

I take a seat between Georgia and Ben. Emory rushes in last, flustered. Annoyed. But my brother is an old school Devil, through and through. They rarely, if ever, show the weakness of emotion. It almost makes me feel a little better that I've been able to crack his armor. Almost.

He doesn't waste time, jumping into the last-minute assignments for the prank. Admittedly, with everything going on, I haven't been totally plugged in to the details. "This is all about coordination and timing," he says, eyes skimming over his notes. "Everything has to be done with surgical precision. It's not just one prank. It's two, set to go off like simultaneous bombs at the dance and the alumni meeting."

I know that last twist had been Carlton's idea. Why waste a good prank on the adults?

"Everything a go with the screens?"

"Yep," Carlton says, kicking back. "Luckily, yearbook had this whole montage they wanted to play. Some lame-ass throwback to past homecomings. It's perfect for both events."

"What if we can't get in the tech room? Or even the building?" Caroline speaks up. "It's always locked up tight on the weekends."

Reyn's smooth voice cuts in, "That's not a problem."

"The biggest issue is linking the feeds and turning off all the security cameras," Ben says. "I don't know how difficult it'll be to get into the network."

"Wait, you tested it right?" Emory asks.

"Yeah." Caroline glares at Ben like he just insulted her mother. "It's not even over the network, it's through a third-party streaming platform that's about as secure as a wet paper bag." She jerks her chin at Reyn. "If he gets us in, we'll get it hooked up."

"Good, good." Emory rakes his hair back, a sign that he's a little nervous. "Afton and Elana, you're on the decorating committee, early access. Do you need anything?"

"We're ready," Afton says. "All the supplies have been ordered. The board gave us such a killer budget that I managed to insert our stuff in with theirs. They'll never notice a thing."

"And you'll have everything at the ticket table?"

"Yep," Elana says. "At both events. Whoever is working the tables will have everything at their fingertips."

Having several of us working the welcome tables is part of the plan. It makes us noticeable and we'll definitely need to be seen.

"Georgia and Tyson will work the table at the school. Vandy and I will be at Preston hall." Emory nods to the boxes stacked by the door, the logo of a company on the side. "Every guest will get a sticker when they enter, and I do mean *everyone*."

He continues, clarifying that Carlton and Sebastian will keep Dewey and the rest of the security team distracted, but I'm hung up on the fact Emory and I are assigned to work with one another. Last I heard, I was helping Reyn. I look at him now and he somehow knows, instantly meeting my gaze. We watch each other for an extended moment, something sure and firm passing between us.

"Are there any questions? Concerns? Confusions. Now is the time to ask." He looks around the room, although notably, his gaze skips right over me.

I raise my hand. "I do."

His shoulders tense. "What?"

"I'd like a reassignment."

Tyson shifts next to me and Elana's eyes flick in my direction, curious.

"Sorry, but no." He shakes his head, turning away. "It's already set."

I give a big, fake smile. "I thought it was all set the other day when you assigned me to help break into the building."

He shoots me a look that's full of warning. "Well, I was wrong. Things change. Roll with it."

"Jesus," Sebastian mutters from his seat. "Does it really matter?"

"Yeah, let her swap out." Ben's dark eyes dart between us. "Who cares, right?"

"I do." My brother's eyes are as sharp as his voice, and when they jerk toward Reyn, his face just hardens further. "The answer is no."

"Em," Aubrey says quietly, but he moves right along.

Or, he tries to.

Voice hard, I interject, "We all need to be focused and on our game tonight. I'm telling you right now, if I have to spend an hour alone with you, I won't be either of those things."

Emory looks at me and everything goes quiet. I know the others are uncomfortably watching our standoff. Among those stares, I feel only the heat of Reyn's eyes settled on me.

"Fine," he relents through clenched teeth. "But I need you on the welcoming committee. Georgia, you're with me. V can go with Tyson." I'm not sure if Tyson feels the threat under the directive, but I know I do. "Now, enough of this. Everyone huddle up."

*Huddle up?* Like a game?

There's a shift of confusion where we all look at one another quizzically, but when Emory sticks his arm out in the middle of our circle, everyone reluctantly stretches their hands out to meet it. It's a cluster of shoulders and arms, and I've never done a huddle before, but when I feel a familiar warm hand settling against mine, I lift my eyes, locking with Reyn's.

"Hail to the Devils!" Emory says, ever the captain.

"Hail to the Devils!" Ben barks.

"Devils!" we respond as a group. It's so stupidly silly that I almost screw my face up distastefully. But Emory is a captain, and he must know how it feels to share one voice as a unit, because as embarrassing as it is, I feel it.

We're one. And we have an epic prank to pull off.

IF I THOUGHT my drama and the looming event would get me out of going to Aubrey's house to pick out a dress, I was wrong. She waits patiently for me in the parking lot by her dark gray BMW. I only get in because she pushes Emory away when he tries to approach us.

"Girl time is for girls only," she explains primly, opening her car door.

I watch her curiously when I settle into my seat. The way she holds herself. How she manages to ignore my brother, who's glaring at us as we exit the parking lot. "You're different," I observe. "From his other girlfriends."

"You mean Campbell?" She raises an eyebrow, nose scrunching up. "God, I hope so."

My laugh sounds lighter than I feel. "Not a fan, huh?"

"She's a fucking tyrant. Made everyone's life miserable." She adjusts the heat and points to the seat warmers. I flip mine on. "I don't hold her against him, though. Emory's spent the last few years trying to find his footing in a world of assholes. I mean, I guess we all have been, right?" She snorts. "Living in the shadow of Hamilton Bates and Campbell Clark isn't easy. For the first time in years, I feel like I can breathe."

I'm surprised. I didn't know the popular kids resented them so much.

"You may not know this," she goes on, "but most of your brother's bad decisions have been made under the influence of impressing those people."

"I do know. That's why…" I run my hands nervously down my thighs, "it's why he and Reyn stole the car that night. It's probably what gave him the guts to do what he did with Skylar," *God*, I'm still reconciling that one, "and the prank with Micha."

"Trust me, we've talked about that, particularly Skylar. It's just…" her nose wrinkles, "gross. Repulsive. And I want you to know I wouldn't be with him if I didn't believe he was truly sorry for it." She glances over. "I'm sure he hasn't told you this, but he did contact her to apologize directly."

I gape at her, stunned. "No, I didn't." *Wow.*

She nods. "It's almost as if being part of that toxic group was like being under the influence of a drug."

Well.

*That* I get.

"But they're gone and he's really determined to run the new Devils in a different direction. Less asshole-ish. More tradition."

"Well, I'm pretty sure he regrets inviting me to join." It's not like I wasn't already aware that he didn't want me to in the first place. That was all Reyn, and only because I'd blackmailed him.

"I disagree," she says, turning into one of the more expensive neighborhoods in our area. The security guard at the gate waves us in. "Honestly, he's liked having you involved in this. He told me himself that it was cool to have you around this year. He just worries so much." She cuts her eyes to me. "I don't think you know just *how* much."

"I have an idea," I mutter. "Did he tell you that he saw me and Reyn together?"

"Yeah." She nods, squinting. "Look, I don't care about you and Reyn. Actually, in a way, it makes total sense to me. Only the two of you know what it's like to have gone through what you did." She turns and heads the car up a long, twisting driveway. "And any idiot could see why you're into him. He's all sexy and cool and strong. A little mysterious. *Very* good at what he does."

My cheeks heat. "Yeah, there's all that."

"I'm just telling you all that so you know," she says, parking in front of a massive brick house, "you can talk to me, okay? I know I'm Emory's girlfriend, but I can be your friend, too." She cuts the car and looks at me, waiting for a response.

"Thanks," I say, feeling awkward. Despite the fact I know she likes my brother and probably wants to get in good with him, the sentiment sounds sincere.

Later, when we're in her room, I'm thinking that giving me this—a friend who doesn't mind me being with Reyn—would probably accomplish the opposite of impressing my brother. She's likely taking a risk here.

"Red would look stunning on you," she's saying, leading me into her closet. Although, to call this a closet would be like calling Lake Superior a pond. It's furnished, for god's sake. "But I'm thinking... red for a Preston girl is so pedestrian, right?"

I perch on one of the wingback chairs overlooking a massive shoe collection. "Uh, yeah. Pedestrian."

If she hears the doubt in my voice, she ignores it, flipping through the dresses. "Black would be nice, but..." She gives me a look. "Too boring."

I blurt, "I had sex with Reyn."

She pauses, eyebrows rising. "Well, yeah, I figured." There must be something on my face that signals this is more delicate than her usual 'I had sex' discussions, because she abandons the dresses, sitting in the chair beside me. "First time, huh?"

I nod, feeling stupid. "Like that's a surprise."

"Eh, people have gotten around nosier brothers." She shrugs, and then haltingly asks, "Was it... okay?"

I know what she's asking. "It was..." I fall back into the chair and try to find words to describe it. I'm still aching with the knowledge that, if we hadn't gotten caught, we could have done it again last night. I can't stop my blissful smile when I respond, "Better than okay."

She meets my smile with a secret one of her own. "That good, huh?"

"You have no idea," and *ew*, if she does, I seriously can't hear about it involving my brother, so I hastily add, "it wasn't like Emory thinks. He didn't talk me into it, or like... manipulate me. We just..." I chew on my lip, trying to choose my words carefully. "We just happened. If anything, I think he was more surprised than I was."

She watches me, forehead creasing in concern. "Vandy, your brother, he just feels betrayed. You understand that, right? The things he might be saying, or the way he might be treating you..." She shakes her head sadly. "I won't excuse it, because I don't know how bad it is. But I think—no, I *know*—that he doesn't mean it. He's just scared. Dating a guy like Reyn? There's a lot of ways for it to go wrong. He's cute and nice, and I like him. But the boy has 'work in progress' written all over him."

"Yeah, well it's not like I'm without my own baggage here." I roll my eyes, fingers reaching up to fidget with the charm around my neck. "We make each other better, though. Emory doesn't get it."

"Talk to him," she says, eyes imploring. "Like, make him talk to you. He's stubborn but he'll listen."

I throw my hands in the air, feeling the floodgate opening. "I tried! He just has the most infuriating god complex. He wants to control me, Aubrey. They *all* want to control me. And like, how is it fair that he gets two girlfriends and no one blinks an eye? I'm not asking for two boyfriends. I'm not a greedy jerk like him, I'll be happy with just the one, but—" I clamp my mouth closed, rueful eyes falling on her. "I'm sorry, I didn't mean to..."

*...bring up Campbell and the fact he's still with her.*

But Aubrey just snorts. "Girl, please. I'll have that boy locked down and exclusive before she comes back for Thanksgiving break. Give me some credit." She leans close, lips quirked. "Between you and me, here's a little secret about your brother. When it comes to you, he's stubborn as hell. But otherwise? He's like putty."

I scoff. "Emory?"

She bobs her head. "Totally. So easy to manipulate. Why do you think Campbell liked him so much? Why do you think he was so quick to impress the old guard? Why do you think he's so terrified that you might be, too?" She raises an eyebrow. "*Putty.*"

I give her a long, searching look, and I realize that she's

completely right. Emory has always conformed to the people around him. This thing he's doing, leading the Devils? It's the first thing like this he's ever gone into without someone else's influence. Seeing it in that light, I think I'm starting to get a part of why it's so important to him. I narrow my eyes. "Should I be worried about you?"

"I really, *really* like your brother, Vandy." Something in her eyes softens, and when she looks like that, it's easy to believe. "I only use my powers for good, but I promise to always respect and comply with your use of the Protective Sister card. God knows it's time the tables turned a bit." She repeats, "You should try to talk to him again. Don't argue or fight. Just talk. If there's one thing I've learned about Emory, it's that you're his weakness. Use that."

I nod, but I doubt it will do much. The whole situation feels hopeless and immoveable—just as steel as I'd felt that morning.

# 34

I've spent a lifetime on a tightrope, balancing over a cavernous pit of shame, guilt, punishment, and fear. The rope sways but somehow, some way, I've always managed to stay vertical.

Pure defiance, mostly.

A touch of stubbornness.

A heavy dose of not-giving-a-shit.

But at the moment, that tightrope is pulled taut, and I'm swaying over a pit of vipers. First, there's Emory, who I know is going to give me my reckoning once this prank is over with.  There also Dewey, who will kick my ass back to Mountain Point—or worse—if he catches me sneaking around campus. There's my dad, who's been counting on me to stay clean, even though every single circumstance pushes me into the muck. Then there's Vandy, the girl I love, who will get hurt the most if I screw any of this up.

It just keeps piling on and on, and I keep juggling and bracing for a fall that I won't let happen. Maybe Dad was right. Maybe this is all adulthood is—facing one problem after another and just dealing with it, because there's no other option. There's a part of me that wants to just run away from it all. To snatch her up and drive her away from all this pretentious, secret-society, prep-school bullshit. But then... I got into this for her. To give her something. Because if I really do end up on the wrong side of this, at least she'll have the club and the relationships she's built. The Playthings like her. They treat her like one of the girls. And she'll have Sebastian, who still some-times makes me want to hear her promise again, but who seems to get her.

There's a long whistle from the doorway, drawing my attention.

"Look at you." My dad leans against the door frame, eyebrow raised. "Gonna break some hearts tonight."

I turn back to the mirror. The suit is ridiculous, but looking the part is a requirement of the job. "It's only for a few hours," I remind myself, even though he's not wrong. I look damn good in a suit.

Even if I can't get this fucking bowtie tied.

He pushes off the jamb and walks into the room, pulling a stack of bills from his wallet. He tucks them neatly into my palm. "Take her someplace nice, pull her chair out for her, chew with your mouth closed."

I blink at him in confusion. "What? Who?"

"Your date, dumbass."

I hand the money back to him. "I don't have a date." I try not to even humor the thought of it—how nice it'd be to do all those things with Vandy. "I'm just going for the team."

My dad frowns at the money. "Didn't you ask anyone?"

"No."

"Not even hickey girl?" He gives me a look that's full of disappointment, muttering, "Maybe your mother was right."

"About what?" This whole conversation is making the back of my neck sweat. Or maybe it's just because I keep fucking this bowtie up.

He sighs, eyes roving around my room. "She seems to think I'm not setting a good example here." His lips press into a grim line. "With how to respectfully treat *women*."

"Christ..." I walk over to the laptop, searching for a tutorial.

He kicks around the room, face tight. "Here's the thing, Reyn. The women I bring home... they know what's in the cards for them. You understand that, right? I don't... *date*... younger women because I prefer them, it's because they're single and not looking for anything serious. It's important to—"

"For fuck's sake!" I can't take it anymore. The man says the word 'date' like he's referring to a backroom orgy. "I'm not you, Dad. I don't sleep around!" *Not anymore*. When the roiling nausea passes, I decide to give him a piece of the truth. "I didn't ask anyone to the dance because the person I want to ask can't go with me. That's it."

His face smoothes out into something slack and surprised. "Oh." His eyes narrow. "Hickey girl?"

I know he's fishing for a name, but all I offer is a terse, "Yes."

He exhales in relief. "For the record, these talks hurt me more than they hurt you."

"I really doubt that."

"I can't watch this anymore," he decides, coming over to yank the bowtie from my neck. "Stand still." His forehead creases in concentration as he loops it around my neck. I only relent, raising my chin, because there isn't much time to fuck around here. He doesn't meet my eyes when he asks, "Is she special?"

I stare at the ceiling, throat constricting with a dry swallow. My hands feel clammy, neck prickling uncomfortably. "Yeah," I quietly confess. I don't do it because of whatever bullshit bonding moment he's trying so hard to actualize. I just can't stand the thought of saying anything else, because she is.

Vandy *is* special.

His fingers stall momentarily, before pulling the tie through the knot. "Ah," he says, grinning. "The firefly pendant was for her."

"Dad," I warn. He's getting too close and it's making me fidgety as hell. That's what I get for having it shipped here. The one day this asshole is actually home to intercept the mail, and it's the day her charm had arrived. "Back off."

He looks taken aback by my tone, but easily recovers, tightening the knot and stepping away. "It'll hold," he decides.

"Thanks," I mutter, trying to smooth over the tension. "It's not that I don't—"

He raises a hand, stopping me. "When you're ready to talk, I'll be ready to listen."

I observe him, this strange man I barely know anymore. He's not quite the same dad I remember. That dad had been firm, but unyieldingly present. He would have pushed. He would have interrogated me about this until we were both blue in the face, and then he would have opened that drawer over there, dumped it out, and given me the third degree about all the things inside.

This dad doesn't know me—not really. But lately, all this space he's given me feels less like a cold shoulder and more of a generosity. This dad is oddly patient, and I wonder if it's the same kind of patience I've grown into. The necessary kind. The sort of patience you've been forced to feel. Sometimes I see the way he walks through the house, eyes averted, like looking at these walls is physically painful, and I feel bad for him. Because maybe the other dad was present and firm, but this is a dad I can relate to.

Somehow, he's become the better version.

"Dude—" a voice whispers from the dark. "You're late."

I make out Ben's face from where he's tucked against the wall in a dark shadow. Caroline is next to him. They, like me, are dressed in formal wear—not exactly my first choice for a break-in. "Sorry. It was this fucking tie. I couldn't find it, then I couldn't tie it, and shit. I know. I'm here."

Caroline assesses me. "The bowtie was a strong choice, McAllister. I approve."

Not sure I was asking for her approval, but whatever. "Are you ready?"

"We've been ready," Ben replies, holding up his laptop. "The cameras are shut off for the next hour—on a loop. Buster shouldn't notice anything."

Buster is old and probably taking a nap in his chair right now. He's not my biggest concern. Dewey, on the other hand, is conniving and wise. He'll be waiting for something to go down tonight, even if it's just some d-bag spiking the punch bowl. That's why we have Sebastian and Carlton, though.

It takes almost nothing to get into the main building. I'd already swiped and traced a key days ago. A little marker, some clear packing tape, an old orange juice jug, and some careful scissor work had provided me with a passable blank, which I'd already tested before the pep rally.

I slip it into the keyhole, using my torque wrench to turn the tumbler.

Caroline grins wolfishly when the door opens. "Radical."

For several logistical reasons, we have to take the long way through the building, sneaking through the east corridor and past the languages wing. Unlike the gym at Thistle Cove, the hallowed halls of Preston Prep are not completely darkened. I feel exposed and jittery under the soft emergency lights, hugging the lockers and walls as we tread quietly.

When we reach the tech room, I pull my kit from my pocket and start testing picks. Swiping a key to the main doors was easy—it's the most worn and accessible key on the janitor's ring. But finding the key to this room in that mess? Fucking impossible.

Ben watches me work while Caroline anxiously surveys the hall, teeth gnawing at her thumbnail.

"So, uh," Ben starts, eyes fixed on my hands as I work the pick through the tumbler, counting pins. "Fair warning and all, if we get through this, Emory has *plans*."

Quietly, I reply, "Yep."

Ben unnecessarily adds, "He's going to kick your ass."

"I'm aware."

Ben is gloriously silent long enough for me to count twenty pins. *Fuck*. That's a lot of fucking pins. "What the hell do they have in here, the crown jewels?" I get to work, trying to be as efficient and methodical as possible.

Ben doesn't even interrupt my concentration when he asks, "You gonna let him? Kick your ass, I mean."

I don't pause. "Haven't decided yet." I get the first cylinder cleared and cut my eyes to him, curious. "Think it'd help if I did?"

He shrugs. "Maybe."

I press my lips together and continue clicking pins. At this point, a mere ass-kicking seems downright optimistic. The thing about best friends is that they have all the dirt on you, and Emory has truckloads of mine. Things I've stolen. Places I've broken into. People I've taken from. If it were anything else but Vandy, I might think he was bluffing about narc'ing on me. But when it comes to her, I'm not so sure.

"He's acting like a pig," Caroline mutters. I guess everyone knows by now. Awesome.

Ben argues, "You don't know the whole situation."

"I know Vandy deserves to make her own decisions and have those respected by the people who claim to care about her."

"I'm not saying she doesn't, I'm just saying there are circumstances, and even though I don't agree with him, I understand why he's—"

She barks out a sharp, "*Ugh*. I can't believe you're Team Emory. Even Carlton's Team Reyn."

"I'm not choosing teams," Ben replies.

"Shocker there," Caroline says. "Football and band. Guys and girls. V and Em. You don't commit, Shackleford."

"I commit!" he hisses. "I might commit to *everything*, but trust me. I fucking follow through."

Caroline doesn't seem to have anything to say to this. "Well, all the Playthings are Team V."

I calmly cut in, "I'm Team 'shut the fuck up so I can pick this lock and not get busted'. Feel me?" There's a long, contrite silence. I take advantage of it, getting lost in the repetitive movements. The longer it takes, the more I can hear them shifting impatiently, checking the clocks on their phones, biting their nails.

When the last pin is in, I pause, wrench still in the tumbler.

This is the point I'd ask my girl to choose a direction—left or right.

I could ask Caroline or Ben, but strangely, the thought of choosing doesn't make my throat all tight and constricted like it used to. It's stupid, because I should be feeling it now more than ever. It'll take me for-fucking-ever if these pins get reset.

Without hesitating, I turn it right.

The lock opens.

I stand, popping the knob and waving them inside. I barely pay attention to what they're doing once they are. I drop into the same desk I'd sat in that day, weeks ago, when Vandy had driven a figurative knife through my gut. I'm thinking of how I haven't had that chest-clutching anxiety in a long time. I'm thinking of how I probably *will* let Emory kick my ass. I'm thinking of how love is so fucking stupid, and yet also fully badass.

Whatever they're doing, it doesn't take nearly as long as getting through that lock had.

"We're good," Caroline says, stuffing cords into her bag.

Ben closes the laptop and nervously darts to the door, checking both ends of the hallways before nodding us out.

Buoyed by the feeling of success, we retrace our steps, going in reverse. Relocking the doors, double checking our blind spots. Caroline giggles nervously behind me, giddy with her own duplicity, and Ben keeps taking his phone out of his pocket, checking and re-checking the time.

Once we get out the door, none of us linger. As planned, we split up, each of us taking different routes back to the gym. Most of my excitement is about getting to Vandy, though. I'm fucking dying to lock eyes on her. I want her to see me in this stupid suit, ridiculous bowtie and all. More than anything, I want to drag her onto the dance floor and show the whole fucking school—Emory included—

that for better or for worse, she's my girl. I know I can't, but it's a nice dream.

"Decided to come after all, huh?"

I skid to a stop, turning to see Sydney leaning against the Devil's Tower. She's wearing a red, skin-tight dress, and might even look nice if not for the smudged eye makeup and the lazy, bitter smirk on her face. I can smell the liquor on her from over here. "Guess I decided to see what all the fuss is about."

Her lean against the tower is slumped and awkward, and I don't really like the way this all looks. Some drunk girl propped against the entrance to the Stairway to Hell doesn't give me the most fun and consensual vibes.

"Are you... waiting for someone?" I reluctantly ask.

She looks at the door, and then up, as if someone might be up there. She gives the stonework a little pat. "Nope. Just little old me." Her smile is overly bright, sloppy. "Getting stood up, as one does."

I pull a face, craning my neck to look toward the gym. "Uh, sorry to hear that." I can see now her makeup isn't smudged, so much as running tracks down her cheeks. This girl is a complete mess.

I nod my chin, gesturing to where her foot is at an odd angle. "Something wrong?"

Her eyes follow mine, and she must be pretty wasted, because she almost looks surprised. "I twisted my ankle on the grass." She extends her leg, giving me a view of her long legs and the sharp, pointed heel of her shoes. "That's what I get for trying to look fabulous for guys who don't show up."

I glance down at my phone. The clock is *literally* ticking. I need to get into that gym. "Do you need me to call someone, or..."

She sniffs. "Maybe a little help getting to the gym? Once I'm there, I can take my shoes off."

I'm not exactly sure why she can't walk across campus barefoot, but the last things I understand are the fine intricacies of drunk girl logic. I run my hand through my hair and glance around like someone else will magically appear to help. They don't.

"Sure." With a heavy sigh, I walk over. "What do you need me to do?"

"Um… how about you wrap your arm around my waist. I can hobble over that way." She looks behind me and then bats her eyes. "Unless you want to carry me."

I look shiftily into the distance. "The waist is fine."

I do as she asks, sliding my arm around her waist to stabilize her. She leans into me, pressing her cheek, and well, her *rack*, into my side. Over the stench of alcohol, a waft of oily perfume passes over me, stinging my eyes. Damn.

We start across the campus, me bearing most of her weight. "This makes twice you've helped me out," she says. "It's like you're my guardian angel."

I stare forward and try not to snort. More of a Devil, really. "Don't sweat it."

We're in the middle of the parking lot when she stops and turns to face me, body still pressed close to mine. "I know everyone thinks you're a bad guy for what you did to Vandy, but I know better now. You're *nice*, Reynolds McAllister. I see who you really are under the surface."

Her fingers are wrapped in my jacket and I try to unhook them. She doesn't budge.

I grimace at the people in the distance. "Uh, thanks, I guess."

She tightens her grip on my lapels, rambling, "You should have come with me, you know. I can show a guy a good time, just ask some of your shiny new buddies. All of you are just best friends now, aren't you? Afton and Bass and Emory. And oh," she gives a low, scathing laugh, "Vandy, of course. Because she's the bees' knees now. Everyone just *loves* Vandy all of a sudden. Vandy, Vandy, Vandy. Isn't she so pretty and prim and *wobbly!*"

I narrow my eyes at the contempt dripping from her voice. "Sydney, you're drunk."

"Yeah, I may be drunk, but I'm not a fucking addict like your precious Baby V." She laughs, dark and mean. "You think all her new friends will like her once they find that out? When they hear she's been gobbling up painkillers like candy for the last three years?"

I look down at the pathetic girl clinging to me. I knew she wasn't a good friend to Vandy, but telling me that? It was intended to hurt her and me. "You want to know why everyone loves Vandy? Because despite having a better reason than most people, *she's* not a bitter bitch."

Her mouth falls slack in affront, but I don't regret saying it. Her eyes jump over my shoulder, and then her jaw sets. In a show of quick dexterity that makes me think she's a lot less drunk than previously suspected, her hand slips behind my neck and she wrenches me down, kissing me hard. Her tongue thrusts into my mouth so forcefully that I almost bite the fucking thing off.

I jerk back hard enough that she stumbles forward on her uneven shoes. "What the fuck!" I swipe the back of my hand over my mouth.

There are tears in her eyes again, but this time her face is twisted up into an ugly, angry snarl. "Fuck you, McAllister. You want a bitter bitch? Maybe I'll show you one."

I knew this girl was a hot mess, but Jesus Christ. I didn't think being nice to her would result in something like that. My phone buzzes, alerting me to the fact we've only got about five minutes before the video goes live. Without another word, I walk away. Leaving Sydney and her drama behind, I head toward the gym to find my girl.

## 35

MUSIC PULSES from inside the gym, along with flashing lights and shimmery decorations. Afton and Elana did a great job decorating for the dance.

My nerves are on edge, and not just because of the prank that's looming over all of us. I'm in a shiny silver-blue strapless dress, and I've never worn anything like this before. It has a slightly debutante feel, with a wide skirt that bunches at the waist. My boobs feel horrifically squished into the tight bodice, but peeking out the top is an amount of cleavage that one hesitates to call modest. Fortunately, we were able to find matching ballet flats, so I don't have to worry about any precarious high-heel maneuvering. Aubrey spent an hour on my hair, curling it into tight little ringlets that hang from a sleek updo. The only jewelry I'm wearing is the firefly, which hangs from a delicate silver chain I pilfered from my jewelry box.

My part of the job is easy. Tyson and I meet and greet every attendee, handing out custom-made Preston Prep stickers. It won't be suspicious, since we're supposedly taking over the duty from a sick pair of boosters.

"What's this?" Corey Markham asks. His date, Sabrina Randolf, stands next to him in a tight, sequined dress. He rocks back on his heels and I wave a hand in front of my face, batting away the reek of rum and weed.

"Wear it all night and you'll be entered into a raffle."

"For what?"

"Uh." I glance at Tyson, the pre-arranged lie stuck in my throat.

He covers easily. "Box seat tickets to the Falcons game next weekend."

The guy shrugs but takes one.

When they enter the gym, I say, "You're good at that," nervously running my hand through the remaining stickers. It's about an hour into the dance, and according to the timeline, about fifteen minutes before shit hits the fan.

"Good at what?"

"Making stuff up."

"Lying, you mean?" He gives me a tight grin. "I guess. I don't get off on it or anything. It just gets easier after a while to make up a story and stick to it."

"Yeah, I get that." I lean my elbows on the table. "I did a lot of lying when I was using."

He appraises me. "But you're better now, right?"

I nod confidently. "I am. I was just... in a bad place, and I wanted an escape. But things are better now. I don't need to escape anything." It'd be a lie to say I don't miss it, in some deep-down, strange way. It's not like I look back on it with fondness, and I have other ways of feeling good. Better highs. The kind that don't hurt me. But the pull never fully disappeared. Sometimes I wonder if it ever will. "The whole thing just got so out of control."

He mirrors me, forearms propped on the table. "I feel the same way. I really do love Presley, you know. And I think she loves me." His face falls. "Or at least the person I'm pretending to be. You're lucky, actually. This thing you have with Reyn? It's—"

I blurt, "You know about that?"

He slants his eyes. "Kind of hard to miss with the warpath your brother's on, isn't it? I'm just saying, I know it's supposed to be a secret. But the two of you are keeping everyone else out. Not each other. You really know him, and he really knows you." He slumps, eyes sad. "I wish I had that with Presley instead of what we're doing now. It kind of makes me want to come clean with her."

I carefully suggest, "Maybe you should," but inside, I'm rippling with the comfort of his words. I've spent so long hiding myself away that, until Reyn, there was no one who knew the real me.

At that moment, the lobby door flings open and in walks the object of my thoughts. It's so cheesy and cliché, but it really is like slow-motion, the way he swaggers through the doors. My breath catches in my throat at the sight of him, and I have to do a double take, because Reyn...

Reyn is in a tux.

I knew he'd dress up like the rest of us. That's not a surprise. I was just somehow harboring this vision of him at the age of twelve, dressed in a wrinkled, navy suit at my parents' anniversary party at the club. That was the last time I saw Reyn dressed up at all. But this?

This is not that grumpy twelve-year-old boy who wouldn't stop yanking off his tie.

Reyn is clean-shaven, hand stuffed casually into one pocket while the other rakes his hair back. He looks like James Dean met James Bond and decided to knick his style. My stomach flips in the best of ways. I'm taken by the sudden and completely obvious thought:

*Oh my god, that's mine.*

*He* is. That guy there. Yes, the sex-on-legs, well-fitted pants, sharp-featured Adonis who just strutted in here. That's my boyfriend.

It's surreal.

When his green eyes find me, they skitter past and then lurch back. I have a fleeting notion that if he busts out the dimples right now, I might actually die, but before the thought can fully form, he does it.

The dimples.

"Well?" Tyson whispers, bumping his knee against mine. "Go on."

"Huh?" My brain isn't really operating at maximum capacity when Reyn looks at me like that.

Tyson leans in to quietly explain, "He can't see your nice dress when you're trapped behind this table. Go give him a sticker."

"Right." I push my chair out and stand. "Good idea."

Reyn watches me with heavy eyes as I round the table, gaze descending to take in my dress. His eyes climb back up, only to fasten on the charm hanging around my neck. I watch as his throat bobs.

"You look..." His mouth works around several aborted replies before settling on, "Fucking amazing."

My laugh is all breathy and embarrassing. "You, too." I emphasize, "Really, *really*." Shaking myself out of the stupor, I grab a sticker out of the basket and pull off the back, placing it neatly on his lapel. Getting close, I catch the scent of a fragrance on his jacket.

"That's a strong choice," I say.

"What?" He seems distracted but it's understandable. We're minutes from either pulling off something epic or going down in flames. Either way, we'll make history.

"Your cologne," I elaborate. "Interesting choice."

He lifts his jacket to his nose and takes a sniff, grimacing. "Caroline's," he grouses. "She must have rubbed on me when we were getting in the building."

I laugh. "Yeah that makes more sense. A little flowery for your style."

"You guys ready?" Tyson asks, pointing to the time.

"Let's do this," I say, feeling brave.

We're about to head into the gym when Sydney and Fiona slip in the side door. My former friend's cheeks are red, make-up wiped away, and the bottom of her red dress looks wet and dirty. I'm caught off guard at the sight of her.

For a moment, I'm actually *worried* about her.

I'm just about to ask her if she's okay when her gaze darts between me and Reyn. She looks at me and makes this sharp, disgusted sound that settles like ice around my spine.

She mouths, "*Delusional,*" and I'm thrown by the contempt there.

"Want me to get them a sticker?" Tyson asks, coming up behind me.

Reyn turns to eye them, ultimately shaking his head. "Fuck it."

Together, the three of us head into the gym. I'm still tossing hurt, confused glances over my shoulder when the DJ cuts the music. Headmaster Collins steps up to the podium and I try to tune out the weird scene with Sydney. I knew she was mad at me, but that was a bit much, even for her.

Up on the stage, I see Aubrey and Emory, glittery crowns perched on their heads. According to Afton, before the traditional announcement of Homecoming King and Queen and their dance is a special presentation.

Or so Collins thinks.

"If you'll direct your attention to the stage," the Headmaster says, standing a little too close to the microphone, "the yearbook committee has created a video in celebration of tonight."

The lights are already dim, but they cut the swirling dance strobes. The video begins, some cheesy Top-40 music swelling in the background. The first scene is of the bell tower, picturesque against Preston's backdrop of ancient oaks. Next is a cheering crowd at the state football championship—a sea of red filling the bleachers.

Abruptly, the music cuts, the lights drop, and the screen turns black. Girls squeal like they always do when the lights go off, the sounds of fledgling confusion feeding itself.

Letters begin slowly fading in, blurry at first, but then becoming crisp, bright.

*Hell is empty and all the devils are here.*

A sinister laugh begins echoing out of the speakers. Up on the wall-sized screen, an image flickers, then another, and another, flashing bold and erratically, no pattern to the casual eye. But I know what it is, and Reyn, whose fingers lace with mine and squeeze, does too. It's a history of the past few weeks, the rites of passage, the new Devils, up there for everyone to see.

It starts with fuzzy images of black hoods and the creepy passage that leads from the lake. Next are the pranks at the rival schools—the swapped-out Viking horns, the removed shield, the other iconography that symbolizes each and every school. The next images come fast and furious—bleeding tattoos, photos of the founders, each located in the upstairs bedrooms of the Preston House—a house all the alumni are currently watching this in. There are the stamps, a shot of the bell tower, the infamous notches. Heat flickers in my belly, remembering being up there with Reyn. My heart pounds at the memory of the other rites. The fear, the adrenaline, the *power*. Over and over, the photos are shown in a turbulent, blurred montage, until the laughter returns along with the Devil's logo. The following words are overlaid:

*The best trick the Devil ever pulled was convincing the world he didn't exist.*

The lights go down completely, sinking the entire gym into a darkness that would be opaque, if not for the stickers. The room is absolutely glittered with them, stuck to each and every chest—pitchforks surrounded by a glow-in-the-dark circle. This had been my idea —inspired by Reyn's firefly, which is glowing even more fiercely than my sticker—but my breath still catches at the sight of the gym. The glows move and shift, erratic yet graceful, just like a blanket of fireflies.

We've marked them all.

"Oh my god, this is amazing," I whisper, leaning into Reyn. He looks down at me and smiles, and I can see the same spark in his eyes.

Things have been so tumultuous the last few days, so full of tense frustration and doom, that being here now is almost like a dream. I clutch onto it as tightly as I'm clutching Reyn's hand, and when he bends toward me, I meet him halfway.

The kiss is soft and sweet and boldly public, even if people can't actually see us. I'm thinking that no matter what comes after this, at least we have this moment. Special. Rare. Shared.

In the distance, I hear the Headmaster's panic. The microphone crashes to the floor while he shouts for the video to be stopped. It's futile, because in a blink, the original content has been restored and the whitewashed pride of Preston is currently on screen, going through the motions like the well-kept, dignified student body that is the face of our revered community.

But the students know what's going on. They're howling with laughter, shouting in alarm, gasping with awe.

Across the crowded gym, our eyes slowly find one another—the Devils and Playthings. In the split moment chaos reigns, I realize I'll never turn on these people. *My* people. It'd be so easy to hold my article over Emory's head, to force his hand, but it'd also be wrong. I didn't join the Devils to get a boyfriend. I joined to bring it down.

But I don't want to.

I want to watch Georgia smile. I want to see Tyson finally show Presley the real him. I want to see Afton and Elana take Caroline under their wing, much like they did for me. I want to see Aubrey get my brother away from Campbell. I want to see Sebastian stop fighting so much.

I want to see the Devils become something better.

COLLINS ACTUALLY ENDS the entire dance, just like that. He instructs the staff to turn the lights up and bathes us all in the blinding gym fluorescents, ordering us to go home. Most of the students look annoyed at this, but they're also so caught up in the melodrama of the reveal that their protests don't last long.

As we leave the gym, Georgia, Caroline, and Ben walk up.

"I wish you could have seen their faces, you guys," Georgia's words come out in a rush. They'd all been assigned to the Preston House. "The alumni were *hilarious*. They didn't even know what to do. Most of them were stunned. A few of the older ones just seemed annoyed, but there were a few who actually looked impressed. A couple were even laughing!"

"Don't forget the ones who were so drunk they didn't even notice," Ben adds.

Caroline snorts. "Or out back smoking cigars. God, they're so disgusting. But all in all, it went off without a hitch."

"Collins looked like his head was going to explode," Afton says, eyes shining in wicked glee. "Elana and I were up near the stage and he was swearing and making threats. Someone," she gives my brother, who's all the way across the quad, an exaggerated look, "cut his microphone during the video."

"I wondered why he was so quiet," Tyson says, grinning ear to ear.

I jump in, "Em was on the drama crew in tenth grade for extra credit. He ran the sound board."

"The stickers were perfect," Aubrey says, looking at me in particular. "It looked like every single person had one on."

"I just hope no one calls me looking for their raffle prize," I say, falling into giggles. The whole thing feels like walking on air. I glance at Reyn across our little huddle and he smiles back.

While everyone talks, my phone won't stop buzzing with videos and notifications about the prank. I have a feeling the next few days are going to be wild, and as if the gods want to show me proof, we start across the quad and abruptly stop.

The branches of the massive old oaks are strung with toilet paper, large looping sheets that hang down like tendrils. Dewey storms around, yelling into a walkie-talkie. As a group, we burst into laughter.

"I guess the boys did a god job distracting Dewey and Buster," Afton dryly notes.

I fall in stride with Reyn, arms brushing. I look up and find him looking down at me. He's been really quiet tonight. Well, he's usually pretty quiet. But right now, everything is loud and happy, and why shouldn't we be, too?

I slip my hand into his, heedless of the people around us. His steps falter briefly, but he quickly recovers, sending me a curious glance as he squeezes my hand.

I notice when his eyes jump in Emory's direction. "Everyone here already knows. What can it hurt?"

We stop when the group does, all of them huddling around Sebastian's muscle car. I spot the car's owner and Carlton leaning against the hood, both sweaty and dirty. They look like they've been having the time of their life. A strip of toilet paper clings to Carlton's shoe.

Reyn reaches up to brush one of my curls from my temple. "You should leave first."

I watch him, head tilting. "Why?"

His jaw twitches. "I just don't want you around for what comes next."

"What comes next?"

He looks toward Emory again, but instead of answering, he gives me a tight smile. "Apparently, there are plans."

Before I can ask what that means, Carlton yells out, "Yo, Reyn!" and waves him over, hands flapping around.

Reyn lets out this little laugh before touching my chin. "Just trust me, okay?"

I let his hand go slowly, reluctantly, our fingertips dragging until the hold breaks. All of our phones shake with notifications. Caroline takes hers out first and we all tumble like dominoes. It's too hard to resist, looking at our success; video after video, photo after photo. The whole thing is documented. I feel a slight weight off my shoulders. The resurgence of the Devils is out there, and I didn't need to publish anything to accomplish it.

"Oh, fuck," Afton mutters to herself. I look up and see her share her phone with Elana. Elana's eyes dart to Reyn, then to me, her lips parted in surprise. My phone buzzes in my hand and I look down. It's Sydney's profile. The first picture I see is of Reyn, dressed in his suit, his bowtie perfectly straight. It's dark, but light enough to tell the Devil's Tower is right behind him.

The second one is a picture of Reyn and Sydney, leaned in close. His neck is bent down and she's straining up. It's not the greatest photo—a little blurry, kind of dark. But there's absolutely no mistaking what their mouths are doing.

It's tagged: *#gotmarked #stairwaytohell*

I stare at it for so long that it has to be burned straight into my retinas. I know the second I look away from it without finding any clue it's a fake, this brittle thing currently invading my chest will shatter.

There are no clues.

Slowly, I look up. All the girls are silently staring back, and the looks on their faces—full of stricken pity for me—tells me they all know. They're not stupid. *I'm* stupid.

Fuck, I'm so, so *stupid*.

I completely lose my breath to whatever's happening inside my chest, the crash and crumble of it. Too full of hurt to cave in, and too empty to expand, I remain suspended in the ugliness of it. It's violent and excruciating and unutterably real, and for a long moment, I don't know what to do. I just stand there with this atomic bomb going off in my lungs. Unmoving, unblinking.

Somehow, I lock eyes with Sebastian, who's been watching me. He instantly slides off his hood, spine going straight. "What's wrong?"

Reyn whips around when he hears it, those green eyes examining me.

It takes me so long to speak that the rest of the guys are turning us, too. Worried. Curious. When I find it, my voice sounds frail and unfamiliar. "Take me home," I ask Sebastian. "Please."

He pushes off the car. "Why?"

"Hey, what's going on?" Reyn asks, reaching out to me as I pass. I flinch away, feel wan and weak-kneed.

Refusing to turn around, I wrap my arm around my stomach, right over the scar, like I could hold my guts in if I just applied enough pressure. "Bass, I need to go home."

His eyes dart behind me, obviously at Reyn. With casual ease, he turns and opens the passenger door of his car. "Sure. Hop in."

I'm halfway in the car when I hear, "The fuck is going on?"

"I don't know." Sebastian sounds just as confused as Reyn. "Guess I'm driving her home."

Reyn leans into the open door, brow furrowed with worry. "Come on, talk to me."

I can't. The words are caught like dust in my throat. With a shaky hand, I hold up my phone.

Sebastian lets out a low, "Shit."

The silence from Reyn is deafening.

I don't look at him, because if I do, I'll break. "It was her perfume, wasn't it." My voice emerges like gravel. "The plans you have tonight are with her."

His voice comes out in an urgent rush. "Vandy, listen to me. That fucking picture isn't what it looks like."

"How is this not what it looks like? You're kissing her." I refuse to cry. "It's not even the first time, is it?"

"What?" I'll give him this, the guy's got acting chops. He actually manages to sound confused. "No fucking way. I've never kissed her before!"

"Just this time then?" My tone, dripping in sarcasm, comes out stronger than I feel. "Are you telling me you didn't drive her home? Go in her hot tub?"

"Yeah, I drove her home. You knew that. She needed a ride, but —" He keeps leaning in closer and closer. "I never fucking went into her hot tub!"

Like an idiot, I do it.

I look at him.

Just like I knew would happen, my eyes instantly start swimming. "You promised me."

"I did," he says, and his voice is a stark contrast to my own. Where mine is weak, his is strong, pushed forward by the anger I see sparking in his eyes. "And if you'd take a second and actually listen to me, you'd see that I never fucking broke it. This is her, V. You fucking know it is."

"Okay, that's it," Sebastian says, stepping between the car and Reyn. His demeanor shifts, instantly turning intimidating. "You need to chill out and stop cursing at her."

I swallow against the rising tide of bile in the back of my throat. "I thought this was Sydney being Sydney, just making shit up. But look," I shove the phone at him again. "That's *you*. Kissing her. Tonight. Right before you kissed me."

"Because that's how she wanted it to look!"

Movement shifts behind Reyn and I see Emory coming our way. His expression is steeled in anger, hands balled into tight fists.

"Sebastian," I say, turning away. "*Please.* Please get me out of here."

"You've got it." He slams the passenger door and I press down the lock. Reyn is caught between trying to get to me and the barreling force of my brother. Emory told him not to mess with me, and in this moment, I understand why. Reynolds McAllister can't be trusted. All he does is take and steal. But most of all he *hurts.*

Sebastian hops in the front seat, cranking the engine before his door is even shut.

I shut my eyes, but not before Emory takes the first swing.

The Ford's engine revs, blocking out any noise, and the hot tears I'd been holding in finally run down my cheeks. I don't look back as we drive away.

THE DRIVE IS TENSE, quiet but for the sounds of my hitching breaths and embarrassed sniffles. He drives carefully, which I know is on purpose. If I weren't so full of this suffocating agony, I might actually be able to appreciate it. As it stands, I'm trying my hardest to gather it all up inside myself until I get home. My abdomen trembles with the weight of it.

When he gets to my driveway, he eases the car to a stop. "I'm really sorry, V. I thought he was doing you right."

It takes me a handful of swallows before I can speak with an even voice. "Yeah, well, I guess people don't really change."

"I won't argue with that. Once a bastard, always a bastard." He sighs, pressing his head back into the seat. "But—"

I swipe at my cheeks before looking over at him. "What?"

"But remember, Syd is the master of game-play, and it really does seem like she wants to hurt you." He taps his temple. "She's a lot more conniving than you think."

"He was kissing her, Bass," I argue. "I don't think Sydney tricked his lips to fall on hers."

He doesn't have a reply to that.

After asking me ten times if he should walk me in, he finally relents and leaves, engine bouncing off the neighboring houses as he goes. My feet carry me unsteadily toward my house, where Firefly meets me on the front walk. He weaves around my ankles with a soft meow. Mechanically, I bend, gathering him up in my arms, holding his soft body against mine. The night is quiet and has a chill. The dry fall leaves rattle in a passing gust of wind that should feel cold on my skin, but it barely penetrates.

I spent the last three years alone, lost. Maybe I've always been alone and lost. Maybe these last few weeks have been some tepid anomaly, and now the universe is making sure I know my place. But now that I know what it's like to be part of something—to love and *feel* loved—the loss is that much sharper. I carry the cat into the house, sneaking past my parents and up to my room.

It's not like I make a choice. I already know what I'm going to do before I do it. I think maybe I knew as soon as my eyes set on that photo. Hell, I've wanted to do it for weeks already, and only *one* thing held me back.

The routine settles over me like an old friend, toxic with its tainted comfort. Like the old days, I lock my door first. I lock the window next—no reason to bother with that anymore. I turn off all the lights but the one by my bed. I yank off the dress, tossing it on the floor, and change into something as worn and ugly as I feel. What's the point of dressing like a princess if you have no prince?

With a pounding heart, the lick of anticipation creeping up my spine, I go around my room, pulling out all my stashes. The baggie tucked in the toe of a sock in my top drawer. The handful hidden inside an aspirin bottle. The six I keep in an envelope taped to the underside of my desk. Pill after pill, hidden in boxes, drawers, pencil pouches, jewelry compartments. I gather them all until I have the full stash. All of them piled on my bed.

Grabbing the bottle of water next to my bed, I pop the first pill onto my tongue and swallow.

# 36

REYN

IN THE END, I do let Emory kick my ass.

But only kind of.

"I love her."

The words come out in a gasp. I'm hunched over my knees, blood dripping onto the ground below. Emory groans a few feet away, still clutching his stomach. I'd punched him—*hard*. But just to get him off of me.

"Fuck off," Em wheezes, grimacing. He keeps his distance, and I'm grateful. Not saying I *couldn't* go another round, but my arms are tired and my lungs are screaming, and we're not actually getting anywhere.

"I'm serious." My head is buzzing and pounding. "I love her. I—" I turn to spit in the grass. "Maybe I always did, I don't know."

He looks up at me with one eye, the other already swelling shut. The Devils left. Apparently, none of them were willing to be witness to the two of us pummeling one another. Aubrey stayed the longest, begging us to stop, but even she knew there was no stopping this confrontation. It's about four long years in the making.

As I stand here, nursing my wounds, it's almost a relief to have it done. There's an ominous, angry rumble of thunder rolling in the distance, and the air feels charged with the coming storm.

"Goddamn it, Reyn, she doesn't need your bullshit!" he says, teeth clenched. "She deserves better than you."

I slump down against a car. I'm not sure whose it is, but it's sturdy against my back when I slide down, settling against its driver's side door. "I know," I agree, raising my face toward the cloudy night sky. "She deserves better. But she deserves what she wants, even more than that."

"How convenient," he sneers, but when he goes to stand, he wobbles, landing hard on the ground against another car. He looks briefly surprised by it, face eventually puckering into a glower. "Vandy doesn't know what she wants."

I shake my head. "You're wrong, Em. She knows, just as much as any of us do."

He volleys back, "And if you love her so fucking much, then what the hell with Sydney? I mean, are you fucking kidding me? This is exactly what I was talking about, you're already screwing around with—"

"That's bullshit!" It almost makes me want to start the fighting again. Almost. "I'm not my dad, okay? You know me better than this!"

"I know there's a picture!"

I bark a humorless laugh that gets stuck in my throat. The picture. That fucking picture. How do I explain that? Sydney was right. She really had shown me a bitter bitch. "She jumped me on the way to the gym. She was pissed off and drunk, saying all kinds of crap about

V. I jumped to her defense, and it just pissed her off more. That kiss lasted a fraction of a second before I shoved her away. There must have been someone else there taking video." I push back my hair, sweaty on my forehead, waiting for the inevitable disbelief. When Emory just sits there, blinking at me through one eye, I wave a hand. "Go on. Tell me how full of shit I am."

Emory takes an inhale that looks painful and releases it in a loud, booming laugh. He doubles over, wheezing, and I'm completely flummoxed as I watch. He raises his head to speak, but it dies off into more of that annoying, wheezed laughter.

I scowl at him. "What's so funny, exactly?"

Still laughing, he points a finger at me. "You," he manages to eke out.

I roll my eyes. "Great."

Eventually, he leans back against the car, wiping his eye. He's still panting, but he sucks in a big breath and says, simply, "I believe you."

I eye him warily. "You do?"

"Completely." He lifts a shoulder. "That's a classic Syd maneuver."

"Well, I'm glad it could amuse you," I sneer. "Because I'm fucked."

"Oh, you're absolutely fucked." He nods. "Totally fucked. Colossally fucked. They don't even make words yet for how fucked you are. Because like I've been *fucking saying,*" his voice roughens to a tight growl, all mirth gone from his face, "V is naïve! She doesn't have experience, Reyn. She doesn't know when she's being yanked around yet."

"I wonder why!" I gesture widely. "You and your parents never let her do anything! Maybe if you'd loosened the fucking reins a little, she'd know by now what an asshole really looks like! But then she wouldn't need you, would she? Her big bad brother, always standing between her and anything even remotely exciting."

"It's not like that." His smile is back, but it's sharper now. Meaner. "You think I enjoy this? You think it's fun staying up all night worrying about her? You think I like the fact my stomach lining is getting eaten away by all this fucking stress? Sure, it's a real party, puking my guts out when she gets into a car with someone else. It's a blast seeing my mom drop everything when V has the tiniest problem, but never even fucking asking me why I can't keep dinner down. Seriously, you think I like this?" He gestures to the space between us. "You think I like beating the shit out of my best friend, even though I can't even blame him?" He lifts a shoulder in a belligerent shrug. "Because I can't. The two people I love most in this world love each other. It's the only thing that's made sense to me in years."

I look at him, my jaw gone slack. "Then why—!"

"Because that's not how this works!" he yells, voice cracking. "You don't get to do what we did, and then just act like we fucking deserve to be anything more." He swipes a knuckle under his nose, head shaking. "Nah, dude. You and me? We made our bed."

"Emory..." I rub my eyes, not unaware of the irony of what I'm about to say. "Vandy doesn't blame you, and even if she did, she would have forgiven you ages ago. Fuck, she's already forgiven *me*."

He peers at me through a slitted eye. "When?"

"That night she fell asleep at my house."

Emory scoffs derisively. "You had no right to ask for that."

"I didn't ask." I shrug. "You need to forgive *yourself*, you can't just —you can't just keep living your life like it's a goddamn prison sentence. It's not what she wants, and the more you do it..." I sigh, head feeling heavy. "You're driving her away, Em."

He rests his elbows on his raised knees, picking at his bruised knuckle. "It's not that simple."

"Don't I fucking know it." Sensing an 'in', I carefully choose my words. "When I got here, Vandy was lonely and isolated, and I get how this all looks. But I was all of those things, too." I make sure he's looking me in the eye when I promise, "I never took advantage of her. In fact, she's the one who kissed me first. I've let her take the lead for every step of this. That stupid fucking destructive protectiveness you feel toward her? You think I don't feel that way, too? Because I do. You have to know that, Em."

"You knew it was wrong," he says, voice rough. "That's why you kept it a secret. You knew, Reyn."

"It doesn't *feel* wrong." My head thumps against the car. "I just knew you'd never listen and—I'm not special here, Em. You would have kicked anyone's ass. Don't pretend I'm wrong. No one could ever be good enough."

He takes in a long, bloody sniff, and doesn't argue.

"But no one would treat her as good as me, Em. *No one.*"

After a long pause, he mutters, "Yeah," and looks away, eyes tight. "I know."

"Then why," and I hate the frustrated pleading in my voice, "why can't you trust me with this?"

He's quiet for a long beat. So long that I begin to wonder if he's even heard me. "Sky's about to open up," he finally says, slowly and awkwardly pushing himself to his feet. "I need a hot shower, an ice pack, and a blunt."

My shoulders fall in defeat. "Right."

He sways on his feet before finding his balance, peering down his nose at me. "If you find a way to make this shit with Syd right," he scoops up his jacket from the ground, "then maybe we'll see."

I blink owlishly up at him. "We'll see?"

He flings out his arms. "It's not a formal blessing or anything, I'm just saying if you manage to unfuck the mess her head is probably in right now, then I'll be a lot more fucking inclined."

I thrust out my hand, and after a long, silent stare, he grips it and shakes.

Ten minutes later, I'm still sitting there on the pavement, thinking over this issue of unfucking the situation. I'm not stupid. He probably thinks there isn't a chance. That's probably why he was laughing so hard before, because in the end, he didn't even need to come between us. But he has to be wrong.

He *has* to be.

The parking lot is mostly empty, save for the car at my back. At some point, the rumble in the distance descends into a spattering of fat, wet sprinkles, but I'm not ready to move yet. I'm guessing most of the people went off to after-parties, which is confirmed when some of them begin returning to the parking lot, collecting their cars, one by one.

That's how I discover who the car I'm currently propped against belongs to.

"Um," comes a haughty voice. "*Excuse* me. You're on my car!" I peer up at the girl standing before me, car keys dangling from one hand, her phone clenched in the other. Her eyes widen when she realizes who I am, shoes clicking against the pavement when she takes a wide step back.

I grin. "Fiona."

~



I DON'T EVEN BOTHER GOING HOME.

The first thing I do is gather up my phone and kit, and cross the driveway to her house. It's raining like a fucking monsoon all of a sudden, little rivers of runoff sluicing down the drive. Emory's truck isn't here and the downstairs windows are all dark. It's not easy pulling myself up onto the roof. There isn't a gutter here, and the water running off the roof slides right down my neck. My muscles are sore and already exhausted from my scrap with Em, and that doesn't help matters, either. The knowledge that he looked even worse than me is a meager consolation.

When I finally manage to heave myself up onto the overhang, soaked to the bone and slumped in fatigue, I sneak to her window. The curtains are closed, but that's no surprise. I grab the bottom of the window and tug, but it doesn't give. Locked. Also not a surprise.

I mutter a low curse and pull out my kit, having anticipated this. Windows suck. I have a crude jimmy stuffed into my roll, so I pull it out and get to work. It takes even longer than the door to the tech room had. The only light I have to work with is the occasional flash of lightning behind the clouds. By the fifth time my swollen knuckles bang against the frame, I'm beginning to think it'd be a less hassle to just get in through a door. I'm soaked through and it's not exactly warm out here, as it is.

I'm just about to give up altogether when the lock finally gives. "Fucking finally."

The window opens without resistance.

I carefully step through the curtains, but it doesn't matter. I'm soaking her floor, either way I shake it. The light inside is dim and soft, and when the window shuts behind me, it's quiet. Warm. A stark contrast to what's happening outside.

Vandy's on the bed, curled on her side.

I take a moment to gather my thoughts, because I have this whole, like, *plan*. If I play this right, I can exonerate myself to Vandy and get Emory's blessing, all in one fell swoop.

"V?" I softly call, not wanting to scare her. The last thing I need is for her to scream. She doesn't move, so I kick off my shoes, shuck off my jacket, and shuffle closer. When I'm standing over the bed, I touch her shoulder and shake gently. "Vandy, hey."

Her eyes are closed, mouth parted as she breathes evenly. She's flaccid when I shake her, like she's out hard, which isn't like her at all. Nights of sleeping at her side have taught me that Vandy is a light sleeper, always on alert. I reach out to brush her cheek, warm and pale beneath my palm.

A curled tendril of her hair draws my eyes to the side.

And then I see it.

There's a pile of pills. A *shit-ton* of them. They're haphazardly gathered into a heap on top of her sheets, right next to where her loose fist rests.

"No." Everything constricts and narrows before exploding into a panicked frenzy. "No, no, no." I don't even care about being heard. I take her face in my hands, yelling. "Vandy! Wake up!"

She doesn't respond.

I try shaking her again, growling out, "V! Come on, baby, come on!" Nothing.

Without thinking, I shove my arms beneath her and wrench her limp body up into my arms. The journey from the bed to the bathroom is completely lost to me in a blur of velocity and my own flooded lungs. Her arm swings floppily when I push through the door, rushing to the bathtub.

I lay her in the tub, but when I go to turn on the water, my bruised fists are shaking so hard that I can barely keep a grip. Cold water bursts from the shower head in a hissing stutter, and I fight to pull my phone from my sopping pocket. But for some reason, the phone won't turn on. I keep swiping and pressing, but the screen remains black.

Swipe, press. *Black.*

Press, swipe. *Black.*

Over and over again, nothing. I'm struck with the impossible notion that I've forgotten how to even work a phone. How long has it been since she left with Sebastian? Two, three hours? Long enough to make a stomach-pumping dubiously effective. Long enough to ignite a spark of resentful anger at Emory for holding me there, for fighting with me, when his sister was...

I hear a wet sputter and my eyes lurch away from the screen.

Vandy's face is screwed up in a grimace, turning away from the spray of water.

I drop the phone, falling to my knees and cupping her cold, wet cheek. "Hey, hey, look at me! Wake up, V! Come on, look at me."

She blinks against the water, cringing away. "Huh?"

"How many," I demand, forcing her chin toward me. "How many did you take?"

Her bleary eyes finally fix to mine, a weak hand rising to block the spray. "Reyn? What?"

"Come on, V, focus!" I give her cheek a firm tap. "How many pills did you take?"

Something in her eyes shifts, growing a little more alert. When it does, her face falls. "Fireflies," she mumbles.

My jaw locks. "Listen to my voice, V! How *many!*"

"Two!" she yells back, feebly shoving my hands away. "I took two! God..."

"Two?" My eyes dart back toward the room, to the pile of pills on her bed. "Are you sure?"

She wraps her arms around herself, shivering. "It was just my normal dose. Think it knocked me out."

Reluctantly, I reach over to turn the water off. My hands aren't trembling any less violently. "Jesus Christ." I slump to the floor, my back against the tub. My heart feels like I've been running laps all damn day. My head is pounding, lungs aching. "Jesus Christ, Vandy. You don't have a tolerance anymore. That's how overdoses happen." The words are rote, mechanical. I can't even bring myself to look back at her. If I do, she's going to see this wild, terrified thing that's not letting go of me.

"What are you doing here?" she curtly asks. I can hear her teeth chattering and I should do something about it, but my limbs are just numb. "Why are you all bloody and—?"

"The plans I had," I let my elbows dig into my knees when I press the heels of my palms into my eyes, pushing against them until I saw sparks, "were that your brother wanted to kick my ass."

There's a loud, horrible squeaking sound from the tub when she shifts, sitting up. Her voice is flat, lifeless. "Because of what you did with Sydney."

"No, Vandy." I finally crane my neck to meet her glazed blue eyes. "Because of what I did with you." She's shivering harder now—just as hard as I am—wrapping her arms around her knees. "There is no Sydney. If you would have given me the chance to explain, I could have told you that it was all a dumb trick."

She blinks at me lazily and I hate it. I hate the flat look in her eyes and the way her head lolls on her neck. "The picture—"

"Was completely fucking staged. And I have the video to prove it." I lift my phone. It hadn't been easy to convince Fiona to send it to me. It had been less easy to force her to permanently delete the copy on her phone, and then the one on ChattySnap.

She repeats a slow, teeth-chattering, "Staged."

I try again to turn on the phone, but it suddenly dawns on me why it won't. "Son of a bitch," I growl, shaking the water from the case. All that rain from the roof had gone straight into my fucking pockets. I deflate, flinging it aside. "Phone's fucked. I might need a little more time to—maybe some rice, or—"

"It's okay." She doesn't look like it's okay. She looks miserable. "Why would she do that?"

"Because she's jealous, V."

"Of me?"

I shrug. "Yes. And me. And the Devils, and the Playthings." I still remember the bitterness in her eyes, and the despair hidden underneath it. "Sydney wanted to hurt us."

"I know." She looks away, chin dipping. "I know she did."

"Where did you get all those pills?"

Softly, she answers, "Around. I had them stashed in... places."

I take a second to wrap my head around that, the fact that Vandy's been sitting on a fucking mountain of narcotics. I point to the space beside the toilet, voice accusing. "You stood there—right there—and promised me that was the last."

I don't hear anything for a long moment, and when I do, it's just the wet sound of a sob. It startles me into finally turning to her, eyes landing on her shivering form, curled in on itself.

"I lied," she says. "I didn't want you to know that I—"

"Hey, no," I gently pry her hands from her face, surprised at how cold they feel. "Fuck, you're freezing." Idiotic statement. I was the one who blasted her with cold water. I'm not faring much better, still dripping wet from the storm outside.

She lets me pull her shirt over her head. Helps me take off her shorts and underwear. Sits there and blankly watches as I run a hot bath, plugging the drain.

Her hand wraps around my wrist when I pull back, though. "You're bleeding."

I only barely caught a reflection of myself as I rushed in here, but I saw enough to know how grisly I must look. "Just my nose." My tongue prods around inside my mouth. "And my lip."

She looks at me with her wet, wrong eyes, pulling in a long sniffle. "Get in with me?"

She doesn't have to ask me twice. I begin peeling off my suit, hissing when the heavy, weighted fabric grazes against my bruises and scrapes. She lets me get into the tub behind her, pulling her into my chest as the tub fills. The water is bordering on too-hot, but it relaxes my aching muscles, and she's stopped shivering. Too much adrenaline for one night, I bury my face into her neck and breath in the scent of her, alive and okay. *God*, if I'd lost her. If she'd taken more of those pills...

When it's full, she grabs a washcloth. "Let me..."

I don't argue when she turns, gently dabbing the cloth over my chin. Her eyes are a little clearer now, watching raptly as she cleans the blood away. Her small sniffle is still loud in the silence. "I'm sorry about Em."

I shrug. "You might not be when you see him."

Despite everything, the corner of her mouth quirks up. Her eyes fall to my chest, her legs all crowded between us. "I think I was... glad." Her forehead creases. "Or not glad, but maybe... relieved? Grateful?"

"Grateful for what?"

When her eyes meet mine, they're full of guilt. "I was talking to Tyson earlier, and I was telling him that things are so much better now. That I don't need the pills—the escape. Because I have you and the Devils, and things are so... so *good* for once. And then I saw that picture..." Her face goes tight, shuttered.

Comprehension dawns over me. "It gave you a reason." I still her hand, gently taking the cloth away. "Maybe Em was right. Maybe you're not ready for this." It hurts like a bitch to admit, but I can't ignore it.

Her eyes fall closed. "Don't say that, Reyn. I can take it from my parents and him, but not you."

"Baby, look at me," I say, touching her chin. When her blue eyes open, so full of fear and sadness, I explain, "I like being the reason you don't need it anymore, but I can't—I *won't* be the reason you *do* need it."

Her lip wobbles and I still it with a kiss, tender and full of things I can't bear to say. "I promise I won't do it again."

"I don't think that's a promise you can make." I gently add, "You have a problem, V."

She blinks and the tears spill over, running tracks down her cheeks. "I don't want to."

"I know." I pull her into my chest, palm cradling the back of her head. "I'm sorry," I say, pressing a kiss into her hair.

"Does this mean you're—" The words get swallowed by a sound that I feel more than hear—a hard jerk in her chest. Her shoulders quake against me, and I hold her tight.

I know what she needs to hear, but maybe there are promises I have no business making, either. "It means that I love you. The rest?

We'll figure it out. But tomorrow, okay? Tonight's been a long... week."

"Will you stay?"

This promise is easy to make. "Always."

The warmth from the bath dissipates the second I reenter her room, seeing the pills on the bed. She's still in the bathroom, pulling on clothes, so I swiftly gather them all up and stuff them into the pocket of my damp coat. I'll get rid of them my-fucking-self.

I ROUSE SLOWLY. Painfully.

There's this ray of sun stabbing right into my eyelids, but when I try to turn away from it, it awakens every single ache in my body. I wonder how Emory's feeling right about now, and I hope like hell it's as bad as this.

I squint against the light, my eyes blearily taking in the room. The spot beside me is cold and vacant, but it only takes a second to find her. She's sitting at the desk, hunched over her laptop, lip trapped pensively between her teeth as she scrolls with a fingertip. There's something hard and determined in the set of her jaw.

I try to sit up, groaning at the tug of my muscles.

Her head whips around first, and then she turns in the chair, angling her body toward me. "Hey. I wasn't sure if I should wake you, but..." The way her eyes rove over my injuries tells me everything I need to know. I must look like shit.

"It's cool."

Her eyes are completely different from the glazed deadness of last night. Here, they're wide and eager, full of that warm spark. "I have a plan," she starts, rushing up from the chair. She must have woken up a while ago, because she's beyond alert as she jumps on the bed, knees tucked beneath her. "I'm going to go back to seeing Doctor Cordell. I turn eighteen in soon, right? So when that happens, I can tell him about everything, because I'll be an adult and he can't tell my parents. In the meantime, there are these groups online, completely anonymous. I joined one, and—I mean, I know it's not ideal. I know it won't cure me. But it can help, maybe. Until I'm eighteen, until I can tell my doctor."

I gingerly rub my eyes, her rush of words pouring through my fuzzy head like a sieve. "Wait, wait. Slow down."

She just charges on, "So I know it's not like a full-on, immediate solution, but this can work for now, can't it?"

I squint. "Work for what?"

"For us," she answers, hitching forward. "So you know I'm ready. So you won't... you won't leave."

The memory of our talk in the bathtub last night rushes back to me, and my face falls. "Vandy." I reach out to cup her cheek. "I'm not leaving."

Her eyes flutter before pinning me with a stare. "I know I messed up. I let Sydney get to my head and I..." She sighs, eyes dropping. "No, I'm not going to blame it on her. It was me." She shrugs, simple. "Because I have a problem. I need you to know, I get that now. I worked past the physical dependence and I didn't understand that there was more to it. But just because I'm still figuring stuff out doesn't mean I'm not ready," she insists, eyes blazing. "I had a weak moment, Reyn, but I'm not a weak person."

"I don't think you're weak." I take her hand in mine, watching as my thumb sweeps over her delicate knuckles. "I think you're strong." I bring her hand to my mouth. "Beautiful." A kiss to the back of her hand. "Smart." A kiss to her knuckles. "Funny." Flipping her hand over, I press a slow kiss into her palm, eyes trapping hers. "Mine."

She breathes, "Reyn," but I go on.

"I'm yours for as long as you want me to be, Baby V." I tuck a strand of hair behind her ear, letting my fingertips linger there. I beg. "But please—*please*—never let me be the reason you do that. Send me away if you have to. Have Emory kick my ass. Do it yourself, for all I care. I'll let you. But don't let me drag you down."

"You won't," she exclaims, face crumbling. "Reyn, you could never—"

Instead of finishing, she pushes forward, pressing our mouths together. I take the kiss without reluctance, tangling my fingers into her hair and holding her close. When she swings a leg over my hips, I steady her, arm wrapping around her waist.

*This.*

This is all I've needed and I take it in greedily, hungrily. The warmth of her skin against mine. The rush of her breath against my mouth. The veil of her golden hair around us, shutting out the world. The feeling of her hand on my chest. The way she rocks against me. I know it can't be this easy—nothing this good ever could be—but even though it's flawed and messy and gut-wrenchingly scary, it's ours.

My busted, swollen lip is screaming, but I hardly notice it, too wrapped up in the push and pull.

She pulls back, only to rip off her shirt. My mouth is on her instantly, tasting the soft skin around her peaked nipple. My hand glides up the other side, cupping her in a gentle palm, and the way the column of her neck looks, head thrown back, draws my mouth upward.

If I thought that wild, feral, hungry thing in my chest had abated since that day in the treehouse, then I was so fucking wrong. If anything, it's just worse, this aching rawness that keeps wanting and wanting.

I help her shimmy her shorts and panties down her legs, baring all of her body to me. My hands can't find one place to settle. They keep making confused circuits over her thighs, tits, neck, the smooth skin of her back, down to her ass.

When she shoves my underwear far enough down my thighs to feel me against her wet heat, I break away from her eager mouth, panting.

"Wait, I don't have anything."

She rests her forehead against mine, chest heaving. "It doesn't matter, I'm on the—I'm on birth control." She's rubbing against me as she explains this, and my cock, throbbing hard, is trapped between my belly and all that hot slickness.

"Shit," I hiss, mindlessly grinding up into her, and maybe it's a mistake. Maybe I need to be heeding the hell out of my dad's 'rubber' advice right now. Maybe Vandy needs to wait and see that goddamned video so she knows, for sure, that me and Sydney never happened.

But when things sort of... slot into place, and she sinks down, I just grab her hips and hold on.

"Oh my fucking god..." I grind my head back into the pillow, eyes sliding closed at the feel of it. She's so wet and tight, skin to skin, pushing down onto me, my face screws up in pure pleasure.

"Reyn," she gasps, rocking down, taking me in slowly. "Is this...?"

I wrench my eyes open to look at her, taking in the crease between her brows, the way her eyelids are low and heavy, how her pink tongue looks when it swipes out to wet her lips.

I grab her hips and roll us over. It's not incredibly smooth and I have to shoot a hand out to catch us before we fall off the bed. She barks a mirthful laugh that she seems surprised by, but it cracks through the intensity and tension. The charged air between us grows as soft and warm as the light coming in through the window.

I bracket her face with my arm and brush the hair out of her eyes. She's looking up at me so happily—so hopefully. "I love you, you know that?"

The mirth in her eyes shifts to something focused and acute. "I know," she replies, running a warm palm up my back. "I love you, too."

I kiss the words away, planting a hand into the mattress for leverage as I rock into her. She whimpers into my mouth, thighs clamping around my hips, nails digging into my shoulder. It's slow and quiet, the way I move in her, hips meeting her body in long, unhurried thrusts. There's a muted, barely-there squeak to her mattress, and everything feels so sharply real. The way her blue eyes watch me, the taste of mint on her tongue, the sound of her hitched breaths, the way that ray of sunlight catches on the fan of her lashes, fluttering against her cheek.

She moves with me, meeting my rhythm, teeth sinking into her lip when she finds just the right way to grind up against me.

I breathe a low, "That's it," watching my girl discovering what feels good like this—with me—against me. My jaw's already tightening under the strain of holding on, fist curling into the sheets beneath my hand. I press a slow, tugging kiss to her lip. "Can you come like this, baby?"

That little divot between her eyebrows is growing deeper and deeper. She nods, eyes glazing over, planting her feet on the bed to rock up against me harder.

It's hard, holding on. I've never done it like this before—without something between my dick and her. It's so good that my legs are trembling with the strain of not just fucking senselessly, *rabidly*, into her. But *fuck*, I want to feel her come around me.

It isn't long before her jaw begins dropping, head thrown back into the pillow, eyes slammed shut as she climbs. I suck a kiss into her neck, twisting my hips forward and forward, and I can feel it before she shudders, the tight clench of her pussy around me, thighs clamping hard around my hips.

She releases this sound—this maddening little cry—that completely breaks me. I slam forward and back mindlessly, grunts trapped in the back of my throat, and come with a hard punch of breath.

She sucks in a soft gasp at the feel of it, but cards her fingers through my hair as I come down, heels sliding lazily down my thighs.

"Fuck, that's," I pant, lungs burning. "That's the best sex I've ever had." I regret saying it as soon as it emerges. Not because it isn't completely true—because it is. But because this wasn't just about the sex.

Vandy is fucking *beaming*, though. "For me, too."

"Well, yeah," I laugh breathlessly, rolling off of her. "Since it probably didn't hurt this time." And then I turn to her, worried. "It didn't, right?"

She curls into my side, fingers grazing over my tattoo. "It didn't hurt."

We lay there for a few minutes, catching our breath, but it grows weird really quickly being naked like this in Vandy's room. Too exposed here, in a place I'm not supposed to be.

"I hate that my brother messed up your pretty face," she says, reaching up to gently graze my bruised cheek.

"Aubrey's probably thinking the same thing, but…" In all the panic and grief of last night, I'd completely forgotten to tell her. "We might have worked things out."

She gets her elbow beneath her and jerks up, eyes wide. "You did?!"

"Might have," I stress.

She doesn't look any less buoyed, dropping onto my chest with a big grin. "That's amazing, Reyn!"

I run my hand down her back. "I need to get home, though. Take a shower. Ice my nose. Find some rice."

"You're hungry," she guesses as I rise, tugging on my shorts.

I give her a look. "For my phone. The video, remember?"

Her face falls. "Reyn, I don't need to see it. It doesn't matter, because I believe you."

I roll my eyes, because as nice as that is to hear… "Look, for once I have some proof that I'm not a fuck-up, and you're going to watch it."

The sounds of her protest are lost behind me as I get my damp suit from the bathroom, grimacing as I pull it on. It's still bloody, only now it's wrinkled and smells like sweat and old water.

"Talk to Em today, okay?"

She wrinkles her nose distastefully but says, "I will."

"I'll call you later," I say, throwing on my jacket and heading to the window. I push open the frame and sling a leg out, giving her one last look. She's adorable wrapped up in her blankets, cheeks still flushed from us being together. Seriously, I'd give just about anything to crawl back into bed with her, but the last thing we need is for someone to walk in on us, or for my dad to notice me missing—if he hasn't already.

I shut the window and look up at the sky, it's pinkish purple, the sun rising over the lake. I get to the edge and turn, placing my hands on the rooftop. The fall is easy and I land with a quiet thud.

"Don't move," someone barks. "Put your hands up, boy."

The voice rattles me, surprises me, yet at the same time doesn't. *Fuckin' Jerry.* Right on schedule.

"Which is it?" I ask with a snort. "Put my hands up or don't move. I can't do both."

"Goddamn smart-ass mouth," he sneers, and a moment later his hand flattens against my back, slamming me against the house. My face hits the siding, banging against my lip, reopening the cut. Blood pours hot and bitter against my tongue. He barks some fast orders into his walkie-talkie before breathing down my neck. "I knew I'd catch you. I knew if I kept watching, you'd finally trip up." His hands are on me, frisking down my sides. As if he has the *right* to pat me down.

"Get your hands off me, Jerry." I glance toward the house. Dad's car is in the driveway. "I want to talk to my Dad."

"Sure, once the cops get here, you can talk to him all you want. Down at the Sheriff's station."

He digs in the front pocket of my pants and pulls out my roll of picks. *Shit.*

Then he goes for my jacket pocket and I twist sharply away. "Get your hands off of me," I seethe. "You have no right to search me. None. You're a security guard, not a fucking cop."

He lunges forward once again and I turn away, but not before he grabs my pocket. Vandy's pills fall to the ground like confetti, dozens of white circles dotting the ground.

Fucking Jerry crouches down to pluck one up, looking like he's about to cream his pants with glee.

"Jerry? What's all this ruckus out here?" a woman's voice calls. *Shit. Shit. Shit. Shit.* Mr and Mrs. Hall emerge from behind the browning hydrangea bush, both disheveled from sleep. Mrs. Halls' eyes flick between us, the scene registering on her face. Mr. Halls' eyes dart to the second floor. I'm bloody and standing beneath their daughter's bedroom window, dropping pills all over the ground. I look away, unable to bear their accusatory expressions.

"Reyn," Mr. Hall says, "what's going on here?"

Before I can even attempt to get out of this shitshow, Jerry jumps in. "What's going on here, Mr. and Mrs. Hall, is that I caught this delinquent crawling out of your upstairs window. In his pocket, I confiscated a set of lock-picking paraphernalia, and—as you can plainly see—he's also in possession of a large quantity of drugs— from the looks of it, prescription painkillers." He plants his hand into the middle of my back, forcing me against the house again. "Where did you get the drugs, boy? Steal those, too?"

"Steal?" Mrs. Hall asks, her face suddenly cast in the flashing lights of the police cruiser screeching to a halt on the street in front of our houses. Her eyes hold mine and I think for a moment she's going to put two-plus-two together and connect that the drugs came from Vandy. The flicker of awareness vanishes as quickly as it came. "I had no idea you were struggling like this, Reynolds."

I swallow back any urge to defend myself. Instead, I say nothing as two deputies approach the scene. Everything that happens next is like sand, slipping through my fingers. Cuffed. Sat on the curb. Asked questions.

I'm not an idiot. I keep my mouth shut. I don't even nod or shake my head, I just look straight forward.

"This one's been in trouble before," Jerry's saying to one of the deputies. "It was only a matter of time before he reoffended. I've been keeping my eye on him. It's my job," he boasts, "to keep this community safe."

Thirty minutes of this bullshit before I'm shoved into the cruiser, ducking to not hit my head. All I want is to get out of here, to get away before Vandy realizes what's happening and tries to intervene. I led her into trouble once before, I won't do it again, even if it means I have to take the fall for something I didn't do.

# 37

Vandy

A SHARP RAP on my bedroom door jolts me awake. In a panic, I reach
for Reyn, but remember that he's gone, having snuck out the window
approximately—I glance at my clock—an hour ago.

"Vandy, open up," Dad calls.

"One sec," I call, scrambling out of bed. I grab a sweatshirt and
pull it hastily over my pajamas. I take a quick, nervous glance around
the room to see if anything is out of place. Nothing seems to overtly
say 'your daughter got high on painkillers last night, had a boy

sleeping in her bed, and then had amazing sex with him', but I do another circuit, just in case.

Smoothing down my hair, I yank open the door. My father's standing in the hall, and behind him are two uniformed officers.

I peer at them with wide eyes. "What's going on?" My mind is instantly a rush of presumptions. Did they find out about the prank? That we broke into the school and did all those things? That we ruined the dance and the fundraiser? Dad's expression is more concerned than angry, but that's a weak comfort. I glance down the hall. Emory's door is still closed. "Dad?"

"These two deputies need to check your room." He steps aside and lets the two officers enter, so I'm guessing I don't have a say. Again, my eyes skim the room, differently this time. Did I leave my bra on the back of my desk chair? What about my dirty laundry? Then, I'm seized by a totally different realization.

The pills.

My eyes jump frantically over my bed, but I don't see them. They were gone last night, when I slid beneath the covers with Reyn. Had he taken them? Had he flushed them? God, did he just stash them somewhere? Will these guys find them?

My heart pounds erratically.

The deputies casually inspect my room, static from their radios echoing harshly off my walls. They note my laptop on my desk, the jewelry scattered on top of my dresser. My phone is charging next to the bed. "Miss? Have you noticed anything missing or out of place?" one of them asks.

The other man walks over to the window, and I watch him fretfully. "N-no." He lifts the shade and opens the window, eyeing the latch carefully. I turn to my dad. "Did something happen?"

He opens his mouth to speak but then looks down the hall. Emory comes into view, his hair sticking up from sleep and a dark, violet bruise swelling under his eye. Dad's jaw drops. "What happened to your face?" he asks at the same time Emory says, "What's going on here?"

"Pick-up game got rowdy," Emory says first, waving it off. Our eyes meet. It wasn't a pick-up game and we both know it.

Dad, distracted by the police, nods in blind acceptance before saying, "Reyn was caught this morning outside our house. Jerry says he was climbing off the roof outside Vandy's window."

"Jerry?" I ask in a hoarse voice. "He caught Reyn?"

Dad frowns. "He had some lockpicks and some other, uh, *contraband* on his person."

*Contraband.*

The heavy thing that's been wedged in my throat finally drops. I press my fists into my stomach, begging Emory with my eyes to help.

I stutter out, "Well he wasn't in here. And I've certainly never seen him with drugs." I hope my voice sounds calm, confident. "You know Jerry is obsessed with him. He stopped him that day when we had our football party. Claimed he was trespassing."

"V's right about that," Emory says, surprising me. "He's always following Reyn around, busting his balls for nothing."

Dad makes a face at the word 'balls' but doesn't argue. Jerry's harassment of Reyn in particular is pretty well known.

"There are scratch marks on the window lock over there," the officer says, walking over. "The kind consistent with being tampered with." He takes a few photos with his phone and stashes it in his pocket. "You sure you haven't noticed anything missing?"

"No." I shake my head rapidly, stomach aflame with nerves. "Nothing."

"Well, contact us if you can think of anything," the deputy says, nodding at the other officer to leave.

"What's going to happen to Reyn?" I ask. "If nothing is missing, he should be okay, right?"

He makes a sharp, amused sound. "Not with the quantity of drugs he had on him. That'll be a possession with intent to distribute charge. That's a felony in this state."

"Reyn's in a lot of trouble, sweetheart," my dad says, wrapping his arm around me to give me a tight squeeze. I remain silent and frozen. This has to be a nightmare. "I know we all thought he'd made a lot of progress, but it doesn't seem like it. Hopefully he can get the help he needs." He walks the officers to the door, and I feel like a statue. Like all my blood has been drained from my body and replaced with something rigid and cold.

When I finally regain my senses—realize what I need to do—I race into the hallway. I barely get a foot out the door when Emory grabs me.

"Don't do it, V," he says, holding me in his arms.

"They were mine," I gasp, struggling against his hold. "He didn't do anything wrong! A felony? He was just..."

He was helping me.

He was *saving* me.

He hisses, "It's possession, Vandy! They're not going to give a shit why he had it on him. Just having it is enough!"

"That's not fair!" I cry, jerking away.

He blocks the door, nostrils flaring. "We need to be smart about this. *Think.* The cops aren't going to let him go, no matter what you tell them. We're past that, got it?"

I press my palms to my cheeks, stunned. "I can't just sit here while they take him to jail!" I've messed up a lot of things in my life, but this?

This takes the cake.

Emory waves at the window. "He doesn't need you going out there, spouting off about shit, and probably incriminating him further in the process. Reyn's not stupid! He knows how this works. He can plead his case in front of a judge. That's his best bet."

"This can't be happening." I pace around my room, but Emory is right. I need to think. I need to be smart about this. I need to take a deep breath and look at this objectively. I turn to Emory and tell him something else I need. "Go get your phone and call Hamilton."

Emory looks at me like I'm an idiot. "What the fuck is Hamilton going to do? Glare the cops to death?"

"Hamilton," I calmly explain, "is a Devil, just like Reyn, and he's going to give me Gwen's number."

~

The call with Gwen Adams is weird and awkward, but she doesn't hang up on me, so at least there's that.

"Your mom," I'm saying, "she does that kind of stuff, right?" Mrs. Adams has a reputation in the community for being both a badass lawyer and a soft heart for charity cases.

"Yes," Gwen slowly says. "But this isn't usually how it works. Usually there'd be a public defender, and then—" She pauses abruptly, voice changing. "You know what? It doesn't matter. This guy is a friend, right?"

"Boyfriend." I haven't had many occasions to actually use that word, and it comes out stilted, unfamiliar on my tongue. My eyes lurch to Emory, who's flopped back on my bed, grumpily prodding his bruised jaw. Upon hearing the word, his head jerks up, eyes narrowing. I narrow mine right back, and when I say, "He's my boyfriend," there's nothing stilted about it.

"Huh." There's a stretch of silence. "Isn't this the guy who... uh, you know. With the accident?"

My jaw tightens. "Isn't Hamilton the guy who tormented you all throughout school?"

Silence, and then, "Fair enough."

"Look, I'm sorry, there are just... circumstances."

"No," she replies. "I get it, I do. Why don't you start from the beginning?"

I tell Gwen about the pills. The addiction. Reyn taking them from me. Getting caught. It's not a nice story and I don't like telling it—especially when Em is there on my bed, watching me—but if it can help Reyn, then I don't care. I don't care what Gwen thinks about me, and I don't care if Emory disapproves. Gwen hums along, making quizzical and consoling sounds in all the right places. I can hear rapid typing in the background, and I won't lie. It's sort of pissing me off. It's like she's not even paying attention to me.

Then she says, "Mom's telling you to keep your mouth shut. Don't admit to anything. Don't say anything to anyone."

My breath escapes in a shocked exhale. "That's it? I can't help him, at all?"

"I didn't say that," Gwen answers. "This is just damage control. Part one. Keep your mouth closed."

I prop my forehead on my palm, staring unseeingly down at my desk. My eyes fill with tears, blurring my vision. "Is there a part two?"

"Yep." There's a few more clicking noises before Gwen adds, "Part two is where my mom kicks ass and takes names."

Emory snorts when I relay this. "Told you so."

I slide the phone away, rubbing a hand over my face. "So I guess we wait." I *hate* it. Who knows where he is right now or what he's thinking, how he's feeling. Freaking out, probably.

Emory pushes himself up, groaning just as painfully as Reyn had this morning. "This is fucking stupid. What the hell were you two thinking?"

I glare at him. "Us? Just what the hell were *you* thinking with that stuff last night?"

"What stuff?"

I fling a gesture at his face. "The fighting, you idiot! You two going at it like that? That's what's fucking stupid."

He rolls his eyes, wincing because of aforementioned idiocy. "This is what guys do, V."

"No, it's what children do." I add, "Actually, I know children who manage to settle their differences more maturely than that."

"Had to happen." He flexes his bruised fist, head shaking. "Reyn broke the bro code. If he really wanted you, then he had to fight for you. So that's how it went down."

"Well, when you say it like *that*..." On second thought, "Nope, still sounds idiotic."

"Whatever," he scoffs. "You got duped by Sydney Prescott and that baby hag of hers. You weren't exactly operating on all cylinders, either."

Well, not much I can say to that.

"Em," I start, remembering Reyn's missive from earlier, before everything imploded. "About Reyn and I..."

Emory groans, flopping back on the bed again. "You two are such a pain in my ass, I swear to god..."

I smile sadly. "I know you think it's... how did you put it? '*Stupid schoolgirl puppy-love*'?" He must hear the hurt in my voice—the same hurt I'd felt when he'd said it—because he cuts his eyes to me, confused. "But it's not. I really do love him." I don't say what I'm thinking. Reyn and I didn't pick one another; fate, tragedy brought us together. It's going to take a lot more than that to pull us apart.

He looks away, reaching up to rub at his temple. "Sometimes I wish..."

When he trails off, I prod, "Wish what?"

He answers, "I wish we could just be a normal brother and sister," and I almost have to laugh. How many times have I had that same thought?

I remember the first time I came home after the months in the hospital, all the surgeries and physical therapy. My parents moved my room to the main floor, to the guest room my grandparents use when they visit. All my things were in there. My stuffed animals and books, the poster of Brendon Urie taped to the wall, my pillows, and the soft comforter I'd missed so much while I was trapped in hell, and I burst into tears.

Not because I was happy to see it all.

I cried because all I wanted was to be back in my room, upstairs with Emory, like normal. *All* I wanted was normal. Being moved to the guest room was just another reminder that everything in my life had changed.

That day, I'd passed out on the couch, exhausted from the trip home. When I woke up, Emory had moved every single thing back upstairs, up to and including perfectly taping the Brendon Urie poster back in its exact place. My parents were furious. "She can't even get up the stairs!" my mother had whisper-shouted.

Emory snapped back. "Then I'll carry her!"

And he did. He carried me up and down those stairs, under my mother's fretful eyes, until I could do it on my own.

I've seen normal siblings. I've seen them bicker, resentment sparking between them. I've seen them shun one another in the halls of Preston Prep. I've seen Heston putting Sebastian in that ring, even though he thought he'd lose. I've seen Georgia and George, who live in the same house and share the same genes—the same *name*—but you'd never know it, because they barely look at one another when they're at school.

I think of normal siblings, and suddenly, "I don't wish that." He looks taken aback when he meets my eyes. "Because I know you love me, and I know you'd do anything if it meant keeping me happy and safe. I can't... I can't imagine not having that. I wouldn't want to try."

He blinks at me for a long moment. "Well... yeah, I guess that's not so bad."

I'm struck by the fact he won't be here next year. It'll be the first time in my life I won't have him down the hall, always there, just in case. "I know you don't need me to carry you up and down the stairs, or scare off mean girls, or throw you parties for silly milestones, but I would. You know that, right?"

"Sure, V." He gives me a sad smile. "I know that."

"Because I love you." I add, "Even though you're an idiot who doesn't use your words."

"You're really buttering me up here."

I stand, walking to the bed and flopping down beside him. He jostles at the motion, but doesn't move. "I'm not asking your permission." My voice is soft, but invites no argument. "It's not yours to give. I just need you to know he makes me happy, and that I'm going to be okay. You don't have to worry about me so much, Em."

"Yes, I do."

"No, you don't," I argue. "And you want to know why? Because I kind of had the best brother ever. He taught me how to get through the hard things. He taught me what kind of people to *not* hang out with. He taught me how to drive. He taught me how to stand up to everyone but him." I slant my eyes at him. "I learned that one on my own."

"Yeah, and you suck at it."

"I think I get by."

"It was my idea to steal the car, you know." It comes from out of nowhere, so much so that I almost feel whiplash from it, from the way his voice sounds, low and monotone. He's staring up at the ceiling, face blank. "I don't know if Reyn told you that."

I stare at him. "He didn't."

"I'm not saying I had to twist his arm or anything," he says, voice dry. "But we never would have done it if I hadn't—"

I grab his wrist. "Hey, stop."

"I'm not a good brother, V." He rolls his head against the bed, gaze locking with mine. "All that shit you're talking about—the party, carrying you, scaring people off? I wouldn't have had to do any of that if I hadn't..." It's subtle, the way his voice breaks, but he quickly looks away. "I'm a shit brother."

I look at the bruise on his jaw. It's swollen and blotted with blue and purple. It looks painful every time he talks.

I jab my finger into it.

"Ow!" He flinches, slapping my hand away. "What the fuck!"

"Don't insult my brother!"

He cradles his jaw, eyes flashing. "You're insane!"

"And you're an even bigger idiot than I thought." I grab his hand. "You're overbearing, you don't respect my boundaries, and you have serious control issues. But you're a *good* brother!" I make a sharp sound when he opens his mouth. "Not up for debate. I'm the only person you're a brother to, so my opinion is the only one that counts. Shut up about it."

My brother is twice the size that I am. He's broad-shouldered and strong. His muscles are powerful, his gait so sure that colleges are willing to pay him to run down their field. We're opposites, but with our palms pressed against one another, our blood vibrates, warm and true.

He says, "I'm sorry if I ever made you feel... lonely and isolated. I was just trying to protect you."

"I know." I look over at him. "But I can take care of myself."

He almost looks bashful when he admits, "It's been nice, having you around this year. Watching you make friends. Being there when you learned to drive."

"It has been," I say, squeezing his hand. "I'll miss it next year."

"Me, too."

The room goes silent and we both watch the ceiling. Somewhere out there Reyn is alone, dealing with my mistakes, because I'm finding this new life I lead is precarious and strange. One part of my life clicks into place just as another one falls to pieces. I realize I couldn't do it. Not without the both of them.

Maybe I'm greedy, but I won't accept anything less.

IT'S LATE when I hear Mr. McAllister downstairs. I've been waiting all day for a call from Gwen or her mom, turning my phone over in my hands, restless and impatient. I don't know what's taking so damn long. But when I hear Reyn's dad, I rush down the stairs as fast as my leg will take me.

He's sitting at the dining room table with my parents, head hung low. He's saying, "... has to be within twenty-four hours, so probably in the morning."

They all look up when I approach. "Did you talk to him?"

Mr. McAllister meets my gaze, giving me a tense, tired grin. "Hello, Vandy. I just came by to apologize for Reyn's—"

"There's nothing to apologize for," my dad insists. "Whatever's going on, we just hope he gets the help he needs."

Mr. McAllister—Warren—bristles visibly at this. "Yes. Well..."

"Is he okay?" I ask, hands wringing.

Warren looks surprised by my concern. "You don't need to worry about him. He's just waiting it out until—" He goes abruptly silent, and it takes me a moment to realize he's staring at my chest.

*No*—thank god.

He's staring at my necklace.

He pushes back into his seat, eyes rising to mine. "Denise, could I... have a word with your daughter?"

My mom looks taken aback, but ultimately says, "Yes, of course."

Even still, neither her or my dad stand to leave. Warren watches them blankly, realizing they don't mean to. "Okay then." He pats the table awkwardly, eyes shifting to me. "Vandy, why don't you have a seat."

My stomach erupts in nervous flutters, but at my parents' nod, I slide out a chair and perch on the edge of it.

He leans toward me, hands laced together, and haltingly begins,

"I want you to know, I... understand. Why it's a secret." His eyes flick down to the firefly, and I don't miss the way his eyes flash in recognition. I reach up to clutch it anxiously in my hand, because somehow, there's a knowing look in his eyes. "But if you know something that can help my son, then—"

My mom cuts in, "I'm sorry. What's a secret?"

His eyes jump to her, flashing in annoyance. Instead of answering, he continues, "I don't want to put you in this position, but you need to know how serious this is for him. Reyn doesn't have any second chances here."

Reyn has his father's strong features. His green eyes. His sharp angles. When Warren McAllister looks at me with those imploring eyes, it's eerie. It's almost like how I felt that first day, seeing Reyn back. Like someone else is walking around in his skin.

"My son told me the girl he gave that necklace to was special," he says. "I really need you to live up to that."

My mom's saying, "What necklace?" and my dad's asking "Warren, what's going on?" but Mr. McAllister is pinning me with his gaze and my heart is banging wildly against my ribcage.

I finally break, "I wanted to tell, but I'm not supposed to."

"What did you want to tell, sweetheart?" my dad asks, looking worried now. "Did Reynolds do something to you?"

Warren ignores him, but I can see the way his jaw goes angrily tight. "Why aren't you supposed to tell, Vandy? Did Reyn ask you not to tell?"

"No," I answer, rubbing my palms nervously over my thighs. "Not Reyn."

"Then who?"

I look nervously at my parents, and there's no way to back out of this. "His lawyer did."

Warren obviously wasn't expecting this answer. He falls back, eyebrows pushed together. "I haven't even had a chance to contact Steven yet." He explains to my parents, "Old friend from college. He's helped in the past."

I shake my head. "Not... Steven. It's someone else. I called in a favor?" I say this like a question, feeling small and guilty.

My mom's face screws up. "A favor to who?"

Warren raises a hand. "Let's come back to that later. Why did this lawyer ask you not to tell?"

I push out a hard breath, not at all prepared for my parents to hear what I'm about to say. "Because I risk incriminating Reyn. And... and myself. She said I should wait and let her handle it, and I know it looks bad." I plead to him with my eyes. "I know it looks *terrible*, but I'm just trying not to make things worse."

"We're not the authorities," Warren says, voice soothing. "There's no incrimination happening here between the four of us, understand? You can tell us, it's okay." He looks at my parents, seeking their agreement. "We'll just keep it right here, in this room."

My parents look both mystified and concerned, but they reluctantly nod along.

So.

This is it, then.

The nervous flutter in my belly transforms into wild flapping. I shift in my chair, trying to look them in the eye, but I can't. I can't look them in the eye when I say it. I look into Warren's instead—into the familiar green—and if I squint, cross my eyes and make everything go fuzzy and indistinct, I can almost pretend it's Reyn in front of me.

"The pills weren't Reyn's." I say, "They were mine."

The dining room is bathed in a tense silence while the confession sinks in.

My mother's face works though a dozen expressions, the strongest being the cognitive dissonance that's been holding her together for the last three years. That I'm still a child. That I'm hurt. That I need help.

My father is a little more connected with reality. "Can you repeat that?"

"The drugs were mine," I say in the firmest voice I can muster. "I'd been hoarding them for a long time. Getting extra prescriptions when I went to the doctor, double doses from the specialists. I talked each one of them into giving me a little bit more so that I had enough to take for as long as I needed."

"But," my mother starts, touching her throat, "why would you need them? You've been past that level of pain for years now." Her eyebrows knit. "Are you still in pain? Do I need to call—" My father's hand rests on her knee.

I fix my eyes to the table, throat thick with shame. "I took them because I liked how it felt. Because it took me away, to a different place. I took them because I was," I swallow thickly, "*reliant* on them. But not anymore," I rush to say. "I stopped, I'm off them now."

"Sweetheart," my dad carefully says, "if you feel like you need to cover for Reyn—"

"I don't need to cover for him. I need to tell the truth." To protect him. To fix this. If it can even be fixed. "Those were my drugs. Reyn found them in my room and took them away from me, but he did it for my safety. He was worried because I'd been upset—"

"Reynolds was in your room," Mom clarifies, face paled. "Last night?"

And a bunch of other nights, too.

"Yes," I slowly say, eyes flicking to Warren. "We'd had a fight earlier and he came over to make sure I was okay. I wasn't," I confess, avoiding their eyes. "I was having a... really bad night. He took care of me."

"And he took the pills away from you," Warren says, looking relieved. So relieved that he breathes a laugh. "I knew there was more to this. That damn kid." Despite his words, I can see a spark of frustrated pride in his eyes, and I'd been so worried about Reyn that I hadn't considered it before—the toll this would take on his dad. I know their relationship is awkward and strained, but that look isn't the reaction of a cold, uncaring father.

I worry my lip between my teeth. "What's going to happen?"

Warren rubs a hand over his face. "Nothing tonight." My parents stand when he does, so I follow suit. "His arraignment's tomorrow, so until then, he has to sit tight."

"Tomorrow," I repeat, nodding. I add in an energized burst, "I can send you the name of the lawyer! She's really good, I think. Becca Adams?"

Warren freezes. "Adams? Christ, guess it's time to borrow against the house." He looks briefly embarrassed by this remark, but I'm quick to assure him.

"Don't worry, this is, like... pro bono or whatever it's called." I explain, "Reyn and I go to school with some of her kids," and I'm babbling and drawing this out, because I know the second this man is out the door, everything is going to crumble.

He looks pleasantly surprised at this. "Well, Reynolds and I appreciate you... calling in favors." He seems to sense my anxiety, the way my eyes keep creeping to my parents. "Tell you what," he adds, pulling out his phone. "Why don't I get your number and I can text you when I have an update."

Despite the coming storm, every cell in my body warms in a flood of relief. "Would you?" I watch as he punches in my number, giving me a grateful smile of his own before walking to the door.

I try to draw it out further, but it's no use. Before I know it, Reyn's dad is closing the door behind him and my parents are turning to me, waiting.

I've been running from this for a long time—too long. Even just yesterday, I would have done anything to avoid this. I can blame Emory and my parents all I want for being so isolated the last three years, but it wouldn't be entirely honest. It's been the secrets—the addiction—that truly pushed me into that dark, lonely place.

I lift my head when I look at them, refusing to go back there. "Let's talk."

Coming clean for Reyn's sake was an easy decision to make.

Now, it's time to come clean for my own.

## 38

I DON'T BOTHER TRYING to sleep.

The holding cell is over-warm, bright, and too quiet, even with the two other guys in here with me. There aren't bunks anyway, just two long, low benches. Against the wall opposite me is a sink and a urinal. There's a drain in the middle of the grungy floor and the whole place smells like old piss and armpit funk. One of the guys is older, maybe mid-thirties, and I've been calling him Big Ben in my head. The other guy looks around my age, surly and quiet. He's absolutely covered in paint.

There are two payphones on the wall, but I've already called my dad. No point calling anyone else, even if I did have their numbers memorized. Which, I don't.

Instead of sleeping, I try to make myself still. This used to be something I was good at—passing long lengths of useless time being still as a statue, avoiding any trouble. Now I keep getting there, into that frozen headspace, and then finding some part of me slowly fidgeting out of it.

I look down at my bouncing knee, forcefully stilling it for the hundredth time.

Big Ben keeps walking to the reinforced glass that neighbors the heavy door and banging on it, angrily pounding his fist. No bars here, just cinder block walls, glass, and that steel door. The sound breaks my concentration, penetrating my brain fog and making my knee bounce in agitation.

"Do you mind?" Paint Guy sneers. He's laying along one of the benches, arm thrown over his eyes.

Big Ben keeps banging. He was already here when I arrived, but Paint Guy was brought in five hours ago, twitchy and radiating energy. Drugs, for sure. Whatever he was on has clearly worn off.

"I've been here sixteen hours!" *Bang bang bang.* "This is unconstitutional!" *Bang bang bang.*

Paint Guy and I ignore this. We get regular updates like these from Big Ben. That's why I call him Big Ben—because he informs us of every hour that passes. Like *clockwork.*

I finally snap, "They have twenty-four hours to arraign you!"

This doesn't slow him down. "Hey! You can't hold me without a charge!"

Paint Guy's arm falls away from his face and he gives me a look. It's full of exasperation and annoyance. "You want to shank him, or should I?"

I jerk my chin toward the camera in the corner. "You shouldn't joke. Anything can and will be used you."

I know how I look. I'm still wearing this grungy, blood-stained suit. My face has graduated from swollen bruising to deep, dark, tender patches. My lip is throbbing. I try again to get into my stillness, closing my eyes and thinking of the way Vandy looked before I left. Laying there in the bed, all nestled in beneath her covers. Eyes bright and soft. Safe. Warm.

My come probably dripping down her thighs.

My knee starts bouncing again.

I better keep that memory close, because the chances of me seeing Vandy again are pretty much nil. Even if my dad bails me out, Mr. and Mrs. Hall think I broke into their house and did God knows what. I'm sure Emory knows by now. My probation officer knows, so the school probably knows. Expulsion is a given. Mountain Point would be too, but I'll be a bit busy, what with the being in prison and all.

They take Big Ben at four in the morning, right after the shift change. No one is as happy as me and Paint Guy, who are finally left in silence. Paint Guy sleeps and I go over it again and again—just how fucked I am.

Mom's going to give up on me. That much, I know. I was already skirting the fringe of her scant tolerance. Coach, the team. They'll be disappointed. The Devils will be one man short. I wonder who they'll recruit to fill my place. Someone better at academics and worse at breaking and entering, no doubt.

When the door opens again, I figure they're taking Paint Guy. Instead, the officer says, "McAllister, your lawyer's here."

"I don't have a lawyer." I'd specifically asked my dad to not call Steven. The guy doesn't give a fuck about me and we can't afford him anyway.

The officer looks at me impassively. "Well, you do now. Let's go."

Reluctantly, I stand, following him out the holding cell and down a brightly-lit corridor, past the booking desk, past the medical office where I'd been seen after being brought in. He leads me into a cold room with a Formica table in the center.

There are no chairs.

I stand behind the table and wait.

The woman who walks in is completely unfamiliar to me, but she's dressed smartly, hair pulled back into a long braid. There's a stack of folders shoved under one arm and a plastic shopping bag clutched in her hand.

"Reynolds," she greets me, holding out a hand. "Nice to meet you, my name is Becca." I reluctantly take her hand. She looks around, noting the lack of chairs, and just shrugs, setting the folders and bag on the table. "I believe you know my daughter, Gwen?"

I watch her, feeling absolutely lost. "I don't think so."

She looks surprised. "Oh, well maybe my twins. You go to school with them. Michaela and Micha Adams?"

The name rings a bell and I'm reminded of the little flippy kid on the cheerleading squad. I haltingly offer, "I think I've seen Micha around."

"He's hard to miss, my boy." She opens a folder, beginning, "So your hearing is scheduled at seven. Your dad sent these clothes," she nods to the bag. "Nothing fancy. Don't want to ham it up too much, but you can at least look clean." She shuffles through the papers. "I have the arresting officer's statement, the security guard, the Halls'. All I need you to do is stand there and look as innocent as possible. Think you can handle that, Reynolds?"

I stare blankly at her in response. I don't look innocent. I look like I just got into a massive parking-lot fistfight.

She seems to sense the vibe I'm putting out. "Well, do your best and let me do all the talking. If things don't work out the way we planned, then you'll need to enter a plea. Not guilty, naturally. That's the only point in which you'll be expected to speak. It's very important that you remain quiet."

She goes on about where to stand and where to look. There'll be a camera—the magistrate won't be physically present—and I'll have to sign some papers.

"Any questions?" she asks.

This isn't my first hearing. The only thing I really need to know is whether or not Vandy is okay. But asking that would invite its own series of questions, and I'm not going to answer them. "No," I reply.

Things go fast after that. The lawyer leaves so I can change into the pair of jeans, shirt, and hooded sweater my dad sent. Shedding the grungy suit is like peeling away a layer of skin. I shove it all into the bag and it just sits there, all crumpled up, looking like crime scene evidence. If I manage to actually get out of here, I might just burn the fucking thing.

The room the hearing is in is cold and eerily quiet. Every breath, every shuffle of paper, every pen click is amplified harshly. I don't know where my dad found this lady, but she sends me the occasional glance, a warm smile softening the concern in her eyes.

I want to tell her not to worry. I know what's going to happen here. I know so acutely that I pretty much space out when the magistrate appears on the screen and the lawyer starts talking. Possession with intent. I brace for the breaking and entering charge, but it never comes. Doesn't matter. Breaking and entering is a misdemeanor. Possession with intent is going to bulldoze right over any hopes I might have had for a normal life here.

I don't really tune in until I hear her say, "...the statement from the minor and her parents regarding the ownership of this medication and the special circumstances regarding his possession of it, we've requested a dismissal from the state, which the district attorney has generously suggested, and with prejudice..."

"Wait," I say, head snapping up. "No, it wasn't—"

The lawyer instantly covers the microphone, eyes shooting daggers at me. "You need to be silent, Reynolds!" She looks beyond pissed as she whispers, "Silent!"

My heart hammers in my chest and I know.

I know Vandy's trying to take the fall.

Before I can think of a plan to save it—to save *her*, her future—the magistrate is dismissing the case. The screen goes blue and I stare at it in numb, stupefied horror.

The lawyer touches my arm. "There's going to be some paperwork, it might take a few."

I look at her hand, throat constricting. "What's going to happen to Vandy?"

She gives me a strange look. "You don't need to worry about her. You need to worry about yourself. You just dodged a serious bullet, young man."

But I hadn't. Vandy had taken it for me.

I'M SO exhausted by the time they dump my bag of personal effects in my arms that I can't even muster any excitement about leaving. The door opens with a harsh buzz and I shuffle through to the sally port. My dad's waiting there for me, hands stuffed in his pockets, propped against the windowed counter. He looks a lot less pissed than he sounded on the phone yesterday. A lot less confused, too.

"Got everything?" he asks, like I'm being picked up from camp instead of lockup.

I hold out the bag containing my wallet and car keys. My picking kit is toast, probably gathering dust somewhere in a seizure locker. "Yeah."

He claps a hand on my shoulder. "You look like shit, son."

I grimly assure him, "The outside matches the inside."

He gives me a small shake. "Let's not keep her waiting, huh?"

I figure he's talking about the lawyer, who'd sat with me over the paperwork. God only knows what her billable rate is. I don't know how my dad isn't foaming at the mouth about it, but he's not. If anything, he looks... settled.

But when we exit the sally port, crossing into a long corridor and entering the lobby of the main entrance, the lawyer isn't there.

Vandy is.

She's right by the door we enter through, eyes fixed to a plaque on the wall. Her blond hair is pulled up into a ponytail, sweater wrapped tight around her, and she looks almost as tired as I feel.

When she hears the door open, she whips around. Her eyes go alight when they land on me, and I'm not expecting it. I'm not expecting her to be here. I'm not expecting the way she looks at me, so full of fear and something soft and assured. She jumps to throw her arms around me, and I'm so stunned that I drop the bags to catch her, instinctively folding her into me.

"Oh my god," she gasps, clutching my neck. Her cheek is smashed against my jaw, but she turns her face to press a quick kiss to it. "I'm so sorry! Are you okay?" She pulls back to take my face in her hands.

"They kept telling us to wait and wait, and the guy who took our statement wouldn't tell us *anything*, and Gwen's mom—"

I cup the back of her head and haul her back into me, squeezing tight. Her hair smells clean and flowery and I bury my nose into it, breathing her in. "You shouldn't have done that," I whisper, voice hoarse. "You're going to have a record now."

I can't stand the thought of her going through what I've had to. Everyone always watching you, waiting for you to fuck up. Watching other kids get away with shit that would send you packing. Knowing that the smallest infraction could topple your house of cards. Vandy doesn't need it. She has enough to worry about.

She makes a confused sound into my neck. "What? I'm not going to have a record."

Puzzled, I say, "But... you told them."

"I did," she confirms, squeezing me back. "I told them everything. I told them they were mine and why you took them, and I'm—I'm not in trouble, Reyn. At least," She pulls away, giving me a look, "not the legal kind."

It's only now that I notice the other people in the room. Mr. and Mrs. Hall are rising from a pair of lobby chairs, watching us. I step back like I've been burned, banging my elbow on the door behind me in the process.

Vandy rolls her eyes, bending down to collect my bags. "Relax, they know."

There is absolutely nothing relaxing about that statement, so it achieves the exact opposite.

Before I can properly indulge in the imminent freak out—her mom does *not* look pleased—Emory barges through the door of the station. He's got a pair of shades perched on his nose and a tray of coffees in his hands. His jaw is a whole rainbow of blues and purples.

"Oh, they set you free," he says, handing the coffees to his parents. "About time. We've been waiting here since the crack of Vandy's phone alarm." He whips off his shades and I suck in a hiss. His eye is seriously fucked up.

Wincing, I say, "Sorry." I think he probably knows I'm apologizing more for the eye than the wait.

"All's well that end well, or however that goes." He punctuates this by pulling me into a one-armed hug that takes me by surprise. He mutters a quiet, "Thanks," slaps me hard on the back, then flattens a sweaty palm to my face and shoves me away. "Idiot."

I bat him away, dragging a hand down my cheek. "What's everyone doing here?"

Vandy's mom opens her mouth to speak, but Emory beats her to it.

"Oh, this one here," he jabs a thumb in Vandy's direction, "could not be contained. Mom wouldn't let her come unless they came," he jabs a thumb in their direction now, "and I'm here because this is all hilarious. Also because it gets me out of school."

Vandy mutters, "Shut up, Em," and laces her fingers in mine. "Maybe we can all get some breakfast. I know Reyn has to be hungry, and we didn't eat before—"

"Before you dragged us all out the door," their dad finishes dryly.

Their mom sees our clasped hands and looks like she wants to flay me with her eyes.

"That sounds like a nice idea, Vandy." My dad looks at Mr. Hall and says a touch too cheerfully, "Wouldn't that be nice, Rob?"

Rob says just as cheerfully, "Very nice," but he's looking at his wife in much the same way someone might approach a wild animal. It doesn't exactly take a genius to get the vibe going on here. Everyone is either cool or, at the very least, down with faking it.

Except Denise Hall.

"So." When I get into the car with my dad, he shoots me a long look. "Vandy, huh?"

I groan, thumping my head against the window. "Yes, okay? It was Vandy." *It was always Vandy.*

He just shakes his head, pulling away from the station. "You don't make things easy for yourself, do you?"

"No," I agree. "I really don't."

~

We all meet at The Nerd.

To say shit is weird is an understatement of epic proportions.

I'm in a booth, wedged between Vandy and my dad. The rest of the Halls are sitting across from us. I'm so tired that the idea of this being some strange lucid dream isn't even entirely out of the question.

I get a cup of coffee and sip it gratefully, because I might be tense enough to feel muscle aches at the strain of sitting so straight, but I've also been in jail for twenty-two hours.

Rob is scanning the menu when the waitress walks up. "I think I'll have the traditional breakfast platter."

Em flings the menu aside, agreeing, "Same."

My dad says, "I'll have the pancake platter."

Vandy smiles tightly at the waitress. "I'm not having anything."

Her mom makes a sharp sound of disapproval. "Vandy, I haven't seen you eat anything in days."

Vandy's jaw goes rigid. "Mom. Leave it. I'm not hungry."

"You need to eat something."

"And you need to get off my back!"

The waitress shifts uncomfortably.

I bump my shoulder against hers, leaning in close. Quietly, I say, "Get something, and whatever you don't eat, I will."

Vandy's lips are all puckered angrily, but she squishes them to the side, abruptly pensive. "Maybe... maybe just the ham platter."

When I shift my gaze to her mom, she's watching me with an astonished expression. I send her a brittle smile, because she is so clueless. Anyone who knows Vandy at all understands that she hates wasting food. I should know, being the recipient of their household's leftovers for quite some time now.

When the waitress eventually leaves, we fall into a tense silence. It's missed by Emory, who's focused on his phone, thumbs flying over the screen. Vandy's got her thigh pressed to mine and she kicks her leg back, hooking our ankles together.

"No," her mom suddenly says. She shakes her head. "I'm sorry, but no. You're not ready for a boyfriend, Vandy."

I carefully put down my coffee.

Vandy doesn't look up from the menu she's still reading. "I wasn't asking, was I?"

"Vandy, *tone*," her dad warns, but it's halfhearted. He looks like maybe this is more the middle of a discussion than the beginning of one.

I share an awkward look with my dad, who seems like he's just trying to stay out of it.

Her mom continues, "Reynolds, this has nothing to do with you. We understand and appreciate that you were just helping her. But Vandy isn't ready to be with a boy, especially not one with your..." She chews on an aborted word before settling for, "Special background."

My dad finally looks up, eyes sharp. "Watch it."

"Now Warren, you know I don't mean—"

"I think you *do* mean," he argues. "And I think I'm done hearing all your presumptions about my son. Reynolds is a good *man*. He's not a boy. I don't treat *my* kid like a child, and I'd appreciate it if you didn't either."

Emory and I look at each other, both cringing. There's no missing that jab. This could get ugly.

Mrs. Hall gives him a look. "I didn't mean it in a bad way." To my surprise, she actually addresses me directly. "You've been through a lot, and although you're not a *child*, you're still young and figuring things out."

"Who isn't?" Shockingly, it's Emory who butts in. "Unless you want her dating a thirty-year-old, you should seriously reassess your expectations."

Mrs. Hall shifts her aggressive gaze to him. "On board now, are you? So, there'll be no more 'pick-up games' between the two of you?"

Emory pulls a face, flinging a hand toward me. "Fine! I beat him up a little, but I can hold my own against Reyn. What about the next one, hm?" He lazily sips his straw, eyebrow raised. "Think about that."

"That's enough!" Vandy hisses over the table. "This isn't up for debate. You don't get to decide what phases of my life I'm ready for!"

"Sweetie, I know you're mad—"

"Emory has two girlfriends!" Her voice is loud enough that its drawing stares. "I'm done sitting on the sidelines, watching him live a normal life while you cage me up. I mean it, Mom. I'm *done.*"

Mr. Hall, who's been pinching the bridge of his nose, holds up a hand. "This is going nowhere good. Vandy, you want to keep seeing Reyn?" He watches her nod belligerently. "Denise, you want to sign her up for that rehab program?" Mr. Hall concludes, "Compromise. One for the other."

Vandy's forehead creases. "You're saying if I do the program, I can keep seeing Reyn?" At her father's nod, her expression firms up. "Deal."

I don't know what the program is, but it must have been a particularly sore point of contention, because Mrs. Hall looks like she's about to faint.

"Oh, Vandy, really?!" Her whole face transforms and she reaches across the table to grab her hand. "It'll be so good for you, sweetheart."

Vandy grimaces but doesn't pull her hand away. "Three weeks, right? Then I can continue outpatient here."

"Yes." Mrs. Hall gives her hand a pat. "I'm so glad that you—" She seems to remember there's a condition attached to this, because her eyes jump to mine. Her lips press into a stern line. "There will be rules, however."

Vandy argues, "Emory doesn't have rules!" and I can see a little part of Mr. Hall's soul die.

"Emory's girlfriend doesn't live next door."

My dad clears his throat. "Neither will Vandy's boyfriend."

I look at him. "What does that mean?"

"I've thought a lot about it, and I've decided to put the house up for sale." He bobs his head. "It's time. You have a lot of problems in that neighborhood, Reyn, and I won't stand for it anymore."

I know he's talking about Fucking Jerry, and I'm just...

I'm shocked.

His eyes search mine. "Are you okay with that? I know they said you needed something familiar, but I think they're dead wrong."

It'll suck, not being next door to Vandy anymore. Not being able to look out my window and into hers. It'll be hard to let all the other things go, too. The treehouse. The spot between our driveways where the three of us had painted our initials in the wet cement. The sidewalks we used to—very badly—skateboard down. The backyard where my dad had first taught me how to throw and catch a football. So many of our childhood moments live there, suspended in time, and some of them were bad. Some of them were fucking *awful*. But most of them were good.

Dad's right, though.

I'll never be left alone there. It'll keep chasing me around doggedly, relentlessly. Like with the pills, it'll only be a matter of time before there's another misunderstanding. Another infraction. Another dumb mistake made in the service of dodging my reputation. If I'm ever going to become someone bigger than my mistakes, then I'll need somewhere new to do it.

"I'm okay with it," I decide.

Vandy's voice is wounded. "Reyn…"

"Hey, I doubt we'll be going far." I nudge her knee with mine. "Plus, there's still school." I'm seized by sudden panic, whipping around to look at my dad. "There is still school, right? Collins isn't booting me, is he? The charges were dropped, but the scholarship is morally conditional and if—"

"I'll handle Headmaster Collins," my dad assures me. "I'm sure we can all clear things up."

Our food arrives just then. We all crowd back into the booths while it fills the table, and I wasn't lying before. I can absolutely eat my food *and* Vandy's. No question.

We're about halfway through the meal when Vandy suddenly bursts, "I want to get my license."

Her dad groans. "Can we not take it one thing at a time? You don't even know how to drive yet."

Emory smoothly replies. "Yeah she does."

Vandy looks at him gratefully. "And I'm good at it, too."

Her mom drops her fork. "Since when?!"

"I taught her," Emory explains, shrugging. "She's right, she's pretty good. I'd rather see her drive herself than be someone else's passenger. Uh, no offense, Reyn. You know how it is, can't help it."

I nod back. "I get it."

Mr. Hall intervenes, "This is something we can discuss later."

But I already know from the look on Vandy's face that she's going to win. Not because she'll be eighteen in four months and won't need their permission for anything, but because I was right. My girl knows what she wants.

And she's not afraid to fight for it.

Not anymore.

ON WEDNESDAY MORNING, I wait for her at my Jeep, rubbing the sleep out of my eyes. Even begging off school and sleeping most of the day yesterday, I'm still working off a massive sleep deficit. It probably didn't help that I'd been up late, video chatting with Vandy. At this point, sneaking through her window would be a stupid move. *Beyond* stupid. So we're resigned to settling.

A sane person would have skipped school again to catch up on sleep, but then that sane person probably isn't on thin ice with the administration for being arrested over the weekend. That sane person also probably isn't dating Vandy Hall, because the sight of her in her uniform skirt tends to make me feel the exact opposite of sane. I prod my sore lip with my tongue as I watch her come toward me, my eyes dragging down to catch a glimpse of the skin beneath her hemline. The way her eyebrow quirks when she drops her bookbag on the driveway tells me she knows.

"Hey," I say, reaching out to tug the waist of her skirt.

She falls into the space between my legs without hesitation, winding her arms around my neck, and if I start every day with her looking up at me like that—head tilted, smiling, eyes shining—then I'll never get tired of it. "Your bruises look better today," she notes, eyes tracking over my face.

I wrap my arms around her waist, trying not to feel nervous about the public display. The driveway is a lot more private than Preston will be. "Emory still looks like shit though, right?"

She rolls her eyes. "Yes, you big strong manly man, you won. Your ego can sleep soundly."

Satisfied by this, I ask, "Did you talk to your mom?"

Vandy frowns, pitching forward until her forehead lands on my shoulder. "I leave next Friday. I'll be back by Christmas, but it still sucks."

The rehab program, I discovered, is out of state and strictly in-patient. That means Vandy has to leave for three weeks. I keep reminding myself that it's a good thing. Vandy needs to get help from people who are qualified to give it. If things were perfect, I'd be everything she needs. But they're not.

I brush her hair back. "We can video chat."

She exhales loudly, pushing back to look at me. "You think we can find time? Like, before I leave? To…" Her cheeks flush a vivid pink and she scans the driveway. "To, *you know*."

"Show you my stamp collection?" She fixes me with a look and I chuckle. "We'll think of something. There's always the treehouse, and failing that, the Kmart parking lot has a certain ambiance that I've found can really get you going."

"This sucks! I can't wait until you move." She got over being upset about me moving approximately the same time she realized how much easier it'd be to come over when my house wasn't in view of her own. She reaches down to straighten my tie, eyes averted. "Plus, I miss sleeping with you. I always have good dreams when you're there."

"Me, too," I admit, aching just as much for that—a long, warm sleep with Vandy beside me—as I ache for *other*, far more naked things. "But hey, at least now we get to do this…" I hook a finger under her chin and tip her face up, pressing a soft, slow kiss to her lips. She curls her hand around the tie, tugging me closer, and our lips part. The kiss is lazy and unhurried, full of her warm breaths and the way I'm clutching at the small of her back like I can mold her to me.

"Okay, that's a hard no." We break apart in a flinch, turning to see

Emory standing at his truck. "We're going to have set some ground rules. Rule number one; no making out in the driveway. It's gross and I don't like it. Rule number two," he goes on, throwing his bag into the truck. "No sex while occupying the same building. Rule number three—"

Vandy groans, "Oh my god," and swipes her bag from the ground. "The amount of times I've had to see you sucking some poor girl's face are unquantifiable."

He barks, "AIS, V!" and climbs behind the wheel, craning out to give me a look. "You and I will discuss rule three later." His eyebrows say that rule three is something meant only for me.

I'll follow it, whatever it is.

I get into my Jeep and wait for them to back out before following closely behind. There's going to come a day when Emory isn't here to drive her to school. When that day comes, maybe I'll be the one to do it. Hell, maybe she'll just do it herself. But for now, this is their thing. I've always known that V and Em are a package deal. Some things might change, but that never will.

Campus is already buzzing with life when we arrive, pulling our cars into neighboring spots. It's hard to imagine that the homecoming prank happened just four nights ago, but I can already tell that everyone's still talking about it, drunk on the melodrama of mystery and mischief.

I get out fast enough that I can open her door, extending a hand to help her down. She doesn't need it, but she lets me anyway, pressing our palms tightly together as she steps out.

Instead of letting go, we lace our fingers together.

"Can I walk you to class?" I already know I technically *can*. My no-tolerance no-contact regulation as it relates to Vandy has already been lifted.

It's just nice to see her smile up at me and say, "Okay."

Emory's behind us, making gagging sounds. "*Barf.*"

"Sorry that some of us have game and you don't."

"Rule three!" he calls from behind us. "No using game on my sister!"

It's hard to tell if the looks we're getting are because I look like I went eight rounds with a hammer, or if it's because I'm holding hands with Vandy. I can tell she feels it too, because she keeps looking down at her feet. I worry at first she's being shy, or worse, embarrassed.

But then I catch a peek of a grin.

"Hey," I say, squeezing her hand. "We forgot about the Stairway." At her confused glance, I elaborate, "You know, as a Kmart alternative."

Her eyes widen. "Yes! Oh my god, Reyn, I have third period free on Wednesdays."

I laugh, because I wasn't actually being serious. Only now that I think about it... "That could actually work."

We run into Sydney on the way into the building. She's standing by a massive stone urn with Fiona, adjusting her ponytail. Her eyes skid to a stop when they land on us, hands freezing in her hair. She quickly recovers, flicking her ponytail over her shoulder and looking away.

But Vandy sees.

She must, because suddenly she's tugging me that way, a determined set to her jaw. "Syd."

Sydney does this little shimmy with her shoulders and turns, plastering a snide smile on her face. "Vandy. Reyn."

"I want you to know," Vandy starts, "that I'm sorry if the way I've disappeared lately hurt your feelings. I was actually really grateful to have you as a friend. And even though you were kind of mean to me and always calling attention to my issues, we had some good times, and I'm going to miss them."

Sydney looks completely thrown off guard by this, that snide look melting off her face. Without it, she just looks big-eyed and... if I didn't know better, mournful.

And then Vandy adds, "But if you ever try to make a move on my boyfriend again, I will make you fucking regret it."

With that, Vandy squeezes my hand and tugs me back toward the building. I can't help the shit-eating grin I send Sydney's way, because *damn*. My girl really sounded like she could back that shit up. I have no doubt she could, either.

One day, I'll tell Vandy about how I've gone back there, to that dark deserted road that almost ended it all. I'll tell her how I parked and listened, waited, coming to the slow, mind-blowing comprehension of just how much the universe had to conspire to get us in that exact spot, at that exact time. I'll tell her how something in my chest all at once shattered and mended at the awareness that maybe we were just...

Just fucking *unlucky*.

We know better than most that all it takes is one blink, one wrong turn of the wheel, one bad decision to end it all. But what people like Sydney and Mrs. Hall don't understand is that the universe conspired —so fucking painstakingly—and we didn't flicker out or fade away. We survived. Call it luck or chance, or really good engineering, it doesn't matter.

I'm calling it *ours*.

# EPILOGUE

VANDY

I HEAR the motorboat entire minutes before I see the dark shape of it gliding across the glassy surface. Running lights reflect off the water the closer it comes, and when it's near enough to make out the driver of the boat, my stomach flips.

The person is dressed from head-to-toe in black, including the ski mask covering his face. It's a guy, I can tell that much from the silhouette. He docks the boat and cuts the motor, looping the tie around the post to keep it in place. He does this all in an easy, casual display of

competence. I stare at that mask, the clothes, and am suddenly overcome by the excitement of this moment.

These are the things I do now. Sometimes impulsive, occasionally
brash behavior isn't such a strange look on me. Not anymore. I don't
always stay home. I read books and I binge watch ridiculous teen dramas
on Netflix, but I also go out. Have a bite with the Playthings. Meet my
boyfriend in a make-out spot. Go to the movies with my brother.

Get initiated into a super exclusive, underground secret society.

The guy steps easily off the boat, takes a few paces in my direction, and extends a large, gloved hand. "Let me see your envelope."

I take one last look at the final missive, found in my locker earlier
that day:

*Initiate,*

*To unseal your fate, meet at the Cedar Shoals boat ramp, 10pm.*

*"You never walk alone. Even the devil is the lord of flies."*

*Elevatio Infernum*

I look up. "What do I get in return?"

My captor pauses, dropping his hand. "Well, what do you want?"

I tap the card on my hand. "Take off your mask."

"Can't." He shrugs. "Said I had to wear it."

I narrow my eyes at him. "Just the bottom half then."

He tilts his head, watching me curiously, but ultimately does as I
ask, hooking his thumbs beneath the mask and shimmying it up to
his nose.

I step up to him, peering into the dark, shadowed eyes that are
watching me, and use a hand on his shoulder to balance myself as I
strain up to kiss him.

"You know," he says, sounding perturbed as he rips off his mask.
"What if it ended up being someone else under this thing?"

I scoff. "Come on, it was so clearly you."

"It was supposed to be Bass." Reyn takes the card from my hand.
"Lucky for me, Em was having one of his moments."

My smile falls. "Is he okay?"

Reyn takes my hand and helps me over the edge, sure hands
steadying my hips. "He is now that he knows it's me."

It really isn't fair. Everyone thinks the aftermath of the accident is exclusive to me and Reyn, but that's not true. Emory's been opening up a lot more about his anxiety and stress. No one's told me directly, but I'm pretty sure he has his own appointment with Doctor Cordell after I leave tomorrow night.

I grimace when I see the hood he has for me.

"Sorry," he says, placing it over the crown of my head. Before he tugs it all the way over, he pitches forward and kisses me again, lips soft and warm. "It's going to be fine."

Masked and cold, I sit on the vinyl cushions, trusting Reyn to get us there safely.

A moment later, the motor cranks. Reyn pushes the throttle so that the boat flies over the water, gliding over the glassy surface. I hold onto my hood with one hand and my seat with the other, and it doesn't matter that I can't see anything, because I have Reyn driving me, and I can feel it all. The crisp winter wind across my face, damp and ripe. The bare tree limbs waving as we pass, rattling in grim celebration. I can't see the moon overhead, but I can feel the pull of it, loud in its magnetism.

*You are alive*, it's screaming. *You are free.*

Mostly I can feel the warmth of Reyn's fingers, curled sweetly around my wrist.

My lips tug into a smile as the wind whips my hair around my arms, fluttering about me like an excited puppy who's missed its owner.

I have too much time to think and feel as we buzz across the water. I wonder how much I'm going to be able to video chat with Reyn while I'm at the facility. I wonder if my parents are freaking out as badly as Emory is about me leaving for three weeks. I wonder if the other Devils and Playthings are excited, and I wonder if we'll get to finally see these Powers That Be.

There's more of that ratcheting thrill when the boat begins slowing, the sound of the motor decreasing to a hum before cutting off altogether. After the roar of the motor, the sudden silence is jarring in its loudness.

It doesn't last long before Reyn laces our fingers together, standing. A low, velvety voice rushes against my ear, "I've got you."

A shiver runs down my spine. "I know."

THE BUNKER DOESN'T LOOK the same. It's been draped in black cloth, shrouding the boundaries of the walls. Dozens of flickering candles cast an eerie, shadowy glow. If they're going for gothic creepiness, it's working.

We stand in a line—Emory included—each holding an unlit candle. No one speaks, although Elana's foot bounces anxiously next to mine and Sebastian has sighed dramatically twice. All eyes shift to the main door when five cloaked figures walk in, standing across from us. Their faces are veiled by their hoods, only the barest sliver of a profile visible at times. Everyone but the person in the center holds something in their hands. They each carry something different. A lit candle. An ornate box. A gold chalice. And a leather book.

The person in the middle steps forward, and I have to admit that the hair on the back of my neck stands on end.

"Pledges," the voice, deep and male and older, says, "welcome to the final night of your initiation. Up to this point you've been working toward the status of Devil, and tonight we find out if you truly deserve the title."

He drones on a little bit, talking of legacy and loyalty. But that's old Devil fare. Us—the new Devils? I look around and know that none of us really care about that stuff. It sounds nice, sure. But we're connected in other ways. In deeper ways. In ways that are going to make the Devils better.

The man eventually reveals, "Each of you fulfilled the requirements for membership. Each of you were successful in all the rites—both individually and jointly. We didn't expect that," he admits, turning slightly to the other Devils. "Too often, arrogance supersedes duty and kinship. To be made a Devil is to make a pact. To break that pact is to fail your brothers."

Elana coughs a delicate, "Ahem."

The Devil inclines his head toward her, and after a beat adds, "To fail your brothers *and sisters*."

All the Playthings lock eyes, grinning.

He goes on, "Rejecting any one of you will compromise the group. We can see the chain formed here. Remove one link and the others will fall." There's a long, suspenseful pause before he announces, "So it's fortunate that you'll all be given membership."

I exhale, the nerves rushing through me.

"It's time for the initiation," the leader says. "When your name is called, you'll approach the first member." He nods for Emory to step forward and directs him to the first cloaked person on the end.

This Devil is the one holding the candle. "The Devil's light represents our undying flame. May it guide you through hell."

The elders all repeat, "May it guide you."

Emory holds out his candle and the flame passes from one to another.

The Devil with the box opens the lid. He pulls out a small, silver object. I squint my eyes and see that it's a small, slim stickpin. A pitchfork. "The pitchfork represents the forked paths of our brothers and sisters. Wear it always. Keep it hidden. May it guide you through hell."

They all repeat, "May it guide you."

The main Devil places the pin on Emory's black shirt and gestures for him to move forward to the chalice. "The cup represents our combined potential and willingness to share it. Drink for luck and wealth—two important tenets of this society. May it guide you through hell."

"May it guide you."

The cloaked figure holds it out and my brother takes a nervous swallow, licking his lips after.

The next person holds out the book. In the crease there's a pen. "The book represents our history and legacy. Sign your name and make your vow. May it guide you through hell."

"May it guide you."

Emory does as he's asked, scribbling his name on the fresh sheet of paper.

"Emory Hall," the leader says, "you are a Devil, for now and for always. Elvatio Infernum."

They all welcome him in with a chanted, "Elvatio Infernum."

Ben goes next, and then Afton.

When Sebastian steps up, he takes a sip from the chalice and pulls a face. "Just wine," he mutters, sounding disappointed.

Caroline is next, and then Aubrey. Tyson sticks himself with the pin and spends his whole initiation rubbing grumpily at his chest. Carlton goes, and then Elana. Reyn brushes my hand when he steps up to get his candle lit, and I find myself mouthing along to each iteration of, "May it guide you."

When it's my turn, Emory sends me a grin, looking excited and important with his dumb candle and pin. I smile back, because this is definitely going down as the most crazy and absurd experience of my life, but at least I'm sharing it with these people—these amazing, kind, ridiculous, beautiful people—who are all ready and willing to call me a sister.

That's one thing I certainly know how to be.

CARLTON THRUSTS his beer into the air, shouting, "Elvatio Infernum, motherfuckers!"

Ben and Tyson raise their beers, whooping obnoxiously.

"I'm not driving you all home," Elana says, sounding bored. "Last time we did this, Tyson threw up in my back seat and I had to get the whole car detailed."

Tyson pouts. "Sorry, El. If it makes you feel any better, I spent the next morning praying for the sweet release of death."

We're back at the lake, celebrating. There's a bright fire roaring in front of us. It's chilly and late, but I feel pleasantly warm. Reyn's sitting on the ground and I'm between his legs, his arms wrapped tight around my shoulders.

Sebastian, just returning from a munchie run, tosses Emory a bag of chips and snorts a laugh when it just falls limply at his feet. "Captain of our football team, ladies and gentlemen."

"I'm the receiver," Reyn says. "Em just throws shit and hopes someone catches it."

Emory points an arm at Reyn, looking anything but offended. "And he usually does!"

From out of nowhere, Aubrey says, "We should go skinny dipping," and all the guys—the *Devils*—turn to stare at her.

"That water is freezing!" I say, gaping at her.

"Eh." She flaps a hand. "We've got a fire going, we can warm up."

Emory instantly jumps up. "I'm in!"

And with that, "I'm *out*. No way I'm skinny dipping with my brother and his girlfriend."

Something must have been in that chalice besides wine, because all these idiots are somehow down to get naked and jump in the cold water. I stay right where I am and Reyn squeezes me tight.

I guess he's missed out on the chalice-induced insanity, too.

Luckily for me, everyone goes out to the waterfront before the nakedness ensues. I like all these guys. I really do. But I don't want to see their dicks.

There's a long stretch of silence before the sound of a loud yelp comes from the distance.

"Was that Caroline?"

Reyn buries a laugh into my neck. "Pretty sure that was Carlton."

"These people are crazy," I say, amazed as more yelps begin sounding out. "We might be the only smart ones. This whole secret society is doomed."

"Maybe leave that out of your article," Reyn suggests.

I stare into the fire, head shaking. "There is no article."

He doesn't sound surprised. "I figured."

To punctuate this point, I reach into my pocket and extract the flash drive I brought along. I hold it up, inspecting it. "This is the only copy left of all the evidence and files." This flash drive is a betrayal of everyone—not just Emory and Reyn. There isn't a lot about the Devil stuff I can take seriously, but the vow of loyalty to all my friends?

That's as real to me as the feel of Reyn's warm kiss on my neck.

It's easy to throw the flash drive into the fire.

Reyn and I watch it burn, the distant sounds of our friends fluttering up the shore to us.

"I'm going to miss you," Reyn says.

I hook a hand around the forearm that's pinning me to his chest. "Me, too. Especially because you'll be gone when I get back." I swallow thickly.

"Hey," he says, nosing my ear. "It's only a seven-minute drive to the new place."

"It won't be the same," I worry.

We're quiet for a long stretch, watching the sparks from the fire. I feel mesmerized and so comfortable—so content—that I'm terrified of blinking, let alone leaving for three weeks. It's my experience that feelings like this don't last long.

Reyn sighs, resting his chin on my temple. "Let's make a deal. We'll meet up every day after school."

I slide my eyes up, even though I can't see him. "*Every* day?"

"Every day," he agrees. "We'll go to The Nerd, or the treehouse, or go get coffee, or... here. We can come here, too. Or we can stay in, even. Wherever."

The sparks from the fire flutter into the sky, rising higher and higher. If I lower my eyelids just so, it's almost like a perfect dream. A dream of me and Reyn, being on the dark, still lake, fireflies flickering around us. I feel the same way now that I'd felt in those dreams. Calm. Happy. Not alone.

"Every day." I test this out in my head, deciding, "It's a deal." And it's an easy one to make.

After all, the very best deals are the ones I make with my Devil.

# AFTERWORD

ANGEL'S ANTICS
READER GROUP

Don't miss out on the complete Boys of Preston Prep Series:
Devil May Care
Touched by the Devil
Devil Incarnate

And for lovers of Dark Contemporary Reverse Harem Bully Romance
check out the Royals of Forsyth U
*extremely dark content. Read the warning!!!*
Lords of Pain
Lords of Wrath
Lords of Mercy

Wanna sneak peek of Touched by the Devil? Scroll down....

Chapter 1
Sebastian

There's something ironic about how the uber wealthy go to tiny, back wood, hick towns for vacation. God forbid we go to one of the five-star resorts that line pristine beaches, or the comforts of a modernized summer home in the mountains. Nope, every year the Wilcox family makes the trek to the little town of Briar Cliffs to stay in our hundred-year old, musty cabin, overlooking the lake that my father has been coming to since he was born, and *his* father came to since he was born. Apparently, it's family tradition to bore the hell out of the Wilcox men, which is just a dangerous fucking move.

It makes us restless, and if history has proven anything, it's that there's nothing worse than a restless Wilcox.

Makes no damn sense. Even my dad hates it, holes up in the makeshift office drowning himself in whiskey and work. My step-mom spends most of her time with the other summer wives, gossiping and trying to show each other up. I pace around like a lion in a cage, trying to find something to do with my hands, going crazy with the ripple of unspent energy sparking beneath my skin. And Heston. Well, Heston is the worst of all. This has never been a quality family bonding experience, is what I'm saying.

It's my sense of restless, energy-rippling boredom that ejects me from the cabin one summer night on the hunt for weed, pussy, and maybe a fight. Three things a determined seventeen-year-old can find pretty easily, even here.

"Yo, Wilcox."

I look up and see my friends Reid and Mitchell walking down the cracked sidewalk. I jerk a nod in greeting. "Thing One, Thing Two. What's going on?"

"In the Briar Cliffs?" Reid asks, bumping his fist with mine. "Jack and shit."

"Except," Mitchell says quickly, "We heard there's a party down at the dock. Wanna come?"

"Let me check my schedule," I joke, pulling out my phone, which predictably has no service. I've had shit-all to do for weeks now. "Yep, looks like I'm free."

We head off, passing the antique shops and pharmacy, taking the turn to the dirt road that heads down to the water. I know this place like the back of my hand, every nook and cranny. The steep cliffs overlooking the river. The seedy liquor stores. The mom and pops shops. The suburbs ten minutes north of here. Parents feel secure in letting their kids roam free around the Briar Cliffs from a young age —the wisdom being that there's not much trouble to get into, and whatever trouble we do find, they'd done it all before.

Reid reaches inside his jacket and pulls out a silver flask. It's pretentious and a little douchey but when offered, I take a swig. The liquid burns like fire down the back of my throat, then warms my belly. I hand the flask back over and ask, "Is this a townie party or summer people?"

There's a distinct difference between the two. Summer people like myself have the kind of parties you write home about. Great booze, big boats, and freaky bitches dying to be the center of some rich boy's attention. Townie parties, though. Those are thrown hastily together on a wish and a prayer. The booze is cheap swill, the boats aren't safe for occupancy, and the girls...

The girls are dicey as fuck.

Not always a bug, sometimes a feature.

"Probably a mix," Mitchell says, taking a drink and then wiping his mouth with the back of his hand. "I got a text from Karen telling me to come."

Karen is a local girl who works down at the marina. She's a sexy ginger that Mitchell had the pleasure of hooking up with last weekend on one of the docked boats. I spent last weekend bare-knuckling it with some douche from Rockport and won two-hundred bucks, a loose molar, and a bag of weed. For the Briar Cliffs, that's a pretty great night.

We reach the top of a rise, and down below is the public dock. During the day, little kids jump and dive off the end, and family's picnic on the beach. At night, it's an infestation of older kids and a few college students. This is the place to be if you're looking for some trouble. I head down the hill toward the crowd that's already gathering.

"Hey, Bass," a girl calls out. I look over and see Madison, a girl who's spent summers here almost as long as I have. Mostly I see her tits pressed tight against the fabric of her tube top.

"Hey, Mads, how are you?"

She walks over, gait a little wobbly. She's already drunk. "Fine, fine, fuckin' peachy."

I slide my arm around her waist, peering down her top. "You sure look fine."

"So do you." Her hand presses against my abs, feeling the muscle. Madison has never been shy, but we've only hooked up once. "I've been wondering something…"

"Yeah?" I lick my lips, thinking I might be ready to raise that number to two. "What's that?"

"Where has your brother been this summer?"

*And scene.*

I drop my arm, but try to keep the easy expression on my face. "Heston didn't come down with the family," I say, trying not to grit my teeth over his name. "Busy getting ready for college."

"Oh," she pouts, "too bad."

"Yeah." I reach out to Reid and swipe the flask from his hands, taking another too-long swig. "Too, fucking, bad."

"Hey!" he complains, rightfully.

I swallow it down and shove it back at him. "Sorry." I reach into my back pocket and pull out a small bag of weed, tossing it to him. "Take it."

He nods appreciatively. "Come on, let's light up."

But I've already started skimming the crowd, looking for something, someone, a *reason* to blow off a little steam. It doesn't take long when I spot a few kids that I'd beefed with a week ago over a parking spot following my last fight. They'd parked too close to my car—my sweet Jasmine—and these motherfuckers showed her no respect. Downright rude, really.

The biggest guy leans against the boathouse, cat-calling a group of clearly uninterested girls nearby. They all shift uncomfortably when he says, "Come on, sweet thing! Don't be like that."

My hackles rise in a familiar way, shoulders going tight, face smoothing out.

"Meet you in a few," I say to Reid, and start toward the dock. I sweep past the huddle of girls—townie's, I gather, from the accents and clothes. Back home, I'm used to conservative uniforms at school and trendy outfits at parties. But these girls have an edgy grittiness that Preston Prep girls can't buy. Frayed, cut-off shorts. Worn boots. Stony expressions. Dark, sexy, eye makeup. I make eye contact with a pair of hard, hazel eyes and dart my gaze down to her lips. They're pressed in a tight line. Whatever she sees in me, she's not impressed.

*Well, sweetheart*, I think, *just wait until I'm done with these fuckwits.*

"Sugar," the big guy pushes off the wall, leering at her, "you know, you'd be a lot prettier if you smiled every once in a while."

Hazel eyes scowls and cuts her eyes at him, jaw setting. She's wearing a loose flannel shirt, which should be universal code for unsexy. Unfortunately, it just makes us really wonder what's hiding underneath. Which is exactly what's got this dumbass up her grill.

She bites back, "You'd be a lot prettier if you fucked off and died, Derek," and the other guys all laugh.

Derek presses a hand to his chest, feigning hurt. "Come on, Sug, I bet I could make you smile for once." He moves closer and the group of girls parts like the Red Sea, giving him berth. The only one still holding her ground is the girl he's harassing. She's tiny, yet her stature implies she's tough as nails. Long black hair hangs over her shoulder, the tips dyed blue. "We've fought this thing between us for too long. Stop playing frigid princess and let me warm you up."

"Sure, I can probably find some lighter fluid," she says, all faux-casually, looking around. "Setting you on fire could get me downright toasty."

I snort, but he takes a step forward, and something wavers in her eye. A flicker of fear. A hard swallow bobbing her throat. I dart between them and look up at the stupid oaf.

"Looks like this girl isn't interested in what you're selling, *Derek*," I say, looking behind me to shoot her a grin. I get nothing back but hard glare. *Okay, then.* "Why don't you move along."

The oaf laughs. He's got a couple of inches on me, and he's big, but it's not the lean mass that I have. I'm fast. Quick. And I already feel the building hum of anticipation in my knuckles, ready to slam into something hard and meaty. Beating his ass would be a pleasure. "Why don't *you* move along, pretty boy. This isn't about you."

I grin. "First, thanks for the compliment. I really am pretty. Second, I've seen how you treat other people's things and it's not great, Derek, it's not great." He tilts his head, assessing me for a minute, like he's trying to place me. "Third—and not to sound egotistical or anything—but *everything* is about me."

Derek narrows his eyes at me and a twisted grin tugs at the corners of his mouth. A moment later he lifts his two meaty paws and shoves them at my chest, pushing me back. The girl I'm defending skirts out of my way, but I keep my eyes on this asshole. He hardly moved me, but he's just given me the opening I need to justify ruining him.

"Thanks," I say, grinning. "This was getting boring." I jerk my elbow back and slam my fist right into his jaw. I barely feel the pain in my knuckles, just the momentum of my arm propelling them forward. I follow through on the punch and then slam a second fist right into his gut. He growls like a beast and swings, but I jump back fast enough that he misses. He tries to barrel into me next, hoping to take me down to the ground, but it's easy to step out of his path and bury a fist into his kidney.

"Oh, so close!" I taunt, seeing some of his boys gathering in my periphery. Fucking classic. Can't take someone one-on-one, just keep adding dudes to the pile. Fine by me. "Everyone can get a turn," I assure them, swiping one of Derek's flying fists.

"Stop!" a girl cries from the growing crowd. "Stop fighting!"

I play for a second like I'm deeply considering it. "Nah. Not until this piece of shit learns a little respect." But Derek's had time to recover. He doesn't lunge at me, taking in my stance—fists up, legs loose and quick. Instead, he shakes out his shoulders and braces himself, mirroring me. The sight of it pulls a laugh from me, high-pitched and crazed. "Now we're talkin'."

No more of this clumsy rage-driven shit. It's too easy.

His fist flies forward but I duck it. I'm not counting on his left fist following it, but it's a messy, badly-coordinated punch. This guy is no southpaw. His knuckles barely graze my cheek. Even though he's not here, I can hear my brother's voice in my head, vicious and taunting.

*You're such a little bitch, Bass. Look at you, gonna get your ass beat by this loser? Typical. Can't even handle a drunk townie. Fuck, you're embarrassing. This is the only thing you're good at and you can't even win.*

It makes my focus narrow tightly on him, fills my head with a violent red and something so chaotic that I can't pin it down long enough to understand it. I just know it makes me want to pound this fucker's face in.

I reach back and slam my fist forward, getting in a solid hook that rocks Derek backward. I don't stop. I plan to keep burying my fist into his face until it's bloody and limp. A flash of movement comes from the side, and I know one of his boys is coming to help him. I react on pure instinct, jerking back and slamming a tight fist into the face coming at me.

The sound is almost sickening—the sharp crack, the loud gasp, the soft sound of a small body hitting the ground.

It takes me so long to realize that it's *not* one of Derek's boys that I'm already turned back to the oaf, fist raised. But I freeze, doing a bewildered double-take.

Because that was not a hard jaw.

That was not a man.

The body on the ground has long dark hair, with blue tips. A girl, the girl I've been *defending*.

My fist drops to my side.

"Fuck," I say, and the crowd shifts, her friends shuffling forward with palms covering their mouths, watching her lifeless body.

I had to have killed her or something. She's not moving, and I don't punch like a little bitch. I follow through. That had been a hard hit—a devastating hit—to someone smaller than me. To someone who's not used to it. To someone with soft skin and a delicate neck. I move forward in horror, looking down at her limp body, but notice instantly that her eyes are open. Unfocused. Squinting, like she's confused.

"Hey," I try, bending down to touch her arm. "I'm sorr—"

Her hazel eyes finally go into focus, landing on mine. She opens her mouth, dragging in a big inhale, and releases it in a bone-chilling scream.

I jerk back first, and then everyone else does. The scream—it doesn't stop. It keeps building and climbing, but it doesn't die. Even when she drags in another breath, it's just to feed that blood-curdling shriek pouring from the pit of her chest.

I look around nervously, but the crowd is frantically dispersing. This is too loud, too much attention. The cops will come. People will ask questions. We'll all be fucked.

Thick with terror and a pain that goes far beyond the punch I'd landed. I stare at her for another for a moment, and then I do the only thing a Wilcox can in a situation like this.

I run.